Praise for the *Bridge of D'Arnath* novels

"A very promising start to a new series."
—*The Denver Post*

"Berg has mastered the balance between mystery and storytelling [and] pacing; she weaves past and present together, setting a solid foundation. . . . It's obvious [she] has put incredible thought into who and what makes her characters tick." —*The Davis Enterprise*

"Berg exhibits her skill with language, world building, and the intelligent development of the magic that affects and is affected by the characters. . . . A promising new multivolume work that should provide much intelligent entertainment." —*Booklist*

"Imagination harnessed to talent produces a fantasy masterpiece, a work so original and believable that it will be very hard to wait for the next book in this series to be published." —*Midwest Book Review*

"[Seri] is an excellent main heroine, her voice, from the first person, is real and practical. . . . I'm truly looking forward to seeing what happens next." —*SF Site*

"Gut-wrenching, serious fantasy fiction for the reader with enough time to appreciate it."
—Science Fiction Romance

"Excellent dark fantasy with a liberal dash of court intrigue. . . . Read this if you're tired of fantasy so sweet it makes your teeth squeak. Highly recommended."
—*Broad Universe*

"Berg excels at strong world-building and complex, sympathetic characters. Her world is realistic and reasonable despite the obvious magical elements, and heroes and villains alike have complex motivations that make them real." —*Romantic Times*

continued . . .

DAUGHTER OF ANCIENTS

Book Four of
The Bridge of D'Arnath

CAROL BERG

A ROC BOOK

ROC
Published by New American Library, a division of
Penguin Group (USA) Inc., 375 Hudson Street,
New York, New York 10014, USA
Penguin Group (Canada), 90 Eglinton Avenue East, Suite 700, Toronto,
Ontario M4P 2Y3, Canada (a division of Pearson Penguin Canada Inc.)
Penguin Books Ltd., 80 Strand, London WC2R 0RL, England
Penguin Ireland, 25 St. Stephen's Green, Dublin 2,
Ireland (a division of Penguin Books Ltd.)
Penguin Group (Australia), 250 Camberwell Road, Camberwell, Victoria 3124,
Australia (a division of Pearson Australia Group Pty. Ltd.)
Penguin Books India Pvt. Ltd., 11 Community Centre, Panchsheel Park,
New Delhi - 110 017, India
Penguin Group (NZ), cnr Airborne and Rosedale Roads, Albany,
Auckland 1310, New Zealand (a division of Pearson New Zealand Ltd.)
Penguin Books (South Africa) (Pty.) Ltd., 24 Sturdee Avenue,
Rosebank, Johannesburg 2196, South Africa

Penguin Books Ltd., Registered Offices:
80 Strand, London WC2R 0RL, England

First published by Roc, an imprint of New American Library,
a division of Penguin Group (USA) Inc.

First Printing, September 2005
10 9 8 7 6 5 4 3 2

Copyright © Carol Berg, 2005
All rights reserved

REGISTERED TRADEMARK—MARCA REGISTRADA

Printed in the United States of America

PUBLISHER'S NOTE
This is a work of fiction. Names, characters, places, and incidents either are
the product of the author's imagination or are used fictitiously, and any resem-
blance to actual persons, living or dead, business establishments, events, or
locales is entirely coincidental.

The publisher does not have any control over and does not assume any
responsibility for author or third-party Web sites or their content.

It's time to acknowledge all those who have helped me bring Seri, Karon, and Gerick to life. First and foremost, Linda, the eternally patient listener and perceptive questioner, Pete, who told me all the right things and consulted on myriad technical issues, and Andrew, who asked the magical question, "Have you written any more of that story, Mom?" Then there are the Word Weavers old and new for being my extra eyes, Markus the Fighter Guy and his henchwoman Laurey and henchman Bob for assistance with combat, and Susan and Di for additional horse lore. Much appreciation to the New York crew, as well: Lucienne Diver, Laura Anne Gilman, and Anne Sowards. And roses all around for my faithful readers all over the world, especially the Roundtable and the Warrior group. You, too, are family, and your enthusiasm and encouragement brighten every day.

PROLOGUE

J'Savan stared, unblinking, at the dark blotch moving slowly across the dune sea, out where fingers of green grass were reaching into the desert. The young Gardener stared, not so much because he was concerned or felt any urgency about his assignment to watch for Zhid stragglers; after all, no Zhid had been sighted in southern Eidolon for almost two years. But he knew that if he so much as lowered one eyelid, the utter boredom of his post was going to put him to sleep. A man could appreciate only so much of the burnt copper sun and the heady scent of moisture, and the cool storm clouds the Weather Workers sent out from the Vales ensured that the blustering wind never ceased. The reawakening desert was beauty transcendent, life reasserting itself over the dead lands of Ce Uroth. But enough was enough.

He squinted into the western brightness. The blotch was likely a wild goat or perhaps a lame gazelle—too slow and erratic for a healthy one. At worst it was a scavenger wolf. The creature disappeared behind a dune, reappeared, vanished again.

J'Savan yawned and stretched out on his back, propping his head on his rucksack. The grassy dune underneath him was warm and comfortable, the day pleasant, but he would have preferred to get back to his regular duties of digging, planting, and coaxing the earth to do his will. He enjoyed his work. Even better would be an early start to his coming leave days and his planned visit to the charming young Singer he'd met at his aunt's house before the autumn's turning. Her waist was plump, her laugh as musical as the patter of spring rain, her spirit tart and flavorful like new-cut limes. Yawning again, he lowered his chin to rest on his chest, closed his eyes, and envisioned her breasts . . . soft . . . curving above the neckline of her gown like a sweet sunrise . . . flushed . . . warm . . .

"Kibbazi teeth!" he yelled, as a fiery sting on his neck startled his drooping eyelids open. "Who are you? What do you think you're . . . wait . . ."

He scrabbled his feet for a moment, but fell still at once when a few warm droplets dribbled down his neck from the sharp edge pressed against his throat. A filthy, ragged woman of indeterminate age hunched over him, rifling his pockets with one hand while threatening his heart vein with the other. A scavenger . . . but no wolf.

She wrenched the small leather tool packet from his belt, sniffed it, and threw it aside, then yanked his rucksack out from under his head. She needed both hands to untie the leather thong that held the sack closed. J'Savan used the opportunity to scramble away, backing up the reclaimed dune like a nervous spider until he was out of her reach.

She didn't seem afraid of him, now she had his things. Greasy tendrils of hair hid her face as she ripped the sack open and pulled out the stone water flask. After yanking the stopper, she cradled the flask in trembling hands and took a sip, no more than a taste. She moaned faintly.

"You can have it all," said J'Savan, peering at her anxiously, desperate to see her eyes. No matter how much he would rather run away, he had to discover if she was Zhid. He was responsible for his fellow Gardeners' safety, for the camp . . . Summoning power, he shaped a simple enchantment of confusion and delay, holding it at the front of his mind lest she attack again.

The woman set the stoppered flask aside and rummaged in the rucksack. She stuffed a crumbling biscuit into her mouth, and after it the bruised pear J'Savan had decided not to eat earlier as he didn't like them so ripe. Only after she'd consumed every morsel, thrown down the empty rucksack, and taken a second sip from the flask did she seem to remember the young Dar'-Nethi. She stood up slowly, clutching the water flask in one hand and her knife—a crudely worked strip of bronze—in the other.

She was tall for a woman, so thin that her sunburnt skin stretched over her bones like silk across the spars of a sailing ship. Sand caked her arms, her bare feet, and her legs that stuck out from her stained, shapeless gray tunic. A dirty cloth bag the size of a man's fist hung from a thong around her neck. She moved toward the Gardener.

J'Savan backed away slowly. "Who are you? Show me your face. I can get you more water and food, but I'll defend myself if need be. I don't mind what you took . . ." His tongue would not be still, as if chattering might set her at ease—or maybe it was for himself. She was so mysterious, so intense. ". . . or where you've come from. I can help. Find you clothes. Are you hurt? Are you . . . ?"

She stepped closer, using the hand with the knife to push the salt-stiffened locks of hair from her face, and J'Savan's voice dwindled away. Her eyes might have been windows on the sky. Huge, blue, limitless. So young, much younger than he'd thought, no older than himself. Her cracked lips moved slightly.

"What? Sorry, I couldn't— What did you say?"

"Regiré. S'a nide regiré." Her soft voice was as dry as the rocky wastes.

She was clearly Dar'Nethi, not one of the warrior Zhid or their Drudge workers. Her eyes said it all. Yet she was not a Dar'Nethi slave, freed by the victory over the Lords, for she wore no collar nor the wide terrible scar from one. Perhaps a Dar'Nethi fighter, lost in the last battles? Surely not. Not after five long years. And her language was unfamiliar, some corrupt dialect, just on the verge of understandable.

"Regiré. Desene, s'a nide regiré." Even rough with thirst, her voice was commanding, urgent.

"I'm sorry. I don't understand you. Look, come with me to the camp. There's water—all you could want—and food. Not a quarter of an hour's walk from here. We'll help you. Find someone who can understand what you're saying." Never quite turning his back on her, he beckoned, using gestures to guide her toward the Gardeners' camp. He breathed easier when she trudged after him, her steps weary and slow, as if she didn't believe he could help, but had nothing better to do.

It was difficult not to run ahead. No one would believe this, someone wandering out of the wasteland after so long. Rumor had it that Zhid still lurked in the jagged mountains of Namphis Rein, the Lion's Teeth, far to the north. But in these first years after the fall of the Lords, the Zhid had been aimless and leaderless. Everyone believed that those not captured were long dead. Was this woman even real?

Quickly J'Savan turned and swept his mind over the woman. Her lank hair had fallen down again, masking her marvelous eyes. But she was no illusion. He sensed no enchantment about her at all.

When the woman squatted down and began pawing at the sand in the middle of the rootling grove, J'Savan averted his gaze, embarrassed to keep staring at her when she clearly needed privacy. He walked through the slender trees more slowly for a few moments, until he heard her plodding along behind him again.

The other Gardeners spotted them while they were still five hundred paces from the camp. Three women and two men stood up from the mounds of dark earth they were working and shaded their eyes. A gust of wind snatched away their calls of greeting.

"Eu'Vian!" shouted J'Savan. "This woman's come out of the Wastes. She's starving and parched. Sun-touched, I think." He ran toward his comrades in fits and starts, slowing whenever he glanced over his shoulder to make sure the woman hadn't vanished, then speeding up again.

A sturdy, capable-looking woman in a dusty yellow tunic and brown trousers stepped out from the other Gardeners and extended her palms to the stranger.

"Welcome, wanderer," said the gray-haired Eu'Vian. "How may we help you?"

"Be careful!" said J'Savan. "She's not Zhid, but she's fierce. Those stains on her tunic . . ." He hadn't noticed the rust-colored blotches earlier. His neck hadn't bled that much.

The woman pushed her straggling hair aside and looked from one kind, curious face to the next. "*S'a nide, regiré.*"

"That's all she's come out with," J'Savan said. "I can't understand her speech."

Eu'Vian crinkled her brow, but did not lower her voice. "It's just an ancient mode. She's asking to be taken to the *regiré*, the king."

"But—"

"Hush, lad." Eu'Vian's face fell into puzzled sympathy.

The warm wind fluttered the strange woman's rags and the wide hems of Eu'Vian's sandy trousers as the Head Gardener spoke haltingly with the woman. At the end of their brief exchange, the stranger dropped the water flask and bronze knife to the grass, closed her eyes, and clenched her fists to her breast. "*Regiré morda . . . D'Arnath morda. . . .*" She sank slowly to her knees and began a low, soft keening.

"I told her we have no king in Avonar, that we honor D'Arnath so deeply that no successor has taken any greater title than his Heir," said Eu'Vian quietly. "Then she asked if King D'Arnath had truly died, and when I said, 'Yes, of course,' the result is as you see. She mourns our king as though he's been dead three days instead of nine hundred years."

As the evening light swept golden bars across the sweet-scented grassland, Eu'Vian crouched beside the stranger, laid her hand gently on the woman's shoulder, and spoke as one does to a child who wakes from a nightmare or an aged friend who has lost the proportions of time and events.

But the stranger shook off Eu'Vian's touch. With her hands clenched to her heart, she turned to each one of them, her very posture begging them to understand. *"S'a Regiré D'Arnath . . . m'padere . . . Padere . . ."*

Eu'Vian straightened up, shaking her head. "Poor girl. Who knows what she's been through to put her out of her head so wickedly."

"What is it she says? What sorrow causes this?" said J'Savan, unable to keep his eyes from the grieving stranger. His chest felt tight and heavy, and tears that were nothing to do with wind or sand pricked his eyes. His companions, too, seemed near weeping.

"It is for a father she mourns," said Eu'Vian. "She claims she is D'Arnath's daughter."

CHAPTER 1

Seri

In spring of the fifth year after the defeat of the Lords of Zhev'Na, our fifth year at Windham, Karon lost his appetite. He stopped sitting with me at breakfast, smiling away my inquiries and saying he'd get something later. Every evening he would push away from the dinner table, his plate scarcely touched. I paid little heed, merely reminding him not to burden Kat, our kitchen maid, with preparing meals that would not be eaten or by untimely intrusions into her domain. Our household was steadfastly informal.

Then came one midnight when I woke with the sheets beside me cold and empty. I found him walking in the moonlight. He claimed he was too restless to sleep and sent me back to bed with a kiss. Alert now, I watched through the next few nights and noticed that he walked more than he slept. In the ensuing days a certain melancholy settled about him, like a haze obscuring the sun.

Though I observed these things and noted them, I did not pry. For the first time in my life, I did not want to know my husband's business. The tug in my chest that felt like a lute string stretched too tight warned me what was happening. Though Karon was scarcely past fifty, a tall and vigorous man with but a few threads of gray in his light hair, I had long laid away any expectation of our growing old together. He had cheated death too many times, even traveled beyond the Verges and glimpsed L'Tiere—the realm of the dead that his people

called "the following life." I feared the payment was
coming due.

The morning of the Feast of Vines was sunny and
crisp, a nice change from our inordinately cold and wet
spring. Though the sunlight woke me earlier than usual,
Karon was already up. From the bedroom window I
spotted him in the garden, walking on the path that overlooked the willow pond. Pulling a gown over my shift
and sticking my feet in shoes, I hurried outdoors to
join him.

I sneaked up from behind and threw my arms around
him in a fierce embrace. "Are you hiding feast gifts out
here for me, good sir?"

He groaned sharply and bent forward, as if I'd stabbed
him in the gut.

"Holy Annadis, Karon, you're hurt! What is it?"

Hunched over, he clutched his belly as if he were
going to retch, his face gray, lips colorless. "Sorry . . ."
He held his breath as long as he could in between short,
labored gasps.

I took his arm and led him across the damp grass to
a stone bench surrounded by a bed of blue and yellow
iris left soggy and bent by a late spring snowstorm.
"Earth and sky! Is this what's had you skipping meals
and walking half the night?"

He sank slowly onto the bench. ". . . was going to tell
you . . . soon . . . I'm not sure . . ."

"Shhh." My fingers smoothed away the tight, deep
creases on his brow and stroked his broad shoulders,
which were knotted and rigid. When his breathing eased
a bit, I pressed one finger to his lips before he could
speak. "Remember there is only truth between us."

He took my hand, kissed it, and pressed it to his brow
before enfolding it in both of his. "I suspect it's a growth
in my stomach." His bleak smile twisted the dagger in
my heart. "I've tried to imagine it's something else, but
all the willing in the world hasn't made it go away as
yet. Not a pleasant prospect, I must say. When I've seen
it in my patients, I've judged it best to leave nature have

its will and use my power to . . . ease the way. Ah, gods, Seri, I'm so sorry."

Of course, Karon would not be able to ease his own way, for the enchantments of a Dar'Nethi sorcerer cannot be turned in upon the wielder for either good or ill. He'd given so much for all of us. It wasn't fair. . . .

The disease devoured him. A fortnight after the Feast of Vines, Karon canceled his long-planned sojourn at the University, where he was to give the first lectures on the history of the Dar'Nethi sorcerers in the Four Realms, an enterprise dear to his heart. And as our frigid spring slogged toward an equally unseasonable summer, he relinquished his healing practice, growing weaker and so consumed by pain that he could not bear the lightest touch.

All that our mundane world's physicians could offer were blisterings and bleedings that would sap his remaining strength and hasten the end. And so I cursed the demands of fate, generosity, and politics that made it necessary for him to live so far from his own people, some of them Healers like himself—sorcerers who might have helped him. But only the Prince of Avonar, our old friend Ven'Dar, had the power to cross D'Arnath's Bridge at will, and only once a year in autumn did he unbar the way between magical Gondai and our mundane world and come to exchange news and greetings. Autumn was months away. Karon would never last so long.

"Seri, come tell him you're going to bed. He won't take the ajuria until he's sure you're not coming back. He needs it badly."

The slim young woman with the dark braid wound about her head stood in the dimly lit doorway to the garden where I walked every evening. When she'd received my message about Karon's illness, Kellea had left her herb shop, her husband, and her two small children and come to stay with us, hoping to find some remedy in her knowledge or talent. But herbs and potions could not reverse the course of such a disease, and though she was Dar'Nethi too, Kellea's talent was for finding, not healing.

I dropped my soiled gloves and stubby garden knife on the bench beside the door, kicked off my muddy boots, and followed Kellea back to the sitting room, the largest room in the old redbrick gatehouse at Windham. We'd converted it to a bedchamber when Karon could no longer manage stairs. Weeks had passed since he'd been able to leave his bed.

Tonight he lay on his side, facing the door, thin, far too thin, like a creature of frost and dew that might evaporate in a warm west wind. Pain rippled beneath his taut, transparent skin in a punishing tide. Kellea had lit only a single candle and set it on the windowsill behind him so it threw his face into shadow. Even so, a flicker of light illuminated his eyes and the trace of a smile softened his face when I came in.

"Ah, love," he said. "I knew . . . the day was . . . not yet done. Not while you can appear before me . . . the image of life itself." Every few words he would have to clamp his lips tight to let a wave pass without crying out.

I pressed my finger to his lips. "I must disagree. This day is indeed done. I am ready for sleep after an exhausting slog about these bogs we call our gardens. Despite the late frost, everything is trying desperately to bloom and needs trimming or coddling. The gardeners do their best, but you know I can't bear to keep my hands out of it. And remember, I was up early this morning answering five thousand letters from friends and acquaintances, and five thousand more from people we've never heard of, asking as to the 'great physician's health,' or the 'most esteemed historian's recovery.' We've had fifty offers of grandmothers' poultices, thirty of herbal infusions, twenty of Isker goats known for the potency of their cheese and milk, and five of pretty young women to 'warm and liven' your bed. I refused them all in your name. It was very tiring."

"Even the young women? I'm always so cold . . . and very lonely here while you sleep in that dreadful chair."

I drew the thick wool blanket over his shoulders, shivering myself in the unseasonable chill. "Most assuredly the young women. If anyone is to warm your bed, it will be me. I will take up my sword and slay the woman who attempts to get there first."

Only you can appreciate the marvels of my mental condition enough to have me now. I felt more than saw his teasing smile. As happened more and more at the end of the day, his words echoed in my head, not my ears. Speaking directly in the mind was far easier for him. *For once I have all of my memories, no lost identity, and no extra soul contained within my own, making me do things I'd rather not. And I'm neither dead nor disembodied— though these days I wish I could be rid of the wretched thing and live without it as I once did.*

Kneeling beside his bed, I laid my head on his pillow where I could feel his breath on my hair.

Tassaye, beloved. Softly. He brushed my damp eyes with his cold fingers. *Life is not done with me yet. I've been in and out of it so many times, you must trust my sense of it. If you can put up with me so long, I'm determined to be here when Gerick comes in the summer.*

"And of course, Ven'Dar may come early and carry you off to Avonar to see a proper Healer, but unless he arrives tonight, you must rest and save your strength. As soon as I've washed my face and hands, I plan to do the same. Dream well, my love."

I kissed his fingers and his eyes and straightened his blankets before I left him. Then I watched from the shadows as Kellea forced him to sit up and drink her sleeping draught. He hated for me to see how hard it was for him to move. Only after he dropped into blessed insensibility did I bring my blankets and pillows and settle in the chair beside his bed.

"Hear me, Ven'Dar," I whispered a short time later, stroking Karon's graying temples to smooth away the lines illness had ground into his handsome features.

"Come early this year." As on every other night, I envisioned my plea taking flight like a red-winged nighthawk, streaking through the airs of the Four Realms and across the Bridge to Avonar, the royal city of the Dar'Nethi, and into the ear of Prince Ven'Dar, Karon's dearest friend. As on every other night, I received no answer.

Kellea nodded a good night and blew out the candle, retiring to her own bed in the room at the top of the stair where she was in range of my call. Not in a thousand years would I be able to repay her service. Karon moaned softly in his sleep. I prayed he did not dream of his terrible days.

Mother . . .

I sat up straight, knocking the pillows from the chair, sleep and shadows and starlight confusing my eyes.

Mother, I'm on my way . . . soon as I can . . .

"Gerick! Good . . . yes . . . soon." Though distant and faint, the voice in my head was unmistakable. I felt more than heard him acknowledge my answer.

I must have spoken aloud, for the light-sleeping Kellea appeared at the doorway with a candle. "What's happened? Is he—?"

"No, no. It's all right." I almost laughed. "Gerick is coming. He mustn't have used any power for three months for me to hear him at such a distance."

"You're sure?"

"I wasn't asleep, only quiet enough to hear him. Paulo must have found my letter at the Two Thieves. I was so afraid. . . ."

"It will be good for him to be here."

Exchanging letters with our son was complicated and unreliable, especially in the past year when a plague of vicious bandits had afflicted the northern roads. Every midwinter at the season of Seille, Karon and I traveled to a barren hillside in northern Valleor. There Gerick would meet us and take us through an enchanted portal into the primitive, shadowy realm he called the Bounded, a land born of his mind and his talent from the chaotic Breach between our human world and magical Gondai. And once a year at midsummer our son would come to us for a week to soak up the sun and revel in a few days' freedom from his responsibility for an entire world. Karon had not been ill when we'd made our fare-wells at the dawn of the new year, and it was still four weeks till midsummer.

Faint light filtered through the window as Kellea touched my shoulder the next morning, warning me that the ajuria was about to abandon Karon for another day. She dared not give him more of the potion than she did already. Though it might ease him longer, it would begin to eat away at his mind so that he could never totally emerge from its cloudy comfort. He didn't want that.

"My ministering spirits," he whispered as I washed his face with a damp cloth. "It's a wonder every man in Leire is not taken to his bed so pitiably as I, just to have the two most beautiful women in the world coddle him so."

"You may flatter all you wish, sir," said Kellea, pulling up a short stool beside the bed, bowl and spoon in hand, the weapons of their daily war. "But I am still deter-mined to get breakfast down you."

"Ah, no . . ."

"Hunger has nothing to do with it, nor do your inces-sant claims that everything tastes beastly, which I will not credit. Seri will tell you why it is more important than ever to take care of yourself."

As I knew it would, the news of Gerick carried Karon through the ensuing days. We talked a great deal of our son's kingdom, marveling again at his odd, deformed subjects who called themselves Singlars. They wor-shipped the young man whose talent had given shape to chaos, creating them a home, and who now struggled alongside them to make their world live. After five years of his leadership, they had created thriving markets and trades among themselves, had embraced the rudiments of schooling, managed their first ventures into the arts, and given birth to their first children. Gerick had not wanted to be their sovereign, but when fate had presented no alternative, he had thrown himself into it, learning what he needed as he went along. Karon and I had watched with pride and amazement as he'd grown into a wise, disciplined, generous, and self-assured monarch at the ripe old age of twenty-one.

It was a slender young man of middle height with red-brown hair trimmed to his collar who strode into the garden on a wet afternoon, only nine days after his message.

"You made decent time," I said, once I'd loosed my embrace enough to allow a look. Dark brown eyes sat deep in his narrow face. You could not gaze into them for long without understanding that this quiet, graceful young man had seen and known things of awesome and dreadful consequence.

"It would have been faster if Vroon could have transported us," he said. "We haven't yet figured out why his 'hops' about the countryside don't work any more. Nothing of the Bounded seems to work quite right lately. Fortunately Paulo can still convince a horse that a league is no more than fifty paces. I had no choice but to ride along."

At the mention of his name, a tall, gangly, freckled young man hurried around the corner of the house into the shade of the rose arbor. I extended my hand. "Paulo! He'll be so happy you've come."

"We worried we'd be too late," said Gerick, as I dragged Paulo into an embrace. "Your weather seems as foul as ours. The roads north are a mess."

"He was determined to wait for you," I said. "Come. He's in here."

With a smile and a handclasp, Kellea yielded Gerick her place at Karon's bedside. Karon's face brightened as our son drew the stool close to the bed and touched his hand. To see the two of them together, bearing such love, respect, and friendship for each other, was everything I had ever asked from life.

A glance over my shoulder took me back to the front hall. Paulo had accompanied us no farther than the sitting-room door and now stood outside on the stoop, facing away. "The horses did more than I asked," he said huskily when I laid a hand on his shoulder. "Like they knew."

"Bless you for getting Gerick here," I said. "And for coming yourself."

"Never thought it would be so bad. He needs someone to do for him what he done for me."

"I keep hoping for it, but unless Gerick can help him, we're out of choices. It's four months until Ven'Dar's autumn visit."

Paulo stepped off the stoop. "I'll be in the stable."

I caught hold of his leather vest. "Go to Karon first. You are his son every bit as much as Gerick. Our groom will care for your horses until you get there."

When I followed Paulo inside a short time later, he was sitting at Karon's bedside, speaking quietly to the man who'd rescued a lame, illiterate peasant boy from a desolate future and entrusted him with his life and the survival of three worlds. Paulo had justified Karon's trust many times over, but the young man had never lost his wonder at it.

Gerick was around the corner in the housekeeper's room, splashing his face with water at the washing table. As he grabbed a towel from the stack and blotted his face, he caught sight of me and motioned for me to stay where I was. He threw the towel in the basket beside the table. Returning to Karon's room, he touched Paulo on the shoulder and murmured a few words to the two of them, then joined me at the door.

"Tomorrow, after I've had a little sleep, I'll see what I can do for him," he said as we strolled down the gravel path between the muddy beds of struggling violets and summerlace. "Kellea says she's already tried all the simple painkilling things I know how to do. So that leaves the soul weaving business. I'll do it, but it's just . . . if I try it now, I might never get back to my own body. We scarcely slept all the way down here."

As the only Soul Weaver known outside of Dar'Nethi legend, Gerick could actually leave his own body and enter another, either taking control of that body or lending his knowledge, skills, and strength to the other person. When his purpose was accomplished, he could slip back into his own skin, leaving his host whole and undamaged.

"Will you be able to help him?"

He shook his head. "I don't know. He doesn't think so. But perhaps he'll be able to guide me into something useful once I'm joined with him. I just don't know."

At twelve, Gerick had been one of the most powerful sorcerers in any world, the prodigy of the murderous Lords of Zhev'Na. But since he had rejected the life they had planned for him, he rarely spoke of sorcery and, according to Paulo, used it even less.

We returned to the house, poked up the fire, and sat with Karon for an hour. Gerick and Paulo fought off sleep and told us of the heavy snows and freezing rain that clogged the roads from the north. Their failure to see a single thriving field along their route boded ill for the coming winter. Their own land's always-unstable weather had taken a turn for the worse in the past months as well. Paulo had been on his way to Yurevan to find someone who could teach them to engineer drainage canals to control the Bounded's unusually severe barrage of storm waters when he'd stopped at the inn called the Two Thieves and found my message.

Kellea soon shooed us all to bed. Everyone needed rest, and she didn't want three more patients to take her time. On that night it was Gerick who helped his father sit up and who whispered comfort as Kellea's herbs worked their mercy.

None of us watched as Gerick left his own body and entered his father's on the next morning. It seemed too intimate an act for public display. I sat in an upstairs window seat with an open book and tried not to hope. Just as well. After an hour Gerick burst out of the front door below me and vomited violently into the undergrowth. For a long while after, he stood beneath a tree, hands clasped behind his neck, his elbows squeezing his bowed head. He didn't need to tell me his attempt had been fruitless.

And so we settled in to wait. As so often happens, grief unleashed a reservoir of laughter. We played lively games of chess or draughts at Karon's bedside where he could listen to the progress of the game.

Kellea astonished us by singing in a rich contralto a variety of Vallorean folk songs, a repertoire she had apparently acquired as a child. She admitted sheepishly that no one had ever heard her sing until her husband surprised her at it when she thought no one could hear.

Gerick and Paulo recounted more tales of their struggle to make the Bounded live. The past months had seen their first large-scale harvest, but also some worrisome failures of the glowing sunrocks that enabled them to grow food enough for all in their sunless world.

I passed on greetings from dear Tennice, Gerick's tutor who had been forced to cancel a journey to visit Karon by a lingering lung fever, and I reported on their friend, our young Queen Roxanne, and her continuing struggle with the Leiran nobility. Four years after her father's death, my old enemy's daughter had at last succeeded in wresting professions of fealty from every member of the Council of Lords, who had once sworn that an ox would rule the Four Realms sooner than a woman. I hated to think of her hard-won concessions tested by a hungry winter.

But all that was before a rain-washed sunset four days after Gerick's arrival, when a sharp knock on the door announced two visitors from Gondai. For a short while, I thought my summoning prayers had been answered after all.

"As soon as he wakes in the morning, we'll take him home." The slender man in robes of dark blue silk gazed down at a sleeping Karon. Though his ageless complexion and fair hair and beard could leave one guessing, Prince Ven'Dar had seen his sixty-fourth birthday. The network of fine lines on his open face had been carved by laughter, but on this night his gray-blue eyes seemed

uncharacteristically shadowed, as if he, too, had not been
sleeping well.

Ven'Dar lifted his hand from Karon's brow. After dis-
patching his Dulcé companion back across the Bridge to
prepare for our arrival, the prince had cast a winding,
an enchantment shaped from the nuances of words, to
send Karon to sleep without the ajuria for the first time
in a month. "Unfortunately, he cannot be in this state
when I take him across the Bridge. As we've found out,
strange things happen when minds lie fallow during a
Bridge crossing. And I am not— Well, walking the
Bridge is difficult of late."

"I'll give him ajuria then," said Kellea, who was settling the blankets around Karon's wasted body. "He'll
need something if you're going to move him."

"No. Whether induced by enchantment or potions, he
cannot be asleep."

"I can take care of it," said Gerick, quietly. "I can't
cure this disease, but I can help him bear it for long
enough to cross the Bridge and get him wherever he
needs to go."

"So be it," said Ven'Dar. "We'll let him rest through
the night—and you as well, lad—then at sunrise we'll
go. Strange for all of us to be together again. Would it
were a happier occasion."

As the stars pricked the deep blue sky outside our
windows, Gerick and Paulo spread pillows and blankets
by the hearth, Kellea retired to her room, and I escorted
Ven'Dar to the bedchamber upstairs. It had occurred to
me, even as the flurry of greetings flowed, that Ven'-
Dar's arrival four months earlier than usual was not truly
a response to my nightly wishing. Even the Dar'Nethi
ability to speak in the mind could not span worlds. And
so, once the matters of towels and washing water and
other rituals of hospitality were taken care of, I paused
at the bedchamber door and broached the question. "So
tell me, my lord prince, what's brought you here? If the
power of my desires can reach all the way to Avonar,
I'd like to know of it."

Ven'Dar stood at the window I had opened to air the

room. "Only a curiosity. I was hoping Karon might have some advice for me. We've had a bit of interesting news in the realm." He turned his back on the window, his arms folded across his breast. "But for now all that must wait. Don't trouble yourself." No amount of wheedling gained me any more than that.

Karon woke before dawn, before anyone else in our suddenly crowded house was stirring. "Who is this lovely wench who comes to warm my bed? I thought they all had been refused." His cold fingers traced the line of my cheek.

"I've set myself to guard against these intruding maidens," I said, trying to waken my tingling arms and ease out of the bed without jarring him. Unable to sleep, suddenly sensing the too-rapid approach of the inevitable, I had slipped in beside him. "Now what of you? How does Ven'Dar's remedy?"

"It lingers a bit. And while I still benefit from it, I'd like to see Martin's gardens once more before I go."

I fumbled in the dark to find his shoes, then helped Karon sit up and get them on. I threw a heavy cloak over his shoulders, and we picked our way around the sleeping Gerick and Paulo, emerging into the predawn stillness. The seasons had gone backward. Instead of the scents of grass and fading lilacs, a frosty mist floated over the garden.

Halfway across a grassy square between two bowers of blighted roses, Karon stopped and closed his eyes, a smile, not a grimace, crossing his features. "How I love this place," he said. "Cold or not . . . feel the life. Smell it. Taste it. You know, sometimes I feel the others here—Martin, Julia, Tanager. I wonder . . ." Holding his arms tight about his middle as if willing the pain to stay away a little longer, he lowered himself to a stone bench. "I've thought it could be that L'Tiere is not so far away. Perhaps the boundary between this life and the next is less formidable than the Breach, and we can find our way back to the places we love most. Who knows? I may come back here again."

I wrapped my arms about his wasted shoulders, unable to answer. Ven'Dar found us there as dawn touched the eastern sky.

"Time to go home, my friend," said Ven'Dar. "Are you ready?"

"I don't promise to be fast. No chance you've a winding to put all but my mind to sleep?"

"Sadly not. But you'll not be alone." He motioned toward Gerick, who had just stepped out of the garden door, conferring quietly with Paulo.

Paulo was drinking something that wreathed his face with steam, and Kellea soon came to us with a similar mug. She sat down beside Karon. "You're not leaving before breakfast," she said in mock severity, holding it to his lips. "Only a little to warm you on your way."

After two sips, Karon took her hand, kissed it, and pressed it to his forehead, a gesture of affection from the land of his youth. "I'll never forget, dear Kellea. Never. Go back to your children and your good sheriff and live in joy."

While Kellea embraced each of us in turn, Karon looked up bleakly at Gerick and Paulo. "If I'm to do this, I'm afraid I'll need an extra hand or two."

"We've come up with a better way. Maybe a little easier on you," said Gerick, hesitating. "If you'll permit me . . ."

Karon understood immediately. "Are you sure?"

Gerick nodded. And so, when Karon signaled he was ready, Gerick laid an arm about Paulo's shoulders. As the first pink and orange sunbeams bathed the garden, Gerick's body slumped, saved from falling by Paulo's firm grip around his waist.

Karon shuddered and sat up a little straighter. Then we stood, and his voice sounded stronger than I'd heard in weeks. "Lead us, lord prince. My wife and my son— my two sons—bear me upon their shoulders, and I would not burden them longer than need be."

Kellea stood watching in the garden, her hand raised in farewell. Her image faded as our strange procession passed into the sunrise. Ven'Dar walked in front, his fair hair shimmering in the light, and behind him a gaunt Karon wrapped tight in his black cloak, leaning on my arm, Gerick's strength enabling him to bear each step. Paulo came next. Over his shoulder he'd slung the slender body that belonged to his best friend and his king, whose soul was temporarily housed elsewhere. A strange procession setting out to journey along the strangest of roads.

CHAPTER 2

D'Arnath had built the Bridge after a magical cataclysm had driven his world of Gondai and the human world apart, separating them with a chaotic void the Dar'Nethi called the Breach. The Breach upset some balance in the universe that drained away enough of the human world's excessive passions that we would not destroy ourselves, while fueling the extraordinary magic—the Hundred Talents—of the Dar'Nethi. Somehow the Bridge maintained this balance, rescuing my world from the consequences of unmitigated violence, and preserving the very souls of the Dar'Nethi, which were inextricably entwined and illuminated with their sorcery. This did not mean that crossing between the two worlds was ever easy.

It seemed so at first on the day we took Karon back to Gondai. The dreadful visions of the Breach seemed to have lost their fearsome reality since the last time I had crossed. The rivers of gore, the bottomless caverns, the legions of the dead, all a traveler's foulest nightmares and deepest fears brought to life in the formless matter of chaos, had less substance than the monsters a child sees in the shifting clouds of a stormy sunset. It was good to think these changes had come about because of Karon and Gerick and some healing that their victory over the Lords had brought to the world.

Yet by the time we stepped beyond the wall of white fire into Gondai, the relentless barrage of enchantment had left my spirit in tatters. Karon was shattered. His breathing was harsh and shallow, and Ven'Dar and I could scarcely keep him upright.

With a grunt of effort, Paulo leaned against a smooth column and set Gerick's feet on the ground, allowing the pillar of rose and gray stone to help support Gerick's limp body.

"I'll put you to sleep. But I'll cast only when you're ready. Do you hear me?" Ven'Dar gripped Karon's shoulders and peered into his eyes, speaking loud enough to be heard over the low rumble of the Gate fire. "Tell me, my friend. Give me a sign."

"Of course, he's ready," I said. I couldn't understand Ven'Dar's delay.

But only after a long few moments did Karon jerk his head, his mouth clenched to suppress a cry. At the same moment Gerick shuddered and stiffened with a sharp intake of breath. Ven'Dar touched Karon's forehead, and my husband slumped heavily in our arms. We lowered him to the floor, and I took his head in my lap.

Gerick breathed deeply, shoulders hunched and arms wrapped about his stomach. He waved his hand and Paulo stepped away, leaving him to stand on his own.

Now I understood. The prince had been waiting for Gerick to leave Karon before casting his spell of oblivion.

The circular chamber was cold; the wall of fire that hurled itself to the pearl-gray dome above us—the Heir's Gate—was enchantment, not true flame. Someone had erected a monumental bronze sculpture in the vast chamber, a rampant lion, the symbol of the ancient king who had built the Gate and the Bridge. The sinewy beast, twice the height of a man and almost growling in its vigorous presence, balanced globes of gold and silver on its upraised paws—symbols of the two worlds linked by D'Arnath's Bridge, I guessed. Though the piece was inarguably impressive and beautifully rendered, it felt out of place in a chamber of such enchanted antiquity.

The door to the outer passage burst open and two men, vastly differing in height, hurried in. "My lord

prince"—the taller of the two bowed to Ven'Dar, and
then turned to me and did the same—"and Lady Seriana, Bareil has told me . . . such a grievous circumstance
for our reunion." He squatted down beside us, took Karon's limp hand, and bowed his head over it, closing his
eyes. "My good lord," he whispered, "I am so sorry."

If someone told me that the sculpted figures that
graced the gates of Avonar, proclaiming the Dar'Nethi
ideals of physical perfection, had taken human form, I
would avow that Je'Reint was one of them. Long elegant
bones defined his features and his tight, lean body. He
was descended from a rare Dar'Nethi family group almost entirely wiped out in the Catastrophe; his skin
gleamed a rich mahogany in color. Even the scar of his
slave collar—he had spent the last three years of the war
in bondage—had faded into his deep coloring.

Ven'Dar had sent Je'Reint to us for a month-long stay
the year before, so I knew that the young man's intelligence and talent were a match for his appearance. He
was a Perceiver, one who could hear and feel the emo-
tional nuances in speech and communicate his own with
clarity. We had been delighted to hear that the childless
Ven'Dar had named the thoughtful young man his
successor.

I took Je'Reint's proffered hand and felt his sympathy
and willingness to be of service take palpable form
around me, building a wall of comfort and inviting me
to lean on it.

Behind Je'Reint waited a neat, diminutive man with a
well-trimmed black beard and dark, almond-shaped eyes.
In Karon's years as Prince of Avonar, the Dulcé Bareil
had served as his madrissé—a repository of knowledge and
wisdom accessible only to his linked Dar'Nethi partner—
as well as his faithful friend and companion. "We've
brought a litter," he said.

Ven'Dar led us up the sloping way of a softly lit passage into a bare, musty chamber. "I'm going to take you
out of the palace," he said. "Though I'd be honored to
have you stay here, you'll be more comfortable and
more private elsewhere."

I understood. To protect our anonymity would be difficult in the bustling royal residence. The Dar'Nethi believed that the last direct descendant of King D'Arnath,
Prince D'Natheil, had been killed in the final battle with
the Lords of Zhev'Na five years before. And truly the
last remnants of D'Natheil's soul had died that day. Only
a handful of people knew that D'Natheil's body still
lived, inhabited by Karon's soul and spirit as it had been
for eleven years now. Karon, stripped of the Heir's powers when he abandoned D'Natheil's soul beyond the
Verges, had joyfully yielded D'Natheil's office to the
man he had anointed as his successor. Together they had
chosen to let the people believe that D'Natheil had died
to save them and that Gerick had remained the Fourth
Lord of Zhev'Na, corrupted in childhood and executed
by his father in that final battle. Unraveling the complex
layers of deception that had been required to lure the
Lords to their destruction would be far too distracting
for a people who needed to remember what their life
had been before the ancient Catastrophe had almost destroyed them. Our public reappearance could not fail to
open old wounds and old fears. Karon needed peace and
care, not to be the center of an uproar.

Ven'Dar scribed a circle on the floor of the chamber
with a beam of light from his hand, stood in its center,
and began working some enchantment. While I sat beside the litter, stroking Karon's brow, Bareil conversed
quietly with Gerick and Paulo. Je'Reint stayed apart,
leaning against the doorway, arms folded and eyes fixed
on Gerick. Je'Reint knew our son's story, of course, and
had expressed an eagerness to meet him, so his coolness
was a bit surprising. To be fair, Gerick did not invite introduction. Our son's nature was anything but gregarious.

After a tedious half-hour, a wavering distortion hung
in the air above the circle. The prince exhaled slowly,
rubbing his forehead. "My apologies for the delay. I
must be more tired than I thought."

Gerick, Paulo, Bareil, and Je'Reint carried Karon's
litter through the enchanted portal.

"Gar'Dena's house!" I said, when I followed them

into a luxurious chamber, uniquely exotic in its decoration. Once introduced to the swathes of enfolding red silk draped from the ceiling to serve as seats, the elaborate fountains, the exotic plants and birds, the bells, the wind chimes, and the hundreds of colorful cushions scattered everywhere, one would never confuse the place with any other.

"Is this room not every bit a reminder of him?" asked the young woman who offered me an embrace as I entered the room. "Would my father lived to offer his own great heart's care in this terrible time."

Aimee was the youngest daughter of Karon's late counselor and friend Gar'Dena. Five years had left the luminous Aimee more womanly than when I'd seen her last. Her sun-colored hair was coiled smoothly at the back of her neck rather than hanging in the girlish loose curls of the past, and a serene confidence imbued her every word and gesture.

"Your father's kindness and generosity live on in his children," I said, kissing her flushed cheeks.

"Many thanks for your hospitality, Mistress Aimee," said Ven'Dar as the young woman offered him the Dar'-Nethi greeting of respect, a graceful bow with hands extended, palms up.

"As always, it is my pleasure to serve you, my lord, and my honor to aid those who have given so much for Gondai." Aimee's countenance expressed her sympathy, though her eyes reflected nothing of what they looked on. She had been blind since birth.

Aimee led Ven'Dar and me to a large, airy bedchamber with high ceilings. Late-afternoon light spilled through its tall windows. The four men had settled Karon on a wide bed, where he lay as pale as Aimee's sheets, and so thin and still he might have been an image graven on a stone tablet.

"My lord prince, I've summoned T'Laven as you commanded me," said Barcil. "He will arrive within the hour."

"Thank you, Dulcé," said Ven'Dar. He stroked his

short beard thoughtfully as he gazed down at Karon,
rare uncertainty clouding his face.

Aimee, who was stacking extra blankets and pillows
on a nearby chest, lifted her head and raised her eyebrows. "But, my lord, have you not asked for the Lady
D'Sanya? I would have thought—"

"No! I've sent for T'Laven. You understand, young
woman, that no word of our guests is to be spoken to
anyone unless I give you leave."

"Of course, my lord." Aimee wrinkled her brow as
she moved to the hearth and blew gently over her fingers
toward the fire. The flames snapped and flared high.

I'd never heard Ven'Dar speak so abruptly to anyone.
And for the recipient of his rebuke to be Aimee, who
had served both Karon and Ven'Dar in many matters
where discretion was required . . . Why would Ven'Dar
doubt her? As soon as the thought blossomed, I dismissed it. He'd never have given us into her care if he
doubted her. Something else was bothering him.

The prince took his leave before I could question him.
"Have no doubt, my lady," he said, meeting my gaze
only briefly as he squeezed my fingers. "T'Laven is a
superb Healer. I'll return this evening to see what he
has to report. I have charged Mistress Aimee with your
comfort and Je'Reint with your safety. Bareil has offered
to assist you with anything you might need."

Je'Reint took his leave at the same time, bidding me
a kind farewell and Aimee an even kinder one. "You
will soon completely overwhelm me with your talents
and mysteries, mistress," he said to her, bowing deeply
and extending one hand in invitation. "Every day I seem
to learn of another."

She flushed and dipped her knee, laying her hand in
his. "Good sir."

Je'Reint kissed her hand, and as he straightened from
his bow, his fingers seemed reluctant to allow hers to
slip away.

Bareil excused himself. The prince and Je'Reint followed him out, pausing at the doorway to confer quietly.

Je'Reint's gaze flicked several times to Gerick, who sat
on the gleaming wooden floor with his back against Karon's bed, elbows resting on his drawn-up knees, the heels
of his hands pressed into his eyes.

Aimee ran her fingers along the edge of the tabletop
and set a glass of wine on the curved-legged table between my chair and Karon's bed. "Here, refresh yourself, my lady," she said. "You must tell me what you
need. I'll have rooms made ready for you and your—"
Her voice dropped to a polite whisper. "Is it your son
here with us, my lady? He has not spoken. And someone
else with him, I think?"

With skill, experience, and some wondrous working of
her Dar'Nethi gifts, Aimee could read some enchanted
books, find her way about her house and the city, and
pursue her talent as an Imager, using her power to create exact images to match the ideas in another's mind.
She used this same power to connect an individual's
presence with an image in her own mind, that is, to
"recognize" the person, but only if the individual had
spoken to her. It was easy to forget she couldn't see
everyone in the room.

"Oh, Aimee, please excuse my rudeness. Yes, my son
is here, and his friend Paulo, who stayed here with me
so many years ago."

Poor Paulo looked as if a brick had fallen on his head
after witnessing Je'Reint's obvious attentions to Aimee.
Karon and I had not failed to note our young friend's
casually placed inquiries after Aimee's well-being over
the past years.

"Welcome, my lord and good sir," said Aimee, bowing her head and extending her palms in their direction.
"May I offer you some refreshment?"

Paulo crouched beside Gerick and whispered a few
words, then stood up again after Gerick shook his
head slightly.

"If we could just have a bit of ale or tea for the young
master. He's had a rough— But he'll be fine if he could
please just have a sip. Or if you could tell me where it
is, I could get it." Paulo's eyes darted between the young

lady and the floor, and his freckles pulsed in a sea of scarlet.

Aimee's smile had the brilliance of raindrops in sunlight. "Of course, I should have thought to bring in ale and water, too. We must fetch Andeluthian ale for Master Karon—it is so nourishing—and a bowl of fresh water to soothe him. And it is very kind of you to offer to help. Though I can carry quite a lot, I do have a problem getting it all set down safely." Much to Paulo's discomfiture, she beckoned him to accompany her through the doorway that Ven'Dar and Je'Reint had just vacated. "Would you prefer ale, also, or water or wine? Or saffria, perhaps? I've some newly brewed."

Paulo's color deepened, if possible, but he was saved from the desperate chance of having to speak to the lady again in public hearing by the return of Bareil with a slight, dark-haired Dar'Nethi man of middle years. The stranger's floor-length tunic was scarlet, trimmed in yellow, and his left arm, bared by the silver brooch that held his draped sleeve, was covered with a network of uncountable white scars. This man was a Healer of extensive experience.

Bareil introduced the stranger as T'Laven, recognized for many years, the Dulcé said, as the finest Healer in Avonar.

T'Laven flushed at this introduction. "No man can hear himself called the finest of Healers when in the presence of Prince D'Natheil. I am honored beyond all telling to be entrusted with the knowledge Prince Ven'Dar has shared with me today and with the care of my noble lord. If it comforts you to know it, my lady, I am one of those who followed your husband when he lived among us, studied his work, and listened to his words as he demonstrated talent not seen since the Catastrophe diminished all talents. Every day of my life I strive to emulate the grace with which he practices our Art."

"Nothing could reassure me so well," I said. "But you must call him Karon now. He no longer answers to your late prince's name."

T'Laven dragged a green-cushioned bench up beside my chair. "Now, lady, if you would please tell me the course of his illness. I see how heavily it lies on him, and I would not rouse him from Prince Ven'Dar's enchantment just to tell me what another might report as well."

The Healer shook his head gravely when I finished my description of the past three months. "So long . . . unfortunate . . ."

"I understand the cost of the delay, Master T'Laven, and I'll not hold you to account for the workings of fate any more than a Dar'Nethi would do."

"I'll do everything I can for him, madam."

As T'Laven stood up and unpacked a small silver knife and a strip of white linen from a leather case attached to his belt, Gerick at last took his hands from his eyes, unfolded himself from the floor, and came to stand behind my chair. The Healer bowed and extended his palms, his expression politely neutral.

"T'Laven, may I introduce our son Gerick. Gerick, this is T'Laven, a Healer sent by Ven'Dar."

I could not see Gerick's expression or whether he offered any greeting in return. The Lords had taught him that the Dar'Nethi were greedy, conniving, and cowardly, unworthy of the great talents they hoarded and constrained. His only experience of the Dar'Nethi beyond his father and Kellea had been as the master of Dar'Nethi slaves during his cruel childhood in Zhev'Na and as their reviled prisoner in Avonar. Knowing that half the population of Avonar would put a spear through his heart and the remainder recoil in horror at the first hint of his identity, one could not expect him to have endearing thoughts of his father's people . . . his own people.

"If my father falters while you do this work"— Gerick's words were soft and cool—"give me a sign. I can sustain him. I don't think it will interfere with you."

T'Laven's sharp gaze told me how dearly he wished to ask how Gerick might do such a thing, but no note in Gerick's chilly offer invited him to make the query.

So the Healer nodded and turned back to Karon. T'Laven made an incision in Karon's arm and his own, and
bound the wounds together to mingle their blood. Whispering the Healer's invocation, he stripped away the barriers of Ven'Dar's winding and created his link into
Karon's mind and body. Karon stirred restlessly but did
not open his eyes.

The evening birds whistled and chittered in the flow-
ered grotto just outside the tall windows. As the daylight
faded, Aimee returned. With a touch of her finger, she
caused an ivory globe painted with delicate brushstrokes
of green to cast a soft light across the expanse of floor.
Paulo accompanied her, carrying in a tray laden with a
crystal carafe of water, three stemmed glasses, a pewter
pitcher, and several mugs. He set the tray quietly on a
small table, filled a mug from the pewter pitcher, and
gave it to Gerick.

As Aimee drew Paulo out of the room once again,
whispering of a light supper for later in the evening,
Gerick sat on a footstool beside my chair and took my
hand. Callused with his work in the Bounded, scarred
by his years in Zhev'Na, his strong hand unraveled the
knots inside me. After a while he closed his eyes. Frown
lines about his eyes told me he was not asleep.

More than an hour later, a pale T'Laven, his narrow
face glazed with a sheen of sweat and his skin showing
the transparent aspect of a Dar'Nethi Healer who has
expended every scrap of his gathered power, untied the
strip of linen that bound his scarred arm to Karon's. I
knew better than to question him right away. He had
lived with Karon's disease for every moment of their
link, delving deep into nerve and muscle and tissue seeking out the cause of the illness and the possible remedies
for it. Dar'Nethi healing was a formidable calling.

After a short while, the slim Dar'Nethi sighed and
raised his head. "It is as he has surmised. To heal such
disease is beyond my skill and beyond my judgment. I do
most sincerely wish I could say otherwise. With Master
Karon's consent, I have temporarily severed the sensory
pathways that cause him such distress, so that for the

moment he may rest in comfort. He sleeps even now, and will do so for another hour or two. But you must know, my lady and good sir, that as long as I maintain this remedy, he will remain paralyzed, unable to move, unable to speak save with his mind. Only heavy enchantment keeps him breathing. He has no wish to sustain his life in this fashion, as I am sure you understand better than I, and so, at his sign, I will undo what I have done."

"And then?" I said, knowing what I would hear, and yet required to ask it in case the universe had taken a left turn and changed its villainous workings.

"He will die, my lady. Not in an hour or a day, but neither will it be so long as a week. Though I will offer what remedies I can, his death will not be easy, but it will be the way of his choosing."

T'Laven started to add something else, but seemed to think better of it. "If another alternative is available," he said, "Prince Ven'Dar must inform you of it. I will return tomorrow morning unless you summon me sooner." He bowed and left the room.

I told myself that I had expected nothing else, but, of course, I had. Gondai was a world of sorcerers. Avonar was a city of power and magic. Anything was possible.

Well, no more of that.

We ate Aimee's supper of cold roast duck, herb-buttered bread, and sugared oranges at Karon's bedside, I in the chair, Gerick and Paulo on floor cushions, and Aimee sitting on the footstool when she was not serving us with her own hands. Our attempts at whispered conversation flagged early on. No one wanted to risk disturbing Karon's sleep, and yet to leave his side was unthinkable. As Paulo followed Aimee out of the room, carrying our still half-filled plates, Ven'Dar returned.

"What news?" asked the prince, beckoning me from the doorway of an adjoining room.

I stood up and then hesitated. "Gerick, perhaps you should come—"

"I'll stay here," said Gerick, who had not spoken a word since T'Laven's verdict. "He oughtn't be alone when he wakes."

I followed the prince into the tidy, efficient study adjacent to the bedchamber.

"So what did T'Laven find?" asked Ven'Dar.

"Nothing more than we expected . . ." I told him all the Healer had said, including his enigmatic conclusion.

"Perdition!" Ven'Dar slammed his hand against the window frame and pressed his forehead to the glass. I had never seen him in such a temper.

"What is it, Ven'Dar? What remedy could you or T'Laven know that Karon himself would not? If you can make it any easier for him, we can ask no more."

"You could ask if I have done everything remotely possible. You so blithely assume such to be true. You think that because he is my friend, I would not allow him to suffer without offering every remedy."

"And would not my assumption be true?"

"No."

Ven'Dar turned his back to the window. In the dark glass gleamed the reflection of two tulip-shaped lamps of amber glass that hung from the high ceiling. They looked like the eyes of a great cat peering around the prince's back. I felt suddenly uneasy, my past experience of the conspiratorial Dar'Nethi undermining my trust.

"Then there must be some good reason for your withholding."

"I cannot see the Way."

"I don't believe that. If anyone among the Dar'Nethi can—"

"I've failed to mention certain alternatives for the same reason I came early to Windham. I need Karon's advice as to whether I should give up the throne of Avonar."

CHAPTER 3

"Her name is D'Sanya, and though she appears no older than Mistress Aimee, there are not five Dar'Nethi in all of Avonar who fail to believe she has lived more than a thousand years. And in five months' time, on the day appointed by the Preceptorate, I must yield the—"

"He's awake." Gerick appeared in the doorway from the other room.

"Go to him," said Ven'Dar, offering me a hand up from the couch where I had just settled. "The world will wait."

I hurried into the softly lit bedchamber, a thousand words of comfort ready. Yet once I'd knelt beside his bed, I couldn't think where to begin.

It's all right, love. He lay so pale and still, his eyes closed, a trace of a smile on his lips. One might think him already dead but for his words that shimmered in my mind and body, bearing everything of him. Comforting me. *You know it's all right. I've been ready a long time.*

Unable to answer, I lifted his cold hand, so limp and lifeless, kissed it, and pressed it to my brow. His chest rose and fell almost imperceptibly.

I can't stay this way, you know.

"I know."

I miss not feeling things. Not the disease, of course. But a lady's kiss . . . to do without for very long would be dreadfully boring.

"Your imagination has always been excellent," I said,

smiling through my tears. Paulo came in and joined Gerick, who stood on the opposite side of the bed. "We'll just have to keep your mind occupied . . . until you're ready."

Not too long, I think. I'm not much use. . . .

"As a matter of fact, Ven'Dar came to Windham to ask your advice." I grasped at anything to stay the future. "Perhaps . . . He was just beginning to tell me about something astonishing. Would you like to hear?"

As someone very wise once said, "Nothing better to be at."

I laughed at hearing Paulo's favorite phrase so dryly echoed. Karon had clearly directed his reply to the other two as well, for a trace of a smile lightened Gerick's somber expression, and Paulo ducked his head and grinned, his cheeks blazing.

"I'll fetch Ven'Dar, and we'll make him restart his story."

When I stepped into the study, I discovered that Je'-Reint had returned. Though I urged them to come in, the prince hung back. "Ah, no. To burden him in these last days . . ."

"He told me not two days ago that life was not done with him yet," I said. "Perhaps it is for exactly this. Let him help you if he can. He'll tell us when he can do no more."

And so we gathered at Karon's bedside—I in the chair, Gerick and Paulo close beside us on cushions, Ven'Dar on a backless stool, Aimee on a settle beside the door with Je'Reint standing beside her—and listened as Ven'Dar outlined his dilemma.

Gerick's face grew stony as the prince described D'Sanya's claim that she had been kidnapped as a girl and held in a prison of enchantment by the Lords of Zhev'Na, the three sorcerers who had rebelled against King D'Arnath and laid waste to nine-tenths of the lands of Gondai.

". . . and so in five months more I am to yield D'Arnath's throne."

D'Arnath's daughter . . . enchanted for a thousand years. How can so many believe such a fantastic tale? Karon's comments sounded clear and sharp in my head.

"She makes no attempt to explain the mystery herself," said Je'Reint. "We subjected her to every test we could devise. The Archivists quizzed her on everything known of D'Arnath's time, but her only 'errors' were to correct perceptions that had never made sense. Our picture of D'Arnath's reign has been clarified immeasurably."

Ven'Dar sighed and settled his chin on his folded hands, far less excited than his heir—his former heir, now. "Ce'Aret gave her the most stringent tests of truthsaying and was entirely satisfied. As Je'Reint, her own grandson, stood to be set aside, one cannot say she was too easy on the woman. We even drew old Ustele from his moldy hermitage long enough to examine her, believing that if anyone could unravel her story, the old skeptic would do it. By the end of it, he was weeping and kneeling at her feet. When the Preceptors voted to vest her, placing her in the direct line of succession, not one dissented. I begged them to delay the anointing a while longer, but in truth, the people would not have stood for it. They are so hungry to put the last thousand years behind them. D'Arnath's name works a magic in the spirit that my best efforts cannot match."

What was written of D'Arnath's children? I recall only sons.

Je'Reint jumped in again. "Very few histories survive from D'Arnath's day—books were a particular casualty of the early years of the war. The most reliable source mentions a single daughter, lost in the war when she was seventeen. We've no record of her name. But D'Sanya led us to a ruined house long buried in the Vale of Maroth—her mother's house, indisputably. She showed us the mark of Garafiel, the most famous swordmaker in Dar'Nethi history, on D'Arnath's sword and claimed that Garafiel was in love with her mother long before she was betrothed to D'Arnath, but they were forbidden to marry because they were cousins. We had never noticed the—"

"By Vasrin Shaper's hand, she showed us how the vines engraved on the sword's hilt hid the letters of her mother's name!" Ven'Dar's outburst silenced Je'Reint. "The Archivists traced Garafiel's lineage and Maroth's, and the kinship was true as D'Sanya had said, though we'd never known it."

Ven'Dar's emotion hung in the air for a few moments, until our silence allowed it to disperse and vanish like smoke in a breeze.

Gerick, did you ever hear of—?

"No." Gerick jerked his head in sharp denial before Karon could finish his thought.

Well then, what of her power?

Ven'Dar sighed and rubbed his brow. "We've seen nothing like it in living memory. She has healed hundreds of Zhid prisoners with her touch. In less than half a year, she has reforested the Vale of Grithna, dead since the early years of the war. The caress of her hand on its soil gave the land such vigor that in a single day the grass was knee-high, the flowers abloom, and saplings two fingers thick stood taller than a man. She lends her power to Builders and Gardeners and Healers, unraveling enchantments and spell traps laid by the Zhid, soothing nightmares and diseases of war victims."

And still Karon continued probing. *Yet you do not believe.*

"I *cannot*"—Ven'Dar shook his head, tightening his lips and squeezing his tired eyes—"and yet I cannot explain precisely why. Everywhere I hear whispers saying, 'Ven'Dar was a fine shepherd, but we have anointed the true Heir of D'Arnath. She should take her father's place.' Ah, my good friend, after her first visit to the Bridge she walked into a palace courtyard weeping, and her tears revived a spring that had been dry since D'Arnath's death. What could it be but my own selfish pride that prevents my belief?" He threw his hands in the air, jumped up from his stool, and paced the length of the chamber three times, like a clock spring unwinding. "My own doubts betray me. The Bridge— To cross these past two days—my first crossings since they anointed her— has been extraordinarily difficult, as if I were a minnow swimming against a torrent, as if my heart knows I don't belong there any more."

There must be something. You have never been driven by pride or greed. Think. Then tell me one thing that makes you doubt.

Ven'Dar folded his arms, closed his eyes, and held still for a moment. When he spoke again, his voice was calmer, uncertainty banished. "She has built herself a great house in Grithna Vale, and in the last two months she has begun to take in people the Healers have judged too ill to benefit from their gift."

Those like me.

"Yes." The prince stepped to the bedside. "A hospice she calls it. Lady D'Sanya uses her power to ease their suffering—suspend their death, as it were. Those who were bound to their beds are no longer; those whose eyes or heart or limbs were failing now have use of them. As long as they do not leave the confines of the hospice, they are as they were before they were stricken . . . except for their talents. They cannot pursue sorcery of any kind. But they feel no pain and do not die. Even after so short a time, public opinion considers those who suggest this result is not a blessing to be, at the least, foolish and self-deceiving. I don't know what's come over them all."

A seductive . . . most seductive outcome . . .

Ven'Dar wandered across the room to the wide windows and back again. "Je'Reint and I have gone over this a hundred times. Dar'Nethi have viewed death as a passage to be accomplished in peace and care when the Way leads us to it, not some fearful event to be avoided at the cost of our innermost being. I have spent my life teaching that the source of our power is accepting whatever joys and sorrows life grants us and viewing them in the larger perspective of the universe. To admit that this woman is D'Arnath's daughter and this hospice a reflection of his philosophy that we have called our Way is to give up my foundation. I cannot do it. Not until I'm sure."

Though he spoke to all of us, Ven'Dar's gaze settled on Gerick, who sat with his chin propped on his clenched fists and his eyes on the floor. "And she has come out of Zhev'Na. How can I trust her? I came to you yesterday to ask if you would meet with her . . . read her . . . and tell me where I'm wrong."

I hear more urgency in you than these events can explain. You've five months before a final decision must be made. You say the woman herself does not push for you to yield, and even the people see how she needs time to be ready for such responsibility. Why the hurry?

Ven'Dar sighed and looked down at Karon with sorrow and affection. "You leave me no choice but to burden you with everything?"

You may have service of all the resources I can muster at present—the paltry few.

Ven'Dar's rueful smile unfolded like a moth's wings, and he returned to the bed, perching on the stool once again. "Despite all, I'm happy you're here, my friend. It is a considerable relief to share all this with you. Can you forgive me?"

Tell me.

"We never knew how many Zhid the Lords controlled. We captured or killed a great number in the year following the Lords' death. Though leaderless and directionless, they couldn't stop fighting. Over the next two years, Zhid renegades drifted in one by one from the Wastes, often starving, weak from lack of power. Still vicious, though. Some of them claimed that thousands more were holed up in the northern mountains. But our Finders could locate no such colonies, so we dismissed their claims.

"In the fourth year, the trickle stopped. Not one more Zhid in the months after. We've kept searching with no result. But half a league from the place the Lady walked out of the desert, we found two dead men—armed and accoutered as Zhid. The evidence of her weapon and the blood on her tunic indicate she was in a fight, though she claims to remember nothing of her desert madness. Then, a few months ago, traders made a regular run to a Tree Delvers' village in the north, a former Drudge work camp that had grown and prospered. It appeared that every resident of the village had got up in the middle of the evening meal and vanished. Some signs of a fight, but no people, either alive or dead. We've seen at least three similar incidents in the past months. In short, I'm afraid we find ourselves facing a new enemy or the revival of an old one."

This news tainted the air like milk gone sour. For a thousand years the Lords had hungered to feed their power by reiving the mundane world and exploiting the chaos of the Breach. Using plots and schemes, mind-twisting sorcery, and war, they had battled to bring down Avonar and with it the Bridge that constrained their power and enabled Dar'Nethi sorcery, for only the Dar'-Nethi stood in their way. We had thought the struggle ended with the Lords' death—Karon's and Gerick's great victory.

Ven'Dar's fine-lined face looked old as I had never seen it. "Factions are developing in Avonar over this succession business. Some think I should serve until nature supplants me. Others—many others—believe D'Sanya should rule tomorrow. We cannot risk division. We are still too fragile. The person who bears the banner of D'Arnath must have the complete trust and loyalty of all Dar'Nethi. If the Lady D'Sanya is what she seems, she should take her place as soon as possible. But if she is somehow . . . corrupt . . . then the danger . . ."

Karon did not hesitate. His words appeared in our minds with all his belief in Ven'Dar's instincts and his honor. *Then the woman must be tested yet again. But I am not the right one to put her to the question.*

"Who then?" said Ven'Dar, wrinkling his forehead.

Gerick.

Gerick, standing now, had retreated to the shadowed corner of the bedchamber as if to physically distance himself from Karon and Ven'Dar. "Ah, no. Don't ask it," he said softly, shaking his head and folding his arms across his breast. "Please, Father. Anything else."

Karon must have spoken privately to Gerick then, for no words appeared in my mind, and Ven'Dar's expression did not change from a thoughtful surprise. Je'Reint snapped his head from Ven'Dar to Karon to Gerick and back to the prince, his back as straight and rigid as the door frame behind him.

My son closed his eyes for a time, and then, with an unsteady breath, he moved to the bed and laid his hand on his father's shoulder. After a moment, his expression as sere as a winter heath, he looked up at Ven'Dar. "My father asks that you summon T'Laven to undo what he has done. Tomorrow we will seek the aid of the Lady D'Sanya and take my father to her hospice if she permits it. Together we'll see what we can learn of her."

Je'Reint strode to the middle of the chamber, his hands spread and raised as if to contain emotions threatening to escape his control. "My lord prince, my lord Karon, the Lady D'Sanya has been forthcoming and modest in all ways. To deceive our princess . . . even if we disagree with her philosophy . . . to set a *spy* on a young woman . . ." He did not need to voice his feelings about the choice of Gerick as the principal in the deception. The set of his dark brow, the direction of his glare said it all. "Surely we can find some other way to discern Zhev'Na's influence on her ideas, to persuade her to study the wisdom passed down through so many generations."

Ven'Dar shook his head, troubled. "I am not easy with deception, Je'Reint. And to take advantage of my friend's pain and to keep Gerick from work that shapes a new world are actions my conscience will not view lightly. But somehow in the months since the Lady's arrival, Gondai itself has felt different to me, as if the very rock and soil beneath us are no longer stable. I've dismissed it as an old man's foolishness, but after my experience on the Bridge yesterday and this morning, I cannot shake the sense that we are racing headlong toward the verge of some great precipice."

"My lord, no one else describes this uncertainty you feel. Rather the opposite. All who work with the Lady feel their own talent enhanced and their power magnified, as if the world is returning to the way it was before the Catastrophe. Yesterday, while working with her to unlock a Zhid spell trap on Ger'Shon's horses, I discovered that I was able to detect the breeding marks buried deep in the bone and tissues of his mares. For centuries every Horsemaster has worked toward such a skill, as it gives us our first hope of breeding out the weak hearts that have plagued our stock. What can that be but the Lady's influence? And how could such service of life be corruption?"

Je'Reint, every line and sinew of his body echoing his words, could have persuaded a cat to rescue a drowning dog. But I was astonished to hear him challenge Ven'Dar so directly, especially with this hint of self-righteousness so uncharacteristic of him—and so ill-suited to a Perceiver.

Even Ven'Dar stepped backward . . . but only one step and no farther. "If the danger I feel is not the woman herself, then we may need her exceptional power to withstand whatever is happening. In any case, we must be sure of her in every way possible before we give her the Bridge. I say this plan goes forward."

In any matter pertaining to the Bridge, the authority of the Heir of D'Arnath was absolute. But I had never heard it asserted so forcefully. Je'Reint inhaled deeply, reining in the further arguments so clearly on his lips. He extended his palms and bowed. "My lord. I respectfully request that you release me from any active participation in this plan. My conscience—"

"Unless the safety of the realm demands it." No doubts softened Ven'Dar's assent. "And you will discuss this with no one outside this room. If my requirement of silence gives you difficulty, I will devise a memory block."

"My lord, your command binds me as always. Again, it is not your purpose, but only the means that gives me pause. If you will excuse me . . ." He bowed again, and

Ven'Dar's gesture gave him permission to go. After a bow to me and a minimal nod in the direction of Gerick and Paulo, he took attentive leave of Aimee. She escorted him out of the room. I squirmed a little, feeling as if I had just barged in on a household of strangers and been presented with their unwashed linen.

Seri . . .

As Ven'Dar spoke with Gerick and Paulo about a story to use—something about old friends of Gar'Dena, come to the city to find better care than that in their town—Karon spoke to me privately, trusting that I understood the reasons why he had to help Ven'Dar, and why I could not go with him on what was likely to be his last journey. He did not reveal what he had said to Gerick to persuade him to the task. A portion of their relationship remained so intimate that I could not be a part of it. I had never grudged that. But in my own secret heart I raged once more at villainous fate, wishing fervently that my prayers had never been answered, that Gerick had stayed with his Singlars in the Bounded, and that Karon could have died as we sat in Martin's awakening garden, believing all his wars had been won.

CHAPTER 4

Gerick

It was a letter from Roxanne that first got me thinking about taking a wife. Not her, of course. Though I'd known her since childhood and we'd shared an adventure or two, the Queen of Leire was not available. She had taken herself a consort less than two years after succeeding to her father's throne, an Isker prince who brought legitimacy to her sovereignty over his conquered land. He also brought no complications of romance or affection to muddle her first difficult years consolidating her authority, so she said. He was only thirteen years old. Her own mother's marriage had been such a political move, and Roxanne conceded to me—and most likely to no one else—that she held out a hope that by the time he was old enough, and she was ready to consider bearing a child, the union might turn out as successfully as her parents' had. But if not, she would find her pleasures where she could. Roxanne was a person of considerable determination.

But it wasn't so much that her letter painted such an attractive picture of matrimony that my current lack of interest in the subject was reversed, but rather that it pointed out that I was doing a terrible injustice to one of the last people I could ever wish to hurt. She wrote that she was looking for a new Master of the Royal Horse, and that it was too bad Paulo wasn't available to take the position, as it would be a perfect situation for him: two thousand of the finest horses in any world to do with as he pleased. *Let me know if ever you decide to set him free of you*, she wrote, *but if I had a captive friend who would do anything in the world for me, from loaning me his body, to saving my life, to polishing my boots, I wouldn't let him go either.*

I didn't like what she'd said. Paulo stayed in the Bounded by his own choice. I'd never asked him . . . never told him he couldn't leave if he wanted. We were friends. He knew how important he was to me.

But Roxanne made me think back to the first time I had joined with Paulo, when I had possessed his body to keep him from being killed by the corrupt Guardian of the Bounded. Amid all his other thoughts and confusions, I had experienced his feelings for a Dar'Nethi girl he admired, and I'd realized that someday he'd have to do something about those feelings. Now five more years had passed, Paulo was almost twenty-four, and I'd not given it the slightest consideration. We'd had so much to do.

While I made laws for the Bounded, heard disputes, set up the Watch, and trained it to protect the people from the wild creatures at the Edge, Paulo taught the Singlars how to make a harness and use it to control a mule, and how to use the mule to help them haul stone and water and to break ground to grow something other than tappa roots. While I worked to convince them of the value of reading and writing and sharing their knowledge with each other, Paulo taught them how to barter for the things one person could do better than another. And it was well known throughout the Bounded that if the king was too busy to hear your petition, or if he'd made up his mind too quickly, then the surest way to see justice done or needs addressed was to find the king's friend where he worked in the fields or the town. If there was merit in your words, the king's friend would recognize it, and the king would hear of it. I didn't see how I could possibly manage without him, but it had been too long since I'd asked him if that life was what he wanted.

It would do no good to ask him outright. He'd say,

"Nothing better to be at," and stay with me forever. And I couldn't just send him away as if I were angry with him or tired of his company. He knew me so well, he'd never believe it. And that was what got me thinking about taking a wife. Paulo and I ate together, worked together, rode together, and when we had any occasion to talk at all, we needed only half the words anyone else might. But if I were to marry, all of that would have to change. It would give him a reason to look at his own situation, and not to have to worry so much about me.

So that became my plan. The only problem was, I had no idea as to how to go about it. I didn't know many women. The Singlars were only just getting used to pairing up with others who cared for them in that way, and I'd never met a one of them who wasn't so in awe of me that she could look me straight in the eye. And beyond that . . . well, the Queen of Leire was taken, even if we'd been willing to try cramming her ambitions and my strange history into one marriage. I didn't know anyone else.

All this was on my mind when I sent Paulo through the portal to the Four Realms to find someone to teach us how to channel storm waters, and he came back the same day with the letter from my mother telling me that my father was mortally ill. And, of course, before you could brush a gnat from your face, we were in Avonar, Paulo stammering his heart out in front of the Dar'Nethi girl he'd worshipped since he was thirteen, and I faced with watching my father die.

I had never planned to go back to Gondai. I had no sympathetic feelings for the Dar'Nethi or their world; the place would just bring back bad memories.

Only my father came close to understanding the things I had been taught in my years with the Lords, the deeds I had done, what I had become when I joined with them. He had kept his promise never to reveal to anyone the horror of what I had been, even to my mother, from whom he kept no other secret. So he knew what it was he asked when he said I needed to use what I knew of Zhev'Na to test this Dar'Nethi woman. But he was willing to postpone his own dying, a release he craved as much as I craved forgetting the past, to make sure that the work we had done together was finished. I could not refuse him. We made a private bargain that day. If either one of us found that his part could not be borne another day, my father would let me go back to the Bounded so I could forget, and I would see him released from his suspended life and let him die.

And so, on our first night in Avonar, I worked with my mother and the Dar'Nethi Healer T'Laven to help my father endure one more night of illness. In order to persuade this Lady D'Sanya that he was willing to relinquish his freedom and his talent in exchange for relief of pain and postponement of death, my father believed it necessary to create in himself true desperation. *I'll not be able to hide that I don't relish her gift,* he said. *But this way, if she reads me, she'll see clearly that I have reason enough to accept it. In truth, feeling* anything *is preferable to the way I am now—neither dead nor alive.*

When the sky turned gray, my father was dozing. T'Laven had left with the first birdsong to summon the Lady D'Sanya, while Aimee brought us cups of something hot that smelled of fruit and spices. My mother took a cup, sighed, and held it in her lap. Since my father had made his decision, she had said very little. Though she agreed that our plan was the only one that made sense, she was afraid of the cost.

I was sitting on the floor cushions, leaning against the bed. Aimee leaned over so I could reach the steaming cup perched on her tray. "Saffria," she said quietly, when I looked up with that very question on my tongue. Her smile was much too cheerful for so early a morning, like a stray sunbeam that strikes your eyelids before you're ready to wake up. "Spiced fruit cider. I seem to have made it especially pungent this morning. I've not been sleeping well of late, and it leaves me more careless than usual."

I took the cup, not so much because I wanted it, but because her tray was tilted at an alarming angle and I

didn't want the scalding stuff in my lap. I was feeling
groggy, numb, and half nauseated, as one does after so
little sleep. "Thank you," I mumbled, holding the cup
with no intention of putting it near my mouth.

"You might try it," she said. "My father always said
saffria cleared his head when he had difficult thinking to
do." Then she crouched down beside me, whispering,
"You must persuade your mother to drink some, too.
She didn't eat anything last night. And your friend . . .
he sat outside that door all night, just fallen asleep in
the past hour. My lord, will he be offended that I've laid
a blanket over him? The morning air is so chill coming
in through the courtyard, even in summer."

"No. Not offended at all." More likely he would go
speechless for a fortnight at the thought of her touching
him. Why was life so complicated?

Aimee hovered over me for a moment before tiptoe-
ing out of the bedchamber. I didn't really believe she
would know one way or the other, but I took a drink of
the saffria to please her . . . and almost coughed it up
again. Far too sweet for my taste, but indeed pungent.
It raced straight upward, eating away all the cobwebs,
dust, and other detritus that clogged my head. "Thank
you," I croaked, even though she was no longer there
to hear me.

I downed the rest of the saffria. Fully awake now, I
was ready to do almost anything to get the matter of
the mysterious D'Sanya over quickly. The sight of my
mother resting her head on my father's pillow made me
hate Healers who had no remedies for disease, hate the
Dar'Nethi who complicated everything with their self-
righteous bickering over their Bridge and their throne,
and hate myself for being unable to help my father in
any meaningful way and for grudging him this single task
that he had set me. Last night had been wretched for
several reasons.

Sounds of doors and voices pulled me to my feet. My
mother kissed my father's brow, waking him gently with
whispered words I tried not to overhear. We all recognized the fact that he was unlikely to survive this ven-

ture. Soon, much too soon for my mother, Aimee poked her head through the door to the side-chamber. "My lady, this way, quickly."

My mother was to watch our meeting through a mys-cal, a Dar'Nethi mirror device that could show her what was happening without her being seen. We had deemed it too risky to expose her as my father's wife when one touch on her shoulder and a simple probe of sorcery would reveal that she was not Dar'Nethi. Everyone in Avonar knew of Prince D'Natheil's remarkable wife from the other world. Our venture would be ended quickly if the Lady guessed our identity. A corrupt prin-cess was not going to reveal the truth to the man who had destroyed the Lords, and an innocent princess was not going to reveal truth to a man who had been one of them.

With a last touch of my father's hand and a kiss on my forehead, my mother hurried out of the room. The door shut softly behind her. Then the Lady D'Sanya, purportedly the daughter of a king a thousand years dead, walked into Aimee's house and eclipsed every thought, every plan, and every caution in my head.

She was every bit of my own height, slender and graceful as a dancer. The planes of her cheek and her jaw were fine and delicate, shaping the light as if its source lay within her. Her dark blue gown, close fitting and banded high at the neck, revealed nothing and ev-erything of round breasts and long, slender throat. Her hands clasped a heavy silver pendant that hung between her breasts, yet my eyes did not linger even in so entic-ing a place, for a pale corona of hair illuminated the most remarkable eyes the worlds had ever produced. They were the sapphire blue of a northern Vallorean lake where the icy water was deeper than the bowl of the sky, yet so clear one could see the gentle movements of the mosses among the smooth rocks at the bottom. She did not smile as she entered my father's room on T'Laven's arm, but swept us all into the sympathetic embrace of those shining eyes . . . and left me breathless and gaping like a fool.

"With blessings of life, I greet you all," she said, in a voice as clear as a snowmelt brook in the highlands. "Gentle lady, good sir, and you, sir . . ." She opened her palms and nodded her head to Aimee, to my father, and then to me.

Despite my every instinct and intention, I could not break the lock her eyes set upon my own. It might have been an hour I stared, discovering nothing I had expected to find in a mysterious Dar'Nethi woman come from Zhev'Na. I had steeled myself to see the Lords' mark on her, the touch of lurid amethyst, emerald, or ruby lurking behind a golden mask, the hint of dark steel behind her soft words, the faint stench of corruption tainting her presence. But all I saw was kindness and wisdom so painfully won I believed I already knew the stories she could tell if ever she could bring herself to speak them. She broke our gaze first, shifting her attentions back to my father, who lay huddled on his bed, fully awake now and quivering with the effort of not screaming with each breath.

The Lady knelt gracefully on the floor beside him, and, after a brief hesitation—perhaps asking his permission without words—laid one hand on her breast and one on his forehead. If enchantment could ever be visible to the eye, then I saw her lay her magic around him like blessed armor against the assault of his ravening disease. His tremors eased, and in a shaking whisper, he said, "With blessings of life, Lady . . ."

She pressed a finger to her lips. "The good T'Laven tells me of your state, Master . . . K'Nor?" My father nodded at the false name we had chosen. "And of your belief that your life's work is incomplete. He has told you of my offer and the conditions of it? I cannot cure this illness. If you leave the hospice, it will come full upon you again with all its mortal consequence. And while you stay with me, you will have no power of sorcery."

"I'll confess . . . that's difficult. But I cannot . . . go on. . . ."

"You have discussed this with your family? Their support is very important."

"My son has accepted my judgment. There is no one else."

"I wish I could offer more. But time and peace are yours if you wish them. Life awaits you."

"Can it be soon? Please, Lady . . ." As he had planned, his desperation was no sham.

"Give me your hand, sir. Your son may come to you five days hence, once you are settled." Though speaking to my father, she nodded at me. "Thereafter he may come whenever he wishes for as long as you stay in my house."

As if lifted from his bed by her slender hand alone, my father rose and stood by the Lady, then stepped with her through the shimmering portal that appeared in the center of the room. As he and the Lady D'Sanya vanished from the room, his voice lingered in my mind. *Until we say enough.*

Until then, Father, I said, staring like a mindless idiot at the spot where the portal had closed in upon itself.

As Aimee and T'Laven hurried off to inform Ven'Dar, my mother returned from the next room. Arms folded, she stood by the tall windows and glared at the bright, empty morning in Aimee's garden. "I expected a demon," she said after a long silence. "A hag, at least, that I could hate respectably."

"She looks younger than Aimee." Trivia . . . while my mind was reeling. Of course her appearance didn't matter. What I saw, what I felt didn't matter.

"How will you begin?"

The very question I'd been asking myself. I had been so sure I would recognize corruption. I would report it to my father and the prince, and then I could run away again and bury myself where I didn't have to think of the past. But all of that changed when I saw her. The Lady D'Sanya had come from Zhev'Na; that part of her story was true. Her eyes had told me. And because of that I could not trust her. But if she was evil, then never had evil been wrapped in such marvels.

"I'm going to tell her I was raised in Zhev'Na."

My mother spun about, her hair glinting in the early

sunlight. "Is that wise? I thought you were going to keep it secret, to try to catch her in some knowledge she shouldn't have."

"I think she already knows," I said. "Just as I would have known she had been there even if I'd never heard her story. I won't tell her all of it, just that I was taken like other Dar'Nethi children, and lived there until I was rescued. As long as no one recognizes Father or me, she won't know everything . . . unless she is even more powerful than Ven'Dar says, in which case none of this makes any difference."

"Walk carefully, love. I need you a while longer." As always, my mother's trust eased my lingering doubts. She took my arm, and we left the empty sickroom behind, walking down the winding passageways of Aimee's house in search of Paulo and breakfast.

CHAPTER 5

I left Avonar in the early afternoon four days after my father's departure. My mother had already written ten letters for me to take to him, and filled my saddlepacks with warm shirts, books, and pastries and tea my father especially liked. She had wandered through our rooms in Aimee's house all that morning, picking up this and that—a pen, a magnifying lens, a small sewn pillow filled with grain that Kellea had been able to warm with sorcery and then tuck in the bed with him to soothe the persistent ache in his back—asking if I thought he would want the things now he would be able to sit up and to walk. Before I could answer, she would throw the object down again in frustration.

"She said I could come and go as I please, Mother. And it's only a day's ride. I'll be back and forth as often as you like. I'll ask him what he wants and needs, and you can send it back with me."

She tossed a pair of boots on the bed, sending two pillows bouncing onto the floor. "You know this has nothing to do with tea or boots."

"I know."

I kissed her and left her in Mistress Aimee's charge. Aimee would need every bit of her cheer and patience to put up with her.

To venture out alone in Avonar felt awkward and conspicuous, so I had asked Paulo to ride along with me, feeling I needed his good eyes and ears to watch my back. If anyone recognized me, matters could get very unpleasant. No one could tell by looking that Paulo was not Dar'Nethi. But if anyone did happen to discover it, we could always say he was a former Drudge, freed by the death of the Lords.

He agreed to go, of course, and we set out with as good spirits as fine weather and excellent horses can lend to a dismal journey. Once we had passed through the gates of Avonar and into the rolling countryside of the Vales, I at least felt that I could breathe again. But the farther we traveled, the more morose Paulo looked. Every time we rounded another bend in the road, he heaved a huge sigh.

"You can go back if you want," I said, after the first hour of it. "But I thought after so many days of inactivity, you might want to get away. Mistress Aimee's house isn't very lively, and when she isn't being excessively hospitable, or excessively cheerful, she is excessively quiet. Worse than me."

He popped his head up, scowling. "She's not at all. Not unpleasantly so. Only refined. And with Master Karon so ill, she wasn't going to—" He caught my look then, but couldn't bring himself to leave the lady undefended. "She's about perfect." Then he nudged his mount to a brisk walk, as if riding ahead would punish my teasing. But I, in turn, spurred my horse deep and left him eating dust.

"Damnable belly-crawling worm-eater!" He raced me down the road until our judgment demanded we slow to spare the horses for the rest of the journey. It was the best thing we ever did together, to ride hard enough we could hear nothing but the roar of the wind and the chugging breath of our mounts, and could think of nothing but staying in the saddle, leaving every fear and worry subservient to speed and sweat and the dust of the road.

We arrived in the village of Gaelie near sunset. The houses and shops were tucked into the heavy growth of trees at the lower end of Grithna Vale as if they were shy of each other. It was a tidy place, everything neat and trimmed and freshly painted, unlike the Bounded, where the Singlars' tower houses were very like the people who lived in them, awkward and lopsided for the most part, and were never the same from one day to the next. Our houses grew, and though most were ugly, every once in a while, on some particular day, you might see a cornice or a window or a section of wall that was extraordinarily pleasing.

Gaelie was large enough to support a modest guesthouse frequented by the families of those in D'Sanya's hospice. The proprietor was a stumpy woman with a face like a granite cliff. Though I was more facile with the Dar'Nethi language, Paulo never seemed to need all that many words. He arranged for a room and a meal without any trouble.

The two of us spent the evening in the bustling common room, hoping to pick up some gossip about the Lady D'Sanya, but there was little to be had. A handful of local fellows pursued a serious conversation about weather working that I might have been interested in had the complex sorcery involved not required immense reserves of magical power. The weather in the Bounded was dreadful and seemed to be getting worse this year. But I only used what power grew in me naturally. Power-gathering carried risks I was not willing to invite.

Across the common room, a large family was celebrating a grandmother's birthday with loud toasts and speeches and much joking back and forth. They quieted only when one of them, a plain, blowsy woman whose fleshy body seemed anxious to escape her clothes, began to sing about sailing ships. I groaned inwardly. The woman's voice was wavering and thin, and it was obvious that her saga was to be a long one.

People settled into their chairs, lit pipes, and let their eyelids droop. Faces took on a look of contentment, even awe, that seemed entirely unwarranted by the talent of the performer. But then, I wondered. . . . My father had told me of Dar'Nethi Singers—his mother had been one of them—but I'd never heard one for myself. He'd said you had to close your eyes. And so I did. . . .

"Close your eyes," I said, after only a moment, slamming my hand on Paulo's arm as he was digging his knife into a plate of mutton and mushrooms.

"You could come up four-fingered doing that," he said, his mouth already full and his knife heading back to the mutton.

"No, you need to experience this. Close your eyes." I closed my own again . . .

. . . and the blustering wind riffled my hair, and the white sails snapped and billowed above my head, sharply outlined against a cloudless blue sky. One of my hands gripped the rough, damp hemp of the bow lines, the other the polished rail. With a wet, booming crash, the bow dipped into a deep trough, and I shivered when the salt spray wet my thin shirt and runnels crept into my boots. . . .

"Cripes!" When I looked again, Paulo's hand was suspended in midair, a mushroom dangling from his knife dripping thick gravy on the table. His mouth hung open for a moment, until he blinked and lowered his hand, staring first at the Singer and then at me. "That's damned marvelous. Can *you* do that?"

"Certainly not. It's one of the Hundred Talents." Which meant that only those born to it, as I was born to soul weaving, possessed the skill. And even if singing was your primary talent, surely you had to have some reservoir of memory . . . of decent things . . . of beauty . . . to make such a vision. That would eliminate me. I sawed off a piece of the stringy mutton, watching the face of the blowsy woman as she sang. Her expression shifted subtly: shadowed, then light again, worried, then peaceful, changeable as I had read about the sea.

"There's nobody in this whole blasted world that's just ordinary," Paulo mumbled. "Singers. Soul Weaver. Horsemasters. Of all things . . ." He dug the point of his knife into the table.

"Don't you start that. She'll see what she needs to see. Just . . . when you go back to Avonar, talk to her. Tell her about all the things you do in the Bounded. No one in this world can do half the things you can. Don't

think you have to race right back here as if I can't get
my feet in my boots without you."

A noisy party burst through the door, informing the
proprietor that they were Gardeners and Tree Delvers
returning to Avonar from the borders of the Wastes. As
the Singer continued her performance at one end of the
room, the newcomers settled around a table, grumbling
at the difficulties they'd experienced in getting their latest project to take hold. A man with a beard down to
his waist joked about harvesting a bucket of Lady D'Sanya's tears to set their trees growing.

A few other people lingered in the corners: a slight,
dark-haired youth huddled over a bowl of soup at the
small table crammed up next the stairs, an old man and
a young couple with their heads bent over ranks of
brightly painted cards laid out on the table between
them.

Not long after the Gardeners arrived, a knob-jointed
fellow in a shabby velvet doublet carried in a heavy
leather bag and asked one of the serving girls for the
proprietor. Pulling a large, well shaped wooden bowl and
a graceful hand-spindle from his bag and setting them on
the table next to Paulo and me, he asked the formidable
Mistress A'Diana if she needed an experienced Wood
Shaper to serve her guesthouse. "Fine repairs or new
work, indoors or out, for little more than my keep, mistress," he said, wrinkling his brow as he drew thumb and
first finger around the battered corner of the table, leaving it smoothed and nicely angled.

"Have you references?" asked the big woman, examining his samples. "I've things need doing, but I don't
hire without references."

"I've worked for a number of guesting houses," he
said to her back, as she bent to see the repaired table
corner. His voice dropped almost to a whisper. "But the
folk who could recommend me are long dead." He
looked wan and anxious, as if the dead proprietors were
waiting to pop out from under the table and grab him.

"Long dead . . ." The proprietress looked up sharply,
then straightened, snatched up the bowl and the spindle,

and shoved them into the man's arms. "Get out of here, *arrigh scheide!*"

Two of the Tree Delvers growled and stood up, and the Weather Worker spun in his chair to look, almost toppling it in his haste. The pale Wood Shaper grabbed his bundle and scurried out of the room. The guests returned to their activities, but the conversation at several tables turned grim and quiet enough that we couldn't understand it.

"What did she call him?" asked Paulo. "Meat-eater?"

I shook my head. "Flesh-eater. It's an old Dar'Nethi name for the Zhid."

"But he wasn't—"

"No. Not any more. I guess some people don't care to do business with those who might have spitted their brothers on sticks." I sopped up the last of the gravy in my bowl with a hunk of bread, but then dropped the soggy bit without eating it.

As his gaze drifted over the other guests, Paulo wiped his knife on the last piece of bread. "But it wasn't their fault. And they don't even remember what wickedness they did, so Master Karon says. Might as well kill them as heal them if you're not going to let them live and work."

I shrugged. "Some of them wanted it. Liked it. They may not remember. But some wanted it." And I wondered if the restored Zhid truly forgot . . . deep in their bones . . . even if they knew it wasn't their fault.

We left before the Singer had finished her tale, as I was dozing in my wine. Anxious and unsettled, I'd not yet caught up with my sleep after sitting up with my father through his last night of illness.

"I can always tell when we're off on another chase," Paulo said as we trudged up the steep, narrow stair. "Always starts with you not sleeping right and me getting dragged off someplace I'd rather not be."

His turn to tease. But I hadn't forgotten Roxanne's letter, so I didn't laugh as I might have another time.

I decided that my first visit to the hospice had better be a careful one since I didn't know the lay of the land, so I left Paulo in town to listen for gossip while I rode alone through Grithna Vale. I wasn't prepared for the Vale of Grithna any more than I'd been prepared for the Lady D'Sanya.

The Vales of Eidolon are a series of broad valleys that seam the mountains ringing the royal city of Avonar. Each of the fifteen Vales has its own character, wild or cultivated, forested or grassy, dotted with towns and villages or sparsely settled. Grithna is a rugged area to the north of the city, one of the "lost Vales" that was destroyed either in the Catastrophe itself or in the early years of the war. Where limestone cliffs had once risen from thick forests and fertile meadows, nothing was left but dead trunks, parched earth, and blasted rubble.

But five months before, so Ven'Dar had told us, D'Sanya had come to Grithna and touched its barren earth with her tears. Now her Vale sported a woodland in its prime. Intermingled with a new growth of rowans and birches, the lifeless trunks of thick-boled oaks and ashes had developed wide, spreading canopies of green. Shrubs heavy with bright red berries grew thickly in any thread of sunlight, massing in colorful ranks along a rutted roadway that led up the heart of the valley.

As always when I saw such a place, my mind went out on its own, assessing where watchers could get the best view of the road, locating the rock piles where archers could take effective cover and harass an oncoming force, noting the crowding trees where warriors divested of noisy armaments could lurk and move unseen alongside their prey until the word was given. Unwary travelers along this road would be easy blood for the taking. The Lord Parven had been a master of military tactics. Though the Lords were no longer a part of me and their voices were long silenced, their lessons had not died with them.

In late morning, I reined in at the top of a long rise. Below me lay a well watered valley surrounded by barren peaks. Broad, green, stream-threaded meadows and a swath of woodland. Some cultivated fields. And a cluster of structures centered by a sprawling white house

with a red tile roof, its walls hung with ten years' growth
of ivy. A low wall of white stone completely surrounded
the house and a vast expanse of the valley floor, some
of the enclosure left in pasture, some carved into gardens and orchards. The wall had only one break, a single
gate with two upright pillars and a stone lintel.

The day was fine and hot as I rode down the hill
and across the half-league of meadow. The glare had me
squinting. After five years living in the ever-night of the
Bounded with its purple lightnings and green stars, I
wasn't used to the sun. I didn't miss it all that much, not
the way Paulo did.

The gate was not guarded. A child jumped down from
her perch on the wall and pushed open the white iron-
work as I approached. Before I'd even dismounted in
the gravel yard, two Dar'Nethi men hurried out, offering
to tether my horse in the shade of a spreading beech
tree alongside two other mounts. If I had not fetched
him in an hour, they would take him down to the stable
to tend him. The Lady D'Sanya herself waited on the
wide columned steps to greet me, a tall, slender, gray-
haired man standing just behind her.

"Blessings of life," she called, smiling. "Welcome, sir."

"Lady." Halfway between the house and the tether
rail, I bowed and extended my hands, and then awkwardly retreated after my horse to retrieve the things
I'd brought. I yanked two bags from my saddlepacks and
held them up as if to explain why I had not rushed to
her feet right away. "Some things for my father." I felt
like a ten-year-old.

"Of course." Her gown floated as she moved, a gauzy
thing, pure white, which set off the brilliant eyes that
almost made me forget my purpose in coming. "Did you
have a fair journey?"

"Quite fine," I said, as I walked across the gravel yard.
Investigators had found two dead Zhid half a league
from the place where she had walked out of the desert
with blood on her tunic and a knife in her hand. I
needed to remember that.

"You're staying in Gaelie? At the Hawk's Bill, I suppose. Mistress A'Diana looks grumbly, but is very kind."

"Yes."

Tongue-tied dolt. I couldn't come up with anything to say. How was I ever going to question her? And I had been giving advice to Paulo!

Stepping aside, her gown swirling about her like smoke, she extended a hand toward her companion. "May I present Na'Cyd, consiliar of this hospice, the dear gentleman who makes my life purest ease and pleasure. I have but to voice an idea, and Na'Cyd executes it more perfectly than I could imagine."

The man extended his palms, and I returned his grave politeness.

The Lady motioned to the wide doorway that centered the porch. Every one of her fingers had a silver ring on it, not gaudy but fine and delicate. "Please come in, Master . . . ?"

"Gerick. Please, just Gerick." Probably foolish to use my own name, but neither my father nor his Preceptors had ever published my name in Avonar, believing anonymity was safer for me. As poor as I was at this spying business, I wasn't sure I could manage a false name.

She smiled, and the sweat trickled down my neck. "I'll have someone bring you wine. Or perhaps cold ale would better suit this warm day?"

"Ale . . . yes. Please."

"Consiliar, if you would . . ." The tall gray man bowed and vanished through the wide doorway.

The Lady smiled and motioned me to follow. "Welcome to my home, son of K'Nor."

I stepped inside, and she led me through a series of rooms and passages.

In my days with the Lords, I'd had the power to take any form I wished and explore the most hidden and remote places of the earth. On one of my journeys, I had taken myself to the deeps of the ocean and swum in the form of a fish through a series of cold stone caves: smooth, clean lines, uncluttered and pleasing, one space

easing into another—that's what I remembered of it—
the dim, green-flecked light sufficient for my fish's eyes
to see my way.

D'Sanya's house had a similar feel. The curved lines
of the smooth white walls, not one square corner anywhere, were simple and pure, uncluttered as you passed
from one comfortable space to another. The peace and
quiet soothed the lingering aggravations of the unfamiliar saddle and the too-bright noonday, and a soft breeze
filtered through the shady passages, cooling the sweat of
the ride.

We came to a round, high-ceilinged chamber with at
least six arched doorways that opened onto long passages. Above the doorways were rounded window openings that had no glass or shutters to filter the bright
sunlight. The narrow dome was a well of light.

The consiliar Na'Cyd was waiting for us, a Dulcé at
his side. "You will find your father in his apartments or
his private garden," he said. "Bertol here will show you
the way once you have refreshed yourself."

I shifted both bags into one hand as the Dulcé pressed
a glass goblet filled with amber ale into the other. I
hadn't even removed my riding gloves yet.

"Whenever you come here in the future, you must go
straight to your father," said D'Sanya. "This is his home
now, and you are welcome in all these public rooms and
gardens. Here, let me show you. . . ."

D'Sanya was already halfway up a short straight stair.
The consiliar and the Dulcé remained behind while I
hurried after her to the top of the stair and onto a
curved balcony with an iron railing. From this vantage
we could look out over the entire compound. Most of
the hospice was built on one level, neat, narrow arms
leading out from this main house and surrounding many
small courtyards and gardens. At the westernmost end
of the place, across a wide green lawn, stood a modest
house of three stories enclosed by its own small garden.

"That's my residence," she said, as if she had followed
my eye across the red tile roofs. "The wings of the main
house are for our guests. Out that way"—pointing with

three ringed fingers, she indicated a cluster of tidy buildings set off from the others out beyond the orderly rows of a large orchard—"are the attendants' quarters, the storehouses, and such. The tall whitewashed structure is the stable, and the square of buildings to the right of them are workshops for metalworking, pottery, and all manner of activities. Even lacking their true talents, some of our residents enjoy pursuing their former occupations, and they enrich us all by their work. In this building you'll find the common rooms, the dining room, the library, sitting rooms, and studies that all may use."

"It looks very comfortable." I clutched the sweating goblet, but didn't drink.

She drew me down the stair again, scarcely giving me time to take in one thing before showing me something new. "The families of my guests are always welcome here. All I ask of my visitors is that they do not intrude on the residents who wish to remain apart."

She guided me through a warren of rooms with comfortable seating, colorful rugs and hangings, and many bookshelves, each room giving onto elaborate gardens thick with flowers, trees, and fountains. Though the consiliar was no longer in sight, the Dulcé trailed after us.

"It is perhaps one of the more difficult aspects of the hospice, that those who live here must inevitably lose a measure of their privacy. I try to help them maintain it as they wish. I share no names unless permitted, and provide each resident with a private apartment and an attendant to see to his or her needs. Only if they desire company do I invite them to join us in the common room to dine, although I do encourage it. Companionship can be helpful at those times when their families cannot be with them. They say the reasons that bring them here are often less clear when they are alone."

"I think—" I tried not to stammer. "I believe it is important to my father to remain private. He was a Healer before this illness felled him, and it makes him uneasy to take this road when he has left so many others. . . ."

"You've no need to explain. I have not and will not

pry into his affairs, though I must confess a slight violation of my own rules already." We had arrived at an
open foyer that I believed was the place I had first entered the house. She tilted her head to one side, and
wrinkled her face in mock dismay. "I did ask your father
about *you*. Only a small misdemeanor. I didn't ask him
about himself, you see. But there was something when
we met the other day. . . ."

I swallowed uneasily. "And what did he say?"

"He apologized profusely, saying that as you had
passed the age of eighteen by several years and had gone
out on your own, he, as any father, must refuse to answer any more for you. He is a most charming gentleman, your father. Tell me"—she laid a hand on my
arm—"would it be insufferably impertinent if I were to
invite you to walk with me this afternoon? You need
not feel obliged."

This was exactly what I had come here for, a chance
to question her, yet those deepest instincts that warn us
away from mortal danger demanded I run away; even
through my sleeve, her touch set my arm afire.

"Perhaps after I've seen my father," I mumbled, my
feet already retreating. I set my untouched ale on a marble table and shifted the heavy bags again into both
hands. "I've brought him some books, and a few of his
clothes."

"Of course, you must go to him first! I'll be in the
library should you decide to indulge me after. Anyone
can show you. Bertol, please show the gentleman to
Master K'Nor's rooms."

The Dulcé stood waiting in the doorway behind me.
I felt the Lady's eyes on my back as he led me down
the passageway, but I resisted the urge to look over my
shoulder. I wanted to make sure I could still do as I
pleased. She could not be trusted. She had come from
the heart of corruption.

We walked across two wide courtyards and down a
marble cloister paved with flagstones that were delicately
carved with vines and flowers. At last the slight, dark-

eyed man bowed and pointed to a doorway tucked behind a vine-covered arbor. The door stood open.

I thanked the Dulcé as he withdrew.

Peering inside, I tapped on the open door and called
out. "Father?"

I stepped from the glaring sunshine into the cool dim-
ness of a spacious room. Before my momentary blindness allowed me to locate the bedchamber door, a
shadowed figure rose from a chair next to the windows.

"No need to look farther. If nothing else, I'm set free
of my bed for the moment."

He wore a simple high-necked robe of dark blue, and
though pale and gaunt, he showed no sign of the pain
that had made even so simple an exercise as standing
unsupported impossible a short week before.

"Are you all right?" I dropped the bags on a settle
and embraced him. He was scarcely more than bones, a
man who had once been a warrior unmatched in the
history of any world.

"I will say it's good to be up and about."

The room was well aired and comfortably furnished:
a wide hearth, a small dining table, several couches and
chairs, and a writing desk set to take advantage of the
large windows. On the left a door led to a bedchamber
similarly appointed. A pair of glass-paned doors opened
onto a walled garden sheltered by spreading elm trees.

"Let's walk outdoors a while," my father said, after
showing me the finely bound volumes in a half-empty
bookshelf and the marvelous plumbing fixtures that
piped water into a small, carved basin and emptied waste
from an enclosed water closet into a series of channels
underneath the hospice buildings. "I can't seem to get
enough of the open air."

We set out through the formal gardens of thick shrubs
and perfectly trimmed beds of flowers and herbs, and
then turned onto a faint path that skirted the paddocks
and led through the fringes of a stretch of woodland.
Before any other conversation, he wanted to know about
my mother. Only after he had wrung my brain inside

out probing for every word she had spoken, every expression that had crossed her face and what I thought it might mean, did we move on to our investigation.

"I remember almost nothing about my first hours here. Candlelight . . . a blur of colorful candlelight. Kind words. A hard bed. She kept me swaddled in hot blankets and her enchantments . . . a blessing, I'll confess, but not so good for precise observation. And then, sometime around the second day, I believe, she and a man named Cedor brought me here and left me to sleep a great deal. I scarcely knew when I was awake and when I was asleep. Cedor brought my meals. He still does, and takes care of my linen and those sorts of things. But he doesn't act like a servant." He drew up his brow thoughtfully.

"A spy?" I said. Something had to be wrong about all this kindness and generosity.

"I don't think so. He's gentle, efficient, does his job, and makes no attempt at familiarity. But he's not . . . servile . . . in any way, either. He is well-spoken, clearly intelligent, and shows an exceptional command of complexities like the plumbing. His demeanor is more that of a physician or a tutor, yet he performs the most menial tasks with good grace."

"You'll need to be careful not to leave Mother's letters lying about."

"Perhaps. But I don't think Cedor's a spy. He's something else. I just don't know what."

"I'm to speak to the Lady before I go."

"She's very curious about you," he said. "She asked me where you live, what you do, how old you are. Does she suspect, do you think?"

"I don't think so. It's . . . When I saw her, I knew she'd lived in Zhev'Na. So *that* part of her story is certainly true. I think she knew the same about me."

We emerged from the woodland path, crossed a grassy lawn teeming with birds and butterflies, and wandered into an apple orchard. I had glimpsed a few other people walking in the gardens, but we had the woodland and the orchard to ourselves.

"And so you've slept in your apartments after all this enchanting?"

"Yesterday, I woke up in the morning as if I'd never been ill. You can't imagine. . . . I rose, washed, ate. Crept about like an infant just learning how to walk, waiting for the onslaught . . . a twinge . . . something. But it never came. For the first time in three months, I could take a full breath without feeling like my gut had a grinding wheel in it. Cedor found me giddy and confused, and kindly reassured me that I was not mad. I supposed they explained the rules of the house to you, as well."

"She told me. So you feel normal? Healthy?"

"I don't feel *anything*. It's so strange."

The path ended abruptly at the edge of the orchard. Beyond the straight line of the trees and across a short expanse of ankle-high grass stood the hospice wall, an unimposing strip of white stone no higher than my waist, stretching in both directions. I was ready to turn back, but my father walked on through the grass.

"Do you sense enchantment here?" he said, running his hand along the top of the wall, where octagonal bronze medallions the size of my palm, each engraved with a flower, bird, or beast, were embedded at intervals.

I brushed my hand on the smooth stone. The hairs on my arm prickled and stung uncomfortably, and I snatched my hand away. "Yes. It's colder than it should be. Active enchantment, certainly."

He shook his head. "I can't sense it. Yesterday afternoon when I was out walking, I climbed over the wall right there by that wild rose. Stupid thing to do. She had warned me. But after thinking of nothing but this wretched body for so long, to have no pain at all . . . I wondered if I was really dead and had just missed the whole thing! Well, I knew right away I wasn't dead. Clearly there is no reversal of disease while one resides here."

"Someone found you?" I hated the thought of him lying in the grass in such pain.

"Cedor. He says everyone tries it in their first days here, so he was keeping watch."

For a while we stood gazing across the grassy spread of the valley floor beyond the wall, threaded with streams, dotted with white clover, meadowsweet, and a few stubby hawthorns. Then we turned back and strolled through the apple, plum, and cherry trees, talking about nothing. Rather than returning the way we'd come, we wandered through sprawling vegetable gardens, encountering an occasional gardener who nodded or smiled as we passed. After a while, a cloud hanging over the distant mountains slid down across the valley and chased us inside with a drizzle of rain.

"How does she do it?" I asked, taking up the only topic of real importance as if we'd never left it.

My father had changed out of his wet robes into the more ordinary shirt and breeches I'd brought him and set about lighting a fire to chase the damp from my clothes. From the mantelpiece he took a small, lidded brass cylinder. A single living flame was visible through the perforated sides, and when he opened the cap and held the vessel next to his tinder, the flame leaped from the luminant and set the dry stuff ablaze.

"The Lady says she doesn't completely understand it herself, but that she has learned how to channel the power we 'residents' gather and bind it to her own, using it to shape the enchantments of the wall. She works the linking enchantment in our first days here. That's why we have no shred of power left for our own use. I can't so much as warm a cup of tea that's gone cold or light a fire." He said it lightly, but I knew that such incapacity was no trivial matter to a Dar'Nethi. "Cedor has to bring me this." He capped the luminant again and set it on the mantel.

"It's like Zhev'Na, then," I said.

He shook his head as if to banish that memory, even as his hand rubbed his neck where the scar of his slave collar was now revealed by his open-necked shirt. "No. Not so crippling as that. I can gather power in the way I'm accustomed. It just dwindles away as fast as it builds.

Truly I feel no evil in the Lady, and the beauties of this place are undeniable. To walk, speak, and eat free of pain, to read, write, and think . . . I never appreciated those things enough. But everything seems . . . different. I can't grasp it. At least in Zhev'Na, I dreamed, but here, not once. Nothing."

He settled into a chair beside the fire and fell silent, staring into the flames. I didn't know what to say.

After a while, he glanced up at me. "One thing we must do each time you come: You must join with me, test me to see if I've changed somehow. My word won't be enough."

"Are you sure?" I hated the thought of intruding on him again. Possessing him. When I joined with a person in that way, no thoughts or feelings could be kept hidden from me. I tried not to pry, but some intrusion was unavoidable. "We don't even know if my ability will work here."

"Another good reason to do so. I know it's awkward. But you mustn't worry; I trust you." He smiled, and motioned me to come nearer the hearth. "Come along. You know I'm right, so get it over with."

We sat on a small couch. Closing my eyes, I gathered what power I had, willing my talent to rise, feeding it with power, and allowing it to swell up inside me until it felt as if my skin would split. Then came the unnerving separation of body and soul, the tearing loss as my detached senses failed, and the moment's disorientation as I abandoned my own body and slipped into my father's. My talent worked without difficulty, but I knew at once that all was not right with him.

When I had joined with him at Windham, again as we had crossed the Bridge, and the third time on that last night at Mistress Aimee's house, I had thought no one could endure such pain as his without madness. My soul had been seared with his longing for release, entwined with his grief at leaving us. Yet even in his torment, my father had been filled with the joy I had come to recognize as his unique gift. He treasured life so very much.

But when I entered his body that rainy afternoon at

D'Sanya's hospice, I thought I might suffocate. He could see, but the colors of the world were flat. Objects had no substance and no meaning beyond their shapes and dimensions, none of the history, associations, nuances, or sensations that a Dar'Nethi absorbs with every breath of his life. I tried speaking in his mind, but he evidenced no sign of hearing me. My father was blind and deaf and mute and numb in every way of importance to him.

"I'm sorry," I said, after I'd left him and come back to myself, sitting on the floor shivering in the suddenly chilly room. "I'll get this done as quickly as I can."

He smiled tiredly and leaned back in his chair. "So it's not just my imagination. That's a relief."

CHAPTER 6

I left my father reading the stack of letters from my mother and retraced my way to the main house. The rain shower had left the sky gray, the cloisters dripping, and the courtyards smelling of damp earth. When I came into the public rooms, I wandered lost for a while, looking for someone to ask where I could find the library. The consiliar Na'Cyd glanced at me over the heads of two men in the dark blue tunics and black breeches that seemed to be the livery of the hospice staff. But he made no move and was soon reengaged in conversation.

I opened a door that seemed likely, only to find a group of five or six chattering people clustered around a confused-looking elderly man. Mindful of the rules of privacy, I backed out of the room in a hurry, only to collide with someone who had walked behind me in the passage.

"I'm sorry," I said, managing not to fall on top of him by grabbing the doorjamb.

Unfortunately, a paper packet flew out of his hand and split open on the floor, scattering its contents down the passage, red juice and pulp smearing the sand-colored tiles. A fruity scent filled the passage—raspberries. With a hiss of exasperation, my victim—short and dark-haired—dropped to the floor, snatched up the ripped packet, and began scooping the remaining berries into it. I crouched down to help.

"You might find walking with eyes front somewhat more fulfilling on the whole."

Not a youth, as I'd thought at first, but a girl. Her

dark hair, lopped off so short around her face and neck, had confused me. She didn't look up. My own surreptitious glance revealed little—a slim untidy young woman wearing a wrinkled linen shirt of dark green, scuffed black leather vest, and tan trousers. I couldn't see her face.

Gathering raspberries enough to fill both hands, I stood waiting stupidly while she stuffed her own gatherings into the packet, got back to her feet, and held out the bag.

"I was trying to locate the Lady D'Sanya," I said, dropping the fruit into the soggy paper. "She said she would be in her library. Can you tell me where that is?"

"Second door on the left, just . . . just beyond . . ." She stared at my hands, which were wet with sticky red juice. "Just beyond the fountain."

I shrugged and held my hands awkwardly away from my clothes. "Serves me right for being clumsy."

Her eyes flicked upward, but only briefly, allowing me a quick impression of dark eyes in a narrow, fine-boned face.

"You can use this to wipe them," she said, almost swallowing her voice completely as she offered a handkerchief she pulled from her trousers' pocket. She kept her eyes averted.

Assuming she was one of D'Sanya's guests who wished to remain private, I kept my own eyes down while I dabbed at my hands. The white linen square was soon sticky and red. Ah, damn . . . I hadn't thought. The scars across my palms were repulsive.

Returning the stained kerchief, I quickly crammed my hands into my pockets. "Sorry again," I said. "Good day."

I felt the woman's gaze on my back as I hurried down the passage toward the door she'd pointed out, pulling on the thin leather riding gloves that I had looped over my belt.

The library was immense: a high, painted ceiling, tall windows of colored glass, at least twenty lamps, and so many books that a staircase reached up to a walkway that encircled the room halfway up the walls. The Lady stood in the middle of the room, hands on her hips, looking from one side to the other as if trying to decide where to start.

She had changed into a long-sleeved red shirt, a gray vest embroidered in red, yellow, and green wool, and an ankle-length skirt of gray leather, split like trousers. A gold bracelet worked like a vine wound up one forearm, bright against her red sleeve.

I greeted her with a bow.

"I keep thinking I should start reading all of these," she said, "so I might understand everything that's happened and everything that's been learned since I was a child. But I never cared for reading books. My mother always said it was because I wasn't grown-up enough. Even yet I can't sit still for it. Do you think that means I've not grown up yet?"

"I don't know."

As a child at Comigor, I'd heard the kind of witty replies men make to such questions from a lady, but I'd never learned the art of devising them myself. It was critical that I make this woman's acquaintance and gain her trust, but I was beginning to think even Paulo was better suited to it than I.

"Do you ride?" I said, unable to come up with anything more clever, and unable to take my eyes off her.

"I've been told I sit a horse quite fair." Putting one finger by her mouth, as if to tell a secret, she leaned her head toward a gray-haired lady who sat frowning over a book. "Mistress S'Nara," she said in a loud whisper, "do you think the young gentleman is asking me to accompany him on a riding excursion?"

"Indeed, Lady, I do." For a moment, the old woman reflected D'Sanya's radiant smile. Her face crumpled into a knot as she went back to her book.

"Well, are you, sir?" The Lady's eyes sparkled with laughter.

"I— Yes." Demons, why was it so hard to talk to her?

"I'd accuse you of reading my thoughts, but I think you might be reading my clothes, instead—certainly from your fixed glance. Or is it just you've never seen a lady's riding skirt?" She spun about until the wide legs of her leather skirt billowed out like a wind flare. Then she patted the reading lady's hand and waggled a summoning finger at me. "Come along, then. Let's ride away."

As we strolled through the hospice and across the yards to her stables, she told me how she'd coaxed the Dar'-Nethi Builders into spreading her house across the meadow rather than piling it up tall as was the usual Dar'Nethi preference. "I didn't want my guests to be stacked one upon the other, and the views are lovely enough from all the windows."

And she talked of the difficulties of bringing seventy people from every part of Avonar into one household and making them feel welcome, yet not compelled to mold their renewed lives into some image of hers. Her experiences made me think of the Bounded and the difficulties we'd had building a life there, and believed that she might be interested in hearing about those things, if ever I could trust her enough to tell her of them. For the moment, I simply listened. She never seemed to stop talking, as if she were trying to make up for a thousand years of silence in one day. Yet none of it was the nonsensical stuff my sometime mother Philomena had spewed endlessly when I was a child.

We passed two elderly men trudging grimly down the path, and she greeted them gaily. "Blessings of life, gentlemen. Was not our rain refreshing after so hot a morning? Good Master Gerard, have you enjoyed the paintings I sent you for your apartments? I tried to find just what you described to me, but I'll try again if they don't suit; the modern styles are still beyond my comprehension."

Just as the woman in the library had, they brightened with her attention, agreeing with her assessment of the weather and the artworks. Neither man wasted a glance on me.

"I thought you didn't use names here?" I said.

D'Sanya waved to a middle-aged woman strolling

among the flowers. "Only with those who have given permission. Most of my guests who come together in the common rooms and grounds see no need for the restriction any longer."

A balding man with a horrid scar on his face met us in the stableyard with my horse. He bowed to the Lady and held open the tall painted door, unrestrained adoration in his gaze. As I mounted, D'Sanya disappeared into the clean-smelling stable for a moment, only to reappear astride an unsaddled gray stallion.

"My brothers taught me to ride," she said, smiling at my surprise. "We were something less civilized in those days." Twining her fingers in the pale mane, she leaned slightly forward as if to whisper in the beast's ear and shot out of the yard like an arrow from a master archer's bow.

I prided myself on my riding. Though not as instinctive a master as Paulo, who became as one with his mount, I had good balance and hands sure enough to convince a horse to do whatever I required of it. But D'Sanya left me feeling awkward and slow, a dead weight in the saddle. She gave a cheerful whoop as the gray soared over a stone fence and landed like a feather, scarcely disturbing the air as he flew, while I jolted my teeth and jerked the reins to straighten our course, wondering who had put lead in my horse's hooves. I caught up with her halfway across the meadow, but only because she reined in, laughing over her shoulder. I halted beside her.

Her cheeks were flushed; her windblown hair settled around her face like a golden cloud; and her clear eyes reflected the sun that poked angled beams through the thinning clouds. "You sit fair yourself, sir. Where did you learn to ride?"

Would that I could have said "in my father's house" or "in my village in the Vale of Maroth" or even "on the bare green hills of Comigor in the mundane world across the Bridge." But I had not come here to make her smile at me. "I've ridden since I can remember," I said, "but I only mastered it in Zhev'Na."

And before I could prevent them, the images filled my head: of Fengara, the Zhid riding master, forcing me to ride my bad-tempered mount between blazing desert scrub, of endless hours in the scorching desert with sand in my mouth and bruises upon bruises from being thrown because she wouldn't let me use the reins or she'd driven the horse mad with visions of slavering wolves. I saw myself riding a gauntlet of screaming Dar'-Nethi slaves who had been lashed until their flesh was in ribbons and their bones bare, just so I could learn how to control my mount when the blood madness was upon it. I tried to concentrate on the green meadow sparkling in the returning sunlight.

"So I was right," she said softly. "I knew it when I saw you. How long were you there?"

"Almost two years," I said. "I was taken when I was ten. Rescued when I was twelve." Though bound to the Lords for four more until my father set me free. But I wasn't ready to tell her about the unique nature of my association with the masters of Zhev'Na.

"Rescued," she said, her lips parted in an expression of wonder, even as her eyes filled with tears that did not fall. "I didn't know anyone was rescued from Zhev'Na. I prayed for it, hoped, wept for it every night for three long years. My father was the High King of Gondai, the most powerful of all Dar'Nethi, and he loved me as the earth loves the sky. But he never rescued me."

"I was fortunate."

Her gaze swept over me with the intensity of desert noonday. "You were not Zhid, not if you were taken so young. And you were not a slave, not if they taught you to ride. . . ."

"No."

She searched my face, her own so filled with sorrow and pity that I wanted to look away for shame at the lies I would tell her. But I kept my gaze steady.

"I heard them plan to steal Dar'Nethi children," she said, "to turn their souls without devouring them as they did those of the Zhid. They said it would be their sweetest revenge. I never knew whether they were successful at it."

"The Lords succeeded at most things they tried."

"Indeed."

She clucked her tongue, and the gray took off at a slow, easy walk up a narrow rift into the surrounding foothills. The path followed a grass-bordered brook that poked like a crooked finger of green through the barren crags. After a last steep climb, we came to a level spot where the stream rose from under the rocks, pooling in a rocky depression before splashing down the gorge we had just traveled. A few willows leaned over the pool, and starlike white flowers on long stalks grew out of the rocks. To one side of the track a jumble of rocks piled one upon the other towered over us. To the other side, beyond the pool and the willows, a huge boulder, cracked by millennia of freezing and thawing, hung out high over Grithna Vale.

"I like to come to this spot to remind myself I'm not there any more." She dismounted and knelt beside the pool, scooping a handful of water to drink. "Fifty paces farther up the trail and you're looking out on the northern Wastes. The sight of it forces you to remember. But here the water is pure and sweet, and you can see only beauty and life."

I slipped from the saddle and walked out on the boulder. The Vales lay like deep folds of green, stretching all the way back to the mountain-ringed city of Avonar, invisible in the distance. Though every instinct told me it was beautiful, the green-and-blue vista of tree and valley and sky repelled me. The Lords had nurtured and honed my senses and instincts for war, nothing more. Nine years of discovering how badly they had warped my perceptions had done nothing to correct them.

However, I had decided long before that I reaped no profit in worrying about such things. The important matter was that if D'Sanya could see beauty where my senses found only ugliness, then what had been done to her was different than what had been done to me. I needed to understand it, and after what I'd already revealed, I had the right to ask.

I turned back to face her, but remained where I was on the rock. "I know everyone in Avonar has asked you questions . . . made you prove who you are. But have you ever told anyone all of it: about Zhev'Na . . . what it was like . . . what happened to you there?"

She trailed her hand idly in the silky water. "How could I? I remember so little. I lived there for three and a half years. Then the Lords tired of me and sent me to sleep for a thousand. And who, except for one like you, could possibly understand what I had to tell? I'm not there any more. I'm not what they wanted me to be. Nothing else is important."

"My father told me that if I kept it all hidden, I could never be rid of it."

Her lips parted and eyes widened. "You told him? The things you'd done, the things they made you do?"

"Yes."

"He forgave you for it?"

"He said no forgiveness was necessary."

"And did you believe that?"

I wanted to answer her. My father was the most generous of spirits, and he loved me very much, a grace I could not yet fully comprehend. But even he could not understand everything. The question hung heavy, like a sodden pennant waiting for a gust of wind to unfurl it.

D'Sanya stretched and stood up, wandering over to her horse and stroking his neck while he nuzzled her pockets. The sun glared behind her hair like a fiery corona. "It's late. I should get back to my guests."

The things I'd done, the things they made me do . . . I gave her a hand up, mounted my own horse, and followed her slowly down the path, wishing she would break the silence so I would have an easier time dismissing the vision of a Zhid warrior I'd lashed until his flesh spattered on my clothes, or the ones with blackened lips and swollen tongues who had died raving in the desert when I withheld their water to test their loyalty.

Neither of us spoke until we reached the bottom of the rift.

"You intrigue me, sir." Tilting her head to look at me, D'Sanya smiled, reigniting the joy and mischief in her eyes. Perhaps she'd been seeing visions, too. "You seem to take it in stride that I am ten centuries old, yet can best you in a horse race. I've met no one else who can do that. I'll have to learn more of you."

"Only if I may request the same privilege," I said, a vibrant warmth spreading like plague to my every bone and muscle. "And I can best anyone in a horse race except my friend Paulo—especially a woman of such advanced age."

I dug my knees into Nacre's flanks and took out across the meadow at a gallop, shouting wordlessly for no reason, relishing the smooth surge of muscled power beneath me and the stretch of thigh and back as I leaned into the wind, winning by surprise what I could never have won by plan. She took the jump over the last fence no more than a tail's length behind me. Flushed and laughing, she almost leaped off the stallion when I offered her my gloved hand.

"When will you return for a rematch?" she said.

"I'll be here every day for a while. I've thought to stay in Gaelie for several weeks so I can be with my father often . . . to be sure . . ."

"Will you see him before you leave today?"

"I planned to bid him good night."

From the direction of the main house, a tall gray man—Na'Cyd, the consiliar—hurried toward us, a Dulcé at his side. "My lady, we have—"

D'Sanya held out a hand to stay him before he could reach us. She fixed her eyes on me, and I felt the blood racing to my face yet again. Her expression was never static, but shifted in subtle ways, soft, engaged, not smiling, yet pleased and filled with anticipation. If a man could grow wings and stand the first time on a cliff top, he could not feel such a mixture of promise and peril as I felt under D'Sanya's eye. "May I come with you? I'd

like to become better acquainted with your father, I
think. Would my intrusion disturb him?"

"Not in the least. He'll welcome it." Surely my father
could do better than I in the matter of investigation.

The stableman took my horse, promising to have him
ready to leave in half an hour. The impassive Na'Cyd
stood beside a grape arbor, arms folded, watching as the
Lady and I left the stableyard. We strolled through the
golden light, across a wide lawn and through the steep
angled shadows of courtyards and cloisters to my father's door.

"I've brought a lady to say good evening, Father," I
called out as I tapped on his door and pushed it open
wider. "I told her you wouldn't mind."

"Certainly not!" He was sitting in the chair by the far
windows again and jumped up as we walked in.

"Your son does not grant you the same courtesy you
gave him, sir," said the Lady, laughing, "but presumes
to answer for you. I only wished—"

The Lady's words fell to the side like a dropped anvil
when my father stepped into the evening glow from his
windows, extended his palms, and bowed to her. Her
hand flew to her throat.

"You were a slave." Her voice sounded dead, all gai-
ety fled in a instant's change.

My father looked puzzled, until his own hand touched
the red scar from the slave collar glaring unmistakably
above the loose neck of his shirt. "Yes," he said softly.
"I was."

"I'm sorry," said D'Sanya, softly. "So sorry. I didn't
know." Tears rolled down her pale cheeks, all the flush
of the day's enjoyment vanished.

"What is it?" I said.

"Please forgive me. I just— I shouldn't intrude. Good
night to you both." She nodded and hurried away, leaving us both staring after her.

I told my father briefly of our ride and our conversation, and we puzzled at her behavior. A great number
of ex-slaves lived in Avonar. Surely the Lady had seen
the scars before. She'd certainly seen the truer horror;

the scars were benign beside the reality of slavery in Zhev'Na. By the time I needed to leave, we'd devised no likely explanation.

"Ride carefully, son."

I bade him good night and set out for the stable and the road to Gaelie.

When I reached the inn, Paulo was loitering about the fringes of the guesthouse's crowded common room, where almost the whole town had gathered to talk about disturbing news. "Another village attacked," he said after working his way across the crowded room to join me by the door. "They're thinking it looked like Zhid work. Do you think that's possible?"

I shrugged and threaded a path toward the stairs. I was here to help my father. Anything else was the responsibility of the Dar'Nethi.

"This time all the bodies were still there." He followed me up the stair. "It was crazy, looked like they'd done for each other: men fallen with their knives in each other's guts, women who'd smothered their children then slit their own throats . . ."

. . . *hangings . . . houses burned with the occupants locked inside . . . murder between brothers . . . neighbors . . . husbands and wives . . . hatred and madness erupted into destruction and slaughter.* I knew exactly what he described. I'd seen it. Powers of earth and sky forgive me, I'd caused such things to happen and then fed on the hatred, terror, and despair I'd caused, until my power was so monstrous I could melt rocks with a flick of my eyelash.

"What is it?" As we walked into our room, he took a breath and examined me. "You look like you've eaten something rotten."

"Nothing. Nothing I can help with."

I was *not* a Lord of Zhev'Na. Twice I had chosen to leave the Three and their gifts of power and immortality behind. My father and I had risked death to destroy them. The last strikes of failing Zhid were *not* my responsibility.

I dropped my packs on the floor. "Tomorrow I've got
to go back to the hospice. See what this damnable
woman is about, so we can go home." I had my own
people, my own kingdom, to worry about.

"What do you want me to do?"

I undid the straps on the saddlepacks and pulled out
a bundle of letters and a list my father had given me.
"If you can force yourself to return to Mistress Aimee's
house, take these letters to my mother and give the list
to Bareil. Ven'Dar said he would send Bareil back to
Windham to retrieve anything my father needed, and
this list describes where he can find all my father's notes
on Dar'Nethi history. He said that as long as he wasn't
dying, he might as well have something to do."

Paulo knew exactly what all of this meant for my father, how he would prefer to be dying than to be sitting
in D'Sanya's house neither dead nor alive. Yet, the
thought of him gone . . . "Shit."

Exactly.

Darkness had fallen as I rode down Grithna Vale
toward Gaelie, but it wasn't as dark as my dreams that
night. As I suspected might happen, they took me back
to Zhev'Na, deep into the heart of the horror I had
lived. When gray dawn woke me the next morning, the
last voice to fade was Lord Ziddari's, repeating the farewell he'd whispered as I left him beyond the Verges:
"Heed my last word, Destroyer. You will never be free
of us. No matter in what realm we exist at the end of
this day, you will not escape the destiny we designed for
you. You are our instrument. Our Fourth. Every human
soul—mundane or Dar'Nethi—will curse the day you
first drew breath."

CHAPTER 7

For three days running, I rode the two hours up Grithna Vale to D'Sanya's hospice, spent the day with my father, then rode the two hours back to Gaelie without so much as a glimpse of the Lady. My father saw her only rarely and discovered nothing we didn't know already: She was beautiful, kind, powerful, generous, discreet, charming. He felt no further change in his own condition, and I detected none. He was numb, and our investigation was going nowhere.

In Gaelie I tried talking to the proprietor of the guesthouse, but the granite-faced Mistress A'Diana could tell me nothing but that those who brought their kin to the hospice were the happier for it. Who wouldn't be, she said, to have a loved one living free of pain and disease when it was thought all hope was past? No, she'd never heard of anyone wanting to leave the hospice once they'd lived there, nor anyone who'd thought they'd made a mistake to send their friends or kin to the Lady. No, she'd never spoken to the Lady, only seen her kindness, and now would I get on with my own business for she, the innkeeper, had a full house of linens to wash.

Every evening that Paulo was gone I spent alone in the common room feeling awkward and useless. The same people were there every day: the parties of Tree Delvers from the Wastes, the two Gardeners, brothers it appeared, who stopped in for supper every night, and the dark-haired youth hunched over his table alone in the corner by the stair. The young man and wife sought endless consultations with endless streams of people

over their painted cards—something about the prospects
of talents in an expected child.

Inheritance was a magical thing to the Dar'Nethi.
Adoption, disinheritance, and mentoring could influence
a child's magical abilities as decisively as blood relationships. That's why my father's revival in D'Natheil's body
had made me the prospective Heir of D'Arnath with all
the power and control such descent implied, even though
I was not born of D'Arnath's blood.

Paulo returned in three days, riding in after I'd completed yet another fruitless venture up the Vale. On the
next morning I was able to take my father a stack of
books and notes from the writing he'd abandoned when
he'd fallen ill and another bundle of letters from my
mother. She must be doing nothing but writing letters.

"Perhaps now I can think about something other than
the state of my belly," said my father as I pulled the
bundles of journals and papers from the bags and
dropped them on his table. "Constant self-examination
is unutterably boring, whether the result is pleasing or
otherwise. At least when I was ill I had people fussing
over me."

As before, his first activity was to read my mother's
letters, the first of many readings, I guessed. He sat in
his chair and broke the seals one after the other. I tied
up my empty bags and poured myself a glass of wine.

"Your mother's not happy being cooped up at Gar'-
Dena's house," he said, waving the current missive at
me, his spirits noticeably improved. "Ven'Dar doesn't
think she should be seen about the city, in case anyone
should recognize her or get too curious about Aimee's
guest. But she's already wheedled Aimee into taking her
to hear a Singer who comes to Avonar next week."

"Mistress Aimee doesn't have a chance," I said, sitting
on one of the hard chairs beside his eating table and
propping my boots on the other one. "She's too nice."

"I don't know. Maybe the girl has more grit than we
know. Your mother's been trying to find out her feelings
about Je'Reint. She says that the cook is certain that

Aimee has an understanding with Je'Reint and that they're just waiting to announce it until 'the matter of the succession is settled.' But Seri can't get Aimee to reveal anything, and it's about to drive her mad. She writes: *'The girl just blushes and says Je'Reint is a noble gentleman whose Way will lead him to great honor, even if he is not to be Heir.'* Poor Paulo."

"Better not tell him. If he gets any lower about Mistress Aimee, he'll have to reach up to shoe his horse." I wanted to shake the woman. "If she could just *see* him . . ."

"I think she sees better than people credit," said my father. "But she's young and generous, and believes she should offer her best to everyone, no matter her personal feelings. And she must be conscious of her position, the daughter of powerful family. For a Dar'Nethi to consider an attachment outside her—"

"To a *mundane,* you mean. A fellow with no power, who can't read, and who'd be happy living in a stable, but who just happens to have the best heart."

"You don't have to convince me, Gerick! It's just something she has to consider, assuming she is considering any attachment at all. You know, I don't claim to understand much of anything about women. Your mother has been challenge enough for one lifetime. Or three for that matter."

A light meal of roast chicken and long peas was laid out on a sideboard, and I helped myself as he went back to his letters, smiling to himself as he read. Then he picked up a page written in a different hand. This one was clearly not so entertaining.

"Ven'Dar writes of another raid in the north. He says that witnesses saw Zhid riding toward the mountains afterward." He looked up, frowning. "The rumor of a mountain stronghold has been repeated for years. If we could only find it . . ."

My father spent the next hour talking about Ven'Dar's news, examining a map of Gondai we pulled from the bookcase, marking the locations of the recent attacks, and speculating on the location of the Zhid headquarters and what could be motivating their actions. Their duty, their desire, the function infused in them from the time they were made Zhid, was to serve the Lords' wishes. I could not imagine them anything but half crazed with loss.

"Perhaps they just can't believe the Lords are gone," said my father. Ven'Dar's half-unfolded letter lay between a basket of leftover bread and a pewter salt dish that held the crumbled bits of wax I had picked off the paper. "They obey the last commands they were given because they don't know how to do anything else. Of course, that doesn't explain the period of quiet and why they are revived at this particular time. You didn't hear of any mountain—"

"I saw only the desert camps and spent time . . . trained . . . in only one of those. I never went into the mountains. Never heard them talk about secret encampments. Please, could we could talk of something else now?" I hated thinking of these things.

He leaned back in his chair and tossed a book onto the stack of maps and papers, looking at me far too closely. "Ah, Gerick, I've always believed that a great deal of this burden you carry is not related to your own past. Somehow, when you were joined with the Three, you took on responsibility for their deeds as well. If only you could touch their actual memories, make use of them to unravel these mysteries, that might make your pain worth something at least."

My fingers played with the edge of his map, rolling it tightly across one corner. I clamped my lips shut and kept my eyes on the paper, waves of heat and chill and nausea leaving my skin clammy.

My father leaned forward and laid a hand on mine. "Gerick, what is it?"

"Don't ask it. Please don't."

He blew a long slow breath of realization. "You *can* touch the Lords' memories . . . earth and sky . . . *all* of them?"

"I tried it that night when Ven'Dar first told us about the Lady . . . when you were so ill . . . to see if I could retrieve some memory of her and avoid all this. Certainly in the few hours I was joined with them, the Lords weren't thinking of her. But I couldn't make myself dig any deeper into their past. You know the risk if I think about that life too much."

To delve too deeply into unhealthy memories, to touch the kind of power I'd had, could waken desires that should stay buried—like digging through a charnel pit and remembering how much you enjoy the foulness, the stink, and the cold heaviness of the dead. And though I chose not to nurture and exploit the talent born in me, I knew I was no weakling child even without my three partners.

"I trust you, Gerick, no matter what the circumstance." My father squeezed my arm and shook it gently, as if to wake me. "You have chosen the right in circumstances far more difficult than examining sordid memory. But the Preceptors and their Geographers and Imagers can pinpoint the source of these raiders far better than we've done here, and for the present the purposes and timing of the Zhid are matters of curiosity, not safety."

For the present. But if they were to find out the Zhid were rising again . . . if they needed to know where the legions lurked or how the warriors could function without the Three, and they came to me . . . "I'm sorry, Father. I just can't—"

A knock on the door interrupted us just then. A stocky, light-haired Dar'Nethi entered at my father's invitation, and with a quiet voice and a pleasant manner asked if we had finished our meal.

"Yes. We're quite fine, Cedor," said my father. "Thank you, as always."

"My pleasure as always, Master K'Nor," he said, sounding as if he meant it.

Once the man was gone, my father pulled out a chessboard and a rectangular wooden box. As he placed chess pieces of green agate on the board, he cocked his head thoughtfully toward the door through which the man had just exited. "I've at last unraveled the mystery of Cedor. Now why do you think a man who once taught natural

history to the children of Avonar spends his days supply-
ing meals and clean linen to a resident of this hospice?"

I shrugged and reached for a handful of the white
pieces, happy we had changed the subject. "No idea."

"He was Zhid. For some two hundred years. I asked
him about the pendant he wears about his neck—a little
brass lion. He said it was a symbol of D'Arnath that
Lady D'Sanya gave him when she restored his soul. Evidently quite a number of the Restored work here."

"Former Zhid here? Is that safe?" Of course, no ex-
ternal marks identified those who had once been Zhid.
I had just never considered that any of them might be
so close. My neck bristled at the thought.

"Quite safe, I think. Cedor was captured in the southern Wastes, nowhere near where I was held. And I've
no contact with anyone else on the hospice staff. You
don't think—" He looked at me as if he'd forgotten until
that moment who I was. "No, no. Even if they could
remember anything of their years as Zhid, they would
remember you as a child, not a man. Nine years it's
been."

Most Zhid were Dar'Nethi who had lost their souls as
a result of the original Catastrophe or in the early centuries of the war, as the Lords drove more and more of
Gondai into ruin. Others had been transformed as the
Lords perfected their Seeking, an enchantment that
could creep through the countryside and even across the
walls of Avonar to capture a person's mind. Few of them
had been given any choice in the matter. Only when my
father became the Prince of Avonar did the Dar'Nethi
come to understand that Zhid could be restored and
take up a normal life again.

"Most of the Restored have long outlived their own
families and friends," said my father, shoving the green
queen's drone forward—his standard opening, though he
seemed to have forgotten that white plays first. "Cedor
says the Lady has given them a chance to earn their
livelihood in a less public setting, and to feel as if they're
making some recompense for their past at the same time.

A generous, insightful gesture on her part. And truly, I could not ask for a kinder or more diligent attendant."

I responded by shoving a white drone forward two spaces, and we talked no more of Zhid.

As my father and I walked in the gardens that afternoon, I caught a glimpse of the Lady, but she was hurrying away from us. I stayed a little later than usual, wandering around the stable and the paddocks, hoping she might reappear. But she didn't.

Just before dusk, I left my father to his books and papers and headed back for Gaelie, wondering what we were accomplishing with all our elaborate secrecy. The journey was slow. Clouds had swallowed the full moon, and without the moonlight, the road was treacherous. Halfway down the road, a thunderstorm broke over the Vale. Having stupidly left my cloak at the hospice, I tried to wait out the rain under the trees rather than riding the last few leagues across the open fields to Gaelie.

By the time I arrived at the guesthouse stable, it was nearing midnight, and I was drenched. The rain had never stopped. The stable lad was just dashing out of the stable on his way home when I rode in, so I told him I would see to my own horse. Once the beast was dry, blanketed, and fed, I hunched my shoulders in my wet shirt and picked my way across the muddy stableyard in the dark and the rain. I wished Paulo had not left for Avonar that morning to take my father's latest batch of letters. I wondered how I was going to proceed with my grand investigation if the subject wouldn't show herself. And I hoped I might still be able to cajole the innkeeper into a hot meal to warm the chill that had seeped into my boots and my skin along with the rain. Halfway across the yard, just as I was passing an abandoned cookshed, a mountain fell on my head. . . .

Probably not a mountain, my fogged brain told me as my arms were stretched almost from their sockets, and my faced bumped and scraped over the rank-smelling roughness of mud, straw, and stones. A rock, perhaps, or a wooden cudgel across the back of the head. Something to knock me senseless long enough for my assailant to lash my hands to this beast that was dragging me through the muck and to bind my legs together so tightly, I could find no leverage to get to my feet.

The restless disturbance of large animals to either side and the change of texture from wet muck to damp straw on my face informed me I'd been dragged into the stable. I considered it a great victory to come up with that conclusion. When I lifted my eyelids, the world was blurry and dark.

The dragging stopped. Yellow light flared just beyond my head, so that if I could have lifted the damnably heavy thing, I might have seen who was ripping the gloves from my hands and holding a lantern close enough that my skin felt the warmth of it.

Dig in your feet and push . . . loop the rope around the bastard's neck . . . Just need a little slack in the rope. Wet rope. Wet boots. Miserable. Conjure something . . . you're a sorcerer. Hungry, too . . . surely the cook made something new tonight . . . hate that green-pea mess . . . A warrior's belly should be lean . . . always on the verge of hunger . . . Swirling thoughts, blurry as the night. Nonsense.

Concentrating, I drew my knees toward my midsection and dug in my toes. The immediate result was a sound that could be nothing but the slap of an experienced hand on a horse's rump. The beast lurched forward. The overstretched muscles in my shoulders began to rip, but when my mouth opened in protest, the mountain fell on my head again. . . .

Drowning! I coughed and spluttered and gagged, fighting for breath. Panic eased when I grasped that the water was knife-edged rivulets of cold rain running down my face and into my nose. *What in the name of sense . . . ?*

My cheek bounced on wet leather. The wind hammered a flap of scratchy wool onto my scraped forehead.

Rhythmic jolts bruised my aching gut and threatened to burst my pounding millstone of a head. The world smelled of wet horse. My disorientation slowly resolved itself into the realization that I was draped over the back of the beast. Upon consideration, drowning sounded quite appealing.

I couldn't see my captor or where he was taking me, for a rag had been tied about my eyes. He needn't have bothered. Everything had been blurry already. I knew better than to give any sign I was coherent, but I had to get the rain out of my nostrils before I puked my guts out—which was going to happen any time now. I cautiously rotated my face toward the rough saddle blanket, and my thoughts blurred as well.

Just when I was convinced that the dark, wet, miserable journey would never end, the horse jolted to a stop. Cold rain soaked my back. Ropes fell slack, and I was dragged off the beast by my feet. My face bumped its way across the saddle, and then I slid all the way to the ground in an untidy heap, unable to catch myself as I was still trussed up like a goose.

Accompanying an ineffective pawing of hands trying to catch me on my way down, I heard the first words from my assailant, not through my ears, but directly inside my head. *I'm sorry. No, not sorry a bit, unless I'm wrong, which I'm not.*

So my assailant was Dar'Nethi. No surprise there.

The fellow dragged me through wet grass and rocky mud, sat me up, and eventually wrapped my arms backward around a broad tree trunk, binding my wrists tightly. At least I was right-side up and somewhat out of the rain. Though my head was clearing a bit, I allowed my chin to droop. Before committing myself to any more serious action, I needed to learn whatever I could. I couldn't see anyway, as the sodden rag was still in place about my eyes. So I listened.

Footsteps. He was light on his feet. The boots hardly made a sound. A soft cluck of the tongue and the two horses walked a few paces away. A rustling of branches . . . soft pats. The horses snorted and blew in a friendly way. The fellow was alone. Small. No strong-armed warrior, else why the head-bashing, dragging me about with a horse, and inordinately tight binding? I wasn't all that heavy.

Footsteps again, back toward me. He crouched on my left side, close enough I could feel his breath on my wet hair. The warmth from his body smelled of horse, damp cloth and leather, and something else I ought to know, something not unpleasant. Fruit—

A sudden movement. Metal sliding on leather. A touch on my chest.

I slammed my head backward into the tree. "Who are—"

Flat, cold steel pressed first on my lips and then across my throat. I understood the implicit command, holding as still as I could, the back of my head hard against the rough bark. No one within range was likely to offer me any help anyway. If this person was going to kill me, there wasn't much I could do about it.

The blade moved away. Not far. His breath came faster. Cold, damp fingers fumbled at my neck. The knifepoint pricked as the blade slit open the front of my shirt, and the fingers jerked the fabric apart. Though I squirmed inside, I held my body still. Pale white light leaked around the edge of my blindfold.

But then he stood up. Footsteps hurried away, quickly lost in the pattering rain. The light was gone.

Stars of night! Releasing a breath held too long, I wriggled and fought to get out of the ropes. No luck. So I was left with sorcery . . . and only a few hours gone since I'd used sorcery to examine my father for the fourth time in four days. In hopes I had recovered, I concentrated and scraped together what power I had left, but no attempt at loosening, breaking, or splitting the rope had any effect. When my fifth attempt left hair and cloth smoldering on my scorched wrists, I quit. Clearly my captor had used exceptional rope, and his prisoner was exceptionally inept.

As the chill and the damp seeped into my bones, the two horses crunched the grass, and the drizzle rustled the leaves above my head. The rain smelled of wet grass and flowers, and we'd climbed since Gaelie. The air was thinner. I was shivering in my wet clothes.

Soon I heard approaching footsteps. Slower than before. And two people this time, the second one heavier, but not by much. His feet shuffled a little in the wet grass, and his steps were uneven. Limping? Light glimmered. Not the white glow of a Dar'Nethi's handlight, but the yellow flicker of a lantern. I stiffened, wary of what might come.

"Oh, child, what have you done?" The soft, chiding voice of a man no longer young.

Cold fingers forced open my clenched fists, somewhere behind the tree beyond my aching shoulders.

"Look here and tell me it's impossible!" Demons and all perdition—a woman!

"What's going—?"

My thick-tongued attempt at participation in the conversation was cut short by the knife pressing a reminder into my windpipe. "Silence, monster!"

"Stop it, Jen!" said the man. "Stop! These are just scars from the war . . . or from any number of things. You have to forget, child. Let it go. And let this poor young man go. Look what you've done to him."

"Look at his hands, Papa. Only one thing ever caused scars like these. Look at the color of his hair. Remember it? Look at these other marks on him." She yanked on my ripped shirt and held the lantern close enough that I could feel the warmth on my clammy skin. With the tip of the knife she traced a scar on the left side of my rib cage, and another on my right shoulder, one on my abdomen, and a long, jagged one on my right arm. How could anyone know of those scars, remnants of my childhood sword training in Zhev'Na?

"It's impossible. He's long dead." But the man wasn't so sure any more.

"He *should* be dead. Justice is a mockery in Gondai while the monster yet breathes. Yet he rides the roads of the world as if he has a right to them. I'll see him dead, Papa. I will. The moment you acknowledge him,

I'll bleed him dry. Only three other creatures in all the world bore these same scars on their hands."

I didn't know who these two were, but they certainly knew me . . . and no word I could say could possibly assuage either the woman's hatred or her fear. Not if she knew what the scars on my hands were.

"Even if . . . even if it were so," said the man, "only the Heir of D'Arnath can condemn a man to death. You must not wager your soul for something so fleeting as revenge. And I can't be sure. It's been so many years. . . ."

"Perhaps if you look on his face, Papa. Look and remember. No one in authority is going to listen to me, but if a Speaker testifies . . ."

The cold fingers pulled at my blindfold, and at last I identified their scent: raspberries. By the time my eyes could filter out the lamplight, I had already cursed myself for a fool, remembering the retiring "youth" in the Gaelie common room and the dark-haired young woman who'd taken such an interest in my hands. Ten paces to my right stood the ghostly white ribbon of the hospice wall.

But my disgust at my blindness was quickly overruled by shock when I saw her companion. An old man with one ruined eye and a villainously twisted back stared at me, droplets of rain trickling down his face like a shower of tears. Even with eyes that refused to hold their focus, I knew him. I had last seen him when I was eleven. He'd been standing in the door of my house in Zhev'Na as I rode off into the desert with a red-haired Zhid warrior who would tutor me in the fine arts of murder, torture, and war.

"Sefaro," I whispered, heedless of the woman's knife. The kind, gentle chamberlain of my household, the slave forbidden to speak unless I gave him leave, yet who always smiled at me. The slave allowed to wear nothing but the vile steel collar and a gray tunic, yet who always told me how well I looked in my fine clothes. The slave fed nothing but sour gray bread, though he always made sure I had my favorite things to eat. The man I came near killing in a child's pique, yet who looked in on me in the long nights when I couldn't sleep, giving me comfort by caring that I was lonely and afraid. I had believed him one of the thousand victims of my training. . . .

Don't get too close; don't get too familiar; don't care about anyone or they'll disappear and they'll be dead. Your touch means their death. Your interest means their death. Knowing their names, looking in their eyes, hearing their voices means their death. And they can expect nothing else, for they are slaves and their only life is to serve your need. To make you strong. To make you worthy to be a Lord of Zhev'Na. Cruel lessons for a child of eleven. Ones I'd learned all too well.

"He condemns himself," said the girl, raising her knife. Dark eyes blazed in her sharp face.

The old Dar'Nethi's remaining eye searched my face, but I could not meet his gaze. Nor could I bring myself to ask the questions that came instantly to mind. How was it that he lived, when the Lords had purposely slain every one of my servants? How did he know of the scars on my hands, caused by an event that happened months after he'd vanished from my life? How had he been set free? I would have given my own eyes to hear that I'd had a hand in his salvation. But I had no right to ask him anything.

"You've used him ill, Jen," said the old man, softly.

"How can you say that? How can you care what harm comes to him—knowing what he is, what he's done? And I had no choice. I couldn't allow him to use his power."

"And did you not think to ask what's become of him? If he is a Lord, then why do you find him riding back and forth to this place and eating in a poor guesthouse in Gaelie? And how is it that we live, daughter, now he's looked upon us? How is it that he's allowed you to use him so and bind him to a tree in the rain?"

Her dark wet hair, hacked off ungracefully short, stuck to her brow and cheeks. She was neither ugly nor beautiful. The features of her small face were fine, but her jaw was sharp, her mouth slightly lopsided. The knife quivered in her hand, but not from fear. I was trained to smell fear. Her outrage was as palpable as the rain. "He can't look you in the eye, Papa."

"Do you think a Lord of Zhev'Na would have difficulty with that?"

"He can wear any face he wants. He must have some purpose in allowing me to take him; perhaps he thinks I'm too cowardly to kill him. He should be dead."

The old man laid a hand gently on the angry girl's shoulder. "He is what he is, daughter. If he is a Lord, you will not damage him, but will be drawn into his evil by your act. And if he is not, then you will bear the guilt of life-taking. I'll not allow it, certainly not for what was done to me. Not even for what was done to you and your mother and your brothers. Release him."

The girl shook off Sefaro's hand and glared at me, tapping the flat of her knife blade rapidly on her left palm. "This is for Avonar, not for me! The Zhid are raiding. He can't be allowed to make it all happen again. Someone has to know. At least we should go back to the hospice and tell the Lady D—"

"No!" I said sharply, jolted out of my silence by her words. I would attempt no explanation, no history or excuses or hollow words to tell one so grievously harmed that I hadn't meant to hurt him. I had no right. I was everything the woman named me. But mention of the Lady, and the sight of the hospice lights beyond the veils of rain where my father lay dead but not dead, forced me to speak. "Please," I said. "I am not . . . what I was."

The girl snorted.

"I don't expect you to believe me. But others whom you might believe would tell you that it could be of mortal importance that the Lady D'Sanya not know who I am."

"Lies! Listen to the flow of them. Why would we believe anyone you would name?"

"Please listen, sir." Though I addressed Sefaro, I could not bring myself to call him by name again. "In your last days in . . . that house . . . where we lived, a woman came to you, a Drudge, and she told you of a boy I'd wounded, hoping you could see to him, and she asked questions that you believed no Drudge would ask. You obtained a transfer of duty for her, so that she would be close to me. Do you remember her?"

Sefaro stepped closer, peering at my face with his soft brown eye. "Eda, the sewing woman."

"You told her I was not evil. Not yet."

"She said that if she could be close to you, she might prevent it."

"Because of you trusting her, helping her, she was able to do what she said."

The girl stepped forward to stand at Sefaro's shoulder. Her hands were small like the rest of her, but they gripped her long-bladed dagger securely. "And that was before he sent you away, Papa, where they burned out your eye for having looked on the young Lord and before they stuck a hook in your back and hung you up like a haunch of beef to teach others to fear the vile beast."

"Hush, child. This Eda was an extraordinary woman. I never forgot her. She wanted to tell me her secret, but I said better not. I knew what was to come. To kill anyone close to him, to make everyone fear him, to keep him alone . . . these were their plan for him. All could see it."

"She never forgot you either. She told me everything . . . later, when I could understand it."

"Who was she? I've always wanted to know."

"She was . . . is . . . my mother."

"Papa! This is madness to listen!"

"No, child. You didn't know the woman. If anyone—"

"But I did see her. You forget, I was there! I watched her weep as he was changed. I saw him step out of the Great Oculus with no human eyes left, and I saw them melt the sword across his palms. I saw him in a gold mask with jeweled eyes just like the others, and I'll never forget it. He is one of them, and they said on that day that there was no going back."

How was it possible? She could be no older than I, which meant she could have been no more than twelve when I was changed.

As if she heard my question, she stepped closer and pulled down the high neck of her tunic to show the angry red scar about her neck. Her eyes glinted in the lamplight. "Surely you remember, young Lord. Usually they didn't make slaves of Dar'Nethi children. They would kill them or bleed them for power or the few special ones they would corrupt. But if it gave them pleasure to torment a particularly powerful Dar'Nethi, one who held great honor before his capture—a Speaker perhaps—then they would seek out his children whatever their age, and they would make him witness their collaring. They would make sure the children were put to work close enough that he could see them often, never able to speak, never able to help, never able to touch them or ease their pain and fear. Surely you remember your pleasures, Lord."

I remembered. It was the first time I ever fixed the seal on Dar'Nethi slave collars, the first time I'd listened to their screams as half of their hearts were ripped away. I had sealed three that night, two boys in their teens and a small, dark-haired girl. The Lord Ziddari had told me the Dar'Nethi forced their children to fight in the war, and Lord Parven told me how those children could kill our warriors with their enchantments just like adults could, so they must be treated like adults as a lesson to their people who used them so. I had done it. And I'd never known the three were Sefaro's children. The girl had served in my house for a time, but I'd never heard her speak, never allowed it, never looked at her when she drew my bath or laid out my clothes. . . .

I closed my eyes and fought to keep from vomiting the bile that churned in my stomach. I didn't want to remember. I'd tried so hard not to remember.

"Release him, daughter. I think your knife can do no worse than your tongue has done. And you—whoever you are now—as a price of our silence, I would like my daughter to meet your mother. She is not here in the hospice?"

"She resides in Avonar at the house of the late Preceptor, Gar'Dena." I could scarcely squeeze words past my sickness. "She cannot come here. For the same reasons—"

"—that the Lady cannot know of your past."

I nodded.

"And the one here? Who lies in the hospice and draws you here?" He suspected what I would say. His eye was wide, his lips parted in anticipation. My slaves had known of my parentage.

Secrecy was vital, but I could offer Sefaro nothing but truth. "My father lies here, the man known in this world as the Prince D'Natheil, believed dead these five years. He is dying now, but has returned to Avonar to perform one last service for his people."

"Vasrin's hand! And does the Lady know this? Or anyone?"

I shook my head. "The Lady does not know, and must not know. Not yet. Only two or three others . . . and now you and your daughter."

"There is a tale here."

"A complicated tale. On the grace of my mother and the honor of my father, I swear to you that we work for the safety of Gondai."

The old man bobbed his head in return, then turned his back to me. "Release him, daughter. Whatever harvest he must reap for what he has been and done, it is far beyond you and me."

With an explosion of disgust, the girl sliced through the ropes, nearly taking a few of my fingers with them. She whispered in my ear with a spit of hatred. "I won't forget. Justice will be done." Or perhaps it was only in my head that I heard it. Then she untethered her horses, and took her father's arm, and with no more word, they headed off toward the hospice lights and soon vanished into the night.

As for me, I huddled alone in the shelter of the tree through a very dark midnight, waiting for my vision to clear and the blood to return to my arms and legs. The cold rain fell for hours.

CHAPTER 8

"You were fortunate to be given a chance to speak," said my father when I explained my shopworn appearance on the next morning. "Seeing that bruise makes my own head hurt."

"If the choice had been left to the woman, the earth would have split in half before I'd have said anything," I said.

I'd only told him an abbreviated version of the night's encounter: how I'd been recognized and assaulted by a woman who had been captive in Zhev'Na, that I'd managed to convince her father to withhold judgment and keep our secret, at least for now. My father would guess there was more, but it wasn't his way to push. I just couldn't bring myself to talk about it.

"I'll watch my back a little closer from now on," I said.

We strolled along a tree-shaded lane that led from the main house to a fenced paddock where the Lady D'Sanya's horses grazed. Though the hour was still early, the sun had already sapped the previous day's moisture and glittered hot through the leaves. When we came to the edge of the shade, our steps slowed.

A horse cantered through the paddock gate on its far side. No mistaking the well-formed gray or the rider's cloud of pale hair.

"I'm not very good at this investigating business," I said, pausing to watch her. "I want to march up and ask her straight off what she's up to."

"You don't think it remotely possible the Lady could be as she claims?"

"She lived in Zhev'Na for more than three years before she was enchanted to sleep. No, I don't believe she could be untouched by it. She was amazed that I'd told you what I'd experienced, and she seems to assume that . . . forgiveness . . . is necessary for anyone who was there. She was not a slave. So what did she do that needs forgiving? That's the key."

As I resumed walking down the path that led past the paddock, my father didn't move from his position in the shade. "I think I'll go back," he called after me. "I want to finish a letter to your mother, and I think the Lady might be inclined to be more sociable without me."

I waved, walked on to the paddock, and soon found myself hanging over the white painted fence, admiring the way D'Sanya slipped from her mount so gracefully and catching her unguarded expression when she turned and saw me. Her face took on a certain brightness, an indescribable clarity. How could such a look, not even a smile, please me so well?

Think, fool. She is of Zhev'Na. It is impossible . . . impossible . . . that she is what she seems.

"Master Gerick! How is it I find you here alone? Is your father well?"

"He claims he's getting lazy and hasn't finished a letter he wants me to take to a friend, so he's sent me off on my own."

Her horse snuffled and crunched an apple she pulled from her pocket. After patting his nose and stroking his neck, she turned him over to a groom who had hurried out from the stables. Then she walked over to the fence. She wore a tan riding skirt, tan boots, and a filmy, wide-sleeved shirt that was either blue or green, depending on the angle of the light. When she stretched out her arm in my direction, I believed she'd read my thoughts and was allowing me to see more of the long pale limb the slightest breeze left bare, but eventually her arched eyebrow and her boot on the fence rail penetrated my thick head.

She laughed as I gave her a hand to climb over. But when she stood before me in the lane, a quick sobriety clouded her face in the way thin sheets of vapor mute the sun. Her fingers twined in a knot at her breast, as if she couldn't quite decide what to say next and didn't like her choices. "I must apologize for my rudeness the other evening," she said at last. "I hope your father was not offended."

"Not in the least. Just a bit—"

"Curious, I suppose."

"I won't deny it. You didn't know he'd been a slave. But you hadn't asked; we assumed there were others here." I clasped my gloved hands behind my back.

"Of course there are. Several others."

She started walking down the road toward the trees, her arms folded tightly now. I walked beside her, not offering my arm. She was no wilting flower, and I needed to keep my wits about me.

"Their slave-taking was so despicable, so wretched." Her head and shoulders moved tautly with each word. "Amidst all their cruelties, it was so absolutely evil. When I see the scars, it makes me feel— I don't know how to describe it."

"Guilty? For having escaped it?"

She glanced up at me sharply, her eyes almost on a level with mine. "Of course. That's it. Yes. I should have known I didn't have to explain it to you."

"My father was in such pain before he came here that he couldn't move, couldn't think, could scarcely speak. You've helped him a great deal."

"And I'm glad of it. But I wish so very much . . ."

". . . that you could go back and change what happened in Zhev'Na. Because those horrors make illness such as his so unfair after what he's suffered already."

"Exactly." Her steps paused, and she crinkled her nose at me. "Do you read thoughts?"

"As little as possible."

"Then it must be that you have the same ones as I."

"I wouldn't wish them on you," I said, resuming our stroll into the trees. "Or anyone." This was not easy banter between us. Not with the ache in my head and shoulders to remind me, and the depths of sadness in her words. Talking seemed easier when we kept moving.

Unfolding her arms, she clasped her hands behind her as if to mimic me. "There's much to be said for sharing these experiences as we do. We can move on to other topics without having to dredge them up and explain."

"What other topics?" Perhaps I was at last going to hear what I needed to hear.

The dappled sunlight teased at her face and shifted the color of her silken shirt to deep purple and blue. Suddenly she stopped walking again and tugged at my arm, forcing me around to face her. "Remembering how to enjoy ourselves," she said. "I think that would be a marvelous beginning. I would state unhesitatingly that you've near forgotten it."

Without meaning to do it, I burst out laughing at such foolish words so seriously spoken. She was so unexpected. "Conceded," I said.

She threw up her hands, more animated by the moment. "I've been so involved in explaining myself, being tested, dragging Archivists about to dig up ruins of my lifetime, and trying to do some good with the gifts holy Vasrin has shaped in me, that I've not had time to remember what I was doing when I was fourteen . . . before the world changed. I know that life was wonderful, and I enjoyed it immensely. But I seem to have lost the skill. So I need to relearn it, and you must relearn it along with me."

"I don't think I ever knew how. I was only ten. . . ." And had lived in terror since I was five years old, when my nurse discovered that I was a sorcerer in a world where sorcerers were burned alive, even if they were five.

"Exactly so! The Preceptors and a hundred town guilds clamor that I must assume my father's throne right away, that it is my duty, my 'heritage,' even though the good Prince Ven'Dar is much loved and admired. But I've put them off. I've told them that I need to learn of the world as it is now and to grow accustomed to being free again. I intend to permit no distraction, not even the throne of Avonar, until I've recaptured the pleasures of being fourteen and grown up to my duties." As if to prove her point, she climbed up on a stone half-pillar, one of a pair like those that marked the roadside all up and down the lane between the paddock and the gardens.

I didn't know what to say to such things. Fortunately, she didn't seem to expect me to say anything, but pointed to the ground in front of her perch, saying "here, here" until I moved to the spot she wanted. Once I was in place, she stood tall with her hands on her hips, looking me up and down. "No child—certainly no girl of fourteen—can exist without a best and dearest bosom friend. I think you'll do nicely . . ."

"Me?"

". . . though before we begin, you must tell me what you've done to yourself. You look as if you've had a disagreement with a bull and a hay fork!" With one finger, she turned my head to the left where she could get a better view of my bruised forehead and the myriad abrasions that extended from eye to jawbone.

"A clumsy encounter with the floor of the Gaelie stables," I said, stepping back as if she might learn the cause of my injuries by touching them. "Embarrassing mostly."

"Hmm . . . so I must pry it out of you as part of our relearning how to be children. Ten-year-old boys are not so easily embarrassed. Tell me, what do ten-year-old boys enjoy? Ah, I've got it. . . ." And before I could answer, she hopped down from the stoop and darted into the woods. The shifting colors of her clothes made her disappear so effectively, I might have thought she was nothing but the laughing voice that echoed through the trees, calling out, "Hide-and-seek . . . and you're seeker!"

I stood stupidly in the lane, trying to decide if it would better suit my purpose to indulge her whimsy or wait for her to give it up. But I concluded that I wasn't going to get any information if I wasn't with her, so I took off through the noonday woodland, stopping every so often to listen and search for her path. She was very good at moving quietly, only occasional bursts of giggling giving her away, and she was very fast. But she knew nothing about covering her tracks, so it was only a matter of staying on her trail and waiting for her to pause too long.

Only at the end did she succeed in throwing me off, when I strode through knee-high stems of fading mayapples and wood-sorrel to the center of a sunlit glade, losing her trail beneath the canopy of a monstrous oak that stood there alone. I listened, but heard nothing. I crouched down to examine the faint trail of crushed grass that ended so abruptly. She must have used some sorcery to hide herself. Or else . . .

I looked upward and a small hard missile bounced off my head. I caught the second one. An acorn. Ten more followed the first in quick succession.

"I thought I won the game if I caught you," I said, peering into the branches over my head, thinking I saw a shifting blue-green tunic somewhere in the leaves. "Not fair to attack."

"But you've not caught me yet. There's a chance I can drive you away with my weapons. And you are down there, and I am up here."

"Easily remedied, if that's what it takes," I said and swung up to the low-hanging branch that had given her entry to the tree.

"There, you see? You know how it's done. You just have to work to remember the rules."

She scrambled up higher in the tree. I followed until we were perched on the last two branches that could possibly hold our weight, a height that left us far above the roof of the woodland, able to see across the leafy green sea to the meadows and mountains, sharp-edged and clean in the morning light.

"Is this not a marvelous tree? I think we should stay up here until sunset," she said. "How long has it been since you were in such a joyful place as this?" Sunbeams danced in her eyes, and her cheeks were colored a deep rose.

"Forever." The answer had formed itself unbidden. I grasped feebly at my purpose. "So what is my prize for finding you?"

She pulled off two leaves, colored the bright green of new growth, and curled them in her fingers. "I'll have to think on that. Boys always have to win and get their prize, don't they? Whether at games or stories. With ten-year-old boys, winning at hide-and-seek is a matter of life's breath."

"I suppose."

"The palace in Avonar was the most delicious place to play hide-and-seek. My brothers and I knew every crack and crevice of it. Even better, D'Leon was a Word Winder, and even at thirteen, he could cast windings that made us invisible to each other, so we had to hunt through all five hundred rooms using only hearing and smell. Once D'Alleyn hid in my father's council chambers during a very serious meeting. D'Leon and I found him just at the same time, and chased him out from under the council table and around the columns and in and out of the room. Imagine ten pompous sorcerers remarking on the change of seasons causing such a disturbance in the air, assuring each other it wasn't evil spirits or evil omens for the times to come.

"But Papa knew exactly what it was, and he sent us to our country house for a month with our tutors commanded to teach us proper deportment, which we thought very cruel. My uncle J'Ettanne told me later, though, that Papa laughed himself to tears at the memory of his hoary-headed counselors looking for evil auras and portents when it was only three children playing hide-and-seek. It was one of our best family legends."

She sprawled out on the length of her branch like a cat stretching, and propped her head on her hand as if prepared to stay there forever. "Now you must tell me of times when you would play hide-and-seek. I know it's still done; children's games do not change over the centuries."

"I wasn't much for games," I said. "I've no brothers or sisters, and we lived remotely, so other children

weren't about very often. My father was away. The war
and all. And my mother . . . I lost my mother when I was
small. I spent most of the time alone or with my nurse."

"So you have no family legends, no games to tell of?
That's so very sad!"

Her expression revealed such shocked sympathy that
I found myself trying to soothe her by spewing out
words. "Well actually, my mother had one story about
playing hide-and-seek in our house . . . the house I grew
up in. Though not so cheerful an outcome as yours, I
suppose. Maybe I shouldn't spoil—"

"No. Now you've started, you must tell the story."

"When my mother was very young, she was playing
with her brother and his friends, and hid herself in an
old cupboard deep in the cellars. The others abandoned
the game without telling her, and she couldn't get out of
the cupboard. She'd been told so many stories of wicked
monsters who hunted naughty children in the dark that
she was too frightened to make a sound, and it was two
days until she was found. It wasn't until she met my
father that she could bear being in a dark confined space
again. My father says it was the only thing she was ever
afraid of."

It wasn't exactly the humorous story she'd told, but I
didn't think it was so awful that it would make her turn
pale. The light and shadow were so tricky, I thought
perhaps I was mistaken. Whatever her judgment of my
tale, she didn't say, but instead, with movement faster
than I could grasp, she shinnied her way down through
the tree branches and dropped lightly to the turf. "I'll
race you back to the house." As she disappeared into
the trees across the glade, she cried over her shoulder,
"The loser has to tell a secret!"

I dropped through the branches, getting well tangled
and scratched, half cursing at her foolery. Though I told
myself I only entered the race to win her secret and
keep her out of mine, I would have run after her even
without the promise of a prize.

Three fences and D'Sanya's loose apparel yielded me
the victory. She had long legs, and ran with the speed

and grace of the fell-deer on the Comigor heath, but my legs were longer, and I could leap the fences without slowing or catching my garments on the fence rails. I was sitting on the garden fence, trying not to appear winded, when she collapsed on the grass just beside it five heartbeats behind me.

"I'm out of practice," she said cheerfully, between deep lungfuls of the hot air. "Give me two weeks and a man's breeches, and I'll leave you gasping in the meadow."

"No doubt of it," I said, grinning at her. "You'd have had me today except for the fences. But I'll claim my prize anyway."

"Hmm . . . a secret. Let me think." She closed her eyes and pushed up her floating sleeves to bare her arms. By the time she spoke again, I'd almost forgotten what I was waiting for.

"I have it!" She popped her eyes open and sat up, and I did my best not to fall off the rail. "It's nagged at me ever since I began hearing everyone speaking of my father with such reverence. D'Arnath—the epitome of a kingly ruler, the symbol of all nobility, the savior of his world. One would think him a candidate for godhood! But—now this is for you alone, my play friend—what would everyone think if they knew that holy King D'Arnath was an inveterate card cheat? He hated to lose more than anything in the world, and even when he would sit in on our children's games, we'd find him slipping a card from his sleeve, or fingering the pile of them, using sorcery to discover the sword trump or whatever he wanted. What do you think of that?"

I could do nothing but laugh.

"Next race, when I win, I shall expect an equally scandalous confession from you, sir!" she said. Then she jumped up from the grass, grabbed my arm, and dragged me into her house.

I spent the rest of the day with her. We ate fruit and drank wine. We unpacked three crates of books she'd had shipped from Avonar, and I climbed up and down the steps in her library five hundred times, commanded to admire each volume and place it exactly where she wanted. Among the new books was a folio of drawings of Dar'Nethi ruins in the most ancient corner of the city. She held that one aside until our tasks were finished, and then spent two hours on the carpeted floor showing it to me, telling me what the places had been like when she knew them, and where the Archivists who'd done the sketches had guessed wrong.

Na'Cyd came in frequently to seek D'Sanya's advice or opinion about some matter of business—food supplies, painters, two possible candidates for admission—but she put him off each time. Each time the aristocratic consiliar bowed gracefully and retired without comment or sign of annoyance. When the angle of the light falling through the tall windows told me evening was near, I mumbled something about her having business to attend to. ". . . and I need to bid my father good night and start down the road to Gaelie."

D'Sanya pushed me back to the floor. "You shall do no such thing. Na'Cyd can see to all my business; he is very wise and needs to assert himself more. As for you, I have decided on your prize for winning the game of hide-and-seek—a picnic supper. I've already given orders as to its contents and delivery, and I really must insist."

Then she left me for a while, saying she was going to change her clothes and rid herself of the dust from the book crates and our adventures in the woods. She offered to send for fresh attire for me, but I said I would look in on my father and perhaps borrow something of his. We agreed to meet in the library in an hour.

As I set out through the garden doors, taking a short-cut to my father's apartments, I stumbled over a small pair of boots sticking out from under the barberry hedge just to the left of the garden doors. The boots were attached to someone's legs. "I'm sorry," I said. "I didn't see you." Before I could glimpse a face, the person scrambled away into the thick greenery. I saw only the

lurker's back. Slight. Dark hair, cut short and ragged.
Was it Sefaro's daughter, keeping an eye on me? I
walked more slowly after that and kept my eyes open.

My father was standing on the little terrace outside
his sitting room, staring into the blue-gray haze that had
settled over the rim of the valley. It took several greetings to catch his attention.

"Can't say what I was dreaming about," he said as he
rummaged through his clothes chest and pulled out a
clean shirt. "Nothing of importance. Your day must have
been more interesting than mine, especially if it isn't
done yet, and you need a change of clothes."

I sponged myself off and changed into my father's full-
sleeved white cambric shirt. Made before he fell ill, it
hung large on me. As I tucked it into my breeches and
grabbed a brush to clean up my boots, I told him of the
day and how we had not spoken a single word of substance since the Lady's apology when I first met her.
"Maybe this evening I can get some answers."

"So she feels guilt when faced with evidence of slavery, yet she was herself a prisoner."

"When we went riding, she said she'd been a prisoner
for three years and was 'enchanted' when they tired of
her. She claims to know nothing of the years between
then and now."

"That may be exactly the truth. Just because her enchantment has this . . . deadening . . . effect does not
mean the woman is evil. Perhaps she's just inexpert in
the use of her power. She was so young when she was
taken."

"She lived in Zhev'Na and wore no collar," I said.
The glimpse of Sefaro's daughter had sobered me con-
siderably. "Her father was the first and most bitter
enemy of the Lords. I'll not believe her uncorrupted
until I hear what happened in those three years. Perhaps
if I consent to this game of hers, I'll get the chance. But
I never imagined this business would involve playing
hide-and-seek or climbing trees."

My father smiled and straightened my collar. "Sounds
as if you'd best get in some running practice, too."

"She's unbelievably fast. I've never imagined a woman could come close to catching me at full speed. And when she rides . . ." I pressed my hands to my eyes and tried to get her image out of my head before I started babbling about how the sun caused her skin to glow golden when she lay in the grass. "I wish we could just get to business, and get it over with. I keep thinking of how the Singlars are getting on; we have so much to do yet. I need to get back. And you're trapped here. Damnation! She can't be what she seems, but I can't get her to speak anything but nonsense."

"Don't be in too much hurry. Ven'Dar still has five months. You've taught your Singlars to care for themselves, and L'Tiere will not vanish before I get there. I doubt I am any more dead here than I will be there. Whatever else she may be, I think the Lady has judged you wisely. It might be very good for you to learn how to enjoy yourself a bit." With a clap on the shoulder, my father shoved me out the door.

CHAPTER 9

The full moon had moved across a quarter of the sky by the time D'Sanya and I arrived at our picnic supper high in the foothills beyond the hospice. The world was so quiet as we walked up the light-washed path, I might have believed no soul existed but the two of us. The path leveled out and in twenty steps more we emerged from the scattered trees and rocks into a grassy meadow. In the center of the meadow, looking like a patch of snow left lingering into summer, sat a low table covered with a white cloth and carefully placed silver spoons and crystal wine goblets. Whoever had set out the plates of roast fowl, the bowls of cherries and plums, the hot, cinnamon-dusted pastries, and the chilled wine was nowhere in evidence.

D'Sanya took off her sandals and looped them over one of her silver-ringed fingers as we walked through the springy grass and took our places on cushions set on either side of the table. Candles in silver holders sat in the center of the table, but we didn't light them. The moon bathed the meadow in light.

"Did I not promise a prize worth the winning?" D'Sanya was laughing at me as I marveled at the perfection of each delicacy I loaded on my plate. "What use to be a princess of the Dar'Nethi if one cannot bring something more to the table than meat and bread? Since I've used my talents for one *useful* thing tonight, I'm now entitled to use them for something frivolous."

The useful thing she'd done had been to heal my lame horse, who now grazed peacefully far below us at the lower end of the moonlit path. We had ridden from the stableyard across the valley to find the stone marker that would indicate our path into the hills. Impatient, I refused to follow the track the long way around and took off across the grass, racing to beat D'Sanya to the path. Halfway across the valley floor, my horse reaped the worst consequence of nighttime riding. His shoulders and head dipped suddenly. As he stumbled to a halt with an ear-shattering shriek, I felt, more than heard, the ominous dry-wood snap of a slender bone. I leaped from the saddle and rolled quickly out of the way, cursing all rabbits, gophers, and blind, stupid riders.

D'Sanya had circled back while I tried to comfort the wild-eyed beast who struggled to his feet, tossing his head and snorting painfully as he tried to put weight on his right foreleg. Paulo would yell at me unmercifully— and deservedly—for ruining a fine mount for an evening's pleasure.

"Are you injured?" asked D'Sanya.

I reached for the quivering beast's neck but he shied and tossed his head. "Unbruised. But Nacre . . . I'm afraid I've done for him."

"Take care of it quickly, then, before the poor creature goes mad."

Take care of it? What was she thinking? That I'd slit the poor beast's throat, then wash my hands for dinner? "Not yet. If I could get a Horsemaster up here to see to him, we might be able to save him for breeding. He's a fine runner."

"Well, of course, I don't mean kill him! How can you let him suffer so? Surely you can take care of a horse's hurts."

My face blazed, and my insides churned. In ordinary times, I used my sorcerer's power not one day in thirty. That way, I was never required to grow my power beyond whatever happened to germinate in me on its own, just by the fact that I was born my father's son. The ways the Lords increased their power were grotesque and cruel, and I refused to use them any more. The ways of the Dar'Nethi were maddeningly slow and impossible to master; my feeble attempts to use them did little but cause an unhealthy craving in my blood. As I'd expended everything I had when I entered my father's body and tested him that morning, I had not a scrap of power left. No ordinary Dar'Nethi would live that way. Gathering power from the experiences of their lives was as compelling to them as breathing.

Well, she was going to find out sooner or later that I was no ordinary Dar'Nethi—not when it came to sorcery. "No, I can't."

"You can't? You mean you won't." She slipped from her horse, glaring at me. But when I failed to respond, her expression of indignant accusation softened into puzzlement. "No, you're saying that you don't have the power; and you don't summon it. Ever?"

"Not since Zhev'Na."

"Of course." She expelled a quick breath of sympathy. "Here, let me take care of the poor beast. Hold him still."

I grabbed the trailing reins, caught hold of the bridle, and held Nacre's head, trying to remember the things Paulo had told me could soothe a pain-maddened horse. But my efforts were unnecessary. D'Sanya touched Nacre between his eyes and whispered a few words, instantly quieting the animal. She had adorned every one of her fingers with a silver band, some plain, some intricately worked, and they glittered and shone in the moonlight as she ran her fingers over Nacre's leg from shoulder to hoof. The depth and intensity of her enchantment almost knocked me off my feet. Though it was over in an instant, I felt as if I'd been sucked up into the heart of a whirlwind and then set down again in the hospice pasture with all my joints put together in the wrong order.

"You were there when you came of age," she said, stroking the now-healthy horse's nose, patting his neck, and fondling his ears, soothing his lingering agitation. "I've heard it said that those who came of age in Zhev'Na have difficulty developing power and never find

their true talent, but I thought that was only those who
were slaves. Crippled as they were . . ."

"I don't know about others. For me, it's impossible."

"Heaven's lights, how do you bear it?"

I was thankful she didn't wait for an answer, or ask
for more specific details, like the nature of my true talent
or whether I even had one. Better for her to assume I
could do nothing. To reveal my true talent was to reveal
my identity, for the only Soul Weaver known to the
Dar'Nethi was the corrupted son of Prince D'Natheil
who was supposed to be safely dead.

She spoke no more of sorcery as we tethered the
horses in a grassy glade and walked up the path. Perhaps
she thought it would bother me to consider the immen-
sity of her own gifts when I professed to have none. I
could think of no subtle way to ask her if she had always
possessed such power or if it was somehow grown larger
since her awakening, so I just listened to her chatter,
which took up again where it had left off.

All through our supper D'Sanya talked of one thing
and another: of her two older brothers, the quiet, serious
D'Leon who had succeeded D'Arnath and then fallen in
battle with the Zhid after only five years, and the wild,
mischievous D'Alleyn who had completed the Gates to
his father's Bridge between the worlds. "You can't imagine how it is to read of my brothers in manuscripts so
ancient they would crumble were it not for the Archivists' enchantments, when it seems only a few years since
they filled my bedchamber with birds on my sixteenth
birthday. To hear that D'Leon died so young and so
valiantly and that D'Alleyn, the wicked tease, ruled with
wisdom for fifty years. I do miss them so."

Then she went on to talk of the hospice, and her plans
to build a second one in the Vale of Maroth far to the
south. "Na'Cyd has three Builders working already. I'll
need to visit the site soon to see how they progress.
They argue a great deal over the design, and I speak to
one and think the matter settled, then another one sends

me a letter telling me the faults of the first, and the third
sends a message threatening to abandon the project if I
can't persuade the other two that arches should be
sealed by a Word Winder to ensure their strength. All
I want is for the building to be completed so I can help
more people. Enough have applied to me in the past
few weeks that I could fill the place already."

"I know exactly what you mean," I said. "The one
who conceives the shape of the building gets insulted
when the one who must lay the bricks says you can't lay
bricks in such a shape. The builder is incensed when the
artist says a better builder could find a way. I've had to
lock them in a room—" I stopped abruptly when I realized what I was doing . . . talking about the Bounded,
which she must not know of.

When my father had taken me out of Zhev'Na through
the Breach, I had submerged myself in the chaotic matter
of the rift between the worlds to escape the pain of separating from the Lords. Somehow, my act had imposed
shape and coherence where there had been none before.
My strange little kingdom would not exist had I not been
a Soul Weaver linked to the Lords of Zhev'Na, had I
not been desperate enough to do anything to separate
myself from them. And my subjects—the Singlars—had
given me just such problems as D'Sanya's as we rebuilt
their tower cities after the war with the Lords.

"Go on. Tell me more of your builders and bricklay-
ers," she said, leaning across the table, lips parted, eyes
shining. "You've said so little of your life. Nothing of
what you do in ordinary times."

I shoved aside thoughts of the Bounded and the Singlars. "Nimrolan Vale is so remote that, in the years of
the war, we had to make sure we could defend ourselves
if the war came to us. For centuries we crowded together
in horrid, cramped towns, everyone on top of one another. So we're trying to replace what we have with
more scattered dwellings, less fortified, open to our
woodlands, the way things once were. I've been
helping. . . ."

Concentrating on the story that Ven'Dar and I had

contrived should the question of my profession ever come up, I evidently said something that convinced D'Sanya I had led a building project such as hers, which of course I had.

I tried to change the subject—I hated lying to her—but she would not let it go. "You must come with me when next I go to Maroth," she said, clapping her hands in delight so that her ten rings glittered. "Na'Cyd has no skill at negotiating. He only makes them argue the more. You can settle their disputes and get the new hospice built for me."

I had no intention of staying in Avonar so long or becoming involved in her projects. Yet it was not a night for arguing. Again D'Sanya was dressed all in white, a loose filmy gown that fell to her ankles. Still barefoot, she wore a slender band of diamonds about one ankle. One side of her pale hair was held back with a diamond clip, while the other curled about her face and brushed at her long, slender neck. Her diamonds might have been stars for all I knew, just as her flesh might have been shaped of moonlight as she held out a glass of wine the color of rubies. At that moment I could have refused her nothing.

"Drink to our pact," she said. "Together we shall recapture the years that were taken from us, and learn again the delights of living free."

I touched my glass to hers. *"J'edai en j'sameil,"* I said in the ancient tongue of the Dar'Nethi, D'Sanya's tongue. It was a traditional Dar'Nethi feasting wish I had learned from my mother, but I was not thinking of my mother as I said it.

"To life and beauty!" Her delight, as she echoed my words, showered on me like sunbeams. "Oh, friend, is it not a magnificent night? The skies of Avonar are marvelously familiar, far more than the people or the cities or even the land itself, which are all as strangers to me. My brothers and I would often sneak out of the palace at night. We loved packing up food and wine and creeping through the city and out into the countryside to have a moonlight adventure. Or we would climb the terrifying stair to the top of Skygazer's Needle—ancient even in our day—and pretend we were looking through the moonstones that revealed the secret movements of all worlds. The city was much smaller then, of course, and unguarded, for the walls were not built until I was older, just after I turned fourteen." Her voice faltered as her chatter led her to this less comfortable place.

"What happened?" I said, pouncing as if I'd seen the first breach in an enemy's wall. "Tell me, Lady. I want to know you."

"Ah, no. You first," she said softly, holding me with her eyes and a smile that had turned wistful. "A secret for a secret. It is part of our game. You agreed."

I nodded, my mind racing ahead, shaping my story for simplicity . . . and safety . . . as near truth as I could make it. "It was an old acquaintance of my parents," I began. "He was turned, and in his enmity chose to torment my parents by turning me. He carried me away to Zhev'Na, gave me a house and weapons and horses and slaves, and treated me as a man instead of a child. He twisted truth into such knots that he made me believe I belonged in Zhev'Na, that I was the cause of all the wickedness I had witnessed in my life, that I had no choices left to me. And then he began my training . . ."

I lay back on the white cushions and fixed my eyes, not on the moon, but on the cold darkness behind it, and I told her of my days in the desert where I learned how to flay a man, and what sound it made when taking a prisoner's eyes, where I listened to the music of Dar'-Nethi screams and the death rattle of empty-eyed warriors, where I studied the manifold aspects of death and suffering and excelled at my lessons. As trailing wisps of cloud drifted past the stars, I told her of my sword training, where young Dar'Nethi slaves and Zhid warriors were brought in for me to perfect the techniques of slaughter.

I kept thinking, *Fool, you've told enough. Now stop.* But I couldn't stop. She would understand my tale as no one I had ever met possibly could. I drank another glass of wine, and the story poured out of me, of how I learned to gather power from hatred and vileness as the Zhid would do, and that to interest myself in my servants or my soldiers or my tutors was to sign their death warrant, so that I came to be what the Zhid had planned for me to be—unfeeling and alone. I told her the part I had never been able to tell my parents or Paulo—of how it felt to watch my soul die, like a paper that when thrown in the fire chars and curls and withers into ash.

She said nothing as I spoke. Though the food grew heavy in my stomach, I forced myself to remember the horror I had left in my wake, renewing my loathing and revulsion for the life I had tried so hard to put behind me. And even then the things I told her were not all. Not the worst things. I didn't mention the spinning brass ring—the oculus, the instrument that enabled me to channel the horrors of two worlds into my empty soul to grow the power I craved—or the jewels in my ear that gave the Lords constant access to my mind, so that my training was at the hands of the masters themselves. And I did not reveal that I had at last become one of them, profoundly evil, and holding a universe of wickedness in my scarred hands.

But I told her a great deal, ending my story by telling her that my father had risked his life in Zhev'Na to steal me away again and how he had healed what he could of my injuries and convinced me that, no matter what I had done or believed as a child, I was not destined to be a monster. I could still choose my own path in the world.

When I was done, feeling exhausted, empty, and far calmer than I had expected, I sat up and poured more wine. D'Sanya sat with her knees drawn up and her arms wrapped about them, staring down at the grass. I filled her glass and offered it to her, wondering if revulsion at my tale would bring the evening to an abrupt end. But all she said was, "Poor, poor child. What evil can compare to corrupting a child?" Then she fell quiet again.

"Now it's your turn," I said. "You can't leave me out here alone . . . so exposed. That's not a fair game."

She lifted her glass and gazed into it, then took a sip and set it down, never looking at me once.

"I was fourteen when the event you call the Catastrophe occurred. I've told Prince Ven'Dar, and the Preceptors, and the Archivists of what it was like to see two-thirds of the world go up in flames, the forests reduced to ash, the cities and villages ruined, rivers left dry in a matter of days, whole kingdoms vanished in a few weeks, thousands upon thousands of people dead or driven mad or transformed into these soulless Zhid. I was young and living in Avonar, so I survived it, and I had no doubt that my father the king would put it all back to rights. But I saw my father weep as he sifted the ashes of the twelve kingdoms of Gondai through his fingers. By the time of my sixteenth birthday, he and his dear cousin J'Ettanne were at work on their plan to restore the world before all Dar'Nethi power was lost forever.

"I rarely saw my father after he began work on the Bridge, or my brothers who toiled beside him. He sent me away from Avonar to our house in Kirith Vale. My mother had died of illness when I was five, and everyone I knew was either dead or at work on the defenses of Avonar, so I was left alone with the bodyguards my father had commanded to protect me. I chafed at being banished, and though I had not yet come into my talent, my father's power lived in me. I tried every way I knew how to convince my father to allow me to help with the Bridge. 'Too dangerous,' he said. 'Too risky. Too near the Breach.' He said he could not concentrate on his work if he thought I might fall prey to the madness that lurked in the Breach, and that at least one of his heirs must stay safe. As for my brothers . . . well, they were older, and it was necessary that the people see young men labor alongside their king."

She laughed ruefully and lay down on her side, propping her head on her elbow. "Almost three years had passed since the Catastrophe. I told no one when I felt the stirrings of true talent at seventeen, and unbeknownst to anyone, I took a man named L'Clavor as mentor. I decided to develop my talents so quickly and to such a level that I would prove how wrong Papa was to leave me behind. I worked every hour of every day to master everything L'Clavor could teach me. One day in late spring he summoned me to his home for my lessons, saying that he could teach me advanced techniques only in his own workshop.

"My bodyguards would not allow me to go, so I sneaked out on my own and rode to L'Clavor's village. Naïve child that I was, I didn't notice how deserted were the lanes of the village. No one in the fields. No one in the shops. I was intent upon my own wishes. Foolish, proud, blind girl. Only when L'Clavor opened his door and I saw his eyes did I know how foolish I'd been. He was Zhid.

"I tried to run. I had protective wards with me . . . things L'Clavor and I had made. But they were not enough. Fifty Zhid were waiting to take me before the Lords . . . the Three. Perhaps you saw them while you were in Zhev'Na. Unnatural, monstrous beings they became, with faces half of flesh and half of beaten gold, and gemstones for eyes."

She paused for a long time, and I didn't know whether it would be better to keep silent or to encourage her to say more. But without anything from me, she took a deep breath and gave me a quick smile. "Though they were not yet masked when I first met them, I could feel them probing my heart, laying bare my soul, searching for any weapon to destroy all that I loved. I could tell them nothing of the Bridge or its construction or even where it was that my father and brothers labored; it made matters no easier to know my father had been right to keep it from me.

"Once their initial questioning was done, I was left alone—a bargaining token. I was installed in a windowless room, comfortable and safe. They would return me uncorrupted, unsullied, in exchange for my father's sworn word to stop work on the Bridge and to destroy whatever was completed of it. I knew he wouldn't do it. I cried myself to sleep every night, for my father believed that the Bridge was the only hope for our world or for the other . . . that strange, mundane place that lies on the other side of the Breach. He would never sacrifice so many for one foolish daughter, no matter how bitterly he grieved for her.

"I suppose I was fortunate that they had not yet learned the skills with which you were molded. Or perhaps because I was a girl, they were less sure of what to do with me. Perhaps they, too, held out the hope that my father would miraculously change character and relent, for it was an entire year that I lived alone and untouched in their citadel. Servants waited on me, and brought me materials for writing and drawing and for sewing my own clothing. I wrote long letters that were never sent, and drew endless pictures to remind myself of my true life. I was not prevented from wielding power, though it did me little good. I wasn't strong enough to combat the Three together. Only mind-speaking was forbidden, and they monitored me closely to make sure I obeyed.

"Every sevenday I was required to appear before the Three. They would examine me to make sure I'd had no secret communication with my father. And then they would tell me stories of him, every time a different one: he was dead, he was captive, Avonar had fallen, the Vales had burned, I was forgotten, I was named a traitor, I was named Zhid. . . . But I was not a child. I was D'Arnath's daughter and carried the strength and power of his blood. I refused to believe their lies.

"After a year of this, something changed. Perhaps my father convinced them he wouldn't bargain for me. Perhaps he tried to rescue me and failed; I liked to think it was that. Perhaps the Lords could no longer withhold their hatred. But there came a night when I was taken from my room and thrown into a filthy pen with the other Dar'Nethi prisoners. My hair was cut off, and I was given rags to wear. I was commanded to clean the quarters of the Zhid warriors, forbidden to speak, controlled with the lash. . . . Well, you know all those things.

"But unlike the other prisoners, once every moon's turning I was taken before the Three and offered release. They gave me three choices. I could lure my father into a trap. Or I could yield control of my mind to the Lords, and they would let me 'escape' so I could spy on him. Or I could renounce my father publicly and . . . consort . . . with one of the Lords to birth a rival to him. All these things I refused, and they could not force me without breaking my mind. Nothing could have persuaded me to betray the hope of the world."

Another deep breath and she sat up again, straightening her back and fixing her eyes on nothing that I could see. "So they devised another use for me." Now there was steel in her voice. "I was to test the loyalty of the Zhid officers. I must offer myself to whatever officer they put in my way, begging for my freedom in exchange for whatever he would want of me. If the officer agreed, they would slay him—sometimes right away, but more often after he had taken his part of our bargain. The Lords said they would tolerate no more refusals. They would slay five Dar'Nethi prisoners each time I disobeyed. And I would have to watch them do it.

"For month after month they forced me to do this . . . and other vile things . . . many other things like it. I could not sacrifice the lives of our people for anything less than the safety of Avonar. It was horrid and cruel. But I couldn't refuse. *You* can see that. *You* understand."

As the moon settled behind the notched mountains to the west, she waited for my answer.

"There was no honor to be had in Zhev'Na." My father had said those words to me a thousand times over.

D'Sanya nodded. "No. No honor. Always I chose the lesser evil. I told myself that for two long years. I would not turn. I would not betray my father or my brothers, and if they were driven to sacrifice me to save Dar'Nethi lives, I could do no less than they. Always the lesser evil . . . and pray that Papa would come to rescue me."

"But then it ended. What happened?"

Even with the steel foundation, her voice was shaking. Her gaze had lost focus again, telling me that she was reliving her horror just as I had. "I was taken before the Lords once again, to their throne room where the floor was like black ice and the roof was like the midnight sky. They were masked now, and their jeweled eyes gleamed hard and cold. They said they were finished with me. I was too 'expensive,' and as my father would be stubborn, he must be taught a lesson. I assumed I was to die and was glad of it. They told me terrible things, all their lies over again. Then they laughed until it violated my soul to hear it, and the world went dark . . . until I found myself wandering in the desert half a year ago."

"You remember nothing in between?"

"Nothing. No. Nothing."

She was lying. Perhaps it was only that I was so conscious of my own omissions that I could recognize it so easily. Every word she had spoken was truth—until the end. Not all of the truth, but at least no lies. But when she claimed to remember nothing between her last visit with the Lords and her release, the very timbre of her voice cried falsehood. I couldn't blame her.

We sat for a long time, letting the cooling breeze brush away the horrors we had spoken and replace them with the cries of night birds, the rustling of the trees that bounded our meadow, and the quiet ripple of a brook that traveled mindlessly from the meadow down the steep hillside. Then, with no more words, I rose and gave her my arm, and we abandoned the remnants of our feast and walked slowly down the path. Somewhere along the way my arm found its way about her waist, and somewhere along the way her head found its resting place on my shoulder, and we kept our darkest secrets, yet drew some kind of comfort from what truth we had shared. Even after we collected the horses, we chose to walk, parting at last in the stable yard. Only then did she speak. Softly. Lantern light brightening her eyes as if the moon had fallen into a mountain lake. "You'll come again tomorrow?"

I nodded. "But tomorrow, *I* choose the games."

CHAPTER 10

I was soon spending most of every day with the Lady D'Sanya. We rode. We walked. We picnicked in the hills. We ran races and told silly secrets. One magical afternoon we explored one of the caves that riddled the mountains of Grithna, D'Sanya casting a light so that we could follow the path to a milky-white underground lake. A forest of stalactites and stalagmites surrounded the lake, the shapes more fantastic than any sculptor could invent.

Some days we stayed at the hospice in D'Sanya's house or in the library or in the garden, looking at books or playing draughts. We tried playing sonquey, a game of strategy played with tiles and silver bars, but D'Sanya found it boring when I would not use enchantment to manipulate the tiles. She said that playing sonquey without the added dimension of sorcery made her feel like a child allowed to use building blocks only in the horizontal plane, forbidden to stack them one upon the other.

On none of these outings did we ever return to the horrors of our past. The secrets we exchanged were innocent and childish. She adored flavored ices and had stolen them from the kitchens before her father's royal feasts so there were never enough for the guests. I abhorred eating green things and had hidden them in my pockets for the washing women to find. She got abominably seasick. I had never kissed a girl. We both preferred being outdoors—riding or walking, running, or just sitting—to any other activity.

My father smiled as I dashed in to greet him and deliver the latest packet of letters Paulo had brought from
Avonar and then dashed out again before ever sitting
down. He insisted that he did not feel neglected, but
rather was pleased that I pursued my investigation with
such vigor. Of course, I had not forgotten our purpose.
We were close to an answer. I already knew more of
D'Sanya than I knew of anyone save Paulo.

Paulo worried more. He accused me of infatuation,
warning that my distraction would reap trouble. I told
him he was just jealous because his own infatuation was
going nowhere, but I did heed his warning and worked
harder to keep my head. That very day D'Sanya asserted
that my mysterious friend who could read horses'
thoughts didn't really exist and begged again to meet
him. Though tempted to agree—wanting to please her,
wanting to make things honest between us—I saw how
blatantly stupid was that idea. I told her he was busy,
taking care of my father's business in Avonar. Not a lie.
Not really.

I never allowed D'Sanya to see the scars on my hands.
Most of the time I wore gloves, claiming that a childhood illness had left my hands persistently cold. She
teased that it was just another aspect of my shyness. I
did not argue with her, just kept my palms out of sight
when gloves would not do. If she saw my scars, then,
like Sefaro's daughter, she would know I had been one
of the Lords. Every day it seemed more important that
she never find out. Whether she loathed the Lords or
served them, I would lose something I had never thought
to find.

D'Sanya teased me about Sefaro's daughter, as well,
saying she must be smitten with me the way she followed
me around. Had I perhaps rebuffed the young lady's
attentions? Professing ignorance, I changed the subject
quickly.

One evening as I was hurrying to meet D'Sanya, I
discovered I'd forgotten my cloak and reversed course
abruptly to return to my father's apartments. I slammed
right into Sefaro's daughter, grazing her shoulder against

a brick wall and stepping on her foot. I started to make a comment about us needing to mark our current positions on a map, but checked my tongue when I met her gaze. Of course, she wasn't going to appreciate levity. "Sorry," I said.

"What meaning can *sorry* have coming from you?" Along one fine cheekbone a ragged scar shone white against her angry flush.

I crowded along the hedge as I passed so as not to touch her again.

She lurked in the shrubbery, in the cloisters, in corners and shadows, her constant presence ensuring I didn't forget the past in the pleasures of the present. Though I tried to dismiss her, I never made the nighttime journey from the hospice to Gaelie without keeping a close watch for mountains ready to fall on my head.

D'Sanya and I spent one long, rainy afternoon in the library reading a book of Dar'Nethi legends. At sunset, Na'Cyd summoned us to dinner. Afterward, D'Sanya wished to take up the story again, so I returned to the library to fetch the book. Sefaro's daughter was leafing through the pages. Seeing me, she threw it on a table as if it had scorched her fingers. "How dare you read of Vasrin and beautiful things!" she said, her cheeks a fiery scarlet. "What are you playing at?"

As usual, I had no answer.

"Before we set out for Tymnath, I have a riddle for you, my play friend." D'Sanya dragged me up from the grass beneath an ash tree where I'd lain waiting for the past hour listening to locusts buzzing in the grass, unable to concentrate on my book for my impatience to be with her. A delicate strand of sapphires set in silver dangled from her wrist, the color matching the flowing tunic she wore atop her leather riding skirt. "Forgive my dawdling, but one of my gardeners—my *stone* gardener—was showing Na'Cyd and me the work he's just completed. Now I want to share it with you."

"*Stone* gardener? That sounds like a riddle itself."

"You'll see." Waving to the ever-present consiliar,

who stood watching us from the gate, D'Sanya led me
across her lawn, up the wide steps, and into her house.

"Does Na'Cyd ever do anything but watch us?" I had
found the consiliar's gray eyes fixed on me four times
that morning: as I arrived at the hospice, as I left my
father's apartments, as I met D'Sanya in her garden, and
now again, when he ought to be off about hospice business. "I'm beginning to see him lurking in my sleep."

"Pay him no mind. I believe the man considers himself
my substitute father, ready to protect me from mysterious handsome fellows who constantly distract me from
my work."

Beyond the sunny sitting room where we talked and
played children's games lay an enclosed garden, lush and
green. It included three apple trees, a small lawn, a
gravel walk lined with beds of flowers, but its heart was
a magical fountain where spraying water sculpted the
misty shape of three swans taking flight from the pool.
On my every other visit to this garden, the solid gate in
the stone wall on its far side had been closed and locked.
D'Sanya had told me it was a part of the house construction that remained unfinished. But on this morning the
gate stood open, and the Lady motioned me to walk
through, into a small courtyard. I gaped in amazement.

Before us lay almost the exact replica of the green
garden behind us, but in this courtyard, every flower and
tree and blade of grass was gray stone, its surface as
smooth and luminous as pearls. Even the magical swans
had been duplicated in stone, their rising wings as light
as if filled with air.

"I've never seen stonework so delicate, so exact," I
said. I ran my fingers over the rose petals. Each flower
was slightly different, just as true flowers grew, and the
artist had captured the fine veins in the leaves, the mot-
ley blights and blemishes of real flowers, even a rose
beetle here and there. The thorns seemed real, as well,
sharp enough to prick my finger when I touched them.

"You didn't guess, then!" She stood behind me, her
delight warming me more than the hot sun on my back.
"But then perhaps you've never seen shellstone."

"No. Never. What is it?"

She dragged me back to my feet and through an open doorway into a long, low-roofed building—a garden workshop. On one side were pots and shovels, barrows, barrels of dirt, and wooden tables on which sat trays of seedlings ready to be set out in the rich black soil of the valley. But one long table was topped with a slab of gray stone, and on it lay a variety of plants and flowers, feathers and twigs, each one partially encased in thin layers of pale gray.

"Do you understand now? Though I knew of it from childhood, I'd never seen shellstone for myself until we found a deposit in Grithna Vale. If you lay an object— anything, a natural object or a model that you've made from wood or clay or steel—on the slab and don't move it, the stone will grow around it, preserving the exact shape. Even as the stone grows thicker, the details are all retained. A fresh and lovely rose will look fresh and lovely forever."

I started to ask if she didn't miss the smell or the color, but I didn't want to spoil her pleasure. The sculptures were indeed marvelous. A natural material of this world—that explained why I'd felt no prickling or coolness to indicate enchantment.

"The gardener, who is truly a Stone Shaper, takes the individual pieces—the flowers, the stems, the trellises, the insects or other creatures—along with sculpted pieces of his own invention, and he arranges and links them together to accomplish his vision."

Once I had expressed sufficient admiration for her "gardener's" talents, we rode out for Tymnath, a sizable town with a bustling market three leagues south of Gaelie. Over the past weeks we had made frequent visits to Tymnath market. With the same amusement, wonder, and delight as the children who ran barefoot through the lanes, we had picked up and put down everything we found there: jewelry and fabrics, cooking pots and music boxes, games, artworks, and magical devices of infinite variety. I had never imagined such magical things existed, invented just to entertain or amuse. We had

eaten every kind of foodstuff that was offered: little pastries filled with bitter fruit, sugared leaves, savory skewered bits of meat, shellfish in butter so spicy D'Sanya
turned red and drank three cups of saffria before dissolving in laughter, and wine so potent I had to sit in the
middle of the lane for a quarter of an hour before I
could walk straight again.

On this day several artisans had set up a display of
painted silks, some already sewn into scarves and gowns,
some raw lengths hung from frames taller than my head.
The designs and rich dyes confused the eye, forming
colors I could not name and shapes that were not imprinted on the fabric itself, but only on my mind.

As we turned to go, I glimpsed Sefaro's daughter leaning against the side of a sausage-seller's cart, watching
us. Did the woman truly travel so far just to spy on us?

I took D'Sanya's arm and led her away from the central market. A woman strolling toward us with a child
at each hand stopped suddenly, staring at D'Sanya, her
jaw falling open.

"Ah, not yet," D'Sanya murmured. "If we could have
just a little while longer to ourselves . . ."

"The Lady!" whispered the woman, trying to be polite
without taking her eyes from D'Sanya's face. Bowing
awkwardly and raising her hands, she elbowed her children, a pale boy and a girl wearing a pink ribbon in her
hair. "Your hands, J'Kor, Ma'Denne. It's the enchanted
princess." The gaping children raised their palms and
bobbed their heads.

D'Sanya nodded quickly and hurried onward, propel-
ling me through the crowded lanes of the market, turning her face toward my shoulder so people could not see
her straight on.

Someone always recognized D'Sanya on our outings.
Word would spread through the market-goers, and before very long a crowd would gather around her, people
begging for help, for healing, for blessings, for relief
from their fears. Some people only wanted to touch her,
or to have her say their names, thinking some wonder
would come of it. She gave everything she could, always

apologizing to me with a glance before delving into their problems: listening, healing, touching, comforting.

I had worried at first that someone would be curious about me, start to ask questions I couldn't answer, and uncover my false identity. But I soon learned that no one ever looked at me if D'Sanya was nearby. When she tired, she would glance at me over their heads, and while she told her petitioners where to apply for more help or when she might return, I would stretch out my arms and make a way for her to retreat through the press.

We hurried into the quieter streets of houses and shops before the word could spread too far. "Perhaps we should just go," I said, slowing her pace. "We could ride back through Caernaille. Stop at the ponds and watch the blue herons." For some reason this day had felt sour from its beginning; I couldn't bear the thought of the reverent, babbling crowd or all the Dar'Nethi magic that would grate on my spirit like sand in my boot.

She smiled up at me and squeezed my arm. "I've never known anyone so shy as you. Behind your gentlemanlike manner you've the reflexes of a cat, the strength of a bear, and the eye of a seer. I've a guess that not ten men in all of Gondai could best you in a test of mundane combat, or even if they brought their own sorcery to bear for that matter. So it cannot be lack of confidence or fear for our safety that frets you so. Your voice neither stammers nor grates. You are ravishingly handsome and so graceful in posture it cannot be uncertainty as to your welcome . . ."

"Lady, you flatter me too much."

She spun around to face me, taking my hands and walking backward down the lane, evidently trusting me to keep her from falling into potholes or tripping over gutters and lampposts. ". . . and certainly no dullness of intellect keeps you back. Your mind is as keen and bright as an enchanted blade, and new learning brings your face to life. I've learned that when you squint in just a certain way, your mind is racing, questioning and formulating answers, all inside yourself. Yet once we're outside the hospice grounds, you never speak a word to anyone but me. I'll wager a year's breakfasts that you would never come to even so tame a place as Tymnath market if I didn't force you."

"Most likely not."

"Well," she said, taking my arm and squeezing it to her side, walking frontward again, "for today I will indulge your fancy, but in the future we shall work on your social skills. You must learn to enjoy yourself in all ways!"

We strolled through the lanes that skirted the marketplace, poking into a luthier's shop to watch the master steam and shape and join the thin slices of wood that would form the shell of a new instrument. We found a jeweler's cart, and I bought D'Sanya a jade comb she admired—a gift she allowed only because it was unlike anything she already owned. She adored jewelry, never leaving her door without three or four rings on each hand, bracelets on her wrist or arms or ankles, and something dangling from her neck. The pieces were most often pure goldwork or silver, sometimes set with gemstones, though never garish or overdone. But she wouldn't allow me to buy her more, saying she had enough.

When we came to the hostler's yard at the edge of the town to reclaim our horses, we found a furor. Twenty people or more were clustered around a small party of horsemen. From the center of the crowd came thuds, grunts, and shouts. A horse squealed and reared. Curses and epithets flew through the air, along with rumbling blasts of enchantment that unsettled my stomach.

"P'Tor, fetch the Winder!" a man shouted. A youth in bright red and green burst out of the shifting crowd and streaked past us toward the center of town, his long braid flying.

A man screamed in pain as a sharp crack split the air above the fight, a streak of darkness that might have been the absolute reversal of lightning. Many in the group drew back. And then came a low, soul-grating hiss that chilled the day, shadowing the sun as surely as a rising storm cloud.

"Sssslay us if you will." The voice that shaped the hiss into words was harsh and brutal.

"They are cowardsss like all Dar Nethi vermin," said a second voice, "sssneaking, binding with their pitiable magics. None dares challenge us with a blade."

Zhid.

I stepped backward into the lane we'd just exited, ready to draw D'Sanya away from danger. But she shook off my hand and hurried across the trampled dirt and grass, leaving me no choice but to follow.

"What's going on here?" she called out. Her tone of command was irrefusable, as I well knew.

Men and women turned to gape at her, stepping aside as she walked into their midst. Five or six men were struggling to force a bedraggled captive to his knees. The Zhid, a thick, shaggy man with blood smeared across his face, was half standing, refusing to go down. Backs and arms strained to retain their hold on the warrior's brawny arms; boots scuffed the dirt as the Zhid shoved his captors inexorably backward. Zhid were wickedly strong and hard to kill. While one townsman held a roll of thick silver cord, two others were cutting off lengths of it to wrap around the captive's wrists and ankles.

I couldn't see the second Zhid, as he lay face down on the ground with two villagers sitting on his back, binding his limbs with more of the silver cord; *dolemar,* it was called, a material enchanted to prevent use of power. While a man in a blacksmith's apron tried to restrain a wild-eyed horse, two women tended to a groaning townsman with a horrific gash in his side. Dark blood soaked the hard ground beneath him.

"Come here, little maid, and tell these brutes to leave off," said the shaggy Zhid, his pale eyes settling on D'Sanya. He snarled and wrenched his shoulders as the townsmen knotted the silver cord about his left wrist and yanked his hand behind him to tie off with the other. "You've a pretty face. Won't you have pity on a ssstarving warrior?"

"Pity, yes," she said softly. "What is more pitiable than a being without a soul?"

"It's the Lady . . . the princess . . ." I couldn't see who said it first, for the words swept through the circle of Dar'Nethi like an autumn wind. Some stared. Some bowed. Some dropped to their knees. Eyes flicked from D'Sanya to the growling Zhid and back again, anticipating.

The burly Zhid scrabbled his feet back under himself and lurched upward, toppling one Dar'Nethi and smashing his captor in the face with his boot. But a wooden club in the gut felled the Zhid warrior instantly and left him in the dirt. The Dar'Nethi rolled him onto his face, jerking brutally on the cord about his wrists and wrapping it around his ankles until his back was arched like a bow.

D'Sanya flinched at the blows and the vigor of the Dar'Nethi captors. "Careful," she said. "He is sick and broken, but not irredeemable."

"I don't know, my lady," said one of the men tightening the cords. "We caught these two at Hy'Tan and J'Kari's house . . . and the two of them and their two little ones murdered. These damnable creatures were drinking J'Kari's blood! If Prince Ven'Dar had not commanded us to keep Zhid alive . . ." His voice broke.

"We'll drink yours as well before we're done," said the second Zhid, a long thin man with a tangled mop of red hair. He lay face down, arms and legs trussed as awkwardly as his fellow's. "We'll savor it . . . sssssssavor it . . ." The Zhid's unnerving expression of disdain issued from him like a viper's greeting.

Unlucky that I had stepped up to stand beside D'Sanya, for when a heavy boot rolled him onto his side, the red-haired Zhid's eyes fell directly on my own. His face brightened in astonishment . . . and then glee. "So it's true—"

I bellowed and pounced on the Zhid, throttling him so that he could not utter the words of honor and greeting that sat so eagerly on his tongue. I gripped his head unmoving and locked my eyes on his, forcing my thoughts into the villainous murk that was a Zhid's mind—especially this *particular* Zhid's mind. *You will say nothing, warrior. You will neither speak my name nor give the slightest hint that you know me. I am your master, your Lord, and my purposes are beyond your comprehension. You will obey me or I will squeeze the blood from your heart.*

Even as Dar'Nethi hands tugged at my arms, trying to pull me off him, I ripped power from the Zhid's exhilaration and his fear, and I squeezed his heart with an invisible fist, feeling its pumping stutter, using his pain and the panic of his failing breath to strengthen my hold on his body and mind. *Acknowledge my command or die this moment, Gensei Kovrack. You will say nothing of me. You will not look upon me. You will not think of me.*

Of course, Great Lord Dieste . . . we hear your call . . . yes . . . yes . . . as you command . . .

My hands were shaking as they dragged me off him, hatred and murder flowing through me like a river of fire. I bit my lip and tasted the blood, and the hunger came near choking me. I required every smattering of will I possessed, every scrap of control I could summon, to take my hands from his throat and release his heart without killing him. By earth and sky and all gods, I wanted him dead—Gensei Kovrack, the red-haired Zhid general who had taken me into the desert and taught me the arts of command and torture.

The eyes of the crowd were hot on my back. An explanation. I needed an explanation. Someone might have sensed the vile enchantment I had worked. No one would guess it mine, not when Zhid were present, but my actions were very un-Dar'Nethi. "I've seen him before," I whispered. I was kneeling in the dirt, five men restraining me. "He slaughtered . . . so many . . . enslaved my father . . . my family . . . so powerful. Don't trust even dolemar bindings to hold him. I'm sorry . . . so very sorry."

"We understand." The hands that held me gradually fell away, a few squeezing my arm tight or touching my back in comradeship and sympathy.

"I'm sorry. I lost the Way." That's what a true Dar'-Nethi would say.

Two fair hands reached out for me, offering to help me to my feet—D'Sanya's hands. "Oh, my dear friend." Her brow knit in worry, sympathy mellowing her eyes, she brushed a hand across my brow. Peace and comfort and care enfolded me . . . smothered me.

Unfortunately her gifts were designed to soothe a sorrow I did not feel. Hatred and revulsion sat heavy in my belly, and my attention remained on Kovrack, a wily and powerful Zhid. Would he obey? Would he suspect I was no longer what he believed?

"I must help here," said D'Sanya, half apologizing.

"Of course," I said. "Do what you have to do. I'll wait. I'm sorry."

As D'Sanya knelt beside the wounded townsman who lay in the profound stillness of mortal injury, the youth in bright red and green pelted across the yard toward the growing crowd. Behind him trotted an older man in purple robes, breathing hard.

I backed into the crowd, feeling an occasional pat on my back or my shoulder. Kovrack's gaze was pinned to the dirt. I did not take my eye from him.

"Stand back," said the man in purple when he came to the center of the crowd. He closed his eyes and threw out his hand as if scattering seeds on a field, and I felt the shivering power of the Word Winder's cast settling over the two Zhid. An extra binding to prevent their use of sorcery, I suspected. As had every enchantment I had sensed since crossing the Bridge, it abraded my spirit like steel on glass.

At the same time the afternoon sunlight flickered brighter, almost garish in its orange brilliance. The chattering crowd fell into awestruck silence as D'Sanya breathed into the mouth of the fallen Dar'Nethi. His chest spasmed. One limp hand moved as if to grip the earth itself, and soon his eyes flicked open and color flooded back into his pale cheeks. The two women swooped down on him again, weeping.

When D'Sanya rose and stepped away from the man, the Word Winder bowed, extending his palms. "My gracious Lady," he said. "Surely holy Vasrin has sent you to us in our need. Those of us privileged to witness your deeds are blessed."

"Good Ka'Ston," she said, returning his greeting. Then she moved to the two bound Zhid.

"We thought to send them to Feur Desolé," said one of the men who had bound the two prisoners. "At the prison, perhaps, a Healer . . ."

"Let me see what I can do." As she knelt on the hard dirt between the Zhid, D'Sanya's eyes met mine. Her expression was solemn, but I could not understand what she was trying to tell me. Then she bent over Kovrack and touched his red hair.

His head popped up. "What is this?" he said harshly, jerking his head away from her hand. "What are you doing?"

"Anything broken must be put right," said D'Sanya, laying a hand on his breast, her gold rings catching the sunlight.

"Don't touch me, witch. I am not broken. I am as the Lords of Zhev'Na made me." He spat and writhed and twisted, his boots scuffing up a cloud of dust as he tried to get away from her, even bound as he was. His attempts at sorcery—virulent, tangled bursts of pain and confusion—fell dead quickly, aborted by the power of his bindings. That he could create anything tangible, even such ephemeral wisps, while under the restraints of dolemar and a Word Winder's binding spoke a great deal about his age and power.

Several Dar'Nethi held him still as D'Sanya placed her hands on his breast and his head and closed her eyes. As her enchantment took shape, the snarling, furious Kovrack riveted his gaze on me . . . expectant. I glared at him, hoping he would remember his oath and my fist on his heart. I dared not plant a thought in his head to reinforce my command, not with D'Sanya so close. And I dared not touch power again.

"Lord, do not allow—" With a gasp and a shudder, Kovrack's eyelids dropped shut, and his body relaxed. No one seemed to notice what he'd said.

Could she do it? Restore the soul of a Zhid as old

and decadent as Kovrack, a general of the Lords' armies, steeped in their corruption for hundreds of years? And what would come next? If D'Sanya could reawaken his soul, his bond of obedience to the Lords—to me—would be broken, and he could betray me. Ironic that he was more danger to me if he was whole. What would happen if he told these people who I was? The Dar'Nethi believed I should be dead, and to use power to save myself might possibly make me into the very thing they feared.

D'Sanya's power swelled, silencing the murmuring onlookers, choking me with her overwhelming enchantment. Unable to analyze the complex threads of her working, I watched her face instead. Intense, devout, passionate. The fiery liquor in my blood began to cool, hatred and self-loathing yielding to feelings that were cleaner, better. Moments flitted past. Almost too soon, D'Sanya straightened her back. If she had failed . . .

"What place is this?" Kovrack had opened his eyes as well, fixing them first on D'Sanya, who knelt beside him, and then sweeping his gaze about the hovering crowd. Lost, confused, searching, his gaze met mine . . . and passed on to the man next to me without recognition. "Why am I bound? Good mistress, I feel so strangely ill."

"Not ill, sir. Not any more." She beckoned the Dar'Nethi. "Come, cut him loose. Care for him."

"Tell us your name!" I called out. "Who is your master?" Better to know right away. Better to be sure. Zhid were allowed only one answer to that question.

The red-haired man blinked and looked puzzled. "P'Var, Numerologist of Gladsea, I am. And though I offer service to many who need my skills, I serve no master save the lord Prince of Avonar." He looked at me and then to the others as if for confirmation.

A Dar'Nethi woman cut his bonds and helped him to sit up. She didn't remove the last windings of silver about Kovrack's wrists and ankles, however, but jumped back to the verge of the watchers. When Kovrack noted the silver cord around his wrists, he jerked his head up and surveyed the crowd again. His sallow face told me in what moment he began to suspect what he had been. Even then he did not look to me. My fists unclenched.

D'Sanya, smiling, pressed something into his palm and folded his fingers over it. "Take this token, son of D'Arnath, and let it remind you of your goodness and strength."

As he opened his palm and stared at a slip of gleaming brass threaded on a silken string, D'Sanya, her skirt red with the dust of the yard, turned to the second Zhid. When we left them a short time later, Kovrack sat alone in the middle of the hostler's yard, his head in his hands. He had refused all help or comfort save the brass lion pendant. P'Var the Numerologist's home village was long destroyed, and his family seven hundred years dead. For all he or any of us knew, he had killed them himself. The other man was sobbing, leaning on the thick arm of the smith who had reluctantly offered him a straw pallet in his forge for the night. The relieved townspeople had withdrawn in a hurry.

D'Sanya and I rode out of Tymnath without speaking. The afternoon light sculpted the green hills around us and stretched our shadows long across the path. When we came to a split in the road, D'Sanya surprised me by choosing the longer way, the way that led to the valley called Caernaille and its ponds with their blue herons. Only after we had sat for a while, watching the herons snare the rising fish, did she speak.

"I'm so sorry it had to be that one," she said, laying her hand on my knee. "Someone who had hurt you so terribly . . . your family . . . your father. Will you tell me of it?"

I shook my head, unspeaking. Unwilling to tell her more lies.

"It's all right to be angry," she said, her fingers squeezing my flesh. "You were a child. It was all brutal and unfair. You didn't kill him today. It's all right."

No, I hadn't killed him, only done a bit of torture and brutalized his mind. She had given him back his soul. Which of us was corrupt?

* * *

One bright morning in midsummer, D'Sanya and I climbed Castanelle, the highest peak in the range that formed Grithna Vale. As the sun reached its zenith, we sat, tired and hot, on a wind-blasted slope of short grass and rock. A rock-pig whistled from a nearby boulder as D'Sanya chattered, reliving every slope and switchback of the climb. We gazed out across the sunlit world and laughed as a wedge of geese flew past below us, and we sat motionless as a flock of goats with curled horns grazed within ten paces of us.

Despite the perfection of the morning, the blustering wind turned sour and sent us down early. The rain caught us halfway down the mountain.

"Look, over there," I said, holding my sodden cloak stretched over D'Sanya's head. "It's some kind of shelter."

Rain splattered and dripped from the trees. The path was swirling mud, and we were soaked to the skin. Our teeth were chattering. Even the half-collapsed shepherd's hut looked inviting.

"At least it has part of a roof," she said.

Only the end next to the stone hearth had enough of a slumping sod roof left intact that we could stuff our drenched and shivering selves into it. I gathered a pile of wet wood; D'Sanya set it to blazing with sorcery; and we huddled together to get warm, laughing at the fickle ways of nature, which had tempted us so high only to abandon us so abjectly. While the rain poured and her flames crackled, she talked and I listened.

It was on that long afternoon, as we grew relaxed and warm in our solitary island in the midst of the storm, that I first realized I loved her. It seemed the most natural thing in the world for my arms to be around her to quiet her shivering, and for her damp, fragrant hair to tickle my nose because her head was resting on my chest. All doubts and confusions were banished with her first sigh of contentment as I held her close.

"Are you awake?" she asked drowsily, without moving her head from the place I wished it to stay as long as I could persuade her to leave it.

"Approximately."

"I leave tomorrow for Maroth Vale. Will you come?"

"If you wish it." She could have asked for me to give her my eyes, and my answer would have been the same.

"How could I not wish my best friend to be with me?" She nestled closer. "But before we go, friend, there is the matter of one of your secrets that I think we must clarify."

For a moment my instincts shouted a warning. But only for a moment . . . until she turned her head just enough that it was the most natural thing in the world to kiss her.

CHAPTER 11

Jen

From the earliest days of my memory, my mother called me her forget-me-not child. I had the annoying habit of remembering every word and image of every story and song I'd ever heard, and neither my parents nor their guests nor their hired Singers or Storytellers dared leave out a single one in hopes of an early release from my attention. This was but an early sign of a certain singleness of purpose which my brothers preferred to describe as "dogged stubbornness akin to that of a particularly unintelligent mule."

I had a number of annoying habits when I was a child. I constantly interrupted adult conversations with sober, if ill-informed, opinions. I drove my family frantic by disappearing for long periods of time into a tree or some other hideaway and losing myself in a favorite book, ignoring their calls until they'd rousted the town Watch to find me. And I never tired of filling my brothers' boots with mud or hiding their school papers or otherwise getting them in trouble, and then playing the innocent girl child while they reaped the consequences of my tricks. My brothers had fond names for me, too, though certainly less polite than *forget-me-not child*.

Fond names for annoying habits are a natural part of a happy childhood, and loving parents always assume that those less-than-desirable traits will fade away as childhood yields gracefully to the passage of time. Perhaps that's why I never lost my annoying habits. My childhood did not yield gracefully, but was aborted, truncated, sheared off in the span of a single moment as I hid in the boughs of my reading tree and watched the Zhid slit my mother's throat and drag my father into slavery. And childhood was buried forever one year later when they came back for me and my brothers, the day the cold-eyed boy with the jewels in his ear sealed the slave collar about our necks, while my weeping father was forced to watch in silence. I had thought my life ended on that day, my heart transformed into steel as cold and dead as the collar itself, and it took me many years to discover it was not. But I never forgot.

It was a true measure of my father's goodness that he was able to look upon the person who had destroyed his children and caused his own savage torture with anything but hatred in his heart. My brothers had been used to train the beast in swordsmanship and then discarded like so much rubbish when he grew more skilled than they. They were sent into the desert camps and died there, I believed, for they were never found after the war. I was nine years old when the collar of Zhev'Na was sealed around my neck and fifteen when it was removed by a Healer who wept when he saw how young I was.

To find my father among the pitiful remnants of the thousands who'd been held captive in the Wastes had taken me three months. He lay in a house of healing in the Vale of Nimrolan, scarcely able to walk for the pain of his deformity. But one might say his grievous injuries were fortunate, for the path of life that led to his torture was the same that brought him back to me.

My father was a Speaker, one who can, with study and observation, divine the essence of a problem and judge its truth so that the parties to it may find a wise or just solution. It is an uncommon gift, and the single Dar'Nethi talent that leaves its wielder immune from transformation into Zhid. The power of a Speaker is immense; thus it was imminently desirable to the Lords, but it is born solely of truth, which left it out of their reach. Even the Three of Zhev'Na could not bend truth to their will. And so they took particular delight in enslaving a Speaker, abasing him cruelly, torturing him and flaunting him before the other Dar'Nethi as a reminder that no one could escape the Lords entirely, no matter what that person's gift. But they kept him alive.

Once free and reunited, my father and I had taken up life in the town of Tymnath. A Speaker's services were always in demand, so we lived comfortably enough. I kept our household, cared for my father, read and studied furiously to make up for missing years of education, and eventually pursued my own profession, facing the hard fact that whatever true talent had been born inside me had been destroyed by the slave collar of Zhev'Na. I had come of age without the Way, and like a seedling buried too long beneath a rock, my gift, whatever it might have been, had given up and died away before it ever saw the light. I could do the few small magics that any Dar'Nethi child could do, but nothing beyond. In five years I had grown accustomed to my lack, just as I had to the red scar about my neck, and I had made my own place in the world.

There was certainly work enough to do—rebuilding Tymnath for a start. I excelled at mathematics and had a good eye, so Builders and other craftsmen throughout the Vale of Hester found it useful that I could calculate their costs and sizes, loads and measures, and remember them exactly from one project to the next. True talent would have been nice, but paper, pen, and my mundane skills served me well enough.

It didn't take long to learn that people were shy of those who had been slaves, as if we had carried something more than our red scars from the desert, and it would behoove them not to get any closer than business required. Their discomfort didn't bother me. I had half a lifetime's worth of reading to catch up on and new skills to learn, and as often as we could get away I would hire a carriage and drive my father into the newly reclaimed countryside. It appealed to us far more than the untouched beauties of Avonar and the Vales. We would sit for hours reveling in the smell of moisture on the wind and the graceful brushstrokes of green newly painted over the healthy land, rejoicing in our survival and our Prince D'Natheil's victory over the Lords. After a few years, Papa said he almost couldn't remember what Zhev'Na had been like. I remembered.

In the fourth year of our freedom, Papa's strength began to fail. He lived with pain every day, the Healers' remedies helpful only in passing. They told him that if he would let them try to relieve the twisting of his poor back, then perhaps he would do better. But the healing itself was so excruciating, he could not bear it, and so it was never completed.

When his condition grew so painful that he could no longer work, he began to look for some other answer. More for me than for himself. He feared he was making my life intolerable. I spent hours alternately packing him in ice, then wrapping him in warm blankets with hot stones near the most painful places, and stretching and bending his limbs when he could not bear to do it, so as to keep his muscles working. Eventually I, too, was faced with giving up my work. The Lady D'Sanya's hospice seemed the perfect remedy. Since Papa could not work as he was, he insisted he would lose nothing by giving up his talent, and he wished to set me free to pursue my life without the burden of his suffering.

Our house was lonely without him, so I would spend one week of every three in Gaelie, where I could see him every day. It was on my third visit that I encountered the living beast in the hospice, and then saw him riding like a king on the very road I traveled and skulking in the guesthouse at Gaelie like a pickpocket hiding in the marketplace crowd. When I recognized him, I vowed that he would die.

My father was wrong about my reasons. It was not a matter of revenge. Nothing could restore my family or my childhood or give me talent, and though I was incomplete as a Dar'Nethi, I had not forsaken the Way. I rejoiced in my life and in the life of everything and everyone around me. But the Zhid were rising in the north, and here was their commander going about his sneaking business right before my eyes. I was a daughter of the Dar'Nethi, and I did not forget. No Dar'Nethi would be enslaved again if I could strike a blow to prevent it.

So why did I not kill him once I had him captive? I fully intended it at first. But my father's questions echoed those nibbling at my own mind. Why was I able to capture him so easily? Why did he not tweak his scarred hand and drive me mad or set me afire? If he'd made the slightest move, I would have driven my knife home, but he did not . . . and so I could not. In the final event, what stayed my hand was not my gentle father's belief that the villain had truly changed, but the sober consideration that someone needed to find out what he was up to. His death might not halt the evil growing in the north. All right. Let him think he had fooled the kind old man and his foolish daughter. Then watch him. That was my plan.

I gave up my profession as a Builder's assessor and became expert at lurking and skulking, at listening at doors and peering into windows, and at diving into bushes. Holding my tongue when he stumbled on me was much more difficult. Once free of my collar and its consequences, I had reverted to the indiscipline of my childhood.

The tall, skinny fellow at the guesthouse caused my first confusion. In the beginning I guessed that the young man must be the young Lord's manservant, but they seemed so easy together, I decided they must be accomplices. But then one day I found my borrowed horse panicked and wild from an inflammation of his hoof. The skinny young man encountered me in the guesthouse stable and was generous with his help and genuine in his concern and care for the animal. Unless he was the finest actor I'd ever encountered, he didn't even have an idea about who I was or what I'd done to his friend. He must be another innocent dupe. So I decided to warn him. But the moment I broached the subject of his companion, he turned bright red, slammed his mouth shut, and said he didn't talk about his "master" to anyone.

As for my quarry, I came to understand what an Imager must feel when he had inscribed a new object on his mind. Given material of flesh and bone I could have reproduced the slender form with the prideful bearing, the musculature so unexceptional until one witnessed the strength and power in the long legs and arms, the straight brown hair with a touch of red in it, the scarred hands he kept hidden from the day I noticed them. I could have sculpted his every facial feature: the wide-set, shadowed eyes, the narrow face and high cheek-bones, the straight nose and slightly jutting chin. I could have stated his weights and measures as if he had been one of my clients' building projects.

It infuriated me that in all my secret watching I could not catch him out of his quiet, serious demeanor—a mask, as surely as the gold and diamonds he had worn in Zhev'Na. Only with his skinny friend and with the Lady did he ever soften his expression, and even then he held his smiles and laughter close-reined as if he were embarrassed to show them. He spent almost every waking hour with the Lady D'Sanya, and I was sure he meant her harm, but the longer I watched the two together, and listened to scraps of their nonsensical conversations, the more confused I became.

"What game does he play?" I threw my ripped and muddy cloak onto the floor of my father's room one afternoon after spending three hours getting wet, scratched, and muddy while watching the two of them gather raspberries in the rain. "He trails after her like a hungry calf; he does her bidding in everything: what he eats and drinks, where he walks, what he reads, what he wears. He cringes in distaste when she drags him to meet her friends, flinches as if he'd been struck when anyone walks up to them at Tymnath market, yet you'd swear he doesn't even know he's doing it. He puts on this never-ending show of mooning adoration, but I can't see who it's for, except the Lady herself, and she . . . Well, I just can't decipher it. He as much as admitted to us that he was planning to deceive her."

My father fluttered the pages of his book with his

thumb, then closed it and set it aside. "Did you ever consider, dearest of daughters, that it might be nothing more than what you see? Is it impossible that the young man has fallen in love with the Lady?"

"He is incapable of love. He has no soul. I saw its last remnants burned away. Remember?"

"And what of the Lady? How does she react to this villainous mooncalf?" His eye smiled in the firelight, but I would have none of it. "Is *she* capable of love?"

"It makes no difference in the world what I think of her, Papa. She must be told who he is."

It's true I didn't care for the Lady. She was beautiful and kind, and the comfort her enchantments had given my father was undeniable, but I thought she talked too much and listened too little, and it seemed to me that every kindness she did was done mostly for herself. She hungered after doing good in the way some crave influence over others or power to feed their talents. And I saw in her the same thing I'd seen in so many when they glimpsed the scars of our slave collars. She wouldn't look us in the eye, and shied away as if we were dirty or diseased.

But I didn't have to like her. She was the rightful Princess of Avonar, and she had been a prisoner, too. I wouldn't wish anyone to fall under the hand of the Lords of Zhev'Na even once, much less a second time.

Papa drew me down onto the couch beside him and pulled my head onto his lap, ruffling my short, ugly hair. "Why this masquerade, Jen? You cannot be your brothers, nor would I ever wish it. You are my beloved daughter, a woman of intelligence and generous heart, and I glorify good Vasrin's creation every day that your path travels alongside my own. But you hide here with me and chase these ghosts of the past instead of finding friends and living your own joys. Why do you treat yourself so slightingly?"

"I wear men's clothes because they are more comfortable and more practical when I work or travel. I keep my hair short because I don't have time to waste. I don't wear rings and baubles like Lady D'Sanya does at every

hour of every day because I don't want to feel like a
jeweler's cart at Tymnath market. I am what I am, Papa.
Letting my hair grow long or wearing silk gowns or smiling at smarmy men who squirm when they see my neck
will not change it. Now stop hiding from my question.
Why won't you let me warn the Lady?"

"Because he asked us not."

"How can you—?"

"Because I have faith in the Way. Vasrin's creation is
not disordered; we just cannot always discern the Shaper's pattern. There is a reason I was sent to serve in his
house. A reason his mother was sent to me there. A
reason we found refuge here and crossed his path."

It was strange to hear him speak with such firmness
and conviction. Since he'd come to the hospice it had
been as if the heart had gone out of him, so that even
decisions so small as to what to wear each day had become difficult. But I still didn't share his belief.

"Perhaps the reason is that we can warn our princess
of her danger."

He pulled my face around to look at him, and his eyes
no longer sparkled, but shone with wonder that stilled
my protests. He dropped his voice to a whisper as if
someone might overhear. "Jen, I have seen the one he
comes here to visit—not the Lady, but the one he names
father. The man stays apart as you've noted for yourself. But one night when I could not sleep, I went walking in the gardens. He was doing the same, and we
came face to face in the moonlight. Though he turned
away quickly, I knew him, daughter. Back when you
were a child, I had a close friend, a Healer named Dassine, one of the Preceptors and a man of great power
and daring—"

"The man who fostered Prince D'Natheil."

"Yes. Back in those days Dassine asked me to Speak
for him, for he was sorely troubled at something he had
done. He confided only part of a very great mystery and
made me vow on my life never to reveal what he had
told me or anything of a man—two men, in fact—that
he allowed me to speak with on that day, though I only

saw one of them in the flesh. But I tell you, girl, the man I saw in the hospice garden was indeed the man who reigned for four years in Avonar as the Prince D'Natheil. The great Healer. The man who destroyed the Lords."

"The one who condemned his son to death saying he was too evil, too corrupt to live?"

"The same."

"It's impossible, Papa. Prince D'Natheil is buried in the Tomb of the Heirs. And clearly he did not do everything we thought. One of the Lords still lives."

But I was very confused.

CHAPTER 12

Gerick

"A fortnight more or less, then I'll be back," I told my father. Outside, the dawn gleamed through a watery mist, the lingering remnants of a rainy night. "Are you sure you'll be all right? Perhaps I shouldn't have—"

"If we're ever to be done with this business, you must be satisfied that the Lady serves no purpose of the Lords. Can you say so yet?" My father sat listless and unshaven in his chair by the open doors. Unable to lie abed on the morning of my departure for Maroth Vale, I'd rousted him too early.

"She loathes the Lords. The least mention of Zhev'Na sets her talking of some new scheme to erase all memory of them. She is . . . exceptional . . . in so many ways, and I can find no fault in how she uses her talents."

On our last visit to Tymnath, D'Sanya had healed, embraced, and listened to people's troubles until well past midnight. Every day she spent at least an hour writing letters to those who worked to restore and rebuild Gondai, encouraging them to persevere. She sent them gifts of tools and materials, even hiring craftsmen to aid those in remote villages.

"But you're not ready to tell Ven'Dar to yield his throne and sleep soundly after." He tried to smile. An effort . . . but a poor one.

"She's still said very little of what they made her do in Zhev'Na. It pains her to speak of it. But most of

my doubts center on her power. I've not yet come to
understand it."

I didn't want to tell him that my greatest concern was
his own erratic behavior; he needed nothing more to
weigh on his spirit. On some days he could converse
with the same insight and intelligence as always. But on
some days, he could not utter three syllables that made
sense together. Why did this hospice enchantment,
woven with such care and generosity, leave its subjects
so empty and joyless?

"She changes the subject whenever I ask her about
power or talent, as if by talking about it, she's somehow
boasting or pointing out my lacks. But she's admitted
that she has little need to gather power the way most
Dar'Nethi do. She says that she and her brothers inherited their father's power directly. Does that make sense?
I'll confess, when I try to analyze her enchantments, I
feel as if I'm being battered by a tidal wave, and the
best I can do is survive the onslaught."

Having so little experience of sorcery and enchantments outside Zhev'Na, I had no feel for the magic
D'Sanya worked. It was incredibly complex, dense, obscure, slightly different in composition every time she
used it. Of course all Dar'Nethi magic seemed somewhat
obscure to me, out of tune somehow, more so than I
remembered from my limited experience of it. Perhaps
I'd been in the Bounded too long, living without sorcery
in a primitive land. But as long as I could not testify to
the components of D'Sanya's magic, I could not declare
our work done.

My father hunched in his dressing gown. No matter
how cool or wet the weather nowadays, he insisted on
keeping the garden doors open, saying he felt suffocated
otherwise. "Inherit power, rather than talent? I don't
know. D'Arnath's power was legendary . . . as was that
of all those of his blood. The histories claim that many
other Dar'Nethi wielded power on an incredible scale
before the Catastrophe. When I first ruled in Avonar,
the Preceptors told me that my workings felt that way
to them. Ah, Gerick, I *do* miss it."

I squatted beside his chair and laid my hand on his knee. "I know, Father. A fortnight with her will surely satisfy our last doubts. You'll take care of yourself while I'm away? Paulo said he would ask if T'Laven might come visit you."

He picked at a frayed corner of his pocket and stared vacantly into the light.

"Father?" I twisted my neck, making sure my face was in his line of vision. "You'll be all right while I'm in Maroth?"

"Yes, yes. I'll be fine." A spark of good humor brightened his face for a moment. "Now, go. A fortnight with a beautiful lady who adores you . . . Who would have thought our stay here would lead to that? Don't waste one moment of it. Not one."

Adding this one more guilt to my oversupply of them, I hurried through the public gardens and took a shortcut to the stable, arriving at least a half-hour early for our departure. F'Syl, the head groom, was still yawning over a mug of saffria.

"Have you seen Cedor this morning?" I asked. Perhaps I could arrange an early breakfast for my father as an apology for waking him.

The balding groom, two purple scars making his round face look inexpertly put together, pointed toward the orchard with a four-fingered hand. "He brought me my cup. Then took off that way as if he'd a bee on his backside."

Thanking F'Syl, I stowed my pack inside the door and hurried down the orchard path. The sweetish odor of rotting fruit—plums and cherries that had been crushed underfoot during the harvest—hung in the damp air along with the scent of ripening apples . . . early, it seemed from what I knew of apples. But then one could say that everything in the orchard was "early." A year ago the orderly ranks of trees had not existed. So many marvels D'Sanya had wrought. Growth and healing. Verdant life. The Gardeners at the Gaelie guesthouse had said the reclamation of the Wastes had almost come to a standstill before last month, when the Lady spent a day on the western fringes. The Lords had never valued growth or healing or verdant life. D'Sanya did not serve their purposes.

I walked all the way to the end of the orchard path before locating Cedor. On the far side of the grassy strip that bounded the orchard, just beside the hospice wall, my father's fair-haired attendant was deep in conversation with a taller man in a green cloak—the consiliar Na'Cyd. I couldn't hear what the two were saying, but their rigid posture and the occasional crescendo of sound indicated it was no morning pleasantry. Rancor and bitterness flowed out from them like fish rings in a pond, making the very air about me venomous. Though discord among the Dar'Nethi was always a matter of concern— Zhid fed on discord—I turned my back and retraced my steps. D'Sanya would be waiting.

Three horses, one of them mine, stood saddled and ready in front of the stable. Wrapped in a light traveling cloak of scarlet, the Lady was supervising F'Syl as he snugged a small bag on her saddle. The bulk of her baggage had already been sent on to Maroth through a portal, but we had chosen to ride on this journey, as we took such pleasure in it.

I stood for a moment at the edge of the orchard, pleased to watch her when she was not aware of me. She was teasing F'Syl about his propensity to oversleep, but when she thanked him for loading her pack, her slim fingers, adorned with two gold rings, touched his maimed hand. Even twenty paces away, I felt the tidal wash of her magic. F'Syl's bones ached terribly in the damp, but he refused to take up one of the precious places in the hospice to ease his hurts. He, too, had once been Zhid and proudly wore D'Sanya's lion pendant around his neck.

When D'Sanya turned to watch the groom hobble away, she caught sight of me. The happiness that blossomed on her face warmed the morning far more than my brisk walk had done.

"When I didn't see Nacre here this morning, I worried

that you had changed your mind about the journey," she said when I joined her at the stable.

"Nacre's a bit edgy since his injury. Probably afraid I'm going to take him running at night again. My friend insisted I take this fellow instead." I patted the chestnut's flank. "My lady, this is Stormcloud. Stormcloud, this is the Princess D'Sanya, who believes she is the finest rider and her Miaste the fastest horse in Gondai. Sooner or later, we shall have to prove her wrong. Again."

D'Sanya sniffed and arched her eyebrows. "Ah, my poor deluded friend, the sad truth awaits you. I've allowed you your few wins on these crude cross-country tracks only to lure you into my clutches. But at Maroth is the most marvelous racing oval . . . lovely, smooth turf . . . and there shall we set our wagers, leave off these saddles, and have a true match. Now give me your hand, and we'll be off." She raised her foot and waited.

I laughed and offered her my linked hands. Her step was so light as she bounded onto Miaste's back, I doubted she needed me for anything but confidence.

"So who is this?" I said, jerking my head toward the placid brown mare, aggrieved at the thought of a third person intruding on our ride.

"This is Savira, who belongs to . . . ah, and here he is."

Na'Cyd came running down the orchard path and swung skillfully into Savira's saddle. "So sorry to be tardy, my lady. I was making final rounds before our departure. I wanted all to be in order for Gen'Vyl. The grain deliveries have come in. The plum harvest is complete. Mar'Kello has taken leave time to visit her mother. Hy'Lattire is uncomfortable with the new resident and asks that she be allowed to serve a woman instead. I've assigned her to Mar'Kello's resident and asked Sy'Lan to take the new man. In short, all is in order."

Still hoping to prompt the breakfast favor from Cedor, I lagged behind for a moment as D'Sanya and the consiliar rode up the road toward the hospice gate, but the soft-spoken attendant did not appear. Kicking Stormcloud into motion, I vowed to make up to my father for my neglect the moment I returned from Maroth Vale.

The weather was perfect, the shady route down Grithna Vale cool and pleasant as the morning warmed. Na'Cyd was at least considerate enough to ride a few hundred paces ahead of us, politely out of hearing.

"He had to come," said D'Sanya, after I muttered some remark about unwanted chaperones. "He is to be the master of the Maroth hospice, so he must be involved in all aspects of its birth. Once living quarters are ready, he'll move there permanently."

I watched the green cloak disappear around a bend. The consiliar sat a horse with a commanding air far different from the watchful deference he exhibited at the hospice.

"I'll be glad when he goes," I said. "He makes me feel as if I've dirt on my face all the time, but is too polite to say it." As if he knew something unpleasant about me. "So is Na'Cyd one like Cedor and some of the others . . . one who's been . . . restored?"

"He is a brilliant man. Excellent at his work. Compassionate and faithful."

"But he was Zhid?"

"Why does it matter? He is no longer. None of them are. Their lives were stolen from them, and they deserve to find peace and forgiveness."

"Of course, you're right. It's just difficult to let go of the past." Did the Restored truly remember nothing of all those years of destruction and murder, centuries for some of them? Why did Na'Cyd watch me so closely? Why had he failed to mention his argument with Cedor when reporting on his "rounds" to D'Sanya? She always wanted to know of anything that might disrupt the peace of the hospice. My instincts told me to be wary of him, but then I could not rely on instincts shaped in Zhev'Na, where compassion and forgiveness were unknown.

D'Sanya chattered as we rode, today about the setting, design, and outfitting of the new hospice. Required only to listen and respond now and then, I could have asked no better amusement on the road. Her enthusiasm was boundless, her thoughtful musings, unending good humor, and colorful storytelling making better music than any I could imagine. I never tired of watching the animation of her face, her eyes far brighter than her rings and bracelets struck by stray beams of sunlight.

But my habits would not remain subservient to my pleasure. My eyes and ears and trained sensibilities insisted on surveying the forests and the fields we traveled as they had not in these past weeks as D'Sanya had consumed my mind and heart. Perhaps it was my father's disheartened agitation that put the thorn in my shoe that morning. Perhaps it was the argument I had witnessed . . . that palpable anger . . . its extraordinary virulence . . . and the purposeful hiding of it. But in the moment I started paying attention, I knew something was wrong.

The sunlight that had shone so gloriously bright after our rainy day on Castanelle felt tarnished, the cool green shade murky. I might have thought I was viewing the world through my father's distorted senses, but for D'Sanya's voice in the background.

". . . though I know you are shy of Avonar, I really must stop in and speak with Prince Ven'Dar. I've ignored him dreadfully these past few weeks, having been so preoccupied." She glanced sideways under modestly lowered brows, the corner of her mouth curving upward . . . not at all modestly. "But as a reward for your indulgence, I plan to show you something truly wonderful that no one has seen in centuries."

Neither her enticing look nor her intriguing promise soothed my growing unease. I returned her smile. It was impossible not to. And I played to her teasing and, as always, felt my skin flush in pleasurable disbelief at my good fortune whenever she turned her eyes on me. But I kept every sense alert and nudged D'Sanya's mount toward the center of the road. I even picked up the pace and followed Na'Cyd a little closer. The consiliar wore a sword, at least.

I probed a little to see if I was alone in my foreboding,

asking D'Sanya and Na'Cyd if they thought a storm might be lurking beyond the forested horizon. Neither sensed anything that might spoil our journey.

The day grew hot. We picnicked by a hidden waterfall D'Sanya knew of that was only a few paces from the road. She talked and I listened. Nothing untoward occurred. By evening, when D'Sanya whispered her name to two awestruck guards, and we rode through the gates of Avonar, I was calling myself a worry-wife. But I could not shake the sense that every aspect of Gondai had slipped out of position sometime in the past weeks when I wasn't looking.

Only my unwillingness to disappoint D'Sanya had persuaded me to come to Avonar. I had told myself repeatedly that no one would look at me when she was near. It was only for one night. I would wear a hat in the streets and keep to my room at the palace, feign illness if need be, while D'Sanya talked with the prince. Ven'Dar would see that I was not exposed. But I hadn't expected the whole world to feel askew, and I hadn't expected the crowds.

The streets of the royal city were teeming with people as the blazing summer afternoon cooled off to a mellow evening. We rode through a succession of small commards, each open space jammed with squawking pipers or blaring horn players and uncountable Dar'Nethi, shoving and pushing, everyone in a hurry. Every bridge that crossed the city's five waterways was packed with well guarded crates that Na'Cyd surmised were filled with fireworks for later in the evening. Just past a troupe of drummers clad in billowing yellow silk, we came on a group of several hundred people seated on cushions and blankets laid out on the grass. They watched a theatrical performance in which the actors sang their parts. The place was suffocating.

Feeling threatened and anxious, I balked when Na'Cyd pointed down a steep, narrow lane he had been told was a less crowded approach to the Heir of D'Arnath's palace. But D'Sanya insisted she was tired, and that anything that would speed us to our destination was welcome.

The deserted lane was little more than an alley between the brick walls of two tall houses, and blissfully quiet. Even D'Sanya was subdued. We reached the juncture where the lane opened into the grand command so quickly, I felt foolish at my apprehension. But when I glimpsed the vast expanse, crammed with enough booths, carts, and vendors hawking sausages, music boxes, card games, and rubbish to make twenty Tymnath markets, the skin on my back crawled. "How did I let you persuade me to come here?" I said.

"Because you are my play friend, who cannot bear for me to enjoy myself alone." She sighed deeply. "I would dearly love to have stopped to hear the Singers' play, but I think supper, bath, and bed in Ven'Dar's house will be the most I can manage tonight. Tomorrow, business first and then our little adventure."

I wasn't going to argue with her. I was not so tired, but I needed time to think without distraction. To feel. Perhaps to have a private word with Prince Ven'Dar, if I could arrange it. Something was dreadfully wrong.

D'Sanya had wrapped a light blue veil about her head and shoulders as we rode into the city, so that no one would recognize her. Knowing we were stopping in Avonar, I had worn a wide-brimmed hat for the journey. Though the sun was long gone and the lingering daylight quickly fading, I tugged it lower to keep my face in shadow.

Just as we nudged our horses to life again, ready to abandon the dark lane for the well lit command, a fiery explosion of blue light engulfed us. Stormcloud balked and whinnied. Flash-blinded, swearing at the Dar'Nethi and their frivolities, I slapped one hand over my burning eyes, while keeping a firm hold of the reins. "Easy, easy, fellow," I said. "It's all right. My lady, are you—?"

But I knew instantly that she was not all right. Grunts and thumps and a woman's muffled scream came from my left. Miaste whinnied in panic. I could see nothing but a blue glare. So I concentrated . . . listened . . .

"Get the rings . . . and that thing on her neck . . . Bind her hands."

Thieves. How many? *Listen . . . feel . . .*

A thud and a groan in front of me . . . Two men grappling. Blood on the air. An aborted cry identified the bleeding, choking victim as Na'Cyd. Four men to my left—all afoot—and D'Sanya struggling . . . Feeble bursts of enchantment . . . ineffectual . . .

"Lady!" Damn these human eyes that would not recover fast enough!

"Hurry," growled a breathless man to my left. "Get her away."

Searing threads of binding magic . . . foul . . . diseased . . . These were no ordinary thieves. Enchantments slowed my limbs . . . clouded my thoughts . . . Zhid enchantments . . .

D'Sanya's cry . . . cut off . . .

"No!" Shaking off the Zhid snares, I dragged Stormcloud's head around, dropped out of the saddle, and slapped his rump, sending the frightened beast toward the two in front. Confusion might give Na'Cyd a chance. "Consiliar! 'Ware!"

Racing hooves, scrambling boots, screams and shouts. I lunged in the direction of that breathless abductor's voice, calling up every scrap of power I could muster to sharpen my senses, thanking my mentors in Zhev'Na for those interminable, hateful hours of practicing hand combat blindfolded. My hands slapped and groped and fumbled until they found a jutting jaw attached to a thick, sweaty neck and twisted the two in opposite directions. The neck snapped.

Shoving the heavy body away from me, I extended my hands and my senses, crouching low as I spun and dodged, caught up in a confusion of nervous horses before I felt the threatening movement to my left. I pivoted on one foot and slammed my leg into a human target, evoking the crack of bone, an aborted cry, and the solid, satisfying crack of a skull hitting pavement.

"Enough! Kill him!" shouted the leader.

I pivoted again, this time with my forearm on a course

for the speaker's throat. But I checked abruptly when cold, edged steel intruded on my inner vision in company with a lady's whimper. Where was D'Sanya? Where was the damnable blade? Blinking furiously as I stood paralyzed for a moment, trying to clarify the hints of form and substance appearing through the veil of blue fire, I was startled to feel the prick of the knifepoint under my chin, lifting my face upward. Pausing. A severe mistake.

I smiled.

"By the winds of darkness!" The awestruck whisper came from a solid blur right in front of me. Even half blind I knew him Zhid. "We heard that you liv—"

I broke the cursed Zhid's hand when I twisted the blade from his grasp and plunged it into his throat. By this time I could see the outline of a fourth man hurrying away up the dark sloping lane, a ripped blue veil and a mass of light hair dangling over his broad shoulder. I raced after him. But before I could catch him, a party of horsemen approached from the direction he traveled. I considered enchantments, ready to lick the blood from my hands to feed my power. They would not have her. They would not.

Before I could do anything so drastic, my clearing vision noted the gleaming white-and-gold badges on the horsemen's mail shirts—Ven'Dar's men. The leader of the party rode toward the trapped Zhid. In one hand he held a sword that shone brightly, casting a green glow on his silver mail and helm. The weapon was wreathed with enchantment that twisted my own bones though it was nowhere near me. "Release the princess, *arrigh scheide*," said the warrior, "or you'll suffer such torments as even a flesh-eater cannot imagine."

"You do not know your peril, Dar'Nethi pig. Zhev'Na will rise, and we will have this one as we will have you all." One of the Zhid's arms was wrapped about D'Sanya's body, holding her on his shoulder. His other arm he held behind his back, fist clenched. Enchantment swelled from it. "She is poison."

I crept slowly toward the Zhid. All the villain's attention was on his growing enchantment and the Dar'Nethi rider. The Dar'Nethi nudged his mount a few steps closer, then slipped easily from the saddle. As he approached the Zhid, he twirled his blade in the air, leaving little green circles of light to tease the eye. "*Zhid* are the world's poison, flesh-eater. We've almost done with you. Think you to give me a fight? Put the Lady aside and use both hands, and even so, I'll stick this blade between your Zhid eyes."

When the Zhid shoved his clenched fist into the air, I knew we were out of time. Forced to choose between his fist and D'Sanya, I lunged forward and gripped his wrist, wrapping my body around his forearm. The Lady could better survive a fall to the pavement than whatever deviltry the Zhid had built. An explosion slammed into my gut. Fighting for breath, I held on and felt the Zhid's arm crack.

Though a violent tug threatened to pull the squirming Zhid from my grasp, I refused to release him. We staggered on the sloping pavement when the tension was released. A second explosion in my gut propelled me backward, smashing my back into the brick wall. Feeling my grip slacken and my senses waver as we slumped toward the ground, I flung one arm around the Zhid's throat, rolled forward, and trapped his writhing body under mine, squeezing. After a while, he lay still . . . as did I for some indeterminate time. . . .

Firm footsteps paused behind me. Moved around my head. Mail chinked and boots creaked, and a body's mass settled close to my face. A firm warm finger felt the vein in my neck.

My jaw was jammed into the hard, uneven pavement. I still couldn't move. Could see only blue-edged blurs. Every bone, muscle, and hair ached, and a small boulder or perhaps . . . someone's head . . . pressed into my breastbone. "The Lady," I mumbled awkwardly.

"She's safe."

The voice was familiar. Through a milky haze, I spied

a green gleam from a sheathed sword. The swordsman. But more familiar than that . . .

"My men have escorted her to the palace. A few scrapes and bruises and a wrenched shoulder; I had to pull her away a bit forcefully. And she's already shaking off the fright. Prince Ven'Dar will see to her." He was cool. Polite. "I've sent for a Healer. Can I move you? Or perhaps I can help until she arrives."

I closed my eyes and considered the state of my health. Wriggled my hands and feet, stretched my neck a bit, and started drawing my knees up underneath me as well as I could with a body crumpled under me. "I think I'm all right. Bruised"—my belly felt as if one of the brick walls had been dropped on it—"but not bleeding."

He offered me his hand, the back of it the color of good earth, the palm lighter. Je'Reint.

I accepted his help, as I was tired of the paving stones digging into my face and Zhid bones poking everywhere else. And I wasn't sure I could get up on my own.

We stood alone in the center of the sloping lane. Two men hefted the bodies of dead Zhid onto horses. A man stood guard at either end of the lane, preventing anyone from happening across the scene. Je'Reint slung his helm on his saddle and watched as I confirmed to my amazement that the blasts of power from the Zhid had not even broken my skin.

"We'd ridden out to escort you into the city," he said, shoving his damp, matted hair out of his eyes. It hung almost to his shoulders. "After this week's raids, the prince was concerned about the Lady traveling with so little protection. But obviously we weren't watching the right roads. Who would have expected you to take back alleys?"

"Someone did." Someone had directed us to this very lane. "The Lady's consiliar . . . how is he?"

"A little rough—a stab wound to his back—but he'll live. Your horse seems to have trampled his assailant at a critical moment. The consiliar was fit enough to ride and chose to remain with the Lady."

Nothing conclusive about Na'Cyd, who once was Zhid. I clucked to summon Stormcloud, who stood fidgeting and blowing alongside Je'Reint's mount. "So how did you find us?"

"We were right on your heels. A young woman witnessed the initial attack and rode for help. Said she had followed the Lady here from Gaelie and insisted that Prince Ven'Dar be notified. Persistent enough to see it done. I didn't get her name." A good thing Je'Reint's eyes were not knives. His examination would have flayed me. "She said the Lady's 'lover' traveled with her."

Sefaro's daughter. That would take some thinking about when I had time and sense to do it.

Happy to have something to hold on to, I fondled Stormcloud's ears and stroked his neck. He was still quivering. So was I, but I didn't want Je'Reint to notice. Five years since I had killed a man with my bare hands. Such an elemental thing. Power for the taking.

"Well, if you ever introduce me to the young woman, I'll have to thank her. And I'll thank the prince for sending you to watch over—"

"Here, my lord. We've found something with one of the bodies." One of Je'Reint's men tossed him a small leather bag. As the soldier returned to his fellows, Je'-Reint dumped the contents into one hand: four silver rings, a bracelet made of entwined strands of gold and silver, and a long silver neck-chain with a plain circle pendant.

"Those belong to the Lady," I said, as I moved slowly to Stormcloud's middle, my belly protesting at the thought of getting up on his back.

Je'Reint lifted a hand to stay me. "While we're here alone, I need to speak with you."

Needed to, perhaps, though he definitely did not *want* to. But I welcomed a longer time to recover. I laid my forehead on the saddle for a moment while a wave of dizziness passed. "Go ahead."

Piece by piece he dropped D'Sanya's jewelry into the leather bag. "Three days ago thirty to forty Zhid attacked a settlement and a supply caravan. Witnesses swear that the Zhid attacked in formation. Not a ragtag few after the same prize, not undisciplined warriors joined together for a raiding party only to kill each other over the spoils, but small marshaled bands that hit swiftly, took only adult male prisoners, and retreated. How is that possible?"

"Marshaled . . ." Organized Zhid acting under tactical command. But the Zhid had never devised their own tactics in Zhev'Na. Every direction, every initiative, every plan had come from the Lords.

I glanced up at Je'Reint, sure he must be mistaken. But his demeanor stated that he was not merely purveying rumor.

"In all the years we fought the Lords, we were never able to extract strategic or tactical information from captive Zhid," he said. "No mind-bending or thought-reading or arcane investigation revealed anything of how orders were passed. Ever. We couldn't even distinguish between commanders and the lowest warriors." He stepped closer and lowered his voice. "You were one of them. They trained you to command their warriors. How did you do it?"

I had trained as a commander for months, and yes, eventually the Zhid had obeyed my voice commands with the same ferocious, terror-laced loyalty they yielded to all their brutal leaders. But I had never learned the final piece—how the Lords deployed so many thousands so seamlessly. "I don't know. I never commanded in the field. Only in training."

"Has someone else learned how to do it? How could they? Do you believe—? Are the Lords truly dead? We *must* know what enemy we fight. We've heard rumors of thousands of Zhid. If you are what you claim, then you must tell what you know."

"I told you I don't know anything."

A blatant lie. As I had told my father, I *did* know the information Je'Reint wanted. Or rather, I *could* know it, if I chose—as I could know everything the Lords had known, everything they had done, every depravity and despicable plot that three beings of corruption had been able to devise over a hundred lifetimes. Even the truth of the Lady. The sum of their memories lived inside of me like another organ, another stomach or heart, only rotted and loathsome.

I hated that it was so. Feared it, as I feared nothing else in my life. To touch their memories was to use that rotted heart to pump poison into my veins, weakening the barriers between the person I wanted to be and the vile creature of power I had once been. I could not afford to pity these Dar'Nethi blithely going about their summer-evening entertainments, or to regret the families who had moved out into the Wastes believing their prince and their small bands of warriors could root out these few Zhid stragglers, because I dared not uncover those memories. Certainly not with the smell of blood on me. Not with the feel of snapping necks still vibrating in my fingers. "I can't help you."

"Or is it that you won't?" He moved in close, where I could feel his breath on my cheek and smell his sweat and leather. "What is your purpose here? To unmask the Lady? You've gone far beyond that. 'Her lover,' this woman said. Does the prince, your father, know how shamefully you use a kind and generous heart?"

Shoving past the big Dar'Nethi, I gripped the saddle rim and Stormcloud's mane and swung into the saddle, anger muting my body's complaints. "You chose to remain ignorant about this matter, Master Je'Reint, and have clearly been successful. I don't have to tell you anything."

"Does your father know that you kill to protect her . . . and how you kill? And is that more evidence of your suspicions or a sign of your good heart or is there some other method in your deeds? Tell me why these Zhid magics left you walking, young Lord, even though you put on this impressive show of killing. Did you not find that strange?"

I clucked to Stormcloud and rode down the lane and through the thinning crowds of the grand command to the palace gates. The enjoyments of the evening had evidently continued unabated, only the late hour sending the people of Avonar home to their beds, unaware that five Zhid had attacked their princess a hundred paces from their city's heart.

My fury at Je'Reint's self-righteous accusations had not robbed me of simple reason. The dangers that concerned him were real, and his last point was well taken. The Zhid enchantments were not designed to kill. Why? Je'Reint believed the Zhid wanted to protect *me*. But evidence indicated that D'Sanya had slain two Zhid before wandering into the Gardeners' camp. She swore she could not remember how that had occurred. It seemed clear that these Zhid tonight wanted to take D'Sanya alive. Take her back.

"I've come to see the Lady D'Sanya," I said to the palace-gate guards. "Please tell her. Or, if she is asleep, please inform Prince Ven'Dar that the Lady's traveling companion begs entry." I swayed in the saddle.

I hadn't needed to send a message. She was at the gate and in my arms before the guards could choose which messenger to send. But as I buried my face in her hair and blessed every kindly spirit that she was unharmed, I could not help but wonder what use the Zhid had for her. I shivered, and the world still felt wrong.

CHAPTER 13

Though bone-weary from the night's events, I was unable to rest in Ven'Dar's palace. Turbulent images of broken bodies, crowded commands, and D'Sanya swooping down on me with empty eyes and a knife in her hand plagued the dark hours. Yet the demands of the body will always win out. About the time daylight crept through the slot windows, I blinked, and suddenly it was hot mid-morning. A tense serving man stood over my head, offering to dispose of the filthy clothing heaped on the floor beside the bed and show me to the guests' bathing room. The Lady D'Sanya was asking after me . . . urgently.

Despite the welcome luxury of a full bathing pool of gloriously hot water, I expended little time before hurrying along the corridor to join D'Sanya. Na'Cyd was standing in the passage outside D'Sanya's door, one bandaged arm sashed to his chest.

"I need to speak with you for a moment, sir," he said. "It's very important."

"Later, Na'Cyd. The Lady is waiting." We had been too tired to talk the previous night. I needed to sort out this strange business: why they wanted her, why she hadn't struck them down with the devastating power she held in her fingertips.

"But sir . . ."

I pretended I hadn't heard him and pushed open the door.

She sat at a small table where cold roasted meat, hot

bread, and an array of fruit had been laid out. "Stop," she said, as soon as I stepped through the door.

Mystified, I obeyed. She jumped to her feet and walked around me, eyeing the palace provision of dark green shirt and tan jacket and breeches.

"I approve," she said at last, tweaking the high neck of my shirt. "I think perhaps Prince Ven'Dar's stewards have a better eye for becoming fashion than you do. You should hire the one who selected these to be your manservant."

"You look lovely, Lady . . . as always." Breathtaking, in fact. A long tunic of deep, rusty red draped down below her knees over loose riding trousers, emphasizing her graceful height. The color set off her light hair and flushed complexion.

She laughed and drew me to the table. "Be quick about your eating. I breakfasted hours ago. I've already met with Prince Ven'Dar and assured him that I am nowhere near ready to relieve him of his office. He wanted to know everything about last night, of course." The flush in her cheeks faded at this last.

I sat in the chair next to her and drew it up close. "Lady, did they . . . your abductors . . . did they say anything that might tell us—?"

She laid a gold-ringed finger on my mouth. "No more of it. Speak of something else." Her voice wavered slightly. She shoved a bowl of plums in front of me.

"For now," I said. "But we *must* talk about it sometime."

And so we talked nonsense as she watched me eat, telling innocent stories . . . until with no warning she burst out, "Oh, holy Vasrin," jumped up from her chair, and ran out of the room.

I threw down my spoon and table knife and hurried after her down a long portrait gallery, trying to think what in the nonsensical conversation about childhood disobedience could have raised her temper. I'd told her of pouring ink on my tutors' papers and putting lamp oil in their tea to get rid of them, not mentioning that

I'd hoped to prevent their learning of my "evil" talent for sorcery.

She stopped in a cloistered courtyard beside a bubbling fountain, one hand pressed over her mouth, the other over her heart. Slowing my steps, I clasped my hands behind my back. I could not breakfast in gloves. "What is it, D'Sanya? Did I say something wrong? Offend you? Please, tell me."

"How could my valiant rescuer offend me?" D'Sanya stifled a sob and hugged her arms, her attempt at a smile failing. "Je'Reint told me what you did. To think you could have been killed . . . blasted to bits . . . destroyed by Zhid magic. For me. As you were telling your story, I thought of how lonely you must have been as a child, yet you have brought me such joy. These past few weeks have been the happiest I've ever known, and I've seen you happy, too, and I could not bear to look at you and imagine . . ."

I drew her close and kissed away her tears, ignoring the serving woman who passed by us gawking. "Then don't imagine it. I'm quite undamaged. As are you. And you see, *I* feel so stupid . . . so careless . . . taking you on the road with no protection. Knowing that Zhid were raiding. Inexcusable . . ."

And everything I said was true. Gods, where had my head been lost? Even with this creeping sense of disorder warning me, I had been unforgivably careless.

"You are my protector, now and—" She pulled loose and whipped around, leaving me standing behind her.

But it was only Na'Cyd who had entered the courtyard and bowed. "Excuse my intrusion, my lady, but you left orders for me to find you as soon as the gentleman was finished with breakfast."

"Of course, Na'Cyd. How are you this morning?"

"Mending well, so the Healers say. This"—he lifted the elbow of his bound arm—"is merely to support the repaired muscle for a day or two until nature strengthens it further."

"I'm delighted to hear it. Prince Ven'Dar has recommended, and I have agreed, that I will journey to Maroth

through a portal. If you would arrange for our horses to
get there with us . . ."

"Of course, my lady. Is there anything else?"

"The prince will summon you in an hour."

The consiliar did not leave, but bowed and watched
as D'Sanya took my arm and drew me back the way
we'd come. His expression, as always, was inscrutable.
Perhaps a little darker than usual on this morning. Or
perhaps that was my own mood.

D'Sanya pulled my arm closer as if to focus my attention. "Now you've soothed my silly megrims, I've not
forgotten my promised adventure. Alas, our time is constrained by this portal business and Prince Ven'Dar insisting that he do the portal-working himself. So we
won't have time to stay long. But what use to keep company with D'Arnath's daughter, if one reaps no wonder
from it? Any Nimrolan maiden might do as well!"

"No other, Lady. No other."

Beaming, she led me quickly through the palace, dis-
tinguishing the new-built parts from the parts she remembered, and telling how the use or furnishing of one
place had differed in the past, or what marvelous events
had occurred there.

"Down that passage is the chamber with cracked walls
from the time D'Alleyn sealed it, filled it with water and
honey, and spent twenty days freezing it, sure he could
make the largest sweet ice anyone could imagine." D'Sanya giggled as she pointed into a low, narrow passage
where a single yellow lamp brightened as we stopped
and peered inside, and then dimmed as we started down
a steep staircase that led into the core of the fortress.
"The three of us would roll ourselves in layers of rugs
and slide down this stair . . . it's the longest in the palace.
But D'Leon broke his arm on it one day, and Papa forbade it after. We've only a little farther to go. Can you
guess where I'm taking you? So few have ever seen it."

Of course, I knew. I remembered the steep, narrow
flight of worn steps from carrying my father's litter from
the Gate. But I said, "Another of your childhood hiding places?"

She laughed, and before I knew it, we came to the lower end of a sloping passage—nothing more than a massive wall of seamless, square-cut stone, darkened with age and smoke. D'Sanya stretched her hand toward the wall. The stone shifted and shaped itself to reveal a pair of wooden doors three times my height. They swung open to reveal the vast chamber, filled as always with cold white fire and billowing frost plumes.

"Now stay close. I am taking you through the Gate and onto the Bridge, where I will show you the most wonderful sight you will ever see! Not even Prince Ven'Dar knows of it. I've been saving my first venture for a special occasion—and what could be more special than being alive and free and keeping company with my bosom friend and dear protector?" She raised her arms, lifted her face, and danced through the doorway, spinning on her toes until she was out of sight.

I made it no farther than the doorway, where I stopped dead and clapped my hands over my ears. Unfortunately the horrid, scraping sensation was inside me, not outside.

The last time I stood in the Chamber of the Gate, I had just returned to my own body after our journey from Windham. I had thought the feeling that my spirit was an open wound immersed in salt water was the inevitable result of soul-weaving with my father's diseased body. But the chamber didn't feel so very different on this morning. Only to be expected, I supposed, as every other Dar'Nethi enchantment seemed to be having this effect on me.

I gathered control and shook off the disturbance as much as possible before D'Sanya could notice. Suffering ill effects from proximity to D'Arnath's Bridge had always been considered evidence of corruption.

When I entered the chamber, the Lady was kneeling on the smooth tile floor in front of the bronze lion, her head bowed and her palms spread wide. After a moment her eyes lifted to the lion's head and the gold and silver globes that some enchantment balanced far above us on the beast's upraised paws. I held back, knowing how she revered her father—the Lion of the Dar'Nethi, his people had called him. The Tormenter, the Talentbinder . . . those were the mildest of names given him in Zhev'Na.

In moments D'Sanya was on her feet again and beckoning me to join her. "Come see. Is this not a formidable lion? I commissioned it as soon as I was permitted to enter the chamber and view the Gate. I had it placed here after they anointed me, and I added the two orbs shortly after—to represent Gondai and the mundane world. It seemed only just that Papa should be remembered forever here beside his greatest work."

"It's a fine piece," I said, knowing nothing about it whatsoever. I would be doing well to keep from banging my jangling head against the thing. The light of the shifting Gate fire reflected off the metal globes—each of them an arm's length in diameter—so that beams of gold and silver light shot randomly across the chamber. The first one that struck my eyes came near boring a hole right through my skull.

D'Sanya tilted her head and examined me, tracing a finger along my cheek. "Are you well?"

"When you do that . . . yes," I said. Wholly the truth. Surely to bury my face in her breast would make the grinding illness inside me go away as well.

"Oh, holy Vasrin, I've dragged you down here on my silly whim, and your poor bones could be fractured from those vile firebursts! Prince Ven'Dar told me you refused a Healer last night. We must go up at once and see to your injuries."

If I had not already experienced the Bridge, my curiosity at her planned adventure might have overruled any physical ailment. But my previous crossings had shown me nothing so marvelous that it could persuade me to remain another moment in that chamber.

"I suppose I'm a little more bruised than I thought." I pulled open the door, wincing as even the vibrations of speaking lanced my spirit. "Will you bring me here another time and show me your wonder? Tell me about it."

"Of course, I'll bring you again!" We started up the sloping passages that took us back to the steep stair. "Papa took me to the Bridge only once. I was so angry with him—I told you that—and he said that to appease me, he would show me something that he would never show my brothers or my Uncle J'Ettanne or anyone else in the world. Something that would be our secret forever. First he showed me how he shaped the chaos beyond the Gate into a landscape of his own choosing, how he reached out with his power and opened a way through it. Then, he shaped a mountain from the matter of the Breach, and he forced the Bridge to lead us up to the very pinnacle—a place like Skygazer's Needle, where we could look out and see the worlds spread out before us, poor wasted Gondai, the mundane world—so marvelous in its variety—and even the horrid chaos and random matter of the Breach. He said that when I came into my power, I would be able to do exactly as he had done. I so much wanted to try it with you beside me . . . to share it with you."

Intrigued at the thought of such a view, I almost bade her take me back. But indeed as my spirit eased with our distance from the Gate, my bones and gut reminded me of the two concussions they had suffered the previous day. I again refused a Healer, though, as well as D'Sanya's offer to see to my injuries herself. I wished to experience no more Dar'Nethi enchantments than necessary that day.

We met Ven'Dar in a remote corner of the palace. He strode out of a columned walkway and joined us in a small cobbled courtyard, where a fountain centered a bed of fragrant herbs. Two men wearing the jewel-colored robes of the court accompanied him. One of them bowed to the prince and remained at the entrance to the walkway. A sword hung beneath his flapping robe. The second man stayed at the prince's elbow, his eyes scanning the upper-floor windows that overlooked the yard. Ven'Dar must be worried.

"My lady." The prince extended his palms but did not

bow. "I hope the night has revived your companion?" I garnered neither palms nor bow, but only a polite nod.

D'Sanya mirrored his gesture of respect, which named them equals, then gestured at me and smiled proudly. "Indeed my dear friend and noble protector finds Avonar more dangerous than his quiet Nimrolan Vale."

"My good lord," I said, bowing deeply with palms extended, as would be expected. My gloves had, of course, long found their way back onto my hands. "Gerick yn K'Nor. An honor to meet you, Your Grace."

Ven'Dar nodded to Na'Cyd as well. The consiliar had been waiting in the courtyard when D'Sanya and I arrived.

Ven'Dar returned his attention to the Lady, expressing polite concern over her safety, offering some of his own guards to accompany her until the Zhid threat was under control. Though I listened to their talk, I retreated a few steps so as not to be too obvious about it. Na'Cyd did the same, ending up at my side.

"Master Gerick yn K'Nor," he said softly, his expression impassive, his eyes fixed on the Lady and the prince. His free arm was at rest behind his back, his back straight as always. "I need to speak with you, sir. Alone."

"In what regard?" I said, maintaining a similar posture, uncomfortable with the intimacy in the consiliar's tone.

"Last night's events. Your mission in the hospice."

My *mission*? "My father is a guest of the Lady, Na'Cyd. I don't think—"

"I am aware of who your father is." His tone did not change. His gaze did not stray from his mistress, who was unsealing a folded paper just delivered by one of Ven'Dar's guards. "It is urgent that I speak with you in private, young Lord."

I snapped my head around. *Young Lord* . . . Earth and sky, he knew. He, too, was one of the Restored.

"Na'Cyd!"

The Lady's call startled me. She clapped one hand to her breast, staring at the unfolded paper as if it carried plague. "Something dreadful has happened!"

The gray man dropped his free hand to his side, all attention. "My lady?"

"Cedor was found dead last night in the hospice paddock. Gen'Vyl says it appears that his heart stopped, though he's found no cause for it. The staff is upset . . . the residents hearing rumors . . . We must go back at once."

"Of course there is no need for you to go back, my lady," said Na'Cyd smoothly. "Your business in Maroth is urgent. The new hospice could shelter so many more who need your care. I shall go back and take care of these matters. It is my place."

"If you're sure . . . and you'll call on me if you have any difficulty. Poor Cedor . . ."

"Of course, my lady. I'll leave at once."

". . . and you must find the kindest, most careful attendant for Master K'Nor." She beckoned me close and examined me carefully. "Do you need to go back, as well, dear friend, to see to your father? Will he be afraid? I would miss you so, but—"

"He will accept it as part of Cedor's Way," I said. "After yesterday, I think I should stay with you."

In a flurry of suggestions, good wishes, and warnings to be careful, Na'Cyd set out for the hospice, and D'Sanya and I for Maroth. As the consiliar had not told anyone of my identity as yet, I presumed he had no intention of doing so. But over the next three weeks, I constantly debated my decision to continue the journey. On one day I felt reckless and cruel to abandon my father and his failing instincts to chance. On the next I played my calculation game again: If D'Sanya was innocent, then she was in more need of protection than my father, and if she was guilty, then I would only discover it in her company. The only fact that gave me solace was that the danger of exposure was more mine than his.

In truth, I had little time to worry about Na'Cyd or wonder what he had been so anxious to tell me. But I sent a letter to my father by way of Paulo, warning him to be wary of the consiliar and to mistrust whatever new attendant was assigned him.

CHAPTER 14

Seri

Never in all the years since I first entangled my life with the Dar'Nethi sorcerers had I felt so useless, so unnecessary, so absolutely incapable of affecting the outcome of events. Even in the ten years between Karon's execution and the day he came back to me in the body of a Dar'-Nethi prince, I had been in control of my own survival. Even in my despair as I had watched Gerick's transformation into a Lord of Zhev'Na, I had refused to let go of him, and my words had woven a thread that helped draw him back from the abyss. Even in these past months while watching Karon die, my days had been filled with purpose—to gather him close and give him what comfort love could provide.

But now Karon was gone, spending his last days in an exile I could not share, and Gerick was off with him pursuing truth and forgiveness. No matter how often Ven'Dar spared a quarter of an hour to ask my judgment of Karon's letters or so kindly inquired what word I'd had from Gerick, I knew I wasn't needed. What use had anyone in Gondai for a middle-aged woman with no talent for sorcery?

I slammed my book onto the table, causing the lamp to flicker dangerously and my young hostess to stick her head into the sitting room. "Is all well with you, my lady? Is there anything I may—"

"No, Aimee. I'm sorry. I'm just unpardonably rude and impossibly restless. No one can do anything for me until I decide on what, in the name of heaven, I'm going to do with myself."

I didn't want to be "done for." I wanted to do something—anything—to get this over with. And, of course, even as I wished it, I understood that I was wishing Karon back to his dying. If I could just be with him . . . But a casual touch by any Dar'Nethi could reveal that I was mundane. My face might be recognized. The sight of the three of us together might trigger a question that would lead to discovery, wasting all these weeks' work.

"A plague on that woman!" I said.

"Surely these matters will not take long to resolve," said Aimee. "With Master Karon's wisdom and your son's power . . . and their friend, Master Paulo, is so capable and devoted. . . ."

"My husband writes that no conclusion is in sight. They've found nothing to prove that the Lady D'Sanya is not everything she appears to be, yet clearly doubts remain. And with these vicious happenings in the north, they must be sure of her."

"Would you like company for a while, my lady? I've slept so ill of late that I keep drowsing over my work. I'm on the verge of feeling entirely useless."

"Of course." I couldn't seem to concentrate on anything.

Aimee carried in a large basket of yarn, sat on the couch beside me, and began winding the yarn into spools. "The Lady D'Sanya seems to have done only good deeds in all these months. My sister writes that she has reforested the worst devastation in Erdris Vale, where the Gardeners believed ten years would be required. And my father's older brother, blinded by Zhid sorcery in his youth, was hired to do the water-seeking for the Lady's new hospice in Maroth. When she saw him struggling to mark his plans so the Tree Delvers would know where to set their saplings, the Lady brushed her hands on his eyes and he could see for the first time in thirty years. He told my sister that he would happily be blind again if fate ordained, for he'd had the chance to look upon the beauteous daughter of D'Arnath and found her worthy of her father's name. Everyone in Maroth marvels at her kindness and her good works."

Perhaps it was my general irritability or just the fact that I had never known anyone to live up to such a singularly virtuous reputation, but as I listened to Aimee's glowing report, I set myself the task to find Lady D'Sanya's flaw. I could not confront the woman, lest Karon and Gerick's subtler efforts come to naught, but I would investigate everything she'd done since she appeared so abruptly. She could not be so perfect as everyone believed.

"So is the Lady a Gardener or a Healer?" I said. "What true talent enables her to do all these things?"

Aimee wrinkled her brow, her fingers pausing. "I don't know that I've ever heard it said. It is most unusual for anyone to display such skills in so many disciplines. Though she cured my uncle's blindness and has healed the souls of many who were Zhid, I've never heard that she uses the healing rite as T'Laven or Master Karon does."

The girl felt through her basket for another length of yarn, and a tickle of enchantment feathered my skin as she tested one and then another until she found a color that matched the rest of the spool she was winding. "Have you asked D'Sanya about your own sight, Aimee?"

"Ah, well . . ." Aimee closed her eyes and dipped her head a little as if to dismiss my question. Speaking of herself always gave her pause, yet she had never been awkward about her infirmity.

"Come, tell me. Have you?"

"My blindness is of nature, not enchantment, and long before I could remember, my dear father tried every Healer in Avonar with no result. Though I've never been other than content with the Way laid down for me, my sisters urged me to speak to the Lady after our uncle's change. And so, one day when I met her at the palace, I asked her to examine me. She neither spoke the Healers' invocation nor used the blood-rite as she tested me, and so I suppose we must conclude that she is not a true Healer."

"And what did she say?"

"She was most profoundly grieved. When she laid her cheek on mine, I could feel her tears. 'Would I could remedy nature's cruelties along with those of men,' she told me. I assured her that it was truly of little matter to me. I could not deem nature cruel, but rather immensely generous to make me an Imager, who could envision things so vividly in my mind, and to give me a talented and loving family to help me develop my skills and put up with my clumsiness."

Aimee—who could not be certain of a person's presence or identity if that person had not spoken to her—was unaware of the new arrival who stood in the doorway of her sitting room, listening as she expressed her contentment with her life. She could not see the thin, freckled face and understand instantly that she need never suffer a moment's unhappiness that a sworn worshipper could prevent. The poignancy of the scene was almost enough to soothe my irritation.

Aimee paused thoughtfully. "The good Lord Je'Reint once said that—"

"Paulo," I said, interrupting before the girl's good-hearted affection for the whole world—and her frank admiration for Ven'Dar's deposed successor—drove another stake into poor Paulo's heart. "A perfect time for you to join us."

"Master Paulo!" As with every visitor, Aimee jumped up to greet the newcomer as if he were the one person in the world she had been yearning to welcome. Three balls of yarn rolled from her lap to bounce and unwind themselves in colorful disarray across the floor.

"My lady. Mistress Aimee." Paulo bowed to each of us, allowing no hint of either awe, admiration, or hopeless dejection to touch his voice. From the leather pack hung over his shoulder, he brought out a single folded sheet of paper and gave it to me. "I've only the one today, ma'am."

Knowing that Paulo and Aimee would forgive my rudeness, I read Karon's letter right away. Two short paragraphs. Nothing he hadn't said five times before. Even his handwriting was listless and straggling. Blinking away the pricking in my eyes, I stuffed the letter in my pocket and turned back to the others.

Paulo had retrieved Aimee's yarn, the colorful mass looking odd in his hard, bony hands. "Here, miss." He thrust the tangle into her graceful fingers. "Sorry. I seem to have made a mess of your thread."

Aimee frowned, plopped the yarn into her basket, and wagged a scolding finger at Paulo. "Never try to fool me, sir, thinking a blind woman cannot see the truth of her own mistakes. My friends know better."

Paulo's breath stopped, and his cheeks paled as if a headsman had just raised an ax aimed at his neck. Though his lips worked, they produced no sound . . . until Aimee covered her mouth with her hand and broke into merry laughter. "I'm sorry," she said, after a moment. "You are just so serious and so very kind . . . and I am a terrible, wicked tease . . . please, come sit and rest yourself from your journey."

Though his face told me he might prefer to bury his head in the cushions piled in the corner of the room, poor Paulo sat down in a straight wooden chair across the low table from Aimee and me. Setting her basket aside, Aimee poured a cup of cold saffria from a pitcher on the table in front of us and offered it to Paulo. A peace offering, I thought, though she could not see that he took the cup with his eyes fixed somewhere in the region of her gold-link girdle and thus could not observe her smile of apology. She tilted her head as if searching or listening, and, after a moment, bit her lip uncertainly.

I went to their rescue. "Paulo, Aimee and I were just discussing the Lady D'Sanya. Has Gerick mentioned her true talent?"

"No, ma'am. He's not said anything about it. And I guess it's not a thing you go and ask right out."

"You're exactly right, sir," said Aimee as she returned to her seat and picked up her basket. "To question a person's true talent is to imply that the person's worth is somehow defined by his abilities at sorcery, which of course it could never be. There are so many qualities of more importance." Rarely had I heard Aimee so earnest in her opinions.

"So what is she then?" I asked the world at large.

Paulo frowned thoughtfully. "She's no Horsemaster. That's certain. She fixed Nacre's leg weeks ago all right, but he's been bothered about it since."

"It's not just that the leg is tender?" Though I cared nothing for Lady D'Sanya's skill with horses, Paulo's observations were always valuable. And I wasn't about to say anything to discount him in front of Aimee.

"No. He's just . . . not himself. Not by a league or ten. He's gone vicious. That's why I've come here in the middle of the week. To bring him back and find another. I sent my Stormcloud with the young master to Maroth, and I thought I could coax Nacre back to himself. But it's no good."

"I've few enough horses in my stable, and they're mostly carriage horses or plodding nags suited only to carry a petrified rider around her little paddock," said Aimee, offering her pitcher again. "But you're welcome to any of them. And if none suit, I'll take you to Master Je'Reint's stables—the finest in Avonar. We can surely find you an excellent mount there. My lord is so generous. He's taken me to his house many times and offered whatever service I need since my sisters moved away. I'll be happy to arrange a visit if you'd like. I'll take you there myself."

"That would be fine, mistress. Really fine." Given the look on his face, one might have thought she had offered him the sun from her silver platter and then told him he couldn't have it after all. He refilled his cup and set the pitcher back on the tray.

"What other news, Paulo? Is Gerick back from Maroth? Three weeks, it's been."

"I've not seen him. Last I heard, the Lady was still away from her house."

"And Karon . . ."

"He says he's not managed to write further on his work nor any more than the one letter. Says he gets distracted too easy, but not by anything that's worth writing about." Paulo's face reflected the worry that accompanied any mention of Karon nowadays. "Things are not right with him, my lady. Though it's a risk to have me sneaking in, he seems to pick up a bit while I'm there. But he's not right."

I knew things were not right with Karon. His letters had dwindled in number and length and substance as the weeks had gone by. I ached for his loneliness and isolation, and without Gerick there to test him, I couldn't even know what was natural and what might be caused by the strange enchantment under which he lived. "He says your visits have been the best thing in his life, Paulo. You must have found something interesting to talk about."

When Gerick began spending so much time with D'Sanya, Paulo had taken it on himself to visit Karon, saying he would sneak through Karon's private garden, so as not to risk anyone inquiring about "Master K'Nor's" new visitor. But what had begun as an occasional hour had expanded into daily visits, so we'd seen little of Paulo for the past weeks. Karon's letters said that he and Paulo were having some *useful discussions* that were the first things to keep his attention since he'd been at the hospice.

"We pass the time. Talk a bit. Not much as would be interesting to anybody else." His gaze followed Aimee, who stood at her sideboard cutting slices of cake and setting them on small plates. When he noticed me watching, he colored and looked away. "He's a deal lonesome since the young master's been away. I'm sure he'll pick up when my lord comes back."

Ven'Dar had told us about the Zhid attack on Gerick and the Lady. Gerick had sent only a brief description of it along with his warning message about the consiliar. If he hadn't needed us to forward the message on to Karon for him, he'd likely not have told us anything.

Since then, Gerick had sent only one brief note from

Maroth, saying they had seen no more signs of Zhid interest in the Lady, and that D'Sanya had kept him so busy, he'd had no time to investigate anything. *Life has changed for me, Mother,* he'd written. *I've learned things about myself I never imagined. And I've come to understand so much about you and my father and how you've been able to survive all that's happened to you. Whatever comes of all this, I hope to be the better for it.*

Karon was intrigued by the Lady's determination to teach Gerick to enjoy himself—an unexpected echo of a wish the two of us had shared for five years. He said I wouldn't recognize our son's manner. *I've seen Gerick pleased or satisfied in the past,* Karon had written a week or two before Gerick left for Maroth. *And when he has joined with me, I've felt his care and love as if they were my own emotions. But never until these past weeks have I seen him happy. When he comes in from his time with her, he exhibits no trace of the burdens he has borne all his life. Though I fear for what we may yet unearth about this woman—and truly those fears lessen every day—I cannot regret Gerick's discovery that he can be happy or my witnessing it before I have to leave him. The paths of life are truly marvelous.*

I didn't like it. Gerick and Karon were like two infants setting out to untangle a family squabble. Gerick had been a hermit for nine years after a completely unnatural childhood, emerging only briefly at age sixteen to offer his life to save the world from the Lords. And nobody in any world was less willing or able to recognize ordinary human wickedness than Karon, who insisted on seeing his own goodness reflected in everyone he encountered. All the more reason for a practical and uninvolved—though not exactly objective—observer to get busy.

I had the beginnings of an idea, and all I needed was a few words with the harried Prince of Avonar to help me decide if my plan made sense. When Paulo and Aimee set out on their excursion to Je'Reint's stables, they took my message for Ven'Dar to the palace. And along with a new horse for Paulo, and a gift of some elegant writing paper sent to me from Je'Reint, they returned with the Prince of Avonar's agreement to meet with me the next morning.

Two days later, I set out to seek my own version of the truth. Though skeptical that I might discover what others had not, Ven'Dar had provided the assistance I requested. He had given me an introduction to V'Rendal, a loyal and discreet Archivist, who could allow me access to the records of D'Sanya's interrogation, as well as provide me with an identity, credentials, and a plausible excuse to be poking around in case I wanted to look further. The woman worked tucked away in a quiet chamber below the palace library—the Royal Archives, a cool, high-ceilinged room lined with tall wooden cupboards.

I began by reading the official report of the Lady's examination by the Preceptorate, and the statements by the Archivists, Healers, and Historians who had questioned her. D'Sanya's knowledge of historical detail, her experiences, and the evidence that could be corroborated from other sources supported the belief that she was exactly who she claimed to be—a twenty-year-old woman who had been born more than a thousand years in the past.

"One thing bothers me, V'Rendal," I said to the buxom red-haired woman who sat across the wide table carefully removing the pages from a tattered book. My finger tapped the crisp vellum of the report that lay in front of me. "Your Historians found only three references to D'Arnath's daughter, all in a single text. The first is merely a date in the record of royal births. The second is in a listing of those attending the celebration when D'Arnath was crowned High King of Gondai. And the third is in the record of the residents of the palace when the great census was taken in the third year after the Catastrophe. He never even mentioned her name. Though he recorded no date of death, in every description of the family's activities after the third year of the war, only the sons were listed. How can we assume that this writer was correct, and all others in error?"

The woman picked up a penlike instrument with a leather-wrapped handle and used the small V-shaped blade set into its tip to cut a stitch in the book's ruined binding. Then she lifted out another fragile page and set it on the stack beside her. "The source is the important thing here. S'Tar was the official Historian of D'Arnath's court, required to be complete and adhere to the strictest standards in his writing, including all lists of the sort you've mentioned. His works are considered unimpeachable. As to his lack of detail about the daughter, I have my own theories. Prominent Historians pay little mind to women even yet."

A fly buzzed around our heads and into V'Rendal's face before settling on her stack of pages. She blew a quick sharp puff of air toward it, and the fly bounced from the stack onto the table, apparently frozen. Then she split another stitch and resumed her work and her lecture.

"Few histories . . . few books of any kind . . . survived those days. Books are so fragile. One of the great tragedies of this pernicious war occurred when King D'Arnath himself destroyed the Royal Library and its archives by mistake in a battle near the end of his reign. S'Tar's work and a few other specialized court histories survived because they had been so widely distributed. Every major library had its own copies. A few lesser-known histories—E'Rind's *Obscure Histories,* Mu'-Tenni's *Ancients,* one or two other texts—had never been added to the royal collection, and thus survived the destruction." She pursed her wide mouth in resignation. "But very few of those works still exist, all reportedly in the same condition as this poor volume and quite scattered throughout the Vales. I've never seen even one of them. After that disaster we began storing our most important histories inside the palace rather than a separate building. Tell me, are women ignored in great events in the mundane world?"

I smiled at her as I closed the bound reports and stacked them. "Dreadfully so. At least Dar'Nethi women have been able to *participate* in great events. In my country we are just beginning to wield influence. So, did the Historian who wrote this report research any of those more obscure histories?"

V'Rendal clipped another stitch and rolled her eyes. "He told me that it wasn't worth the trouble to look further, when S'Tar had provided the necessary confirmation of the girl's existence. The stories of her in the more obscure texts would not likely be reliable. And in truth . . . he was probably correct."

I hadn't expected much from the public record— clearly the Preceptors and the Dar'Nethi people had been satisfied—and so I was only slightly disappointed by my initial lack of results. If the opportunity arose, I might hunt down the more obscure histories, but I was more interested in the D'Sanya of my own time. The ancient Historians would not have known what happened to D'Sanya in Zhev'Na anyway.

"To be confined 'asleep' for a thousand years . . . how is that possible?"

"I don't know of any way. For short periods, yes. Everyone assumes the Lords could do whatever they liked—blatantly ridiculous, of course, else how would Avonar still stand? Yet it's true we don't know half their works."

"So no one investigated the nature of the Lady's enchantment?"

"No. I've wondered myself. Believed it should be a part of the records. Only one other person ever asked about it, one of the Restored. The man came in here every day for a week, reading the entire history of the war and how it all ended. A quiet man and most polite, but"— she shuddered—"I had M'Qeti from the Royal Library come here every day the man visited, so I didn't have to be alone with him. I suppose he had been Zhid for a very long time. It is so difficult to imagine that they don't— Well, I told the fellow I might speak to a friend of mine about the Lady's enchantment, but I've

had so many other things to work on these past
weeks . . .''

V'Rendal paused in her activity, setting aside her cutting tool, her thick fingers lying quietly on her book. "I
suppose *you* could speak to my friend. Garvé's an odd
man . . . and friends tell me he's gotten a bit unstable.
I suppose that's the nature of being an Arcanist."

"An Arcanist?"

"When a Dar'Nethi boy or girl comes of age, it is
usual for the child to be gifted with one of the hundred
named talents." Her speech reverted to the precisely
pruned simplicities of a nursery tutor. "That particular
talent comes on them over a period of years and eventually dwarfs the smaller skills that all Dar'Nethi—"

"I know all about the Hundred Talents and coming
of age."

"Hmm . . . well . . .'' The woman cleared her throat,
disgruntled at my interruption. "Perhaps you also know
that enchantments of great difficulty and complexity
often cross the boundaries of the hundred?"

I bit my tongue and held patient. "No. Please go on."

"Well, Arcanists are gifted in such matters. They are
quite powerful . . . unusual . . . and often become dangerous, as I've said. Garvé is our only living Arcanist. He
happens to be off investigating the site of these Zhid
attacks just now, but he returns in a few days. If you
like, I could ask him to see you."

"Yes, I'd like that. That would be very kind."

"I'll send a message to Mistress Aimee's house. I
should get on with my work now. Everything seems to
be taking longer than it should of late."

"Certainly. You've been most helpful. Just one more
question before I go."

V'Rendal had bent her head to her work again, brushing a stubby finger delicately about the ragged border
of a page. But she didn't say I couldn't ask more.

"I want to speak to those who first encountered the
Lady." Those who witnessed her return to the world of
the living might have insights or impressions that had
been suppressed by later evidence.

Sighing and pulling a sheet of paper and an ink bottle close to her, V'Rendal wrote out several names. "These are the Gardeners who first spoke to the princess. Come back tomorrow morning, and I'll send you to their present location—assuming they've not pulled out. I've a book to send out that way, so I'm having a portal made. Easy enough for the portal-maker to send you on as well, assuming he can get the thing to work at all."

"Thank you so much for your help, Mistress V'Rendal."

As the workroom grew suddenly chilly, the Archivist nodded, but did not speak. Enchantment filled the space like a shower of unseen feathers, and the brittle edge of the thin sheet beneath her hand seemed to soften and flow together, as if it were knitting itself together again. But then the shower of enchantment came to an abrupt halt, and she swore at her clumsiness. I pulled open the door and hurried out, closing it softly behind me.

V'Rendal's portal left me at the dusty village of Megira, a deserted cluster of whitewashed mud-brick buildings once used as a watch post where Dar'Nethi warriors could keep a wary eye on the desert. No permanent settlements existed out so far as yet. The Dar'Nethi had abandoned the security of Avonar and the Vales only slowly after the war, and talk in Avonar said the recent attacks had brought that movement to a halt. V'Rendal's information said the Gardeners were working somewhere out past Megira, and that I should take the road straight west to find them. I set out walking down a cart track that showed signs of recent use.

The day was warm and windy. Megira sat in gently rolling hills of grass and rock and scrubby trees, but the cart track descended quickly into wide expanses of grasslands newly claimed from the desert. I wasn't worried about the Zhid. The recent attacks had occurred far from this region.

Evidently in ancient times, few cities or towns existed in the twelve kingdoms of Gondai beyond the royal cities used for governance. The Dar'Nethi had preferred large, sprawling dwellings sprinkled randomly across the landscape. With the ability to make portals for urgent travel, journeys were for exploration and pleasure, and long guesting was the custom. Dar'Nethi householders had thought nothing of having fifty guests at a time staying a month or more. Those who desired solitude had built themselves retreats in the woodlands, mountains, or open spaces, and warded them with enchantments so that no one would happen across them uninvited. Only since the Catastrophe had the people felt the need to huddle together tightly for safety and survival. And as their talents declined through the centuries, complex skills like portal-making and mind-speaking became beyond most people's abilities.

After an hour's walk I caught sight of blue tents billowing and flapping in the warm, gusty wind, small figures moving around dark mounds, and many flat wooden structures. Closer approach showed the dark mounds to be piles of rich earth, and the wooden structures long, rectangular trays of small plants, filled ones scattered all over the area, empty ones piled one upon the other. A number of people were unloading . . . no . . . loading three half-filled wagons with the seedling trays.

"I've come to see the Gardener Eu'Vian," I said to a dirt-streaked young woman who came out to meet me. "My name is Ser . . . S'Rie, and I've been sent by the Archivist V'Rendal to interview her."

"Ah! About the Lady." The girl offered me one of the water flasks tied to her belt, and I accepted gratefully. "Poor Eu'Vian will be happy when everything is written, and she can retire from celebrity. Usually she's hounded only when she goes into the city; you're the first in a while who's come all this way to meet her. I'm K'Tya."

The young woman reattached the water flask and tied a red scarf around her hair as she led me into the busy Gardeners' camp. Sweating men carrying picks, shovels, and small trees nodded as we passed, and women wearing brightly colored shirts, trousers, and scarves bade me a good day as they wheeled barrows filled with dirt and plants out into the dunes.

I hurried to keep up with the young woman. "Archivist V'Rendal is hoping for something—"

"—to make her history superior." K'Tya finished my thought with an accompanying sigh. "Some new fact. Some new clue. We know. But you'll find that Eu'Vian is not the kind of person to remember things unevenly. She'll tell you only what she's told before. I'll warn you not to waste her time. We're awfully busy just now."

"I saw the wagons."

She nodded. "Preceptor L'Beres has sent out a notice to forward parties like ours, recommending we pull in at least as far as the nearest settlement. We're trying to get enough done that our newest plantings can survive our absence for a while. Can't say I'm not a mite nervous with these awful reports coming in so fast, but it tears you apart to leave your work at such a vulnerable stage. The last half-year has been such a struggle." She slowed and waved to a sturdy woman who was stacking seedling trays onto a small handcart. "Eu'Vian! You've a visitor!"

K'Tya's prediction was exactly correct. The square-jawed woman with whom I sat in the shade of a dusty plane tree quickly demonstrated that her mind was highly organized, and she was unlikely to have forgotten anything. In no more than a quarter of an hour, Eu'Vian had recounted her tale of the young Gardener J'Savan bringing the starving woman with the incredible blue eyes to her camp, where the poor soul grieved for the long-dead king she claimed was her father.

". . . We fed her and cleaned her and put her to bed. She carried nothing with her but a primitive bronze knife and J'Savan's water flask. She bore no scars—none visible at least—and no evidence of beatings, torture, or enslavement. We were sure she was mad, yet she touched us so deeply that we wept to see her sorrow."

"And you took her back to Avonar right away?"

Eu'Vian sat up as straight as a child reciting lessons, her hands folded around a gray stone water flask. She did not fidget as so many do when questioned. "Not for three days. Though we had no Healer among us, she was so weak, you see. We woke her only to give her water and nourishment. On the third day, her madness seemed behind her, and she was already picking up our modern speech. She called for me and asked if she could hold my hand while she asked me a question. Of course, I agreed."

"And what was the question?"

"She asked how many years it had been since King D'Arnath had died. I hesitated, fearful of her delicate state, as you can well imagine. She spied my reluctance and smiled at me so sadly. 'Good mistress, I promise I will not retreat into madness,' she said. 'As I have lain here enfolded in your kindness, I have searched my memory and concluded that something extraordinary has come to pass. If I am to confront my fate, whether it be truth or enchantment or some disease of my mind, I must know its full compass. So—you spoke of D'Arnath as if he were a being of myth, his life and passing well beyond your own span of years. Tell me, Eu'Vian, how far beyond?' "

"And when you told her?"

"She wept, but did not falter. 'So there is no one living who knew him, or his sons, or his children's children. No one who could tell me of his dying words?'

" 'No, gentle lady,' I said to her. 'Unless they are written in our histories, no one could tell you that.'

" 'But you've told me you have a prince . . . a successor. . . . Is he not of D'Arnath's line?'

"I told her how the direct line of D'Arnath had ended so honorably with Prince D'Natheil and so tragically with his demon son, and I told her of good Prince Ven'Dar."

"And how did she react to that?"

"With resignation, I would call it, as if my news had met her worst expectations. All she said was, 'I would dearly love to have met my great-great-grandnieces and-nephews to the hundredth degree, but I suppose I shall have to be content with your prince. Am I right that my identity will be a great sensation in Avonar?' When I confirmed that it was already, she laughed sweetly, but with her sadness yet entwined with it. 'It is a wonder, is it not? I cannot explain it.' That's all she said of the matter to me. As we escorted her back to Avonar, she asked ten thousand questions as to matters of our history, exclaiming over each revelation as if it were a wonder in itself."

My fingers traced the sun-faded patterns of the woven blanket, feeling the malleable firmness of the warm sand underneath. My mind was racing. "You say she asked about D'Arnath's dying words. Did you not think that strange?"

Eu'Vian glanced at me oddly. "Not if one considers the traditions of our past. Did your family not—? Well, I suppose so many died in the war that some families have forgotten the old ways."

She seemed to be waiting for me to respond. I didn't want her wondering about me or examining me. "My family was never traditional," I said. "No one had time for it."

She shook her head, not quite in disapproval, but in disappointment. "How will our young people ever grasp the value of our Way if those of us with graying hair forget? That's why our enchantments continue to weaken, even though the Lords are gone. No one remembers. Well, it was long the custom that a father's dying words would make a family whole: settling grievances, resolving disputes, setting recompense for offenses, finalizing judgments. The family left behind was required to adhere to the dying man's saying. Before a battle, a man would set his words in writing or hold them in his weapon or a ring or something that could be given his family."

"Ah yes. Of course, I've heard of that custom." Only a small lie. "Just one more thing. Did the Lady ever give any hint of her true talent?"

"No. Certainly not to me. I've never even thought about it." Few Dar'Nethi would ever have asked the question. She puzzled over it for a few moments, but shook her head.

"What of the youth, J'Savan? Did he ever refer to it?"

"I never heard anyone speak of her gifts—except in the months since that day, of course, when they reported of their astonishing magnitude. Do you think there is some . . . significance in the direction of her talents?"

"Most likely not. We would just like to have the records complete. So, I'd like to ask J'Savan about it, and about other small things he might remember from the first encounter. Mistress V'Rendal says that no one has spoken to J'Savan himself since those first days, as you are the leader of your group and you've been so clear and reliable in your reports. But every mind remembers small things so differently. Would it be possible for me to speak to J'Savan? I promise not to take much time from his work."

For the first time Eu'Vian looked a bit uncomfortable, shifting her position on the blanket and brushing away gnats or hair from her face. "J'Savan no longer works in our group. He—" She shifted again, frowned, and pressed her water flask to her mouth for a moment without drinking from it. "It is very sad about him, as he is so young. No one knows quite what happened."

"What is it, mistress? I would really like to speak with him."

"J'Savan fell ill several months ago—a terrible disease of the mind. I ask after him frequently, but no one has yet been able to help him. He is confined in Feur Desolé, the prison house at Savron. You could learn nothing from him."

"You're saying he's gone mad?" Dread crept into my soul, roiling and growing and thickening like yellow winter fog.

"Indeed. He slaughtered three members of our work group and tried his best to murder us all."

CHAPTER 15

Any jailer in the Four Realms would have scoffed at the Dar'Nethi idea of a prison. No dank dungeons, no chains, no whips or rats or moldering foulness, no starvation or torture. Not even very many prisoners compared to the bulging horrors in Leire and Valleor. Even Gerick, the most dangerous prisoner the Dar'Nethi had ever held captive, had been imprisoned in a cell that was clean and dry. And though confined deep in the palace in Avonar, he had been given comforts of blankets, food, writing paper, and wine.

The Dar'Nethi philosophy discouraged imprisonment. For most crimes, the convicted offenders were subjected to spells and enchantments that would make repetition of the crime physically or mentally intolerable. Only for the incurably violent was confinement required, along with a host of powerful enchantments. A Dar'Nethi who threatened innocent life forfeited all claim to his own existence. Although executions were extremely rare, he would never again walk free unless society was given compelling evidence of his change.

Yet any house of secure confinement could not but burden the spirit. The Dar'Nethi had not learned how to avoid that.

The prison house of Feur Desolé stood about five leagues from Avonar, an old fortress with thick walls and few windows, but clean and dry inside. The wardens were men and women of varying talents who were willing to serve their sovereign and their fellow citizens in a work that was quite against their nature. Most of those confined to the prison were Zhid captured at the end of the war, warriors of such great age and power that no Healer had yet been able to help them recover their souls. A few of the inmates, like the unfortunate J'Savan, had fallen prey to some disease or perversion of mind that, while not the profound corruption of the Zhid, had turned them on their own kind.

A stooped, gray-haired man led me down a long corridor, his wine-colored robe whispering over the warm yellow of the stone. Lamps hung from the high ceiling every few paces, the light swelling as we approached and fading behind us, as if we traveled in a carriage made of light through a tunnel of night.

"No need to be afraid here, mistress," said the man over his shoulder. "None can escape their chambers in Feur Desolé. Look in the door glass. They've no way out."

Several of the doors that lined the passage were scribed with a name in silver lettering, and above the name was fastened a round glass that gleamed in the light as we passed. A morbid curiosity slowed my feet, and I peered into one of them. The palm-sized glass was not a window, but a myscal—one of the magical Dar'-Nethi mirror glasses. If you looked long enough, your own reflection faded, and you could see into whatever place the enchantment had linked with the glass. In this case, I glimpsed a windowless room of ten paces square, its whitewashed walls and ceilings reinforced with bands of silver—dolemar, no doubt, the "sorcerer's binding" that prevented any use of power by those held captive within. The cell's only furnishings were a water basin that was a part of the wall, a single chair of thick white wood bolted to floor and wall, and a pallet laid on the floor. On this pallet a large man in a brown tunic lay on his back in the image of sleep, his slack face as craggy and rough as a granite boulder. The chamber was dark, the soft light that illuminated the stark scene some factor of the enchanted glass that moved with my eyes.

"He looks dead."

"He's not," said the warden, motioning me to keep moving. "We keep the prisoners under heavy enchantments that allow no freedom to move or speak. We treat them with dignity—often more than they deserve—feed them, clean them, and rouse them when Healers or others come to pursue a remedy for their problems."

If the inmates could not be healed, they would continue to age until they died, so V'Rendal had told me. For the Zhid, this could be a very long time. The enchantments that had taken their souls had also made them incredibly long-lived. For J'Savan, a young man of twenty-three, life would stretch only an ordinary life span—long enough when facing those years without hope.

The warden paused at a door. "Are you sure you wish to do this? I'll warn you that the sight will wrench your heart. And it will be no small danger to sit with the boy. He has no control of his tongue or his limbs. Three of his friends lay dead and five others wounded before he was taken captive, and you wouldn't want to know what he'd done to them. He was sitting calmly in the midst of the bodies like a rock in a river of blood."

"I must try, Warden. Our histories must be complete, even if the tale is painful."

The stooped man bobbed his head. "All right, then. I must bind him before I can leave you." He passed his hand along the smooth edge of the door, which swung open silently. A snap of the man's fingers illuminated the cell, and we stepped in.

It was indeed heart-wrenching to see the handsome young man, so near Gerick's and Paulo's age, lying in the sterile cell unmoving. A lock of his dark hair had fallen over his boyish face. No sound or smell or breath of movement stirred the dead air.

From the warden's belt hung a variety of slender bars, wooden sticks, cups, and keys. He unhooked one of the wooden sticks, unfolded it into a backless stool with a gray fabric seat, set it beside one wall, and motioned me to sit still. As I watched, he lifted the youth's limp body into the chair and secured it there with leather straps, binding his hands and feet with silver cords as well. *"Tan y sole, J'Savan,"* he said, not unkindly, laying a hand on the young man's forehead.

J'Savan's eyes blinked open. Flicked to the warden and then to me. Lost. Confused. His gaze encompassed the bleak walls. The leather straps on his arms, thighs, and breast. A slight movement as if to test that they were real. He glanced up again quickly . . . frightened.

My heart knotted. Surely someone had made a terrible mistake.

But even as I opened my mouth to protest, a hard-edged gleam erased the baffled terror in his eyes. His pale skin darkened, first red and then purple, dark veins popping out on his forehead and neck, and he strained at his bindings until blood spotted his yellow tunic, and the flesh of his arms turned black where it bulged between the silver cords. "Well, well, well," he said, half singing, his voice soft, playful. "A woman comes calling . . . a scholarly woman. Wise perhaps. Are you wise? Not young, not old. Come to see me, have you? Are you not afraid? Afraid, afraid, afraid. Be afraid . . ."

"Are you sure you want to be alone with him?" asked the warden. "I've duties to see to, so I must lock you in. He can't get free, but it'll not be pleasant to see or hear. You're not going to get sense from him."

"Yes," I said. "It's necessary." My conviction was stronger than ever.

"Knock on the door when you're ready to go."

The warden closed the heavy door behind himself, setting the magical wards on it, too, no doubt. The walls glowed with a flat yellow light, leaving no shadows. I swallowed hard.

J'Savan writhed in his bonds. "Talk, talk, talk. Going to heal me, lady? Put my head together? Going to kill me, kill me, kill me? Burn it away. Burn it. Dig it out . . ."

Then followed such a stream of epithets and vileness that would have made my ears burn when I was a girl of seventeen, even though I'd grown up around soldiers.

Oddly enough, as the young Dar'Nethi spewed forth this verbal sickness, his body fell limp, his eyes gone dead and his limbs flaccid, his jaw slack and drooling. It was as if a demon had been trying to get out through his skin, but only succeeded when it found his mouth.

"J'Savan!" I said softly. "J'Savan, can you hear me?"

I'd come here to see him against the recommendation of everyone who knew of his case. The boy who had encountered the Lady was gone, they said. Better to let the one who remained sleep away his life and bring no more horror to the world. The Healers had found no disease in J'Savan, no cause for the transformation that over the space of a single day had changed a handsome, friendly youth who loved his work and enjoyed flirting with girls into a monster. Of course there was no connection with the Lady. His madness had struck him more than a month after his encounter with her.

But my unspoken fears, the remote, nagging belief that there were no such things as coincidences, had forced me to come and see for myself. I would stay only long enough to ask one question that I knew had not been asked of the youth.

"J'Savan, did the Lady D'Sanya do this to you?"

The young man's sky-colored eyes fixed on me, and I thought I saw in them one brief flash of perception in the storm of his madness. But I could have easily been mistaken, for his face grew hard and vicious, and he wriggled and strained against the cords and straps, taking up his odd singsong. "Dig, dig, dig in the garden. Make the desert live. Draw the spring, but not too close . . . not too close. Stay away, away, away. Speak tenderly to the rootlings. The roots go deep, deep, deep into the darkness. Bury it deep. In the dark where the springworms dwell. Dark, dark, dark. So dark. Ah . . ." As he struggled, a groan of such agony came from him, one would think his body was on the verge of disintegration.

The Healer who had worked with J'Savan had said she'd come near going mad herself in the chaos of his thoughts. This violence that wrenched his body was the most devastating pain she had ever encountered. Even the Lady D'Sanya had been unable to ease him. The Lady had recoiled in horror at a single touch, almost ill herself when she saw his condition.

J'Savan shook his head and twisted and his cry dissolved into words once again. "Lady, lady, lady. Most perfect lady. Perfect eyes. The desert blooms with eyes. Not grass, not trees, not vines. No, no, no. What grows so deep where the roots delve? Such eyes. Old, old shining. Eyes in the desert. Bury it. Bury it. Nurse the rootlings. Tender, tender, tender. Make them live. Draw the water from where the springworms dwell. Danger, danger, danger . . ."

With an explosion of spittle, the meandering words were replaced by mumbled curses, by descriptions of the defilement J'Savan's hands wished to perform on me and the mutilation and murder they could wreak on the warden or anyone else who fell within their reach. And as he spewed this filth, those same hands fell slack once more, his body still and his face numb. Dead.

I raised my voice so perhaps he could hear beyond his own mumbling.

"J'Savan, I'm sorry this is so hard for you, but I must know about the day you met the Lady. You were afraid until you saw she was not Zhid. You gave her water and offered her more, and you took her back to Eu'Vian and your friends at the Gardeners' camp: C'Mir, D'Arlos, Kedrin . . ."

I was floundering, grasping at will-o'-the-wisps. To put this young man's body and mind through such torment for my whim was cruel. But in the moment I spoke the names of the dead Gardeners, I knew that somewhere within the wretched being before me some spark of J'Savan yet lived. Even as the stream of muttered obscenity flowed from his drooling mouth, tears welled up in his dead eyes, rolling unfettered down his cheeks.

I knelt in front of him. "What is the danger, J'Savan? You're trying to tell me. What happened to you?"

Again the transition, again the instant of awareness, of pleading, I thought, of horror as his face shriveled into the snarling mask and his body pressed against the cords of dolemar, craving release. His voice was harsh and desperate now. "Round and round and round. Danger, eye of danger. Deep in the roots. Rootlings dying, dying. Eyes shining in the darkness. Ah, it burns, burns, burns. Round, round. Bright eyes in the dark. Danger, danger, danger . . ." Gasping, fighting, wrenching his head in frenzy, J'Savan battled his madness. Blood dribbled from his bound wrists. His tears mixed with the rivulets of sweat coursing down his snarling face.

Then, just as abruptly as they began, his struggles ceased and he slipped into his obscene deadness once more. He was trembling, exhausted, as the abominations fell from his lips. My own tears flowed unchecked. Unable to justify his torment any longer, I hammered on the door to summon the warden.

"You are not abandoned, J'Savan," I said, as I listened to the approaching footsteps and the clicking of the lock. "I know you're in there, and you must hold on however you can. You are not responsible for what happened to your friends. I believe that as dearly as I believe anything in this world."

As the Dar'Nethi warder invoked the words of enchantment that would drop blessed oblivion over the wretched youth, the whisper faded. "Danger, danger, danger. Bury it deep. . . ."

Was there any meaning in what I'd heard? The wardens, Healers, and Archivists thought not. Nothing of his condition or his ramblings were included in the report I'd read in the Archive. The investigators would have considered him unreliable, V'Rendal had said. Why include the ravings of a madman?

But on my journey back to Avonar, J'Savan's words scribed themselves on my thoughts, refusing to be dismissed until I set them down with pen and ink in the serenity of Aimee's firelit sitting room. Not every word, not the exact order, but I believed I captured their essence. When I laid down my pen late that night, I sat back in my chair and contemplated what I had written.

On the next morning, I dispatched a letter to Eu'Vian

by the first messenger Aimee could summon, and I could not settle to any task for the two days until the answer came back from the edge of the Wastes.

To my diligent acquaintance S'Rie, greetings,

In answer to your questioning: On the day he was stricken with his terrible affliction, J'Savan had gone out alone to tend a small grove of trees he had planted. The trees were dying after taking a vigorous, healthy start. J'Savan thought they might have root rot—perhaps he had drawn the groundwater too near. He was planning to inspect the roots to learn the problem. As I told you, he did not return until nightfall when he attacked us with murderous intent.

Yes, as it happens the grove was very near the place where he first met the Lady D'Sanya. She remembered it when she came to visit us after hearing of J'Savan's terrible illness, even visiting the spot for a time to mourn the boy. Her gentle soul was much affected by J'Savan's state and our tragedy.

You did not ask, but if the other matters are of interest to you—which I do not understand why, but presume you have reasons—then you may wish to know that the rootlings fare well. J'Savan must have done his work before he was affected, as his grove thrives. He was very good at his work and a cheerful spirit. We miss him sorely, as well as our brothers and sister who lie dead as a result of his affliction.

I hope your history work proceeds well, and that Mistress V'Rendal is satisfied with my saying.
Eu'Vian

What had J'Savan found when he went to tend his rootling trees? What danger had he discovered that had so shattered the harmony of his life that he was driven to acts against nature? And what was the connection to D'Arnath's daughter? The answer was close. Though I could not find it in the rambling words of the mad Gardener, I knew it was there, and I had no doubt that it mortally threatened my son and my husband, and the worlds at either end of D'Arnath's Bridge.

CHAPTER 16

A few days after Eu'Vian's letter, I received a message from V'Rendal saying that the Arcanist Garvé would be able to see me that evening. She warned me yet again that to seek out an Arcanist for minor inquiries was most unwise. She herself had not visited Garvé in many years. But the sight of the poor young Gardener had hardened my resolve.

Garvé's house surprised me. I had assumed that such a powerful sorcerer must have a fine and formidable residence. But the little stone house was squat and ugly, set in the midst of a ruined part of the city, an area of fire-blackened rubble thickly overgrown with weeds that had not been cleaned up since the end of the war. With the Dar'Nethi drifting out of the city, the space wasn't yet needed, and a great many things had higher priority than cleaning up a thousand years of debris. The house seemed to fade in and out of sight in the oncoming dusk.

The man who appeared at the door to answer my knock was as disheveled as his surroundings and almost as dirty. His scholar's ankle-length robe hung open, revealing a baggy shirt and trousers of indeterminate shape. Layers of food, wine, soot, paint, and other unnamable stains prevented one from guessing the original color of any of the garments. The limbs that protruded from this unappetizing garb were stick-thin, and his hacked-off hair resembled nothing so much as a boar's-hair scrubbing brush well past its usable lifetime. I couldn't see his face, as his nose was pressed into a ragged-edged book he held in one hand.

"Well?" I wasn't sure if this greeting was directed at me, at the fat one-eared cat he kicked back into the house when it tried to squeeze between him and the door, or at the tattered volume from which he had not yet removed his eyes.

I reread the slip of paper in my hand to make sure I'd got the location correct. This was the only likely place. "Master Garvé? I am S'Rie. The Archivist V'Rendal has sent me to see you."

"Well?" The low, throaty rumble seemed out of proportion to his slight frame. His eyes had not yet moved from the book.

"Have you a few moments to speak with me about a matter of interest to V'Rendal?"

"It's not hot is it? Won't work when it's hot."

Hot? "Excuse me, I've come to inquire about an enchantment, Master Garvé." I knew I wasn't making a good start, though I felt it would be a lot easier to make sense of things if he would just look at me.

"The sallé that you've brought. V'Rendal always remembers it. It mustn't be hot."

Sallé . . . "Oh, yes, of course!"

I pulled a finger-high, frost-rimed green bottle from my pocket. It almost froze my fingers to touch it. V'Rendal had informed me that Garvé was immoderately fond of sallevichia, a rare, expensive and violently spicy condiment made in the Vale of Nimrolan. Aimee had helped me find some of the stuff to bring him as a consideration. "No. It's still quite cold," I said.

Still without looking up from his book, Garvé snatched the bottle from my hand, whirled about, and disappeared into the house. As he had accepted my gift and had not shut the door, I felt only slightly awkward about following him inside. Although the house seemed quite a bit larger on the inside than it appeared from without, I could scarcely find a path between all the boxes, baskets, and furniture. Chairs and tables had been piled with every sort of item from birdcages to harps, spools of thread and wire to wheelbarrows, and unending stacks of books, reams of paper, and boxes of pens,

tools, trinkets, and feathers. The soft blue light of evening through the uncurtained windows kept me from
tripping over any of this clutter as I followed the gangly
figure through the house.

We emerged in a stifling, brick-floored kitchen that
looked as if a whirlwind had recently passed through it.
Alongside a huge, soot-blackened baking oven of red
brick lay a disarray of dented kettles, spilled flour, and
mounds of dubious vegetables. Long worktables had
been set around the periphery of the room and piled
halfway to the ceiling with more books, broken pots, at
least five sleeping cats, bottles, wooden boxes and glass
jars of every possible size, and what appeared to be endless piles of scraps: of fabric, metal, glass, leather, rock,
leaves, twigs, dirt, paper . . . Yet around and above the
disorder hung the savory smell of baking bread. My
stomach growled.

By the time I squeezed through the half-blocked doorway, the odd-looking man was pulling a long-handled
plank, bearing two perfectly shaped loaves, from his
oven. With one elbow he shoved aside enough of the
clutter on one of his tables to make a space before tipping the bread off the heat-darkened plank. The bread
teetered precariously on the edge of the table before
settling down beside the green frosted bottle. Book still
firmly in hand, the man snatched a small, chipped crock
of butter and set it down beside the hot bread and the
bottle of sallevichia.

He pulled two wooden stools up to the table, dislodg-
ing the disgruntled feline occupants. "Hurry," he said.
Though he had not yet looked at me, I assumed he was
speaking to me. I sat on one stool while he plopped
himself onto the other.

Whatever he was reading must be fascinating, I
thought, for he laid the book on the table and kept his
head bent over it closely while he grabbed a knife from
the table. He sawed one loaf into great hunks, slapped
a thick layer of butter on one of them, and dribbled a
few drops from my little green bottle on top. Instantly
the butter sizzled and gave off a small puff of greenish

smoke, and a dark green film formed over the entire
chunk of bread. When Garvé crammed this somewhat
unappetizing artifact into his mouth and tore off a large
bite, his eyes fell shut and his shoulders sagged in pleasure. In only a moment, he picked up his book again
and read furiously as he ate the rest of his green-
filmed bread.

Only when he had demolished the entire piece did the
man afford me a scrap of attention. For one instant, he
peered over the top of his book. My stomach lurched
inexplicably and I felt a bit wobbly as I glimpsed his
face, which made no sense at all. He could have been
anywhere from twenty-five to eighty-five, his skin smooth
and unmarked except for a web of fine lines at the corners
of piercingly intelligent gray eyes. I guessed him close to
my own age, mid-forties, and not only did his appearance
belie the dry knot of apprehension in my throat, but also
he displayed a smile of sublime cheerfulness.

"Well, you must have some! Before the bread cools
or you won't get the full effect."

"But I didn't—"

Before my protest had even taken shape, he had already snatched another hunk of bread, slathered it with
butter, topped it with the green nastiness, and shoved it
into my hand. "Quickly!" All this while his gaze darted
back and forth across the pages of the book he'd set on
the table.

I looked askance at his offering. All the warnings
about the dangers of the Arcanist clamored in my memory. Was it riskier to eat something of his making or
to offend his hospitality? Holding the impression of his
pleasant face, rather than the unsettling jolt I'd felt at
his glance, I took a small bite.

"Sword of Annadis!" I thought the inside of my
mouth was dissolving. I blew out a quick breath, terrified
to inhale, lest I blister my lungs. Sweat popped out on
my forehead. My skin felt as if it were on fire. Sometimes politeness must yield to survival. Yet just as I
made ready to spit it out, the taste of the warm bread
and melted butter mellowed the fire and blended the

spice into the most remarkable combination I have ever encountered: pepper and lemon, sunlight and frostbite, wood smoke and green leaves, seared with the very essence of flame, and everywhere the richness of the butter and the nutty flavor of the chewy bread.

Once I had swallowed and inhaled enough to assure myself that my throat and lungs were not scorched away, I looked doubtfully at the remaining green-glazed bread in my hand. Before I could decide what to do with it, Garvé exploded into laughter, holding his stomach until I thought he was going to fall off his stool. His laughter thrummed in the walls and ceiling. How could so much hilarity come from one so thin?

"Should have known. Should have known." Tears streamed from his eyes. Blotting them with his sleeve, he prepared another small piece of bread. "What a constitution you must have, madam! Should have guessed when you didn't know."

He popped the bite into his mouth, and then shoved a cup of dubious cleanliness and a carafe filled with something dark and foaming across the table, while wiping more tears from his cheeks with the hand that held the book. My head resonated with his booming laughter.

"How could I know V'Rendal would send me one who was not Dar'Nethi?" he said, once he had swallowed his next bite and calmed his laughter enough to put a whole sentence together. "Are you quite well? Uninjured?"

My tongue throbbed, my voice croaked, and my mouth watered excessively. "I've never had anything quite like it."

While I poured the liquid from his carafe and took a grateful drink—beer, it seemed, with a touch of fruit in it—he laid his book on the table again. Still reading, he hacked at the second loaf with his knife, wrapping each piece in brown cloth and throwing it in a basket he had pulled out from under two pots and a skillet.

"Well, of course you haven't! And no Dar'Nethi since the first one who tried to eat sallevichia has either. To ingest it without protection . . . Birds and beasts, I'm surprised you have a tongue left!"

"Protection?" The cool, strong beer was slowly soothing my throat.

"Here. Try this." Without looking, Garvé reached over and passed his bony hand across the green-filmed bread that still sat in my other hand. "Go ahead. I promise it won't hurt."

Tentatively, I raised the piece to my lips and felt a frosty kiss as if I'd just inhaled a huge breath of wintertime. I took a bite of the bread and, though I still tasted the potent fire and marvelous mix of flavors, my tissues remained intact.

"Better, yes?" He didn't look at me for the answer, but busily prepared and ate another piece himself, all the while studying the pages of his book and running the fingers of his left hand over the faint script as if committing the letters to memory.

"Better. But I don't think I'll trade it for strawberries or cheese."

"Not many people savor it as I do. And it is dreadfully expensive, so you're quite well served not to acquire the taste." He popped the cork back into the sallevichia bottle, blew on it, which immediately coated it with frost again, and set it carefully on a high shelf. Settling onto his stool, he quickly became entirely engrossed in his reading, abandoning me like another piece of his furniture.

At first I had thought the sallevichia was making me dizzy as we conversed, and causing my head to throb so sorely. But when Garvé's attention was diverted, I realized the sensations had more to do with the man himself. Every word he had spoken was like a blast of wind, each sentence the force of a gale. His movements and his speech were immensely larger than his person, so that I didn't like to think what his anger might be like. But I didn't like being ignored.

"Excuse me, Master Garvé, should I come back another time?"

"You're welcome here any time, with or without the sallevichia. I have few . . . very few visitors. Messages arrive at my door, but few bodies. Almost two months I think since the last. Age seems to be making me less capable of civilized behavior rather than more. I'm surprised you weren't warned off."

He turned a page and continued his reading. I would have sworn that the brick floor vibrated when he spoke. I couldn't decide whether to be frightened or angry or insulted at his inattention. I was certainly perplexed, so I decided to try once more. "Sir, I've come to ask you some questions about the Lady D'Sanya. Would you mind very much answering?"

"Not at all. What a lovely young woman she is. Such power! Awesome in magnitude and depth, complex, as if she has taken all the dark and dreadful things that happened to her and wrapped them in her own special brilliance—quite unlike the power of any other Dar'-Nethi I have ever examined. And so much good she has done with it, I hear." He still didn't look up, yet his comments were not the type of distracted mouthings of one wholly focused elsewhere, and his tone was not at all forbidding. "I don't know what questions I could possibly answer about the Lady, but forge ahead as you will."

"V'Rendal has sent me to ask about the enchantment that kept the Lady alive for so very long unaged. V'Rendal says she's never heard of anything quite like it."

"Ah, yes. The Lady's ensorcelment was indeed unusual. True stasis. The body alive, but held in preservation. I've thought about it quite a bit." He turned another page, read for a bit, looked back at the previous page as if to check something. Then he continued his reading . . . and the conversation. "We can delay the disintegration of things that once lived: flowers, fruit, bread, wood. That's easy enough, though we cannot stop their decay entirely. We can send a living being into sleep, shallower or deeper, and prolong it for some fixed time beyond the normal span of sleep or waking. Not indefinitely, though. Sleep rhythms will reassert themselves. We can reduce their needs for food and water, cloud their minds. More difficult, but still possible. They continue to age, however. Slowly, perhaps, like the Zhid. The Lords themselves were near immortal, but they sacrificed much of their human state for it. We've never learned how to prevent aging in a fully human person. To weave all these things together in a single enchantment would require a great deal of power and skill. For the Lords of Zhev'Na, perhaps just possible."

"So you believe what she says about it? And you can make some reasonable guess as to how it was done?"

He dug a pen and inkpot from the debris on his worktable and scratched some notations in the margin of his book. "Oh, yes. I have no doubts as to her tale. But I have not the least desire to know how it was done."

Though his desires were not relevant to my inquiry, the absolute surety of his statement pricked my curiosity. "Why not? As an Arcanist you study complex enchantments, do you not? How can you resist knowing of this one?"

For a brief moment he glanced up from his reading and the force of his full attention was like the pressure of a powerful hand, only released when he turned away again. "Because it is a savage cruelty," he said.

"I don't understand. Certainly to imprison an innocent girl, separating her from family and friends, is terrible and wicked. But the enchantment itself seems no more cruel than sleep."

"But this enchantment was not sleep, madam-who-is-not-Dar'Nethi. One thing I have learned in my years of study is that it is impossible to completely suspend the activity of the mind. No matter how deep the enchantment, no matter how long the span of it, one would retain some awareness of the world beyond oneself. Perhaps the Lords learned to deaden the mind completely. But mercy was not in their nature. No, as long as the body lives, the mind lives. Therein lies the cruelty."

He turned his pages more and more rapidly, his eyes

devouring the words. His free hand grabbed a fistful of grapes from a wooden bowl and popped them into his mouth one at a time.

"Do you mean that during that thousand years, the Lady might have been awake . . . or at least aware of time passing, of her surroundings, of all that had happened or was happening?" The thought of it left me breathless with horror.

Garvé nodded and swallowed a grape. "Not a pleasant consideration, is it? But considering the Lords is never pleasant. They must have set her mind wandering far from where she was, as we do with those poor souls in Feur Desolé, or she could not have survived it so well."

Savage cruelty indeed. Garvé's words bounced off the unpainted walls like pelting hailstones. Indeed all his words seemed to have more substance than those of anyone I'd ever met, and they lingered about his house with all his other scraps, as if you could pull open a drawer in one of his shabby bureaus and have whole conversations fall out.

I had heard what I'd come for, and I stood up to leave.

"Have you no more questions, my mysterious not-Dar'Nethi?" he asked, even while pulling a second book from a tottering stack of them and opening it in the clear space on his worktable, flicking his eyes back and forth from one to the other.

"I've a thousand other questions," I said. "But it appears I should not bother you with them today."

"I'd like to hear them. It's little disturbance. No one comes here." He glanced up ever so briefly. "You must understand, I cannot hold you in my attention as others do. My control seems to be slipping far too easily of late. But I am listening, and very curious myself as to what brings a lovely not-Dar'Nethi woman of amazing constitution and sensible intelligence to call on someone of my reputation to inquire of D'Arnath's daughter."

I couldn't help but like the strange man, though I was indeed coming to fear the quivering atmosphere surrounding him as I feared nothing else about the Dar'-Nethi world. V'Rendal had warned me that no one knew the limits or the directions of Garvé's power, as by its very nature it crossed the boundaries of all talents and grew as it touched each one. He never expended his own power except when gaining more from other people.

"I am interested in everything about the Lady," I said, settling back on the stool. "Her reappearance after so many years. Her story. The fact that she was in Zhev'Na for so long and appears . . . untainted by it."

"Creatures of the deeps! I know you!" In the space of a heartbeat, I was lifted from my stool and slammed against the wall by an invisible fist, my ribs creaking and groaning with the strain, though Garvé had done nothing but lift his head from his books in surprise and stare intently at my face.

"Ah, sorry . . . sorry . . . Forgive me." He jumped off his perch, dropping his books on the floor and toppling his inkpot, so that my blurring vision saw a great dark blot pooling on the sooty brick floor. But instead of coming to peel me off the wall and check on my state of health, he grabbed an armful of pots and jars and spoons from his shelves, lined them up on yet another worktable, and began to measure and pour ingredients from one to another of them.

Gradually the monstrous unseen hand that pinned me to the wall was released, and I took a deep breath. Ascertaining that my ribs were intact, I returned to my stool and watched him work.

"Sorry"—almost a quarter of an hour had passed— "my Lady Seriana of the world across the Bridge."

"How is it you know me?" My instincts demanded that I be afraid, but for once I didn't believe them. I didn't think he meant me any harm at all, and in fact was doing his best to preclude it. I watched his fingers moving furiously in a frenzy of mixing and stirring and measuring. I wasn't curious about what he was making. I had come to think it didn't matter in the least what he was doing, only that he was doing it.

"I was called in by the late Prince D'Natheil after your injury those many years ago, when you were dying and he brought you to Avonar because he could not heal you. I was unable to help. I never knew you had recovered. We heard . . . well, clearly we heard much that was not true. Prince Ven'Dar has tried to explain to me what went on in those days with D'Natheil and his son and his wife, but I'll confess, I've never really listened."

One hand paused briefly, as if an idea had occurred to him. Then he quickly bent to his work again. "Now, perhaps, I understand. Of course you would be interested to hear of the Lady D'Sanya's return from Zhev'Na because of what happened to your son there. I saw the boy, too, after his capture. I—" He shuddered slightly, and the floor trembled until he found a tarnished brass balance and began weighing miniscule portions of leaves and herbs, wrapping them up in small packets, labeling them, and tossing them into baskets already full of such things. "I created the enchantments with which your son was confined before his execution. So much sorrow. So much pain. To bear such grief . . . And here you are in my house after so many years, asking about the Lady and Zhev'Na, and I will not ask why, for I sense—I know—that if V'Rendal sent you, it is because someone of importance has questions about the Lady. I think it behooves me not to think of it too very much."

"Your discretion is appreciated."

He nodded even while keeping his back to me, his hands moving so quickly as to be almost invisible. "Ask what you will. As I've told you, I believe the Lady's story. She was cruelly used, but she is strong as you are strong, and she survived it as you have survived the injuries done to you and the path of sorrow that is the Way laid down for you."

"Is the Lady an Arcanist? She seems to have so many talents. So much power. I've been curious."

"An Arcanist? No. No. I don't think so. The Lady D'Sanya does one thing at a time and the power is her own. The nature of an Arcanist is to bind many things together: I can take the herbs from a Gardener, infused with the force of his talent, and bind them into a paste to smear on the eyes of a Sea Dweller so that she can permeate it with her own power, so I can then use the paste to penetrate darkness in the way of an Imager, seeing the colors that radiate from the mind of an Artist, so we can understand why his talent has failed him. So am I Healer or Gardener or Sea Dweller or Imager? No. None of these. I only use their talents. The Lady is not one of us."

"Then what, Master Garvé? We must understand her before she takes the throne of Avonar, and how is it possible to understand a Dar'Nethi without understanding her talent? Your tradition says it is rude and unworthy to ask the question, as the qualities of the soul are so much more important. Yet I have never met a Dar'Nethi whose soul was not shaped by the gift born in him: the talent that guides his fingers and the power he brings to serve it."

Garvé's hands slowed, and I felt the shifting of the air, the chest-crushing pressure that was his notice. Only when he forced his hands busy again and started speaking was I able to breathe without conscious effort. "You have seen us at our best and worst, my lady, and at many levels in between, I suspect, and of course you are correct. We profess that we see beyond our talents, but we cannot. As for the Lady, I do not know. I might have thought her a Word Winder, but even in my brief examination I noted that she uses words carelessly—and far too many of them. I would guess she is something like a Devisor, one who creates physical objects to accomplish certain tasks. It is why she can do some things that seem like healing, yet not everything, and things that seem like a Gardener, but not everything. You understand? A Word Winder creates enchantments from the power of words, a Devisor from the physical properties of nature. She makes things to carry her power—a little portion of herself contained in each one."

"I see. Yes, I've been told she carried protective 'devices' that she made with her mentor in his workshop."

"She spoke of a mentor?"

"Yes. A man named L'Clavor."

There are moments between sleep and waking when you feel a slightly nauseating sense of falling, as if you go in and out of time and the body can barely manage it. Whenever I managed to distract Garvé with something unexpected, the room wavered a bit.

"L'Clavor!" Rapidly Garvé pushed his mixing aside and set up a brass oil burner on the workbench. Into a flat copper dish he spilled the contents of one after another of the little twists of brown paper he had tossed in his baskets, and then he set the dish on the burner and hovered over it, stirring the contents rapidly with a copper spoon while dribbling in a thin stream of oil from a glass cruet. "Odd I had not heard this from the earlier investigations. You're sure of your source?"

"Absolutely sure."

"The name answers your question, my lady. L'Clavor was the most famous Metalwright in all of our history."

"A Metalwright . . ."

"Yes. The Lady would be able to create devices of silver, gold, and such to carry the mark of her power. And because she was mentored by L'Clavor, who developed the technique, she would be able to link her devices with each other to make even more intricate enchantments."

I puzzled over this revelation, as Garvé bustled about with his never-ending activities. It seemed so incongruous—totally unexpected. I had always thought of the Lady as being involved in the more nature-oriented talents, like Healer or Gardener, or the more abstract ones like Balancer or Speaker, but never as one who could shape metal into jewelry or teapots or door locks, weaving her enchantments into them.

I was ready to ask more, but Garvé had set down the cruet and was attempting to read while stirring his nasty-smelling concoction over the burner. He'd already come near setting his book afire at least twice as colored flames shot upward from the contents of the copper pan. Though his voice held calm and steady, his hands were trembling. "Madam, it has been a delight, and I would take great pleasure if you were to grace my home again, but for now . . . I think it would be best if you were to leave. And I would recommend you be quick about it."

"As you wish. Thank you, Master Garvé. I'll think on—"

"Go now!"

I ran. As I darted through the cramped rooms, the floor shook. Several boxes tumbled from their piles, and a basket of pinecones toppled into the pathway. I bent to pick them up but thought better of it when the shaking grew worse and I could scarcely keep my feet under me. I ran out the front door, and from behind me came a noisy rumble in the earth and a clamor of falling metal and breaking glass. Red smoke puffed from the chimney and the door.

When the shaking ended and silence fell, I considered going back into the house to see if Garvé had survived. But from the dust-filled darkness behind the doors and windows, I heard a huge, groaning sigh. Perhaps my absence might be of more help than my inquiries.

I pulled up the hood of my cloak and walked the streets of Avonar for hours, twisting my mind into knots with everything I'd heard from Eu'Vian, from poor mad J'Savan, and from the gently violent Garvé. I could make no sense, no connection, though I knew it was there for me to find.

Exhausted, I touched the bellpull hanging by Aimee's front door—a white cord with a simple ring of brass at the end—and the ring began to spin slowly, catching the brilliant gleam of the small white lights that blossomed in Avonar's streets at night like stars fallen to earth. The movement caught my eye and focused my distracted thoughts upon it as I listened to the silvery jangle of the bell. Then, in an instant, it was as if my own small earthquake shook the pieces until they fit together. I knew what D'Sanya had buried in the rootling grove, and what J'Savan had found there when he dug to see what was killing his precious trees—the burning eye in the desert. *Oh, holy gods . . . Gerick . . .*

CHAPTER 17

Gerick

"Are you hungry? Should I call Vanor?" I picked up the book that had slid off my father's lap unopened and set it on the table, then crouched down in front of him in hopes he might look me in the eye and show some spark of life.

"Wine, perhaps. I don't know." He propped an elbow on the arm of his chair and rested his head in his hand. "It's just so difficult. . . ."

I jumped up to pour a glass of wine from the carafe on the sideboard. "We could take a walk if you like. It's a fine afternoon. Have you been out while I was away?"

"I don't remember." He waved away the wine without touching it. "No taste. I told you I don't like it."

On returning from our three weeks in Maroth, I had been eager to hear my father's observations about Na'Cyd, and Cedor's death, and his new attendant, a cheerfully attentive man named Vanor. But, though he insisted he felt no pain, no change, no anything, he could not seem to carry on a conversation for more than three sentences.

"Come on, let's go out. Fresh air will do you good."

I offered him my hand, but he just huddled deeper in his chair. "Leave me alone."

"Father . . ."

"Go on. I just need—" He couldn't finish it. "Come back later."

I threw a blanket around his shoulders and told him

I would be in the garden, but would return to eat dinner with him. "Send Vanor if you need me."

Despite his dismissal, I felt guilty at leaving him alone. I didn't know what to do about his condition. I had pressed him to rest and to eat; I had shoved books into his hands and started a hundred games of chess. On the previous day, he complained that I was driving him to distraction and ordered me to leave and not come back until I could sit still.

It was true I had been extraordinarily restless in the two days since our return. D'Sanya was occupied with the hospice: visiting the residents, catching up on business with Na'Cyd and her stewards, and interviewing and welcoming a newcomer. I couldn't settle at anything. Words and images from the past weeks lived more vividly in my thoughts than the food I ate or the roads I traveled. My mind and body were consumed, filled, alight with D'Sanya.

Unable to do anything about either my father or the Lady, I was about to burst.

I pulled the door closed and hurried down the cloistered walk toward the gardens, only to discover Sefaro's daughter sitting on a shady bench where she could observe my father's front door. Another uncomfortable problem.

Since our unpleasant encounter in the hospice library, I had spoken not a word to the woman. Her constant surveillance had kept me on edge—not a bad thing—and I certainly had no right to complain about her violation of my privacy. Any attempt to offer amends for the past was ludicrous. Though I had wished to ease her mind about my intentions, the knowledge that even common courtesies from my lips would rightly disgust her left me tongue-tied. Yet, after the events in Avonar, justice demanded certain acknowledgments, no matter how uncomfortable their delivery made me.

I stopped in front of her bench and extended my palms. "Mistress, please excuse my intrusion. I wanted to thank you for your help in Avonar . . . on behalf of the Lady. Your bringing help probably saved her life."

Her short hair askew as always, the woman just sat there with her mouth open, looking absolutely astonished. I'd never noticed the dusting of freckles on her nose.

"I didn't tell anyone it was you." I rushed to get everything out before she caught her breath. "Not even Lady D'Sanya. As you didn't give Je'Reint your name, I thought perhaps you preferred to remain anonymous. And I want to thank you for not revealing my father's identity to anyone, despite your reservations about me. To be questioned . . . besieged . . . to have demands made of him would be very hard right now. He's not well. Not right. I hope . . . I sincerely hope your father fares better."

Her eyes were the darkest of the Dar'Nethi blues, such a deep midnight shade that only in the brightest sunlight would you see their true color.

I prepared to bolt. She had closed her mouth and now glared at me in her accustomed manner. But at least her first words were quiet. "Some days he is better, some worse. . . ."

Trying to preserve this moment of civility, I bowed and backed away before turning to head down the garden path.

". . . not that you have any right to ask," she called after me, sounding more like herself. "I'm still watching. Don't think I've given it up because I wasn't in Maroth."

Silly that I felt like grinning as I hurried away.

On the fourth day after our return, D'Sanya sent me a message that suggested I stay the night in my father's chambers on the promise of a dawn ride and breakfast with her. I needed no persuasion. But when I arrived at the stables the next morning, a messenger delivered a note asking to postpone our ride until dawn the next day, as she needed more time with the new resident.

. . . and lest you think this delay is some willful neglect, know that I grieve for every moment we spend apart. The future is mysterious and uncertain, and yet one hope and resolution has fixed itself in my heart. One thing I choose

from the realm of all possibility, my dearest friend, and if I must forego all other pleasure, duty, or destiny to do so, I will have this thing I choose, if you but grant it. Ponder this and bring your heart to our next meeting so you may give me answer.

Lost in a confusion of indefinable hopes, I thought to go riding to sort out what she might possibly mean by such words. Yet when I stopped in to tell my father of my aborted plans, he seemed so happy at the prospect of my company for the day, I could not bring myself to leave again.

His mood was much improved from the previous days, and he seemed more alert, more interested, more his usual self. I chose not to discuss my concerns about Na'Cyd, who had not approached me since our return, or tell of the Zhid attack in Avonar. The omissions made me feel guilty, but I didn't know how well my father's erratic temper might deal with new worries and new secrets. Instead I spent the morning repeating the stories of my visit to Maroth, of how I'd been able to get D'Sanya's Builders to agree on a single vision of the new hospice, and how, despite the Lady's incessant words, we'd never gotten around to anything more substantial in our conversations.

"And she truly had you dancing?" He showed no signs that he had heard any of my story before.

"Night after night. She receives more invitations than she can possibly accept. As she's sworn that I must learn to enjoy company as she does, she made sure that we had some dancing party to attend every night we were in Maroth." Perhaps she had guessed she'd best keep me occupied. If we'd had time alone . . . if I'd had hands of flesh to touch her with . . .

"A most determined young woman."

"She's nothing like I expected," I said, sudden heat sending me to throw open the windows.

When my father's smirk broke into a chuckle, I suggested, somewhat resentfully, that we play a game of chess. I did not tell him the full contents of D'Sanya's message. But it was good to hear him laugh.

I won the chess game handily. In ordinary times he would have bested me in ten moves, considering the image that ruled my thoughts—D'Sanya's shoulder, left bare by the dark blue gown she had worn on our last evening in Maroth—but he could not seem to strategize more than one move at a time. "Perhaps a walk will clear my head," he said, as if he'd never heard my repeated urging of the past days. "I don't get out enough."

Activity suited me as well, and we left by his back gate, taking a path that led into the wood. Even within the enchanted bounds of the hospice, the grounds were extensive and varied. After a while, the path began to look familiar.

"It's good to see you smile, Gerick. I suppose I shouldn't ask the cause."

I felt the blood rise in my face yet again. "It's nothing. It's just nice to be out." The place should be just ahead.

But I decided I must have been mistaken about our location. The oak in the center of this sunny clearing lay rotting, its ancient trunk split, and its roots exposed nakedly to the sun. This was not the clearing where D'Sanya and I had played hide-and-seek.

Our walk was the kind I liked best, where you didn't need to say much of anything, not because you had nothing to say, but because the other's presence and companionship and shared appreciation of the moment were enough. By the time we wandered back into the hospice garden, I felt a little more rational than I had all week. "I've just time enough to ride down to Gaelie and fetch any letters Paulo's brought from Avonar," I said, calculating that I could be back well before my dawn ride with D'Sanya. "I could take any you've written for Mother, as well. Would you like that?"

"I've nothing to send." Though the day was warm, my father hunched his shoulders and drew his cloak tight as if the sun had gone behind a cloud. "Must you leave again so soon? You've things to do here. You've not tested me since you've come back."

"You've seemed so much better today." At least until that moment. "I hate to keep intruding on you."

"It's why I'm here, Gerick. We have to know. You were away for a long time . . . days . . . weeks . . . And the past few days have been wretched." He shook his head and rubbed his brow tiredly.

"Of course, I'll do whatever you want." I took his arm and turned back toward his apartments, dreading what I might find inside him.

This fretfulness tainted his thoughts—a restlessness, a chafing at confinement. The deadness of his senses was, if anything, more profound. Colors flowed together, one almost indistinguishable from another. I felt no variation in temperature, unable to tell whether we sat by his fire or in his garden. Sounds seemed flat, harmonies impossible to hear, and if his memory spoke true, he could no longer tell the difference between wine and water in his mouth, or bread and paper.

But as I withdrew, I couldn't decide if these were truly changes in him, or if they were the result of my own perverse vision. Only my image of D'Sanya remained fixed, while the rest of the world seemed more distorted by the hour. I said nothing of what I found. "Not much change," I said. Of course it was so. I willed that it be so.

These joinings were never easy. It took most of an hour to let the insistent hammering of my blood fall silent. Paulo always said it was only right, as "bodies and souls weren't meant to get taken apart and jumbled back together." I couldn't help but agree, especially when I was trying to ease back into my own body and felt the raw abrasion of flesh and bone as my mind reconnected with my own senses.

On this particular day, as I sprawled on his couch trying to remember how to pump air into my lungs and blood into my heart without thinking about it constantly, my father riffled listlessly through a pile of papers on his desk. "Do you think . . . would you stay a while longer and help me organize the papers Bareil sent from Windham? I need another pair of hands and eyes."

"Of course. Whatever you want." I massaged my temples with fingers that obeyed my wishes only reluctantly.

"Bareil is a dear friend, but rather than getting only

the papers I put on the list, the silly fool sent me every scrap of writing in my study. I keep putting off sorting them. It seems such an overwhelming task. But if I could get it done, then perhaps I could move on to something useful. Do some writing. Something.''

To hear my father falter in his struggle to keep living distressed and unnerved me. He had always been so sure of himself, so easy and generous with his immense talents, so at peace and good-humored with his limitations. In that moment I began to believe that we were going to lose him, no matter the outcome of this venture. A detestable thought.

I jumped up. "I'll be happy to help. Show me what you want me to do. Anything.''

For the next few hours we sorted out the five hundred or so pages of my father's manuscript. Words and phrases kept leaping out of his bold handwriting, snatches of the story he'd set down, the history of his—our—people and their life in the world where we were born. He had taken his own experiences and the stories he'd been told as a child and woven them together with the tales he'd learned from Dar'Nethi Archivists here in Gondai and the written histories of the Four Realms. The narrative was unexpectedly fascinating, and I was soon reading more than sorting.

"So what do you think?" asked my father, noting my distraction. "I wasn't sure you would find the story all that interesting.''

"I'd never really understood about the Rebellion, that our problems in the mundane world were our own fault.''

Hundreds of years before, the Dar'Nethi Exiles had actually ruled in the Four Realms for a few years, claiming they would bring justice and enlightenment to the kingdoms. But instead they had turned into worse despots than those they had supplanted, using terror and sorcery to bend the people to their will.

"Well, not entirely our fault, of course," said my father, "and it wasn't all of us . . .''

"You give such a different view of the Dar'Nethi," I

said after he'd talked for a while. "It's hard to imagine that the Exiles, who came to live the Way so generously and so well in our world, came from this same Gondai."

"You've had no experience of ordinary life among us. How could you appreciate our better parts? And here . . . the long war affected souls as well as talent and power. They'll recover, though. Now the Lords are gone, of course they will. Power and passion . . . the balance of the worlds. Dassine once told me . . ."

Somehow touching on these subjects so close to his heart seemed to stimulate his faculties, so that we conversed as if his torpor had been only my imagination. The afternoon passed quickly into evening and dinner, and by the time I looked up, the sunlight told me it was too late to return to Gaelie. So we kept talking about what I'd read, and whether or not the manuscript could ever be safely published in the Four Realms, and about the excerpts he'd prepared as university lectures before he'd fallen ill.

"From a time when I was younger than you, I dreamed of telling the story of my people at the University," he told me, staring at the red wine swirling in his crystal goblet. "I believed that those lecture halls housed the summit of all learning, lacking only the single discipline that was the most important to me—this history that even I knew so little of. Who'd have thought I'd come so close to accomplishing it?"

I knew better than to answer such melancholy with false hope. I wished I could say, "Perhaps you still shall. Perhaps another miracle will occur." It wouldn't. Not this time. I knew that now.

"If only someone could take these notes and do it for you."

A whimsical smile drifted across his tired face, and he settled back in his chair. "I've been wanting to talk to you about that. I stepped over the wall again while you were gone."

"Father!"

"No, you mustn't worry. I've not given up on our investigation . . . or our agreement. It's just . . . something caught my eye, and I wanted to use a bit of sorcery. To see if I still could. I stayed only long enough to accumulate the power and spend it. A good thing I didn't need much. So I was able to step back before I became a gibbering idiot. Look in the top of that chest. You'll find a bundle wrapped in silk . . . yes, that's it. I've an idea about what to do with it, and I'd like your help . . ."

He had wrought a gift for my mother, and wished to surprise her with it at exactly the right moment. His plan was marvelous, its inherent charm and rightness dimmed only by the fact that it must come to fruition after he was dead. We spent the next hour deciding how to go about it.

As I was pouring the last of the wine from the flask we'd shared at dinner so we could toast our plotting, we heard a quiet tapping on the door to his private garden. I had closed it earlier when the wind disturbed his papers. But his attendant always came from the public courtyard, never the private garden. Curious and careful, I pulled open the door.

"So you *were* holed up here. I hoped that might be," said the voice from the moon shadows. "The innkeeper said you'd not slept in the room for two nights running."

"What are *you* doing here?" I asked, hauling Paulo into the room and quickly closing the door behind him. "My not sleeping at the guesthouse for two nights does not constitute an emergency."

My father dimmed the lamps and made sure the curtains were drawn, then smiled and clasped Paulo's hand. "Gerick doesn't know you've been coming regularly to see me, Paulo. Though it's not your usual time. I thought you were off in Avonar."

"Not a regular visit tonight, my lord." He pushed my hand off his shoulder. "And it wasn't just the empty bed, though if you'd been whacked on the head again by whoever is the mysterious somebody you won't talk about, you might not take it so ill I'd taken note of it." He pulled a folded paper from his shirt and gave it to my father. "I've brought this from Prince Ven'Dar. He said it was important enough to send me right back with it before I'd so much as had a biscuit. That Je'Reint was with him"—Paulo always referred to him as *that Je'Reint*—"and he was worried as well."

While my father sat in his chair to read the letter, Paulo started casting his eyes about the place in a way no one who knew him could mistake.

"There's half a chicken and some plums left from dinner," I said, "and from the generosity of my heart, I'll sacrifice the last of the wine for you." I handed him my glass, which he drained in one swallow.

"Nub like you got no business drinking too much wine anyways," he said. "Lucky I grabbed a pie at Gaelie. Just need something to tuck around the edges."

"So you've been coming up here while I was gone?" He hadn't mentioned that last time we'd talked. What else had I missed in my distraction with D'Sanya?

"No use staying around Avonar with that Je'Reint in and out of the house every hour of every day. And Master Karon and I . . . we've had some business to see to. He seemed to think no one would notice me coming in or out of here if I was careful."

I waited for him to continue, but clearly no other explanation of their "business" was forthcoming. The chicken and fruit were gone almost as quickly as the wine, and Paulo had stretched out on the floor in front of the fire with his hands under his head and dozed off before my father looked up from the letter. I could tell from my father's troubled expression and his anxious glances at me that I wasn't going to like what he was about to say.

"So what is it? Has Je'Reint decided to reveal all to the Lady? Or perhaps set the Preceptors on me?"

"Another marshaled band of Zhid attacked a town in Astolle Vale," he said, folding the letter and tossing it on the table. "And they've had three independent reports of a massive force in the north. Reliable witnesses. Veterans of the war, who knew what they saw."

My dinner suddenly sat very heavily. "And Ven'Dar wants me to tell him how it's being done."

"Gerick . . ." He rubbed the tips of his fingers over his brow. "The Preceptors are at the end of their patience. They claim they need D'Sanya's power, her own formidable talents joined with the Heir's power that is hers by right, to put a stop to the Zhid rising, and so they're demanding that Ven'Dar abdicate in favor of the Lady D'Sanya now before his time is up."

"He mustn't do that! Not yet. She has secrets. And she isn't ready, even if everything is . . . honest . . . with her. She needs time. I need time. . . ." My words limped off into silence.

My father looked at me thoughtfully, closer than I wished, and I made some halfhearted attempt to put the remnants of Paulo's supper to rights, stacking greasy plates and bowls in the basket we left out for the attendant to take away. I had to explain.

"She wants to get the other hospice built. She's driven to help all these people and hasn't been interested in anything that might slow that down. When the time comes, she won't hesitate to take D'Arnath's chair. She believes it's her responsibility, but just now it's more important to her to . . . get her life in order . . . to feel right about it . . . find her place . . ." What had she meant in her message about foregoing her destiny?

"What does she say about the raids?"

"She doesn't like to talk about them. She wants to believe the Lords are defeated. She hated them . . . still hates them. She trusts Ven'Dar and Je'Reint."

"And if she were to be convinced that Ven'Dar is not capable of handling the Zhid? What would she do? Where would she start?"

"She doesn't like to run things by herself—detests having to choose between different ways of doing things. It's why she had so much trouble with the Builders in Maroth. One Builder would tell her one thing that made sense, and she'd do it, and then another Builder would tell her another thing. And that made sense, too. But she wasn't even sure enough of her decision to tell the first one she'd changed her mind. She understands this about herself, though, so I believe she'd get people to

help her . . . like Ven'Dar and the Preceptors. Take their
advice. But she believes . . . she *is* . . . D'Arnath's daughter, and if she decides she must take his place, she won't
shrink from it. That's what I think. But I can't say for
sure, of course, or we'd be finished here. I don't know."
Could she forgo duty for anyone . . . for me?

My father nodded and picked up the letter again.
"Ven'Dar's best minds, those who've studied the Zhid
for their entire lifetimes, cannot explain these attacks.
No one can find the villains. Fear is growing. Trade in
the remote Vales and the new settlements is grinding to
a halt. The recovery and resettlement of the Wastes is
paralyzed. If you could come up with anything to help
them understand it, you could give the Lady and
Ven'Dar—and us—more time."

Time wasn't going to solve anything. Only truth. I had
begun to need certainty as I had never needed it my life.
"All right. I'll try."

"I know what I'm asking of you, and if there were
any other way . . ."

"I said I'll manage."

I didn't dawdle. It wouldn't do to think too much. I
set the basket outside the courtyard door, a signal for
the attendant not to intrude, locked both sets of doors,
and then I shook Paulo, a mug of hot saffria from the
pot on the sideboard in hand. "Come on, I need you
awake. Drink this."

"What's wrong?" he said, after the saffria and my
prodding had him alert again.

"I'm going to try to remember some things. It will be
hard, and I'll have to . . . concentrate . . . on some
bad times."

He sat up straighter, no more traces of sleep.
"Zhev'Na, then."

"I need you to make sure I don't take too long about
it—no more than an hour—and that I'm . . . all right . . .
myself . . . when I get back. It might take both of you.
Father, you'll need to look me in the eye and command
me to speak my name"—Paulo's eyes widened when I
stuffed the handle of the poker in his hand—"and *you*

make sure I answer the right thing. I mean it. Be sure. Don't let me see you before you do it, and don't hold back."

Paulo exhaled sharply as if he had stopped just short of speaking. I felt their dismay. But I didn't want to see it on their faces or give them any opening to argue. So I kept my eyes averted as I propped several big cushions beside the brick hearth step and sat against them on the floor, positioned so the two of them could watch my face. I had to trust them.

I had come to need answers as much as Ven'Dar did. It wasn't any good telling myself I didn't care about Dar'Nethi history past or future. What I had just read and heard that afternoon from my father confirmed everything I had felt since coming to Avonar. I wanted to find something to explain why the world felt wrong and what was happening in the Wastes . . . something that had nothing to do with D'Sanya or me. And I had to find out the truth about her. *You will not escape the destiny we designed for you. You are our instrument . . .* Had Lord Ziddari said those things to her as well?

And so, on that quiet evening in my father's pleasant sitting room, I closed my eyes and ever so slightly relaxed the guards I had erected against the bitter record of the time I had spent as Dieste the Destroyer, the Fourth Lord of Zhev'Na. Only an hour had passed from the time I had stepped into the Great Oculus, the man-high brass ring that was the focus of the Lords' power, spinning its web of light and shadow in the depths of their fortress, until I had stepped out of it again, my eyes burned away, my soul withered, my mind and being one with the Lords. Scarcely more than a child, in one short hour I had become very old in the ways of evil.

For all these years my father had tried to convince me that the guilt with which I lived was not mine, that because I had been so young and inexperienced, I could actually have done very little evil on my own. But when the memories are a part of you, you cannot easily separate the things you actually did from the things you only remember. And now I needed to reduce this vague barrier even further, to explore that part of myself where I could not distinguish Gerick from Ziddari or Parven or Notole. The Three. The Four.

As I called on my senses to prod the memories awake, it was as if I entered a long tunnel, and the light that was my current life—the healthy one that my parents and my friend Paulo and my trusting Singlars had so generously returned to me—slipped farther and farther behind me, rapidly dwindling into a pinprick until all I could see was midnight. I remembered midnight. . . .

The hour had come. I was to go to the Lords in their temple. Smokes . . . fumes . . . the stench of burning slaves . . . burning Dar'Nethi . . . drifted through my windows. . . .

Pleasure seeped through me, prickling my skin like a feather. Smell is the most vivid of the senses, the most evocative of memory . . . of obscene pleasure. I remembered the day of my change. . . .

I/we stood inside the whirling oculus, my body on fire with the joining, with the tearing down of my mind's walls, with the infusion of darkness like acid in my veins, with the impossible bloating of my power. As my human eyes were torn away, our heightened senses encompassed all of Ce Uroth: the sounds of battle and torment, the feel of the lash on recalcitrant flesh, and the smells. . . .

Call them what you will. The smells of Zhev'Na are the savory incense of victory: the fragrance of the slave pens where D'Arnath's grovelers lie rotting in their own filth . . . the sweet perfumes of blood and putrid, broken flesh after a battle exercise . . . the exudation of fear that flows with the sweat of the damned—the Zhid, the Drudges, the Dar'Nethi, all who stand in subservience to us. The smells hang thick on the hot desert air. A heady brew. Taste it! Let the stench fill our nostrils, seep into our pores, for this is our desire, and nothing . . . nothing . . . will stand in its way.

Pleasure . . . such groaning, writhing pleasure in the scent.

The withered hand caressed my mind. Welcome to your

*new life, Dieste. Survey your/our domain through the
cold, blue-white gems that perfect your sight. See the
camps of the soulless ones as far as these immortal eyes
can travel, leagues upon leagues beyond the horizon, tents
fluttering in the hot wind like the wings of locusts, swarms
ready to descend upon the fields of Avonar and devour
them. What delight it is to turn a weakling into a perfect
warrior—to rip away his soul and eat it, to lick the blood
from his cringing flesh, to crush the softness and hear his
screams fade into whimpers of helplessness, to grind the
bones of his life under your foot, and build them up again
into a creature of your own design. To see a man turned,
so that a flick of your thoughts will cause him to mutilate
his wife of fifty years, or to whisper commands that force
a woman to strangle her newborn infant and relish her
infamy. What can compare with power over the souls of
your enemy?*

Push harder. Keep looking. What do you seek here in
the pleasures of the past?

*In the tents are the thousands of our commanders, each
one a weapon to be controlled, each one ready to lead
his troops into battle to devour the soft lands, to wrest
the final victory from the blight of dead D'Arnath's grip.
The war plans are drawn . . . centuries in the making.
The circle of D'Arnath's control has grown steadily
smaller and soon it will be obliterated. The power is at
hand. The boy/I, our Fourth, will bring the power, for he
is D'Natheil's spawn, Lord of Avonar and all Gondai,
Lord of Chaos. He/I will fit the key in the slot and unlock
the fountain of discord that will be our feast, that we may
take our fill of the horrors we feed on, so that our will
may be unleashed upon every world. . . .*

Further. Deeper. Go back before the hours of our
joining. Parven of the amethyst eyes sits his black stone
chair in the Hall of Thrones, the shapeless stars cold in
the void overhead. Without voice, he speaks, and I
remember. . . .

*Today's assault . . . the Dinaje Cliffs, the last stronghold
of the Dar'Nethi's western penetration. Take the cliffs and
they have no shelter, no refuge. On the dune seas we can*

pick them off at leisure . . . the bodies sun and desert do
not devour first. The decisions have been made, the warnings sent, the avantir made ready. . . ."

The avantir . . . remember . . . broad as a tabletop, a
bronze mime of the land from mountain to watercourse,
from plain to pebble. . . . How is it used to touch the
thousands . . . to direct the commanders? I remember a
battle morn. . . .

So which of us shall play the music of the avantir this
day? Sister Notole? No? Well, indeed you will have occu-
pation enough with the storm—a charming notion to
complicate a battle. You, Brother Ziddari, are you ready
to play your own sweet music of war after so long away?
I'll guide you . . . the plan is set . . . just touch the device
here and here. . . . We'll bring the boy here soon enough
and teach him how to play. He's done well in the desert.
Charmingly cruel. Now, brother, draw the power through
the Great Eye and into the avantir, so it echoes in the
Vault of the Skull. . . .

The avantir was so clean . . . requiring inordinate
power, of course, but making it so easy to bring death
in a thousand forms. Always precise as I/we wished.

Now to the other matter . . . D'Arnath and his child.
. . . D'Arnath the Tormenter . . . the Imprisoner . . .
the Unjust . . . vengeance everlasting . . .

Deeper. Not the man himself, but his child . . . the
girl . . .

. . . Could we have but made him immortal, so he
could know his pain forever . . .

. . . He knew, brother . . . his petty triumphs were
never more than ash in his mouth . . .

. . . Even when he dwells in the realms of death, the
King of Pride shall feel our victory . . . such hatred as
we bear cannot be bounded . . . to rape his world is to
rape his child . . . to use his child, to ravage her, is to
ravage him . . . destroy him. . . .

Time . . . time . . . hurry . . . What did I/we do with
her? Think of the girl . . . the captive . . . go back, if
you must . . . all the way back to the beginning. . . .

We have her! The pride of this king's blood is too stout

a liquor for his children's veins . . . it makes them fools. Thou art wise, O King, to keep thy sons close. . . . But this soft one will rend thy heart and mind and soul. Keep her safe, Brother Ziddari . . . for now. If he refuses to bargain, then we shall force her to live under the knife. . . .

. . . Damnable insolent man . . . if he will not give, then we must raise the wager to induce him. . . .

We flaunt her . . . bargain her . . . but the proud bastard will not bend. . . .

Everlasting be thy torment, King of Deserts, Prince of Rubble, Sovereign of Corpses! So be it! We will degrade thy innocent . . . use her talents . . . break her . . . destroy her . . . but thou shalt take no comfort from her death. We will bury her, but she will yet live, undying for as long as we breathe the air of this prisoning world you have left us. We shall unmake her and remake her in our image, our daughter, not thine. Woe and ruin will be thine only grandchildren. If knowledge could stretch to five thousand years, thou wouldst know she was yet in our hands . . . our undying captive, subject to our whim . . . Before and after thy death, even until the world's ending, thou shalt curse the day she was conceived for the reiving of her. . . .

"Come back. Leave it, son. It's been far too long. Can you hear me?"

The voice grated at my ears like a buzzing mosquito, and I slapped it away, cursing the interruption. My hand met solid flesh. "How dare you interfere with me?" I roared. "You will be a smear on the face of the deep!"

Lamplight pierced the darkness, glaring in my face. On the floor by my feet sprawled a man grimacing, a rapidly darkening bruise on his forehead. But his eyes did not leave my face. "What is your name?" he said. "Speak your name."

"My name . . ." I was trembling, my body clenched into such a knot that my teeth ground against each other, and my skin felt like to rip. Easy to see why my fist throbbed. The room wavered and shifted. . . . No black glass floor . . . no columns of ice . . . no man-high torches . . . just soft chairs, green carpet on a tile floor, a brick hearth with its spitting fire, and an injured man. . . .

"Demonfire, Father!" I uncurled myself and started to get up.

"Answer him!" Paulo stood beside me, something . . . a poker . . . raised over my head. "Say it."

I held up my hands. "Gerick . . . of course, my name is Gerick." And as I said it, the world settled a little further into its more familiar pattern.

My father's head sagged to the floor.

"Stars of night, Father! Forgive me."

Paulo heaved a sigh, threw down his poker, and together we lifted my father into his chair. I was not much help, as I could not stop shaking. "I'm sorry. Your head . . . we need something. . . . Gods, I'm sorry." My tongue fumbled at finding the right words.

"A little bruise is no matter," he murmured. "But you . . . we were afraid we were losing you. Almost an hour we yelled and shook you. You were scarcely breathing. I thought you were going to burst."

"I'm all right." I sank to the floor at his feet, trying to regulate my breathing and slow my heart.

Paulo poured wine for my father. "Do you want something?" he asked me. "Ale? Saffria?"

I shook my head. Nothing would taste proper or settle for a while. I just wanted to get this over with. "There was a place in Zhev'Na called the Vault of the Skull . . ."

The Vault was a stone chamber buried under the fortress, I told them. It lay close to the Chamber of the Oculus, where they kept the Great Eye, the largest of the spinning brass rings. In the vault were kept the Lords' greatest artifacts of power: the three smaller versions of the oculus, one for each of the Lords, a large bronze map of Gondai called an avantir, and the gold and brass earrings. Every Zhid wore an earring, its sharp spike thrust through the earlobe and locked securely on the other side. I had worn one from the day I pledged my childish fealty to the Lords, though mine, of course, had been unique. Jewels of ruby, emerald, and amethyst linked me directly, constantly, to the minds of the Lords until the day I became one with them.

But in the Vault of the Skull were hundreds of the common ones: the gold that were given to the commanders, and the brass for the ordinary warriors. Everyone had seen the earrings worn by the Zhid, but no one in Avonar could have known they were linked to the Lords through the avantir, a broad, cast-bronze map of Gondai that was played by the Lords as a musician might play his harp.

Paulo had brought a damp towel for my father to hold on his forehead. Regrettably, I had no scrap of sorcery left in me to chill the thing and help keep down the swelling.

My father leaned forward in his chair. "So they used the oculus to gather the power, focus and enlarge it, and then used the power to manipulate this avantir."

"That's right," I said. "Everything necessary for the Zhid to know would be communicated from an avantir through the earrings: the battle plan, the tactics, who should be taken prisoner, who was to be turned. Everything."

My father grimaced as he shifted the wet towel. "But we always examined the earrings when we took prisoners and never found the slightest enchantment on them. We thought them only a talisman, like a battle flag or a badge on a tunic."

"There would have been no trace," I said, shivering. Paulo grabbed a blanket and threw it over my shoulders. I felt no warmth from the fire. "As soon as a warrior was captured, the connection to the avantir was severed. It's why you could never learn anything valuable from a captive Zhid. They really didn't know much of anything. Only the Lords and their generals knew."

"And when we destroyed the Lords . . ."

". . . all connections would have been severed. The oculus that Radele used to control me—Notole's—was destroyed at the same time. Mother saw it happen. Witnesses have told Ven'Dar that the fortress crumbled at the same moment. The temple, the statues, the Great

Oculus . . . supposedly all the magical artifacts were destroyed along with it. That makes sense. The statues and the Great Oculus could not have outlasted the Lords. Their substance was so intimately bound with the Lords' existence."

The black stone statues of the enthroned Lords had been so large three men could have stood in the carved palm of Ziddari's hand. I could still feel what it was like to inhabit the one made to my likeness . . . the huge, heavy, solid sensation, as if my bones were granite, my flesh impenetrable. The sense of permanence . . . of power . . .

When my nails bit into my flesh, I forced my fists to unclench.

"So what does it mean that these things are happening?" said my father, watching me. Worried.

I could not stop trembling, nor could all the wine in Avonar have diluted the foul taste in my mouth. "They had three avantirs, Parven's the master. At least one of them must have survived, and someone out there knows what it is and has power enough to use it. You have to understand—that would be a great deal of power, equivalent to that the Lords derived from using the Great Oculus."

"Earth and sky!" My father stared at me. Paulo's eyes were on me, too.

"It's not me doing it this time," I said, smiling at them. A weak effort it seemed, as their shocked expressions didn't change. "I promise. And it's not D'Sanya. I went looking for the answer to her, too . . ."

At every echo of D'Arnath's name, I had been filled with hatred so bitter I could have clawed the sun from the sky. The Lords would have eaten the king's flesh if they could have gotten their hands on him. By the time I was one with them, the malevolence that filled their minds at the mention of him left no room for other thoughts.

". . . and so I had to go back to the beginning to remember the story," I said. "When D'Arnath's warnings were proven right on the night of the Catastrophe, the Lords focused all their fury and frustration on him, and when the king set himself and his heirs the sworn duty to stand between them and the power they craved—the hunger for power made insatiable by their workings—they swore everlasting revenge. And so they set out to trap one of his children."

I closed my eyes and allowed myself to believe. "Every element of D'Sanya's story was confirmed. Her year of safety while they tried to bargain her. The two years of abuse and degradation . . ."

She had told me only part. They had treated her like an animal, using every humiliation a depraved mind could think of, every demeaning task, constant taunting . . . in a systematic attempt to destroy her identity . . . to destroy her soul. That she had survived with so much human feeling . . . so much compassion . . . such appreciation for beauty . . . and any power at all . . . was a wonder beyond telling.

". . . and then they buried her in a stone chamber and did not let her die, planning to wake her every few years, allow her to remember who and where she was, and force her to do whatever they desired before burying her again. They wanted D'Arnath to go to his death knowing that his child would live forever in torment. Father, she was their prisoner. . . ."

Their prisoner, not their pupil, not one of them like me. I hoped, beyond anything I had ever hoped, that I remembered truth.

"And what of the thousand years since? Did they carry out that plan?"

"That . . . I don't know . . . I presume they did. You woke me up."

CHAPTER 18

By the time my father was halfway through his reply to Ven'Dar's letter, telling him of my conclusions, he was asking me to repeat everything I'd said. The third time he scratched out an entire paragraph and asked to whom he was writing this letter, I took the pen from his hand, helped him to bed, and promised to write the letter myself so that Paulo could take it back to Avonar first thing the next day.

"Do you think the knot on his head will heal, here in this place?" Paulo asked.

"I hope so. But I don't know whether it's my fist or this place that's affected him tonight."

"I've seen it. Some nights when I come, I can't get him to talk at all at first," Paulo said, shaking his head. "Most nights, after I've been here a while, he gets back in his head. But sometimes not."

"Now I'm more sure of D'Sanya, I'll ask her about it," I said.

If I could ever persuade D'Sanya to talk about sorcery, I had a number of things to ask her. My mother had written to ask about D'Sanya's true talent, and I wasn't familiar enough with most of the hundred talents even to make a guess. The Lords' memories had told me only that they planned to *discover her skills and find a proper use for them*. Had anyone ever hired a sorrier spy?

Paulo returned to his place in front of the fire and, with the ease I had always envied, was soon snoring. My hand steady again, I wrote the letter for Ven'Dar, sealed it with my father's ring, and then wrapped the blanket about my shoulders and thought about sleeping. It was impossible.

An avantir had survived the Lords' death. That was hard to swallow. But I had told Ven'Dar everything I knew. I had done what I could, and survived the remembering. He and D'Sanya would have to deal with it as best they could. That should be reassuring.

Of course I dreaded what was to come with my father if we declared our mission satisfied. But I could not wish him to linger here as he was. Was it the hospice enchantment that had such terrible effect on him, or was it that by living here he had abandoned the Way of his ancestors? Having read his manuscript, I could not but think the latter as likely as the former. That same could be true of all the hospice residents. The Way was more important to them than I'd ever understood.

And D'Sanya? Though concern for my father and the news of the avantir dampened my elation, I treasured the discovery I had made. The Lords were dead. Their plan for her had come to naught. The power of life she held was stronger than they had ever imagined. I believed her. Tomorrow held the promise of the future. We had come so far already, the rest would take care of itself.

So, why could I not sleep?

As I stared at the dwindling fire, loathsome images swirled in my head like the scum stirred up from the bottom of a very old cistern. Hoping to make them settle again, I focused my mind on pure flame . . . on clean nothingness. . . .

A sharp stab through my earlobe. Whispers . . . Power awaits you, young Lord. Dip your hand in the blood; the slave doesn't need it any more. Taste it . . . the world exists to feed your hungers. . . .

I jerked awake, shuddering, the flat coppery taste lingering on my tongue. No good. An empty head would not do. *So think of something else. Something beautiful.* My eyes sagged again, and I imagined D'Sanya riding. . . .

*. . . her hair streaming out behind her, cheeks flushed
with the wind and the joy of her freedom . . . I caught
her, and we laughed and ran across the garden, the
shower driving us inside. The rain hammered down as
we sat by the fire, the flames made more beautiful by their
reflection in her eyes. I inhaled her scent, of new grass
and clean air. Felt the comforting weight of her head in
the hollow of my shoulder, and her soft fingers as they
traced the line of my jaw and then reached for my
hands. . . . No, she mustn't see. Where are my gloves?
Gods, no! She turned my palms up, ready to kiss them.
But instead she pulled away, fear and revulsion twisting
her face. "You're one of them . . . one of them . . . one
of them. . . ."*

I sat bolt upright, heart pounding, sweat pouring from
me, my body clenched in a confusion of desire and terror. But the echoes of her horror and disgust did not
fade. Throwing the blanket aside, I let myself out the
garden door into the soft midnight, hurried through the
public gardens and into the paddocks and fields, then
leaped the wall, moving ever faster, so that by the time
I came to the meadow I was running.

For a blinding hour I raced through the patchy woodlands and the tall grass of the open valley under the
black dome of the sky, pushing harder and harder so
that the remnants of dreams and memories might be
flushed from my head. Stumbling over rock and exposed
roots, refusing to slow down, I pushed up the steep rift
where D'Sanya had taken me on our first ride. At last
I dropped on my knees by the pool, plunging my entire
head into the water trying to cool the pounding,
throbbing ache, fighting for some clarity of reason if I
could not find oblivion.

What had I been thinking these past weeks? That the
scars on my hands would go away? That because I wore
leather gloves when we rode, and silk gloves when we
danced, and hid my grotesque telltales in my pockets or
behind my back unless we were in the dark, I could
pretend that they didn't exist?

I loved D'Sanya more than I had loved anyone in my

life; I desired her so passionately that I cried out there by her quiet pool. She had lived in the place where I was formed. She understood the helpless desperation you feel as your soul grows tainted and withered, as corruption steals away first one bit, then another, of your honor, your beliefs, and your values. My parents and Paulo were immeasurably precious to me, but they could never share it, never understand completely the dread of losing your soul and the certainty that it was accomplished. D'Sanya had been stronger than I. She had resisted for longer and come out with more of herself— still able to see beauty where it existed, able to embrace the fullness of life. But she had lived where I had lived. If any person in Gondai might comprehend the meaning of the scars on my hands and be able to forgive me for them, it was D'Sanya. But I was mortally, desperately afraid that she would not.

And so I had named it at last. The root of my fear. Spent and hollow, like a log burned out to make a shell boat, I began the long walk back to the hospice.

Today. I would tell her . . . show her . . . today. We would meet at dawn, and I would savor the rosy light on her hair and relish the welcoming in her face when she saw me coming. I would cherish her laughter as we rode out across the green meadows, and listen to her unending words of wonder at the ways of life. But when we returned, before I kissed her or held her in my arms, I would strip off my gloves and show her who it was loved her.

Satisfied in my resolve I climbed over the hospice wall and slogged through the vast parkland. The silence hung heavy as the night dwellers retreated into their sanctuaries, the dawn greeters not yet ready to begin their business. Less than an hour remained until sunrise. As always, the darkness demonstrated the fullness of its power, holding deep and black and still before approaching daylight could dilute it. I dully weighed an hour of exhausted stupor on my father's couch against an excursion to the kitchens to find something to quiet the gnawing in my stomach. I chose the latter, afraid that if I fell asleep, I would never wake up in time.

But on my way across the lawn, I glimpsed a light in D'Sanya's house. Was she awake preparing for our ride, or was she finishing her mysterious workings to bring her new guest under the protection of her enchantments?

The image of her awake shattered my plan. I could do nothing until I talked with her. I hurried around the side of her house to the narrow iron gate half hidden in a flowering hedge. Wreathed in the cloying scent of honeysuckle, I spoke the words she had given me weeks before, which allowed me to pass through the gate and into her private enclave. I crossed the lawn and the garden and rounded the corner to the front of the house. A diamond-paned casement on the second floor stood open. I imagined her face appearing in it, filled with pleasure at my declaration that I could wait no longer to be with her. But for what I had to say and to show, I needed to be at closer quarters. So I entered her front door and walked through the ghostly gray of the high-ceilinged, uncluttered rooms that during the day were drenched in color and sunlight.

Her workroom and her bedchamber were up the winding stairs, but I had never been invited into either one. She had always blushed and said a lady needed her privacy . . . for a while . . . until the time was right . . . until we were sure of the future . . . of ourselves . . . I started up the steps. For this, I could not call out to her. She would run out of the room, throw her arms around me, kiss me, and start talking, and I would never be able to do it. I needed to be able to press my finger to her lips and say, "Wait. Let me speak first this time. . . ."

I walked softly down the passageway, shapes already emerging from the darkness as a round window at the end of the corridor lightened. There—the second door on the left. A light shone out from under it—an odd light, wavering between green and blue. My neck tingled uneasily. Then from beyond the door came a soft voice, silvery, the essence of moonlight and summer. She was singing.

Come autumn gold harvest, thy kisses delight
Come winter, thy bright tales do fill my long night
Come spring, and I'll dance with thee, greeting life's call
Come warm summer nights, and I'll love thee for all

My uneasiness vanished, and I could not help but
hope. She'd told me that since the day of our climb to
Castanelle, she always woke up singing. The blue-green
light from under the door shifted into dark red and violet as I took a deep breath, pulled my hands from my
pockets, and knocked on my lady's door.

She pulled open the great slab of oak, and her tired
face blossomed into loving radiance at the sight of me.

I felt as if I were tumbling into the crater of a volcano.
Stupid, fumbling, scarcely able to speak. "D'Sanya,
what's that in your hand?"

The question was nonsense. I knew what it was.

"This? It's only the instrument I use to set enchantments. Are you as impatient as I for this morning? Give
me a quarter of an hour, and I'll be ready to ride." She
tilted her head and wrinkled the pale skin between her
brows, brushing my chin with one finger. "Whatever is
the matter?"

"Where did you get it? You must get rid of it . . .
destroy it."

"Nonsense." With a puff of air, she set the brass ring
spinning on her palm, and then lifted it into the air and
walked back into the room. When she removed her
hand, the sphere of light hung above a man sleeping on
a table-like bed in the center of the room. The shadows
of her workroom danced with purple and green and gold
light. Mirrors on the side walls reflected the light, min-
gling it with the fire of candles that burned everywhere
on tables, benches, and walls.

"You don't understand." The fire of the oculus was
already searing my eyes, burning in my belly, gnawing
at my soul with promises of power. "It is of Zhev'Na.
It's their tool . . . the Lords' tool . . . and *cannot* be
used for good."

"Not true, foolish boy!" She stroked the temples of

the sleeping man. "No magical device is good or evil of itself. It's only in how you use it. This poor gentleman is dying of brain fever. Half his body is paralyzed, but when I've done with this enchantment, he'll walk again—run if he chooses—read and study, do kindnesses for others, and love his wife. She comes tomorrow and will be able to embrace, not mourn him."

I ran my fingers through my hair, tugging at it until my eyes watered, pleading with fate or gods or the uncaring universe to let me wake up beside my father's hearth.

"I know you believe its effects are healthy, D'Sanya, but you're wrong. If you look around you—" Stupid, stupid that I'd ignored what had screamed in my face for so long. Was there ever a bigger fool, so enamored of the first woman he ever kissed? "I've seen the results, but I didn't understand why it was happening, and I never believed that you— Your forest is dying. Aging too fast, choked with too much growth. Go down there and look at it. The oak we climbed in its prime eight weeks ago is already dead, fallen, rotten at its heart. My horse that you healed has gone wild, and we've had to put him down."

"You're wrong."

Her cheeks were flushed, and I refused to heed the rising note in her voice. Rather I plowed ahead because I could not bear the thought that she knew what she was doing.

"Talk to the guests in your hospice, D'Sanya. Ask them. Listen to them. My father is dying a cruel death every moment. The pain he suffered before is nothing to the pain he feels now as everything of importance to him fades. He is empty. This enchantment has ripped up the path he walks, and he cannot find his Way."

The words kept coming. Surely if I said the right words, she would listen. Even when her eyes reflected the spinning brightness as if they were another mirror like those on her walls, I kept on.

"The oculus was created by the Lords, D'Sanya. Its construction is so perverse . . . gods, how can I convince you? It devours life and spews out power. It taints everything it touches no matter how kind, how generous, how beautiful the hand that wields it. Please, you must believe me. Destroy it. Get it out of your life. I'll help you. We'll call in Healers to help these people return to the life or death they're meant to have."

Anger bathed her cheeks like the dawn light. "You know nothing of these devices. How dare you call them evil? An oculus is just a focus of power—used for evil, yes, by the monsters who buried me alive, who brought me out of my tomb only when they had use for me. But they didn't make the rings. I did."

The world stopped turning. Lungs and heart ceased their functions.

"Why do you look at me that way? I saved lives by making what they wanted. Five Dar'Nethi would die every time I refused them. I always chose the lesser evil."

"The lesser—" I thought of what the Lords had done with the rings . . . what I had done. Thousands of lives destroyed, cities and villages brought to ruin, thousands of souls in two worlds twisted or brought to despair. "You used their enchantments to make them? They told you how?"

"Of course. I had no training in such complex workings, but I learned quickly. And I did what small things I could to thwart them. I made the oculus painful to look on. Using it . . . wanting it . . . destroyed *their* eyes, but not mine. They had me create masks for them with jeweled eyes, and I made them horrible, grotesque things that molded themselves to their flesh. They stole my childhood, took everything from me, made me do terrible, awful things, but someday . . . someday . . . I knew I would have a chance to build a device for myself. Then I could make up for all of it. I would use my oculus for good and heal everything they'd done."

But it had been a thousand years, and for some things there was no healing. I knew too much.

"D'Sanya, you must listen to me. The oculus is not just a focus. It bears the mark of the Lords . . . even this you make today. It tears into me even now, because

I know what to look for, what to feel. The Lords used them to eat souls, D'Sanya. They created terror and hatred, discord and murder, then used the oculus to draw all of it back to themselves to feed their power. The touch of an oculus is fire that consumes the reason and the heart and everything worthy and honorable, replacing it with hunger for power. You *must not* use it ever again."

I gripped her shoulders, trying to make her understand, but she was angry and afraid, shaking because she knew she'd buried everything so deep: her guilt, the horrors she'd lived, seen, and done, the things she'd suspected and denied. And I was forcing her to dig it all up and bring it into the light.

She jerked away from me, screaming at me now, trying to drown out her fear. "How do you know this? How could you possibly know?"

In no way would she believe me unless I told her all of the truth. So I pulled off my gloves, held out my uncovered palms, and spoke the words I'd come there to say. "Because I was one of them."

CHAPTER 19

Jen

A scream ripped through the soft dawn of the hospice like a sword through flesh. I sat up abruptly, bumping my elbow on the chair where I'd drifted off in the dark hours. "Earth's bones!" Rubbing my elbow, I stepped over my discarded books and shuffled across the cluttered room to peer out the open window, expecting an uproar. But the only noise beyond Papa's quiet breathing was the screech of two magpies arguing with a squirrel outside the window.

Shadows still lurked in the cloisters. A sleepy attendant carried an early breakfast to her charge. Her demeanor was so ordinary, her purposeful steps so slow and steady, that there was no need to ask her what was the alarm. She hadn't heard it.

What poor wretch had reason to produce such a cry? If the sunlight had not been filtered through the dark green leaves of the cherry tree, and if the warm air had not smelled of moisture and roses, I might have believed I was back in the desert, listening as another slave was sealed into his collar. I shuddered. Must have been dreaming.

So, shake it off then. But as I pulled on my boots and jacket and slipped quietly out the door to play the next round of my spying game, that scream clung to my spirit like a wet cloak.

I squeezed through a laurel hedge and wedged myself between its thick tangle of branches and the trumpet-flower vines that covered the stone wall surrounding a private garden. *The wall is not at all high,* I reminded myself as I dug my knees and the toes of my boots into the mortar and eased upward, keeping my back firmly against the thick hedge. *You're as like to fall off as you are to sit in D'Arnath's chair.* I detested heights.

The heavy dew on the dark leaves quickly soaked my trousers and tunic. From the top of the wall, only slightly more than my own height, I could have scrambled into the sheltering branches of an elm tree and looked down into the private garden of the resident the young Lord came to visit, able to observe surreptitious comings and goings at the garden door as well as hear what might be spoken thereabouts. But I had never made it farther than halfway to the top, so I never saw anything. I could only listen.

In two months of listening, I'd heard not a single admission of evil at that door. No hint of treachery or nefarious schemes. I'd heard more laughter and good wishes than curses, and not a single instance of torture or murder. Indeed, the only devious plot I had discovered was the man who lived in the hospice secretly teaching the young Lord's skinny friend to read.

A pair of robins fluttered into the elm tree, and a rabbit or a squirrel rustled in the old leaves. After half an hour of listening I was ready to move on to my next observation post. But just then I heard the garden door open.

". . . supposed to meet her at dawn. I'm surprised he didn't wake you." This was the older man, the one who lived here, the man my father swore was—or had once been—the Prince of Avonar.

"No matter. My guess is he didn't sleep much after last night's work. If I'd not been hammered flat, he'd likely have had me out riding like in the days at Verdillon." This was the skinny young man from Gaelie.

"A foul business, Paulo."

"Aye, my lord. I'll get the letter where it's going. Any other messages?"

"Tell her . . . tell her I'll try to write her this week.

And now Gerick's helped me get organized, perhaps I'll get some work done on the manuscript. But she shouldn't depend on it. It's so difficult. . . ." His words were laced with the same weariness I'd heard in my father's voice.

"She understands, my lord. You know she does."

"Take care of her, Paulo. And watch out for yourself. If what Gerick's guessed is true . . ."

"I will, my lord. With my life as you know."

I held still as hurrying footsteps crossed the grass. As always, he bypassed the gate that opened into the public path and slithered over the wall not ten paces from my position. Only when he dropped into the grass and hurried away did I breathe again. I heard what might be a sigh from the far side of the wall and nothing more.

One question answered. The young Lord . . . Gerick . . . wasn't there. I had been surprised when I first heard his name. I'd never thought of him having one. *Gerick* seemed quite ordinary, quite human, for a person who was neither. It fit the mask he showed to the world. But what lay under that mask was the mystery that was driving me balmy.

I had intended to follow the young Lord and the Lady to Maroth, staying with a cousin of my mother's while pursuing my mad quest, but the Zhid attack in Avonar had scared the sap out of me. I had lurked about the side lanes until I saw the Lady safe in the palace, and then I rode back to Gaelie and the hospice and Papa as fast as I could get there. I would do what service I could for Gondai, but I could not face Zhid.

The attack presented me with more unanswerable questions . . . such as why the Zhid would risk killing one of their "gods." And why could D'Arnath's daughter, a woman with unparalleled power, not defend the two of them? She seemed more concerned with getting back the jewelry they stripped from her than defending herself or her lover. As for the young Lord, he had fought like a man defending his soul.

I had long given up on sorting out his motives at woo-

ing the princess. Marriage would give him no power over
the Bridge. I had suggested to my father that the devil
might be planning to corrupt the next Heir as a child,
the same way the Lords had corrupted him. But my
mouth often said things I didn't believe. Papa asked me
why I refused to countenance the only thing that made
sense of the evidence: the handsome young man was
head over heels in love with the royal young lady. Pig-
headed, as always, I didn't deign to respond. Some answers were just impossible to accept.

No sooner had the young Lord returned from Maroth
than he caught me off guard with his little speech of
gratitude. Furious with myself for letting down my
guard, I trailed him up and down the road to Gaelie
until I thought I would scream if I saw that guesthouse
one more time. I was convinced his presence posed a
danger to Avonar, but, in truth, my heart was no longer
in the hunt.

Papa's condition had deteriorated severely. He'd become irritable and snappish, complaining that I was gone
too much, or that I was hovering over him as if he were
a child. He called the food tasteless and the wine foul.
When his irritation grew almost to the breaking point,
he would collapse into sleep for long hours at a time. It
was almost impossible to rouse him. Throughout all the
agonies he had suffered over the past five years, he had
never issued the least complaint, but when an afternoon
storm blew raindrops through a window onto his book,
he threw the volume across the room and let flow a
stream of invective that should have made the air turn
dark about his head.

Both Papa's faculties and his spirits did seem to improve the longer I stayed with him. After a few days I
asked what had been bothering him so. He had no memory of the incidents at all. A few more questions told
me he remembered nothing of the past weeks, and, in
fact, believed I had only just returned from Avonar!

I sat with him for a long time after he'd gone to bed
that night, exhausted from a day of nothing, and I
watched his sleep grow restless and uneasy. My mulish

conviction that I could change the course of villainy felt incomparably ridiculous as I looked upon the only person in the world I actually cared about.

Tomorrow, I'd said to myself. *Tomorrow I'll tell the Lady about her lover, and I'll ask her what's wrong with my father, and then I'll put aside everything but what's most important.*

I stayed the night at the hospice, so I could go to D'Sanya first thing in the morning. And that was the morning I woke to the man screaming.

I lowered myself the leg's length back to firm ground and wandered over to the stables. That's where they most often met—the young Lord and the Lady. But only F'Syl the groom was about. On most days I would spend an hour talking to F'Syl, just to prove his ferocious appearance didn't bother me, even though it did. Today I just waved at him, wandered casually along the path around the stable, and poked my head into a little-used back door. The Lady's gray stallion stood in its box, and in the next one over, the young Lord's latest mount, a powerful chestnut gelding. So he hadn't ridden back to Gaelie.

The rest of the day at the hospice proceeded little differently from any other. I moved through the quiet activity as if I were invisible. Spying was easy there. Eyes were always controlled. No one wanted to intrude. As in any great house, the kitchens were always busy, the attendants carrying meals to those who preferred to keep to themselves, while a few people made their way through the cloisters and gardens to the perfectly appointed dining rooms. In the afternoon one or two of the residents meandered over to the library or the artisans' workshops in hopes of finding amusement, but they rarely stayed for long. Not one of the residents could pay attention to an activity for more than a few minutes at a time. Most stayed close to their apartments.

"Excuse me." I accosted the consiliar, who stood beside the dining-room door. "When might I be able to speak with the Lady in private? I have some urgent news for her."

"Her day's schedule has changed somewhat," he said, polite and concerned as always. "I'll inform her that you wish to speak with her, and she'll summon you when she has time. Will that be satisfactory?"

"Of course." A few more hours' observation might be useful.

A small carriage rolled through the gates about that time, and the Lady went out to greet newcomers. She wore her filmy white gown and her ever-present bracelets and rings, smiling as if they were the only people in the world and bestowing on them the favor of her unending conversation. Nowhere did I see or hear any evidence of a disturbance. Though the heart-twisting scream still echoed inside my head, I became convinced it had been a nightmare—the screeching magpies, perhaps, entwined in my sleep.

The young Lord did not show himself throughout that day. Five visits to the stables assured me that his horse was never taken out; nor was the Lady's. The Lady attended a musical performance in one of the public gathering rooms in mid-afternoon. She listened attentively to the musicians plucking at citterns and harps, but never once looked about to see where was her constant companion of the past eight weeks. She never sent any messages to his father's apartments. Never asked for him. Never received any message. So she, at least, knew where he'd gone.

The day passed into evening. Where was the man? I'd never seen anyone so efficient at killing. Four severely broken corpses left in the alley in Avonar, and he carried no weapon larger than an eating knife. Had he killed his father's attendant, too, the man found sprawled in the paddock like a starved rabbit?

By the time the hospice settled for the night, I had received no summons from the Lady. Unable to face my bare room in Gaelie with the sagging bed and flyblown window, I chose to spend the night in my father's apart-

ments again. He fell asleep early on. I went walking in
the sultry night. I'd left my horse tethered in a grassy
copse of alder and oak saplings. So, as my thoughts and
fears churned, I led her to a stream and let her drink
and graze.

I had to give over this responsibility. How big a fool
was I to think I could decipher the plots of a Lord of
Zhev'Na on my own—I, who bore no talent, only suspicions and a paltry skill for sums?

The moon hung low in the east, blurred by a drifting
cloud, and the wind was rising, making the dark outlines
of the trees thrash and bustle as I hurried back toward
the hospice buildings. My feet headed directly for the
Lady's house. I didn't care that it was late. Her lamps
yet burned, and she had always encouraged her guests
or their families to come to her at any time.

Unlike on most nights, the Lady's front gate was
closed and locked. But I knew another way into the
grounds, through a service gate on the east side of the
garden. It had been very convenient for spying, buried
discreetly as it was in the hedge and the wall. Though it
was normally kept locked, I had discovered that by sticking my narrow blade through the iron scrollwork, pushing in with my hand on the smooth bar on the outside
of the gate, and lifting up the bottom with the toe of
my boot, I could dislodge the mechanical latch on the
inner side. Tonight the small gate stood wide open.

Of course, I wasn't planning to barge into the Lady's
house uninvited. But as I climbed the wide steps at the
main entrance, ready to tug on the bellpull, I heard fragments of conversation from a second-floor window open
just above me. One speaker was a woman and the other,
fainter, scarcely hearable, was a man.

"Please, D'Sanya . . . must listen . . ." In an instant I
knew that the scream that had waked me that morning
had been no dream, and that this hoarse and desperate
speaker was the one who had made it. Who was he?
What had happened? I had to know.

". . . deceived me . . ." The woman was furious.

Finding a secure foothold on a ground-floor window

ledge, I scrambled up to a second-floor balcony, then crept along a stone ledge toward the open window. A deep violet glow illuminated the windowpanes.

Only when I stopped to catch my breath did I even realize what I'd done. I jammed my face into the stone wall and suppressed a moan, promising myself that I would listen only for a moment and then scoot right back down to the safe and solid earth.

". . . time has come. I've decided on your sentence." My spine shriveled when I heard the tone of the Lady's voice, my own fears seeming quite small all of a sudden.

"Beg me," said the Lady. "Grovel, so I can scorn you. Weep, so I can ignore you. I will bury you in the place where you were hatched, and you'll live forever with what you've done."

Not for the first time in my life I wished I were taller. My toes clenched inside my boots as I willed them to stay on the narrow ledge while I stretched for the windowsill just above my head. *Come on,* I told myself. *Reach. The ledge is plenty wide enough. You won't fall.* The flagstone terrace seemed very far . . . wickedly far . . . below me. But I was determined to see.

I levered myself upward. When I poked my head around the lead-trimmed glass and peered over the sill, flickering beams of sapphire and violet light dazzled my eyes. My stomach curdled—height-sickness surely—and I closed my eyes and rested my head on the sill, gulping air to fight my nausea.

By the time I could open my eyes again, the colored light had vanished. But fifty guttering candles left murky yellow pools on the tiled floor. The illumination was sufficient to identify the chamber as a lectorium—a sorcerer's workroom. Long tables lined the walls. Alongside rows of jars, flasks, small tins, and boxes lay piles of silver and brass rods, blocks, and sheets. Off to my right, in the corner of the outer wall, stood a massive hearth.

In the center of the room stood another long table. On it lay a dead man. I believed he was a man from the shape and size of his boots, which were pointed toward the window, and I believed he was dead from the way his arm drooped from the side of the table, his flaccid hand sporting three elaborately jeweled rings that glinted dully in the candlelight.

For a moment I debated whether I should try to climb through the window and take a closer look or perhaps raise an alarm. Surely the Lady knew he was dead. Perhaps she'd gone for help, yet no Dar'Nethi would leave a dead man abandoned. Before I could decide what to do, my toe slipped off the ledge.

I clung to the windowsill, scrabbling to find the invisible strip of stone below me. The only visible foothold was the outsloping edge of roof tiles to my right, across an impossibly wide gap of stomach-churning emptiness. Desperate, unable to find the ledge, I stretched my boot toward the roof, wedging myself between the edge of the roof and the opened casement. With a jolt, my boot slipped once more, breaking off a piece of a red clay roof tile and sending it crashing to the terrace below. I hung there breathing heavily.

"Get out of here."

For a moment I thought the harsh whisper came from the man on the table, but I knew every aspect of death, and there was no possibility that person was anything but dead. Someone else was inside the room, deep in the shadows where the dying candlelight no longer reached. Though he spoke quietly, I knew at once that he, not the man on the table, had been the one arguing with the Lady, the one who had waked me with his cry of anguish that morning.

"Hurry. Go," he said again.

"Why?" I suppose his whispering convinced me that he had no more authority in the Lady's house than I did.

"You've no business here with your spying."

"And you? What are you doing here? Nothing good, I'll wager."

"I am no concern of yours."

"I can judge that for myself." I twisted around, pulled up, and hooked my elbows over the sill, my boots relinquishing the slight reassurance of the roof edge in favor of imaginary footholds on the smooth-dressed stone.

"What's happened here? Who are you?" I refused to make any guesses as to the identity of either the dead man or the voice from the shadows.

Just then, I heard footsteps crunching on the gravel paths out in the gardens, and a few shouts. A woman's nasal voice called out, urgently. ". . . something breaking . . . an intruder . . ."

From inside the room, the man whispered again. "Get away from here. Not down. Go over the roof to the southwest corner. Where the roof joins the downslope from the cloistered walk, you'll find a rain gutter. It drains into an overgrown corner where the dustbins are kept."

His breathing was harsh and unhealthy, and I wondered again if the speaker was really the man on the table after all, but just on the *verge* of death.

"Do you need help?"

"Demonfire, will you just do it? I won't have you— Just go. If you value your life, do as I say."

Torches flared into life around the corner of the building. Someone shouted that the side gate had been left open. More shouts of warning. I was becoming more interested by the moment in the escape route he described, though truly, I told myself, I had nothing to fear from the Lady. Only embarrassment at prying into her business. Only a reprimand for violating the single strict rule of the hospice. Vasrin's hand, what if my father was dismissed from the hospice or I was forbidden to visit him again?

I glanced downward and swallowed hard. "There's only one problem. . . ."

"What now?"

"Heights. There's no possibility I can get from here to the roof, much less traipse about on it. I'm about to toss my dinner just where I am."

"You're about to— Earth and sky!"

The shouts were coming closer. I clung to the wall, praying they wouldn't look up. My right boot started to slide slowly down the smooth stone, and my heart slid upward into my throat along with my stomach contents and a choking moan. A well dressed man carrying a torch jogged to a stop far below me. But just as my fingers quivered and slipped, and my knees turned to mush, I experienced a mind-ripping reversal.

All at once every sense screamed at me: my skin was on fire, my ears deafened by a roaring tumult that could have been an avalanche on Mount Siris. My vision went out of focus, and then slammed me with a blinding cascade of images until I thought my eyes would be torn from their sockets. Worst of all, my hands screamed in pain as if the cool stone windowsill had been converted in an instant to molten steel. Their strength ebbed until I knew I must let go and fall to my death.

But these sensations passed more quickly than I could encompass what was happening, and then they were replaced by . . . something else. With a burst of strength I gripped the sill, halting the treacherous sliding of my boots. Then I lowered my feet slowly until they touched the narrow ledge below. I astonished myself with my own facility, flattening my face against the wall, clinging like a spider and creeping along the ledge until I could reach for the roof edge and swing my legs up onto it silently. Unfortunately this action resulted in my face pointing downward, right off the edge of the roof. I suppressed a moan of terror.

But the sight of a second servant conversing with the first and not yet looking upward gave me a motive to retreat and incentive enough to try it, though it was not at all the route I would have chosen with the slightest sober reflection. I slithered backward up the rough clay tiles, gradually rotating until I was pointed up the pitch of the roof. Then I crawled upward, catching the buttons of my tunic on the arced edges of the tiles, cutting my hands on a broken one, holding my face close to the curved tops that stretched before me like a miniature mountain range.

As soon as I was out of sight of the guards, I scrambled to my feet, and, not believing my own temerity, I ran lightly across the roof. I didn't seem to give even a thought to which direction was southwest, but my in-

stincts were right as I found myself in the valley between
the pitch of the Lady's roof and that of the cloisters that
stretched off toward the main house. I followed the
white stone rain gutter, and with no more care than if I
had been taking a walk in a garden, I dropped off the
low-hanging edge of the roof into the dark, weedy corner where the sickly-sweet smell of rotten fruit and
stripped bones told me the dustbins lay. I landed right
in the center of them, the only place I could have landed
without knocking them over in a servant-attracting din.

I sped out of the wood-fenced enclosure and through
the waning night, taking a long way around the gardens
until I was sure I was not pursued. Not wanting to wake
my father, I huddled in the corner of his garden and
waited for the pounding of my heart to subside. Not too
long afterward my knees turned to water and my bones
to porridge, and I felt sick and weak and wholly unable
to explain how I'd done what I'd done. I'd heard of the
surge of the blood that makes men and women capable
of deeds well beyond the limits of their strength and
endurance when faced with great danger to those they
love. But I had been in no such extremity of dread, only
a cowardly fear of heights and a yearning to avoid the
embarrassment of breaking my neck in a place where I
had no right to be.

I rolled over and heaved up my well-churned dinner
into the well-tended begonias. Somewhere in the midst
of this humiliating collapse, I acquired the idea that I
had to go to Avonar and tell someone about what I'd
seen. But it seemed so ludicrous, I didn't pay it the
least attention.

When the sun came up, I went in to Papa. He was
still sleeping soundly, so I warmed the water in his bedside pitcher and cleaned myself up a bit. The night had
been so strange; I was almost surprised to see my own
ordinary face in the glass. How could I ever have run
across a roof? I got height-sick when I climbed a tree
any more. I knew exactly when it was I had lost my ease
with heights—on the day I sat quivering in the highest

branches of my favorite reading tree, mortally terrified that I would fall from my perch and land in the pool of my mother's blood.

My father slept late. Unable to contain my curiosity long enough to submit my adventures to his sensible review, I wandered into the public rooms of the hospice, watching and listening for any sign of the Lady. Or any alarm about screaming men or dead ones. Or anything. I saw nothing but the usual busy morning of a great household, servants and attendants bustling about, a few residents and a few visitors, all with averted eyes, settling in their accustomed spots in the library or the sitting rooms.

After an hour of drifting about the place, keeping my ears tuned for any interesting word, I started across a small courtyard only to encounter the consiliar Na'Cyd speaking to a tall distinguished woman who stood twisting a kerchief in her fingers. In the ordinary event, I would have turned back to respect their privacy, but on one of her hands the woman wore three rings— elaborately jeweled rings identical to those worn by the dead man in the Lady's chambers. I hurried past them to the doorway on the other side of the courtyard. Once through the door, I stopped and pressed my ear close to the door opening so I could hear what was said.

". . . only this morning," the consiliar was saying. "She'll be away for a fortnight or more, but said to tell you that she will certainly join you in Avonar for G'Dano's funeral rites."

"The Lady was so kind," said the woman, sobs making her speech breathy and uneven. "Insisting it was not my fault, even though I was the one who hesitated to bring him here. He was so brave in his illness, I thought, perhaps—as Prince Ven'Dar says—we should accept it as a part of his Way. But when he could no longer speak to me— If I had only brought him here a few days earlier."

"You must have no regrets, mistress. The Way still winds through this gentle place. Even the Lady cannot help everyone who comes to her door. Come, permit me to stay with you as you stand vigil with the good G'Dano." He took her arm and led her through the cloisters into the house.

All right, so the man on the table had been gravely ill and died before the Lady could help him. That was reasonable enough. A great number of those who came here were on the brink of death. Why had I been so quick to assume foul play? Why had I allowed someone else . . . someone who wouldn't even show his face . . . to convince me to run away like *I* was some sort of criminal? I needed to tell the princess why her lover kept his gloves on all the time. *A fortnight* . . . perhaps I should ask Na'Cyd where the Lady had gone, so I could follow her.

Uneasy and exhausted from my adventures of the sleepless night, I dragged myself back to my father's apartments. It was almost midday. Papa was sitting in his garden absentmindedly dabbing at a bowl of soup with a soggy piece of bread. When I bade him good morning and kissed his thinning hair, he didn't even look up.

"Papa, I need your advice . . ." I told him what had happened. He nodded and made murmuring noises of interest.

"So, what if the man in the room was *him*? What if he was stealing something or doing something awful and he's trying to make *me* look like the thief? If I find the Lady and warn her . . . what if he's there and accuses me?" I stopped pacing and knelt in front of my father. "Papa, what should I do?"

"I'm sorry, dear one, what did you say?" His face was loving and sympathetic, but absolutely uncomprehending. "Will you stay for supper, then? Is something wrong?"

I laid my head on his lap, and he patted my ugly hair. "Of course I'll stay, Papa. Nothing's wrong. I just need to sleep for a while. Then we'll have supper and play sonquey." Or perhaps we could pull out a pack of lignial cards and explore what vagaries of Dar'Nethi inheritance could explain why a Speaker's daughter could not unravel the simplest puzzle without coming to the conclusion that she was dreadfully worried about a monster she had vowed to expose.

I threw myself on Papa's couch and dropped off instantly, thrust without delay into an incredibly vivid dream. I was frantically trying to climb a mountain of red clay, and had a constant, unshakable sensation that someone was looking over my shoulder, but every time I'd turn to look, no one was there.

Just after sunset I awoke to find Papa dozing by the fire. I emptied the basket of bread from his untouched dinner tray, laid a brightly woven blanket over his knees, and then kissed him and left by way of his garden. Cramming the bread in my mouth, I slipped through the deserted courtyards to the Lady's house. If she was truly gone away, and no one could or would answer my questions, then I had no choice but to seek answers for myself.

Though the thin clouds to the west still showed golden edges, the house was dark. I reached for the teardrop-shaped crystal that dangled from a silken cord, waiting to chime a magical bell somewhere within the house. But after a moment's consideration, I drew my hand away without touching it. A fiery abrasion of my skin when I tried the door latch informed me that even my mechanical skills weren't going to get me into the house by way of the door. The upstairs window was still ajar, though tonight it was as dark as all the other windows.

Telling myself that my feats of the previous night had proven that I needn't be afraid, I started the climb. My knees wobbled like reeds in a storm. As I clung to the stone wall like a terrified leech, I couldn't even imagine how I'd been able to muster the strength or nerve to lever myself from the windowsill to the corner of the roof.

Toes on the ledge, fingers gripping the sill, I raised my chin above the sill. The long table in the center of the room was vacant. No one was inside that room. I hoisted myself up the rest of the way, threw a knee over the sill, and tumbled most ungracefully through the window. Various body parts hit the tiled floor with a thump. I hissed as I straightened one knee and discovered I'd overstretched it in the fall. With a muffled clank a metal candlestick toppled onto some cushions that I had knocked from the window seat. Otherwise the house was as silent as a crypt.

I sat still for a moment. Convinced I was alone in the house, I cast the weak light from my hand and looked around. The proportions of the room seemed designed to deceive the eye. The walls and ceiling were painted a deep forest green that drew the walls close. Yet the measure of the floor was generous, and huge mirror glasses hung on each side wall so that where I had seen fifty candles on the night before, there might actually have been only ten. The corner hearth was actually a small furnace.

I poked around the neat ranks of jars and bottles and boxes that sat on the dark wooden tables that lined the side walls under the mirrors. Scattered across the table were a number of tools—chisels and files, shaped metal pincers, and engraving tools—various items of gold and silver jewelry, and some odd narrow strips of bronze bent into shallow arcs half the length of my forearm. A lovely bronze figure of a horse in full gallop, about as tall as my hand, had fallen to the floor in between open sacks of sand and powdered plaster. Its flying tail was sadly bent.

On the wall opposite the window was a broad door I assumed would open on a passageway, and there was another, smaller door on the right wall. Each had an intricately engraved brass lock that refused to yield to touch or knifepoint. There was little else to be seen, no further answers to be found, and no way to leave except by the way I'd come in.

Foolish to come here. What had I thought to find? My skin burned just thinking about what I could possibly say if the princess came to the door: "Have you no abandoned dead man here, my lady? Have you no tortured ghosts who can reach out with immaterial hands to show me across your roof and into your dustbins?"

Hurriedly I put the toppled candlestick and disturbed cushions to rights. When I raised my handlight high to make sure I'd left nothing out of place, a glint of metal caught my eye from the farthest corner of the room. A thick, heavy chain dangled from an iron ring embedded in the high ceiling, the end of it well above my head. Still and somber, the dull, brutish chain looked out of place beside the fine and delicately worked ornaments lying about the room. As I drew closer, it seemed to point like a warning finger at what lay below.

I crouched down and held my light close to the blue-black tiles. Directly below the chain lay a clotted pool the color of ripe blackberries with a pale seepage around it. Smaller spatters had already dried to a deep rust color. A few steps away lay an oddly shaped wire device—a small frame with five protrusions, each having a small sharpened blade on the end. I picked it up to examine it. The blades—fingers on the palm-sized frame—were stained dark. I dropped it on the floor and clamped my hands tight under my arms, screams echoing in my soul, my head like to burst with darkness.

A crumpled paper lay in the corner. I retrieved it gingerly, only to discover it was no paper, but a wadded pair of gloves, a man's fine leather riding gloves, stiff with dried blood. That the gloves belonged to the one who had cried out in my mind, the same voice that had whispered to me from the shadows, insisting I leave the Lady's house, I had no doubt.

Before the lingering glow in the west had faded, I found myself astride my horse again, heading toward Gaelie—only I didn't stop there, but rode all the way to Avonar.

CHAPTER 20

A thin strip of moonlight was not sufficient to illuminate the dark room where the long-armed man shoved me to the floor. A wool rug burned my cheek as I skidded over it, and tickled my nose when I lay still, fighting to get air into my burning chest before the whole world went dark.

"Aimee, is that you?" a woman called from across the room. She sounded as breathless as I felt, as if she'd been running. "What's going on here?"

Small hard objects clattered onto· a hard floor from another direction entirely. "My lady, what's wrong? And who else is here?" This was another woman. Younger. "Someone's come through the garden door, my lady, one or two people, but they've not spoken, so I don't know who they are."

Who else is here . . . a good question. Whose house was this? Whose knees were digging relentlessly into my back?

I had ridden down from Gaelie as hard as poor Pesca could run and flown to this place as mindlessly as a hummingbird streaks for a scarlet saber-flower. But in my fever to get inside—a fever as terrifying as it was inexplicable—I bumbled over a garden wall and tripped over a step. Long arms had wrapped themselves around me, and no matter how hard I fought and scratched and kicked, they would not let go until we were inside, and they had deposited me on this floor.

The person kneeling on my back snatched away the dry wad of leather I'd clutched for the past six hours and was futilely trying to hide under my breast. I felt a sharp jerking movement, and then a hand grabbed a fistful of my hair and bent my neck backward almost to breaking. "I'll kill you. By the Holy Twins, if you've harmed so much as a hair on him, I'll kill you."

"Paulo, who is this?" asked the first woman, the older of the two.

"It's a god-cursed thieving assassin is my guess." Mercifully, he let my head drop before my scalp tore, and then lifted his weight from my back. When he shoved a boot into my middle and rolled me onto my back, I didn't have enough breath to resist.

"Could we have a light, Aimee?" asked the woman.

"Of course! I'm so sorry."

Yellow light blossomed from someone's fingertips and sprang like a stray bit of lightening to one lamp on the wall and then another. The high ceiling was painted with a scene of a forest glade. I wished I were in that peaceful, uncomplicated place. *Paulo*, the woman had said. The skinny friend from the Gaelie guesthouse. I should have known. I shifted my gaze to the bony face hovering somewhere between my battered body and the painted forest. His expression was nothing I wanted to see on someone whose heavy boots were a handsbreadth from my face.

Where was I? And what in the name of sense was I doing here? A nasty creeping sensation fluttered deep in my head, like a moth that had been stuck there squirming itself free and flying away.

"I've found this lot—a damnable sneaking *woman*"— he was surprised at that—"creeping about the garden." Paulo gave my legs a shove with his boot. "She'll be dead if she can't explain herself."

Far across the room a tall, striking woman of middle years pulled off her cloak and threw it aside. The young Lord's mother, no mistaking it. The red glint in her brown hair, the gold cast to her flushed skin, and the dark brown eyes would have told me, even if I hadn't seen her on that long-ago day in Zhev'Na. "We don't have time to worry about thieves," she said. "Gerick is in terrible danger."

"I've figured that out already. See what I found on her." Paulo tossed the wadded gloves across the room to the older woman. Then he looked at me again. "What have you done with him? Where is he?"

"I don't know where he is." Able to take a full breath at last, I attempted to sit up. Paulo shoved me flat again with his boot on my shoulder.

"So it's only by chance you're carrying his gloves with his blood on them?"

"I don't know whose gloves those are, much less whose blood is on them, and"—I jammed my elbow into Paulo's knee so hard he bellowed and stumbled backward—"I'll tell you nothing else until you get your filthy boot off me."

"Heaven and earth!" The young Lord's mother stared at the bloody wad in her hands.

"I'll give you anything, she's the one attacked him in the stable," Paulo fumed. "He wouldn't never say who it was, but this one's been sneaking about the guesthouse for weeks—even asking me about him. Dolt that I am, I never made the connection until now." He looked so fierce for a moment I almost laughed. "If you've harmed him, I'll—"

"I've not touched him—not that he doesn't deserve worse than I could do. My father lives deformed and half blind because of him. My brothers died in the desert after he used them for his sword training. My mother lies murdered these twelve years at the hands of his friends, the Lords."

I clung madly to the things I believed lest the very earth shift out from under me. I was terrified to hear what these people would say of the young Lord. If he owned the gloves, then he was not only the voice who had warned me off, but the one who had been chained in that corner bleeding. I couldn't bear the thought of that.

"I've sworn to protect you, my lady," said Paulo. "Let me find out what she's done."

Lady Seriana—so I'd discovered was her name, not Eda as my father had known her—squeezed the blood-stiffened leather in her hand. She was having to work at staying calm. "You must have a story as to how you come to carry my son's gloves marked with such stains as these." I opened my mouth, but she didn't give me an opening. "Don't try to deny they're his. I gave them to him, and their maker lives a very long way from here."

Paulo, angry as he was, wasn't going to move without her approval. Taking advantage of his restraint, I jumped to my feet and tried to recapture some dignity. I straightened my muddy tunic and brushed away the damp leaves stuck to my cheek. Paulo came near attacking me again when I touched the leather belt that held my knife sheath, but I just looked him straight in the eye and pulled it around straight. But I kept my hands well away from the hilt that protruded from the sheath. I wanted to demonstrate that they didn't intimidate me, but I wasn't stupid.

"I've no cause to explain myself to you or to anyone," I said. "I've stolen nothing and harmed no one. Unlike others you know." Why were they all so tall? My head was on a level with Paulo's shoulder. Even the two women gave me a full handspan in height.

"Did you attack Gerick in Gaelie?" asked the lady.

"Yes. I saw a Lord of Zhev'Na walking free. Any faithful daughter of Gondai would have done the same."

"But you let him go," she added. "Your father, Gerick said, a resident of the Lady's hospice persuaded you to leave him be."

So he hadn't told his mother who Papa was. I wasn't sure what that meant. "My father is the kindest, most trusting of souls. Far too trusting. I honored his speaking because he is my father, but I don't . . . didn't . . . agree."

"So if you didn't harm my son this time, and you don't wish to tell us anything, then why did you come here? Presumably not to harm Mistress Aimee."

And, of course, that was the difficult question. Part of me wanted to spit at these people, willing dupes of a fiend. Part of me still wept at the cry I had heard, shaken to my very bones by despair that spoke the death of love and joy. Part of me trembled in fear, craving to deny my father's certainty that these events signaled something far larger than we knew. "I don't know why I'm here. And that's the truth. I found those gloves . . . somewhere . . . at the hospice. I should have thrown them away. I've no cause to do him a service. But I couldn't— I want to go." Part of me wanted desperately to run away.

"Perhaps we could sit down, have some refreshment, and come to better understanding. Let me make more light. I've such a bad habit of leaving my house dark when I'm here alone." I had almost forgotten the other woman—Aimee. She glided about the room, lighting the rest of the lamps from the magical glow of her hand, threading her way among numerous objects of dark green stone scattered about the floor—small statues of birds, it appeared—and a broken wooden box from which they had spilled. Her presence was like the first breeze of evening after a hot day. "I'll bring saffria and ale," she said.

When Aimee lit a lamp that hung in the air behind me, the Lady Seriana's stare settled on my neck. My skin burned under her gaze. And my blood grew hot as well. "He did it, you know. With his own hand, he sealed my collar. Did he tell his mother of his pleasures?"

She didn't get angry. Rather her brow wrinkled thoughtfully, and her gaze dug deeper, searching my face. "Stars of night! I know you. The child who served in his house . . ."

Yes, the slave child who scuttled about his house in bare feet and iron collar, terrified for every moment of every day for six endless years. Forbidden to speak, forced to scrub out night jars and empty vermin traps, to lay out his clothes and run his bath, my face scarred by one of his swordmasters, a Zhid who wore a jeweled ring and got impatient when I didn't summon the young Lord to his lessons fast enough.

"No wonder he couldn't bring himself to say more of your encounter!" Abruptly she motioned me to a green-brocaded footstool. "Sit down."

Her command was inarguable. I sat.

"Listen to me," she said. "I don't know why you've come here, and for the moment we'll put it aside. But you are wrong if you think my son is still what he was in Zhev'Na. The danger you fear—the betrayal you feel—as you watch him go about freely when the world believes him safely dead . . . that danger does exist, but in someone else."

"You think the Lady D'Sanya is the danger." I sounded like a petulant schoolchild.

"Yes. Just this evening, I've come to the conclusion that she possesses one of the Lords' devices—a brass ring called an oculus . . . like the ones you saw in their house. I think she makes them."

"Demons of the deep, she's got an oculus?" Paulo sagged against the wall. "Master Gerick knew someone had power of that kind—I've just come from Prince Ven'Dar, delivering his letter about it—but he never guessed it was her. Never. Even to think it would kill him. Demons take the woman!"

An oculus! I jumped up and retreated, my back against the garden doors, all my bravado made laughable. My knees felt like mush; my mind screamed. I had seen what the Lords did with their ghastly rings of light—what the young Lord did with them. Mind and body remembered pain and helpless fear coursing through my veins like liquid ice. I laid my hand on my dagger, not thinking what I could possibly do with it, only that I needed to be as far away from this house as I could get. "You can't hold me prisoner. I can't be here." Not if an oculus was involved.

"Sit down, young lady." His mother pointed sternly toward the stool I had deserted. "In the name of the Prince D'Natheil—my husband and Gerick's father—who set you free of your collar, in the name of every Dar'Nethi who has suffered enslavement to the Lords as did you and that same prince, or who died fighting the Lords as did Aimee's dear father, and in the name of every man and woman of my own world who lived in bondage there as did Paulo and I, I insist you sit here and listen to me."

Grim, determined, she took my shaking hands and drew me back to the stool, pressed on my shoulders until I sat down again, and crouched down in front of me, her stern face softening only slightly. Her eyes were just like his, dark and deep, filled with so much terrible knowledge. "We must know what's happened to Gerick and whatever you can tell us about the Lady. If telling you something of our history is the only way to gain your trust, then that's what we're going to do."

She stayed right there in front of me, sitting on the rug of bright blue wool, and she told me the tale of a mundane girl who had come to love a sorcerer in a land where sorcery was forbidden, and how she had borne him a son two months to the day after he was burned alive, only to believe the infant, too, had been executed. She told me how her son had been hidden away from her and how he had come to believe he was evil, the tragedies of his childhood giving the Lords a sure weapon to twist and corrupt him. As the story of her husband's rebirth in the body of Prince D'Natheil filled me with wonder and astonishment, my shaking eased and my fear receded.

When Lady Seriana stopped to drink a mug of saffria Aimee brought her, the story continued uninterrupted in the soft voice of the young man on the other side of the fire. Unschooled in his speech, yet pouring out a measure of devotion as any man or woman would give a fortune to command, Paulo told how in the stables of Zhev'Na he had discovered Gerick's fight to retain the last shreds of honor, even when he believed his soul hopelessly lost. He told me of his friend's long struggle to be free of the Lords, and his final, dreadful conclusion that the only way to save anyone was to persuade his own father to kill him. Gerick's resolution had rid the world of the Lords.

I was mesmerized by the tale of his battle with the Lords . . . the tale of his talent . . . Was that what had happened to me? Had he taken me away from danger when I could not do it myself? And if so, then he had been closer to me than anyone had ever been in my life . . . and there was nothing of evil in the memory. Could he have masked it from me so completely?

Yet, in the end, it was not for the young Lord that I yielded my past and present anger, but for the woman and the friend and the dying man in the hospice. If these three had been so masterfully deceived, then what hope had any of us to resist the demon son? And if not—if he was truly what these good people claimed—then the land and people I loved stood in mortal danger once again, and I had no choice but to fight.

A log snapped in the fire, showering sparks into the air like a cascade of stars, and as if it were a signal, I inhaled deeply. "Yesterday morning at dawn I woke to the sound of a man screaming . . ."

It was as well I chose to fight, for just as I finished my own story we heard shouts from the street and a hammering on the door. Aimee hurried out to investigate and returned moments later with the news that war had returned to Gondai.

CHAPTER 21

"They say the flames can be seen for thirty leagues," said Mistress Aimee, whom I'd learned was the owner of this house. She whisked the breakfast things from the table as she delivered the newest details of the night's dreadful events. Without warning, a massive force of Zhid warriors had fallen on Lyrrathe Vale, slaughtered or captured every inhabitant, and left the fertile wheat fields of the easternmost Vale of Eidolon an inferno. The imagining left my flesh cold. I knew all about Zhid raiders.

"Prince Ven'Dar has commanded every seasoned warrior to take up a weapon and find an untrained youth or maiden to stand beside him. He is riding out himself with Preceptor W'Tassa and six hundred guards to take their stand at Lyrrathe Vale, and he dispatched another five hundred fighters—all that he could summon in the middle of the night—to the northern borders. Je'Reint has been charged to defend the city and to muster more troops to send to Lyrrathe as soon as possible."

"Ven'Dar must be told she's taken Gerick," said the Lady Seriana—Seri she said to call her, but I wasn't ready for that kind of intimacy with the family of a man I'd once sworn to kill. "He must hear what I suspect about D'Sanya, as well."

"I'll see the message sent," said Aimee, handing a stack of plates and bowls to a wide-eyed girl who was evidently the only servant left in the house. Everyone with talent had been summoned to the aid of Avonar.

"Je'Reint has summoned me to the palace. I go to him within the hour."

Paulo perked his ears up at that. "He wouldn't send you out with the fighters? Not a lady like you." His face took fire as it did every time he addressed Aimee. Not difficult to see how the wind blew in that quarter.

For her part, Aimee gave him a smile that could have melted a boulder. "Certainly not, sir. Master Je'Reint is very wise. He knows that my skills are of far more use in planning strategies than in executing them." She then proceeded to demonstrate that very fact by tipping a tray of cups just far enough that three of them fell off, splattering her white gown with tea. Paulo jumped to her rescue, snatching up the cups and gently removing the tray, while Aimee threw up her hands in good humor. "I can help them lay out an image of the terrain or the placement of troops without being on the battlefield. I'll be quite safe and out of the way, so I don't risk upsetting anything more important than teacups!"

It had taken me more than an hour to realize that Aimee was blind. I had just thought her clumsy. It didn't seem to bother her all that much, even her awkwardness. Indeed she was fortunate—intelligent, talented, well provided for, and with a naturally gracious disposition and the kind of face and figure that made men forget their own names. She even spoke of her family with love. I decided that it would be very easy to dislike Aimee.

But then again . . . she couldn't see the way Paulo wrapped his eyes around her. And she was the daughter of a Dar'Nethi Preceptor, while Paulo was . . . well, I still wasn't quite sure what he was, other than a friend such as anyone might wait a lifetime to have. But I would guess that he could never aspire to a woman of prominent family in his own world. And the secret reading lessons hinted that he had never told Aimee of other yearnings she could not see. Perhaps he never would, and she'd never know. I'd always thought there was a goodly bit of perversity in the turnings of the Way.

"Clearly we'll have to find Gerick on our own." Lady Seriana's mind was fixed neither on war nor romantic attachments. "Could she have taken him back to Maroth?"

While Aimee busied about her household, preparing to answer her summons to the palace, Lady Seriana and Paulo worked on strategies for tracing Lady D'Sanya's movements, and for searching the hospice—just in case I might be lying about him being gone—and the second hospice in Maroth. They even discussed hiring a Finder to help them discover him. They seemed to have forgotten about me.

I sat on the little footstool with my chin on my hand, my ugly, serviceable clothes stiff with dried mud because I had been too stubborn to yield to Aimee's offer to have them cleaned for me. What in the name of sense was I was doing with these people? Their concerns were corrupted souls and wars for control of the universe; their acquaintances were Princes, Preceptors, and Lords, and men who visited the land of the dead and came back again. Vasrin had shaped no such path for me. I needed to be on my way back to Gaelie. Papa would be wondering where I was. As soon as they stopped talking long enough, I would take my leave.

I stopped listening, wandered over to a tall window, and stared out at the deceptively peaceful sunlight bouncing off the garden walls and the city towers beyond them. The air wasn't peaceful . . . not by a long way. War. The Zhid. Avonar's fear was thicker than the daylight. I could feel it in the way you feel the coming of the first storm of winter.

"You've never told us your name."

I almost jumped out of my skin. Aimee had come up just beside me. Her eyes were closed as the sunbeams bathed her smooth skin. "I'd be pleased to know you better before you leave us. And Lady Seriana will wish to tell Master Karon of you. It will give him heart to hear that Gerick was able to help you . . . that he retained some power the Lady could not control."

"Is it truly Prince D'Natheil who lies at the hospice? The very same?"

"It is, though he goes only by his other name now. I

served him with my Imaging in the years he reigned in Avonar, and once I have imprinted the image of a person on my mind, I cannot mistake him. He is the noblest gentleman I've ever known save my own dear father who has passed on to L'Tiere."

"It hardly seems possible."

"Their story is astonishing, is it not? I'd never heard it told all at once until now. Had I not been privileged to witness a small part of it, I'd never believe it."

"I need to get back to my father."

She nodded, understanding. "And then to answer the summons of your own talent in this coming war?"

"No summons comes for such as me. Oh, I've useful skills, but no true talent. It seems to have been lost along my Way."

I waited for the effusive sympathy and subtle aversion that was the usual when a kind person finally made the connection. It probably just took Aimee longer because she couldn't see the ugly telltale about my neck.

Though her voice could not have been heard across the room, she bent closer to my ear. "Someday you and I will have to decide which is easier on those around us: your skills with no true talent, or my true talent with so little skill at anything truly useful."

I had to laugh. She spoke with such sincere good humor as to make me forget my usual bristling at discussions of true talent.

"My name is Jen'Larie," I said. "But I've always been called Jen."

"Jen'Larie—what a beautiful name! I've never heard it." She extended her hand. "May I?"

I wasn't exactly sure what she wanted, but I wasn't afraid of her. I took her hand and felt the warm flow of sensation up hand and arm that accompanied a touch of sorcery. She squeezed my hand as she released it a moment later.

"Now I shall be able to recognize you should we meet again. You are so strong and lovely and delicate all at once, just like your name!"

Now I believed Aimee was blind. No one in all the

world had ever called me lovely. "It was my mother's name, too," I said. "Everyone shortened mine to tell us apart."

"My mother shared my name, as well, but we didn't have much confusion," she said. "She did not survive my birth. It came too early and was very difficult. Many weeks passed before the Healers were sure I would live, with or without sight."

"And your father?"

"The Lords destroyed him. Their sworn traitor used one of these horrid rings of power to control the Prince's son, trying to convince the Prince—Master Karon—that Gerick had murdered my father and betrayed the defenses of Avonar. But all of it was the Lords and their puppet. I offered Prince D'Natheil my talents afterward. I cannot permit such horrors to happen again."

Aimee might have been the very incarnation of Vasrin Shaper in that moment, the stern and flawless female half of our dual god, whose image graced the gates of Avonar to warn away those who would violate our peace. And I had only thought her pretty and kind.

"So you believe this son is worthy of his father and his mother?"

She clasped her hands at her breast and crinkled her brow. "I wish I could find the right words. I don't know Master Gerick well. He is very quiet and shares little of himself in company. But I've witnessed the feeling he bears for these three who have shepherded him from the darkness into the light, and no being of evil could devise it. When I write the image of love on my mind, Jen, it is Gerick's care for his mother and his father and his friend that I model."

"And theirs for him?"

"Indeed. I would give a great deal to help them find him. Master Je'Reint says my Imaging helps him locate Zhid sentries and outposts—he is very kind, of course. But my studies of military history and strategy and the geography of Gondai give me the basic material to work with. I've no such grounding that could tell me where Lady D'Sanya might have taken Gerick."

I propped my back on the window frame and watched Lady Seriana and Paulo shaking their heads. "She said she would bury him in the place where he was 'hatched.' Surely they don't think she would take him across the Bridge."

Aimee turned toward the others, as well, as if she could see them puzzling over this dilemma. "No. Lady Seriana has concluded that D'Sanya will take him to Zhev'Na—that it was his 'birth' as a Lord to which the Lady was referring. But reports say that the temple where he was changed and all the fortress buildings have fallen. Now they're trying to determine the location of the desert camps where he was trained to command."

"I'd think it more likely the Lady meant the underground chambers at Zhev'Na: the Chamber of the Great Oculus or the Vault of the Skull or Notole's den right next to it. Those couldn't have 'fallen' like the rest of the fortress."

"You know these places?"

"I know every place in Zhev'Na. I lived there for six years. In the Lords' house itself for a good part of that time. I've a very good memory, even in cases where I'd prefer not."

"Perhaps—"Aimee bit her lip. "I know you're anxious to leave, but if you could help them make a map . . . You see, it is . . . Master Gerick's friend . . . who is to go after him. He was only in the Lords' house one time. It will be such a danger. What if these Zhid have occupied it again? Or if the Lady herself is there? He must be quick and sure."

"They can't mean for him to go alone. And him not even Dar'Nethi. It's lunacy."

"But they've no one else. With the Zhid on the march, no one can be spared. Prince Ven'Dar, who would gladly have found someone trustworthy to accompany Master Paulo, is gone away, and Commander Je'Reint is burdened with the defense of the city and the raising of troops. No Dar'Nethi would be willing to help Master Gerick, and we've no time to explain the truth to them."

"Well, *I'll* go then. A mundane can't bumble into

Zhev'Na alone." Only when the two at the table fell instantly silent, staring at me as if I'd said I was going to eat the moon, did I realize that I'd blurted out this absurdity at full volume.

Aimee's face blossomed with a radiant smile. "Bless you," she said, quietly enough that the others couldn't hear it. I wasn't sure I was supposed to hear it either. She took my arm and dragged me across the room to join the others.

Why in the name of sense had I done it? As Aimee repeated my offer and, after asking my permission, explained why I was not summoned to war, Lady Seriana and Paulo acted as if I'd taken leave of my senses—or as if I had some less-than-benevolent purpose.

"You're good to offer," said the woman. "But I couldn't ask it." The room was suddenly so chilly, I needed a cloak and gloves.

"It's not just so I can kill him, if that's what you think," I said.

"No, of course not." But her cheeks flushed just enough that I knew she'd considered it.

"And it is not a matter of your letting me or not letting me. I choose for myself. But if all you say is true, you can hardly refuse my help. You believe the safety of Avonar depends on finding out the truth about the Lady, which could depend in great measure on finding your son. I am a true daughter of Avonar. I lived in the Lords' house. I know where to look for him."

"I can find my own way about." Paulo wasn't happy, either.

"Fine," I said. "But will you be able to tell if spell traps have been laid? The ruins of Zhev'Na are not a place to blunder in with great big feet and kick over the stones to find what you're looking for. I've more experience and skill than you'll get from anyone else available."

"Indeed, you must let Jen help you," chimed in Aimee. "I've heard frightful reports of the ruins. Some say they're haunted, that those who venture within never return, or if they do, then they're never the same. You mustn't risk your safety by going less than fully armed, good sir."

Well, he wasn't going to refuse a plea like that. But he scowled at me, and I could guess what he was thinking.

"Indeed, thanks to your friend and the Lords, I have no true talent," I said. "But I do have the same capabilities as every Dar'Nethi: I can call fire, detect enchantments, and hide things—and people—reasonably well if I have no wish for them to be seen. As you can't do these things yourself, you're probably the only person in Avonar who could find my paltry skills useful. Therefore I shall suit you very well. And, of course, whether or not you wish me to come, I shall follow you anyway."

What a silly thing to say. Sometimes I wished I could stop talking altogether.

Lady Seriana warmed a bit at my outburst, smiling as if she understood exactly what I was feeling, which I found quite annoying just when I was doing my best to understand that very thing and having no luck at all. I was determined to go and couldn't say why. But like the mule to which my brothers had so often compared me, I plodded ahead. "And someone ought to be making plans for all those people in the hospice. If the power that keeps them well comes from Lady D'Sanya, and if we believe her power is a danger to Avonar, whether she intends it or not—"

"I am going there myself," said Lady Seriana, all her smiles vanished. "From what you've told us, Gerick's game is up, and therefore Karon's, too. I need to be with him whatever comes."

"You mustn't go there before your son is free, my lady," said Aimee without the least trace of embarrassment at contradicting the formidable Lady Seriana. "Lady D'Sanya must have no reason to suspect we know what she's done. Difficult though it may be, you have to wait."

Lady Seriana folded her arms in front of her as if she were going to argue. But instead she looked at Paulo, who was still tracing a finger over a map. "Twenty-one days," she said. "That's the least, you said?"

Paulo glanced up. "Aye. It's still desert between here and there."

"Twenty-one days and I go to Karon."

He agreed and went back to the map.

"I'll send the Healer, T'Laven, to tell Karon what's happened," she said to Aimee and me. "If you wish, I'll have him take a message to your father as well. And when I go, I'll do whatever I can for his well-being."

"That would be very kind."

I drew her a map of the hospice. Paulo showed her how to find her husband's apartments, and I showed her how to find my father. "He'll be happy to see you," I said. "He's been waiting a long time."

She looked puzzled.

"Perhaps you remember him. His name is Sefaro."

It is always a pleasure to astonish someone so proud as the Lady Seriana.

CHAPTER 22

Gerick

"D'Sanya . . . please . . ." My tongue felt like a lizard, rough and too thick for my dry mouth. "Don't leave me with the oculus." Even before she had transported me through the quivering air of a portal to this unknown prison, I had been unable to see anything but the brass ring, the burning, nauseating swirl of purple-and-gold light that she had made the entirety of my visual world.

The determined chink of hammer on stone ceased. "You must have sufficient time to know the horrors you've wrought on Gondai. It is the only justice fit for a Lord of Zhev'Na. And only the oculus can focus my power enough to contain a Lord. Yet another crime to your tally: The hospice in Maroth will be delayed for months and months until I can make another one." Her voice stayed soft and calmly reasoned as she meted out her mad justice. "Now try to move your arm."

I lay on my back on cold stone, my arms straight at my sides. Indeed, some degree of control had returned to my left arm, paralyzed for this immeasurable time. A physical restraint about my wrist had replaced the enchantment, however, and I needed no prompting to test it thoroughly. But the struggle to break free of her binding was no more effectual than my protestations of love or my reasoned arguments had been.

I should have been prepared for her reaction to my revelation. No sooner had I told her that her thousand-year dream of redemption was a myth, than my scarred hands gave her evidence that I was the very architect of her ruin—I, the Lord of Zhev'Na. Her power was tremendous even without the oculus, and when she used the device to focus her rage, my meager defenses were smothered like a flea in an avalanche. I was soon hanging in the corner of her lectorium, listening helplessly as she prepared the first of my punishments. And what came after . . . I kept thinking, as far as I was capable of thought, that if I could only push her a little further, she might kill me outright. But goading had only made matters worse.

She patted my straining arm. "Good. Now to ensure that your attention stays on your crimes."

A sharp stab in my open palm sent a flood of fire through my right hand and wrist and up my arm. Odd images, fragments of memory—faces, book pages, a castle parapet—flashed through my inner vision, distracting me for a while from the hammer that was now chinking away on my left side.

"I would have confined you in Skygazer's Needle—a perfect prison—but I thought it more fitting that you lie here with the ghosts of your mentors."

Another stabbing pain, this time in the left hand. Another flood of fire. More images . . . so vivid . . .

Riding through the frozen fields and forests of Leire, clinging to Darzid's back on my way to Zhev'Na . . . a child filled with unchildlike hate . . . the winter air freezing my hands . . . my soul. . . .

The waves of enchantment from right and left clashed somewhere between my ribs, searing my lungs and threatening to stop my heart. I fought for breath. "Lady, what are you doing?"

Blood and flesh spattered on my face as I wielded the lash for the first time. I could not falter . . . could not show disgust. I was to be a Lord. Inflicting punishment was my right. My duty . . .

*   *   *

Scrabbling my way out of the insistent vision, I grasped at reality—the swirl of brilliance hanging over me and the chinking inevitability of D'Sanya's hammer as it forged my prison. Even if I had been willing to gather power in the way of the Lords, D'Sanya's enchantments had left me incapable of sorcery. That I had been able to aid Sefaro's nosy daughter and plant in her the compulsion to go to my mother was only a virtue of my soul weaving. D'Sanya's constraints did not seem to affect that talent, perhaps because she did not know of it, or perhaps a talent detached from a body could not be fully bound by physical constraints. But here, wherever we were, my feeble attempts to touch another soul came up empty. And I dared not enter D'Sanya. She was too strong. Too angry. More than half mad.

"D'Sanya, wait . . ." Chinking by my left foot. What was she doing to me? Every moment that passed made it harder to think clearly. Piercing fire blossomed in my foot and washed up my leg and through my groin and my gnawing gut.

As I climbed the jagged cliffs high above the war camps of my warrior Zhid, the desert sun seared my back. I was horribly thirsty, but I could not show weakness. . . .

A stab in my right foot. Leg, back, and belly flushed with the stinging enchantment. At the same time, the lower perimeters of my limbs and torso and the flesh at the back of my neck tickled as if an army of ants milled about beneath me, burrowing into my skin. The chinking hammer next to my ear tugged at a binding that crossed my forehead. . . .

I tightened the leather strap until it cut into the tanned flesh. We had bound the insolent warrior to four posts in the center of the encampment, where the sun could bake him slowly over the next days. Someone pressed a whip handle into my hand.

"They writhe so charmingly when the sand spiders bur-

row into their open wounds, do they not, young Lord?"
Pleasure prickled my spine. . . .

Gasping like one drowning, I tried to escape that
voice, those sensations.

The voice that whispered in my ear so seductively was
Lord Parven's, as clear as on the day of my change.
Visions . . . memories . . . so real . . .

"Lady!" D'Sanya had threatened to bury me alive,
but terror rooted deeper than even so dread a fate exploded in my gut. My struggle drove her sharp pins
deeper into my hands and feet, triggering relentless
waves of fire. The Lords were five years dead, but if my
soul weaving could give coherence to chaos and create
the Bounded, what could it do to the memories I
carried . . . and in the presence of the oculus, the very
agent of my corruption? *You will not escape the destiny
we designed for you. You are our instrument. Our
Fourth.*

"D'Sanya, listen. To leave me with them . . .
memories . . . the Lords . . . please . . ." I could not get
out half the words. Lips and tongue flaccid. Numb.
". . . will break my mind . . . make them real . . ."

"Your pleas are false, Lord." Her breath tickled my
ear. "The tongue of Zhev'Na is ever lying and must be
silent. You must remember the crimes you've done and
know that you will never be free of them. You will not
sleep. You will not die. You will not forget."

An exquisite pain stung the center of my forehead,
and I was engulfed by the past. . . .

"This land is called Ce Uroth . . . and it is indeed a
barren land—stripped of softness and frivolous decora-
tion, its power exposed for all to see." Lord Ziddari,
dressed as always in impeccable black, smiled at me in
his too-familiar way. "If he wants to accomplish his pur-
poses, a soldier must be hard like this land, not decked
out in a whore's finery, or wallowing in weakness or
sentimentality. . . . This slave Sefaro will be your cham-

berlain. He—as all Dar'Nethi slaves—must have permission before he speaks or you must cut out his tongue. Command him as you will. Kill him if he does not please you. . . ."

The tale of my training in evil, of my childhood of fear, of the treacherous dreams of my youth played out unceasingly in my mind. I smelled the stink of the slave pens. My hands felt the solid give of human flesh as my sword pierced the bodies of my sparring partners, and my chest and back ached with bruises as my combat masters pummeled their teachings into me. My enjoyment of power grew into incessant craving. I lived my past again entirely, not as an observer but as participant, swept along like flotsam in a spring torrent, drowning in the raging current of profane memory.

One might think it a blessing to be lost in the past when the present is so dreadful. But deep in the core of my being, in the small part of me that knew the days I lived were but memory, I was frantic. This punishment would not end as my wardress believed. The Lords had designed the oculus. If I were to lose myself in the Lords' memories, I would learn how to control it, how to use the oculus to grow power and get free. But by that time the Three would live again in me.

Fight it, said that resilient core, *you can choose as you have chosen before.* But the memories flowed freely, choking me, drowning me. . . .

"How fare you, Lord?" Like the balm of rain on parched earth, the woman's voice cooled the scalding river that had flowed from my extremities for an eternity.

Darkness swallowed the glare of desert noonday. Here in the real world, even the sinuous streams of color from the oculus were scarcely visible. I must be going blind again as I had when I was twelve; the oculus burned away the eyes of those who dwelt in its shadow, hungering for its use. And the bonds on my limbs and head were no longer my only restraints. I lay in some kind of

trough shaped to my form. Panic choked me. I could
only gargle an answer.

"Do you feel your tomb, Lord?" Soft fingers traced a
line through my hair and along my arm where I felt the
new constriction. "The shellstone grows well. Only a
week gone and already it reaches for your ears. No
sound after that. Never again. And here"—tender sadness flowed through her fingers pressing on my throat—
"only a few days more and the first layer will enclose
your neck. When it covers your face, you will feel neither the movement of the air nor a human touch ever
again. No light. No sky. Never again will I have to look
on your eyes and see the truth of your black heart. Ah,
Vasrin Creator, give me strength."

"Kill me." My parched voice sounded like the dry
gourd rattles the Drudges used to celebrate a victory of
the Lords. Fear forced the words through the barriers
of her enchantment. "The oculus . . . madness . . . will
make me the thing you hate . . . please . . ."

"You *are* what I hate!" She was sobbing. "And you
made me love you. I spoke to your kind father and discovered how you gulled him as well! Did you cause his
horrid illness so you could get close to me? I told him
that you were trying to kill him by destroying the hospice. I told him you were dead."

No! Father!

While I yet reeled from her news, her fingers brushed
my feet, my wrists, and my forehead, setting them on
fire again.

*Hold on . . . you can choose your path. You are a man
now, not a child.*

But still the visions came. . . .

*A caravan brought a new crowd of Dar'Nethi captives
to the encampment, fresh from our victory in Erdris Vale.
The new slaves cowered in their collars and slave tunics,
lamenting their vaunted power. Always delicious to watch
as the truth settled into their spirits. I/we lined up twenty
of them in the warriors' courtyard in front of the rest. I
stepped down the row and commanded each to kiss my*

boots, slitting the throats of three as a price of one man's refusal. Not the impertinent man's throat, of course. I/we never allowed slaves to escape their fate with disobedience.

As I dismissed the slaves, a small ragged figure blundered into the courtyard, carrying an armful of weapons—broken ones, it appeared—and dangling scraps of chain. I would have thought the person a Drudge—a single mind-touch revealed no Dar'Nethi power—but she wore flapping brown rags, not proper Drudge attire. She stopped and gaped at the scene as if the courtyard was not at all what she expected. When she spotted me, she backed away. Her shock and terror were so ordinary, they weren't even amusing.

"Yervis!" I called. "Clean up this mess." We couldn't have such oddments wandering the fortress uncontrolled.

The warrior posted in the corner of the courtyard trotted toward me, only now noticing the quivering interloper. At my gesture, he spitted the creature on his lance. I turned away. . . .

That wasn't right. Nothing like that had ever happened. I shuddered and grabbed hold of a scrap of reason, pricked awake by the discontinuity.

My eyes opened to complete darkness. To immobility, not paralysis. To a stricture that pressed on my throat with every dry swallow. I tried to cry out, but my mouth, stiff and crusted like plaster, produced no sound. Panic threatened to undo me.

Breathe. Inhale. Feel. You are alive. Your name is Gerick. . . .

A whisper of air moved above my face—the oculus, of course, spinning out my corruption. The place smelled of old stone and the dirt that accumulates in unused cellars and dungeons. I tapped a knuckle on the table, hoping the sound might give me a sense of my prison's size, but the movement caused the pin in my palm to burn and send its scalding wave up my arm. Fighting off visions, I forced myself to lie absolutely still so as not to trigger the rest of the pins, an effort that required every scrap of self-discipline I had ever learned.

So move your mind, if you daren't move your body. I extended the fingers of my soul outward, as I did when soul weaving. *There . . . someone!* Carefully I eased into the soul I found . . . and fled right back out again. *Breathe . . . don't move . . . hold on . . . it's not your fault. . . .*

But I jerked and the poisonous enchantment engulfed me again, dropping me into more days of war and cruelty. Deep in my true self, though, I knew more of the truth. I was buried in Zhev'Na. And the poor dying wretch whose soul I had touched had stumbled into the ruined fortress in search of treasure, only to be speared by a warrior who had stepped out of my dreams. Living.

D'Sanya visited me again, weeping as she tormented me with talk of love and light, air and sky. She was happy that I was mute, saying she could not bear to hear my voice as it made her think of a man she had once loved. When she touched my bonds and left me, I fought to hold on to my conscious mind.

Alone in the dark. I could hear the echo of my own breathing now; the shellstone had covered my left ear. I could no longer feel the brush of air on my left arm, only a warm stillness. What would it be like when the stone covered my face? I forced that thought aside and did not move.

If I could just endure for a few days . . . a few weeks. Someone would come for me. Surely my father would not believe I was dead. Surely. Paulo would not believe it . . . not until he saw my corpse. My mother would guess where I was; she had unraveled much more difficult puzzles. But what if they came when I was dreaming?

If I had possessed more capacity for fear, the consideration that my own dreams might kill my rescuers would have overflowed it. *Don't move. Don't panic. Don't think.* It could be weeks until they came. It could be a lifetime.

I prayed for an earthquake to bring the roof down to crush my head. I prayed for starvation or thirst to kill me quickly. But they didn't and they wouldn't. She would have seen to that. Always the oculus burned in my mind, speaking to me of power. Gather power enough and I could escape this place. . . .

Father . . . help me!

Over and over my father had assured me that I was strong enough and decent enough to withstand the lures of the Lords' power. But he lay in D'Sanya's hospice, and if he stepped over the wall she had forged with her devilish oculus, he would die in agony far worse than anything I was experiencing. It wasn't fair. He had already died in torment. Burned alive . . . how had he borne it?

"I had to let it happen," he'd once told me, "to feel it, not trying to ignore it, but to accept it and embrace it . . . and the terror and despair right alongside. I told myself that this was my life, and if it was to have meaning, then that meaning would only be made manifest by experiencing every part and portion of it, even the very end."

I inhaled the sour air of my silent prison, the stink of my fear. The oculus spun, cooling my sweat. Did I have that kind of strength? Not to fight, not to endure, but to embrace?

Carefully I exhaled, trying to imagine that tiny plume of breath rising through a room of unknown size, leaking through its cracks and pores into the vastness of Gondai's desert. I imagined my mind floating upward with it, and from that lofty height I looked down upon myself and considered all that had happened to me.

The desert wind blew outside this chamber. The flat silver sun wheeled across the flat silver sky. I could not see or hear or feel these things. But I believed them. Accepted them.

The shellstone had crept to the corners of my eyes. Instead of shoving that marrow-deep dread aside, I inhaled and exhaled, breathing my fear, understanding that it was and would ever be a part of me. My only task was to explore it and see what it might reveal about the world. Next, consider thirst. . . .

I worked at this for hours. Eventually I moved—breathed too deep or trembled with fear or thirst or longing—and my visions came ravening. But eventually I fought my way out once more and worked again at experiencing and embracing my life and death, hoping to discover my place in the universe. The exercise gave me some semblance of balance, some semblance of peace to leaven my terror.

Unfortunately, upon each subsequent waking I found it more difficult to maintain my state of quiet, not less. The periods of control grew shorter and shorter, and the potency of my visions seemed multiplied by each respite, so that I worried that my efforts were speeding my inevitable disintegration. But I clung to this semblance of sanity, even when I felt the burning rush that signaled the onset of my dreams. Madness. . . .

As these cycles of unsleep and waking passed, something new began to grow inside me, an immense and subtle potency, half familiar, half strange, that filled the cracks and crevices of my flesh and spirit. After a while its sheer enormity itched my skin and stretched and strummed my idle muscles like harp strings. Power . . .

Delirious with terror, I lay in that everlasting darkness trying not to move for one more heartbeat, trying to delay the inevitable. It might take one hour or one day or one turning of Gondai's moon, but I knew I would soon be quite mad and quite invincible, Dieste the Destroyer, the Fourth and only Lord of Zhev'Na, and I would destroy D'Arnath's Bridge and everything it protected. How would I be able to embrace that?

CHAPTER 23

Jen

Paulo and I had been on the desert road for seven days before he allowed himself to go completely to sleep. As he was so much taller, stronger, and more experienced, it was gratifying that he took my capabilities so seriously. I wasn't bothered by the lack of conversation as the white-tipped mountains and the last pale swathes of green slipped farther beyond the horizon with each day's journey. I already knew he wasn't a particularly talkative person, and I had a lot to think about.

Lady Seriana had agreed to get a letter to my father for me. I didn't want him to worry that I was embarked on a journey of vengeance. Discovery was a far better word. Sometime in the past days I'd begun searching—not willingly, not without diversion, not without error—for truth instead of evidence. Papa would like that. A Speaker lived for truth. But I didn't like changes going on inside me without my direction. I wished I had time to talk to him about them, but time was precious. Paulo and I had set out within a few hours of Lady Seriana's command.

For a thousand years the road to Zhev'Na had been hidden, masked by the power of the Lords so that one could wander the trackless desert for a lifetime without happening upon it. After the fall of the Lords, Geographers had found the remnants of the fortress within a few days. By Paulo's reckoning it should take us a little less than three weeks to get there.

A portal would have been very nice. But, even believing the Lords were dead and their lair in ruins, no
one had felt comfortable opening a permanent portal
between Avonar and Zhev'Na; a thousand years of terror could not be discounted overnight. And, now that
the Zhid were on the attack again, no one would dare
risk it, nor would anyone be fool enough to expend so
much power on an uncertain mission. Portal-making,
while not one of the Hundred Talents, and thus theoreti-
cally possible for any Dar'Nethi, was the province of
those with exceptional power and a special knack for it,
something like those who can mind-speak or those who
have a bent for geometry. Aimee had said that the few
people she knew who had power enough had already
gone off to serve the prince or Je'Reint. So Paulo and I
were left to cross the barrens on horseback and on foot.

Had we been on a mere riding adventure, I would
have relished the journey. The Wastes were changing.
Beyond the last green outpost of the Gardeners, the land
remained a desolation of stark red cliffs amid stretches
of shifting dunes, dry, cracked lake beds, and a mix of
hard-packed dirt and rock. But where once only a few
kibbazi and an occasional lizard had survived, we saw
numerous hints of renewal: a small herd of oryx, pockets
of tough grayish grass, an occasional fox. Day after day
we saw thornbushes blooming—ordinarily the tiny white
flowers were visible only on the one day in five hundred
that rain came to the desert. The sun was still voracious,
but not as severe as in the days of my captivity. Wispy
clouds drifted overhead. The cool of morning lasted a
bit longer, and the afternoon heat waned earlier. On one
or two days I caught the scent of rain on the evening
wind, and saw the gray rain-veils hanging over the horizon behind us. But the moisture did not touch the
ground.

Paulo pushed us hard. I knew why. The bloody gloves
were very much in my thoughts, too. But finding myself
in the desert with five dead horses and a hostile man was
not something to anticipate with any pleasure, either. So
I kept yelling at him to slow down to spare the beasts.

But I learned very quickly that horses would do whatever Paulo asked of them.

One morning just after sunrise, when the heat was already murderous, and the beasts and I were flagging after a long night's traveling, Paulo stroked his horse's neck and bent forward, whispering something that made the horse lift his head and step smartly up the hard-baked trail. The simple marvel of it made me break our usual silence. "I wish you would tell *me* whatever you're telling him. I could use a bit of encouragement right now."

"Nothing special. Only things as a horse likes to hear."

I shifted uncomfortably in the saddle. My backside felt like raw meat. Pounded raw meat. "I would think that knowing what a horse likes to hear is fairly special in itself. How did you come by such knowledge?"

"Had it since I can remember."

He wasn't going to make this easy.

"I'm not going to kill him," I said, grimacing as I urged my horse upward until we were alongside him.

"No. You're not."

This was clearly a statement of incontrovertible fact, having nothing to do with my intent. I found that most annoying.

"What if you had evidence that he'd turned—that he was one of the Lords again and you were the only one to prevent him having his way? What would you do then?"

Paulo's glance could have split granite. "I *had* evidence once. Evidence from my own eyes. If things had been different by five heartbeats, I would have killed him, and you would still be wearing your collar—or you'd be dead. The evidence was wrong. He will never be one of them again. Never. And the one that touches him without his leave—anyone—will pay for it."

"How does one earn such love?"

"You give everything," he said. "No matter what the cost."

His knee moved ever so slightly against his horse's flank, and I was soon looking at his sweat-soaked back again. But I couldn't think of anything else to say anyway.

We'd come more than a hundred and fifty leagues from Avonar. Our maps said we were within a night or two of the ruined fortress. When the sun was halfway to its zenith, we found a bleak outcropping of barren rock and stretched out our square of lapaine for shade, spreading our blankets on the sand and pretending we were sleeping through the worst of the heat. I tried to arrange my limbs so that no part of my body had to touch any other. The sweat still dribbled off of me, tickling and itching, stinging the places where the saddle had rubbed me raw.

A hot wind billowed the strong, gauzy lapaine. We had tied the fabric high enough to let the air move underneath. Tired and drowsy, I held perfectly still with some vague hope that the breeze would bring some relief.

Odd. Even when the lapaine shelter fell limp, I heard a soft, purposeful rustling somewhere beyond my feet. Paulo's hard hand crept over my own, and I brushed his thumb to let him know I was awake. While my right hand moved carefully toward my dagger, he poked three fingers firmly into my open palm. Then he tapped one finger, two fingers. . . .

As his three fingers struck my palm, we rolled in opposite directions and leaped to our feet. Sunlight glinted on metal just beyond our patch of shade, and I yelled, "To your right!" Paulo leaped onto a bent, dusty figure as it scurried out of our tent. Keeping my back to the rock pile, I shifted left, holding my knife ready and scanning the shady shelter and the sunny strip beyond its border for other lurkers.

Though a great noisy clanging accompanied the combat, Paulo seemed to have no trouble with the invader. Only moments elapsed before he dragged a bundle of brown rags into the shade. He dropped his captive onto the sand and stood there breathing hard, bent over with his hands on his knees, sapped more by the oppressive heat, I guessed, than the ferocity of his opponent. His sunburned face was beaded with sweat. "Others?" he said harshly.

"No sign of any."

"Scavenger." He waved his hand tiredly at the sand beyond our shelter. "Half a kitchen spread over that dune out there, including our cups and pots and who knows what all. Other junk, too: bits of chain, harness, broken blades . . ."

The heap of rags on the earth before us quivered as if it were freezing instead of baking. I had yet to see just which portion of the dusty mound had a mouth that might answer a question or two.

"We won't harm you," I said. "Tell us who you are."

The heap's quivering subsided a little.

"Do you need water?"

The quivering took a distinctively negative turn. Good enough.

"You're hunting for metal. Why?"

A pair of dark eyes peeked out of a totally unlikely spot, and one knob of rags was revealed to be a tangled mass of brown hair. A dusty voice said, *"Shan t'sai."*

"Ghost metal?" I wasn't sure I'd heard it properly.

"The demon lords return to the dark fortress. The metal is to bind them."

Paulo and I glanced at each other, for once sharing a common sentiment—profound disquiet.

"The demon lords . . . you mean the Lords of Zhev'Na?" I said carefully. "The Lords have been dead for five years. Who's telling you they've come again?"

The heap of rags and hair had slowly resolved itself into the figure of a toothless woman, withered to leather and bone. Not as old as she looked by a long way. No gray in her mat of hair.

"They've come with their legions. We've seen their death fire. We find metal for the kaminar, hoping she will return and forge chains for binding the demons."

"A fire spirit?"

Kaminars were creatures from our creation stories. Legend said that Vasrin Creator had brought forth be-

ings of flame to cleanse the world of imperfections—
chaos, ugliness, and skewed, misshapen, or corrupted
matter—before Vasrin Shaper formed the earth and the
sky and those of us who peopled it. Many believed that
the detritus from this cleansing had collected in the
Breach when it was formed after the Catastrophe. Storytellers always included kaminars in their tales, ensuring
their visions were replete with color and light, fire, glory,
and innocent frights.

"When we freed the kaminar from the demons'
prison, she promised to protect us always. We brought
her offerings, and once she returned to us in her garments of blue fire to thank us. But now we've seen the
demons and the Worships. We're so afraid, and she's
not come again."

"Worships," I said, wishing our tale could be as innocent and hopeful as a creation story. "Were you a
Drudge then?"

The Drudges were servants or laborers long descended from those who had wandered by accident into
Gondai from the mundane world, back in the days before the Catastrophe when there were many portals between. The Lords had used the Drudges for mindless,
menial tasks, breeding away curiosity, initiative, and intelligence. Only Drudges called the Zhid "Worships."

The woman nodded, and I offered her a waterskin.
"What's your name?"

"Nim."

"Tell us about the kaminar, Nim, and about the
demons and the Worships."

"Many turns of the moon since we found the
kaminar . . ."

After the fall of the Lords, most Drudges had chosen
to stay on their desolate farms or to continue working
the mines in the Wastes under the more benevolent direction of Dar'Nethi supervisors. But some had wandered away into the desert, scrabbling for a living as
they could.

Nim said that she and several companions lived in the
ragged ridge of red cliffs that lay between us and the

hard-baked plains where the ruined fortress and the deserted war camps lay. While scavenging in the ruins, they had come upon a stone vault with a broken hasp. They had thought the vault might hold treasure, as it was buried deep beneath the fallen stones, but to their amazement they had found a woman sleeping there in the darkness, not dead, though she wore the very likeness of death.

". . . and when we touched her, she woke and broke Mut's arm with her wildness and burned Dila with her eyes. She kept saying not to kill her, please not to kill her; she was sorry, sorry, sorry. We offered water and food, but all she wanted was metal. To bind the demons, she said. To give her power that was lost. When at last we made her not afraid of us, she said she was a kaminar, and if we would bring her all the metal we could find, she would use it to bind the demons so they could not harm us ever again."

"And you did so?"

Nim sipped from the waterskin. "Three turnings of the moon she stayed, living as poorly as we do until we found her the metal she wanted. It made us sick to touch it. Fal went blind from it. Kyrd burned for three turnings of the sun and died in madness. Cith went screaming into the desert, and we could not find her. But the kaminar said the sickness was caused by demons that didn't want her to have it. She took the bits of metal, and when she had enough, she went away. But she said that someday she would return to comfort us."

I described D'Sanya to the woman and asked if she could be the one they called kaminar.

Nim's sunken eyes were filled with wonder. "You've seen her, too, then, with her noon-sun hair and eyes like sky-waters. She came back to us one night in blue fire so that we knew she was a fire spirit, and she blessed us with food and wine and water. But now the demons have come to the fortress. Mayhap if we gather more metal for her, she'll come back again and chase them away. Perhaps if you see her, you could tell her of our gathering and she'll come."

The story seemed clear enough, though Nim's time estimates did not fit. She insisted that two full "star cycles"—two years—had passed since they had first found D'Sanya and that she had stayed with them exactly three turnings of the moon. But the Lady had wandered out of the desert only eight months ago. Even Princess D'Sanya's power could not have kept her alive in the desert for more than a year; sorcery could not produce food or water, either one. But of more importance to our current mission, we gathered that the hauntings at the ruins, the return of the "demons," had begun just about the time the young Lord had disappeared from the hospice.

"I just can't believe the Lady D'Sanya could be in league with the Zhid, " I said to Paulo, once we'd traded some strips of dried meat and dried fruit for the return of our pots and cups and Nim's promise to return at nightfall. "She is D'Arnath's daughter. She's healed hundreds of the Zhid, and she cares for the sick and restores the land. None of this makes any sense."

"He said she had secrets," said Paulo, twisting the thongs that held the panniers closed until I thought he would shred the leather. "He said she couldn't have lived in Zhev'Na as long as she did and not have been changed by it. When the Prince had him search his memories of the Lords, he figured out that somebody must have a device called an avantir to be making the Zhid work together and power enough to work it"—Paulo paused, shaking his head firmly, his jaw set, his lips a firm line—"but he didn't think it was *her* running the Zhid. Even that night. He said she'd been a prisoner, not one of the Lords like him. If I'd not been so beat and fallen asleep on him, maybe he'd have told me more. But I know that if he'd thought it was her, it would have half killed him."

I didn't mention that from the cry I'd heard the next morning and the blood I'd found, it might have done exactly that. He knew it.

Just after sunset Nim returned as promised with one of her comrades—a bent, dusty man named Rab, thin as a stick. The two of them were terrified when we said we wanted to go into the ruined fortress. But we promised to give them food and water and whatever metal we could spare—I made an initial payment with three metal buttons from my jacket—and we swore to let them turn back if things got too dangerous.

They led us up the eastern slopes of the red crags, a wide well trampled roadway. Bones lay scattered along the way. This was the slave road. I tried to keep my mind focused on the route so we could get our business done and leave this cursed place.

Halfway to the summit, Nim led us away from the road and onto a path that climbed steeply through the broken slabs of rock. About the time the trail started looking too risky for goats, we found a niche with a mostly level floor, a gray stubble of grass, and a few thornbushes. "Beasts stay here," said Nim. "Too steep ahead."

Rab stayed behind with strict instructions as to which of our possessions could be touched and which could not. I started a little fire with a snap of my fingers, and the two Drudges dropped to their knees and put their heads on the ground. Misusing what little power I had to frighten them made me feel unclean. But I believed they would obey me.

Paulo and I each shouldered a rucksack loaded with two days' supply of food and water, and we set off with Nim toward the top of the ridge. Dry wind gusts whipped through the jagged pinnacles. The moon shone swollen and misshapen through the swirling dust. Paulo's shirt flapped about his lean body.

I dismissed the upheaval in my stomach that worsened as we neared the place of my captivity, calling myself a fool, though I took every opportunity to brush my fingers against my neck, breathing in relief each time I felt flesh rather than choking iron. As we approached the top of the ridge, the wind sighed and moaned, gnawing the gritty rocks into ragged, grotesque shapes that loomed fearfully in the night. I trod lightly, as nearly soundlessly as I could, though I could not have said why.

Paulo was doing the same. When Nim held up her leathery hand and pointed, trembling, to a last steep pitch across a flat boulder, we crept up it on our bellies like snakes.

Uttermost dismay stilled my heart as I gazed down on the plains of Ce Uroth. From my companion came a single whispered curse expelled on a breath of disbelief. Stretching to the farthest horizon, the plains teemed with warriors. As numerous as maggots on a dead beast, the legions of the Zhid marched past glowing campfires, surged against each other in mock battle lines that stretched for leagues into the darkness, built earthen fortifications, waved swords, and pumped bellows that flared the monstrous orange flames of their forges. The smell of blood was on the wind, and the acrid stench of coal and molten steel, and the stink of fear. It wasn't until Paulo laid his hand on mine that I realized I was shaking.

In the center of the crawling expanse was a huge, dark mound. As we watched, Zhid warriors threw torches all around its base, setting the mound afire. The black smoke coiled and billowed in the bilious moonlight. Flesh . . . burning flesh . . . the reeking death fog of Zhev'Na rising to blot out the stars. And in the towering blackness appeared a monstrous face straight from nightmare, gross and swollen, covering half the sky. Its eyes flamed red, and its bloated tongue licked cruel lips.

But even the sight of such horror did not sicken me as did the stench of burning slaves. Too often I'd smelled it and thought of my brothers, wondering if it was they who burned, or my father, or when it would be my turn. And the cries that rose from it . . . Not all the bodies in the mounds were dead. I buried my head in my arms, laying my face against the lingering warmth of the rough stone, trying to block out the foul smoke.

Nim whimpered in terror. Paulo tugged on my arms, trying to drag me down the sloping rock face. "It's looking this way," he whispered. "It's coming. We've got to get out of here."

"No! Wait!" Something was very odd. In the moment

I had hidden my face, the screams and wails and drum-
beats had fallen silent, and I could hear only the wind,
and smell only my own stink and the hard, sandy warmth
of the rock. I glanced up quickly, and all was as before:
the eye of flame looming above us, the gross nostrils
flaring as the red demon eyes hunted us, the surging
warriors, the burning . . . I buried my face again, and
all was silent.

What was the truth? This time I looked more carefully
at the sights on the plain. The campfires and torches
burned steadily, not a flicker or a bend in the wild wind.
The endless movements of the warriors had no
purpose. . . .

"Look away," I said. "Turn your back. It's not there."

Paulo did look away . . . to stare at me as if I were a
lunatic. But as he did so, a streak of wary curiosity
crossed his face. I was right. He flicked his gaze back
and forth from me to the monster I could no longer see
or hear, then he turned his back on Ce Uroth, sat up,
and grinned. "Cripes!"

Nim was sure we were driven mad by the demon, but
I grabbed her hand before she could crawl away. "It's
all right," I said, pulling her to her feet and holding on
firmly. "We can protect you from this particular demon.
My power is quite sufficient."

I hefted my pack and led the way down the rocky
path onto the plains of Ce Uroth.

CHAPTER 24

My confidence wavered as we abandoned the cliffs and gullies of the ridge and walked out under the demonic face in the sky. The foul smokes had us gagging, and the agonized screams of the captives and the hissing contempt of the Zhid curdled my blood. But, as I had guessed, neither demon nor captive nor Zhid took any note of us whatsoever.

We walked right through the chaotic war camp. Two Zhid wrestled in the dust to our left, cursing and spitting, slashing at each other with bloody knives. An entire troop marched past on the hammered roadway, their empty-eyed commander with red hair and thin lips riding a coal-black charger, and ten warriors dodged between the dusty tents answering a shouted summons. But not one of the Zhid challenged us.

The faster we walked, the more space there seemed to be between us and the vision, and when we were forced to slow down because Nim was paralyzed with terror, the specters brushed closer. I wrapped my arms about the woman and forced her to move, telling us both over and over that none of it had as much substance as the chill wind that swirled sand into my face.

Paulo slogged along beside me, his face grim, scarcely looking right nor left. But halfway across the plain he took my arm and spoke quietly in my ear as we walked. "Did you ever see stars in Zhev'Na?"

"No. Never." The odd question made me look up, of course. The demon apparition hung in the sky overhead, his eye of flame still pointed at the ridge behind us. But everywhere else the sky had taken on a deep purple cast, and the stars that hung suspended there were green. "Especially not green stars."

"*I've* seen green stars. In the Bounded, the young master's kingdom, we have a dark purple sky and green stars. He's here. This is his work."

"Then he's turned . . . become one of them again." My feet slowed. A ghostly Zhid rider barreled down the path toward us and, by reflex, I dragged Nim out of the way, forcing myself to move forward again.

"No, he cares for the Bounded. If he'd turned—and I told you already, he wouldn't ever—the Bounded wouldn't mean anything to him any more. He knows I'll come after him, and other than his parents, I'm the only one would know about the green stars. But if he's using his magic to tell me he's here, then why would he make all this other wretched business?"

The dark blight of the ruin grew larger in front of us, like a jagged hole in the night. I could see only one answer. "To frighten people away. To warn *you* away."

He nodded and walked on. "We'd best watch our step then."

In the moment we climbed over the cracked and crumbled slabs of black granite that had been the walls of Zhev'Na, the smoke demon and all the rest of the vision vanished. Behind us the plains lay barren and quiet. In front of us was . . . night. If darkness could be said to have bulk, then it was a thick, palpable darkness that hung over the ruin of Zhev'Na and gathered in the shadows cast by the bulbous moon.

We picked our way past the fallen walls, through burned beams and shattered paving stones, all that remained of the armories and barracks that had nestled beside the walls like evil chicks to a monstrous hen. A line of broken columns indicated the remains of a covered walkway, five years of wind-tossed thornbushes piled up in it.

"Where do we start?" Paulo stopped and surveyed the place. The piles of broken stone seemed to stretch forever.

I squeezed the quivering bundle of rags in my arms. "Nim, show us where you found the kaminar."

Her terror-dulled eyes roamed the ruin, peering out from under her mop of tangled hair.

"We'll protect you. You said it was a vault . . . buried deep . . ." Perhaps the Lady would consider it proper revenge to put the young Lord in her own tomb. "Please. We're afraid our friend is a prisoner here. You are so brave to help us. So kind."

Nim jerked her head and pulled me in an unexpected direction, not toward the Lords' house where one would find the deep chamber where the Great Oculus had spun out its evils, but instead through the Drudges' courtyard of workrooms and kitchens, and past the long, low barracks to the slave pens.

"Are you sure?" I asked.

"Just there." Her dusty whisper was almost indistinguishable from the wind. She pointed to a tangle of bent metal rods and broken stone. Wind and sand had scoured the filth from the warped black cages where those slaves used in fighting practice had been kept. In the ruins just beyond the cages, Nim showed us a huge crack in the stone floor. Great sections of paving had buckled as if the earth had heaved up the foulness that had been done there and pushed up against the fallen roof, leaving a gaping hole in the floor and a broken stair descending into blackness.

I cast a light, and Paulo and I knelt to peer over the edge. Nim squatted beside us and pointed to a rectangular opening at the bottom of the stair. Beside it lay the broken pieces of a stone door and tarnished brass hasps and hinges. I pressed the back of my left hand to my mouth and backed away, dizzy and sweating. The Lords had buried her here under this building. So deep . . .

Suddenly wary, I raised my handlight higher. Over my left shoulder stood a huge stone hearth and a broken brick chimney, blackened with centuries of use. Two broad shards of granite lay beside it, part of a single slab cracked down its middle and broken apart. Echoes of agony rang in my memory: my brothers struggling not to scream as the hot metal was dripped on the back of their necks to seal the slave collar, failing when the pain became too much to bear, and sobbing in despair as half their lives were torn from them. I had been so young I had not even tried to contain my wailing.

"It was here," I whispered, pulling my hand down to shrink the span of the light. I didn't want to see any more.

"What was here?" said Paulo.

Arms crossed on my breast, I wrapped my hands about my neck to remind myself of freedom. "They sealed us here. My brothers and me. In this very room."

"Oh, demonfire, I'm sorry, Jen."

Yet the echoes of past screams bared another part of the truth. "Think of it, Paulo. D'Sanya was held captive just below this place, where prisoners were sealed into the collars. If she couldn't sleep, D'Sanya would have heard their cries. For a thousand years. You were here. You know what that sound was like."

Paulo looked gray. "She's mad. However she's been able to hide it, she couldn't be nothing else but mad."

Truth unraveled its knots as I explored its windings. "She made the slave collars. That's why she can't look me or my father in the eye. That's why she begged Nim and her friends not to kill her—because she thought they were slaves, and she knew what she'd done to them. She's a Metalwright, and she made the collars, and then she had to listen to them being used every day of her life." Poor, poor D'Sanya.

"The lesser evil. That's what she told him. They'd kill five slaves whenever she would disobey. She told him she always chose the lesser evil."

The young Lord, Paulo's friend. The handsome young man with the lifetime of guilt in his eyes. The one we'd come to find.

"He's not here," I said, standing up. "She's put him somewhere else. This is the place of *her* guilt, not his."

Paulo glanced up at me. "We've got to go down and look, though. Before we go. In case there's something we can't see from here."

Conscience, ethics, kindness said I should go along to check for traps and spells and to protect Paulo. But remembered pain was palpable in the air. The stair was almost straight down, a sheer drop of almost two stories. "I can't go down there. I can't. I'm sorry."

"Just wait here, then." He looked at me carefully and laid a kind, very ordinary hand on my arm. "I won't be gone but a bit. Will you be all right?"

I nodded and forced my light as bright as I could, shaping it to illuminate the yawning pit as he descended the broken stairs. Then, cowardly, I looked away before I got dizzy and fell in after him.

Nim looked back and forth between me and the hole in the floor, chewing her fingers with stained teeth. "Can't stay here. Not here. Demons will come for us here. Worships will come."

I pulled her close, hoping I would have more success comforting her than I was having with myself. "No demons live here, Nim. Only shadows of demons."

"But some shadows are more substantial than others." The grating voice boomed from behind us.

I whipped my head around as Nim whimpered and collapsed into my arms. A massively built Zhid wearing bloodstained leather armor stood smiling at us with pale, soulless eyes. In one hand he carried a leather whip, studded with metal barbs, and in the other a long, curved dagger that glinted sharply in the soft light from my hand.

Truth? When the whip sliced the air a finger's breadth from my left cheek and cracked into the broken stones at my feet, raising a spurt of dust, I came to the sickening conclusion that this illusion might be real.

"It is most unseemly for such a one as you to exist uncollared," snarled the Zhid. "At least you kneel, as should Dar'Nethi vermin before their betters. Yet clearly you do not remember all your manners."

The whip cracked to the other side of me, ripping the shoulder of my tunic and leaving a stinging warning underneath it. The next one would be on my hands. I knew what he wanted, and I was not about to do it.

I jumped to my feet and dodged the ripping slice of the whip, trying not to trip over the cringing Nim as I shifted to my right. I needed to move away from the pit—force the warrior to turn his back to the steps where Paulo would appear at any moment.

"The days of my servitude are over," I yelled, hoping Paulo would hear. "I kneel to no one, and I spread my arms for no one, especially not a pitiful Zhid who acts as if one mindless brute can stand against a free Dar'Nethi."

"Then we shall have to see about that *free* part," he said, smiling.

"I am not nine years old this time. I don't even think you're real."

Farther . . . only a little farther. Make him turn away from the stair. Another step to the right. A thick, charred beam and a heap of crumbled stones blocked my way, forcing me to move within reach of the Zhid's hairy arms, unless— I quenched my handlight.

"Vermin's teeth!" growled the warrior as I pelted him with shards of stones that clattered harmlessly on his leather armor. In the dark he had no idea they were harmless, and I smiled as I heard him crash into the debris from the caved-in roof while scrabbling to get away. An unstable flickering of red light gave away his position, and then I bolted, grabbing Nim and yanking her back past the pit and the stair, where I hoped Paulo was biding his time in the dark.

We hurried through a maze of rubble, and then dodged into the shadow of a half-broken wall. "We're going to go separate ways to deceive him," I said to the quivering Nim. "You must run back to Rab. As soon as you can, no later than first light, the two of you must have the horses at the place where we crossed the walls of the ruin."

The warrior cursed and bellowed for someone else to join him. I had only moments.

"But the demons, mistress . . ."

"The only dangerous demons are these inside the

walls, and I'll take care of them. You saw my magic light, remember?"

Nim nodded, her face a portrait of indecision.

"Well, I have much more power than that. Just be careful and quiet until you are well away from the fortress. You have been so brave to bring us here. Here—" I pulled a gold coin from my pocket and closed her palm around it. "This is my talisman. It will protect you as you cross the plains. I kept you safe before, did I not?"

"Yes, mistress, you did, but—"

"Then you shall be safe going back. We're going to make sure that you and your friends are safe always. No burning metal to hurt or blind you. No demons to frighten you. But at first light . . ."

"We will be at the wall as you say."

"Thank you, Nim. Bless you. Together we'll bind these demons forever. Now be off with you. Hurry."

Without looking back, I sped in the opposite direction, angling away from the flicker of red light cast by the angry Zhid. Nim had shown us far more than I expected. If the young Lord was to be found, I knew where he had to be. But first, Paulo . . .

"She's heading back for the pens!" The shout was far too close. Another red light flared in exactly the direction I was running. I shifted my course, hurrying across the broad practice yards, risking the exposed route in the need for speed. Paulo would have to fend for himself.

By the time I reached the dark, upright, bony fingers of the broken colonnade, ten more red flares had sprung up behind me and to the sides. My luck took its usual course and a squat, barrel-shaped Zhid warrior with a bald head stepped from behind a toppled statue of a gryphon. The warrior's long sword gleamed wickedly in the scarlet light cast from his hand. Chuckling in satisfaction, he edged around the giant paw of the gryphon, waving the tip of his sword in a tight, controlled circle.

I could not retreat. I had some thought of circling, then taking off and outrunning the broad-beamed Zhid, but my hopes were not encouraged by his bellowing laugh when I began the move. My neck prickled. Worse and worse. Armor clanked from my left in the direction of the barracks, along with the unmistakable whisper of swords leaving their sheaths.

Before I could think what else to do, a thin black shadow leaped off the gryphon's crumbled wing and onto the warrior's back, yelling, "Go!" As I ran, the two fell to the pavement, grunting and grappling.

To my right, just beyond a tumbled wall, a tower of fire belched high into the night, blistering my exposed skin as I picked my way through the fallen columns, into the Drudges' courtyard.

This time keep to the shadows, fool, I thought.

I sped down an alleyway between the servants' latrines and a collapsed guardroom. I'd had to shovel out those latrines and haul food, water, and lamp oil to that guardroom. Slaves learned all the back alleys. If you stayed out of sight, you were less likely to be detained by random cruelties—like the two Zhid holding a knife to my eyes, threatening to cut them out if I blinked too soon, and then laying bets as to how long I could hold them open. The passage was almost blocked by a fallen slab, but I crawled under and emerged in the courtyard of the Lords.

An unnatural cold crept out of the rubble into my shuddering bones. What forces had Gerick and his father unleashed to shatter the slender towers that had soared so high? The gigantic carvings that had flanked the tall black doors had toppled, and one of the beast heads, double my height, stared at me with dead black eyes from the center of the court. The great fire bowls that had once sat atop the parapets were now cold and broken, the giant shards protruding from a mountain of broken granite.

For a moment the shouts and snarls of the chase seemed distant, muted by a sighing wind that crept about the ruins and curled about my feet, grasping with dead fingers at my trousers. The wind whispered in my ears of evil upon evil, lingering remembrances of pain and fear, of souls lost and wandering, cruelly, everlastingly separated from the Way of light and hope and joy.

It was all I could do to go forward. My blood pounded. A warning blazed in my head like a beacon: *Begone from this place!*

He was here. I knew it with a certainty I could attach to nothing else. I half expected to feel his strength moving my legs again. I could have used it; my knees would not stop shaking.

Yet the fortress where I had lived in constant fear was a shattered shell, while I stood here alive and uncollared. The Lords who had terrorized me and tormented those I loved were dead. Whoever these warriors were, whatever this cold terror might be, they were only an echo.

I ran for the gaping maw where the entry doors had stood. From beyond the dark mouth came murmurings, weeping, curses and hoarse, mocking shouts.

The roof of the temple hall was open to the night, the wind howling through cracks wider than a man. Yet no rubble, sand, or thornbush cluttered the polished black floor, so like a lake of black ice. Nothing remained of the giant statues of the Lords—the fearsome monoliths carved in black stone that had been alive with the Lords' presence behind their masks of gold and gem-studded eyes. Far across the cavernous space was the way I had to go, the downward passage into the bowels of the palace. My pattering footsteps mocked my false courage as I sped across the shining floor, while in my head the warning blazed louder, desperate: *Begone from this place! You have no business here!*

As I hurried downward into the oppressive darkness, I cast my light again. It flickered feebly. I'd not be able to maintain it for long. I sped down flight after flight of broad steps, not daring to look anywhere except into the pool of light at my feet. When I at last faced the smooth black door that led into the innermost heart of Zhev'Na, I stopped to listen. The warning hammered in my head with the certainty of mortal danger. *Go back! Do not come here!*

But I couldn't change my mind because of some cowardly palpitations about cold stone and memory. Paulo had put himself in jeopardy to get me this far. I pushed open the door.

The walls and columns of the vast chamber showed gouges and great charred and jagged rents as if damaged in a cataclysm of fire. In its center lay the sculpture of a man resting on a bed of stone, very like those you see atop a coffin lid or carved in relief upon the face of a standing tomb. But before I could examine the sculpture or the damaged walls, a bolt of lightning flashed from the palm-sized ring of brass that hung spinning in the air above the sculpted man, drowning my handlight in such brilliance it forced my eyes closed. And when I opened them again, I was in a different place altogether. . . .

CHAPTER 25

*Silver moonlight bathed the snowy forest. The pine trees'
needles, sheathed in ice, tinkled softly in the frosty breath
of the wind. My cheeks tingled with the cold, and the
comforting scent of wood smoke lured me through the
quiet to a lamp-lit cottage nestled in the trees. Merry
laughter and the plinks of a harp being tuned drifted
faintly on the curling smoke from the chimney. Imagining
the Singers and Players readying their costumes and the
feasting table laden with delights for family and guests, I
thought to draw closer and peer inside to see who it was
made merry on a winter's night. But from behind me
came the soft crunch of horses' hooves in the snow. No
jingle of harness. No hail of greeting. No sleigh bells. A
silent coming.*

*Something wasn't right. Dread crept up behind me like
a cloud across the moon, sending the merry harp strings
out of tune again, and I opened my mouth to cry a warning. Too late. Across the snowy glade flew a lance—flame
at its tip—that shattered the lamplit window, silenced the
harper's music, and turned the laughter into shouts. Dark
figures rushed out of the moon shadows and burst open
the unlocked door, while more fire-lances flew from every
side, striking roof and walls. The shouts turned to
screams. The innocent lamplight burst into orange flame,
and the merrymakers were dragged from the cottage and
their blood steamed as it stained the pure white snow.
Some were slaughtered. Some were hauled away in
chains. Some turned, empty-eyed, upon their friends and
family, laughing at their screams.*

I cried out. But just as a pale-eyed warrior spun on his heel, sword raised, his blood-smeared face searching, an invisible hand clamped itself over my mouth and dragged me deeper into the trees. The one who held me would not allow me to move until the horsemen were gone and the wolves' eyes gleamed from the darkness—waiting. As the flames moved into the woodland to consume the trees, the house fire died into glowing ash. The wolves would finish what the evil had begun.

Released, I turned and ran through the forest. Others lived among the trees, homes and towers scattered in the most beautiful places, in dells and glens, by streamsides and waterfalls, families who welcomed long guesting and souls who hungered for solitude to grow their gifts. What need to crowd together when the whole of the world was welcoming and beautiful? I ran, but always too late, finding only ash, bloodstained snow, and the horrific echoes of death and captivity.

One after the other, hundreds of homes were hit on that winter night. I did not even question how it was I could see them all. The terror and pain grew into something huge, something awful, like a plague or a storm that lived inside me and spilled out into the vastness of the world. I was filled with it and revolted by it, and I wept because I could not make it stop. . . .

I clenched my fists and hammered at my head, fighting to return to my own thoughts, to dangerous reality . . . the ruins . . . the search. I blinked and the ring of dark stone columns took shape on every side of me. Yet the events that had unfolded before my eyes had borne the surety of reality as well, the truth of lived memory: the beginning, the Catastrophe, the night that terror and war had come to Gondai. On that night a hunger had been born whose feeding would ravage the world for a thousand years, for Three had lurked in that darkness and fed upon those screams.

I could not have warned them. The voice inside me was bent with pain. *I could not have stopped it. It happened long before I was born. . . . Before I knew . . .*

I hurried toward the center of the chamber where the lurid light of the spinning oculus shone down on the sculpted body of a man stretched out on the stone slab. No! He was part of the stone, yet not part of it . . . bolted . . . Vasrin's hand, he was fastened to the slab with bolts through his hands and his feet. Strips of iron across his wrists, ankles, and forehead were also bolted to the stone, fixing him in place. And the stone had molded itself about his body in thin brittle layers that over time would grow thick and solid until he was indeed a sculpture of a man. It had climbed up his sides and halfway over his shoulders and face. His arms, legs, and neck were already enclosed, every scar and sinew, every wrinkle in his torn shirt and breeches sculpted in delicate detail.

The lightning flashed and blinded me again. . . .

. . . and a crowd surged forward, carrying me with it. Never had I been in such a crush—stinking, ragged bodies, warm on the bitter winter's day, faces distorted with vices I did not know and hatred I did not understand.

"Burn him!" The cries were deafening, and as mindlessly angry as the roaring of beasts.

From above me came the insistent beating of banners flapping in the cold wind, red banners woven with a gold dragon stark against an ice-blue midday sky. The mob flowed from the narrow street into a wide open plaza fronting a squat fortress of gray stone. In the midst of the sea of jeering faces rose a high platform with a wooden post in its center and a man chained to it—a slender, dark-haired man clad only in rags, shivering in the cold, though he stood straight and calm while the storm of hate raged around him. His eyes were burned-out sockets, his face battered and bleeding, and in horror I watched as red-clad soldiers set torches to the wood piled at his feet. The crowd let out a monstrous cheer of satisfaction.

No, no, no . . . this was not me! The voice inside me cried out in agony. *Oh, gods, not this!*

* * *

I couldn't understand it. The woman next to me, her teeth green and rotting, her breath foul with drink, grabbed my arm and pointed to the balcony high on the castle wall. "It's her! The witch what married the devil." And indeed a young woman dressed in plain white robes, her hair a ragged stubble, stood on the balcony watching the man. But as the flames grew, she sank to her knees and covered her eyes and ears until the man let go his agony in a single dreadful cry. The death scream echoed inside my head. . . .

Father! Despair and grief and denial ripped through me like lances of fire. *It was not me. I was not yet born. . . .*

Searing lightning yet again. Only an instant's glimpse of the still figure on the table and I was no longer in the winter forest or the city of horror, but in the desert. . . .

The heat sapped the last residue of moisture from my lips; the sun hammered on the back of my head.

"Here they come."

"About time. The Slavemaster'll be fit to eat someone for 'em being this late."

The voices were below me, Zhid warriors standing guard duty on the hard-baked desert road, peering into the dust haze to see the gray unwieldy shape resolve itself into a ragged column of half-naked men roped together. Their skin was burned dark by the sun, their lips blackened and cracked, most of them scarcely able to lift their raw, bloody feet. Flies buzzed and stuck to backs streaked with garish mementos of the lash.

"Move on!" shouted the guard with a crack of his whip.

The dolorous column passed by my hiding place, and the doors of the cages slammed behind them with a metallic clang. I knew what came next. My knife was in my hand, and I scrambled down from my rocky perch and sped down the cracked earth of the road. Any child with power could undo the lock. If I was fast, the guards would never expect it—an uncollared Dar'Nethi in the middle of the camp.

The first despairing screams came from the building beyond the cages as I reached for the gate. And then a hairy arm, slick with sweat, wrapped itself about my throat. "What is this? Did we miss one? Shall we drink its blood or collar it with the rest of them?"

"Never again!" I shouted. "I'll not allow it."

"Not allow? Let us show you who will allow what. . . ."

My hand that held my knife was wrapped around behind me, until I was forced to drop the weapon to make them stop . . . only they didn't stop. I screamed as my shoulder snapped. But the warrior was dragged off my back and I lay in the dirt sobbing. . . .

Get away! Run! I cannot hold!

. . . only to wake again to a roaring blast of heat from a fiery furnace. I was stretched upon the tilted slab as a wide strip of glowing metal was pulled from the fire, but before they could wrap it about my neck, the Zhid who held me down was jerked away and thrown to the ground.

Get away from here! Run! Their collars are real. Their knives are real. You'll be trapped here if you stay. . . .

The desert noonday blinded me as I stumbled out of the smithy, cradling my arm, tears of pain and frustration running from my face. . . .

The sunlight vanished. I moaned with the pain of my torn shoulder, which did not vanish with the fire and the Zhid. Clutching my arm, I crept closer to see if the man on the table was truly flesh or stone, alive or dead or only another vision. He looked dead. No trace of color in lips or cheeks, his skin with the waxy pallor of those who have lost an inordinate amount of blood. His eyes were open, one of them half occluded by the stone. They were sunken and hollow, wholly black, as they had been when he was a favored guest of the Lords of Zhev'Na and would return from his nights of sorcery with his hosts. I did not believe he could see anything in the world I walked.

"Can you hear me?" I whispered.

Get away from here. His lips did not move, but it was

not the voice of my own fears that spoke in my mind, nor had it been throughout that wicked day. *Go. I cannot hold for long.*

"We've come for you, your friend Paulo and I."

No! A surge of fear, grief, and despair came near knocking me off my feet. *Get away! You can do nothing for me. Tell them . . . tell my father . . . Ah . . .* A groan resonated in my thoughts, and blood ran from his blackened eyes like tears of horror. Spears of brilliance shot from the spinning ring once more. . . .

. . . and I was standing on a tower in Avonar, watching as the Zhid swarmed over the city walls. The empty-eyed warriors slaughtered the Dar'Nethi one by one as the desperate defenders fell back through the streets. Warning bells rang. Balefires burned on the heights like scarlet demon eyes. Behind me refugees streamed out of the rear gates, while below me, all around, and everywhere, Avonar, the City of Light, was in flames. The night had come. The last night. Unending slaughter. Unending darkness. Unending pain . . .

Truth held me in its steady gaze and left me no alternatives. While watching the destruction of all our hope, seeing wave upon wave of the soulless enemy pour through a ragged breach in the white walls, I fumbled for the dagger at my belt. My right arm unusable, my awkward left hand did the work in a place far distant from the nighttime battle that held my senses in thrall. The deed must be done before I could return from this place to the bowels of Zhev'Na.

"I'm sorry," I whispered, tearing at flimsy fabric, feeling for the right place. His flesh was already cold when I struck. As warm blood gushed over my hand, the vision of terror flickered and faded, and I stood once again in the Chamber of the Oculus, looking down on the tortured young man with my dagger in his heart. From the doorway behind me came a cry of dismay.

"Liar! Murderer! You'll die for this!"

My dagger clattered to the floor as a ragged, bloody Paulo pulled me away from his friend with a roar. Darkness fell as his fist proved to me the power of love and grief.

"He won't die. He won't die." From somewhere in the thrall of midnight, I willed the words past my thick tongue. I had to be fast or the matter of Gerick's dying would be of no importance next to the matter of my own. Was my timing always to be so wretched? I grasped for a handhold that would help me drag myself upright. *Fool, not the right hand or you'll be flat out again.* Darkness toyed with my senses until I was motionless long enough to banish it.

Now, again. Left hand on the cold, broken stone this time. When the streak of painful fire split my aching head, I thought I might be transported back into the young Lord's visions . . . or dreams or memories or whatever were these unending horrors to which he was condemned. But my distorted vision seemed to be only the result of the brain-rattling blow Paulo had laid on me when he saw me stabbing his dearest friend and king. Fortunately, he was so much stronger than me he felt no need to consummate his murderous intent before attending to the young Lord. My handlight had died out, leaving the lurid gleaming of the oculus our only illumination.

"He won't die." This time the words took shape in the air, though heavily distorted by my swollen lip. "She'll have worked it so he can't—even if he wants to."

The lanky figure whirled about, his freckled face ravaged with unashamed grief. "You meant to kill him all along. I knew it."

He hadn't heard me, and it hurt so much when he grabbed my hair and wrenched me to my knees that I wasn't sure I could say it again. His knife reflected the purple-green-and-gold light as he bared my throat, all the time the tears running down his grimy face. "I told you you'd die for it."

"Listen to me if you want to help him," I croaked. "He won't die from what I did. But I had to stop him.

His visions were going to kill us. I think my shoulder's broken, and not from falling down the stairs."

"You're a cursed traitorous liar. Why would I believe you?"

"He's breathing, Paulo. I stabbed him in the heart, but he's still breathing."

The blood welling out of the knife wound slowed, the red droplets rolling down the cocoon of shellstone that covered Gerick's flanks. But his chest still moved.

"We don't have much time," I said, clutching my throbbing arm and easing my aching body upward, bracing myself on the fallen slab. "We've got to get him out of this before the wound heals. Whatever she's done to him makes the things in his head come alive. He tried to save me from getting hurt by them, but it wasn't easy and not always successful, and he may not be able to protect us any longer. It's why he's been trying to frighten everyone away. Don't you see?"

Paulo shook his head. I didn't envy him his dilemma.

"Trust me, Paulo. I'm telling you that he's doing exactly what you say he's done before. He's trying to save us. Trying to save everyone by creating that illusion of terror out on the plains to keep them away from here. No matter the cost to himself. These things inside the fortress are walking out of his nightmares alive, and he can't control them."

"I won't leave him here."

Feeling a momentary reprieve, I pressed my advantage and moved in for a closer look. "We've got to break away the shellstone where it holds him in—and undo the straps. That's the trickiest, as that's where D'Sanya's enchantment will be held. And we'll have to time it just right. Once he's free of the enchantment, if the knife wound isn't healed yet, he'll bleed to death, but if it heals before we've got him away, his visions will start coming alive again, and we'll get skewered by some Zhid."

"Shit."

"I couldn't think of any other way to make him stop. He has no control of it."

Paulo closed his eyes and tugged at a clump of his

sandy hair, as if to focus his thoughts. "I've got linen bandages in my pack."

"Good. You can bash away the shellstone while I look at the bolts. But first"—I really hated to ask him—"you've got to tie up my arm, or I'm going to pass out and be no help at all."

He did it, and gently enough, considering the circumstances. Fortunately he appeared to be uninjured. From the blood decorating his shirt and breeches, I didn't have to ask about the other fellow.

"What about that?" he said, pointing to the spinning ring. "If I was to stand on the table, I could grab it . . . stop it maybe . . ."

"No! Don't touch it. Don't even look at it. I once saw a slave touch one of the rings back in the Lords' house, and it withered his hand. We don't have power enough to deal with it. We just have to get him away from it."

To my relief, what I'd seen as bolts through Gerick's hands and feet were, in fact, long spikes attached to the metal straps, like those I'd seen in D'Sanya's lectorium. Barbed, I remembered, thus wicked enough. Only the straps were bolted to the rock. If we could get them loose, then the spikes could be eased out of his flesh. With luck, there would be no damage to his bones. With luck, we could stop the bleeding. With luck, removing the straps and the shellstone and getting him away from the oculus would leave him free of enchantment. With luck. I had never considered myself a particularly lucky person.

Warning Paulo to stay back, I touched one of the metal straps with my finger. The gut-wrenching slap of power convinced me instantly that we needed a tool with which to get them loose. D'Sanya's enchantments were far beyond me. Setting Paulo to chipping at the thin layers of shellstone with a fist-sized rock, I cast my handlight again and explored the adjoining rooms.

Several of the rooms had collapsed walls and were completely filled with rubble. One was littered with piles of old bones. I spoke words of peace sending and apologized for having no incense, then left quickly.

A skull sat in a niche above the doorway of the innermost chamber. The lintel was cracked and the doorway
skewed to one side, the heavy wooden door hanging by
one hinge, but the room itself was intact. I had never
been inside the Vault of the Skull when I lived in
Zhev'Na, only heard tales of cruel and restless spirits
who inhabited it. But someone more substantial than a
ghost had been here . . . and fairly recently, too. A torch
in a wall bracket still smelled of oil. I whispered the
spell to set it aflame, then let my handlight die. I'd best
hoard power for the spikes.

The chamber was a Metalwright's workroom, con-
taining tools and materials similar to those I'd seen in
D'Sanya's lectorium. I dared not touch the shaped scraps
on the worktable, but in one corner lay neat stacks of
metal bars of all lengths and sizes. They looked fairly
innocent. I grabbed a long flat bar of black steel and a
few of the tools and stuffed them under my arm. Grabbing the torch from the bracket, I then hurried back to
the larger chamber.

Paulo had created a mountain of stone chips. His face
was coated with chalky dust. In a few places the sweat
held enough of the shellstone dust that a thin white glaze
had formed, like the skim of ice on a still pond. He
wiped his face with his upper arm. "He's bleeding
again," he said as I came in, "but the knife wound has
started to close. As you said."

"Good. I knew she wouldn't want him to die. As long
as he doesn't heal too fast . . ."

I found a bracket for the torch on a nearby column,
gave Paulo the steel bar, and warned him again not to
touch the metal straps with his hands. "When you get
the straps loose from the rock, I'll get the spikes off
him." He nodded and set to work, levering the black bar
under one wrist strap and prying with all his strength, his
shoulders bulging. I took up his rock and carefully
chipped away the brittle stone that had molded the
young Lord's cheekbones.

After a seemingly interminable time, the bolts holding
the strap to the rock finally gave way.

Paulo wiped the sweat from his face and moved to the other side. I took D'Sanya's pincers and sharp little trimming knife and, swearing at the uselessness of left hands, awkwardly removed the barbed spike from Gerick's cold flesh. Foul-smelling black fluid gushed from the wound in his palm, and only when it ran healthy red again did I bind his hand tightly with a strip of linen.

It seemed to take us an eternity to free his wrists, head, and right ankle. The torchlight was wavering. Paulo was straining at the last strap, his body shaking with the effort, and I was trying to stanch the flow of blood from Gerick's right foot, when my vision blurred and a musty scent enveloped us.

"Hurry," I said. A quick check of the knife wound revealed only an angry, seeping scar on Gerick's chest. With a furious growl, Paulo pressed again, and I tied off the ankle wound.

"This way! They've trespassed the fortress!" The shouts filtered down the stair. Boots trampled overhead.

"Ignore whatever you hear and see," I said. "You've got to keep working even if you can't see the strap."

Footsteps on the stair. "I'll sup on their entrails!"

The strap snapped loose. We were out of time. Reality was flickering before my eyes and I didn't know how long Gerick could hold back his lethal visions. Without skill or delicacy I slit the flesh around the spike and ripped the vile implement from his left foot. Paulo tied off the wound without waiting for the poisonous flow to end.

"We've got to get him away from here," I whispered. "Away from that." The ring still spun its evil magic overhead.

"Lead the way," said Paulo. "He won't die in this place at least."

As Paulo hefted his friend into his arms and then over his shoulder, the torch guttered and died. The faint gleam of the oculus danced on the shellstone rubble, but on nothing else.

Stale, fetid air . . . a whispering evil that crept around us, moaning, sighing . . . Entombed with madness . . . danger . . . You are our instrument . . . Destroyer . . .

As panic threatened to choke off the wail rising in my throat, one small part of my mind continued to function. *Where is the door?* I felt my way forward, waving my uninjured arm ahead of me . . . holy Vasrin, how did Aimee manage this every day of her life? Ten paces . . . fifteen . . . how large was this chamber? *Think.* I crashed into the stone door frame, almost knocking myself senseless.

Light . . . you've got to have light, idiot girl. Cursing my stupidity and my incapable sorcery, I cast a feeble handlight. It wouldn't last a quarter of an hour.

On our way up the stair we had to step through piles of moaning wounded, begging us to stop and give aid, clawing at our legs with handless arms, weeping with the dreadful wails of lost souls. "Not real," I mumbled. "Not real." The farther we got from the spinning oculus, the more transparent the visions became, until they faded away altogether. No murderous apparitions awaited us at the top of the stair.

Stepping out of the ruined temple into the desert air was the closest thing I'd ever felt to having my slave collar removed, a burden of vile oppression lifted so that the world came to life once more. The sky curved above us pure black and studded with stars, and the wind that rolled the thornbushes through the ruined courtyards was the natural cold of a desert night.

Nim had kept her promise, and she and her wrinkled friend were waiting beside the fallen gates. When they glimpsed Gerick, eyes sunken, skin pale, body slathered with drying blood and shellstone dust, it was all we could do to keep them from abandoning us. Only my threat to bring back the smoke demon kept them with us.

Paulo draped Gerick over one of the horses and tied him securely. Pesca's back might have been the surface of the moon for all the likelihood of my climbing so high, so I took the reins and started walking away from the ruin, my left arm wrapped tightly over the bound right one.

"Wait!" Paulo grabbed Pesca's halter and dragged the two of us toward a granite block, fallen from the broken wall. "Step up."

I stepped onto the knee-high block, and Paulo grabbed my waist and leg and heaved me into the saddle. I almost passed out. The stars smeared across the sky as I wrapped my left arm about Pesca's neck.

The desert dwellers led us across the plain and up a steep, twisting path into the jagged cliffs, outlined like dark teeth against the stars. For every jarring step of that journey I prayed that my arm would fall off. After the mostly invisible track through the cracks and hollows of the ridge leveled into a wide trough between two high walls, Nim stopped and pointed into a small pocket of night on our right. "You can stay here."

I bent my head down to Pesca's mane and sobbed in gratitude and terror. Though happy to stop moving, I just couldn't comprehend how I was going to get off of that horse without coming completely apart.

By the time Paulo had taken Gerick deeper into the dark hollow in the cliffs and laid him on the dirt, Nim and Rab had pulled my feet out of the stirrups and, as gently as four trembling hands could manage a cursing, weeping wreck of a woman, dragged me from my mount and sat me down. They pointed at a muddy waterhole under a rock overhang and shoved a pile of thornbush scraps at us. "The *riake vontu* can make fire, yes?" asked the old man, his voice quavering. Before I could answer, they scurried off into the night.

I felt nothing like a *demon vanquisher*, but did feel my humiliating performance of the last hour was somewhat balanced by the wan yellow light that still glowed from my numb fingers. As Paulo settled Gerick on the sand and whipped two blankets out of our saddle packs to bundle around him, I managed to spit one small spark from my handlight to set the dry brush afire. Hiccupping, trying not to moan too grotesquely, I rolled onto my left side and let my light die. I would leave it to Paulo to organize the blaze, while I concentrated on not moving or screaming.

"Here, let me look at that," said Paulo after a moment, dropping to his knees next to my face.

He touched my shoulder, and I threatened to gouge his eyes out amongst other things. From out of the blinding red haze, I heard him say that my arm seemed to be pulled out of its socket instead of broken, and that he had helped some stableman aid a fallen rider who had the same condition. I heard myself sobbing and saying something like, "Well then do something about it before I take an ax to it!"

"All right, then. Hold on." And he held my wrist firmly, bent my elbow, and did something that seemed to plant a hook in my stomach and draw that organ right up through my chest and out through my shoulder. I yelled and collapsed in a gibbering heap. All in all, a fortunate outcome for both of us. The pain was miraculously reduced, and I had no strength left to kill him.

CHAPTER 26

Over the next hours, the wound on Gerick's left foot swelled horribly and oozed thick black fluid that smelled like putrefying flesh. He lay in a feverish stupor, and, despite Paulo's application of the healing salves Aimee had sent with us, black streaks stretched up Gerick's leg, farther by the moment. I had seen a number of such wounds . . . all of them made by blades forged in Zhev'Na.

"You must let me try this," I said to Paulo, once I had regained my composure and a measure of lucid thought. "You're right that I'm not a Healer, and I've little enough power, but an enchantment of purification might help neutralize the poison. By my father's head, I mean him no harm."

"He hates magic being done to him as much as he hates doing it himself. You wouldn't understand."

No, I didn't understand his argument, but I felt the heat of Gerick's fever even from several body-lengths away. "You lived in Zhev'Na, Paulo. You saw the results of Zhid poison. Putrefaction. Sepsis. A mortification of the surrounding flesh that kills more often than not. Purifying such a wound is more likely to help him than easing the pain, and it certainly won't make things worse. He won't ever have to know I did it."

I edged closer, scooting my backside across the sand and gravel, and laid my left hand on Gerick's chest. His heart was fluttering wildly. Calling up the ritual steps my mother had taught me in a childhood when I was forever falling out of trees and tumbling off the rocks behind our house, I reached out for the three purest elements I could find—the starlight, the sharp wind of the heights, the clean strength of this odd fellow Paulo's love for his friend—and I drew them close to hand and wove them together, infusing their essence with the meager scraps of my power. The simple enchantment that my mother had called "hurt's ease" smelled like clean soap and, if I did it right, should settle on the young Lord's swollen left foot like a Healer's balm and a soft bandage.

Paulo didn't stop me as I laid my thumb on the bandaged wound and let my other fingers enfold both thumb and ankle to focus the little spell. "Why is the Lady's enchantment like Zhid poison?" he mumbled as he jabbed at the blazing brush. "Don't make sense."

He had retrieved my cloak along with our packs and laid it over my shoulders. Once my pitiful spellmaking was finished, I pulled the garment tighter and lay down by the fire, only to find myself too uncomfortable and too overwrought to sleep. I lay watching Paulo drip water on Gerick's lips and bathe his friend's face and arms with a grimy rag dampened in the mudhole. Every hour for the rest of the night he repeated his ministrations. Gerick did not wake.

Daylight revealed that our shelter was not truly a cave, but only a shallow concavity scooped out of the gritty red rock by a long-vanished river. A few scrubby plants and a stand of stiff gray grass survived in the old riverbed, thanks to the shade of the overhanging cliff and the sluggish mudholes underneath it. All we could see from our location were the silver sheen of desert daylight and more layered red rock.

While refilling our water flasks from the slow-to-replenish mudhole—a task that looked to occupy the entire day—I spotted something metallic protruding from a notch in the rocks across the riverbed from the overhang. Closer investigation revealed a jumble of metallic rubbish: old nails, rusting harness, bent shields, and broken tools. The scavengers' treasury.

Paulo had not left Gerick's side all night and demon-

strated no intention of falling asleep, despite my admoni-
tions and avowals of good intent. He paced; he
hammered his hands on the rocks; he fumbled with
cooking pots and tack and spent hours grooming the
horses we'd tethered where they could crunch the stiff
grass. Gerick was never out of his sight.

As Paulo wouldn't allow me to do anything more for
his friend, I had little to occupy my time once I had filled
the water flasks. Thanks to his skillful manipulation, I
could pretty much move my right arm as I wished, but
I had him bind it tightly to my chest again to ease the
constant ache. My fingers were only gradually regaining
sensation. Being one-handed for very long was going to
drive me to distraction.

The sleepless night and my aching shoulder made our
ration of dried bread and greasy meat, no matter how
well preserved, singularly unappetizing. I tried again to
sleep, but could not find a comfortable position. Not a
wisp of a breeze found a path into the old watercourse.
The afternoon was stifling.

Only after the wretched day had long expired did
Paulo succumb to exhaustion. His head lay wedged between two rocks—an entirely appropriate place as far as
I was concerned—and his long body blocked the way in
and out of the sheltering overhang. He would have been
more comfortable farther back under the rocks where it
was sandier, but I couldn't move him by myself, and I
had no heart to wake him.

Though Gerick's fever yet burned, the sepsis in his
foot had not worsened in the past few hours. I kept the
water going down him, and soaked the rag in the smallest puddle and laid it on his forehead. With too little to
distract me, I thought a great deal about the rescue and
about what we had left behind in the ruins. No matter
how I tried to convince myself otherwise, no matter how
terrified I became at the thought that insisted on planting itself in my head, I could not shake the sense that
our work was dangerously unfinished.

On the next morning, while Paulo yet slept, I rummaged through Nim's hoard of metal objects and picked

out a shovel and a sword with a broken tip. Then, with
much swearing and difficulty, I unstrapped my arm and
saddled my horse.

"What do you think you're doing?" A bleary-eyed
Paulo stood at the edge of the overhang as I fastened
the implements to my saddle. He looked more filthy and
bedraggled than threatening—though I would have
thought more than twice before challenging him.

"I'm going back to retrieve the oculus. We can't just
leave it there where anyone can find it. Innocent people
like Nim—I promised to protect her—or others like real
Zhid, or the one who put it there . . ."

"Absolutely not. You can't—"

"I'll not bring it anywhere near him." I jerked my
head toward Gerick. "I've no desire to participate in
your friend's nightmares again. I'll take it down, bury it
where no one can find it, and be back by nightfall."

I verified that the two water flasks in my rucksack
weren't leaking, crammed an empty bag of thick canvas
in beside them, and fixed the pack on my saddle, anxious
to get going before he got some notion of stopping me.

"I thought a person couldn't touch the thing," he
called after me, stepping out into the sunlight. "I thought
it would hurt you. I thought you didn't have power
enough to deal with it."

"Then you won't have to worry about me killing him
any more, will you?" I yelled back at him.

Neither phantom nor villain came anywhere in sight
as I descended the ridge and crossed the searing plain
into Zhev'Na. Yet even with no imminent physical
threats, I felt jittery and sick as I entered the charred
chamber with the rubble-strewn stone block in the center of it. The oculus still spun in the air above the stone
table, weaving its horror from the light of my torch. All
the bravado I had donned for Paulo evaporated. I had
no confidence at all that I could do this.

With only one able arm and no talent to work with,
everything took far longer than it should have. I tried
every simple unlocking and detaching spell I'd ever
heard of to loosen the enchantment that held it sus-

pended, but none of them seemed to work. Finally I climbed onto the table, kicking some of the debris onto the floor. Taking as firm a stance as I could hold, I held the broken sword in my left hand and used my right arm to brace it. Then I stabbed upward to snare the ring, fighting to keep the thing from sweeping me off the table. I held on, and after a few moments, it dropped onto the sword with a clang. I pointed the sword downward and let the ring slide to the floor. Shuddering, I bashed the sword hilt against the shellstone that had already formed a brittle rim around the sole of my boots and jumped down from the slab.

More than ready to bolt, I slipped the oculus into the canvas bag without touching it or even looking at it more than necessary. I didn't start breathing again until I had left the ruin behind, and even then I whined and moaned with each exhalation like an ailing child. No use muffling it. No one was about to hear me. The vile device shredded my spirit like an overseer's lash. Cringing and shuddering in the saddle, I managed to get only halfway up the ridge before I yanked Pesca to a halt in a rubble-strewn clearing. Though still within sight of the ruins, I unstrapped the shovel and began to dig. I had to be rid of the thing. Though I, as every Dar'Nethi, knew the basic steps to destroy an object of enchantment, the power required was well beyond my poor capacity.

Two sweat-soaked hours later the oculus lay buried in a deep hole in the gravelly dirt. Feeling much relieved, I sat on the shield-sized plate of red rock that I had heaved, lurched, shoved, and levered over the spot, and took a few lukewarm sips from my water flask. Suddenly, the rocks beneath my feet shuddered. A few pebbles danced down the cliffs.

Pesca whinnied anxiously. I jumped up and stroked her neck, speaking soothingly as I'd watched Paulo do. After making sure her reins were still wrapped securely around a narrow column of rock, I scrambled up a boulder pile to get a good look at the sky. Desert storms could be fierce, the lightning deadly, and the track across the ridge to where Paulo and Gerick lay was steep and exposed. The desert sky was cloudless, but across the plain a thin column of dark smoke rose over the ruins of Zhev'Na. A broken tower crumbled into dust just as a flash of blue lightning blazed from the heart of the ruin. Moments later another muffled rumble shook the earth again.

"Miffed, are you?" I said.

But my bravado was only skin-deep. I slid down the boulder pile and drew Pesca into a deeper notch in the rocks, huddling there until the tremors had ceased. Only after making sure the sky over Zhev'Na had cleared did I ride up and over the ridge. By the time I got back to the ancient riverbed, the shadows were long and my hands had finally stopped shaking.

"Well?" said Paulo, after giving me a decent time to flop on the ground, pour the brackish dregs from my water flask on my head, and let the throbbing in my shoulder ease.

"The device is safer than it was," I said. I curled up on one side and supported my arm on my rucksack, despairing of finding any position that was comfortable. "Hidden. No one's going to happen onto it by chance." No one who could cause minor earthquakes with her anger.

"Where is it?"

I glanced over at the sleeping man behind him. "You don't need to know that."

Trust wasn't any easier for me than for Paulo.

By the third day in the dry riverbed, I was getting anxious. We needed to be on our way back to Avonar while we still had food and water. The vision of the city's fall festered in my heart the way Gerick's wounds inflamed his flesh, and I would not rest until I saw the city again, walls intact.

Our patient continued to sleep like the dead. Neither dressing his injuries nor pouring water down his throat prompted him to open his eyes. I couldn't blame him for that. He wasn't going to wake a happy man. Assuming he ever woke. Paulo refused to talk about that possibility.

If we couldn't rouse him soon, though, he was going to starve. Taking him away from the oculus had surely broken the heavy enchantments intended to keep him living without nourishment, but the only thing I could get down him was tiny portions of bread, soaked in our gritty water until they became almost liquid. Thus I was delighted when Nim and Rab arrived near midday with three large bundles of brush to burn, a stone crock of reasonably fresh goat's milk, and the slightly ripe haunch of an oryx.

Relieved to see that Paulo and I were still intact after spending two days with a demon, the ragged scavengers decided to stay for a while. They squatted in the shade, picking their teeth with long splinters, and watched me set the oryx haunch to boiling in a large pot I borrowed from their metal cache. They must have pulled the splinters from the charred beams of Zhev'Na, for their activity gave them slightly dusky smiles as I thanked them again for their hospitality. The old man, Rab, never said a word, but he pulled up a few of the spiky gray plants growing near his bare feet and gave them to me, gesturing at the boiling pot. The root smelled a bit like moldy onions . . . very like Rab, I realized. I smiled at the toothless man, peeled the sandy outer layers from the plants, and slipped the things surreptitiously into my pocket.

While the oryx meat slowly disintegrated into a strong-smelling broth, I soaked a bit of bread in the milk and spooned it down Gerick's throat. Perhaps the milk and the meat broth would give him strength to travel if we could ever get his eyes open.

Evening brought encouraging signs. Gerick's skin had cooled, and Paulo had drained his suppurating wound without sending the fever shooting skyward again. Once he had the foot bound up in our last clean bandages, Paulo sat for a moment, his head drooping, his hands dangling in his lap. He hadn't slept since I'd gone for the oculus. "Might you . . . I hate to ask it . . . but could you see to his hands? I'm swiped."

"Of course I will. And I'll wake you if there's any change."

I was proud that I resisted any sarcasm in my agreement. But then, he likely wouldn't have noticed. He was asleep before I finished speaking.

The red-gold light faded, and the wind picked up, skirling sand through the rock gorges. Nim and Rab had slept the hot afternoon away, and scurried off as soon as the sun set. I sat by my little thornbush fire steeping a few eutonia leaves, hoping the tart, bracing tea would keep me awake and perhaps reduce the swelling in my shoulder. All the digging and rock-moving to bury the oculus had set my own healing back several days.

"Thank you."

I jumped, almost upsetting my little pot, when the soft voice came from the shadows.

"Heaven's lights," I said quietly. "You scared me out of a year's growth. How are you feeling?"

"Empty. Stiff. Damp. Alive."

With no small trepidation, I cast a faint handlight and peered across the rock floor to the pallet of sand and blankets where our patient had managed to raise himself on his elbows. His skin color was definitely improved— no longer graveyard white—and to my intense relief, his eye color had reverted to a deep brown, and only in the part of his eyes where there should be color. The ugly mark on his forehead where I had taken out the smallest of the barbed spikes was only a greenish bruise with a ragged black line through it.

"Well, you look a thousand times better, and if we can get a little more food down you, maybe we can fill you up again. You lost a lot of blood, and who knows how long it's been since you've eaten anything substantial."

Neither food nor water would cure the worst of his emptiness. But no one was going to be able to do anything about that part of it.

He eased himself the rest of the way to sitting, stretched out his neck and shoulders, and then shifted around and slumped against the rock wall as if the small movements had exhausted him. "How long has it been?"

"Four days since we brought you out."

"Since the day I was . . . taken."

"Almost four weeks."

"Earth and sky . . ." He closed his eyes, and for a few moments I thought he'd fallen asleep. But after a time he opened them again, and peered at the motionless body sprawled on the ground on the other side of me. "Is Paulo all right? He's not—"

"Just worn out." I stretched my hand toward Paulo, hesitating. "I ought to rouse him. I promised to if you woke."

"No! Don't. I don't think I'll be awake long."

"Well, then. You must drink, and you ought to eat something if you can."

I lurched to my feet with only a small grunt of discomfort and grabbed a waterskin.

"You shouldn't—"

"You have to drink," I said, stuffing the pouch in his hands. "Sorry the water's a bit gritty."

He drank long and gratefully.

"So what do you think? Can you stay awake long enough to get some broth down? It's already made. It would only take a short while to warm it."

"You don't have—"

"Vasrin's hand, I *know* I don't have to do it! But if I were to come up with something, could you eat it?" Were there two more exasperating men in the universe than these?

"That would be very kind."

Stiff. Formal. But on the whole, things could be far more awkward, considering our several encounters of the months just past. I had whacked him on the head, come a hair's breadth from killing him, and pried relentlessly into his private affairs. He had avoided me like a disease for half the summer, and then he had done . . . whatever it was he did when I was stranded on D'Sanya's roof, an incident that still sat in my stomach like undigested meat.

As I busied myself heating up the broth we had stored in a clay jar, I wished I'd gone ahead and waked Paulo. He could occupy his friend so the man would stop looking at me. What did you talk about with someone you'd just rescued from an eternity of horror?

"Why?" Gerick's quiet question was such a perfect echo of my thoughts that at first I didn't even realize the source. But a glance his way confirmed the depth of his interest in my answer.

Fundamentally, I was still without an adequate answer—certainly without any explanation I was going to voice to *him*. So I handed him the mug of broth and said the first likely thing that came to mind. "Your mother is very persuasive."

His face, so determined in its sobriety, broke into a soft smile at that, eyes brightening with amusement and affection. "I've noticed that myself," he said. The smile fell away quickly, and he dropped his gaze to his cup.

He said nothing more, and drank perhaps half the broth before his eyelids drooped and I had to rescue the cup to keep it from spilling onto his blankets. As well as I could manage with one hand, I eased him down onto his back again, and then resumed my tea-making, as tired and relieved as if I'd just survived a battle.

Only later, as I cleaned and dressed the wounds on his hands, did the thought occur that those very hands had sealed my slave collar.

Disgusted, nauseated, I tied up the bandage, then went out into the ancient riverbed and used every paltry bit of power I could summon to shatter a brittle shelf of rock high on the cliff. The sharp bits rained on my back—an unfortunate miscalculation.

". . . all bloody hell, thinking she's played me for a fool and done for you after all. I can't figure the woman. Not a bit. Gutsy, I'll say, though. Smart. It's a good thing for you I didn't leave her in the desert any of the fifty different times I thought of it."

"Don't ask me to explain her. I resign from all investigations for any matter whatsoever."

The quiet voices drifted over my head along with the odors of burning thornbush and scorched barley. Though my mouth was full of grit, my eyes stung with the acrid smoke, and my shoulder throbbed unmercifully, I wasn't about to give away the fact that I was awake. There was always a possibility of hearing something interesting when people thought you were asleep—an annoying childhood habit I had perfected while in captivity. And too, these two were friends and deserved some time together without an interloper or the immediate business of the day to disturb them. I shifted ever so slightly so that both of my ears were exposed.

"And she really got you over a horse, up the Vale to the hospice, and tied to a tree without you getting loose? Damn, she's such a scrap of a thing."

"I don't think I'm cut out to deal with women. Especially ones who don't think well of me."

"Ouch! Damnable, useless . . ." Tin pots and spoons clanked untidily. "I don't know how she keeps this stuff from burning. Here, take the part that's not black. Tomorrow *you* can cook."

"It's fine. Don't worry. I could eat a raw kibbazi."

Thoughts of breakfast set my own stomach rumbling, and I considered sitting up.

"So . . . the other one . . . how did the Lady find out about you?"

The morning's easy humor fled as quickly as the morning chill. I held still.

"Stars of night, Paulo, I'd decided to tell her who I was. I thought . . . well, after what I had learned that night when I looked into the past, I convinced myself she was innocent. I wanted to believe it. Things had changed . . . were changing . . . between us, and I couldn't lie to her any more. So I went to her house and knocked on the door of her lectorium, and she opened it with an oculus in her hand. I swear, if there were a god of dunces, I would be his most exemplary servant."

He paused for so long, I thought he had said all he

was going to. But I felt more than heard him inhale and breathe out again slowly, as a warrior does when trying to ease the pain of a battle wound. "She tried to pass it off as something new. Something innocent . . ."

He told Paulo of his brief struggle with the Lady, and the long, dreadful hours that followed, ending with him bolted to a slab of shellstone, forbidden to sleep. And he told of the ordeal of the past weeks as he had feared he was going mad and of his horror that he might become what others named him. What I had named him.

If I hadn't already learned how close these two were, that morning would have taught me. Constrained by philosophy and custom that forbade us to measure our fellows by which of the Hundred Talents they bore or the strength of power they could bring to their gifts, we Dar-'Nethi spoke very little of sorcery. And we certainly did not dwell on our personal lacks or our feelings about them, unless we were talking with someone closer than kin. Gerick did not detail the torments D'Sanya had inflicted on him in her hospice workshop, but he was astonishingly frank about his humiliation at being so speedily and so roundly overcome, and about his terror as he lay helpless to avert his own disintegration.

". . . The worst point was when I felt the power growing," he said, "this huge, overwhelming, monstrous disease inside me . . . and I knew it was the same vile thing I'd grown when Notole and I worked with the oculus in Zhev'Na. But this time, instead of feeling horrid, the power felt . . . right. Even when I was twelve, I loathed their power at the same time I craved it. But now I lay there knowing I was going mad and knowing the consequences if I did, yet feeling as if I was whole for the first time in my life. If I hadn't discovered that I could expend some of it by manipulating my visions, I would have used it to get free . . . focused it through the oculus . . . used the damnable device . . . and that would have been the end of me. Earth and sky, Paulo, I was so close—"

"But you didn't."

"Not yet. But I'm still not safe. . . ."

He paused, and I tugged the corner of the blanket slightly to uncover one eye.

He had stretched his bandaged hands out in front of him. They were trembling, and he glared at them as if they were diseased. "I feel like a siege cannon with the fuse burning."

He was afraid of sorcery. I could not have been more surprised if someone had snatched me out of my own skin and set me down in an entirely new Jen. It had never occurred to me that a Lord of Zhev'Na could be afraid of anything, much less his own past or his own power. To look at him, ragged and filthy, unexceptional in size, picking up his spoon and gratefully devouring our daily slop of porridge as if it were sweet cream, having just heard him say he'd come a finger's breadth from retaking his place as a Lord . . .

I deliberately shifted weight onto my shoulder just so the sharp little warning would ensure I was awake.

Jen'Larie yna Sefaro, incapable ex-slave, involved in matters of such universal consequence . . . The thought came near choking me. Vasrin Shaper must find great humor in implausibility and incongruity. Yet, somehow, listening to Gerick's admission of his own fears and incapacities led me to analyze his experiences with more clarity than I'd been able to thus far.

He was probably right about the oculus having a particular hold on him. The Lords had deliberately molded him to be susceptible to its lure. I had been an unwilling witness to that. But about sorcery and power . . . he didn't have the least idea what he was talking about. Truth lay right in front of him, as bald as the rock, truth that must set our course over the next hours. He couldn't see it. And it seemed I was the only person available to do something about that. I just wasn't sure how to broach the subject.

Feeling a bit resentful, I threw off my blanket, sat up, and sniffed the dry air. "Is it truly impossible for a man to cook a meal without charring it beyond recognition?"

CHAPTER 27

Seri

"Someone's here to see you, my lady," said Aimee, knocking on the door of my bedchamber and poking her head inside. "She says her name is V'Rendal, an Archivist."

"One moment," I said, tugging on the leather strap that bound my small case.

Twenty-four wretched days had passed since Paulo and Jen had set out for Zhev'Na, three more than I had sworn to wait. Aimee had arranged for a cousin to drive me northward by carriage, believing it the best way for me to travel discreetly now that the roads in and out of Avonar were so heavily guarded. Unfortunately this night was the first the carriage had been available. Every vehicle and animal that could be spared was being used to transport men, women, and supplies for the Dar'Nethi army being assembled on the northern borders. An enormous force of Zhid had been sighted in the northern Wastes, marching toward the Vales and Avonar. But nothing more was going to delay my going to Karon. Nothing.

T'Laven reported that Karon seemed confused and disoriented, one moment asking where Gerick was, the next incapable of communicating his own name, and the next overcome with grief and guilt, recalling the Lady's report that Gerick had been executed for treachery. The Healer had chosen not to tell Karon of our belief that

Gerick lived or of Paulo's mission. He was concerned that Karon might inadvertently reveal our secrets to others at the hospice. If we were to have the smallest chance of saving Gerick, we could not let D'Sanya know what we were doing. But imagining Karon grieving alone for Gerick tore my heart.

"Supper is laid, as well, and Qis'Dar will be here with the carriage within the hour."

"Thank you, Aimee. Any word from T'Laven?"

"He says he will meet you at the Nightingale, the new guesthouse just outside the north gate. I'm to dispatch a message stone when you leave here. And do take your cloak, my lady; the weather seems to be taking an ill turn." Even as she spoke, the night sky outside my window flashed with lightning, and thunder rolled over the mountains in a constant grumble.

"I'll follow you down." The whole universe had taken an ill turn as far as I could see.

The young woman vanished back into the dark passage. With her servants called up to war, Aimee was having to mind the magical house lamps herself and was rarely home to do it. Her house had become a patchwork of darkness and lamplight.

I snatched up my cloak, the small case, and a soft bag that held my journal and some coins that Aimee had supplied. With no hand free to carry a lamp, I navigated the unlit passage and stair by the flashes of lightning that brightened the windows.

An imposing figure wearing a sweeping green satin cloak and a glittering silver comb in her red hair waited at the bottom of the stair, next to one of the house's garden alcoves. "Good evening, madam," she said. "I had no idea you were preparing to depart."

I dropped my bags and cloak beside the door and reached for the Archivist's hand. But she extended both hands, palms up, and bowed stiffly, and I cursed myself for my distraction. I was in Avonar. Dar'Nethi, who could probe bodies and souls with their magic, did not touch each other without invitation.

Turning my own palms up, I returned her bow. "It's a pleasure to see you again, Mistress V'Rendal. What can I do for you? I've a little time before I need to go."

"I have always admired Gar'Dena's exotica," she said, twisting her neck and peering into the thick little jungle of ferns and blooming pink orchids. "I seem to remember some fine bird specimens here."

"Mistress Aimee has sent the birds to an Aviaran, as she has no one to care for them right now. Please, come sit down." I gestured toward the small sitting room door, trying to restrain my impatience.

"Yes . . . everything is disrupted with the Zhid attacks. And now these new dangers in the east and south— Astolle Vale preparing for a siege by a force of thousands, and Seraph under warning. I've heard the palace is in complete confusion tonight. The Preceptors have officially summoned Prince Ven'Dar back to Avonar to answer questions."

She straightened up and examined me as if I were one of her rare books. "I need not stay so long as to sit down. I am on my way to a musical evening at another house along this road; even in perilous times, we must feed our souls. But when I passed this house, I thought of you."

"Yes?" Dismayed by her news, I was only half listening. Astolle Vale was far to the east, so the attackers could not be the same force seen in the north two days previous. There could be two Zhid armies . . . or even three, if the southern rumors were true. And Ven'Dar recalled. Only in the gravest circumstance could the Preceptors assert their authority over the Prince of Avonar. What was happening?

"On that day we spoke of certain history books that survived the destruction of the Royal Archive," V'Rendal continued. "I told you they were rare and—"

"I remember. But I don't think . . ." The woman's heavy brows knit and her mouth turned downward when I interrupted her. "Pardon me, V'Rendal." I clamped my mouth shut.

"Madam, I have ever been willing to believe the best

of those who inhabit the mundane world, but you might find that a modicum of patience and good manners will cause your investigations to bear more fruit."

"Of, course. It's just— Please go on." I hated wasting time. History books were of no moment now. I could not have been more sure of D'Sanya's treachery if I had seen the oculus or the avantir for myself. I needed to be with Karon.

"As I was saying . . . the Archivist Fel'Tiega, an annoying, boneheaded man, sent me a letter this morning asking if I knew about some woman who had come to Avonar claiming to be D'Arnath's daughter." She rolled her eyes. "The indiscriminate clown has ever been an embarrassment to our profession. But, having come up with this astonishing news a mere three-quarters of a year after the event, Fel'Tiega informed me that he possesses a copy of Mu'Tenni's *Ancients,* one of the few surviving histories written in D'Arnath's time. Did I think the Heir or the Preceptors might be interested in the volume?"

She flipped the edges of her cloak over her shoulders so the dribbling moisture would not wet her shoes.

"I responded that they would be quite interested," she went on, "and I sent along the information to Prince Ven'Dar and Preceptor L'Neysine, along with an offer to review the material myself. Though I am quite confounded with all the work I have to do, I would certainly not trust *Fel'Tiega* to analyze the work properly. He accumulates a great deal, but *analyzes* nothing. But I've not heard back from the palace and have no mandate to lay aside my own work. Thus, as I come to my friend's house this evening, my thoughts turn to you. You seem to have the ear of Prince Ven'Dar. You seem an intelligent woman. If you were to read the history, you could perhaps digest the information and pass it on to those who would be interested."

"I don't know, V'Rendal. I've urgent business away from Avonar."

"What could be more urgent than the truth of history? Mu'Tenni has been proved an extremely reliable histori-

cal writer. He was actually a Speaker who preferred to
dabble in the historical record rather than adjudicate
current disputes. This means that his historical practice
might be weak—not collecting all viewpoints or tracing
all relevant threads of his information—but the truth of
his observations would be impeccable."

"So, where would I find this Fel'Tiega and his book?"
I had no intention of being diverted, but perhaps Aimee
could pick it up or I could send my own message to . . .
someone. Suddenly awash in hopelessness, I almost re-
tracted my question.

"A bookshop near Bridge Lane, so I understand. I'm
sure anyone in the area could show you. The man is
infamous for his oddity." She brushed a water droplet
off her gown and drew her cloak around her again. "I'd
like to know whatever you discover. Perhaps we shall
find that our sex has played a larger role in great events
than has been acknowledged."

"Thank you for coming, V'Rendal. Of course, I'll let
you know if I learn anything important."

Another exchange of bows, and the Archivist swept
out of the house and into a large carriage, even as a
smaller closed carriage came to a halt in front of the
stoop. Raindrops pattered vigorously on the paving.

Aimee gave me a quick embrace, a traveler's blessing,
and a magically warm packet of our uneaten supper before stowing me in the plain cushioned seat of the small
cab. Under the pudgy and purportedly expert hand of
her sixteen-year-old cousin Qis'Dar, the large-wheeled
carriage rolled out of the circular courtyard and into the
streets of Avonar.

Pink lightning flickered constantly over the lower city.
Thunder rattled the carriage lamps. And the rain hammering on the roof sent my spirits plummeting even further. Before we had reached the end of the street, I had
inadvertently crushed the food packet flat, and it was
leaking on my hand. I threw it out the window.

Aimee's house stood on a hillside in the center of
Avonar, just below the citadel of D'Arnath's Heirs. To
reach the northern gates, we had to travel down to the

center of the city to cross the Sillvain River and its eastern arm, called the Minor Sillvain or just the Minor. Sheets of rain lashed the city, so that by the time we reached the city center, the paved streets looked like newborn tributaries of the Sillvain.

Though the evening was foul, people were everywhere. They crowded the doorways of every guesthouse and gathering place, shouting news and rumors, or huddled over Avonar's printed news-sheets that stayed marvelously dry no matter the weather. But the bustle was not pleasant. Many of those abroad were armed with bows and spears, hurrying in the direction of the palace. Parties of horsemen, helmets and swords dangling from their saddles, raced past our carriage. Many house windows were dark, as well, and the carts of street vendors were shuttered, rain drumming dully on the flimsy canvas roofs. In one alleyway, two men wrestled under a cascading gutter. Violence was an unusual sight in Avonar, the most peaceful city I'd ever known. Fitting on this awful night.

I pulled my own cloak tight against the damp, shrank into the corner of the seat, and closed my eyes. Tonight I would see Karon. Hold him. Tell him how dearly I treasured our time together, how his touch had revealed the innermost workings of joy, how sharing his life had changed me in profound ways. That his son was not dead.

The carriage bucked along the brick streets. Yet what if Paulo and Jen had not found Gerick? What if they found him too late? What if D'Sanya had decided to question Karon more thoroughly or to turn her vengeance on Gerick's father? Why had I not taken this journey weeks ago?

Shouts rang out from the road ahead of us, interrupting the downward spiral of my thoughts. The carriage slowed, and I pulled up my hood and peered out of the window into the driving rain. The yellow light of torches and the white of enchantments illuminated a scene of chaos.

A drenched mob blocked the roadway, fifty or more

men and women waving swords and clubs and enchantments as they surged toward the two graceful stone
towers that guarded the Sillvain Bridge. The river itself
was dark and swollen; on this night no charming reflections of the white lights that decorated the city's towers,
bridges, and trees danced in the roiling water.

Two men jogged past us toward the crowd. Qis'Dar
shouted at them, but the ensuing exchange was garbled
by thunder, shouts, and cheers and jeers from the mob.
The carriage shook abruptly, and a round face haloed
with sodden yellow curls appeared at the window. "Man
says the bridge tower guards are Zhid!" said Qis'Dar,
eyes flicking anxiously over his shoulder. Raindrops cas-
caded down his high forehead and smooth cheeks. "He
heard they were causing the Minor to flood. These folk
have gathered to pull the guards out. Kill them, he says,
though I can't believe such a thing would be done without the prince's leave."

Indeed some in the crowd were raising tall ladders to
lean on the slender bridge towers. Men swarmed upward, clinging to the rungs, even as the people at the
bottom positioned the ladders at the towers' narrow window openings. More people ran out of the lanes and
alleyways to join the crush.

"Hold, there!" I hailed a woman as she passed just
behind Qis'Dar. Her hair straggled out of a wet scarf,
and she carried an unsheathed blade in a manner that
indicated she knew how to use it.

"Best get home," she said breathlessly, without waiting for me to speak. Her eyes glittered in the light of
our carriage lamps. "Zhid in the city!"

"Are the city walls broached?" I said.

The swordswoman didn't listen to my question. "It's
the Lords come back!" she shouted as she trotted onward. "Don't trust anyone!"

Water sloshed into my boots as I burst the carriage
door open, jumped to the street, and grabbed the next
passerby, a scrawny boy of fifteen or so. "What news
have you heard?"

"D'Natheil's devil son is alive! The Fourth Lord walks

in Avonar." He wrestled out of my grip and ran to join the shouting mob.

Arrows flew from the bridge towers and burst into flame. Many fell harmless, hissing as they struck the river or the flowing water in the street. A few found marks in the crowd. A woman screamed as her skirt flamed high, and shouting people swarmed around her until the garish light was gone and her screams fell silent.

I queried three more passing Dar'Nethi, and each had a story much the same. The Lords were back. *Three witnesses vouch that a man killed near the north gate was Zhid. . . . The Lady D'Sanya has published a description of the Fourth Lord and announced that he is roaming the streets stealing souls. Every citizen should be armed and alert.*

Hearing rumors of Gerick—even ugly ones—fueled a fleeting hope. Had Jen been wrong about D'Sanya's captive? Perhaps he had managed to free himself.

"We should get away from here," said Qis'Dar, urging me back to the carriage, as one of the men on the ladder plummeted screaming into the mob. The ladders were clogged with men wielding swords that gleamed blue in the night. Lightning flashed and streaked overhead, thunder crashing almost in exact time with it. "We should go back to my cousin's . . . something . . ."

Shoes soaked and hair dripping, I ducked back into the carriage and pulled the door closed.

"Is there no other way across the river?" The thought of returning to Aimee's was intolerable.

The young man's thick fingers gripped the window edge. "Second Bridge is a bit south, out of our way. The streets between are low. With so much rain and so many of the city administrators called up to fight, high water's a worry. . . ."

"Please try it. If the way gets bad, we'll turn around. I must get to Gaelie tonight."

"All right, then." The youth vanished, and the carriage frame jerked as he climbed onto the driver's seat.

Soon our wheels splashed through the narrow lanes of the riverside district. Rubbish floated on the water

that reached to the front stoops of many shops. Half of
the white lamps mounted on the corners to light the
dark lanes were out, the deluge overwhelming even their
enchanted fire. Many shops and houses sat closed and
dark. Two men, hunched under dripping cloaks, hurried
past us and hammered loudly on a green door.

"Is Second Bridge open?" Qis'Dar shouted after
them.

"We've just crossed it," yelled one of the men. The
green door opened and the two bustled inside.

A few harried householders were loading crates and
furniture onto wagons, ready to move to higher ground.
One wagon blocked the entire roadway, and shouted
inquiries revealed that the overloaded vehicle had a bent
axle. As the lane was too narrow to turn our carriage
around, Qis'Dar volunteered to repair the axle. Mean-
while, the woman and her three daughters tied canvas
coverings over her bags, boxes, and chairs, a task that
needed experienced hands and dryness spells.

I sat staring out the carriage window, feeling useless.
We were near the river. Perhaps . . .

"Is Bridge Lane anywhere close?" I shouted to one
of the girls.

"Not far," she called back, pointing down the lane.
"Two streets south and take a left on Bywater and you'll
come to it."

"And Fel'Tiega the Archivist's book shop . . . do you
know it?"

"Aye. It'd be the fourth or fifth shop on the left, I
think. Isn't the weather dreary enough for you, ma'am,
that you must seek out that oddment? Gives me the
jibbers to be around him."

"Better than this carriage, I think, as I've no skill to
help you here. Would Fel'Tiega be there this time of
night, do you think?"

She rolled her eyes. "He's *always* there."

Welcoming a productive alternative to waiting in the
soggy carriage, I told Qis'Dar where I was going. The
girl's instructions were approximately correct. The sev-
enth house on the right side of Bywater Street sported

a peeling signboard: FEL'TIEGA, ARCHIVIST, BOOKSELLER. Painted on the red door were the words STEP IN. I lifted the heavy brass latch and stepped in.

I felt as if I had stepped out of Gondai and into a wholly different world, for I could no longer hear the rain or thunder, only the soft rustle of turning pages or the scratch of pens. Every wall of the little shop was lined with bookshelves crammed with books. Bound in leather, cloth, paper, wood, even copper and pierced tin, they filled every crack and crevice, books stacked flat on top of standing volumes, stuffed between the wooden shelves. More bookshelves divided the rooms into tiny enclaves where only a single chair, stool, or small writing desk could fit among the shelves and still allow a person to pass through into the next room.

Almost every chair and stool was occupied. Most of those who occupied the nooks and crannies read by the white light radiating from their hands; the rest had to rely on a few weak, sputtering lamps. As I squeezed past a woman working intently at a small desk, the whimsy possessed me that the sheer weight of words interposed between these rooms and the outside world had prevented the city's anxieties from penetrating this astonishingly quiet place. No wonder this Fel'Tiega had taken eight months to learn of D'Sanya!

"Excuse me, are you Master Fel'Tiega?" I asked the first male reader I encountered.

"Room number eleven." The young man pointed deeper into the warren, never looking up.

A quick examination revealed a little brass plate beside the far door, engraved with the word FIVE. As the current room was the fourth since the front door, I hurried through six more rooms, past the brass plate that said ELEVEN, and into a brightly lit circle of book stacks. All I could see of the man who sat in the stuffy eleventh room was a tidy knot of black hair atop a large head.

"Master Fel'Tiega?" I said, peering around a shoulder-high bookshelf.

"Find it yourself. Every work has a locator spell attached."

V'Rendal's vague references to the man had conjured an image of an ancient, birdlike fellow, wizened and dusty. Fel'Tiega demolished that image. His deep voice resonated like the thunder I could no longer hear, and from what I could see of him above the desk where he was poring over a thick sheaf of papers, he was neither wizened nor ancient nor all that dusty. I judged him no more than thirty. His beard was thick and curling, and dark hair made a thick mat on his well-muscled shoulders, arms, and chest—all of these parts devoid of clothing. When I moved around the bookshelf, I was relieved to see that he at least wore breeches, stockings, and shoes.

"I've been sent here by V'Rendal the Archivist," I said, wondering if all V'Rendal's acquaintances were odd. "She sent me to fetch a rare book you recommended to her."

"V'Rendal? Oh, yes, the Mu'Tenni history. I thought she might be interested in that, what with this astounding news about D'Arnath's child. The time period is the interest of course. V'Rendal thinks it's going to tell us that some *woman* built the Bridge instead of D'Arnath or that everything would have turned out differently if more of the Heirs had been women. She's always going on about women, women, women, as if the world couldn't get along without them." He glanced up at me, then looked back at his papers, only to look up again immediately, his great wiry brows making a single line across his face. "Do I know you?"

"I don't think so. My name is S'Rie. I've not visited your shop before." I extended my palms and nodded to him. "I like to think both sexes have their importance." I resisted adding any remarks about his own existence bearing witness to the value of women.

"Ah, the world can get along without anyone, even you, I'll wager. As we're such a wretched lot, the place'd be better off without most of us. You're wet."

I swallowed a sarcastic reply. I had no time for this. "I'll be careful to keep the book dry, if that's your concern. I'm in somewhat of a hurry to be off, if you please."

He waved his meaty hand around the room. "Have you read all these?"

"Sadly, no. I've been—"

"Then you oughtn't be in such a hurry. You never know when Vasrin will declare your own path ended. I've set myself a goal to read every volume in the shop before the year is out."

He rose from his chair, a bear of a man, wearing a green sash about his ample waist. His thick black top-knot looked as if it might brush the ceiling, and the tips of his beard were tied with green ribbons that dangled over his bare chest. Silly-looking man.

But when he turned his back to rummage among the volumes on the cluttered shelf behind his table, bile rose in my throat. His neck, hidden in the front by his beard, bore the red telltale of a slave collar. His back was deeply ridged with purple and red scars, not the common marks of a slavemaster's lashing, but wide gouges that had been meticulously carved through flesh and muscle in an exact crossing pattern.

I swallowed hard and considered how to respond to an outlandish young man who had survived such calculated brutality. "Which year?" I said at last.

He dropped a heavy leather volume on the table, glanced up at me, and grinned slyly. "One year or the other. If I live longer, I'll give some thought to what I've read and, perhaps, soothe my professional detractors such as the broad-beamed demon-Archivist who sent you here."

"Have you read Mu'Tenni's book?" I asked, deciding that such deliberate goading as this man practiced was perhaps something other than bad temper. "An Archivist should be aware of all views. Perhaps this book could open your mind to things of importance that other Historians prefer to ignore, such as the value of both genders or the worth of people in general."

"Perhaps it could." He bent down, drew a wad of

thick fabric from under his table, and tossed it on top of the book. "Keep it dry. And make sure Mistress V'Rendal returns it. It's not a gift."

"And if Prince Ven'Dar asks to keep it?"

His grin fell away like a dropped hat. "I am ever at my lord prince's service."

I wrapped the book in the thick-woven fabric and bowed. "Good night then, Master Fel'Tiega."

He bowed, and before I had squeezed through his book stacks to the door marked TEN, his dark head was bent over his reading once again.

CHAPTER 28

Qis'Dar had told me to wait at the bookshop and he would bring the carriage around as soon as the blockage was cleared. And so when I peered out the door of Fel'-Tiega's shop and saw naught but night and rain, I pulled up a chair where I could keep an eye on the street through a small round window. No point in fidgeting. I unwrapped the book.

The elaborate lettering of the title, *Ancients*, was worked in gold inlay that was almost entirely worn away. I traced the patterned leather with my fingers, marveling at the finely detailed tooling and at a work so old that proclaimed its subject matter far older yet. In Leire our oldest artifacts were fortresses and weapons, nothing of such exquisite fragility.

The Dar'Nethi Archivists had done their job well. The edges of the fine vellum pages were quite smooth, the pages themselves only slightly yellowed with a few brown stains here and there. Though the book's text was unornamented and unillustrated, the sweeping script was bold, elegant, and quite readable.

Leiran scribes had crammed the pages of our oldest books with tiny characters to conserve precious paper, but the Dar'Nethi copyist had bowed to no such restriction. Or perhaps the subject matter had justified the expenditure. The brief opening text indicated that rather than a historical narrative, this work was a compendium of short biographies of important personages in Dar'-Nethi history, each cross-referenced to pages on other subjects who were related by blood or particular events.

The entries had been organized by the twelve kingdoms of Gondai, though the author allowed that these designations would likely lose their meaning, as only the kingdom of Avonar had survived the Catastrophe. A fierce and sad determination infused the author's declaration that future generations of Dar'Nethi must not forget those who had made their world and its people marvelous.

I thumbed through the pages quickly, unwilling to expend the concentration necessary to parse more of the archaic language until I came to the entry headed *D'Arnath yn D'Samos, Avonar Regiré, Gondai Audde Regiré*—D'Arnath, son of D'Samos, King of Avonar, High King of Gondai. Even then I did not read the pages devoted to the most famous son of Avonar, but turned immediately to the end of the passage, where the cross-references were noted.

Excitement quickened my breath as my finger touched the list of names. Just below *Maroth yna L'Tonil, Avonar Resiné*, D'Arnath's wife, was *J'Ettanne yn D'Savatile*, D'Arnath's cousin and Karon's ancestor, who had led the Dar'Nethi Exiles into the mundane world. And then came *D'Leon yn D'Arnath, Giré D'Arnath, Avonar Regyn*. D'Arnath's eldest son, the first to bear the title Heir of D'Arnath and Prince of Avonar rather than King, was followed by his younger brother *D'Alleyn yn D'Arnath, Giré D'Arnath, Avonar Regyn*. And then, glaring from the page as if waiting for me all these years, was the name I was looking for: *D'Sanya yna Zhulli*. Odd.

Dar'Nethi women were given a patronymic just as men were, their family connections designated by their fathers' names, not by their fathers' estates as we did in Leire. So D'Arnath's daughter should have been listed as *D'Sanya yna D'Arnath*. *Zhulli* wasn't even a name; it meant . . .

"Excuse me, please," I said to a refined-looking woman who sat in an adjoining nook of the bookshop leafing through a large folio of drawings. "What does it mean when *zhulli* is used in a name, such as T'San yna Zhulli?"

The woman glanced up briefly from her book. "Means exactly what it says—daughter of no one. Means the girl has been disowned. Have you lived all your life in a cellar?"

Fires of heaven!

Dar'Nethi kinship was more elastic than family relationships based solely on blood. Gerick had been acknowledged as the successor of D'Arnath's Heir and would have inherited all powers reserved for that Heir, because he was the son of the man whose soul occupied D'Natheil's body, even though he was not born of Prince D'Natheil's own flesh. Ven'Dar was now the Heir of D'Arnath because Karon had acknowledged him as his spiritual successor in a ceremony that paralleled Dar'Nethi adoption. Family kinship was a matter of spirit as well as blood and flesh, and Dar'Nethi inheritance involved much more than titles or land or blue eyes. Inheritance was talent for sorcery. Inheritance was capacity for using power. In some families, inheritance meant property or land or wealth. In the royal family of the Dar'Nethi, inheritance was the Bridge.

I leafed rapidly through the book to the page indicated and found the passage relating to D'Sanya. It was brief, detailing the date and place of her birth, the participants in her coming-of-age celebration at twelve, a list of her childhood accomplishments—riding, drawing, singing—and the popular perception of her: *a child blessed with bright virtue and a sweet cheer who brought joy to all.* She had been tutored alongside her brothers, but in the author's view had not been merely equal with them: *For after the Catastrophe made grim the days, the King's favor rested upon his youngest heir above all others in his realm for the solace she brought him and the hope for the future.*

In a few short paragraphs Mu'Tenni sketched out the story of her rebellion and abduction, much as Gerick had reported it. But here the author revealed the rest of the story—a dreadful miscalculation on the part of the High King of Gondai.

> *. . . The very structure of the Bridge was to be forged of D'Arnath's power and blood so that he and his three heirs would be the supports on which it rested, bound to each other by oath and enchantment, their fates forever linked, their power shared and grown and passed on to their children, a mighty shield for Gondai and its mirror world beyond the Breach of chaos. When the time came for this link to be forged, his sons had come into their own power, and they had learned to wield their father's enchantments as would be their right and duty when the King was dead, one following the other in orderly succession. The girl child, though, had not yet come into her own gift, yet the King would not leave her out of his design. To proceed before she was ready was a risk, yet he believed her joyous spirit would give birth to talent beyond his own and was confident that her good heart would grow into the mature power essential to his plan. But he hid the girl away, depriving his own heart of her sweet company, to keep her safe until her power should arise, lest the design of the Bridge be compromised.*
>
> *On the day the Lords lured his daughter from her hiding place, D'Arnath's great gamble was lost. He could strike no bargain to free her, for her price was the safety of two worlds. And after two failed attempts, his weakened kingdom could afford no more lives to steal her back. Yet the King dared not allow the Lords' captive to inherit his power and the fate of the Bridge. Indeed her talent had come mightily as he had foreseen, and she had become a sword in the Lords' hands, striking at the very soul of the Dar'Nethi. Came the day when D'Arnath saw the vile neck binding the Lords used to enslave his people and reive their souls, and knew that his own child had devised it, he wept bitter tears for that child of his heart and struck her name from his life and descent forever.*
>
> *All this have I learned from Prince D'Alleyn on his deathbed, revealed when I asked him of the girl child lost in the great war. He called on an aged serving woman to*

reveal the girl's name, refusing himself to speak it. Thus even in death the child remains outside the embrace of family. May holy Vasrin maintain the Heir and his successors forevermore.

Only the girl child had not died. She had remained a sword in the Lords' hands . . . just as they had intended.

I bundled the ancient book in its wrapping and dashed out of the bookshop into the rain, heading back the way I'd come. Ven'Dar and the Preceptors had to know that D'Sanya was not the legitimate Heir of D'Arnath. If need be, I would unhitch one of the carriage horses and ride to the palace to deliver this news. Fortunately, Qis'Dar and the carriage materialized out of the rainy night before I was halfway to the corner.

"We must return to the palace," I said to the lad. "To the western gate, I think. I'll explain later. We've no time to waste."

"Whatever you want, ma'am." The sodden youth gave me a hand up into the cab and climbed back to his seat.

We took a different route back through the city, avoiding the mob at the Sillvain Bridge. Though the weather had not relented, and the hour was late, even more people were abroad.

The western gate was smaller and more private than the grand southern entry to D'Arnath's palace. Friends, family, and close associates of the prince and the Preceptors would enter here, people well known to the guards. Yet even as the carriage rolled to a halt, I wasn't sure how I was to gain admittance. I had no assurance Ven'Dar had returned to answer the Preceptors' summons, and too many questions at the gate would cause more delay. Aimee had too little influence to get me inside, and to explain my presence to the Preceptors or any other influential person would take far too long and betray Ven'Dar's confidence besides. Only one person I knew would have the influence and willingness to get my information in front of Ven'Dar quickly and would know who could be trusted if Ven'Dar was not here.

"Tell the gate guard that Commander Je'Reint's

mother is here on a critical matter and will see no one but him," I told Qis'Dar when he popped his head in the window to get my instructions.

I knew Je'Reint was in the palace tonight because Aimee had been expecting to work late with him, mapping out supply routes for the coming battle in the north. As I watched Qis'Dar being shuttled from one guardsman to the next, I clutched the book and prayed that Je'Reint would forgive my impertinence at impersonating his twenty-years-dead mother. That lifetime ago when he had stayed with us at Windham, he had joked that I was very like her.

"They've sent a messenger inside, ma'am, so we just have to wait," said Qis'Dar, propping an elbow on the carriage window. "The guard is tight here tonight, I'll say. Thought they might strip me naked just so I could give a message. It helps that I'm sizable. I had to bluster a bit." He examined me quizzically, his round face reminding me in that moment of his uncle, Aimee's ebullient father Gar'Dena. "You're not really . . ."

Though avowing that her young cousin was trustworthy and discreet, Aimee had not told him anything of our secrets. I managed a smile. "No, I'm not Je'Reint's mother. And anyone who sees me in the flesh won't believe it for an instant. But I've discovered something that Prince Ven'Dar must know right away, something I can't trust to just anyone, and I think Je'Reint will help me deliver the news. Once I've done that, we'll be back on our way to Gaelie."

The rain slacked off from downpour to drizzle as we waited. I invited Qis'Dar to sit inside the carriage with me, but he said he couldn't get any wetter staying out, and he'd as soon not have to dry out the carriage so much before he returned it to its owner. He waited beside the carriage door.

Without light enough to read further in the book that sat so heavily on my lap . . . and on my mind . . . I watched the armed Dar'Nethi stream into the sprawling courtyards. They mustered in small bands here and there, and once a group reached a certain size—twenty or twenty-five—they marched into a brightly lit, cordoned-off area in front of the main gates. Fifty, a hundred, two hundred fighters. Where were they all going? The palace gates never opened. But, of course, we were in Avonar, a city of sorcerers. Someone in that brightly lit area must have opened a portal and be transporting the fighters out of Avonar. Into the northern Wastes? East to Lyrrathe and Astolle? I shivered. Waited. And still the warriors came.

"I think we've got our answer," said Qis'Dar, softly, through the window.

I returned my attention to the west gate. A small party of men, clad in the white-and-silver tabards of the palace guard, marched purposefully toward the carriage. All were armed. Je'Reint was not among them.

"Qis'Dar, perhaps you'd better . . ." But before I could send the youth away, the leader of the party shouted at him to hold his position.

"Your name, boy," snapped the soldier as soon as he arrived.

"My name is Qis'Dar yn Gar'Feil," said my young friend, his head held high, "and I do yield that name willing to a servant of the Heir. I'll say, though, as a citizen of Avonar, having it demanded so rudely in sight of D'Arnath's house tempts me to refuse."

The soldier, a grim, spare man wearing the silver chain of a guard captain, was not chastened by Qis'Dar's dignified protest. The captain nodded to one of his companions, who yanked open the carriage door. "You, madam, will please step out."

I had little choice. The cab had no secondary exit, and I couldn't see anything to prevent these men from coming in after me. Cursing my naïve assumption that Je'-Reint would either hear me out or send me discreetly on my way, I took the soldier's proffered hand and climbed out.

"Your name, madam?"

I considered giving the Dar'Nethi name I had been

using, but I believed this man already knew who we were. "My name is Seriana Marguerite, widow to your late Prince D'Natheil."

As I had surmised, the guard captain was not at all surprised. He nodded, but neither extended his palms nor bowed. An ominous sign. "Lady Seriana Marguerite, by order of Commander Je'Reint on behalf of Her Grace, the Princess of Avonar, you are under arrest for conspiracy against the kingdom of Avonar and its sovereign Heir. You will follow me."

While I grappled with the implications of his warrant—*Her Grace, the Princess of Avonar*—his men quickly positioned themselves on either side and behind me.

The captain was not yet finished. "Qis'Dar yn Gar'-Feil, you are dismissed, remanded into the custody of your parents. Get yourself home immediately, and do not stray. Be warned that if you are seen again in the company of these certain conspirators, you will be liable for criminal charges. If you are found in company with the Fourth Lord of Zhev'Na, you will be executed."

"But I've done nothing wrong!" protested the youth. "Only driven this lady—" He turned to me, eyes wide in his pale complexion. "Prince D'Natheil's lady . . ."

"You've been coerced into matters far above your head, boy. Give us the lady's belongings, then take your rig and get yourself home."

One of the guardsmen nudged Qis'Dar away from me and toward the carriage. The youth unloaded my case and the small bag holding my journal and passed them to the guard. "My lady, I'm sorry. I didn't know. Did you have anything else in here?" He stuck his head inside the cab.

"It's all right, Qis'Dar. You've done nothing wrong. I'll have this straightened out soon enough. Oh, and the book on the carriage seat is one I borrowed from your cousin to read on the journey. Please see it's returned right away before it's damaged by the damp."

"Of course, my lady," he said. He stood alone and

forlorn beside the carriage as the soldiers grabbed my two bags and marched me toward the gate.

I'd not considered being arrested as a way to get inside the palace, but as the iron gate clanged shut behind me and I hurried my steps to keep up with the guards, I decided it was as good as any. At some time I would be taken before someone in authority and could tell what I knew. If D'Sanya was present, she would have to explain in front of other people what it meant that her father had declared he had no daughter, and how it could be right that she had taken what her own father would forbid her.

We emerged from the wide tunnels under the gate towers into a broad, bustling courtyard. Torches blazed on every side, hissing and smoking in the continuing drizzle. A small party of armed horsemen clustered at the far end of the court, while aides and armorers splashed through puddles, carrying newly polished weapons and breastplates. Grooms led more horses from another gate and other men and women loaded panniers and packs. A hundred or more soldiers formed up in ranks, water cascading from helms and shields. Across the courtyard was a columned doorway into the palace proper, but instead of leading me there, the guard captain halted beside a carriage with horses hitched and motioned me to climb up.

"Wait!" I said, dismayed as the guardsmen surrounded me and forced me into the carriage. One of the soldiers tossed my luggage in beside me and slammed the door. "Where are you sending me?"

"To the Princess D'Sanya's hospice," said the captain. "The princess has graciously forbidden retribution on those who have conspired against her. As she herself was so thoroughly duped by this inheritor of Zhev'Na, she refuses to condemn others who were taken in by his wiles, especially those of his blood who are understandably blind to his evils. She cannot, of course, allow you to roam freely, lest you persist in your support of Avonar's enemies. But Commander Je'Reint has vouched

for your character and suggested the hospice as your
place of confinement. He says that your sworn word that
you will not leave the hospice grounds will be sufficient
bond to keep you there. Do you so swear or must we
constrain your movements in some òther fashion?"

They were sending me to Karon. But I couldn't go . . .
not until they knew about D'Sanya. "Captain, I must
speak to Commander Je'Reint or Prince Ven'Dar before
I go, or to one of the Preceptors. Please, I have information of vital importance to Avonar."

"Commander Je'Reint is on his way to the battlefront.
No one else is available." The captain stepped aside and
spoke quietly to the man who had climbed up to the
driver's bench. The other soldiers had withdrawn.

I scanned the busy courtyard for some familiar face,
someone I could entrust with what I knew, but everyone
had hoods drawn up against the rain . . . except a small
group silhouetted against the now-open entry to the palace at the top of the steps. A tall, graceful man with skin
the color of mahogany genuflected before a statuesque
woman. The woman's hands were extended palms up,
offering her service and support to her subject. And in
acceptance of her trust and her commission, Je'Reint
laid his hands atop hers, a pledge of fealty the Dar'Nethi
considered as binding as the presentation of a sword
in Leire.

Je'Reint rose, bowed, and sped down the steps to a
horse held by a waiting groom. He bounded into the
saddle, wheeled his mount, and shouted an unintelligible
command, then led the horsemen and the ranks of soldiers through the gates.

"What of Prince Ven'Dar, Captain?" My voice sounded
weak. Defeated. Somehow the small ritual I had just
witnessed riveted my heart with fear . . . for Gerick, for
Avonar, for the Bridge. For all of us.

The soldier stepped back into view. "The Word
Winder Ven'Dar is no longer Prince of Avonar. The
succession has been restored. And he—"

"Prince or not, I must speak with him."

"That will not be possible. When the Preceptors

learned that Ven'Dar yn Cyran permitted a man condemned by the law of Avonar—a Lord of Zhev'Na—to
walk free in Gondai, they declared him in violation of
his oath." It was not difficult to interpret the guard captain's sympathies. "Neither they nor our princess can
ignore blatant treason on the part of the Heir of D'Arnath. The former prince has been placed under arrest.
Pending judgment, the traitor is permitted speech with
no one. And now, madam"—he slapped his hand twice
on the side of the carriage—"you will go."

"Captain, the Lady is not what she claims. She cannot
be allowed—"

But he wasn't listening to my panicked babbling. The
hair on my arms rose as the captain swept both hands
in a circle encompassing my conveyance. I rattled the
latch, but the carriage door refused to open. The receding view of the wet and deserted courtyard grew hazy.
I sagged back onto the padded seat, my mind reeling.
The carriage rolled slowly toward the western gate.

CHAPTER 29

Gerick

As the sun rose higher, turning our little shelter into a baking oven, Paulo watered the horses and set about examining their hooves, picking out rocks and checking for cracks and bruises. He was worried about the lack of water and good forage leaving the beasts too weak for the journey ahead of us.

I leaned back against the already warm rock and tried to convince myself to get up and help him. We had to get back to Avonar as soon as possible, but I couldn't even keep my eyelids up.

"I need to look at your foot." Sefaro's daughter dropped onto the sand at my feet and began untying the strip of linen that bound my left foot.

Paulo had told me how the woman had come to be involved in my rescue, and I didn't know what to think about it or how to behave. It felt damnably awkward to have one of my victims cooking for me and tending my injuries.

"Just leave that," I said, as she unwrapped the damp, discolored bandage. She had to tug and peel it away from the crusted blood and fluid. Though the surrounding skin was sounder and not so dark as the previous day, the wound started seeping again and hurt like the devil, which probably made my comments sharper than I intended. "Paulo will tend it later. I don't want you—"

"What do I have to do to convince you two that I'm

not going to put poison in your tea?" Her face flamed, and she threw the wadded bandage in my lap.

Why was she so annoyed by my attempts to be civilized? I just didn't know how to apologize for something so trivial when the greater matters between us were beyond apology. Bereft of ideas, I held my tongue. Her flush deepened.

Paulo handled the situation much better than I. As he gentled Stormcloud and lifted the horse's right front foot onto his knees, he asked the woman how she had slept and inquired after her injured shoulder, saying that he knew it had hurt something awful, but now it was put back right, it should heal up pretty fast. Evidently the two of them had reached an accommodation in my rescue. I just wasn't a party to it. When he asked her to explain again what she'd done to make my septic wound improve so rapidly—some Dar'Nethi spell-working, evidently—I shut my ears. I didn't want to hear about Dar'Nethi magic.

I wasn't ready to wrestle the wild rimcats that prowled the Edge in the Bounded, but with a little more rest and food, I'd be able to travel well enough. Then I would decide what to do about D'Sanya and her cursed devices.

As I drowsed through the rest of that day, Sefaro's daughter scrupulously avoided touching my food, water, or bandages. Every once in a while my eyes would drift open to find her staring into nothing, her brow drawn up tight, as if she were trying to decipher something complicated. But after only a moment, her eyes would flick toward me as if she felt me looking at her. When she met my gaze, she tightened her mouth and looked away, busying herself with cleaning her boots or making another futile attempt to strain the muddy water through a scrap of canvas.

The sun angles were well stretched when I awoke with urgent proof that my body was functioning in a most human manner again. As I pulled on the spare boots Paulo had cleverly thought to bring along, the woman announced that Paulo was off scouting for something to shoot with his bow. She stuck out her chin and folded her arms quite deliberately as I hobbled off into the rocks on my own.

I sagged onto my blanket when I got back, distressingly tired after the short trip, and so hungry I thought my belly might cave in. I pressed my face into the sandy wool and thought longingly of the boiled tappa root my friend Zanore cooked back in the Bounded. Though boiled tappa was the most boring and tasteless food in any world, a vat of it would be a feast right now.

"The rest of the milk Nim brought is in the green flask." Water dribbled into a pot, and the strong smell of slightly rancid meat broth wafted over my head. "You should drink it before it spoils. I haven't breathed on it since yesterday."

"Thank you," I said. Then I wondered if she would believe I was thanking her for not breathing on the milk. Avoiding a glance at her that might reveal such a mistake, I lifted my head and spotted the painted flask that sat in the smallest mudhole. "I think I could drink the mud."

"You'll need your strength. We should leave as soon as you can travel. It's at least four days back to the next spring. These sinkholes aren't refilling as fast as they were, and we can't leave Nim and Rab with nothing."

"I'm ready to go whenever you say," I said. "Most everything is functioning now, my appetite certainly. I'll crawl if I have to." I drained the last of the milk. Even warm and slightly off, it filled some of the hollow places. I laid my head on the blanket again, happy to have gotten through this exchange without an argument. For such a slight person, the woman certainly filled up a place.

Paulo rode in a short time later, his game bag empty. As soon as he had gotten a drink and rubbed down Stormcloud, we shared out the last of the increasingly gamy oryx broth, softening a few bits of rock-hard bread in it. We spoke inanities. The future was like a fourth person at our fire that night, and none of us wanted to acknowledge her.

Paulo was too practical to let us get away with that for long, though. After scooping up the last of the stringy overcooked meat from the pot and dividing it among us, he tapped his spoon idly on the edge of his cup. "While I was out hunting, I kept thinking about all you told me this morning. So is it true . . . ? I mean . . . I guess the Lady's running the Zhid after all."

Sefaro's daughter flinched and glanced at me, rolling her eyes at Paulo as if he were mad to say such a thing outright. But I had always appreciated Paulo's frankness and tried to honor it with the same in return.

"No, I don't believe so," I said. "Not intentionally at least. She created the other things: the oculus, the slave collars, the masks, so I have to assume she made the avantirs as well. But as to who's using them now . . . I don't think it's her. And not just because I was . . . infatuated."

Did I still love D'Sanya? Certainly my body still desired the woman who had nestled close to me as the rain fell on the shepherds' hut. But that woman did not exist any more, if she ever had. The woman who had laughed at my pain and terror as she ripped my flesh with metal claws, then healed up the lacerations so she could do it all again, who wept and scolded as she condemned me to an eternity of madness bolted to a rock, was someone else entirely.

"But she's the only one with power enough," said Paulo. "You've said no Zhid could run the avantir."

"Somehow she's feeding them the power they need. That's what I think. The timing of their rising . . . everything points to it." I concentrated on the puzzle. On cold reason. "The avantir is a receptacle: it enables the propagation of enchantment, but it needs an immense infusion of power to make it work. But if D'Sanya isn't manipulating the avantir directly, then one of her devices must be channeling her power to it in some way—the oculus at the hospice or the second one she used to hold me in Zhev'Na or some other device I haven't seen yet. In that case some powerful Zhid—one of the gensei most likely—could use the avantir himself."

"So destroy the vile things," said Paulo. "Then we'll see what's what."

"Someone else will have to do that." I dropped my cup and spoon into the blackened pot and wrapped my arms around my knees so I wouldn't feel as if I were going to fly apart at any moment. "Ven'Dar . . . Je'Reint . . . the Preceptors . . . someone who can touch a cursed oculus without losing his mind or worse. And they'll need to persuade D'Sanya to see what she's doing, but it can't be me. I told you what she did to me and how easily—"

"Her jewelry!"

Paulo and I jumped at this outburst and stared at the woman.

"What's that?" said Paulo.

She looked from me to Paulo and back again, her chin poised in that particularly stubborn set that I was coming to know. "Have you ever seen the Lady without her jewelry? I've only seen it once in all these months—on the day you were attacked in Avonar. The first thing the Zhid did on that day, before she could possibly recover from the surprise, was take every piece of her gold and silver. They weren't thieves. Why would they bother if they were taking her with them anyway? Did you notice? Didn't you wonder why she worked not one spell to defend herself or you? And what do you think was the first thing she did when the prince's men rescued her—even before she went to see to you? She pulled rings and bracelets from a saddle pack and put them on."

I remembered the bag of jewelry Je'Reint's man had shown me, and of course it was true she wore such things all the time . . . adored them . . . wouldn't allow me to buy them for her. And of course I, too, had wondered why she hadn't put up more of a fight that night.

"She's a Metalwright whose mentor taught her to link her devices together." The woman leaned closer to the fire, the firelight licking at her small face and fierce eyes. "Perhaps all her adornments focus power as an oculus does, working together like the avantir and the Zhid earrings to create some more intricate enchantment, something larger than a single device. Perhaps her power is not so strong as she claims if she must always enhance it with her metal toys. I think she puffs herself up too much. She's lied to you all along. Destroy her devices and you'll have her."

Anger rippled through me. "You're wrong. She is not doing these things on purpose. And I've already said I can't—"

"I know what you said." She attacked instead of retreating. "And you think you know everything about evil and corruption and doom, not to mention being the world's first and only man who ever fell in love to see his heart betrayed and to discover that his holy beloved wasn't so holy. So you're feeling sorry for yourself and sorry for the world, and I'm very glad to hear that you care about all of us, but you can't just retreat into whatever strange little hole you've found to hide in for the last five years. For once you just need to listen to someone who knows a few things that you don't."

"I don't know what you're talking about."

"That's exactly the truth," she snapped. "And so I intend to teach you a few things about Dar'Nethi power."

"*You* teach *me*? I know enough about power to choke you!"

But like a stinging fly on a hot day, the damnable woman would not stop. "Of course, you're angry. You have every right. And yes, an oculus does terrible things to you. But this power that's grown in you is nothing of the Lords'. Don't you see? I heard you describe what you did when you lay on that stone table, how you followed your father's teaching—your father, proven the most powerful Dar'Nethi sorcerer since D'Arnath himself. For what did he do when he died on a pyre before you were born? He reached across the universe and opened the Gates to the Bridge that had been closed for centuries! You have to understand . . . what you did in that tomb . . . what you described to Paulo this morning . . . was exactly what *my* father taught me was the greatest mystery of our world—how we Dar'Nethi transform life in all its aspects, its wonders, its horrors, into power.

"Here—" She thrust the last clump of thornbush into my hand. "Put this in the fire and slow its burning so it will last the night. A simple spell for a Lord of Zhev'Na, isn't it? It takes hardly a thought to strip the essence of life from a bird or a tree or a slave, infuse that power and your will into a bundle of dead brush, and make a fire burn as you please, whether it consumes anything or not. Well it's a simple spell for a Dar'Nethi, too, but one that takes thought if you've not been trained to it. A spell that transforms matter into light and warmth at a rate that you decide. So, step one: Consider the dry thing, the life it once held, the place where it grew, the cycle of its life and death and seed and germination."

The thorny wad pricked at my hand, but not as the woman's words pricked at my spirit. What did she know about anything?

"Step two: Consider the need." She wouldn't stop. "Tonight will be cold in the desert. Your body needs warmth to recover its strength and warm food to heal and nourish it. And your friend Paulo and this ugly stubborn woman you can't quite trust need to sleep warm so they can care for you and lead you out of this cursed desert. But brush will burn too fast if you leave it to flame at its will."

I had seen thornbushes burning in Zhev'Na. From dry lightning. From intent. They burned hot and fast, snapping and spitting gold sparks.

"Step three: In your mind, use your need to transform the essence of the thornbush, and then take one tiny portion of that monstrous power you fear and let it flow into your creation. Do it, and then feel what you have done and tell me whether it is good or evil."

As she counted off her steps, I found myself obeying her commands, resisting the old habits I had developed in Zhev'Na in favor of this new way of thinking. And when I tossed the dry bundle onto the fire and carefully let power flow into the spell I had made, I did not create a holocaust, only a small hot fire that would burn bright through a long night. I felt whole, and the world did not end.

"Didn't I tell you?" She leaned back on her rock and nodded. Without smirking. But her chin was ready to challenge my least hesitation.

"The water," I said. "I could make it more palatable . . . get the grit out of it . . ." Was it possible?

"Settle the sand to the bottom, perhaps," she said, tossing me a muddy flask. She looked at me sidewise, out from under half-lowered eyelids. "A little more difficult than a slow-burning fire."

Consider the water. . . .

I went through the steps again. Felt an anxious hitch in my breath as I released a dribble of power. But the working felt right. I opened the flask, drank, and passed it to Sefaro's daughter.

She took a sip, cocked her head to one side, considering, and passed the flask to Paulo. "What do you think? How did he do?"

Paulo, who had been crouched between the woman and me as if ready to leap into the breach when flaming arrows started flying between us, took a sip, stared at the flask, and then proceeded to drain it. "Cripes! I've not tasted anything cold in a year . . . I'm sure of it. And no sand in my teeth!"

"Well, we can't afford to do that any more," said the woman, snatching the flask back again and tossing it onto the sand beside the sinkhole. "He doesn't have time to learn how to pump more water from the earth into Nim's puddles. And he has more important matters to deal with."

My astonishing feeling of well-being fled in the face of the future. We needed to get back to Avonar. "So, mentor, how are you at making portals?"

She looked up sharply. Her small face hardened like cooling lava, leaving her features rigid and pointed and angry. Paulo was sitting behind her, and he immediately shook his head vigorously, giving me a bleak wince that was some odd mixture of embarrassment and sympathy.

"Portal-making is not exactly in my list of skills." She could have frosted the desert. "If it were, I wouldn't have been fool enough to spend four weeks riding through the Wastes to find you, now would I?"

"No, no. I can see that. I wasn't implying— I just—" What had I done to offend her now? As ever, it was impossible to come up with the right thing to say, especially with Paulo making unintelligible faces in the background. "I understand true talent doesn't imply the ability to make portals, but I thought you might know what was needed. I've likely power enough to do it. You've shown me that. But just . . . I don't know how." The Lords never traveled physically, and so had no need for portals.

The woman tilted her head and wrinkled one side of her face. "So you just want me to *tell* you how to make a portal?"

"As you did with the other things. I could take us back to Avonar tonight. We could find some help."

"What about this oculus? If it is possibly empowering the Zhid, you can't just leave it. You likely have power enough to destroy it, if you'll just try."

I tried to hold patience. "I told you. I can't go near an oculus. I daren't touch it. It doesn't matter what I want or what I intend. All the power in the world isn't going to enable me to destroy it."

Flushed and silent, she sat by her rock, digging her boot heel into the sand so ferociously one might have thought her worst enemy buried there. She was thinking about something she didn't like at all, and I didn't want to blurt out anything else until I had a clue about what was making her angry this time.

"So this soul weaving," she said at last, "that's what you did to get me off the Lady's roof?"

Was that what this was all about? Gods, she must have been disgusted when she realized what I'd done. "I'm sorry. It's just . . . D'Sanya was so angry. So dangerous. There was no time to explain or to ask you. If she'd seen you . . ."

"I'm not asking for an apology. I want to know how

it works. If you can make me scramble across a roof and race off to find your mother"—her glance was as pointed as her chin, and I felt my own skin heat up—"can you make me work sorcery as well?"

"Yes. But I—"

"And do things I might not be . . . capable . . . of otherwise?"

"He had me writing words one time." Paulo spoke up. "There's no bigger magic than that. He can take or give what's needed . . . allow you to do what *you* need, as well. He won't trespass where you don't say, neither. He could, but he won't. I think it could work."

Paulo had clearly heard something I hadn't. I puzzled for a moment, watching the woman biting her lip and grinding her heel. I thought her hand might crush her cup.

Then she stuck out her jaw and kicked a last rock out of the hole. "There's daylight enough left. We can be to the place I buried it within the hour. You can stay well out of the way while Paulo helps me dig it up. Then you can do whatever it is you do, and we'll destroy it—with my hands, not yours. I wish I could do it without your help, but I can't."

Earth and sky! "You want me to join with you . . . come into you . . . and destroy the oculus?"

"There's no other way. We've no assurance Prince Ven'Dar will be in Avonar or that he even has the power to destroy one of D'Sanya's devices. You do. You have no idea . . ." She shook her head and mumbled to herself. "And now you have my body to do it with. Let's just get it over with and don't let me think about it too much."

Paulo was already up and saddling horses. I sat speechless, my mind running through five chains of reasoning at once, none of them concluding she was wrong.

"Some day you're going to understand how lucky you were to have me along," she said, scrambling to her feet and running her fingers through her shaggy hair vigorously. "Every Dar'Nethi child is taught complex skills such as how to make portals and how to destroy objects of power. Not one in five thousand can actually do such things, so not one in five hundred remembers more than half the steps. But I—" She dropped her cup into the pack that sat at her feet. "I never forget anything."

CHAPTER 30

Jen

Paulo did the digging. He said he didn't have much to contribute to the night's activity but common labor.

Gerick had remained with the horses two hundred paces up the hill. His spirit had closed up like a slamming gate as soon as we crossed the top of the ridge and started down the track to the burial place, and I made him stop right there. I didn't want any "imaginary" Zhid poking spears into Paulo and me while we did this thing.

A slight chink interrupted the steady crunch of the shovel.

"Ouch! Demonfire!" Paulo threw down the shovel and clenched his hands to his chest. "Shovel hit metal, not rock. Cripes . . ." He bent over, his fists flying to his head and grinding into his temples.

"Time to change the guard, then," I said, jumping up from the flat rock, grabbing his elbow, and dragging him back up the trail toward Gerick and the horses. "Any damage that won't heal?"

After a moment he walked a little straighter, but clamped his fists under his arms grimacing. "I saw a man struck down by lightning once. I'm not smoking, at least. Listen—" He halted at a bend in the track where we could see the desert stretching out behind us, the ugly scars of the Lords' reign a blight on the land. "What you're doing . . . are you sure?"

"Not sure at all. But I've some sense. We'll start

slowly and see if it's possible before he— I just don't see any other way. I'll tell you this: He has power enough."

He nodded and started walking again.

Indeed, I couldn't believe Gerick doubted himself. Even in the small workings he'd used to brighten our fire and clear our water . . . I'd never sensed such power, even from my father in the days before Zhev'Na. I issued a fervent prayer that the Lady Seriana was right about her son's heart.

Gerick was perched on a rock, his arms and legs drawn into a knot, when we walked into the little grotto where the horses were tethered. His head popped up. "So you found it."

"Just where I left it," I said, taking far too much time and effort to take a drink and loop my water flask's cord back on my belt so it wouldn't fall off. I didn't want to look at him, to think about him. "Let's get this done. Do I have to touch you or anything? Stand anywhere in particular? Well, I suppose not." I emitted something halfway between a laugh and a bleat. "The last time we did this, you were dangling in a corner, and I was flailing on a window ledge."

He unwound his arms and slid off the boulder onto his feet. His eyes were so dark in the failing evening.

I had to see . . . I stretched my hand out so my weak handlight would reach his face. "There . . . I'll stand over there," I said, offering a pitiful explanation for my waggling finger.

Ridiculous. His eyes were their natural color. And concerned. I walked over to a boulder near him and propped my backside on it, facing away so I couldn't see him anymore. "Get on with it."

"How can you do this?" he said quietly from behind me. "How can you bear asking me to come inside you after the things I've done to you? Aren't you afraid? Don't you remember?"

And I answered what I had been repeating to myself for the past two hours. "Memory has no power but what the soul chooses to make of it. I choose this. Now will you please just do it?"

His boots scuffed on the dirt. Paulo murmured something. I tried not to think of anything at all. How was I supposed to let him know where not to *trespass,* as Paulo put it? How was he supposed to know the part I needed him to play? Did I have to say it out loud? *Yes, I can tick off steps and form complex enchantments, but a rabbit could bring them to life sooner than my stunted soul will, so you'll have to supply all the real magic.*

Looking upward, to where the first sharp-edged stars poked through the deep blue, I inhaled deeply, relishing the clean, dry air and the oncoming night. No longer did an everlasting pall of smoke and dust haze hang over Ce Uroth. That happy circumstance soothed me a little. I smiled and imagined green stars in a stormy purple sky. Gods, I wanted to snatch Papa from the hospice and go home. Strange . . . "Will you just get *on* with it?" I said to those behind me.

"Jen." Paulo's soft call drew me to look around. He was crouched beside Gerick, who was sprawled on the ground, eyes closed, body limp as a dead man.

"He's already . . . ?" I suddenly felt hot all over, my face pulsing. *Green stars* . . . I should have known.

"He said he'd try to stay back as much as he could until you need him. He knows he was clumsy when he helped you before. Are you all right?"

I stared at my hands. Breathed. Peeked into my own thoughts. And they *were* my own thoughts . . . but, of course, he could likely hear them if he chose. I resisted the urge to ask him, for fear I would hear that quiet voice bouncing around in my skull or coming out of my own mouth. *Good Vasrin show me the Way. . . .* "I suppose I'm all right."

"You holler if you need me. I'm going to stay here to watch out for him. You know what needs doing."

I moved slowly down the path, assuming for some reason that I had to tiptoe. If I stumbled, jostled, or thought too hard about what I was doing, something in the world was surely going to break or explode or crash down on my head. Or perhaps inside it.

I focused on the job at hand. Indeed I knew exactly

what was required to destroy an object of power. As with so many things I could never use, the steps sat right there in my mind, dusty and neglected: *consider need, assert ownership, disrupt containment, trigger the destruction . . .* The triggering, yes, that was where I'd need help.

The implements lay where I'd left them on the flat rock I'd used to cover the hole: the shovel, the broken sword, Paulo's hand ax. I quickly added a few items from my pocket: the sweat-crusted scarf I had tied on my head in the desert crossing, the tight-wound measuring cord I used in my work, my mother's coming-of-age ring that I always carried, my knife, and its sheath that my father had tooled for me.

The oppressive enchantment of the oculus was already deadening my limbs, making it an effort to lift the broken sword. But I carried the sword to the hole and poked about in the dirt at the bottom, probing to find the ring. A muffled clink, another stab, and I snagged it, scooping it out of the loose dirt. As I raised the broken tip, the brass oculus slid down toward the hilt and clanged into the guard.

Trying not to look at the thing, I carried it back to the flat stone and let it slide off again to lie simple, round, and perfect in its evil, gleaming in my pale handlight. My simple invocations of protection felt quite pale as well. I could try to invoke power for strengthening them, testing this joint working, but my mind was already growing sluggish. *So begin. You can do this.*

Step One: Consider the object to be destroyed . . . the need . . . the use or misuse that justifies destruction. That was easy. While visions of ravening Zhid, of Gerick without eyes, and of my father's confusion of mind created a solid hateful shape in my head, I proceeded to the next step, arranging my possessions around the brass device—the knife, the sheath, the little gold finger ring, the scarf. I unwound the measuring cord and wrapped it carefully around them all, making sure it touched each of my four possessions. And then I passed my fingers around the cord, releasing just enough power to assert my ownership of this boundary and everything within it. Unless D'Sanya showed up to break my circle and thus dispute my claim, the oculus was now mine.

The brass circle pulsed and glared as if it knew what I was doing. Its physical shape did not change. My mind knew that. Yet it seemed to grow larger, occupying fully half of the world I could see. *Concentrate, Jen.* I forced my eyes to see the rock and the other things on it, to feel the night air and hear the distant howl of a wolf.

Next step. I considered the casting of the artifact . . . the mold fashioned with care and skill . . . the molten metal running into the mold, skinning over as it cooled . . . the careful burnishing and whispered enchantments that had made it. I thought of all I knew of its designers and its maker . . . envisioning them in all their horror, beauty, and betrayal, a necessary step to encompass the existence of the object. "I'm sorry," I whispered as I concentrated on the Lady. But I dared not slide over the requirements, even the ones that might be painful for either of us to dwell on.

My spirit clamored warnings, and my hand trembled as I picked up the hand ax we'd borrowed from Mistress Aimee's stable, its sharp steel blade properly venerated and cared for by Paulo on our trek across the desert. I raised the tool, and my shoulder howled in protest. Foolish . . . I couldn't possibly muster the physical strength to do this. The oculus had surely been cast with spells to make it impervious to casual damage. Perhaps I should call for Paulo. Confused, dispirited, I lowered the tool.

No! I shook off the leaden sensation. *Focus on the steps. Disrupt containment. What you feel is only enchantment—the object trying to preserve itself. Strike!*

I raised the hand ax high, strength surging into my limbs like a river pushing into the sea. The blow landed square on the oculus and hard enough to mar the perfection of its gleaming surface with a small dent. I had never struck such a blow. So hard. So accurate. Blood rushed to my skin again. I was not alone. . . .

Unsettled, I threw down the hand ax as if it were the

evil instrument. Mistress Aimee's blade would need some tender care; shards of rock had flown everywhere when it struck.

The unity of physical form and enchantment that made up the oculus, the containment of the spells within the physical object, should have been disrupted by the blow. Only a small breach was needed, a flaw in its construction that I could exploit to break it. And so I proceeded through the mental exercises of desire and transformation, shaping them with the simple sorcery nature had left to me.

Once those were completed, assuming I'd done all correctly, only one step remained. The most difficult. The least certain. Hold the desire in the mind, incorporating every sense, and feed it power enough to accomplish the breaking spell. Closing my eyes, I felt the solidity of the enchantment I had constructed, envisioned its accomplishment, hearing, tasting, smelling, feeling the shattering I desired. And then I reached deep into that most intimate place of a Dar'Nethi's soul, and in that reservoir where my Way had left only dust and rubble, I found magic.

My eyes flew open, and every object in my sight—sky, stars, rocks, desert—became more comprehensible, more real, its color richer, its texture, shape, and solidity, even its flaws, delights to the eye and the mind. The bluster of the wind and the screech of a hunting raptor sang with tones and harmonies that extended far beyond those of ordinary hearing, and with such clarity that I could understand the slightest nuances of wild nature bound up in them. For one instant I was admitted to the heart of the universe, its intricacies and truth laid bare for my soul to devour.

Always I had read of the exhilaration of Dar'Nethi enchantment, and how the intensity of the experience grew in proportion to the power of the enchanter. Now I knew that all I'd read was true. Gerick's power left me breathless, speechless.

But before I could even encompass the wonder, the oculus pulsed and shot off beams of light, blinding me, choking me, devouring the bright moment and spewing out horror that overwhelmed every sense—tortured screams, billowing darkness, the reeking smoke of burning corpses. The brass ring gleamed through the murk.

I fed power into the enchantment I had built, more and more, until I feared that even this ocean of magic inside me must be drained dry. And always the circle of brass stayed whole. I knew only one way to divert more power into my enchantment—make the link with its object more direct. Furious at a creation that could convert such beauty into horror, terrified that we would fail, I could not consider the danger. And so I stretched out my hand and touched the oculus itself.

First my hand, and then my arm, shoulder, and neck felt as if I had submerged them in burning oil. But I held on, binding my enchantment ever more closely to the physical object, even as dread and cold darkness crept through my inner vision. I cried out shamelessly, determined that neither pain nor this insidious despair would force me to release the spell. I would not fail. I would not . . . I would not. . . .

Let go. It's all right. It wasn't so much words that penetrated the pain and darkness, but rather an overwhelming, insistent assurance. The world was unbroken. I was unbroken. My injured shoulder had gone into spasms because my fist was clenched so tightly, causing this pain in back and chest. And of course it was dark, because my face was pressed into the dirt and my eyes were closed. This knowledge flooded into me before I could assess these things for myself. And then the tide went out, leaving me sprawled, aching but content, on the shore of life.

Eventually I moved. I tried for a while to loosen my fist, but nothing in my right arm wanted to obey me. Then I lifted my head and opened my eyes only to find that it was still dark. Night. Quiet, except for pelting, skidding footsteps on the dirt behind me, and the anxious call, "Jen, are you all right?"

Impossible to answer yet, of course. Supporting my

right arm with my left, I scrambled to my knees, trying
to persuade my eyes to focus. No chance of a handlight.
Even the thought made my head ache, like trying to
vomit when you've nothing left inside. But I patted my
left hand on the dark shapes scattered on the surface of
the rock. My knife, the sheath, the now-tangled measuring cord, and a few shards of metal, cool and inert. I
peeled open my recalcitrant fist and found more of the
same.

"Jen?" The voice was closer. Kind. Worried. Paulo.

"I'm all right," I called over my shoulder, as I jingled
the bits of metal in my left hand and threw them gleefully onto the rock. "I think we did it!"

Paulo arrived and crouched on the gravel beside me.
"I heard you cry out. And then nothing."

I looked up at him and grinned. "A little yelling never
hurt anyone."

"It wasn't yelling so much as screaming. I thought you
needed help, though I wasn't sure it was even you!"

"Well, I suppose it wasn't all me." I swallowed hard
and squirmed a bit, trying to gather in my thoughts and
feelings that seemed scattered over the landscape like
my other possessions.

Paulo grinned and jerked his head back up the path.
"He's back there where he belongs. Takes him a bit to
get sorted out. And after something like this . . ."

"I probably need sorting out, as well," I said, feeling
an uncomfortable moment of mingled relief and regret.
But as soon as I remembered the magic, relief, regret,
pain, and despair were all forgotten. I could have run,
leaping and dancing, all the way back to Avonar. I
grinned back at Paulo. "Let's get out of here."

While Paulo picked up the shovel and the broken
sword, I gathered my belongings, fixing my knife sheath
to my belt, winding up my measuring cord, and patting
my hand on the ground in a moment's panic until I
found my mother's ring. The scarf was nowhere in sight,
but it was the least valuable by far and I left it go. I
gathered the shards of the oculus and considered what

to do with them. I needed no power to tell me their bitter enchantment was broken.

"You don't think your friend would want these?" I said. "A memento?"

Paulo nodded toward the hole. "Throw them in there and I'll bury 'em. No one needs a piece of that thing."

He had it done faster than I could take stock of all my limbs and other parts and decide that I was in one piece. We started up the track together. "It was all right then," he said, flicking his eyes to the top of the ridge. "With him?"

"He's done it with you?" I said.

"I was his first. Before he even knew he could do it. Felt like a wildcat had gotten into my skin with me. But he saved my life that day, and the lives of a whole world full of people. We did it again later when he was hiding from his da. At least that time he'd learned to keep quieter, and he wasn't trying to kill anybody."

I flexed the fingers of my right hand. As we walked, sensation was returning. "You're a good witness, Paulo. The way you trust him. I might never have gone through with it otherwise."

"But I was his friend already. Don't know as I would have had the nerve to do it, feeling as you do about him. You ever need a witness that you're the damndest woman this side of the Lady Seri, I'll stand up for you."

I laughed, and we climbed up the hill to find Gerick.

We slept under the rocks again that night. The knowledge that we were only a portal away from real food, real beds, and a bath was a fine torment, but the first sight of Gerick at the top of the track had told me we were going nowhere until we'd had some rest. He'd been sitting with his head on his knees, unable to speak, utterly and completely drained. His breathing was erratic, his limbs and shoulders twitching every once in a while as he inhaled with a great whoop. Making portals would require learning and practice, even if he had power left after what we'd just done. We would have to wait until morning.

Paulo boosted him onto his horse, and we rode back to the riverbed and our shelter. Our little fire was still burning, and I used the rest of our water and all the good herbs we had left to make tea. We drank some ourselves and forced the rest down Gerick until he just shook his head and rolled over on his blankets. He hadn't said a word, and I wasn't about to broach the subject of the oculus or our strange partnership. I supposed he knew that we'd been successful.

That night I dreamed of wildcats tearing their way out of my skin.

My eyes fluttered open to see Nim and Rab squatting quietly in the narrow band of shade and staring at me. The sun angle claimed it was almost midday.

"Spits," said Nim, incomprehensibly, as she laid a handful of hard green fruits about the size of plums on a rock. "Clean the nose and throat."

It took me a moment to realize that *spits* referred to the fruit. "Oh. Thank you," I said.

Gerick lay on his side, still sleeping. It looked as if he hadn't moved the entire night or morning. Paulo lay flat on his back under the deepest part of the overhang, snoring peacefully. He had packed up all our gear the previous night, except for our blankets and a few things I'd set aside.

I divided the last of our cheese into five chunks and offered a portion to the two scavengers. It was so dry and hard that droplets of grease ran off it as the morning warmed. Nim kept gesturing me to take one of the green fruits, though I noted that she ate only her portion of cheese. I picked up one and sniffed it. It just smelled green.

"We're leaving today, and, as we can't carry everything, we thought perhaps you'd want some of our supplies." I pointed to the stack of pots, cups, and spoons. "You've been very kind to us."

While the two of them knelt in the sand, patting and stroking each piece, Nim sighing with pleasure, I bit into the little green fruit. "Vasrin's hand!"

Rab grinned, showing his few brown teeth, and in sheer excitement started banging a spoon in one of the pots.

Gerick shot up to sitting. "What's wrong?"

"Nothing's wrong." My assertion came out as a whimper. My nose was running, my eyes watering, and my lips puckered. Now I knew why they called these things spits. "It's just time for you to wake up. We're going back to Avonar today."

He ruffled his hair tiredly and looked around at Paulo's packing job and Rab carrying our scorched pots off to the cache across the gully. "Earth and sky. You two have a lot of confidence in me. I feel like an empty barrel."

"You must be blind." I swallowed the sour fruit and smiled—or grimaced—at Nim, who had appeared a bit worried at my outburst. As soon as she went back to her admiration of our spare water flasks, I lowered my voice and continued. "At the least, your perception of your own gifts is a bit skewed. As long as you make a habit of what you've learned these past weeks, use the technique to replenish your power, you can do anything you wish. Eat something, consider the universe for a while, and then we'll start your portal-making lessons. And be polite, but don't eat those green things unless you enjoy having your tongue curled."

After a brief trip out of sight, he took a long pull from a water flask, ate his square of cheese, and pocketed two spits with admirable diplomacy, indicating he planned to hoard them for his journey home. Nim and Rab bobbed their heads, but didn't look at him. They had called him "the sleeping demon" and had never addressed a word to him for the entire week. As soon as he turned away, they whispered to me that they urgently needed to go hunting.

While I saw Nim and Rab on their way, promising to

leave everything we didn't need tucked into their cache in the rocks, Gerick rolled Paulo onto his side. The sleeping fellow didn't wake, but he did stop snoring.

I sat with my back to the most comfortable rock in the grotto. "Ready for your lesson?"

Gerick stood with his arms folded, looking at nothing. His face, shadowed with several days' growth of reddish hair, was sober and worried, older somehow, and the cast of his skin—a natural red-gold—was deeper than usual. "Before we begin . . ."

I had the sinking premonition that he was going to apologize for something. "Portals are complicated," I said, pointing to the sand in front of me. "We need to get busy if we're going to get out of here today."

"Not until I've— After last night—" He blew softly, rubbed the back of his neck, and then clasped his hands tightly behind his back. "I'm not good with words. You've seen that. All these months I've tried to think what to say to you, and I've come up with nothing but sentiments you would rightly scorn. But I just— Everything you've done, especially last night— You've made me think differently about Dar'Nethi. I have to tell you that. I know it changes nothing about the past. Not many people would even understand what it means, but I think you do."

"Well . . ." Moments passed as I tried to come up with something to say that did not expose the absolutely disproportionate happiness I felt. I had to be quick. Gerick looked as if a knife were slowly sliding across his throat. ". . . that's good then. I'm glad. Though, as a compliment, it's not quite up to the one I got last night when you were falling out of your saddle. I was told that I was 'the damnedest woman this side of the Lady Seri.' "

He laughed then. Deep. Heartfelt. Resonant with health and good humor and hope as only the laughter of those who know the truth of pain and grief can be. I laughed, too, and for once tried not to analyze or question, but just to enjoy a moment of quiet grace.

CHAPTER 31

After an hour of listening to a lecture on Dar'Nethi enchantments and power-gathering in general, another discussing portal creation in particular, and another of intense questioning about particular aspects of defensive and offensive combat spells about which I could offer little information, Gerick began to work on his portal-making. After two hours of exhausting practice to get each step perfect, four false starts, and a trip into Paulo's mind to borrow an exact image of Mistress Aimee's sitting room and the garden just beyond it, he had created a shimmering doorway that hung in the still air of our desert hiding place. The sun was already down, but the brutal heat of afternoon had not yet yielded its sway.

Without seeming to notice the sweat rolling down his brow or the traces of fresh blood streaking the dirty bandages on his hands, Gerick gazed solemnly on his work. "Do you suppose it goes where we intend? Damned awkward if I've mucked it up."

"You were holding back," I said, fanning my face with a tuft of gray grass. "I've told you fifty times: A Dar'Nethi spell-working will never come together perfectly if you starve it. Portals are immense."

"We used everything I had last night. Now we've this portal to make, another oculus to destroy, and who knows what else. I've only been awake a few hours. I can't possibly think or . . . live . . . enough in a few hours to replenish what we'll need."

"You have to open yourself completely when you draw power. Use everything. Not just experience. Not

just the world around you at the very moment you're
thinking of it. But everything you feel. Everything you
are. Everything you remember. You are not a simple
Grower who's done nothing but plant seeds his whole
life! Your capacity is enormous. The 'fuel' you have to
fill it is enormous. Use them."

"I'll try to do better. But there's only so far I can go."
He had closed himself off again, just when I thought he
was beginning to trust me.

Annoyed, I was more blunt than I intended. "Then
sooner or later you'll fail."

Exchanges like this, with half the conversation unspoken, exhausted me. Sometimes I knew what he was trying to say, and sometimes I was completely at sea. No
wonder D'Sanya had done all the talking.

While he and Paulo peered into the night beyond the
portal, I grumbled to myself that anyone stupid enough
to take a Dar'Nethi without talent as a mentor deserved
no better teaching than he got, and I tried to convince
myself that I was not at all unhappy that Gerick had no
need to use my hands for portal-making. The residual
effects of his power drifted on the hot air like a shower
of cherry blossoms, but nothing would ever compare to
the exhilaration of wielding his enchantments with my
own hand.

Only the faint orange glow of a small fire gleamed in
the darkness beyond the portal. But Paulo swore he
could see through the garden door to the blue couch
where Aimee had once sat drinking tea, and the low
table where she had set the book she could read so
amazingly with her fingers, and the tapestry footstool
where she had set her foot—her most elegantly perfect
foot, his expression reported. Mercifully he restrained
himself from speaking it aloud.

Gerick listened soberly as Paulo finished his earnest
description that had so little to do with accurate memory, then shook his head ever so slightly as his friend
stepped through the portal. I stood right behind Gerick
to watch, and I couldn't help myself stretching up on

tiptoe and whispering in his ear. "He needs to tell her, you know."

Gerick peered over his shoulder, frowning as if I'd reminded him of a step he'd missed. "What's that?"

"How he feels. She can't see it, and he doesn't talk enough for her to hear it. She doesn't know."

The wrinkles in his brow smoothed. "I think he could as easily claim the throne of Avonar."

I considered pointing out that perhaps he could advise his friend, as it seemed he'd found ways to say such things himself. But it would perhaps not be a wise thing—and certainly not a kind thing—to tweak the bruised heart of a powerful sorcerer who had once been a devil.

Before my wayward tongue could get me into trouble, Paulo stepped back into our cave, grinning. "Nobody about, but it's the right place and a fire's lit in the hearth. We'll give the ladies a right surprise when they find horses in the garden and us three filthy travelers sitting there drinking tea!"

"Let's go, then," said Gerick.

He snatched up the loose packs, I took the cloaks we'd set ready, and Paulo grabbed the horses' leads, then we stepped one by one through the tremulous doorway.

Passing through a portal is a sensation something like that of jumping off a cliff, I've always thought. Your stomach seems to take a certain amount of time to catch up with you. And the other place—the place beyond—slams into your mind exactly like the hard earth at the end of such a leap. I don't know that even a Dar'Nethi mind is supposed to make such an abrupt shift from one place to another. It must have been the anticipation of seeing Aimee that had allowed Paulo to come back grinning. Or perhaps the whole experience is more pleasant for mundanes.

The house was indeed dark, and the air was cold for a late summer evening, even in the highlands of Avonar. Heavy mist floated through the soggy garden. They must have had days of rain. Though it would be just past the dinner hour, the house was silent, and no noise at all came from the street or neighboring houses. Odd.

The oppressive quiet muted the three of us, as well. Paulo clucked softly and led the horses through the back gate into the stableyard. I unlatched the garden door that opened into Aimee's small sitting room, and by the time Gerick and I walked through it, Paulo was back at our sides. He couldn't have taken time even to unsaddle his beasts.

The wan fire in the hearth scarcely made a dent in the chill. No one was maintaining the house enchantments. The dining room and the kitchen beyond were deserted, and the grand drawing room with its fountains and chimes, birdcages, plants, and gaudy swathes of colored silk hanging from the ceiling felt like a gathering place for unquiet spirits.

"They must have gone out," I whispered, once we'd poked our heads into every room on the lower floor and found no sign of mistress, guest, or servant. "Lady Seriana is surely at the hospice as she planned. Perhaps Mistress Aimee is busy with Commander Je'Reint." Perfectly sensible explanations.

"A fire's lit and her cloak is laid by it," said Paulo, his anxiety setting my own stomach aflutter. "She never goes without it—not on such a cool night as this. And she promised that someone would be here close until we sent word. One of her serving girls if not her."

Perhaps it was Paulo's worry that kept us whispering and creeping about like thieves.

"We'll search the rest of the house," said Gerick. "I'll go up; Paulo, you to the cellar. And if you'd—"

"I'll look in the back garden," I said.

"If no one's about, we'll leave a message and be on our way."

We tiptoed into the entry hall where a grand stair led upward into darkness . . . no, not total darkness. A pinpoint of light hovered on the third-floor landing, then began moving slowly downward. Gerick's gesture commanding our silence was unnecessary. We crowded into a niche filled with aromatic plants.

Three dark figures moved down the stair, and the single candle flame that led them gleamed unmistakably on a steel blade. I felt, rather than heard, Paulo's long knife come free, and my own dagger found its way into my hand. Gerick carried no weapon, but I would not have called him unarmed. The touch of his lean body, pressing me backward into the shadows, filled me with unreasonable dread. I shifted away from him . . . and bumped my head into a dangling wind chime. The merry tinkling rang through the silent house like a trumpet call.

"Who's there?" called a man's harsh voice.

"Hold, mistress!" commanded another, and the candle was raised high and a brush of enchantment made it flare up. Two well-armed Dar'Nethi, dressed in green and yellow livery, held the arms of a pale, worried Mistress Aimee.

A deep rumbling came from Paulo, but Gerick quickly laid a hand on his shoulder. At the same time I heard . . . or felt . . . Gerick open his mouth to speak. But before he could reveal himself, I slapped my hand over his lips.

"Mistress Aimee, are you all right?" I called. "It's only Jen."

Something strange was going on, and I didn't think Gerick ought to be bumbling about in front of anyone. And Paulo was so intent on rescue, it likely hadn't occurred to him that the men could just as likely be there to protect Aimee as harm her.

"I've just stopped in to . . . tell you that my grandmother is much better, thanks to the Healer you sent and the soup and everything. We've brought her to Avonar to recuperate. But when I came to your door, I saw the light creeping about through the windows, and I was afraid. . . ."

"Jen! So soon! I . . . I've wondered if you and your grandmother escaped your village in time. Ha'Vor, D'Kano, have no fear. This is my dear friend from Tymnath. Everything is quite all right . . . well, as right as it

can be in such a terrible time." After the initial stumble,
Aimee's voice was as pleasant and confidant as always.
"I'll be right down, Jen. I'm so anxious to speak with
you, and find out how you got away."

Her strange comment made me think we were right
to be discreet. What did she mean *escaped*?

The two guards relaxed only slightly, but their candle
flame died down again to a normal size. I shoved my
elbows backward to restrain my two companions, who
had relaxed not at all. But whether it was my direction
or their own judgment, they remained out of sight as I
stepped well away from the niche. Aimee sped lightly
down the stair and embraced me.

The scowling guards examined me thoroughly. Rum-
pled and unwashed after a month of desert adventures,
my turnout was certainly not what one might expect of
Mistress Aimee's friends. "How did you get in here,
miss?" demanded one well-armed man. "What's happened to you?"

Aimee interrupted before I could answer. "Excuse
me, D'Kano!" she said indignantly. "Jen knows she is
always welcome in my house. She's had a harrowing
journey through all the checkpoints and uncertainties on
the roads, and I'll not send her off without a rest. If you
gentlemen will take up your watch at the front and back
entries, I'll retrieve my cloak, let Jen warm herself at
the fire you so kindly made me, and learn what news
my friend has brought me of her dear grandmother."

"Mistress, you should return to the palace at once.
Your mission . . ."

Aimee held up a green velvet pouch. "My official business is done, Ha'Vor, but I cannot send on what I've
gathered here until tonight's courier leaves the palace
anyway. So we are truly in no hurry, and Jen's story
might give me valuable news to send along. Only a short
while, and we'll be on our way. Commander Je'Reint is
fortunate to have such steadfast loyalty as yours *and* that
of so many friends such as Jen. I'll call you when I'm
ready to go."

How could any man refuse such a command, issued

as it was with Aimee's usual charm? Utterly innocent. Utterly sincere. Utterly unshakable. The two men could not bow and scrape and hurry off to do her bidding fast enough. I needed to make a study of Aimee.

Once the soldiers had retreated toward the front and back entries, Aimee raised a finger to her lips for caution and took my hand. Her fingers felt half frozen. "Come this way," she said quietly and pulled me into the small sitting room. My two companions glided along behind us.

Aimee closed the door behind us, drew her finger over the latch—setting a common ward—and then whirled about. "There are three of you here. I beg you speak, so I may know you all. I dared not hope—"

Gerick glanced first at Paulo, who stood just inside the sitting room door, apparently struck witless, and then at me, his lips twitching at the edge of a smile. "Good evening, Mistress Aimee," he said softly, bowing to the lady. "It seems I've been rescued yet again with the aid of Gar'Dena's house."

Aimee clasped her hands together fervently as she dipped her knee to Gerick. "And I can hear that you're well. Oh, my lord, welcome." It took me a moment to recall their claim that Gerick was a king in his own land.

"And your third . . ." Aimee's whole being strained to guess the answer, a fruitless yearning until Gerick gave Paulo an elbow in the ribs.

"Uh . . . pardon, mistress . . . I'm here as well. Paulo, that is."

Paulo's state was not going to improve, for Aimee graced him with such a smile as might melt a steel post.

"What's going on here, mistress?" said Gerick, his good humor already set aside. "Where is my mother?"

"Come sit down." Aimee settled on the couch nearest the fire and quickly drew us close: me beside her, Paulo on the floor at her feet, Gerick a few steps away, standing by the hearth, his elbow propped on the mantle, his curled fingers resting lightly on his mouth. Each of us had one eye on the door.

"A great deal has happened over the past weeks," she

said, her voice scarcely above a whisper. "Our plan to discover the truth of the Lady has been exposed. It pains me to report that it is your involvement, my lord, that has caused the greatest disturbance. I'll tell you all, but I must be quick about it. Ha'Vor and D'Kano are good men and very kind, but they don't wholly trust me."

She leaned forward confidentially. "Most importantly, my lord, your parents are safe. Four days ago, your mother was arrested and charged with conspiracy"— Gerick jerked his hand away from his mouth, but Aimee held up her own to keep him quiet—"but she was not harmed. She was allowed to join your father by giving her word not to leave the hospice. Your father's identity has not been revealed to the public, and, as he is her guest, Lady D'Sanya refuses to allow him to be disturbed or questioned. You see, the Lady has taken the throne . . ."

In a concise summary, Aimee described Ven'Dar's arrest, the new attacks on the eastern Vales, the massive movement of fighters and arms to the northern Wastes, and Je'Reint's oath of fealty to D'Sanya. ". . . for he claimed that his oath to his prince bound him not to report our activity. She accepted his word, and has entrusted him with command of the northern troops. He vouched for me and T'Laven the Healer, as well as your mother. These men with me are Je'Reint's own guardsmen, sent to protect me on any foray outside the palace."

"Protect you?" said Paulo. "If there's such danger about, then you should stay somewhere safe and have guards that serve you alone. I would— There's those as would give anything to keep you from danger."

Aimee's cheeks could have ignited a mud puddle. "Thank you for your concern, good sir. I've slept safely at the palace since the Lady Seri was sent away. I've only come here tonight to retrieve some gems that were my father's. We need every artifact of power we can gather for the war."

She laid her hand on my lap and nodded to the other two, lowering her voice even more. "You must all take great care in the streets. Rumors of Zhid fly everywhere. And rumors . . . terrible lies . . . of you, Master Gerick. I *must* warn you: You are in the most dreadful danger every moment you stay here, as is anyone seen with you; your description is everywhere and the Lady has commanded that you be hunted down. This city is choking with madness . . . riot. Two men were killed when the mob named them Zhid."

A mob . . . killings . . . madness . . . Avonar. In all the days of my life, even the most wretched and terrible of my captivity, never had I felt the weight of catastrophe that settled over me with Aimee's news. Avonar was the heart of the world. Our bulwark against everlasting darkness.

"With Prince Ven'Dar confined no one knows where," she continued, "Commander Je'Reint fighting the Zhid in the north, and Preceptor Mem'Tara and her advisor N'Tien sent to retake Astolle and Lyrrathe in the east, the walls of Avonar have never been so poorly defended. The Preceptors have talked of evacuating children and the sick."

"How can they think of ignoring the city defenses?" I burst out. "If Avonar falls, the Vales can be partitioned! And one by one, they'll fall, too."

Amid the ebb and flow of Dar'Nethi history, only a few things could one hold as incontrovertible fact: the sun would rise in the morning, the yellow jeffiri would wing their way to the Lydian Vale on the spring equinox, and Avonar—blessed Avonar, the City of Light—would endure. How could the city that had withstood the worst assaults of the Lords for a thousand years be brought to its knees so quickly now they were dead?

Aimee hushed me again. "Just today, the princess sent most of the city guard north, as reports have Je'Reint facing ten thousand Zhid with more on their way. We hear the Zhid are savage—far worse than in the past. Their numbers increase overnight, and they seem to think as one mind. The Princess has taken on the security of Avonar herself, saying she will shield us in the same way she shields the residents of her hospice."

"She'll fail," said Gerick, ferociously quiet. "They mustn't rely on her devices. Surely they've kept *some* capable warriors among the defenders."

"Certainly. The core of the palace guard remains, and a thin reserve on the walls. She has enlisted a number of untrained volunteers from the city, but also many capable warriors that the other troops have refused."

"Who would refuse a willing fighter?" I said. "Have we so many to spare?"

Aimee ducked her head. "They are the Restored. She's put them in their own band, called the Lion's Guard, and because they are experienced in war, she's set them to command the defenses."

At that, Gerick's head popped up. "The ones who were Zhid? The ones she's healed?"

"Even if the legion commanders were willing, too many Dar'Nethi refuse to fight beside them. But they are good and loyal—"

"If her healing enchantments fail like all her others," said Gerick, "she's as good as put Avonar in the hands of the Zhid."

Aimee blanched. "Are you saying the Restored could lose their souls again?"

"I've not seen it. But yes . . . everything she's done has gone wrong, bent or twisted in some fashion."

"But there are hundreds of them." Aimee's shock left her stammering. "The two men killed by the mob were two of the Restored. We assumed it was just people's fear . . . prejudices against those who had been turned . . . making people see Zhid where there were none. Commander Je'Reint . . . the Preceptors . . . must be told of this possibility. We must convince them to send reinforcements—"

Brisk footsteps, the jangle of chimes from the entry hall, and the hiss of a triggered door ward sent Gerick and Paulo ducking behind furniture. I was hard-pressed to keep my seat, but Aimee held my arm and leaned her head close. When she started to giggle and babble something about people I didn't know, I gaped at her. "You remember," she said, "it was the silliest thing she ever did, and I never thought to tell her mother." A firm finger poked my side. "You remember, don't you?"

"Of course," I blurted out. "The silliest thing. I didn't tell her mother either." I was unable to muster any giggling.

"Mistress Aimee, should we not be on our way?" The man's voice came from the doorway. "We would have you safe behind the palace gates before the night gets late. They're hunting the Destroyer house to house tonight. Perhaps your friend should accompany you to your quarters."

"No!" I said, much too loud. "No, I have to get back to my grandmother. Will you be seeing Commander Je'Reint, Aimee? He is so kind, and was so concerned about my grandmother when she fell ill. He'd come to oversee her favorite stallion's breeding and ended up spending the entire day with her. You know she loves nothing better than her horses. And if you were to see him, you could give him *all* my news."

"Certainly . . ." Aimee's expression shifted in the firelight, growing intensely thoughtful. After a moment, she nodded decisively. "Certainly. But alas, my lord will be engaged in the north for a long while until this Zhid threat is quelled, as they've seen only the first skirmishers. If you were to write him a message, though, I could ensure that he received it. A bit of cheerful, everyday news would surely give Commander Je'Reint joy at such a time, don't you think, Ha'Vor?"

"Of course, mistress."

Her smile blossomed into brilliance as she jumped to her feet and pulled me from my seat. With a grip like an iron pincer, she dragged me across the room to a writing desk. "You'll find paper and pen in the slots. Write your message for Je'Reint, and I'll deliver it myself. I was consulting Preceptor Ce'Aret yesterday, and though she is retired, she is still so wise. She suggested that I should join my Commander Je'Reint in the field as soon as possible. Though I'm so much trouble to have around, awkward and clumsy as I am, the rapid shifting of our forces makes accurate Imaging difficult at a dis-

tance, and my images have not been resolving clearly
of late."

She stood right behind me, laying her hands on my
shoulders as I pulled out a sheet of smooth notepaper
and unstoppered a silly-looking ink bottle shaped like a
rinoceroos. I wasn't sure what she wanted.

"And you know, Jen," she went on, scarcely taking a
breath, "I was thinking that your brother who cares for
your grandmother's horses could join me at the battlefront next week if he can be spared. Je'Reint needs
every hand, does he not, D'Kano?"

One of the guardsmen, an intelligent, dark-browed fellow, nodded. "If the fellow can kill a Zhid or aid those
of us who can, he's needed."

"An excellent thought. His Horsemaster's skills would
be of immense use, and he could, perhaps, relieve these
two gentlemen of this tedious duty to shepherd me everywhere. Even better, he could contribute his immediate knowledge of the situation in the Vales and many
other important matters to the next image I work for
Commander Je'Reint. Speak to your brother, Jen, if you
will, and I'll consult those at the palace, to see if this
might be possible."

As Aimee engaged the guardsmen in conversation
about the best route through the tense city and whom
she should contact about taking her Horsemaster friend
directly to Je'Reint in the battlefield, I scratched some
nonsense about grandmothers and horse-breeding on the
notepaper and tried to sort out what she had just told
me. The bold plan hidden in her sideways conversation
finally emerged clear and sharp, leaving me in awe.

Imagers could weave a witness's knowledge and memories into a visual testimony to be presented at a judgment. The impact of such vivid testimony was
inarguable. Paulo's knowledge of Gerick's case against
D'Sanya, of her use of the oculus, of Gerick's beliefs
and fears about the Zhid would be a mesmerizing tale.
But of course, the integrity of the image was valid only
so far as the integrity of the Imager and that of the
witness, and in serious cases a Speaker would be called

in to judge their veracity. Aimee believed enough in Je'Reint and enough in Paulo and enough in herself to risk her life to bring Je'Reint the truth.

As I gave her the folded paper, her hand brushed mine, and in my mind appeared the faintest of voices, a mind-speaking that the most skilled Dar'Nethi spy would have difficulty detecting. *If he agrees, have him meet me at the north gate of the city when the bells ring third watch. Bring a fast horse that can carry two. If we're to win this race, we must ride faster than I can manage alone.*

And while her words yet gleamed in my mind, she kissed my cheeks. "And now, dear Jen, give your grandmother a kiss for me, and consult your brother about my idea. He is so very brave and honorable, and I delight in his company. I look forward to meeting him again soon."

"I'll speak to him. And I'll set the door wards as I leave," I said, bending casually over the hearth and making curling sweeps of the hand as if to cool and bank its flames. "Be very careful on your journey, Aimee."

"I've no worries. Zhid would find me a poor bargain." She swept her cloak over her shoulders. A vase crashed to the floor. "Goodness, what a mess! Well, perhaps those who come searching this house for the devil Lord tonight will clean it up for me. Come, good fellows, let's be off before the streets get crowded. May your own Way be safe, dear Jen!"

No sooner had the front doors shut firmly behind the three than Gerick emerged from the draperies and Paulo popped out from under a couch.

"Demonfire," said Paulo, staring at the door through which Aimee had departed. "She wants me to come with her?"

"Why would she want Paulo to go to Je'Reint?" said Gerick. "And we can't wait until next week. Her heart is good, but—"

"She's going to convince Je'Reint to send troops to Avonar," I said, still marveling at what had just occurred. "Tonight, if Paulo's willing to take her and be her witness . . ." I told them the pieces of Aimee's plan that they could not have known. ". . . and so she's taken this upon herself and Paulo, leaving you free to deal with D'Sanya and her oculus and her avantirs and whatever else she's made."

"My good lord," said Paulo softly. I'd never heard Paulo address Gerick so. Yet this was no mere formality of address. Never had I imagined that a statement formed of three simple words could bear the weight of a loyalty and friendship so far beyond my understanding. I surmised that it had been a very long while indeed since Paulo's Way had left him anywhere but steadfastly at Gerick's side.

"Stormcloud is the strongest," said Gerick, answering. "He'll carry two and still outrace the wind."

Paulo dipped his head and turned briskly to me. "How far will we be needing to ride?"

Though Aimee would need to direct him to a specific destination, I found paper and sketched out the route to the Wastes north of Erdris and the Pylathian Vale, reviewed the questions Paulo might be asked at the city gates in time of war, and stuffed every other warning and precaution I could think of into his head.

Without interrupting, Gerick found us a flask of wine and brought cold meat pastries from the larder. Paulo and I ate and drank as we talked. Gerick unwound the dirty bandages from his hands and threw them into the fire, then sat on the hearth stool, sipped wine, and watched us. His own meal remained untouched. Just as the clocks chimed nine times—the hour before third watch—lights flared and a clamor of voices rose on the far side of the garden wall. I hoped we hadn't waited too long.

"Sounds like I'd best be off," Paulo said, pulling on his long, dark cloak. "Can't keep a lady waiting."

"I can't make a portal for you," said Gerick. "I would, but—"

"You need to save everything for what needs doing. You know I'd rather ride anyway. You know. . . ."

Paulo extended one hand, but Gerick had already moved to the garden door and cracked it open, alert to the moving lights and activity beyond the garden walls. After a moment, he motioned urgently to Paulo. "Go now. They've moved around the corner to the street that fronts the house."

"Have a care, Paulo," I said, taking his hand and squeezing it. "We'll do the same."

He tore his gaze from Gerick's back and transferred it to me. His worried expression communicated a great deal more than his words. "You do that, Jen. I trust you."

I followed him to the door and watched as he hurried toward the back of the garden and vanished into the night. As the stableyard gate clicked shut, I cast a small diversion spell, the most powerful enchantment I could work, a child's favorite, easily countered by alert parents. But the watchers abroad tonight would be looking for Gerick's lanky friend who had been seen frequently at Aimee's house and the guesthouse in Gaelie. I didn't want him followed.

Gerick spun around and stared at me. "What did you just do?" he snapped. "If you've harmed him . . ."

"Nothing! Only a child's diversion spell. If anyone notices him as he rides out of the alley, they'll think he's much smaller than he is. More my size. And if that observer allows himself to be distracted and look away, he'll forget which way Paulo's gone. Those two guards weren't happy about leaving me here, and I'm thinking they might have left someone to watch."

I went back into the house and dropped onto the couch, muttering as much to myself as to him. "What do I have to do to make *you* trust me?"

He followed me in, stopping just inside the door. "I'm sorry. Of course I trust you. Paulo trusts you."

He shut his mouth and I thought that was all he was going to say. But after a moment, he leaned his back against the door, brushed back a lock of dark hair that had fallen into his eyes, and ran his fingers through his hair. "It's just . . . ever since I've come to Gondai, Dar'-Nethi enchantments have felt wrong to me, distorted, like hearing music that's too shrill or biting into a sugar cake to find it salty and bitter. I've assumed it was just me; Zhev'Na skewed my perceptions of sorcery, of people, of the world. But I hoped that now I understood more about the Dar'Nethi . . . all I experienced with you in the desert . . . things might feel right here. But it's even worse. Something is wrong in this city. Every enchantment here is wrong. The air is wrong."

Well, something was certainly wrong. My spirits, lifted by daring plans and successful diversions, had fallen as flat as street paving. I felt angry and irritable, and I wanted to yell at him that he was indeed a Zhid-mentored bastard, because no one else would send a friend like Paulo into mortal danger without even looking at him.

But we didn't have time to explore Gerick's peculiarities or his megrims or my own. The street noise was getting louder.

"I've too little sensitivity to enchantment to tell you anything," I grumbled. "But I do know we need to be on our way. Are you ready?"

He threw me my cloak, stepped to the center of the room, and picked up a kitchen knife from the tray of dishes, turning the blade over and over in his hand and staring at it. After a moment, he looked up at me. "Will Paulo and Aimee make it to Je'Reint, do you think?"

"Nothing's certain. But Aimee will watch out for him, and he for her. They are two people easily underestimated. A good match, I think." Unlike certain other incongruous pairings.

I drained my wineglass and stood up. "So where are we going first? The Lady or her device? By foot, horse, or will?"

The last was one of those smug Dar'Nethi expressions that avoided asking, *How talented are you?* Those who could travel at will, of course, were those powerful enough to make portals. Those who could do magic enough to keep such fragile, beautiful beings as horses would travel that way. Those like me traveled on foot . . . unless they were in more talented company.

Gerick squatted down in the middle of Aimee's bright blue rug, extended his arm, and touched the point of the knife blade to the weaving. "The hospice first. The oculus is there. And perhaps we can find something to give us a clue about any other device she's made. She told me many times that she could work only in her own lectorium."

Pivoting smoothly on his feet, like a clock spring unwinding, he scribed a circle of split stitches in the rug with the blade. "We'll have to hope *she's* not there. I didn't do so well facing her last time. Even with a bit more power to hand . . ."

He threw down the implement, and I watched his mind turn inward and focus on the task. *Mark the left-hand orientation. Then the right. Stand exactly between, in the center of the circle.* He had learned well, even remembering what I'd told him about making tight circles and quick progress through the steps if you wanted a portal that would open and close quickly. No trace of the portal must remain for D'Sanya's searchers to find.

Ah, good Sefaro, you fathered an idiot! I had forgotten to set the door wards as I'd promised Aimee. Anyone in Gondai could walk into this house without warning or hindrance. Leaving Gerick to his work, I ran through three dining rooms and the silent kitchen, where tall ovens and broad tables, ghostly in the dark, stood sentinel for their brave mistress. Not daring a handlight, I hurried to the end of the back passage. There I passed my hand over the thick wooden door—two half-doors, as it happened—hunting for the ring or knob or swatch of fabric that would hold the protective enchantments. During the war years every householder in Gondai had ready door wards, available for the least talented occupant to set. There . . . a loop of braided silk that felt cool and prickled my arm when I touched it. A tug, a word of attachment, and it was done.

I raced back through the house, glancing through the sitting-room doorway as I passed. Gerick's dark form was scarcely visible in front of a dark oval outlined by a silver thread. His hands stretched toward the developing portal, palms facing each other and slightly apart. Not long now.

But too long perhaps. Fists hammered on the great double doors that led to the street. Frantically I searched for the ward trigger.

"Open in the name of the Heir of D'Arnath!" yelled a man outside the door.

"Just push in," snapped a woman with a voice like a stone grinder. "She's harbored the devil."

While one of my arms swept carefully over the expanse of the door, my other hand fumbled around the elaborate door frame. Ridiculous, I'd thought when I first saw it: birds, beasts, dips and swirls carved into the wood; smooth pieces of ivory, faceted gems, and rounded nubs of brass, inlaid as eyes and tusks and the contents of magical treasure chests. *Come on, Jen, where is it?* Surely they wouldn't have put the trigger at the top of the door, out of my reach. The metal inlays were cold, chilled by the outside air leaking around the doors.

"But this is Gar'Dena's house," the man protested, "one of the oldest families in the city. Just one of his daughters—the blind girl—lives here."

"The devil was seen here," said the harsh-voiced woman. "His mother, too. Old families can be turned, and the Lady commands us search this house in particular."

My hand stopped on a small faceted knob that felt like glass or gemstone, colder by far than all rest of them. It moved at my touch.

Hands rattled the door latch.

I slid the glass knob left, spoke an attachment word, and the door panels grew warm.

"Ouch! By the holy Way, it's burnt my skin off!" The man outside was growling. "Bring G'Ston to deal with the door wards."

I relaxed, sighing with relief and resting my back against the doors, just warm to one on the inside. Now if Gerick would just hurry.

"We don't need G'Ston," said the woman. "See who's coming!"

"Make way!" someone cried amid a welcoming clamor.

"Your Grace, the door is warded. It will burn—"

"Is anyone inside?" You could not mistake the Lady's voice. Her speech floated through the air like gossamer, telling every listener that he or she was the most important person in the world.

"We've had no answer, Your Grace. But I've—"

"Stand aside." Her mind's fingers reached through the door and through my skin and bones, searching for a beating heart or thinking mind—powerful, angry fingers, belying the kindness in her voice. My spirit drew up into a hard little knot and shrank into the darkest corner of my soul as if I were a slave child again. The fingers grabbed nothing and passed on. But Gerick was focused on enchantment, not defense. She would find him.

I wrenched my back from the door and ran, resisting the urge to scream for Gerick to hurry. Distracting him at this point was the last thing I wished. He just needed time to finish. I paused for a moment, peering about the dark entry hall. Across the cavernous place stood a bronze statue of Vasrin, a sinuous body half again Paulo's height, the head cast to show the traditional opposing male and female faces. In the right hand was uplifted the flame of the Creator and in the left was the distaff of the Shaper—a nice long rod that stood loosely in the graceful bronze hand. The bronze winding of "wool" at one end would make a nice club.

I yanked the distaff from the curled bronze fingers and sped to the sitting room. The oval portal boundary shimmered in the darkness; objects in the distant place . . . trees, shrubs, a brick wall . . . were just beginning to take form in a whirling murk. Gerick stood with his hands upraised.

From the front of the house, the entry doors rattled and thundered in their frames. Gerick's head and shoulders jerked slightly, and his arms stiffened, but his hands did not fall and he did not turn around.

Good! Hold your concentration. I stood where I could see both Gerick's portal and the passage from the entry hall, raised the bronze shaft, and . . . felt ridiculous. What did I think I was going to do with my weapon? Bludgeon D'Sanya in the head after her fingers had torn into Gerick's mind? Cursing my foolishness, I closed the sitting-room doors carefully and jammed the bronze distaff through the door handles. Then I pressed my body against the doors, gripped the staff firmly with my hands and my will, and prayed Gerick to be done quickly. I hadn't power to hold a hiding spell for more than moments.

"The Fourth Lord is here! Find him!" D'Sanya's command could have pierced the prison walls of Feur Desolé.

Clattering boots. Shouts. Jangling chimes and crashing pottery. A quick probe of sorcery pushed into my enchantment like a sword tip bulging a tent canvas. And my shield gave way just as quickly as that canvas would succumb to a honed blade. All I could do now was hold the door shut.

"Now!" shouted Gerick from behind me. "Come on!"

A crash shook the door, jarring my head and neck. "Step through," I said through my teeth. "Start shutting it down. Remember the count. Do it!"

Remember the steps. For speed, keep the rhythm steady and fast. One, encompass the portal. Two, sweep the hand . . .

"Move aside." The woman's voice on the far side of the door was deadly.

Five, draw power . . .

Cracks appeared in the fine wooden door, and my bones felt as if they must crack as well. My will softened like hot wax. The fingers of enchantment reached through me, but Gerick should be out of range by now.

Six, infuse the enchantment . . .

On seven, I released the bronze staff and bolted for the fading portal. My stomach lurched as I passed through. The new reality slammed into my mind. Thorny branches entangled my flailing limbs. And as I glanced over my shoulder at the fading image of Aimee's favorite room, a livid Princess D'Sanya swept into the sitting room and screamed, "Destroyer!" Then the image winked out.

I sagged into a heap. My ragged mind whirled: *scratched skin, hammered head, torn clothing, unlikely scents of roses, of smoke, of wine, of night air. Indoors, outdoors. Tangling branches, cracking wood, smooth bronze . . . cold . . . hot . . .* My face was very near damp earth. A lovely smell. And faded roses. Thorns stabbed my stomach and my neck. I seemed to be suspended in a giant rose bush.

"Ow!" Someone ripped away a thorny branch that took part of my sleeve with it and then another that took some of my hair, evoking tears that dribbled across my forehead. *Long past time to hack the hair off again. Gets tangled in everything.* Hands reached under my arms and effortlessly hauled me to my feet. Why couldn't I haul people out of tangled messes without effort?

"A good job, do you think?" He spun me around and picked the dead leaves from my wretchedly filthy, and now ripped, tunic. "Tight circle to make it short-lived. Oval for fast closure. Counted the steps. Steady, as you told me. Brilliantly done on *your* part, I'll say. I don't think she saw where we were going."

"A good job," I said, trying to step backward to distance myself from the formidable enchanter who was brushing the dirt and tears from my face with a gentle hand. The rosebush pricked steadfastly at the back of my soggy knees. "The closure was perfectly timed, but a faster opening would have saved us some bother."

His laughter was genuine, but brittle-edged, his body as tight-wound as a soldier's on battle's eve. His eyes roamed the dark little garden—a garden that smelled like old leaves and fading blooms, withered and dry though it was only summer's end. Behind him rose the charming brick edifice of D'Sanya's house, where an oculus spun out its web of corrupt enchantment. The moon bulged above the hills behind the house, gleaming as if the vile implement itself were coming out to meet us.

"We should find a place to rest," I said. "I could catch my breath while you go warn—"

"I can't warn him." His movements as brisk and tight as his speech, he stepped aside so I could detach myself from the rosebush. "My father can't hear me speak in his mind, and we daren't delay. D'Sanya could be here at any moment."

"But—"

Before I could articulate my disagreement, a long thin hand fell on Gerick's shoulder from out of the rose bower. "Indeed, young Lord, the Lady has sent word for me to be vigilant and notify her immediately should I see her one-time lover sneaking into her house. And now here you are!"

The shadowy figure was tall and lean—Na'Cyd, the consiliar who once was Zhid.

CHAPTER 32

Having watched Gerick's training in Zhev'Na, I was not surprised to see how fast he took down Na'Cyd. He clamped one hand on the consiliar's wrist, spun, and ducked under their linked arms. A firm two-handed lock on Na'Cyd's arm and shoulder, a violent shove, and the lean, gray man was on his belly before I could ensure my toes were out of the way. Gerick straddled his back, twisting the consiliar's arm upward at a wholly unpleasant angle.

"Tell me the name of your master," Gerick said, as he locked Na'Cyd's neck in the crook of his elbow and wrenched it backward.

Gerick would not be able to see Na'Cyd's thin lips stretch into a smile. "You've given me an unwinnable test, young Lord," he wheezed. "You are the Fourth Lord of Zhev'Na. If I name *you* as my master, does it not prove I have no soul? On the other hand, if I name D'Arnath's Heir as my . . . mistress . . . will it prove I am restored? I am not a good liar. So, if I say I serve only Gondai, you will detect the lie and will not trust me. If I say that I serve only my own purposes, you will detect no lie, yet you will not trust one who cannot declare loyalty in this war. A conundrum to be sure."

"You twist words."

"But Zhid are not allowed to twist words in answer to your particular question, are they? And so, my twisted answer proves me. I am not Zhid. Who is *your* master, young Lord?"

Gerick dragged the consiliar's head back even farther

and jerked it sideways, so that I could see the sinews in the man's neck straining even in the dark. "Look into his eyes, Jen," said Gerick through clenched teeth. "They cannot mask their lack of a soul when they're this close to death."

I knelt in front of them. The rising moon lit Na'Cyd's face. Though he struggled to breathe, the consiliar's expression remained unafraid. And from his light gray eyes, an angry and defiant soul stared back at me.

"He is not Zhid."

"Then what *are* you, Na'Cyd?" Gerick loosened his grip only enough that the man could speak.

"I am a man who should have died in his bed six hundred and fifty years ago. The universe, in its perverse humor, did not permit that. Allow me to get up, and I'll tell you more. Or kill me. It's all the same to me."

"You killed Cedor."

"Yes."

I was still trying to remember who Cedor was as Gerick released Na'Cyd's hands and head and climbed off his back. "Was that what you were trying to tell me after the attack in Avonar?" asked Gerick.

The consiliar rolled over and sat up, his face impassive as he gazed up at Gerick. "I owed your father a favor. I thought that killing his attendant, whose reclaimed soul was reverting to its corrupted past, was fit recompense for your father's reversal of my own vile state. And I wanted him to know why the killing was done."

Gerick was startled. "Then my father . . . not D'Sanya . . . restored you."

"In the first year of his reign in Avonar." Na'Cyd rose and briskly brushed the dead leaves from his dark jacket and breeches, seemingly none the worse for his encounter. "I had hoped to share two pieces of information that morning, the first, as I said, for your father, the second for you. You, or at least your horse, saved my life in that same attack. You had no way of knowing I valued my life so little, and so, you, too, had earned some compensation. I had observed you besotted with a woman who never bothered to speak your name, and thus blind to certain truths that lay in front of your nose."

He reached into a pocket and pulled out something that he dropped into Gerick's hand with a faint chinking noise.

With one finger Gerick lifted up a thin chain from which dangled a gold pendant, shaped like an animal. "D'Sanya gives these to the Zhid she heals," he said, puzzled.

"Indeed," said Na'Cyd. "And this particular one I yanked from the neck of the man I fought that night in Avonar."

Gerick let the chain drop into his cupped hand. "So those who attacked us were more of D'Sanya's Restored who had reverted."

"Perhaps, perhaps not," said Na'Cyd, folding his arms in front of him.

The two of them might have been discussing next week's dinner menu at the hospice.

"Actually I don't think the fellow had ever been restored," said the consiliar. "His emptiness was . . . profound. What I tried to tell you was that when I hung this pendant about my neck later that night, trying to understand its decided allure, I felt an immediate compulsion to retreat . . . to regroup . . . to take a position with the rest of my cadre on the north road out of Avonar for the purpose of taking the Lady prisoner if she should ride out of the north gate. Do you understand? The need to obey this instinct was very difficult to resist. It took my entire being . . . my soul, if you will . . . to refuse."

"And when you removed the pendant . . ." said Gerick, eager now, obviously comprehending something I did not.

"I no longer felt obliged to obey."

"The commanders are marshaling the Zhid through the pendants," Gerick said. "They can issue orders to each general, to each cadre, to each warrior if they choose."

"That's why they wanted her prisoner: to make even

more of the pendants for those Zhid who do not yet
have them. For Dar'Nethi they plan to turn." Na'Cyd
pulled a sharpened bit of wood from his pocket and
scraped dirt from under his fingernails. "I felt that
compulsion . . . understood it . . . while I wore the pendant. She enables the revival of the warrior legion."

Indignation rose up in my chest like steam in a spewing geyser as I grasped the enormity of this news. I
wanted to throttle the man, so coolly grooming himself
while Dar'Nethi fought and died in the desert. "Why
haven't you told someone, you bastard? It's been
months!"

Na'Cyd tilted his head to the side. A smile played
around his lips as if I were some toy, wound up for his
amusement. "You don't grasp my intentions even yet,
Mistress Jen'Larie. I care nothing for Avonar or Gondai
or the Bridge or the mundane world beyond it. Once,
long ago, I lived a life that I believed was of some value,
and the universe proved to me that what I valued did
not matter. Through no choosing of my own, I became
everything I loathed for more than six lifetimes. I owed
Prince D'Natheil a debt because he ended that loathsome part of my life. And I owed this young man some
small thanks because he offered me a mortal service
even though I did not want it. Beyond that, I owe nothing and desire nothing."

"But you care for the people in the hospice. I've seen
you do great kindness. . . ."

"I keep order in the place I've chosen to live out
my days."

Gerick snatched the little nail scraper from the consiliar's hand, tossed it aside, and gripped the older man's
jacket at the shoulders, almost lifting him off the ground.
"Do you know how power is fed to the avantir and
the pendants?"

"No."

Gerick's voice remained deadly calm. "But you know
of the oculus that creates this hospice, don't you? You
know how and why the Lords used such devices. Does

the oculus in this house channel the Lady's power to an avantir?"

Na'Cyd did not change expression. "I've seen the oculus, yes; I was to head the hospice at Maroth, so, of course, I had to know of the device that holds the enchantment and links it to the insets in the hospice walls. And I recall that the Lords used such devices to enhance and focus their power. As to whether some of Lady D'Sanya's power goes astray as it passes through this particular device . . ." He inhaled deeply and shrugged.

"I must know," Gerick said, shaking the consiliar. "If you can't tell me yes or no, then I have to destroy it and everyone in this place who depends upon it. Tonight."

Na'Cyd shook his head without sympathy or regret. "I don't know."

"Then live or die as you choose." Gerick thrust him away and stepped back.

"Wait!" I said. "You can't allow him to—"

Gerick plowed a fist into the man's head. The consiliar toppled to the ground.

Gerick crammed the lion pendant in his pocket. "We need to get on with this if you're still willing."

"I'm ready," I said. Why was I shaking? As we hurried through the garden and up the steps, I tried to get my thoughts in order. *Knife, sheath, ring, measuring cord* . . . I had lost my scarf, but could use the soft leather purse looped onto my belt. "We'll need a tool or weapon to damage the oculus. We don't have Aimee's hand ax."

"The Lady has all manner of tools in her lectorium. You'll have a good selection." He tried the door latch and it opened readily at his touch. D'Sanya must not have expected him to visit her again.

The inside of the house was as dark as a Zhid's heart, the shuttered windows of the lower floor barring even the moonlight that had enabled us to see each other in the garden. Gerick took my hand and led me through the rooms and up the stairs. His hand was cold, his movements sure. A terrible thing to be sure of such dreadful doings. I was porridge on the inside.

The lectorium was as I remembered it: tall casements opposite the doorway where we stood, dark mirrored walls on right and left, the cluttered worktables, the hearth and its forge looming in the far left corner. She hadn't even removed the chain in the near left corner where she had hung Gerick to suffer and bleed.

"Where does she keep it?" The fact that we had walked through the house unhindered and unnoticed did not prevent me whispering.

"In there." Gerick pointed to an innocuous little cabinet that sat on carved legs in the center of the room. The black lacquered doors caught a beam of moonlight from the window. "She doesn't lock it. The oculus is not something just anyone could steal. Certainly not I."

Vasrin's hand, I'd forgotten! I peered into the shadows as if living phantasms might be creeping up on me. "Should you be so close?"

"Just don't open the cabinet until I'm out of this body." He released my hand and crossed the room to the windows, taking a route which kept him as far as possible from the cabinet. Arranging the cushions to support his back, he drew up his legs and wedged himself crosswise in one of the window seats. He opened the casement a crack and peered out before settling against the cushions. The moonlight sliding through the glass panes left his face all angles and shadows. It looked almost as if he were smiling at me. "I'll try not to fall out of the window. Are you ready?"

Neither of us had doubts. D'Sanya's implements of power had to be destroyed, no matter which of them was fueling the Zhid uprising. My father would suffer for this particular destruction, but I'd come to believe that he would be set free by it as well. But my father wasn't going to die from what we did here. Others would. I believed Gerick should take the time to warn his father—for both of their sakes—but I was too afraid to insist.

I felt him join with me this time. Perhaps because I

saw his body fall so abruptly and so profoundly still, lacking the familiar animation that marks even human sleep. At the same·time my churning emotions were soothed by a warm solidity and a self-assurance rooted in the core of my being. How had I ever believed such feelings were my own? I also felt a renewed urgency. The Lady would follow us here at any moment. I needed to move fast.

Consider need, assert ownership, disrupt containment, trigger the destruction . . . Oh, yes, and first acquire the object itself.

I cast a faint handlight. A quick trip to the worktables netted a pair of sturdy tongs with a wooden grip and a short metal-cutting saw. I swept a brass bar across the table to make room to work. Laying out my possessions in the cleared space, I made ready to encircle the oculus and assert my ownership.

Despite Gerick's lack of concern about locks and spells, I used the tongs to take hold of the porcelain knob on the lacquered cabinet and pull open the door. At first I couldn't see anything inside, only sense a quiet rush of air and the dread settling in my belly. I pulled open the second door, and the brass ring caught the pale illumination from my hand and swept it into a small orb of light.

But just as I opened the jaws of the tongs to grab the oculus, the air of the lectorium shivered. Instantly, I slammed shut the doors of the cabinet, tossed the tools aside, snatched up my belongings, and dived under the worktable in the deep shadowed corner next to the window. Stunned by the oncoming enchantment, I didn't think about these things, didn't plan them, or even understand why I'd done them. But then the fiber went out of my bones, and I was abandoned, shivering and terrified in my hiding place, watching Gerick gasp and sit stark upright on the window seat only a few steps away from me.

"Sorry, sorry," he whispered between shaking breaths. "Stay hidden. No matter what." After a moment, shaking his head vigorously, he jumped up from the window seat and positioned himself between the oculus cabinet and the sheet of gray-blue light taking shape in the corner of the room opposite me.

Another burst of enchantment split the air and a portal yawned. D'Sanya, wearing the trousers, shirt, and mailed vest of a Dar'Nethi woman warrior, strode through the shimmering oval, halting a few steps from Gerick. Though she wore knife and short sword at her side, her hands were empty. At first I thought she'd brought a cadre of other women with her, but soon sorted out that I was seeing the multiple reflections of the opposing mirrored walls. The Lady was alone.

"In one place or the other," she said, cold as hoarfrost on a steel post. "I knew I'd find you ready to destroy what I've built for Gondai. And here you are, ready to bear witness to your name. Dieste the Destroyer—that's what the Three named their newest partner, was it not? That was the destiny they designed for you."

"Yes." Gerick's hands were empty, too. Though I doubted steel would win this battle, I wished my knife were in his hand. "But if you've learned that much of history, then perhaps you've learned, too, how I walked away from them. How for four years I failed to understand that they still held me captive and how I wrought havoc without realizing that I did their work. A hard lesson, that: Just because you choose to walk away doesn't mean you're free. But you *can* be. Let me help you."

"Ah, your tongue is still sweet, Destroyer." As her portal vanished, the Lady swept a finger around the room, and fifty candlewicks burst into flame, confusing my eyes with myriad reflections of light and shadow. Her anger was cool and righteous. "Yet you speak with one voice, while your deeds speak with another. I know what you plan to do here this night. To think I was ready to abandon my father's legacy, betray the duty to which he bound his heirs, because I believed that you, my shy, gentle friend, would shrivel and die in so public a place as my father's palace. Yet even now your demon warriors converge on Avonar, ready to destroy everything of beauty in this world. Did you call them to Zhev'Na to release you from my justice?"

D'Sanya drifted to her right toward the door to the passageway. Gerick pivoted, matching her movements to keep himself between her and the oculus cabinet.

"The Zhid wear your pendants, D'Sanya. They found you in the desert after the scavengers set you free, didn't they? They forced you to make them an avantir and the lion pendants that link them together . . . the tools of war . . . the tools of the evil you thought you had left behind in Zhev'Na. Until you escaped again eight months ago . . ."

"You lie!" How quickly her cool reason burst into flame. "I am D'Arnath's daughter, born to be his Heir. It is my father's power, my rightful inheritance, that I use to make the lion tokens and to heal the poor lost Zhid and to set my people free of pain and war. His power could never be bent to evil."

Did Gerick feel what she was doing? His gaze seemed fixed on D'Sanya's face as she shifted farther to the right until her back was to the door. But from the angle of my hiding place I could see the reflection of her hands clasped behind her back, her silver rings gleaming brightly in the murk, pulsing with power.

Incapable of focused mind-speaking, I couldn't warn him without revealing myself. And I feared he was right that I needed to stay hidden. Someone had to carry the tale of what we had learned to Avonar.

"Your Restored are reverting to Zhid, D'Sanya." Gerick took a few steps toward her. His voice had taken on a mesmerizing timbre, and he fixed his eyes on hers. "As with everything else you've done, your healings fail. You are poisoning Gondai. Listen to me. . . ."

But his ploy was too obvious. She broke the lock of his gaze. "How dare you speak to me of evil!" she said. "You've come here to kill your own father. Who but a Lord of Zhev'Na could do such a thing?"

She cupped her hands in front of her. A ball of silver flame took shape within them, and with a twist of her wrists, she flung the ball straight at Gerick. Beams of

silver shot everywhere. The panes of the windows behind
him shattered, the crumbling shards reflecting the light
crazily through the lectorium. A howling wind swept
through the room; bottles toppled and shattered on the
tile floor. I had to cover my eyes as the flying splinters,
dust, and particles of glass bit my face and arms. When
the whirlwind calmed, and I dared look up again, Gerick
had raised his hands and a curtain of blue-and-gold light
enveloped the two of them, flaring so brightly I could
see nothing but his back. Their strange duel played out,
not in slashes and spins and footwork, but in hand movements and sweeps of the arm and small steps—forward,
back, now staggering, now braced for an onslaught that
was roaring red light rather than flashing metal.

Enchantment piled upon enchantment, causing waves
of cold fire to blister my skin and still my blood. I
thought my skull must surely crack, and all I could do
was cower in the darkness and pray that Gerick had
learned enough of power to save himself at least.

A few steps away from me, in front of the broken
windows, the air rippled. Another portal took shape and
spit out three men, one of them drawing a bow aimed
directly at Gerick's back. D'Sanya had shifted away from
the mirrors. As long as his attention was focused on her,
he couldn't spot her allies.

I snatched up a palm-sized shard of glass and sent it
spinning toward the thick-necked bowman with a word
to set its course true and another to make its impact
hard. It struck him in the calf just as he lofted his arrow.
His arrow flew high, striking the curtain of light and
bursting into purple flame.

"Take him!" shouted D'Sanya.

Two men rushed forward, while the cursing bowman
threw down his weapon, dropped to his knees, and
wrenched a long splinter of glass from his leg. Shouts
and grunts and bursts of light flared from the other end
of the room. I must have flinched or twitched or made
some noise, for the bowman's head jerked around, and
he looked me straight in the eye.

"Well, see what we have here!" he said. "Something hiding in the corner! Is it a nasty Zhid girl?"

A huge man, whose neck was the same width as his head, he lurched to his feet and reached under the table. I considered removing his hand with my knife, but better judgment prevailed. Unless Na'Cyd had reported us, they had no evidence against me. Remembering the blow Gerick had laid on the consiliar, I chose to gamble that Na'Cyd still lay tucked under the rosebushes.

"Please, sir! I'm no Zhid!" I said. "I saw him sneak in here . . . the devil himself. I thought you and your fellows had come to help him against the Lady!"

The bowman grabbed my hair and dragged me from under the table, just in time to see Gerick smash the heel of his hand into a man's chest. The fellow collapsed. A third man, a long-limbed, wiry fellow with gray-streaked hair, spun and staggered against a worktable when a blast of light from Gerick's fingers ripped his upraised sword from his hand and flung it across the floor far out of reach.

The wiry guardsman snatched a metal bar from the worktable and swung it at Gerick's head. Gerick threw up a hand to block the blow, but the bar must have grazed his temple anyway, for he dropped to his knees, his hands fallen limply to his sides. His gold curtain of light faded. The man kicked him in the belly, and he fell prostrate.

Breathing hard, D'Sanya sagged backward against the solid door and the blue lightning faded. "Bind him," she said harshly, "and then fix his hands to the chain in the corner." Her head dropped back against the wood and she closed her eyes. "Quickly!"

The wiry man knelt on Gerick's back, tossed his metal bar to the floor out of Gerick's reach, and unhitched a coil of silver rope from his belt. The bowman dragged me across the room and shoved me to the floor. "Stay right there until the Lady can deal with you."

The two of them soon had Gerick bound with the silver cord. They dragged him to the corner, and one man lifted him up while the other looped his bound hands over the hook at the end of the chain. The position raised Gerick's arms so high behind his back that his head drooped below his waist.

Only then did D'Sanya move. She walked slowly to the corner and ran her fingers over the links of the chain until it glowed red. Then she lifted his head and spat in his ear. "Oh, what I would give to slay you now, Lord Dieste, lest villainous chance snatch you from my fingers yet again. But my people's fears demand that your execution be a public display, and so I must follow the proper forms. Even so vile a creature as you will not force the Heir of D'Arnath to corrupt our law. But that should cause only a small delay."

He could not have heard her. I wasn't sure he was alive.

D'Sanya let his head drop and turned to the fallen guardsman. Bending over the dead man, she closed his eyes and smoothed his forehead. "I thank you for your loyal service, good Mi'Tan. May your Way lead swiftly beyond the Verges." Her voice was all tears and kindness.

She wiped her eyes as she moved on to the oculus cabinet. As she opened the lacquered doors, the candles flickered, their flames taking on a dark red core. My shoulders sagged under the now-familiar burden of the oculus enchantment, and my own inner being felt as if it burned crimson as well. I must have moaned, for only then did the Lady take notice of me.

"Jen?" The Lady's chin lifted, and her eyebrows, reclaiming a self-assurance that appeared badly shaken by the combat. "Whatever are you doing here?"

"Blessings of life, Lady," I said, scrambling to my knees. The eerie light from the spinning globe only a few steps away tickled my skin. "Your Grace, all my thanks for saving me. I've been so afraid."

She motioned me up, her frown showing no sign of royal indulgence. I bounced to my feet.

"I followed him, Lady," I said, as if my fondest wish

was to open my soul to her. "All these weeks, I've suspected him. He seemed so like the boy the Lords trained to become one of them. I was a slave there, Lady, as a child in his house, and I've been waiting to catch him at something to tell me whether or not my eyes were deceiving me. You've seen me spying, I know, but I meant no disrespect for you. And when I saw him sneak into your house tonight—"

"Why did you not tell me what you suspected?" She grabbed my chin and lifted it up so I could not ignore the dangerous storm in her great eyes.

"Your Grace, no one believes those of us who were slaves when we bear witness to the wickedness of the Lords. They want to put the war behind them, and we are accused of stirring up hatreds and imagining old fears come to life. You . . . Dear Lady, you cared for him so, I began to think I must be wrong. I was so young when I lived in Zhev'Na. But after you proclaimed that the Fourth Lord walked in Gondai, I swore that if ever I caught sight of him again, I would deliver him to you. Tonight when I came to visit Papa, I glimpsed the villain in your garden. Please forgive me my cowardly hesitation that left you in such danger."

I thought my skin must flake away with her examination. "Have you no respect for your father that you come to him in such disarray?" she said after a moment. Her fingers picked at my hair, pulling out dry rose petals, and she brushed at the red dirt ground into my leather vest. "And have you no consideration that you come to him so late of an evening?" Her voice was cool . . . like shellstone.

I shivered. "My lady, call on a Speaker to verify my truth. The young Lord sealed the slave collar on me, and for his training was my father tortured and my brothers murdered. I witnessed the Three devour his eyes and his soul. You cannot believe I would serve him."

"I don't know quite what to believe. And I've no time to deal with you." She stepped away abruptly, as if I had vanished from the room. "Ri'Isse, P'Tor, keep the girl here with the Destroyer. I'll return for him as soon as I've declared his condemnation to the Preceptorate. They are expecting it, so matters should move swiftly."

The bowman bowed. "But we've no more dolemar for the girl, Lady. Have you—?"

"You've no need to bind her. Her physical prowess can scarcely match the two of you, and her own father admits she is not competent in any true Art. She's likely just another gull. At worst, she's his Drudge. Just secure the chamber and keep her here. It is the devil Lord you need to watch. My binding chain held him well before, but his power has grown."

Extending one hand, D'Sanya pointed a finger at a glinting arc of metal embedded in the tiles. The narrow silver band formed part of a complete circle—a permanent portal frame—and she stood in its center. "Be alert, Ri'Isse. I'll reopen this portal when I'm ready for him."

Sweeping her hand around the gleaming circle, she constructed her magical enclosure, and in only moments, a tremulous oval appeared. Even depleted by her struggle with Gerick, the surging power was startling, disorienting, nauseating. As the portal vanished, I felt hopeless as I had not in days. What, in the name of sense, was I to do now?

The two guardsmen, wearing the white-and-gold livery of the Heir, moved efficiently to their duties. While Ri'-Isse the bowman took up a guardsman's stance beside Gerick—hand on his sword hilt, feet apart, balanced, relaxed, and ready—his older companion shot the two sturdy bolts on the door to the passageway and applied some magical working to them. My flesh stung as if I'd been struck with a riding crop.

P'Tor moved across the room to the window, shoved the half-ruined casements open wider, and leaned out. "All's quiet. No one abroad," he called over his shoulder.

I moved toward the corner where Gerick hung suspended like an abandoned string puppet. I was not quite sure why I did so, except that I needed to get farther away from the oculus. The spinning sounded like the contemptuous hiss of the Zhid, evoking images that made my blood run hot and cold.

"Just sit right there on the floor, girl," said Ri'Isse, pointing to the dark-colored tiles at my feet, halfway between Gerick and the oculus. "Give us any trouble, and we'll chain you up like the devil."

"Please, sir, I feel . . . sick. . . ." I stepped closer to him.

Truly my head was horribly muddled. The world felt wrong. The older man was working some protective magic on the gaping window openings, and it grated on my skin like a carpenter's rasp.

Only two of them. They perceive no threat. Certain advantage . . . Another step. I pressed the heel of my left hand to my forehead; pain pierced the spot between my eyes like a lance, as I imagined lightning bolts shooting from my fingertips . . . *The soldier dropped the metal bar on the floor. Where is it?* My right arm lay across my stomach as if I were sick. My fingers flexed. *Death lies in these hands . . . power for the taking.* Something monstrous and horrible burned in my belly. *No! You know other ways . . . stay in control. Move.*

What was happening? What was I thinking? Another step closer. "Please, sir, I just need . . ." I slammed my knee into the bowman's groin.

He yelled and doubled over. The other man streaked toward us, one hand holding a knife, the other fumbling at his sword. Poor Ri'Isse was still retching when I grabbed his tabard at the shoulders, straightened him up, spun him a half-turn, and shoved him into his comrade. The two crashed heavily to the floor, the heavier bowman square atop the smaller man.

Staying clear of their flailing limbs, I kicked the wiry man's knife from his hand, retreated a few steps, and snatched up the brass bar from under the edge of the worktable where it had rolled when discarded. Gripping it with two hands, I raised it over the fallen men. "Stay down!"

But the pale bowman had caught his breath at last, and with a murderous glare he lunged forward and up, growling through gritted teeth. Before he could get to his feet, I crashed the bar into his forehead. Insensible, he sagged back onto his unlucky partner.

The wiry P'Tor had managed to roll sideways and get to all fours before Ri'Isse flattened him again, but despite the bowman's dead weight, he kept scrabbling forward and would soon break free. I dropped my own weight onto the pile, straddling the unconscious bowman's belly. Retrieving my knife from Ri'Isse's belt, I plunged it into the back of the squirming guardsman's thigh. He cursed and fought harder to extricate himself from the pile, but I twisted the knife until he screamed and fell limp.

I released the knife hilt and stared at my bloody hand. How was this possible? I had never stabbed another person in my life . . . never made such moves. My shoulder ached as I climbed to my feet. My fingers tingled, half numb, yet I had no sooner persuaded them to wriggle than my vision blurred and I felt completely disoriented, as if someone had thrown sand in my eyes and spun me around. I staggered forward trying to keep my balance. This was not the oculus enchantment, but something new. Rubbing my eyes and forcing them to focus, I whipped my head around to see the bowman's limp body rolling off the wiry guardsman's back.

"Down on the floor," I yelled, stomping on P'Tor's outstretched hand as it wove his pitiful enchantment. "On your face! Now!"

"Damnable, traitorous witch . . ."

I slammed my boot into his wounded thigh, close to the knife. He screamed and dropped to his belly, his magic withering.

"Don't think to use any trickery on me," I said. I wrenched away the short sword gripped in his left hand and pulled my knife from his thigh. "Stay down and keep both hands where I can see them or I'll cut them off."

A quarter of an hour later, after a number of threats and a few persuasive kicks, the two guardsmen were bound securely with straps from D'Sanya's bundles and bags, and I was cutting the silver cord that bound Gerick . . . that bound me. For the truth had dawned on me at last, that I was once again both of us.

CHAPTER 33

Gerick

Even if D'Sanya hadn't brought in reinforcements, I had been very unlikely to best her in hand-to-hand sorcery. My power had surprised her, giving me leverage in the combat just as an ambush gives an early advantage in a physical trial. But by the time a flaming arrow flew over my head, warning me that someone had attacked me from behind, I was already in serious difficulty. At that moment I would have sworn my skin was melting and the underlying tissue oozing away in great greasy globs.

The only dueling enchantments I could manage as I juggled this new kind of power-gathering were rudimentary magical simulations of standard weapons combat: stabbing, hacking, grappling, and so on. And though I felt as if I could generate power enough to support these workings, the flow as I fed them was rough and uneven, leaving both attacks and defenses ineffective and easily countered.

I felt the first man come up behind me, and while attempting to hold a defensive screen between me and D'Sanya, I spun around and slammed the side of one hand into his throat. The heel of my other hand smashed into his chest, silencing his strangled bubbling and sending him to the floor. D'Sanya, ready and waiting for me to be distracted, picked just that moment to entangle me in an enchantment I had no ability to counter. It blurred my vision so that I couldn't tell whether there were four men or forty coming at me. The battle was lost, and I knew D'Sanya would make sure of her threats this time. I had to withdraw and try something else, and I had best be quick about it.

Jen's body didn't give me much to work with, and to accommodate her different shape and balance challenged my ability to adapt. But her spirit . . . I was already in awe of that. How could such an unkempt sprig of a woman, possessing no true talent and all the magical power of a nine-year-old child, goad, coerce, or sting me into wielding a kind of power I had believed myself incapable of?

When I abandoned my soon-to-be-captive body and joined with her again, I found her ready to take on D'Sanya and her soldiers, whether I was with her or not. That made it easier to do what I had to do—take control of her slight limbs, infuse her with my own skills, and batter two men insensible. Though she had no power to deny anything I demanded of her body, and though my instincts and training insisted I make sure of our captors, I couldn't kill them. Not with Jen's hands.

To yield control of a body once I had taken full possession was always difficult. The mind clings to the senses, to breathing, to a beating heart. The same fundamental urge that drives a soul to hold on to life through pain and peril demanded I stay where I was, not shrink into a quiet corner of Jen's soul and allow her to use my capabilities as she chose. But we had yet to destroy the oculus. And whereas Jen sensed the oculus enchantments as an iron yoke laid on her shoulders and a pall upon her mind, I felt a fiery liquor in my veins. The smell of the guardsman's blood brewed an intoxicating poison that threatened to erase all sense of decency and moderation. Afraid that I might falter in our task . . . or relish it . . . I gave Jen back her will.

Time to begin . . .

Hurry. No time to waste. The Lady could return at any moment.

We can't rush . . . we must be sure . . . make no mistakes. Is he doing this or am I?

Don't think about the results, only necessity.

Our thoughts collided and bounced off each other like raindrops on pavement. My urgency. Her steadiness. My dread of the outcome. Her shame at her lack of talent and her determination to overcome it. The time of transition between full control and simple joining is when it is most difficult to keep the two souls separate and to avoid intrusion.

Consider need, assert ownership, disrupt containment, trigger the destruction . . .

Unsure if we were yet joined, she looked down at the body she had released from D'Sanya's bindings. Infinitely strange to see myself lying there like a dead man who just happened to inhale now and then. Jen wasn't afraid of me any more. But the fighting revolted her.

I tried not to listen to her thoughts, only observe through her eyes and stay afloat in the tides of her emotions, so I would know if she needed me to take a more active role. She laid out her possessions on the worktable and retrieved the tongs and the saw. Fear and dread surged through her as she used the tongs to snatch the oculus from its cabinet. Her skin felt scored by knives. But I felt no faltering of will. She dropped the shining ring on the worktable and began shaping her enchantment. Deliberate. Careful.

Assert ownership . . . Consider the making of the object . . . Consider the reasons for this destruction . . . Hurry . . . Careful . . . Make each element of the working complete. Replenish your power. . . .

Trying to control my impatience, I considered the things Jen had done in the desert and at Aimee's house. Her courage and determination humbled me. So many Dar'Nethi feared me, but few with so much reason as this woman. And she had uncovered my own worst fear. I could not rid myself of the image of the Zhid armies in the north and east, marching toward Avonar marshaled by an avantir, answering the call of the Lords. Were the Three truly dead if their desires yet moved their servants . . . their instruments? *Destroyer . . .* The name had festered in my soul for five years.

Jen fixed a U-shaped clamp from D'Sanya's tools to

hold the oculus and took up the metal-cutting saw. The defenses of the oculus battered her with uncertainty and doubt. I offered what confidence and strength I could, and forced her to keep her arm moving though it pained her shoulder. Once the saw had bitten a notch in the smooth ring, I retreated again and allowed her to complete her magical construction, encompassing desire and will and transformation . . . and a resonating grief for the pain and death we would cause. As she reached for power to accomplish it, suppressed sobs shook her slight body.

I stopped her. *Let it go, Jen'Larie,* I whispered in her mind, trying not to frighten or overwhelm her with the direct contact, trying to mute my urgency and allow her to choose what I was prepared to insist on. *Relinquish your enchantment so that I can wield it. Please. This I must do myself.*

After all, I was the Destroyer. What was one more holocaust to my account?

To my relief, she did not resist. When I felt her release the solid weight of her enchantment—truly little more than an immensely complex thought bound to a physical object with simple threads of magic—I held it carefully, envisioned its accomplishment, hearing, tasting, smelling, feeling the shattering to come. And then I reached for power. . . .

I thought my soul might be sucked out of Jen's body as the power rushed out of me. The lectorium candles winked out, leaving the swelling oculus as our only illumination, a lurid pulsing red glow. Much more than an enchanted metal ring of the Lords' design, this oculus had been bound with the talent and power of every hospice resident. Bearing the substance of their lives and their sorcery, of their pain and diseases, the device existed with the same formidable presence as a phenomenon of nature—a glacier or a forest or a sea—though tainted always and ever with the most unnatural poison of Zhev'Na.

I fought to slow the rush of power and to focus our enchantment on the weakened structure of the brass circle. No rough or halting application of power here. Jen grasped the ring, her physical contact allowing me an unhindered path to the oculus, even as it threatened to tear her apart. She trembled, sobbed, and swore, but her small hand did not release the burning ring. I could not help her, for I had to devote every particle of my strength and concentration to control, to ensuring that I drew on everything of myself that I could safely give. Thoughts and memories swept me down and down, faster, tumbling, choking as if I were caught in an avalanche. . . .

"Look deep and search for the truth. . . ." The man seated in D'Arnath's chair in the center of the council chamber leaned forward, looking at me as he plunged the knife into his own belly. The red stain raced to saturate his white robe. . . .

I wrenched my thoughts away from my father. My mind darted here and there: to riding horses . . . to the storms of the Bounded . . . backward to my childhood in Leire . . . to the day my mother came to Comigor, long before I knew she was my mother . . . before Zhev'Na . . .

The voice echoed in the temple of the Lords, with its floors of black ice and its dome of cruel stars. "The cursed D'Natheil . . . who would have thought he would become the second D'Arnath, the Tormentor, the Preserver of Prisons, the enemy of all our works? We'll have his child, Brother Parven . . . the boy already knows he is evil . . . we will keep him alone, teach him our hate, blind him and warp him until he carves out his father's heart. In one stroke he will destroy the Tormentor's Heir and the Tormentor's Bridge . . . he is made for it . . . the universe has brought forth a Destroyer to be our vengeance. . . ."

No! Rage and terror yanked me out of the whirlpool of memory. That memory was not mine. *Not mine . . . not mine . . . not mine . . . shut it away . . . I am not what they made me . . . I have chosen. I am not evil. I will not be their instrument..*

I slammed the door on memories. *Concentrate. Focus.*

The world feels wrong. The avantir sings of war to D'Sa-nya's lions. The oculus pulsed like a diseased heart, refusing to yield. I released my attachment to Jen's vision so I could no longer see the cursed thing. The power rushed out of me . . . leaving me parched. . . .

Hollow. Empty. Why did I care? Care, like joy and sorrow and worry and honor, was only a word, thin and spidery and gray, unattached to anything of substance. I plummeted into a well of gray. Shrunken and withered, I huddled in its depths. Voices . . . weeping . . . invaded my gray world, one and then another.

"What's happening? Mistress S'Nara is ill."

"Lady, where are you? I feel so strange!"

I tried to ignore them.

"My eyesight fails!"

"What is she doing up there in her house? I heard thunder . . . explosions . . . great sorcery."

"Old Gerard has fallen and cannot rise. Lady! Are you there? Help us!"

I didn't want to hear this. I turned inward.

"Gerick! You must listen to me." Jen's voice, strained and harsh, shouted above the fading clamor. "D'Sanya betrayed these people. She used the Lords' magic to deceive them and rob them of their Way. Don't hide. Listen to them. Embrace them. We're so close: Her enchantment—the oculus—is failing. But you must give just a little more to break it. Don't hold back. For your father, Gerick. Have mercy. Let him die."

Her pleas pulled me out of the dry well. But I refused to think of my father. Rather I returned to thoughts of the Bounded, of the Singlars, of their strange place in the world. What would happen to them if D'Sanya gave this world to the Zhid? What would happen to them if I withered away here in this hole in the desert of spirits? They weren't ready. The power poured out of me. . . .

The world exploded in red-orange light.

". . . on and get up. You can't . . . here. D'Sanya . . . sense what's happened . . . come and . . . you."

The woman wasn't speaking in fragments. I was hearing in fragments. Seeing in fragments as well. Darkness. Wavering light. Swimming reflections. And my chest was on fire . . .

Panic gripped my gut. Suffocation. *Inhale, fool.*

The inflow of air cleared some of the cobwebs from my head. The floor was hard. An overpowering scent of lamp oil filled the air. Somewhere people were clamoring. Anger. Confusion. Fear. Panic . . . But I wasn't sure whether it was inside of me or out.

Breathe again. Keep it up this time.

"Can you get up? We must get away from here. I tried to break her circle on the floor, but I can't. Her portal exists there, just waiting for her to trigger it. She can be here almost as soon as she thinks of it."

Forcing myself to breathe, forcing my eyes to focus, I convinced my arms and legs that they were mine and pushed up to all fours. Only then did I feel control enough to raise my head and look at the person crouched in front of me, exhorting me to move. Dark, dark eyes, pools of shadow, too large for a face so pale and exhausted and afraid. Behind her the lectorium was in shambles. Broken glass, sheets of twisted metal, barrels of sand and dry plaster spilled across the tiles. Tools and implements scattered everywhere. Scorch marks clouded what remained of the great mirrors.

"We did it," she said, dropping crumbled nuggets of brass on the floor in front of me.

"Must . . . destroy . . . this place. Fire." The words would have been easier spoken by a newborn infant.

Jen smiled faintly. "We will. One or the other of us developed that idea about the time the world exploded. But we must get these men out before we torch it. Not to mention I need a spark. All the candles went out. I'm flat. I don't suppose you could manage it."

I gasped again, when my starving lungs and wobbling joints reminded me to keep breathing. "Madwoman."

A gut-twisting rip of enchantment, a crashing blow that ripped the bolts from the wood, and the door to the passageway swung open. I sat up on my knees and fumbled for a nonexistent knife with fingers that could scarcely distinguish between steel and leather.

Na'Cyd, the elegant angularity of his high forehead marred by the bruised swelling on the left side, stood in the doorway holding a small lamp and surveying the wrecked lectorium. "No need for weapons, Master Gerick," he said, sniffing the fume-laden air. "I'll not interfere with your activities. As I said before, I merely keep order in the place I've chosen to live. My duties include ensuring the safety of guests and visitors at this hospice, as well as investigating mysterious explosions in the Lady's house."

He set his lamp on the nearest worktable and wagged a finger at the three fallen soldiers. "Are they dead?"

"Only one," said Jen.

As the consiliar moved toward the nearest man, Jen grabbed her metal rod and bashed his lamp with it. The glass panes shattered and flames rippled outward across the table. She held the rod stiffly between herself and the Dar'Nethi. But Na'Cyd just sighed and bent over the dead guardsman, pressing a finger into his neck. Emitting a matter-of-fact grunt, the consiliar moved to the other two. He hefted the one with the bloody thigh onto his shoulders. As he exited the broken door, he called back to us. "I'll return for the other one."

His boots clumped heavily on the stairs. Popping glass on the burning worktable released little geysers of colored flame, reflecting eerily in the broken mirrors.

"Come on." Jen offered her arm to support my shoulders.

I refused her help and stumbled to my feet. "Did you see anything that might hint of the Lady's other works?" I said.

"Nothing I could recognize. The pieces at the far end of that table are strange. But they're not metal."

Jen grabbed two tall candles from sconces by the door, lit them in the increasingly eager flames, and used them to set off the oil she had spilled on the other worktables and the cushions scattered on several chairs. The fire spread quickly to a stack of paper packets that billowed scented smoke.

The items she had mentioned were broken chunks of plaster, scorched and smudged as if they'd fallen into a fire before someone threw them into this heap. Most were roughly boxlike, each piece having five relatively flat sides and one with a design pressed or carved into it—a coin, a galloping horse, a key—and patterns of straight slits cut into the plaster face. Several larger pieces were broken, but when I assembled them revealed only simple round hollows scooped out of them. Again the patterns of narrow channels radiating from the concavity. Other pieces had a rounded bulge left in relief that would fit inside the scooped out sections like an egg in a nest. Molds, of course, for casting her metal objects. I rummaged through the stack, looking for something that would tell me which of these designs might channel her power to the avantir. I found a small one for the lion pendants, but nothing else that seemed significant.

Voices rose outside the house. I tossed aside the mold in my hand and peered out of the broken window. Men and women were streaming across the lawns toward D'Sanya's garden, carrying lamps and torches, calling one to the other, some of them supporting each other, pointing their fingers at the window from which I looked down.

The bound guardsman groaned, drawing my attention back to the lectorium. To my left a burst of flame shot toward the coffered ceiling. Who knew if Na'Cyd would actually choose to return?

"We'd best get this fellow out," I said, my eyes watering from the smoke filling the room.

By the time Jen and I had carried the heavy man across the room, out the doorway, and to the head of the stairs, two explosions had shot flames through the roof. Billowing smoke set us both coughing, and the heat scorched my back. We rested our arms on the banister, and I considered the merits of rolling the man down the steps and tumbling down after him.

But Na'Cyd bounded up the stairs just then and, with

only a steadying hand from us, lifted the bulky guardsman onto his shoulders.

"Thank you," said Jen, as we stumbled after him.

"I don't burn living men to death. Not any more." He staggered across the foyer and out the front doors.

Brown smoke filled the graceful rooms where I had learned to be a child again. The paint on the ceiling bubbled, charring at the edges like evil flowers blossoming and dying all at once. Another explosion, and the rumble of flames above our heads grew louder.

"We should leave through the back garden," I shouted over the din, restraining Jen as she tried to follow Na'Cyd.

She jerked her arm away. "I need to find Papa. Help him. And you—"

"We can't delay here, Jen. Did you hear D'Sanya? 'One place or the other.' She knows the Zhev'Na oculus is gone. So she must have another device. And then there's the avantir itself. There could be several of them. The Lords always had three."

"You must speak to your father." She sniffled and coughed and wiped her eyes with her sleeve.

"There's no time." I pulled her face into my chest and dragged her toward the back hall. But a great cracking noise and a sudden burst of heat sent me backward, just as the upper stair landing collapsed into the passageway in front of me. Flames licked at Jen's cloak, and I yanked her back and slapped at the sparks glowing in the dark wool. A massive burning beam crashed to my right, raining fiery debris on our heads. Jen and I ducked at the same time, but in opposite directions, and I lost my hold of her.

"Watch out! Ah—" Jen's cry was aborted, and she collapsed to the smoldering carpet, a sooty gash on the side of her head.

"Jen! Jen'Larie!" I scooped her into my arms. Reversing course, I ducked around the blazing beam and hurried through the front doors, only to meet a sea of faces.

Fifty or more people crowded the garden, the eerie light of the flames shifting on pale cheeks and flashing in worried eyes. Behind me the flames roared, but the people had fallen silent, save for hissing breath and moaning misery . . . or perhaps that was the wind wrought up by the fire or perhaps it was entirely in my imagination. Somewhere in the crowd a woman sobbed. They did not move to let us pass.

"Where is the Lady?" demanded an elderly woman with tightly curled hair and a voice like a trumpet. She stood in the front ranks, supported by a pudgy youth of twelve or fourteen years, whose handlight was tinted orange by the flames behind me. "Who are you?"

"The Lady is gone and won't be back," I said. "The hospice is closed. Now, let us through."

Murmurs and exclamations and questions surged quickly into shouts and cries of dismay.

"I know who this is." A bull-necked man shouted above the horrified clamor. "He's the Fourth . . . D'Natheil's demon son . . . just look at him! Haven't you heard his description? He's killed us!"

"The Lord . . ."

"It's true. I've seen him here with the Lady!"

Some wailed in terror. A few fled. Others joined in the man's accusations, feeding their growing anxieties with information and rumor—some true, some ludicrous. The clamor grew, torches and handlights waving. Jen moaned softly and squirmed in my arms as if fighting to wake. I hefted her over my shoulder and gripped her waist with one arm. First one then another of the crowd moved toward us. A stone ripped through the air from the back of the crowd and glanced off my cheekbone. Hostile enchantment softened my knees like strong spirits on an empty stomach.

"Keep away!" I shouted, holding out my free hand as if five fingers could stay them. "You don't understand what you're dealing with." And this wasn't a good time for lengthy explanations.

The advance halted. Though most retreated a step or two, the boldest ones—a youngish man with a twisted shoulder, the woman who first questioned me and her young companion, the bull-necked man—stood their

ground. I tried to summon some kind of power. Though
the effort was like drinking dust, I eventually conjured
a wavering gray gleam about Jen and me. It would do
no more than cause a burst of sparks if anyone touched
it. "Move aside if you value your eyes."

"Where are Na'Cyd, F'Lyr, the others?" called the
curly-haired woman, standing her ground even as a gap
opened on my right. "They could take him down . . .
protect us."

"Come on . . . surround him . . . can't kill all of us."

". . . careful of the girl . . . she's an innocent. . . ."

"What do you want here?"

Somewhere a sword rasped on leather. Knives slipped
free of their sheaths. Some passed stones from the rock
garden from hand to hand, the sly motions rippling
through the mob. I edged to the right. Words and illu-
sions were not going to stay these people for long.

"Hold!" The command silenced the crowd and had
the men and women craning their necks to discover its
issuer, not because it was loud or harsh or portended
evil, but because of the sheer authority that weighted
each word. "For the office I once held, for the life and
service I have given to Gondai, hear me."

On my left a few people shifted aside to reveal a tall
man in a deep blue robe, his fair hair gathered into a
silver clip at his neck. My father stepped slowly into the
circle of light, his back straight, though the line of his
shoulders was rigid and his face scribed with pain.

"Who are you?" demanded the bull-necked man.

"Can you fools not see?" A small man with a twisted
back pushed his way out of the crowd on my right. Gripping his walking stick with two hands, he lowered himself onto one knee. "My lord Prince D'Natheil. All
praise to Vasrin Shaper, who has laid down a Way that
leads you back to Gondai in our time of need." Sefaro.

A murmuring tide of astonishment, wonder, and recognition washed through the mob. A few others genuflected or stepped back, marveling at the apparition of
one they believed five years dead. Where was my
mother?

My father held up his hand to quiet them. "This man before you is indeed my son," he said. "And it is no accident that the enchantments that shielded us from our pain—yes, mine as well as yours—have been shattered by his hand. But his power and his destiny are far beyond our control. We cannot hold him here, and I would not have your griefs compounded by violence this night. His concerns are elsewhere, so I believe he will not harm us further. Let him pass."

I felt the strength of his will holding him together. He could not smile. He could scarcely speak. Yet the faces of those around him changed. Apprehension, uncertainty, but no fear. Many of the people drew close to him, some with defiant faces as if to protect him, some with an awed trust, as if seeking the safety they had always believed rested in his arm.

But I was not comforted. Why didn't he tell them the truth? Why didn't he use his authority to tell these people that I had saved them once and was willing to do so again? Did he really think I wanted to hurt them? Gods, did he believe D'Sanya's charge that I wanted to kill him? I had counted on him understanding the imperative to destroy the oculus . . . forgiving me. Surely . . .

I searched his stern face for one hint of softness, one flicker of acknowledgment, of comprehension. But my father's expression revealed nothing . . . which revealed everything.

My spine stiffened. I backed away from the waiting Dar'Nethi, moving slowly toward a widening gap in the crowd, where the thick-growing rosebushes made it awkward to stay close to one's fellows. My eyes roamed the mob, straining to pick out faces and forms in the shifting light. Somewhere I would find the answer.

There! F'Lyr, the scar-faced stableman who wore a brass lion about his neck, stood with two shadowy figures at the back of the crowd near the gap. Three Zhid ready to close off the escape route before I could get through. Now I understood my father's ambiguity. He well knew the choice waiting for me at the edge of the shadows. My yearning to hear my father declare before

witnesses that I was not the destined instrument of the
Lords was a matter of no importance whatsoever. I
would have to prove the truth or falsity of that prophecy
for myself.

In an instant I considered all that had happened in
the last weeks and months, all that I feared about myself
and the doom facing Avonar, all that I knew of D'Sanya
and the others who would be involved in the dreadful
hours to come. The wrongness of the world tore at my
spirit as fiercely as the flames ravaged D'Sanya's gracious house and garden. By some whim of fate or gods,
I was the nexus, the center of everything, but I was dry
and empty, and my father was dying and every being in
three worlds was at risk. I would not survive another
hour without power or understanding. The evidence was
laid out in front of me and all I had to do was put it
together in the span of three heartbeats. And to do so,
I would have to go back; I would have to remember.

My hesitation emboldened the crowd. "If the hospice
is closed, I'm a dead man anyway," said the bull-necked
man, now brandishing a fence rail.

Others moved forward, rocks and knives in hand. I
retreated a few more steps, poured the dregs of my
power into my gray curtain to give me one extra moment
to accomplish what I needed to do. The slight body in
my arms stirred. I gripped her hard to hold her still and
wished fervently that I could keep her safe. Jen had told
me that memory had no power but what the soul chose
to make of it. Why was I so tempted to believe her,
when for so long I had doubted those infinitely wiser
than either of us? Perhaps it was some magic hidden
deep in her. Perhaps it was because for the first time in
my life, I cared about living another day. I had only
begun to taste possibility.

Wishing Jen were awake to tell me in her brittle tutor's manner that I did it right, I breathed deep and
embraced the distorted world, along with the wholeness
of past and present, what I was and what I had been,
what I had seen and done and felt, both good and
evil . . . everything I/we remembered.

The closures of my mind wrenched and tore. Images and voices and sensations both wonderful and terrible surged exuberantly into my conscious mind like a dammed river allowed at last to fill its natural channel. My bones screamed and my flesh cried out, as if I had changed form and dimension, stretched and bent into something else altogether. Power surged into my arms, pushed on my ribs, and scalded my eyes.

Sooner than I could have imagined, pain stripped away the veils of hope and desire and uncertainty, leaving only the stark ruin of truth. And in that startling moment, I understood which of the molds in D'Sanya's lectorium was significant and I knew what D'Sanya had done. Three worlds were in my hand. Truly, there was no choice to be made.

"Be off to your long-awaited grave, Tormentor's Heir, Prince of Dead Men, Sovereign of Desolation!" I screamed at my father as I retreated briskly toward the gap. "You are correct that my power and purposes are beyond your weakling fingers. Tonight as your pain devours you and tomorrow as the worms feed on your rotting flesh, you will know that I am indeed Lord of Destruction, Lord of Chaos!"

I shifted the woman higher on my shoulder, turned my back on my father and the gaping mob and a shadowy figure with red-brown hair who now stood at the verge of the crowd watching me. I sped through the gap toward the three Zhid who stood waiting. "In the name of the Lords of Zhev'Na, take me to Gensei Kovrack," I said, thrusting the woman's limp body into F'Lyr's burly arms. "We have a city to destroy."

CHAPTER 34

Jen

The cellar walls were black with mold. And only a blind optimist would call the brown liquid seeping through the cracks in the stone floor and soaking into my filthy breeches "water." I let my handlight die. I didn't need to examine the sagging roof beams or the rotted grain sacks to know how many years had passed since any Dar'Nethi had maintained enchantments of dryness or health in this dismal place and thus how unlikely it was that anyone would find me here. F'Lyr said I was to be left here, nicely out of the way while Lord Dieste and his Zhid could see to the destruction of Avonar.

"I won't believe it," I shouted upward in the dark. "I'm not that stupid!"

Yes, Gerick was strange and powerful and kept nine-tenths of his thoughts and feelings locked away where not even Paulo could find them. But he had lived in me. He was *not* a Lord of Zhev'Na.

The moldy stone smothered my protest. No one was going to hear me. The clammy wall made me shudder as I leaned back on it.

The three Zhid—F'Lyr, Gen'Vyl, and Hy'Lattire, two men and one woman, once generous, kind servants of the hospice—had fended off the weak pursuit of the hospice staff and residents long enough to get us to the stable and mounted. They pulled my hands about F'Lyr's thick waist and bound them there, and then we rode hard up and over the ridge behind the hospice. I'd not been able to see much of anything with my nose jammed against F'Lyr's back. I'd let them believe I was still insensible in hopes of hearing something enlightening. Not that listening had done me much good.

Whenever the Zhid began to question—Why had the young Lord not revealed himself earlier? Why had he courted the Lady? Why had he destroyed the oculus?— Gerick snapped at them to be silent. "Do not presume to judge my purposes. Just get me to your commander."

The sun was not yet up when we rode down into the camp. But I could smell the dawn, and the dry air was the color of ash. A peek from under my drooping eyelids revealed a few tents and fifteen or twenty men and horses tucked into deeply seamed foothills, the rubble-and boulder-strewn slopes where Grithna Ridge met the Wastes.

A tall, lean warrior with thin red hair combed back from a high forehead stood waiting for us. Diagonally across his chest he wore an elaborately worked leather strap, the mark of a gensei—a general in the warrior legions of Zhev'Na. An ascetic face, sharp-edged and hard like the granite crags. His lips curled in anger and suspicion. I did not need to examine either his costume or his eyes to know him Zhid.

"I know not how to greet you after our last encounter," he said, as Gerick reined in at the boundary of the encampment. "I know not what you are. No master of Zhev'Na would permit his loyal servants' strength to be stripped away by a woman who was once a slave—the Tormentor's brat, at that."

Gerick dismounted easily. He gave his horse's reins to Gen'Vyl, then clasped his hands behind his back and strolled toward the red-haired man as if he had come here for a month's guesting. Though still wearing torn and bloodstained clothes, his body moved with the confident grace of a king born. He turned his head as if to survey the camp, fixing his attention on the red-haired Zhid only when he stood directly front of him. Then, in a movement so swift I could almost feel the air shatter, he grabbed the neck of the Zhid's tunic and twisted it tightly, forcing the man to bend his knees and drawing the Zhid's face close to his own.

"I am your Lord," he said in a voice that could have frozen the southern oceans. "Your master. The Three of Zhev'Na chose me to be their Fourth, their instrument, their Destroyer. Their glory resides in me, and your proper greeting is to pay me the homage and obedience they demanded of you for seven centuries. Do otherwise and I will draw your bowels out through your ears. Or shall I throttle your heart once more to still your insolent tongue?" Gerick's left hand pointed at the ground. "Kneel and look into my eyes, and then tell me again of your beliefs."

The red-haired Zhid dropped to his knees, whether from fear, from deference, or from lack of breath, I could not determine. No, not deference. His nostrils flared as he raised his eyes to meet Gerick's. For a moment the air felt as if the sun had winked out, never to return. Then the Zhid fell prostrate in the dirt.

From the quivering stiffness of F'Lyr's spine my custodian, at least, had no further doubts. I forced myself to remain slumped against his sweaty back, keeping my jaw slack and my eyelids open only a slit.

The gensei's groveling apologies came with gasps and shudders. "We could not see your plan, Lord Dieste," he babbled. "We heard so many tales of the last day— the day of our shame. Tales of your death. Of your treachery . . ."

"On the day my brothers and sister fell, I was weakened as well," Gerick said, "and forced to go into hiding. But let me be clear. I *will* have my vengeance and retake my inheritance. I've spent these years regaining my strength and studying my enemies, and now I am ready to reveal myself to both Dar'Nethi and Zhid. Patience and stealth. Subtlety in hatred. Thoughtful vengeance. Are these not the virtues you taught me in the camps of Zhev'Na, Gensei Kovrack?"

"Aye, Lord. I beg you allow me to serve you. Command me, Lord."

Gerick nudged the Zhid's shoulder with his boot. "Before I can regain my rightful place, we must recapture the Tormentor King's spawn."

"Of course, Lord Dieste." Kovrack squirmed up to his knees. "But she serves us well as she is. She made the avantirs for us, and imbues them with such power that we can use them ourselves. When you destroyed the oculus, it fueled our doubts. . . ."

"I will tolerate no rival to my power." Gerick spoke to all the Zhid who had gathered behind their gensei. Though his back was to me now, I could see the progress of his gaze as it roved over the cadre—a quailing shiver and then a stiffened spine as his notice passed to the next warrior. "The Dar'Nethi witch has attuned her devices to her own enchantments, not mine, so I will destroy them all and have her begin again . . . in *my* service. Our first priority is to take her captive. Your inept attempt in Avonar forced me to kill five of my own warriors. Such incompetence will reap an unhappy reward should it occur again. Once the woman is mine, she will cast me a new oculus and new eyes, and this world will recognize its master. Now, show me the avantirs."

Gerick ordered F'Lyr and his two companions to remain as they were and vanished into the largest tent. Several Zhid came and went. One scurried away and returned with an armload of scrolls; another fetched a dark bundle that might have been clothes. An endless hour of frightening nothing. The sun burned off the dawn haze and roasted my back. F'Lyr had to fight to steady his restless horse. When a woman warrior carried two frosted pitchers past us and into the tent, I could not suppress a moan.

"Are you awake, girl?" F'Lyr twisted his head around, but couldn't have seen much.

"She must've taken quite a whack on the head," said Hy'Lattire from behind me. "Don't know why he keeps her." Her spirit was no warmer than that of any other Zhid.

"He told me that he desired her to be his first collaring." F'Lyr's voice rumbled through his sweaty back. "She was his first collaring when he came to Zhev'Na, he said, and she squealed so pleasantly. Says it will repay her for her incessant whining."

I squeezed my eyes shut and did not move again.

The day grew hotter. I was horribly thirsty and dozed off several times. Having received no permission from their Lord, the three Zhid did not drink either.

When Gerick stepped out of the tent, he was dressed in sleek black—a sleeveless shirt, tight breeches, and knee-high boots. A light cloak fell from his shoulders, and gold armrings glinted in the sunlight. One by one, every Zhid in the camp came to pay him homage, kneeling before him to kiss his scarred palms, pledging blood and bone to his cause.

"It is time to rebuild Zhev'Na," he said when they stood in ranks again, Gensei Kovrack at their head. "Time to grind this Avonar to dust. Time to obliterate the Bridge of Bondage once and forever."

The Zhid cheered. Gerick did not acknowledge them, but motioned sharply to Kovrack.

The gensei drew a circle in the dust with his sword. Faster than I could believe, Gerick had created a quivering rectangle in the air. How had he recovered so much power since we had destroyed the oculus? I shivered. Perhaps he was just getting better at it.

"Send out word," Gerick said to Kovrack. "I will see every commander and adjutant before nightfall. Senat and Felgir first. Then will I play the music of the avantirs and set the hounds of war on the Lady and her minions. Remember who commands you now."

With a motion of his hand he raised a whirlwind of dust, and the camp, the Zhid, and the wasteland vanished behind us.

I hadn't believed a word Gerick had said. I wouldn't. I couldn't, because I could see no way for Gondai to survive if he had betrayed us after all.

We had ridden through the portal from the bright sun through the blinding dust storm into a dim, cavernous space near a river. The smell of fish and river wrack had overpowered even F'Lyr's steaming aura of stable sweepings and unwashed flesh and my own ripeness. I had been almost grateful when they dropped me into this slime pit before I could blink the grit from my eyes. I didn't want to see where we were.

I drew up my knees and wrapped my arms around them, shivering as the dripping seepage marked the passing time. Surely not Avonar. Surely Gerick had not opened a Zhid portal into the City of Light. . . .

Creaking floorboards above my head jogged me awake. No way to know how long I'd been asleep. Groggy, the bump on my head throbbing in time with my sluggish heart, I sat up, wiped the slime off my cheek, and cast a handlight. I didn't want to be blinded if they opened the trap above my head. But after a while, I let the light dim again. Evidently more important business than me was going on up there.

Heavy footsteps came and went. I paced the length and breadth of the cellar, trying to work out the cramps and stiffness, trying to be ready for whatever came. But it only served to make me feel filthier when I sat down in the slime again.

As the hours passed, my light faded completely, and the chill and damp became one with my bones. Shimmering at the edge of remembrance was the image of a block-like structure—a warehouse?—nestled on the bank of the Sillvain, tucked between the stone support pillars of a graceful bridge in the heart of Avonar. First Bridge, I thought. Perhaps Second.

I could neither recall the significance of the place nor estimate what brought it to mind just now. Perhaps it was the damp or the river. Perhaps it was the building above my head. Yet I hadn't seen the outside of my prison. The portal lay inside this building. More likely my brain was bent from all the mental contortions of the past two days. I was fortunate not to be a raving idiot after touching an oculus.

I lay on my side, curled up in a knot with my head

buried in my arms, sick with hunger and the stink. When the image of a spindly tower at one corner of the Heir's palace settled itself in my head like a gently falling leaf, I sat up again, my heart picking up speed. *All right*, I thought. *I see it.*

Ven'Dar. The name floated in the dank darkness like a new constellation along with an overpowering urgency.

I was incapable of mind-speaking, but that wouldn't prevent someone else from speaking to me in that way or listening to what I might be thinking. Though truly, what I perceived was not so much direct speech, which could always be detected by other capable sorcerers, as occasional, concentrated reflections of another person's thoughts, something like the sun-glints off a gold coin flipped in the air. I couldn't even be sure the contact was intentional. I closed my eyes and made sure I left no barriers to further communication.

A short while later I envisioned a ruin—broken columns and walls set in the heart of a maze of overgrown shrubs, broken arbors, and ponds that held only weed-choked puddles. A deserted bathhouse by the look of it. The view of Mount Siris just behind the structure located it in the neglected lower-east quarter of Avonar. *Portal*.

This image was immediately supplanted by another, this time a quiet shrine where, in ancient times, a massive representation of Vasrin had been carved directly into the white cliffs. Some centuries past, a section of Avonar's city wall had been moved outward to encompass the shrine, so rather than creating a straight barrier across a gradual, treeless slope, the wall took several awkward turnings through a forested gorge and up a steeper, rocky hillside to join the older wall. Even one unschooled in warfare could see the danger of the shadowed gorge and the cliffside looming so close to a defensive bulwark. *Compromised*.

The bustle of activity in the room above my head lessened, replaced by the pervasive pressure of enchantment. Whatever this working, it left me as sick and anxious as the oculus had. Now I understood Gerick's description of his perceptions: the world felt profoundly wrong.

An hour passed. No more images intruded on my thinking, only doubts. It was well known that mold, rot, and unmaintained enchantments carried fumes and diseases that could cause madness. But I preferred to think that someone had been trying to tell me something important. Though I recognized nothing of Gerick in these visions, I clung fiercely to the belief that he was responsible.

Truly, what more sign of madness did I need? Despite every protestation of the past weeks, the gnawing terror in my belly was not solely care for Avonar. Back at the hospice when we were joined, when he took the burden of destroying the oculus from me, he had spoken my name. He had given life and meaning to those common syllables as if they defined something unique and important.

I pounded a fist on my head to jar my thoughts into sensible paths. Crazed or not, I needed to describe these visions to someone who knew what to do with them. I cast my handlight as bright as I could manage and began to hunt for a way out of the cellar.

The cracked stone walls offered no escape, so I quickly turned my attention to the ceiling. My captors had used no ladder or stair to deposit me here, but dropped me through a hole in the floor. The rusty hinges and the outline of the square trapdoor were easily visible. A man of average height stretched on his toes could have touched them.

I dragged the sacks of moldy grain into a pile underneath the door, climbed up, and stretched high. The tips of my fingers brushed the hinges. Then one of the sacks gave way. I lost my footing and crashed facedown on the disgusting floor. Three times I restacked the stinking mound, but the rotted sacks disintegrated underneath me. I never even touched the door again.

"May holy Vasrin unshape your balls, *arrigh scheiden*," I yelled, kicking the pile until the blighted grain became a putrid muck on the seeping floor.

Trampling footsteps overhead sent me cowering to the corner. But the door didn't open. Instead, as if the contents of my skull had been excised to make room, an explosion of images slammed into my head one after another: a vast chamber . . . a dome of light . . . soaring columns of pearl gray and rose . . . a towering beast of bronze . . . a curtain of blinding white fire with a woman—D'Sanya—standing inside it. No sooner had these resolved themselves into a coherent whole than came the holocaust—fire and death, the columns cracked and fallen, the white fire quenched in blood, the glory shattered. The walls crumbled and fell in a deafening thunder and beyond I saw Avonar a reeking ruin. Trailers of smoke rose from charred rubble into a sooty sky. In all this vast expanse of horror only the bronze beast remained whole.

In moments, the vision was gone, winked out as if it had never been. The footsteps died away; the enchantment that had made my teeth hurt evaporated; and I sagged to the fouled floor, sobbing in the empty silence. The world was going to end because I was a wretched runt.

I might have fallen asleep again. It was difficult to tell in the endless dark. But a soft scrabbling noise above my head prompted me to my feet, as much so I wouldn't feel a rat scutter across me as with any further pretense of being prepared to defend myself. Though I saw no light, a soft infusion of fresh air set my heart racing.

A muffled grunt, a slow sliding of wood on wood, and a dark shape invaded my prison and came to rest on the pile of grain sacks. A ladder. Even if the stealthy approach had not signaled an ally, I would not have hesitated to scurry up. Better to die in the open than in such a foul hole.

Lungfuls of clean, damp air and a firm hand were waiting for me when I emerged from the hole and crawled onto a wooden floor. The hands indicated I should help pull the ladder up. Once we had the heavy thing up, my shadowy companion took it away. I carefully closed and latched the hinged trap that had held me prisoner. The room was large, long and narrow, and at one end thin strips of gray light outlined shutters. Before I could determine what were the dark columnar shapes that filled most of the place like crude statuary, my rescuer returned.

"Who—?"

"Shhh." The hand gripped mine, and we sped through a maze of stacked boxes and crates toward the end of the room away from the shutters. My companion cracked open the door and peered out, then pulled it open a little further. Outlined in the lingering gleam of a rainy twilight, dressed in a man's breeches and shirt that were too big for her, was the Lady Seriana.

She closed the door carefully behind us and motioned me to follow. We sped across a muddy flat to a set of wooden steps, half buried in mud and the soggy debris of a riverbank. As I followed her down the steps toward the rush and slurp of the dark ribbon of water, I glanced back and saw the front of the low, block-like building we had just abandoned. It was tucked between two thick stone pillars that supported an arched bridge. Exactly as I had seen in my vision. And though the evening was eerily quiet and no starlike lights adorned the trees and buildings outlined against the night, we were most certainly in Avonar.

An armed man, strolling around the building, paused and turned his head our way. I ducked.

Lady Seriana led me a short way upriver to a spot where the swirling water had undercut the high riverbank. "I think we can talk here," she said, keeping her voice low as she crouched under the bank. "I'd hoped to get you out hours ago, but only in the last hour did they leave the place to just the one guard. You're uninjured? They had to carry you. . . ." Her words poured out as if she couldn't get them out fast enough.

"I'm not injured, but very confused," I said. "How ever did you come to be here? And how did you know where I was? Aimee told us you'd been arrested and confined to the hospice."

"I followed you from the hospice to the Zhid camp,

and slipped through the portal in the dust storm. When I came through, Gerick was having them take you off the horse and put you down the hole. None of the Zhid saw me."

"My lady, do you know what he's doing? Were you able to see those who came here today?"

To make out details in the failing light was difficult; Lady Seriana's eyes were like dark blots. But the strain in her voice told me a great deal. "Twenty or thirty different people came here by ones and twos, most of them men. All of them armed. I couldn't see their eyes, but they gave me the feeling . . . so cold . . . I'm sure they were Zhid. They left the same way in ones and twos. When I thought all of them were gone, I peeked through the window. Ten or twelve men remained, bent over a bronze thing the size of a tabletop—"

"An avantir." Of course, that was the enchantment I'd felt. Here in Avonar. And I had thought I couldn't feel sicker. "The red-haired man wearing a gensei strap across his chest. He was there?"

"Gensei?" She pushed her wet hair out of her face. "Gods, yes. That's what the belt was. I couldn't remember. Yes, the red-haired man was there. And two more with the same kind of belt. Almost all of the others wore the oval badges. . . ."

"Wargreves, then." So many officers. Not just Zhid rabble.

"I couldn't watch," she said. "Every moment I stayed close, I felt sick. Those men—and Gerick, I suppose—must have left by way of the portal, as I didn't see anyone else ride out."

Lady Seriana's hands were long and slender. Though scars and rough patches evidenced her years of hard work, age had not yet coarsened their shape or withered the skin. But as we spoke she twined her fingers into such a knot that the blood completely deserted them, leaving them little more than fleshless bones.

"Jen, I've found out something dreadfully important about the Lady, and I've not been able to tell anyone. Last night, when we realized what had happened to the oculus, Karon and I assumed . . . hoped, I suppose . . . that Gerick was responsible, that he was alive and close by and doing what he thought was necessary to remove her threat. Karon insisted I find him and tell him this information, no matter what I had to do. But before I could go, we heard the commotion, and Karon felt the violence coming and knew he had to intervene, while I found Gerick. But Gerick went off with these Zhid. . . ."

"You say no Zhid saw you. Did *Gerick* see you, my lady? Could he possibly have known you were here?"

"I believed so at first. I thought he raised the dust storm so I could follow. Now, I just don't know."

A damp wind gusted along the river, making me wish for my long-lost cloak. The rills and curls as the water raced around the rocks to join the slower main current shone white against the dark water. "Tell me, my lady, did your son touch your mind today?"

"Mind-speak?" She shook her head wearily as she rested her forehead on the knot of her hands. "No. I didn't hear him."

"Not speech. I don't think he dares mind-speak, not if he's determined to deceive the Zhid. They bend to his power, but they don't trust him completely as yet. Listen, my lady. While I sat in that cellar, I saw several vivid images: this building and another one where, I think, the Zhid have a portal to infiltrate the city; a section of the wall where Avonar's defenses are dangerously weak; and an ancient tower where Ven'Dar might be imprisoned. I think Gerick wants me to free Ven'Dar. Ven'Dar could call in people to block the portals, if I tell him where the Zhid assault will come. Then, if Paulo and Aimee can bring Je'Reint and reinforcements . . ."

As I gave her a brief history of the past days, my mind raced to sort out Gerick's plan. He was taking charge of the Zhid assault, knowing he could not prevent it, but hoping to turn the tide somehow. He had made sure we knew our vulnerabilities, but what more could he do to affect the outcome of the assault? He couldn't divert them with flawed strategies. The Zhid commanders were experienced in war and would know. He couldn't destroy the avantir; if they had more than one, they would kill him and use the others. The moment he betrayed them openly, he was a dead man. . . .

I had to be missing something. *Dead man . . . dead man . . .* The words nagged at me. That's what he had done when he was sixteen—offered his death to thwart the Lords. But he had relied on his father to finish the job five years ago, and this time he had no one to count on but himself.

"Did you see any image, any hint of what he might have in mind for you, my lady?"

"Perhaps . . . I don't know. I imagined you in that awful place under the floor. I couldn't leave you there"—her voice shook, and she pressed her hands harder against her forehead—"but then all I could think of was Karon dying. Alone. Oh, gods, such horrible things Gerick said to him . . . and I know it must be to some purpose . . . I've always had faith in Gerick . . . I still have faith . . . but it is so hard . . . And this time I can't see any way to help him."

I put my arms around Lady Seriana as she fought the sobs that racked her strong shoulders. "Your son is still what you believe, my lady, what your faith has made him. And you've seen how mule-headed I am, not at all easy to convince. He destroyed the hospice oculus because he feared it was channeling the Lady's power to the avantir and thus strengthening the Zhid. He saw no other choice. But I know how difficult it was for him. And even so, he insisted that his own will accomplish the deed, taking the guilt on himself, not leaving it to me. How many people in any world would do such a kindness at such a terrible time? Few that I've known. And he's gone with the Zhid"—the echoes of my own words illuminated the truth—"because he wants to stay alive! He needs time to recover his power and a way to survive until he can confront D'Sanya. His death will not protect us this time, but his life just might."

I pulled her head to my breast and let her weep there in the dark where no one could see. Rain dripped on the muddy bank, a few drops here and there, quickly accelerating to a steady downpour. Time pressed.

"So. I think it's clear," I said, when no longer able to resist necessity. "Gerick wants you to go back to the hospice. To give his father his love and to assure him that he will do whatever is necessary to save Avonar. The thought of the two of you together will sustain him—the thought of your love for him and faith in him. I won't abandon Gerick, my lady. I swear it. Tell me your information and then we'll find you a way back to your prince, if we have to abduct a Preceptor and force her to conjure you a portal."

We couldn't find anyone to conjure a portal. Aimee had been right about that. Even old Ce'Aret, the retired Preceptor so feeble she could not sit a horse, had gone off to Astolle to stand by our warriors with enchantment and determination. But we did find Mae'Tila, an assistant to the Healer T'Laven, gathering a supply of newly formulated medicines to take to the northern battlefront. Lady Seriana, evidencing no further sign of her breakdown on the riverbank, persuaded the anxious, skeptical Mae'Tila to spirit her out of the city in her well-protected convoy. Seri would leave the medical convoy at the Gaelie road and head for Grithna Vale alone. I drew her a map, so she could not mistake the way, but I didn't worry about her. No one who had heard her story could doubt her capability.

An hour after the small, heavily armed convoy passed through the east gate of Avonar, the rain started up again. I ducked under the colonnade on the outer approaches to the palace and pulled up the hood of Mae'-Tila's spare cloak, sorely regretting the prospect of getting damp and filthy so soon after donning my first clean garment in weeks. As I surveyed the patrols guarding the palace gates, I swallowed the last bite of the sausage tart I had snatched from T'Laven's larder and began to believe my legs might hold up under me for another hour.

In the adventure stories I loved to read, the heroes seemed able to go days at a time without food, drink, or sleep. They knew instinctively what to do next and what spells would get them past every locked door and into every treasure vault. Not for the first time, I wondered how I had managed to get involved in Gerick's life. If I didn't eat, I collapsed. I cowered in corners, whimpered at the slightest discomfort, and fell asleep when I should be escaping or standing watch. I couldn't even climb up his father's garden wall. And I had been paralyzed for the past hour trying to decide what to do next.

Was I betraying my own people because I had never heard a man speak my name as Gerick had spoken it when he was inside me? And if I held to this mad belief in him, how was I to do what he asked of me—get past the palace gates and release Ven'Dar? This astonishing information about D'Sanya . . . how was I to pass it along to the man planning the Zhid assault on Avonar?

Disowned. Disinherited. The implications of Lady Seriana's news were monumental. D'Sanya had been purposely removed from the legitimate line of succession, and her anointing had undone that removal, returning her power over the matter of the Breach and the structure of the Bridge. Gerick believed her innocent of ill intent, but I shared his parents' conviction that he needed to know these things before he confronted her. Yet even if I knew where to find Gerick, I could never get near him. Either the Zhid would kill me for being a Dar'Nethi spy or the Dar'Nethi would kill me for being a Zhid spy.

So I had decided to go after Ven'Dar first, and hope that he could contact Gerick.

I drifted from one column to another. On either side of the wide steps and gated portico of the formal entry into the palace precincts were the more businesslike gates, where riders and carriages were admitted to the inner courtyards. And beyond these "riders' gates" to right and left extended the curved colonnades like open arms embracing the vast expanse of the public gardens and markets in eye-pleasing symmetry and grace.

At the ends of the colonnades nearer the palace, single rows of columns fronted curved sections of the actual palace walls, which were carved in relief with scenes from history and legend. But at the point where the walls angled away from the marketplace, the mosaic-tiled walkways became open colonnades. Sheltered gardens, fountains, and walkways filled the space between the receding walls and the fine buildings like the libraries and performance halls that had grown up around the palace. I had never seen the gardens, markets, or colonnades so empty, so early of an evening. Plenty of guards, though. No fewer than fifteen heavily armed men patrolled the approaches to the riders' gates and at least that many more were on the steps before the central gates. Who knew how many others stood atop the walls and in enchanted spaces invisible to the untrained eye?

I arrived at the point where the right-side open colonnade yielded to the palace wall. A few hundred paces away, a guard passed through a rainy pool of torchlight. I hugged the wall and slipped from column to column, approaching the gates, pondering frantically how I was to get past the extra guards, not to mention the protective enchantments and the locked gates themselves.

A thunderous explosion split the night, making the tiles beneath my feet tremble. Flashes of light reflected from the pale stone of the columns and walls. At first I thought these but a violent escalation of the storm. But the guards pointed off to the south, and I peered around the column back toward the lower city. There, where the ramparts of Avonar had held fast against the Lords for a thousand years, the sky had burst into shimmering blue-and-white flame. The wall defenses had been triggered.

"What are you doing, Gerick?" I mumbled, aghast. I had never expected him to go this far with his deception. "Give me some time."

The alarm pierced the rumbling thunder in gut-twisting suddenness and spread like fire in a haymow.

Trumpets blared from the palace walls. Bells rang from the palace towers, soon echoing from clock towers and watchtowers, from great houses and schools. Atop the wall towers that rose behind the opposite colonnade, fonts of scarlet flame burst into life—balefires. Soon they would burn on every tower and wall throughout Avonar and the Vales as they had not since victory quenched them five years ago.

I had not witnessed that signal of Prince D'Natheil's victory over the Lords, but I well remembered the day—the day the thunderous bellows of the Lords had sent their slaves and servants cowering into cracks and corners lest our bodies be flayed by their anger, the day the brittle towers of Zhev'Na cracked and shattered over our heads, the day grown men had wept and women danced as we slowly emerged from the rubble and realized we were free. And now the balefires were lit again. The scar on my neck burned as if ignited by the warning.

The right-side riders' gate burst open and a troop of horsemen rode out at a gallop, racing across the deserted parks and streets of the central city. At their head, astride her gray stallion, rode the Princess of Avonar, clad in silver ring mail, her yellow hair flying. She raised her sword, and it blossomed with blue flame, causing her band of riders to burst out in a cry of joy and defiance. Two bands of infantry followed them out of the gate, marching double time.

I sped through the colonnade, sacrificing stealth for speed, hoping to slip through the gates before they were closed. But I was too slow and too late. The portcullis had dropped, and the iron-banded gates slammed shut before I reached the last column. Guards held pikes and lances at the ready; whatever lethargy had settled over them on a cool rainy evening had been well banished. I sagged against the smooth, damp column, banging the back of my head against the unyielding stone. What now?

The tower I'd envisioned in the warehouse cellar was not one of the great defensive works of the Heir's citadel, which stood as lumbering giants about the palace perimeter. This one was as slender as a spindle and had a slightly bulbous top with a steep-pitched conical roof of slate. The gray conical roof indicated the tower was part of the original structure of the palace in the north-east corner, and the unusual shape should be easy to spot.

As I retraced my steps down the colonnade and took a shortcut through the sheltered gardens behind it, Avonar rose to war. Peering down Mount Eidol between the Mentors' Library and the Hall of Music, I glimpsed the lights of the lower city flaring bright, and at every succeeding opening I saw lanes alive with boys collecting horses, with armed men and women loading wagons with water barrels and bags of sand, with running messengers, identified by their bright blue handlights.

How many defenders remained in the city? How many of D'Sanya's Restored held positions on the walls? How many of those had met with Gerick in the riverside warehouse preparing to betray us?

I ran.

CHAPTER 35

Once I rounded the southeast tower of the palace walls, I threaded my way through narrow lanes of fine shops, shuttered and deserted on this night, and across the slopes of the grassy apron that skirted the walls. The palace was built on the south-facing slopes of Mount Eidol, and the higher I climbed, the less uniform the walls, some sections built of the rose-colored, clean-dressed stone of recent centuries, some sections the age-mottled gray blocks of D'Arnath's time.

When I reached the northeast corner of the citadel, I was surprised to discover that the newer wall cut straight through this ancient quarter of the palace. The steepness of the apron slopes in this area had prevented the Builders from enclosing the entirety of the original structure with the thick new wall. Those parts left outside the wall had fallen into ruin. And among the collapsed walls and crumbling foundation stones stood the spindly tower like a bony finger with a swollen tip, pointing at the sky.

Though a scarlet balefire burned on the great wall, and palace guardsmen would certainly be patrolling the wall and the hulking northeast tower, the object of my search displayed no lights and no guards. This tower would have existed when D'Sanya was a child, far more imposing before the taller towers were built. Perhaps the tallest of its time. And certainly no potential rescuer would ever look for the dethroned Prince of Avonar in such a place, outside the palace enclosure. Everyone would assume he was confined in the prison block in the bowels of the palace itself.

Excited, I crept up the steep apron through a wet, grassy gully, staying low, avoiding any sound that might attract attention from the walls. Once atop the long hill, I caught my breath, then slipped from one ruined structure to another until I pressed my back to the side of the spindle tower that faced away from the palace. Raindrops dribbled down my nose and cheeks, and had long ago soaked through the back of Mae'Tila's cloak.

Though my feet were planted firmly on the ground, a glance upward left me a bit dizzy. The smooth, regular facing stones that had once sheathed the tower's exterior had long fallen away, leaving a mottled outer skin. Numerous stones protruded from this exterior like warts on a finger. Far above, the ruddy glow of balefires outlined the slight bulge of the top. I eased slowly around the base of the tower, marveling at its compact dimension and imagining the steepness of the stair cramped inside it. When I reached my starting point again without encountering a door, I was disconcerted.

I circumnavigated the tower base again, eyes upward this time, assuming that the doorway must be just above my head, its entry steps just broken away. When I returned to my starting point, my heart was in my throat. I leaned my head against the tower stones, closed my eyes, and let the rain pour over my face.

I had seen no doorway. But I *had* seen the way to get inside. The stones that protruded from the face of the tower were no Builder's whimsy, but an open stair— widely spaced nubs of stone that spiraled up the outside of the tower to the very top. If Ven'Dar was held prisoner in this tower, I would have to climb to get him out.

"Great Vasrin, do you amuse yourself in the eternal nights by devising these wretched tests?" I mumbled through gritted teeth as I set my foot on the first excruciatingly narrow, rain-slick step. "Or perhaps you think to force us to accept your existence." Surely godless fortune could produce no such perfect horrors.

I pressed my left shoulder to the rough wall, found a precarious handhold in the crumbling stone, and extended my left foot over the gap of open air to the next weathered protrusion, not daring to think what that gap would look like when I was five stories from the solid earth. Using my hand on the tower wall to brace me, I brought my right foot up beside the left. Again. Left foot forward—the part of the step nearest the wall would be the most solid. Secure a handhold. Push. Bring up the right foot. Again . . .

Twice I came near turning back. Once when I came to the first broken step, so narrow a stub that I could not rest both feet on it at once. I had to take an immediate second step with my right foot, trusting that the outer edge of the second stone would hold my weight while I brought the left foot up beside it, hoping not to get my boots tangled, praying that no watcher from the palace walls would see me perched there, paralyzed, for of course this had to happen on the side of the tower exposed to the balefire. The second time I faltered was when I came to the first missing step.

"No, no, no," I whispered, trying not to look down into the impossible void between my current position and the next relatively whole step, a span large enough that I would have to completely overbalance to shift my weight upward. "A plague on all Builders who believe their works are eternal."

I stood there for a year, it seemed, considering retreat, considering my purpose, trying to convince myself that I felt Prince Ven'Dar's life in that cold dead tower so this would not all go for naught. I wished for courage and longed for Gerick's strength and agility to shore up my own. *Give all of yourself*, I had told him. How pompous! How easy to give such advice when not staring your own demons in the face. And now Gerick was off with the Zhid, treading the very brink of his fears. And truly, he had a great deal more to fear than I did. Death was simple. Had he fallen from that brink or did he hold true?

I stretched my left foot toward the next worn stone, barely able to touch it with the ball of my foot. Pushing off with my left hand and right foot, I lunged forward and up. Though my stomach remained somewhere behind me, I got my weight over the step, fell forward, and grabbed the next step, bringing the right foot up beside the left.

Keeping my eyes narrowly focused on the next step, convincing myself that the handholds in the cracks and crevices could truly prevent a fall, I half climbed, half crawled up that devil's staircase in the dark and the rain. For every interminable moment, I told myself that if Gerick could make accommodation with his deepest terror to accomplish our purpose, then I, a daughter of Avonar, could surely deal with mine.

After a while, the cold rain washed all such considerations out of me. That staircase became my whole world.

My cold left hand clawed at the stone wall as I stared at the step in front of me, pressing my numb mind to tell me why things looked so different. I dared not turn my head to look in any direction but forward. The wind whipped my wet hair into my eyes. The next step was wider. Longer, too. The curve of the wall to my left was less pronounced. And the sound of the rain had changed. A lower, more solid sound than the pattering of drops on my head and shoulders. Holding absolutely still, as if the shift of an eyelash would upset my balance, I flicked my gaze upward. A roof! Emboldened, I flicked my gaze left. An armspan from my scraped knuckles was the threshold of a roughly rectangular opening.

Carefully, refocusing my eyes on the step, I moved my left foot up and forward. Shifted my hand to the edge of the door opening and stepped up. Clutching the ragged stone, and taking my first full breath in at least an hour, I peered into a tiny dark room. The three rectangular window openings had no shutters or panes, and gusts of rain splattered on the stone floor.

"If you tell me you've traversed the Skygazer's Stair to rescue me," said the hoarse voice from the interior, "I shall sing your praises from every mount in Gondai."

The poor man was drenched and shivering, chained to the wall with a steel shackle about one ankle, his limbs bound so tightly with dolemar rope that I doubted he'd been able to make use of the wine flask or the basket of sodden bread that sat on the floor an arm's length away.

"Best save your singing until we've got you down from this place, Your Grace," I said, as I dropped to my knees and set to sawing at the tough silver cord about his scored wrists.

"You're not just an illusion, telling me what I want to hear? Last I heard I was no longer anyone's prince. More disgrace than grace, one might say."

"I've a number of things to tell you that you're not going to want to hear. You might rather I were an illusion." I freed his hands, throwing the scraps of rope across the room.

He shook his hands and worked his fingers, smiling and grimacing all at once. "Ah, no, mistress. You are a most welcome reality. If you had come by way of a portal, the Lady's enchantments would have prevented your seeing me. So even if anyone had thought of searching this place, it would have done me no good. I was beginning to fear I would be but more dust in these crevices before some adventurous child attempted the stair and . . ."

He suffered a coughing spasm that he finished off with a huge sneeze before he could go on. I handed him the wine flask and applied my knife to another set of bindings.

After a long drink, he pushed the dripping hair from his eyes and rubbed his wrists. "Some weeks ago the perceptive Mistress Aimee told me a story of a young woman of strong opinion who had arrived at her house uninvited and left it as a most valuable ally, astonishing even Lady Seriana into speechless wonder. Might you possibly be this person of startling reputation?"

His kind humor held no trace of mockery. Though I could not forget that this man had ruled Avonar for five years and walked D'Arnath's Bridge, I felt no awe in his presence—not as I had when Gerick's father had parted the crowd at the hospice. Perhaps because I still thought of Prince D'Natheil as a dead hero come to life

in our need. Perhaps because Prince Ven'Dar wore only
a bedraggled dressing gown. "They arrested me straight
from my bed," he said when he saw me staring at his
bare, dirty feet.

"For better or worse, I am that same Jen'Larie, a stubborn Builder's assessor who got involved in affairs far
beyond her capacities." I sawed at the turns of silver
cord about his legs as he pulled away the five turns of
rope I'd cut through at his thighs. "I'm sorry I've nothing warm or dry to offer you. Only bad news. And I
don't know enough about matters of succession to say
if you're still a prince or not."

"I believe I know the worst," he said, his smile fading.
"I saw the flares when the wall defenses triggered, and
I heard the bells. The balefires burn?"

"They do." I eyed the shackle that linked his left
ankle to the wall. "I'll try to pick this lock, but if it's
heavily enchanted . . ."

"No need to spend your time or effort," he said,
throwing off the last bindings I had cut from his legs.
"Give me a moment, and stand back a little." He laid a
hand on the lock and closed his eyes.

Of course. Now he was free of the dolemar, he could
call upon his talent and power.

I moved toward the doorway, then thought better of
it and stepped over to one of the three square window
openings. Better to have something to hold on to when
I looked out. But my discomforts soon paled to
insignificance.

Avonar was burning. Not just scarlet balefires or the
illusory blue-white sheets of triggered warnings, but
pockets of garish orange flames and billowing black
smoke throughout the lower city. At least three of the
Sillvain bridges were alight, and the armory—the great
warehouse where enchanted swords and ever-sharp
lances and pikes had been stored for generations—
burned as well. From the dark line of the city wall,
marked by the balefires on the five towers, pinpricks of
light—handlights or torches—spread southerly into the
night for as far as I could see, an ocean of warriors.

Though impossible to see at such a distance in the night and the rain, I knew the eyes of those warriors were cold and empty, and I knew the tide had only just begun to run.

"Hurry, my lord prince," I whispered. "For Avonar and Gondai, hurry."

Sprink! The sharp rattle of metal made me jump.

I helped him stand, a matter of such difficulty I began to wonder if I would have better spent my time finding Gerick or searching out someone else to help us.

"Ah, that stings," he said, resting his hands on his knees and letting his head droop. "It will take a little time to get the blood flowing in my more remote parts. Time you must use, brave Jen'Larie, to tell me how you found me, why you could possibly have doubts about my status, and what you know of the precarious state of this kingdom."

I told him briefly of Gerick's rescue, of destroying the oculus in the desert, and of the events at the hospice. He twisted and squatted and stretched as he listened, peppering me with incisive questions all the while. By the time I told of Lady Seriana's news, Ven'Dar stood beside me, and we watched a wedge of orange flame penetrate the boundaries of the city wall, an arrow aimed straight at the heart of Avonar. The last vision of Gerick's captivity was taking on reality right before us.

Warmth pulsed from Ven'Dar's compact body as he gripped the window edge and gazed out on the end of the world. "Stories say that ancients who came to Skygazer's Needle kept moonstones here that they would use to view the stars and planets and so unravel the strange movement of time and events. You tell me that young Gerick, once a Lord of Zhev'Na, leads the Zhid assault on Avonar, but has no intention of destroying us. And you say that D'Arnath's daughter . . . is not . . . and is leading our defense which *will* destroy us. I am perhaps or perhaps not a Dar'Nethi prince, though surely bereft of any subjects save a courageous young woman lacking power or talent. And we are relying on a blind woman and a mundane to bring us help because our own defenders are Zhid." He shook his head slowly, the creases of his forehead carved deep. "We could use the Skygazer's magic right now, could we not?"

I dabbed at my tears with the back of one hand. "Aye, my lord. But it's all true. I swear it."

Ven'Dar aborted another bout of coughing with another swallow of wine. "Every instinct of history names me fool and traitor to even consider your beliefs. If we're wrong . . . if this goes any further . . ." He waved the wine flask at the horror below us before passing it on to me.

"We're not wrong." I was soaked through to my bones, and the relentless wind slapped my wet cloak against my legs. The wine in the flask left a scalding trail down my gullet. But I would have wagered the lives of everyone I loved that what I said was true. "Gerick sent me to set you free. He's afraid, my lord. Afraid he is not enough to take her down alone. Afraid of what the attempt might do to him. His father is dying, and you are the only person with any power or influence who might choose to aid rather than kill him. He trusts you and desperately needs your help."

"Not as much as he trusts you, I think, Jen'Larie. Even if he is as I wish to believe, I don't know that I will be able to help him." He laid his hand on my shoulder. "Before anything, I must decide whether these 'visions' of yours are warning or misdirection and see to the defense of Avonar. He could not expect me to do otherwise. There will be a few souls left in the city that I can trust to carry out my orders. Once I've done what I can, we'll see if we can find young Gerick."

"I don't know exactly what he intends except to confront D'Sanya," I said, "but I know where he is." I pointed to the wedge of fire. At its apex flared a swirling column of blue-and-purple light. Had I the skills to feel and hear and sense enchantment at such a distance, I could not have been more certain.

"Tell me, my lord, what does the Chamber of the Gate look like?"

He looked at me quizzically. "A large circular room.

A dome of light supported by columns. A wall of white fire—enchantment to set your heart soaring . . ."

He didn't have to describe the rest. I had seen it in Gerick's last vision while sitting in the cellar.

Every Dar'Nethi child learned that if not for D'Arnath's Bridge, our power for sorcery would fade, because of the Breach that separated us from the mundane world. The mundane world, its passions pent up like the roiling ingredients in an Alchemist's glass, would succumb to chaos and violence. The Bridge was the link that bound us together, that allowed our worlds to nourish each other and that gave us hope for the day the Breach would be healed. Without it, the worlds would die.

As strange muted lightnings flared in the long-neglected southeast quarter of the city where a certain bathhouse stood, and a sinuous river of light began to flow out of the Zhid ocean toward a quiet shrine of Vasrin north of the city, the wedge of fire moved slowly, inexorably toward the Heir's palace. Toward the Gate. Toward the Bridge.

CHAPTER 36

Gerick

"The southeast portal has been opened, Lord Dieste, but the legion has not yet moved through it. Gensei Senat asks if he should prompt Wargreve Pavril?"

Somewhere to the east my warriors blasted another structure to rubble. The messenger's horse snorted and rolled its eyes, dancing backward and sideways, forcing the chinless warrior to shout even louder than the scattered combat and the roar of destruction required. My own mount had pretensions to the same kind of indiscipline. I quashed his hopes with a heavy hand on his mouth and insistent pressure on his flanks.

"Absolutely not," I said. "Pavril will answer his command at the proper time. Clearly he has not yet seen the triggering movement from the Dar'Nethi. Tell the gensei his Lord commands patience and attention to his own orders."

"Gensei Senat says his wing is almost in position, Lord."

"Then he will wear his skin for another hour, won't he?"

An explosion of blue-and-gold light and a sour gale from the advance curtailed further discussion. The messenger raced off toward the northwest, or perhaps his terrified steed decided on its own to return the way he'd come and the messenger just rode along.

Another blast of sound and light came from the eastern bank of the river, and a jagged crack split the sides of a stepped wall. Great shards of masonry crashed to the sloping ground, exposing a modest house with a wide porch—a fragile structure, sad and drooping in the continuing drizzle.

The porch exploded in orange flames. I choked up on the reins and shoved my heels deep in the stirrups. "Steady, beast," I said, through clenched teeth, trying to concentrate.

Beyond the visible combat another battle raged, warring enchantments that writhed in the ether, eroding flesh and spirit, driving warriors to desperation. On the rugged western bank of the river, a screaming man threw himself into the water, his skin glowing with yellow and silver sparks. If I remembered correctly, that particular enchantment felt like a rain of biting spiders.

My recalcitrant horse and I sat atop First Bridge, the grandest of the six promenades across the Sillvain. As it was entirely built of stone, incendiary spells posed little threat to me there. My bodyguards had riddled the structure with enchantments that would slow incoming arrows, were there any competent archers in Avonar to loft them, and would divert spears and lances from their courses, were there any Dar'Nethi fighters who could approach so near as to launch them. My retinue comprised three cadres—thirty warriors—under orders to protect me from intrusive enchantments. When I chose to move forward and my banner was no longer seen over the river, my warrior Zhid would crush First Bridge into pebbles. The power was in my word.

To wield such power, to see my banner flying again, was intoxicating. We'd had no sewing women to make the pennon, but an aide had conjured one as it had existed in Zhev'Na, its field black, its device very like the shield of D'Arnath: two golden lions rampant supporting the arch of D'Arnath's Bridge and the starry worlds it joined. But on the Fourth Lord's banner the arch was missing its center span, and in the gap stood a beast engulfed in flame, crushing the starry worlds in its hands. Lord Ziddari had said the beast was me.

Gensei Kovrack was doing his job well, driving our advance through the city virtually unhindered. Ironic that after a thousand years, all it had taken was a few of D'Sanya's Restored to open the gates of Avonar to the warriors of Zhev'Na. The Dar'Nethi defenses were in tatters. Without their walls to protect them, the shop-keepers, boys, and cowards could not face our soulless legions. When their commanders—more of the reverted Restored—turned on them, they broke and ran. All to the good. Wholesale death had never been our objective. Slaves yielded more lasting pleasure.

Only where D'Sanya led the defense did we have to fight. I had caught sight of her twice, racing from one end of the front to the other, beautiful and valiant, rallying her straggling, inexperienced fighters, conjuring barriers and shields of enchantment, expending her extraordinary power without thought for the cost. Somewhere in the morass of tangled feelings I embraced upon this night, I pitied D'Sanya.

All I had to do to counter her workings was to send word of the new obstacle to Gensei Felgir, one of my five senior commanders, who was ensconced safely on the ramparts of Mount Siris. He would touch the master avantir in the way I told him, and a hundred Zhid would veer from their present course, tear down whatever she had built, and savage those foolish enough to rely on it. She could not stay to defend her workings, as she had already moved on to counter another assault. No matter how strong, how powerful, or how valiant she was, the Lady could not fight the entire battle on her own, not when her own perverse sorcery gave life and coherence to her enemies through the avantir. Eventually we would wear her down. I was counting on that.

Against custom for a Zhev'Na high commander, I kept close behind the front line, moving from one watchpost to another as we advanced. The Three had never been physically present in combat. But I could not afford to be far away when D'Sanya broke and ran for the citadel. Though vast swathes of the city remained in

Dar'Nethi hands, our wedge of fire and destruction had reached almost to the grand command. We would have both palace and princess before midnight.

No Zhid questioned my loyalties any more. In less than a day, I had brought the plans of five contentious gensei together. Over the past few years, the five, strong enough and wily enough to survive the passing of the Lords, had quietly gathered the remnants of their legions into the deep and hidden places of Gondai's wastelands. The only circumstance that had preserved Avonar for so many months was the lack of a single will to lead them. If Kovrack had not been temporarily diverted by D'Sanya's flawed healing, he might have risen to it. But what they had needed was a Lord's will. Now Dar'Nethi were fleeing and Avonar was ours for the taking. If I were to unleash the warriors at my command—those here, those aimed at the northern Vales, those in the east—no blade of grass in all of Gondai would survive two days longer.

I spoke in Gensei Felgir's mind and had him touch my three armies through the avantir, reminding them that their only duty was my desire. I reiterated my simple strategy: First, I would take the palace of the Tormentor King and recapture his daughter; second, I would destroy his Bridge; and only then would I unleash the holocaust upon the Dar'Nethi and their land.

"Lord Dieste, Wargreve Raskow begs confirmation that you wish every house destroyed along the watercourses. His cadres cannot give chase to the escaping Dar'Nethi if they are required to attend these enchantments." The grevet with blood streaks on his arms stood with bowed head at my right.

I examined him closely. His fouled weapons were still warm. The full lips smirked at his own clever depravity in finding ways to trap and kill fleeing Dar'Nethi. His tongue had licked the salt of terror from Dar'Nethi skin not half an hour ago. Minor officers such as grevets always overvalued themselves. I closed my eyes and reached out through the avantir into the murky ocean of Zhid minds until I found the man . . . and I touched him.

His pupils dilated with horror, and he slapped a hand to his face. His scream emerged as only a gurgle in the sea of blood that gushed from his mouth.

"Tell the Wargreve Raskow . . . or show him, whichever you wish . . . how I rebuke those who question my commands. Remind him that with increasing rank my rebukes grow more severe."

Still mewling, the grevet backed away, raced down the span of the bridge, and vanished into the night.

And so I waited. Listened. Watched. It was almost time to move forward again.

An hour before midnight, the bells of Avonar stopped ringing. I stood at the foot of the sloping parkland fronting the Heir's palace, and signaled the aide who held my horse to bring the animal closer. I tested the girth straps and had the aide tighten them and shorten the stirrup height. An occasional rumble of the ground and frequent flashes signaled skirmishes to east and west of my position.

D'Sanya had withdrawn to the palace gates after her battle lines stretched too thin. I had forbidden my warriors to pursue for the moment, commanding our forces to solidify their positions on the corners before taking on the Lady. And so she and some hundred fighters had taken their stance before the gates of her father's citadel, sheathed in her blue-and-green fire. The archers atop the palace walls were skilled, diffusing the light about their positions so that we could not return fire accurately or see where they moved next. But they were forced into this tactic because their numbers were far too few for the expansive front of the palace. The archers were not a concern. Nor were the clustered fighters. Only D'Sanya could face us.

Gensei Kovrack and three hundred Zhid fanned out across the command behind me, swords and axes blazing with blue fire, enchantments of rending and destruction hovering about each man like the stench about a three-day corpse. The gensei chafed at my withholding, especially now the bells were silenced, as near rebellion as he dared go with my eye on him and my fist wrapped about his heart.

Another half-hour passed. A horseman raced toward my position.

"Lord Dieste." He dropped to one knee and bowed his head. "Gensei Senat reports a hardening of the defenses at the shrine. A shield wall has gone up, interfering with communication, and obscuring sight. He asks that you hasten the summoning of his reserve troops."

Warmth flooded my skin, but I permitted no change in my demeanor. "Tell the gensei that my plan was flawless. If his own weakness gives breath to the defenders, he must deal with it."

"Of course, Lord Dieste. As you say."

Not daring to consider what his report signified, I glared at the warrior as he slunk away. If I could but get a confirmation . . . "Grevet Gen'Vyl!" I called.

A tall man with a knobby bones, one of the Restored from the hospice, separated from the cluster of aides standing ten paces away. He hurried to my side and genuflected, his cold eyes devoid of the kindness he had shown to D'Sanya's guests for so many months. "Lord."

"Have we new reports from Wargreve Pavril?"

"Only that the ruined quarter around the bathhouse appears to be abandoned. He believes the last Dar'Nethi have withdrawn, and he is hastening his troops' passage through the portal. He will be ready when your signal is given. We didn't think such a minor matter—"

I backhanded the babbling Zhid, shoved him to the dirt, and swung into the saddle. "You are not commanded to think. Nor are you qualified to judge what is minor."

"Now!" I yelled at the red-haired general who sat his pied stallion on my left. And into the dark void where the gnarled Gensei Felgir fingered our instrument of doom, I screamed the same command, all the while praying to gods I had scorned that I didn't mean what I was about to say. "Onward to the world's end!"

My mount, free at last, raced gleefully across the commard toward the palace. Timing was everything. And yet timing was the least certain of all the elements of this battle. Out of harsh necessity, some of the participants fought blind. But the defensive hardening at one entry point and the suspicious quiet at the other indicated that someone had heeded my message.

I rode as I had never ridden, flying ahead of the assault, trying to dodge the initial defensive shock that would be aimed at Kovrack and his warriors, a huge enchantment laid far enough from the defenders themselves that their eardrums and night vision would remain intact. Explosive light and shattering noise erupted behind me. Zhid and horses died.

Plowing through the perimeter of the defensive arc, I allowed the force of my charge to part the unmounted defenders. I hoped that my horse would survive long enough to get me through. My primitive diversion spell worked well enough that the Dar'Nethi defenders' eyes slid past me, and I carried only a knife in my boot, a weapon small enough and far enough from my hand that it would not trigger their perceptions. The Lords had taught me that trick. As with everything they taught, I had learned it well.

The few of D'Sanya's little band who noticed me could not afford to confront a lone, unarmed rider, as the bulk of Kovrack's assault force swept across the command like a hurricane right on my heels. I dodged a few late strikes, my enchantments misdirected a few more, and I was through.

D'Sanya stood at the top of the palace steps, her golden hair standing out from her head with the charge in the air. Her silver rings and pendant gleamed in the murky light as she wove enchantments meant to give her warriors strength, accuracy, far-seeing, and steadfast hearts. Even now, after a long and terrible day, her strikes blasted and scraped both spirit and flesh like a desert whirlwind. Horrific death lay in her wake.

"Stand fast," she shouted. "We will hold this gate until the end of all—"

Her startled eyes met mine. "You!"

Her hand flew to her breast as I leaped from the saddle and raced up the steps. But I ripped the silver pendant from her grasp before she could invoke its particular violence, snapped the chain that circled her neck, and flung the pendant into the melee behind me, wrapping it in a spell that would cause anyone who touched it—even D'Sanya—to throw it away. As she clenched her fists to focus power, I gripped her waist and spun her in my arms, relieved to discover that her mail vest carried no enchantments more dangerous than any warrior's protections. Crushing her wrists to her breast, I snatched the knife from my boot and pricked the pale skin of her throat. "I would not slay you, Lady. But I will not hesitate if you disregard even the least of my commands."

"Kill him," she screamed, as I dragged her backward, pressing my undefended back against one of the gate towers. "Kill us both."

But there was no one to aid her. Throughout the past day and night she had been their rock, the commander who had needed no protection, for hers was the overwhelming power that had shielded them all from fire and wrath. And now her tired, brave warriors were desperately engaged with two hundred and fifty Zhid who slavered at the promise of accomplishing the destruction I had promised them.

"Strip off your rings or I will remove your fingers." She writhed in my arms, but I tightened my grip on her wrists and my knife bit deeper into her smooth flesh. "Now!" I screamed in her ear. I could yield her no time to think or plan. I was already relying far too much on exhaustion and confusion to slow her reactions and dampen her power.

"Lady!" A horrified Dar'Nethi warrior saw what was happening and ran toward us, only to be cut down from behind by a bellowing Zhid.

D'Sanya cried out as if the slashing blow had cut her own flesh. "Curse you forever, you soul-dead devil!" she spat over her shoulder. "I'll never—"

I whipped my blade across the back of her graceful

hand, leaving a trail of bright blood, as I felt the first fire of her magic sear my flesh and claw at my heart. Her cry of pain almost caused me to lose focus. But her enchantment cooled, and my heart kept beating on its own.

I dug the knifepoint into one of her knuckles. "Remove the ring and drop it to the ground."

Sobbing softly, she pulled off the delicate band of silver and let it fall to the ground. I wrapped it in my own power so she could not use it again. I had to hurry. The Dar'Nethi were steadfast . . . but they would not hold for long. I could smell their blood. Their fear. Their despair. My veins pulsed with blood-fever as my warriors hissed in contempt. *Focus. Remember who you are.*

I shifted my knifepoint to the next knuckle. "And now the next. Quickly."

When her hands were bare, I dragged her toward the center of the steps. "Open the gate."

"Never!"

I pulled her ear close to my mouth. "If you open it now, I will allow you to lock it again behind us, secure until my warriors break it for themselves. And once inside, you will have only me to deal with. You might even get the better of me. But if you wait, I will bring five thousand Zhid into your father's house alongside me, and no hand in any world will stop what is to come. Choose the lesser evil, D'Sanya."

"I will not serve you, Destroyer," she said, trying again to wrench free.

I summoned a wind to clear the smoke for one moment. From the steps we could see down the great slopes of Mount Eidol, the foundation of Avonar. Tongues of orange flame ate their way through the darkness in every direction. Dense plumes of smoke bore the thunderous cries of the dying city into the lowering clouds.

"Look on Avonar, D'Sanya! You have served destruction since the first day you yielded to the Lords' will. You know this. You've always known it. This day is your doing as well as mine, and no hollow swearing will alter what we have done. We were children, and they corrupted us. We are their instruments. But our choices this day can change the destiny they planned for us. Lay your hand on the lock. You are the anointed Princess of Avonar. The locks of your palace gates know you."

Her weary body betrayed her. After only a moment's struggle, I pressed her hands onto the great steel plates that centered the leftmost gate. The wood-and-steel slab had scarcely begun to swing open when I dragged her through and shouted to the confused guards to slam it shut behind us. When they saw my knife at their sovereign's throat, they jumped to obey.

The closure of the palace gate triggered the next wave of Kovrack's assault as I had designed it to do. At the shrill bleating of the Zhid warhorns and the trumpeting of the Dar'Nethi alarm, every Dar'Nethi in the palace precincts was summoned to the walls. Shielded by the distraction of battle and the simple spell of not-seeing that I'd learned from Jen, we left the battle behind and entered the palace.

The routes to D'Arnath's Gate were not guarded. My father had told me that in a thousand years, the ancient king's palace had been broached only by individual treachery, never by war, and never at the Gate itself. The wards opened only to the Heir's command. The confusing passages were untraversable by any who had not been shown the way to the Chamber of the Gate. Centuries of safety had left the Dar'Nethi complacent about the greatest treasure they possessed.

As the battle for the palace raged, I dragged D'Sanya down the path and forced her to open the wards. Shoving her toward the brass lion, I slammed the doors behind us. The wrongness of the Bridge enchantment threatened to rend my spirit.

"Why have we come here?" she asked, clutching her bleeding hand, backing away from me, her eyes blazing. The light of the Gate fire—no longer the searing white purity of D'Arnath's enchantments, but the livid color of dead flesh—made the edges of her hair gleam. "You daren't touch the Bridge. Only the—"

"What did you do here, D'Sanya? Were you so mad

to repair your crimes that you had to pervert your father's marvel? Did you even think what you were doing? Did you even consider the consequences, the risk?"

"I don't know what you mean." Hoarse. Defiant.

With a roar of rage, I summoned the power of a battering ram and slammed it against the bronze lion. The deafening crash as it toppled to the rose-and-gray stone might have been the gates of doom closing behind us. The gold orb and the silver, the villainous baubles she had cast in her lectorium, dropped from the air, then clattered and bounced across the cracked floor.

Anger filled me to bursting, fed by the soul-shredding dissonance of the perverted magic, fed by the blood-thirst that raged in me and my horror at my deeds of this day and their unyielding necessity. "Every artifact you create is connected to every other, D'Sanya. Each ring and pendant, each lock and statue and slip of metal that you place in walls and floors and doors is imbued with your power. Some objects focus power. Some devour it. Some pieces are of your own design. Some are of the Lords' contrivance. But *you* are the Metalwright, and your magic binds them to you and to each other as L'Clavor taught you. All of them, am I right? So that you can make larger workings than each device would support."

She retreated until her back rested against the fallen lion. Her expression of confusion infuriated me. "Yes, but I don't know—"

"You didn't have enough power for all your good works, did you? And so you made the orbs and put them here, and then you worked some magic to link them, and thus all of your devices, to the Bridge itself—the artifact of your father's power to which you believed you had a right. You've drained its power for your own uses."

"I did no such thing. How could I? The lion . . . the orbs . . . are to glorify him, so that none who come here forget who made all this. I am my father's Heir, and I bear the power he gave me. Of course I have the right to walk the Bridge and to maintain it as he taught us.

But I would never use it for myself. I wouldn't know how to do that." She knelt on the floor and scooped up the golden ball. Her mail shirt was streaked with blood, her trousers stained with mud and soot. "How dare you touch these things?"

"You made the oculus and the avantir, knowing full well they were artifacts of Zhev'Na, designed by the Lords. As you used the Bridge to feed your own power, you empowered those devices as well. D'Sanya, you've linked the Bridge to the Lords' devices. That's how the Zhid have risen. That's why the enchantments of this world crack my skull, why they twist back upon themselves and go awry."

"Designs cannot be evil." Her denial was weaker now. "I had so much work to do. To heal the things they did. The things they made me do . . ."

Feeling her soften, I pressed on less brutally. I had to learn what kind of link she had forged. "I read my father's history of the Dar'Nethi, about their joy, their kindness, their grace even after such horrors as the Catastrophe in Gondai and the Extermination in the mundane world, about their largeness of mind and heart and their willingness to build the Bridge and suffer this war to keep the universe in balance, to shield the mundane world from the Lords. You told me of your father's strength, his courage, his love and good humor in the most terrible of times. But what do we see now? This passionate hatred of those who were Zhid, whose restoration once caused purest rejoicing. The suspicion and mistrust of those who were slaves—unthinkable a year ago or ten centuries ago. Look anywhere in Gondai and you'll find fear, jealousy, despair, madness even to murder, people abandoning the Way that has sustained them for centuries. And the worst of it has happened since your return, so subtle, so pervasive, the Dar'Nethi themselves cannot see or feel their change . . . because you've tainted the foundation . . . the Bridge itself."

She set the golden ball carefully back on the floor and wrapped her arms about her middle. Her radiant skin had gone gray in the morbid light. Her extraordinary eyes seemed the size of my palms. Perhaps she was beginning to understand what her willful blindness had caused . . . so I wouldn't have to force her to the next step. Earth and sky, how I had loved her. "You have to stop it now, D'Sanya. Break this link so we can undo what you've done. Please, you must—"

Her dagger struck me in the left shoulder. My wards had triggered a warning and made me twist at the last moment or it would have pierced my heart. I staggered backward, fighting to breathe through the pain, through the enchantments that flooded my chest and limbs and caused the muscles to spasm uncontrollably. As I yanked the enchanted weapon from my shoulder, the room began to spin lazily, the air thick and glassy like cold honey.

"You are wrong, Destroyer. *You* are the being who poisons Gondai. I'll prove it. But I'll take your suggestion. I'll walk the Bridge and draw upon my father's magic to save Avonar. I'll destroy you before you and your demon Zhid destroy the world." She adjusted her belt where the empty sheath hung. Then, in a flash of silver mail and golden hair, she vanished beyond the Gate fire.

I fell back against the wall of the Chamber of the Gate, fighting for clarity, commanding my body to obey my will. *Can't let go now. Too much to do.*

I had joined the Zhid assault on Avonar in hopes that I could live long enough to bring D'Sanya to the Bridge and force her to repair what she had done. If I could break her link to the Bridge, perhaps I could end the war for good. But I wished fervently that some other Dar'Nethi could see what was happening. Why couldn't they feel it?

Fighting to control the painful spasms that wracked my limbs and heart and back, I pushed away from the wall and staggered toward the fallen statue. I worried about what D'Sanya might be doing on the Bridge, but first things first. If fortune was kind, I could cut off the flow of power to the avantir within the hour.

A quick probe revealed that the lion itself was magically inert, so I would need to destroy only the orbs. I was grateful for that.

First, consider the need. No difficulty there.

Second . . . I used the bloody dagger to draw a circle around the golden orb. My blood was the only possession I had available to assert ownership.

By the time I had shattered the two orbs, my hopes of a quick resolution were demolished as well. Woozy, nauseated, I knelt on the blood-marked floor, ripped a wad of cloth from my cloak, and pressed it to my bleeding shoulder, strapping my belt around to hold it in place. Nothing had changed. The Gate fire still pounded and thrummed, making my teeth ache, my bones ache, my soul ache. The fading light in the chamber was not some visual consequence of my injury, but a further discoloration of D'Arnath's enchantment . . . now a sooty gray. One test to be sure . . .

Felgir! I called.

Master? Where—?

Maintain the assault according to plan. Gensei Kovrack is field commander for the present.

As you command, Lord Dieste.

No question. No hesitation. The avantir yet held. So I had accomplished nothing. I wanted to scream.

I threw D'Sanya's knife to the floor and tried to take a full breath without passing out.

"Are you mad?" The door crashed open and Prince Ven'Dar strode into the room, his fury surrounding him like an army. But his only companion was a bedraggled Jen, wet hair sticking up, dark eyes wary, darting between the prince and me.

"D'Sanya has damaged the Bridge," I said, as I rose to my feet amid the gold and silver shards. "She's been drawing its power through the lion and the oculus and her other artifacts, linking it to the Lords' devices. I just don't know how. We must—"

"You've destroyed Avonar! Zhid are in the citadel. Dar'Nethi are dying." Ven'Dar held folded hands in front of his breast, as if in pleading or prayer, but I was not fooled. A Word Winder's hand could move quicker than lightning, and the former Prince of Avonar's cast would not be gentle.

I extended my own hands in front of me, pale flames flickering eagerly from my fingers so he would not mistake the blood on my shirt for a sign of weakness. "I've blunted the Zhid attack as best I could, Ven'Dar, and we've no time to discuss how I might have done that better or differently. I took away D'Sanya's jewelry and destroyed the magic of this lion, but I must have missed something else. She's on the Bridge, saying she's going to draw on its power to stop the attack. We must stop her."

He circled between me and the Gate fire as if to see what I might be hiding behind my back. I shifted my position as well. Only a fool would allow Ven'Dar at his back.

"I should slay you here and now," he said, as if he'd heard no word I'd spoken. "The Fourth Lord. The Destroyer. Since the beginning I have relied on your parents' testimony as to your motives and objectives, your feelings, your character, all these things you keep so tightly reined. But what if we've *all* been wrong about you? The immortal Lords can bide their time to take us down paths of seeming truth. Look at you! Look at what you've done! Do *you* even know what you are?"

And of course his question pricked my own remaining doubt. All this—the Lady and her folly, my father's illness, the necessity of war—had proceeded with an aura of inevitability, and now I stood at the Bridge with the fate of Avonar in my hands. After strenuously avoiding power and memory for nine years, I had slipped quite easily into this role, the very role designed for me when I was ten years old. *You are our instrument . . .*

For that moment, a chasm yawned beneath my feet, revealing a bottomless night where the deceptions of reason and intent formed in the light would be stripped away, yielding to a more fundamental . . . and less welcome . . . truth. But then another spasm wrenched my back and shoulder, sending jolts of pain down my spine—D'Sanya's poison. I was certainly not immortal.

I had relinquished that along with all the rest of the
Lords' gifts.

"You've not misjudged me, Ven'Dar," I said, clench-
ing my jaw so as not to reveal my vulnerability. "I still
choose the light. Every day, every hour is a new choice,
and sometimes the choice is easy and sometimes it in-
volves more pain than seems bearable. But since the day
I followed my father out of Zhev'Na, I have denied the
Lords, and if a man cannot determine his fate by his
own choice, then what hope is there for any of us? Believe what I say about D'Sanya and the Bridge, or cast
your winding and let us decide the matter that way. But
by all that you value, do it quickly."

Ven'Dar paused in his circling, the graying fire of the
Gate behind him. His presence was enormous and
dangerous—righteous anger and royal authority and the
power of a Word Winder of prodigious capacity and talent. I felt his indecision. How could I blame him, when
I fought this incessant battle with my own doubts? His
fingers twitched. I raised an enchantment ready to flat-
ten him.

"Speak your name!" The clear command halted the
gathering violence. A small person to so fill a room, like
a skittish bird who fluttered between walls and ceiling
and the two of us, shoving aside doubts and uncertainties
with her pointed chin.

I almost smiled as I answered. "My name is Gerick
yn Karon, known in my own land as the Bounded King."

Jen jerked her head, as if she had expected nothing
else. "Now speak the name of your master."

This, too, was easy. "In the world of the Bounded, *I*
am sovereign, with right and honor and the service of
my people as my guidestones. In my birthplace of Leire,
my sovereign mistress is Roxanne, queen, ally, and
friend. In the world of Gondai, my only master is the
rightful ruler of Avonar, the Heir of D'Arnath—at present the Princess D'Sanya, whose ill judgment and scarred
mind are hurling us all to ruin. As her loyal subject, I
must prevent her from destroying this realm she loves so
desperately. Everything—everything—I have done these

few days, whether vile or foolish or praiseworthy, is to serve that end. On my father's life and my mother's spirit, I swear it."

Jen looked supremely satisfied. She would be most annoyed when I told her that only Zhid and slaves were bound to truth in answer to those questions. The Lords' memories had taught me that they/I could ignore even the binding of names and heart's loyalties. But the clarity she demanded seemed sufficient to serve the moment. Though he did not soften his grim visage or move from his position, Ven'Dar lowered his hands.

Jen stepped between Ven'Dar and me, grabbing my hands without regard to the flames dancing on my knuckles. "But, as it happens, D'Sanya is *not* the rightful Heir," she said.

I quenched my enchantment before setting her skin or clothes afire, and she proceeded to pour out the news my mother had given her.

"Listen to the exact words," she said. "Truth is power, Gerick, and you'll hear it. This is the writing of Mu'-Tenni the Speaker, bound to Truth, in the matter of King D'Arnath's girl child: *After the Catastrophe made grim the days, the King's favor rested upon his youngest heir . . .*" She recited the damning passage, fixing the words in my mind as if she had scribed them on my skull.

The puzzle rearranged itself again. D'Sanya's power was linked to the Bridge, not by an artifact, not by some shaped enchantment of her design, but by the very structure of the Bridge. D'Arnath had disowned her to prevent her corruption from damaging his creation, but the Dar'Nethi, as hungry for redemption and healing as D'Sanya herself, had anointed her anyway . . . had brought her back into D'Arnath's family and undone her father's warding.

Existing in the giant statues under the cold stars of our temple, reveling in the ponderous weight of power, I/we contemplated our enemy . . . Unsearched-for memories floated out of the past. *"We will degrade thy innocent . . . use her talents . . . break her . . . destroy her . . . We shall unmake her and remake her in our image, our daughter, not thine. Woe and ruin will be thine only grandchildren. . . ."*

I remembered: I/we had corrupted her power and twisted her heart with death and despair so that everything she touched might service our desires. When I had embraced the Lords' memories at the hospice, I had examined the past and confirmed that it was only D'Sanya's enchantments, her metalworking, her loving that we had tainted. But we hadn't known about her link to the Bridge. D'Arnath had kept that dreadful secret well; surely no accident of battle had destroyed the Royal Library. Throughout this thousand years of war, the seed of our triumph lay buried under our fortress, growing, blossoming, bearing its wicked fruit, given life by the Tormentor King himself. All we'd had to do was keep his corrupted child alive to reap the harvest of his folly. We had done it for our own reasons, but had accomplished more than we ever understood.

"We'll go after her," said Ven'Dar, facing the steadily darkening fire. "I can still protect us. We'll bring her off the Bridge, assess the damage. Once the Preceptors decide the succession, the new Heir can set out to repair it. But you *must* stop the assault first, Gerick. No one will believe you. *I* cannot believe you—even after your declaration—if Zhid under your command are killing Dar'Nethi and destroying this city."

I looked up at him as if he existed in a different world . . . as he did, in a way . . . the world of past belief. Everything was changed now, made clear by this new information. Ven'Dar, the most perceptive sorcerer in Gondai, didn't feel the danger. Didn't see that it was far too late for Preceptors and judgments and repairs.

Once upon another day, Ven'Dar had told my father how sorely the Dar'Nethi were diminished since the time of D'Arnath. The goal of Ven'Dar's reign, of his generous heart and talented hands, had been to return his people to their glory. But the deterioration of the Dar'-Nethi that had begun in D'Arnath's time had never truly been reversed. And since D'Sanya's arrival and accession, it had accelerated. Five years ago Ven'Dar had been able to read my truth for himself, had witnessed and understood what my father and I had done to destroy the Lords. Now he couldn't even perceive that his mistrust, his difficulties with power, his flawed enchantments, and his inability to reverse the disharmony and prejudices among his people were not temporary aberrations, but signs of his own corruption . . . as they were signs of a pervasive, fundamental corruption in the world.

At last I could put a name to the wrongness of the world: the hopeless confusion, the creeping evil, the soul-scraping enchantments, the bondage of the spirit that destroyed peace and trust, the withering dark lurking just beyond every object in my sight that made ugly what should be beautiful. It was Zhev'Na. It was the Bridge.

"What is it, Gerick?" Jen laid her hand on my bare arm, her touch and my name connecting me for a moment to the old world.

"I can't stop the assault yet," I said, averting my gaze as I gently pushed her hands away. No explanation could possibly suffice. "I'll go after D'Sanya. I'll do what has to be done." And if I failed, my Zhid would have to do the work for me.

Ven'Dar spun to look at me, as if he read my thoughts. But before the horrified Word Winder could raise his hands again, I released my waiting enchantment. He crumpled to the floor, stunned, eyes still wide open.

"Gerick! Wait! No!"

I closed my ears to Jen and to my own doubts and fears. Taking a firm grip on my mind and soul, I stepped through the Gate of fire.

CHAPTER 37

"D'Sanya, where are you?" The rain-battered plain stretched in every direction. Nothing moved. No monstrous birds or ravening beasts. No shrieking spirits or vicious skeletons. Nothing but unceasing rain. A mudhole sucked insistently at my boots. I could not lift either foot without sinking further.

I didn't panic. Instead of fighting such horrors as pits of quicksand, I had learned to shift my direction, to fear something else that would then manifest itself as the world. I turned to my left and found a desert, so bleak an expanse of sun-blasted rock that I knew instantly that D'Sanya was nowhere within earshot. I took a step into the scorched barrens, my feet free of the vanished mudhole.

For hours I had searched down paths of mud and slime, across rocky wastelands, and into desolate valleys, hours of holding my mind together, of resisting the insistent madness of unreality. How did one organize a search when every new direction opened up a different landscape of death? Chaos . . . the Breach.

Yet even the quality of madness in the shifting dimension of the Bridge was changed from my previous experience of it. How was I able to think at all or to travel this realm without the protection of D'Arnath's Heir? Rather than vivid horror—spiders' eyes the size of shields, bats with wingspans broader than kingdoms, tumultuous riots of naked warriors with razored fingers or barbed tongues—I perceived only deadness.

Occasionally I believed I heard sharp breaths or panting over my shoulder. But when I turned, I merely existed in yet another, equally desolate place. Alone.

"D'Sanya, I've something I must tell you." No one answered, not even an echo. A single, rasping locust shot into my face. I brushed it away, detritus no more living than the rock beneath my feet.

I changed course again and this time trod a barren shore. The charcoal-colored lake reflected only bleak storm clouds and sunless sky. At the far end of the lake a mountain peak rose into clouds that flickered with blue-and-purple lightning. The mountain . . . the shaping D'Arnath had taught his beloved girl child . . .

I ran, soon abandoning the graveled shore for a smooth track that wound across the mountainside, relentless in its upward bent. The path steepened, but I would not slow. A hot rain, the droplets sharp like tiny blades, left blood streaks on my arms.

She stood on the rocky pinnacle, hands upraised, wind gusts whipping her hair, sleeves, and trousers. Her fingers were spread wide as if to reach the thick clouds threaded with darkening fire. As I struggled up the last near-vertical pitch, a faint white glow pulsed from her fingertips and faded to gray wisps, indistinguishable from the cloud. A despairing sob racked her slim back.

"D'Sanya."

She whirled. "How can *you* be here?" she cried, as if fate had betrayed her once too often.

She cupped her trembling hands between us, but no ball of fire appeared, only a smudge of gray that drifted upward. Tears and raindrops dribbled down her cheeks.

"I don't know how it's possible." I climbed the last few steps, treading carefully on the barren rock, the wind a constant threat to my balance. "Perhaps because I am not your enemy. Please believe I'm not here to hurt you. We must talk, just for a little while. Find a solution to this disaster."

"They're all dying," she said. "You took my rings and pendant, destroyed the oculus and the orbs, too, and now I can't help them. The worlds . . . the people . . . are my responsibility. If I could just clear away this storm . . . the chaos . . ."

She raised her hands again. A thin, wavering thread of white fire stretched from her hands to a looming cloud. The thick gray wad exploded into more droplets of mist that pricked my exposed skin like needles. Yet, for the moment, I could not heed anything but the landscape that sprawled before us. It halted my breath.

From the base of the mountain to the horizon unfolded all of Gondai, the ocher-and-bronze wastelands centered by the lush green and brilliant white of the fertile Vales and the snowcapped Mountains of Light. Blue-gray oceans rippled at its boundaries. In its very heart huddled the dark blight of Avonar, burning and dying. From that once-bright center dark veins of poison spread into the green lands and the red-brown desert, carrying sepsis to the whole of the land.

If I turned a little to the right, I saw what was surely the mundane world spread out as far as I could see, uncountable cities and villages, mountains and plains— a land trapped in unending winter. Tree boughs sheathed in ice and bent to breaking, grain fields buried in snow, mill wheels frozen, cattle and sheep dead or starving. Bands of ragged men and women rampaged through villages and towns, tearing, burning, killing, ravaging cellars and grain stores. Whole cities were ablaze.

Yet another turn and I gazed out on my chosen homeland of black-and-purple sky, the dark landscape jeweled with golden light—the precious sunrocks that signaled life and growth. Torrential rains battered my virgin world. A cliffside gave way, drowning a cluster of towers in an ocean of mud. One by one the points of light winked out.

In the gap of gray sky cleared by D'Sanya's work another cloud already swelled with coming chaos. I wished desperately to turn my back on this wondrous and terrible display, for I had no faith that even my dreadful solution could heal any of it. "D'Sanya, you must stop. The Bridge is broken. Irretrievably corrupt—"

Her fist gripped my heart. Searing, grinding pain began in my chest and threatened to encompass the universe. As I countered her spell, forced to focus all my power to stay living, the distant, brilliant heart of the Bounded, a yellow ocean of living light, dimmed and faded. "Lady, wait," I gasped. "Please listen to me. . . ."

"This is all your doing!" she yelled, sobbing angrily while blasting another cloud from the sky. Immediately a new cloud bulged in its place, darker and thicker. The rain scalded my skin. "You're destroying my father's work."

I had to stop her. But even after all she'd been through, her power was daunting. Choking on bile and blood as heart and lungs struggled, I struck with the only weapon sure to draw blood. "Do not call D'Arnath father, D'Sanya. Didn't you guess? He disinherited you. Disowned you. Struck your name from the—"

"Liar!" Her hand cracked into my cheekbone. The shrill edge of her scream spoke of long suspicion and denial.

I grabbed her wrist and held her tight, gathering power and weaving enchantment into the words Jen had given me. "This is the writing of Mu'Tenni the Speaker, bound to Truth, in the matter of King D'Arnath's girl child lost in the great war . . ."

To my surprise, the words came not in a choking rasp, but in a stern, clear voice that sounded more like my father than like me.

"For after the Catastrophe made grim the days, the King's favor rested upon his youngest heir above all others in his realm for the solace she brought him . . ."

A story undeniable in its truth. Did my enchantment make it so, or was it the power of the words as the Speaker had written them or, perhaps, some magic of the one who had passed the words to me? D'Sanya stood paralyzed, one hand pressed to her lips, her hair limp and streaming with hot rain.

". . . Yet the King dared not allow the Lords' captive to inherit his power and the fate of the Bridge. Indeed her talent had come mightily as he had foreseen, and she

*had become a sword in the Lords' hands, striking at the
very soul of the Dar'Nethi. Came the day when D'Arnath
saw the vile neck binding the Lords used to enslave his
people and reive their souls, and knew that his own child
had devised it, he wept bitter tears for that child of his
heart and struck her name from his life and descent
forever . . ."*

As I described Prince D'Alleyn's refusal to speak her
name on his deathbed, D'Sanya sank to the ground at
my feet, her hands clamped over her ears, flinching as if
each word were a blow. When I finished, she drew up
her knees and bent her head over them.

"Papa . . . why won't you come for me? I said I'm
sorry. So sorry. I did my best. For so long I wouldn't
listen to their horrid tales. I sang and I wrote and I drew.
But the days were so long . . . so lonely . . . and you
didn't come. . . ." She raised her head and peered into
my face, twisting her own countenance into a childlike
puzzle. "The Three made me do dreadful, disgusting
things with them . . . and with the Zhid . . . and do other
horrid, wicked things that made people scream. They
said that if Papa truly loved me, he would come and take
me home where I wouldn't have to hear the screaming. I
tried so hard. . . ."

"I know. It wasn't fair at all." I crouched in front of
her and grasped her cold, limp fingers that had woven
white fire. "D'Sanya, we have to destroy the Bridge. The
worlds are dying."

She shook her head and wrapped her arms about her
knees, shrinking from me. "I won't betray him. I won't.
I won't. I won't. He'll come for me. He is the High King
of Gondai, and he loves me as the earth loves the sky.
He would never leave me in this awful place. . . . Papa?"
Blood leaked from the cuts I had left on her hand. She
licked the blood, leaving scarlet smudges on her lips,
shuddered in pleasure, and rested her head on her arms,
releasing neither sobs nor wails, but a low keening that
was the very essence of misery and madness.

I had run out of time to think or to analyze or to seek
counsel or solace or the encouragements of love and

faith that had carried me through my most difficult decisions of the past. D'Sanya's anointing had changed the course of our decline from a downward slope to a precipice, and we were very close to smashing against the hard bottom. I had to choose.

Standing on that mountaintop in the driving wind and knife-edged rain, I looked out on the lands joined by the Bridge and saw no alternatives.

Destroyer . . .

I ignored the sly whisper and bent my mind to the work, focusing instead on a clearer voice, one given its rich timbre by strength and courage and a trust uncolored by blood ties or friendship. A voice that spoke truth. *Consider the object to be destroyed . . . the need . . . the use or misuse that justifies destruction.* Not difficult at all. I had been thinking of nothing else for two days.

Now, ownership . . . I, who had been born in one of these encircling worlds, nurtured and corrupted in another, and given, in the third, the first inkling of the reason for my own being, could well assert my ownership of this place.

Disrupt containment. The flaw in the Bridge was already there for me to exploit. I settled myself on the ground beside D'Sanya and touched her hair. *Forgive me, Lady.*

She did not look up.

My soul moved quickly into her body, reaching through the harrowing morass of guilt and denial to find the hidden link with the Bridge—a silver thread buried deep, long tarnished, the bent and broken fragment of her father's working. I took it from her and felt her last defenses crumble. I wove that flaw into my spell of breaking, then withdrew, grieving for the cold and lonely barrenness of a spirit once so bright.

As soon as I had reclaimed my own senses, I gathered power. *Yes, Jen'Larie, as you taught me—everything I feel, everything I am, everything I remember.* I reached into the deepest places of my soul and fed power into my enchantment. . . .

The air about me shimmered as if I viewed the triple

landscape through the heat haze of the desert. I opened
my arms and spread my legs and raised my head,
allowing the power to flow through me unhindered, a
torrent sufficient to drain an ocean of magic. Too quickly
I was struggling with the effort, my extended arms quivering, my knees threatening to collapse. And nothing
had happened.

Gods, had I not worked the spell correctly? I'd been
so sure I could do this. The enchantments of the past
days, of the battle—portals and threats and deceptions—
had been so easy once I had opened myself to the past.
Yet D'Arnath's Bridge had taken twenty-one years to
build . . . the extent of my whole lifetime. How could I
imagine I could destroy it in one moment or one hour
or one day?

Best be ready for a long siege. Using the discipline I
had learned in Zhev'Na, I spread my fingers, angled my
feet, and settled more deeply into my position. With eyes
closed, I set free memories and visions to come and go
in my head. *Comigor . . . Verdillon . . . Zhev'Na . . .
the Bounded . . .* I felt and lived and embraced past
and present.

*Creeping darkness threatened to suffocate me. . . . Mad-
ness lurked in the shadows. . . .* I held on. Gave more.
There passed what seemed like an age of the world. . . .

Cold . . . As you can only feel when exhaustion saps
the last of your inner fire. *Dizzy . . . and so thirsty . . .*
I'd not had a sip of anything for hours. The rain had
stopped, but a warm flow tickled my chest and side—
my shoulder bleeding again. Would the end of the world
be halted by a damnable puncture wound?

I croaked and gasped in some grotesque semblance of
laughter at the irony, terrified to the marrow that I might
fail and equally fearful of success. Then a blast of wind
almost collapsed my knees. The mountaintop trembled.
A skull-cracking barrage of sound, like the cannon fire
of a year-long siege compressed into a single moment,
had me fighting for composure. Yet the noise did not
stop after that initial blast, but grew louder, a grinding

cacophony. D'Sanya flung her arms about my ankle and wailed.

The gale howled in concert with the Lady; the sky itself spun. Fragments of color broke away from the landscape—the bright green of new grass . . . the red-gold of autumn leaves . . . the translucent blue-green of forest ponds—each of a thousand shadings one by one, and a many-textured darkness began to close in over the sprawling worlds. Destruction . . . chaos . . . the terror, panic, and madness of thousands of souls tore my flesh and shredded my mind. . . .

Rent . . . shattered . . . I could not breathe. My bones cracked; my blood surged through its course like liquid fire. Once, in some other age of creation, I had experienced such agony. On my twelfth birthday, as I escaped Zhev'Na. On that day I had abandoned this physical shell when it became uninhabitable.

Coward, not to face what you've done. Despite the exhortations of conscience, I could not hold, and yet again my soul fled my body, seeking the oblivion I could not grant my victims. Alone . . . groping through the chaos of unending night to find some anchor . . . I touched something wet and gritty . . . mud . . .

. . . and saw two Singlars climbing a steep, spiral stair and clutching their casket of sunrocks as roiling floodwaters crept up the stair behind them. One of them tall and dark-skinned with silver hair. The other short and oddly shaped with only one eye. My friends, Zanore and Vroon, and my kingdom, the Bounded, in all their awkward newness . . . how I loved them. Hold on . . . don't die. . . .

I reached farther through chaos and touched ice. . . .

. . . and glimpsed a woman with dark braids wound about her head, huddled with a man and two feverish children in a tiny, snow-covered house beside a frozen river—Kellea, who had helped rescue me from Zhev'Na and who had cared for my father. And a little farther on I found Tennice, my tutor and second father, coughing blood from his lungs in ice-bound Verdillon. And Roxanne, riding through drifted roads to succor her frost-

wracked cities and towns with bread, ale, fire, and courage . . . giving . . . giving . . . Friends who gave their gifts so generously for love and duty and right, expecting no reward but hope. The mundane world, filled with monumental cruelties that made its passionate kindnesses so savory. . . . I loved it, too. Hold on. My mother's world . . .

Where was she? Clutching my connections to these two worlds, I returned to chaos, letting it flow in and out of my disembodied soul, searching. . . .

. . . and found a tall man and a golden-haired woman who clutched his waist, the two astride a strong-limbed bay that raced through the night toward a burning city, leading a dark-skinned warrior and his army of sorcerers. Ah, Paulo . . . long past time for you to take your own road . . . ride swiftly . . . safely . . .

"Your mother was very persuasive." Jen'Larie . . . a force of nature inducing me to smile in a time I believed I would never smile again. Power lay hidden in her that she herself could not see. . . .

Hidden power . . . my mother, too, had her own magic, as on that day in Zhev'Na when the Great Oculus scalded my eyes away and I heard her voice, distant, but clear: "You were beloved from the day your father and I first knew of you. . . ." Mother? I shaped a talisman of that voice and spirit until I found her.

She sat in the grass under failing stars. He lay huddled in her strong arms, crying out his agony. Dry-eyed, she whispered comfort, building a shield of love around his pain.

Ah, Mother, do you know how you are loved? I've lived inside of him. I know. If I could but feel half that love for someone . . . Whatever else, D'Sanya had taught me possibility.

And, Father, how I wish I could make this easier for you. . . .

As if he had heard me, an ember of my father's spirit flared in the darkness, penetrating chaos as it had once penetrated the Breach, as it had echoed beyond the Verges, as it had touched my soul on the day I became the Fourth. The memory of those words still gave me strength. *I will fight them until the last day of the world to set you free.*

How could I do less? I embraced my mother and father, along with Paulo and Aimee, Jen and D'Sanya, and through them all the world of Gondai—Dar'Nethi and Dulcé and Zhid, good and bad together. I enfolded all those spirits, together with the Singlars and the mundanes and the other two worlds, and I held them tight and fought to set them free, wishing I could do more as the last of my power drained away and I became one with chaos.

CHAPTER 38

Jen

"I'm over here, my lord. All of a piece, I think." I crawled across the floor toward the mumbled curses and spitting. Indeed, I felt tangled and out of proportion, as if mind and body had been stretched as thin as silk thread, and then released to clump back together again in whatever way natural forces saw fit. To find myself with an extra ear or missing fingers would not have surprised me in the least. "Are you injured, my lord?"

The floor was littered with sharp fragments of metal and stone that I brushed out of the way as I crept through the absolute dark. I had already tried to make a handlight and could produce not so much as a spark. I tried not to think what that meant. I knew what Gerick had gone off to do.

The Gate fire had vanished in an eyeblink at the height of the earthquake. The Bridge had fallen, and we were left to be grateful the sky had not fallen in on us as well. Or the ceiling.

My stomach curdled at the thought of how deep under the palace we were, of the narrow passages that could be so easily blocked by rubble, or of the fires that had already raged through the palace when we raced down here to intercept Gerick. I hadn't expected to survive this long.

"I wish you would speak, sir. Ouch!" I stopped to extract a metal splinter from my left hand.

The spitting stopped. "Well, I've a knot the size of a

turnip on the back of my head. My sudden meeting with the floor has knocked out at least two of my teeth. And I cannot seem to raise a light. What more can be said?"

Much more. But his breaking voice expressed it, not his words. The surrounding dark was despair.

"The Bridge . . ." I said.

"I've a gap in my soul the size of the sky. What am I to think?"

I was not a good witness. Having never felt the fullness of power, I could not miss it. But if this was the end of everything, the end of power as we had always been taught, it seemed odd that the skills innate to Dar'-Nethi bodies would be gone as well. Only true talent had been served by the Bridge.

Clothes and limbs rustled in the dark. Metal chinked softly. A whispered sigh came, not from the direction in which I was creeping—the direction of Prince Ven'Dar's coughing—but from behind me.

"Who else is here?" I sat up and spun in place, eyes straining to see in the dark, dizzy until I glimpsed a pale white glow. The light moved slightly and expanded, shining on silver ring mail . . . on bodies . . . on bloodied flesh banded by a gold armring . . .

My throat swelled. *Gerick!*

The light jerked and grew, illuminating the Gate chamber. Gerick huddled on the floor beside one of the great columns, eyes closed, trembling violently, so pale he was almost transparent. A blood-streaked, disheveled D'Sanya knelt beside him, one finger touching his shoulder, the white light streaming from her hands. And behind them . . .

"My Lord Ven'Dar! Do you see?" I croaked, not sure of my own senses.

"Aye." The prince, a mere ten paces from me, stood craning his neck to stare in wonder at the section of the curved chamber wall where the Gate fire had once burned. D'Sanya's light danced on a crystalline barrier comprised, not of one smooth face, but of pinnacles and facets, corners and ridges and man-high crevices that might have been the Gate's white fire frozen in time.

"He's so tired," said the Lady, her finger touching Gerick's damp hair. "He hurts wickedly and is so sorry, sorry, sorry. Will he die?"

"Don't touch him, witch!" I snapped, heedless of her power, wanting to strike her, wanting to weep, wanting to tear out my hair in confusion. What was she playing at?

D'Sanya flinched at my command and scrambled away from Gerick toward the crystal wall. But when she touched the translucent surface, she cried out and jerked away, clutching her right hand. Moaning softly, she retreated again and soon cowered on the floor beside the toppled bronze lion. Light still glowed softly from her left hand. I was astonished.

Keeping one eye on the Lady, I hurried to Gerick. Blood saturated his shirt and his bare left arm, oozing slowly from a wound in his shoulder close to his collarbone. A narrow leather belt and a wad of wet, bloody cloth hung tangled uselessly about his upper arm and his neck.

I touched his right arm. His entire right side spasmed sharply, but his eyes did not open and his trembling continued unabated. His skin was clammy. Reason told me to be frightened of the one who had wrecked the universe, but reason was upside down and inside out.

When the Gate fire went out, I had expected to die with it. But the uproar had been only beginning. Throughout the long hours in the dark, as the earth rumbled and groaned, as every deafening crash above my head threatened the end of all things, a certain warmth had spread from my head to my feet, a strength that held me together inside, an assurance that if I could just endure, the world would not collapse. Only now was I left cold and empty and truly afraid.

As I slit Gerick's soggy shirt, peeled the flap away from the sticky wound, and replaced the wad of cloth and the belt to keep it snug, Ven'Dar approached the princess. He moved slowly and crouched a few steps away as if not to frighten her. She looked mainly at the floor, only glancing at Gerick now and then.

"So we are not entirely incapable of sorcery," said the prince softly, taking her hand and examining it before laying it back in her lap. "Lady, what's happened? What did he do to you?"

"They were dying. I broke them and they were dying and I'm so sorry, so sorry. He"—she drew her arms tight and curled her legs underneath her, nodding her head toward Gerick—"held them. Loved them. Saved them. Don't let him die. He carried me through the wall."

"Who was dying?" said Ven'Dar. "I need to understand."

Though he had not raised his voice, she flinched and wrapped her arms about the bronze lion's neck, burying her face in her sleeves so we could scarcely hear her. "The worlds. Everyone. I'm sorry. I'm sorry. I wanted to make things right. Don't be angry. Please don't punish me. They kept screaming and I wanted to silence them. But I just made it worse and worse. They won't stop screaming and Papa won't come."

"My lord, she's—"

"I see it." He laid his hand gently on her shoulder. "No, Lady, we're not angry with you. And there'll be no punishments. We'll find someone to care for you."

D'Sanya's light faded away, but the crystal wall still glowed faintly, as if it retained some memory of the white gleams. Ven'Dar walked over and touched it, snatching his hand back immediately. He examined its entire length, peering into its glassy depths, probing its cracks and crevices and smooth faces, finding nowhere he could rest even a fingertip on its surface. Worry had ground channels in his brow, but the reflection of the crystal wall revealed a growing curiosity on his countenance, not despair.

"I don't know what to believe," he said. "This is wholly unknown to me, and yet . . . But I cannot linger here. We must learn what's happened to the rest of the world."

He pulled a kerchief from his pocket and dabbed at blood that leaked from a bruised corner of his mouth. After stuffing the stained kerchief away, he held his hands out in front of him, turning them to one side and then another as if they were some oddments he'd picked up in the market.

"I feel so strange," he said. "None of the awareness of power I've had since I can remember. No sense of connection to the world. I can see nothing through this wall. I can't bear to touch it, yet it is not pain that repels my hand, but something more profound than enchantment. I can't say what. And I feel neither dead nor mad nor . . . empty . . . as I felt at first. Only different." He met my gaze, face alight with a hint of bleak humor. "Well, shall we see, then?"

A brilliant white light flared out from his hands, almost blinding me.

"Hand of Vasrin!" he said, as the crystal wall took fire with his light. Pale green, rose, blue, and yellow danced through the peaks, facets, and crevices of the wall. "I scarcely gave it a thought!"

He closed his eyes, narrowed his brow and cocked his head as if he were listening. "What's that? I hear . . ." His eyes popped open. He grabbed my arm and dragged me to my feet. "We must get Gerick away from here. I don't know how to judge him, but others are coming in search of the Destroyer, and until we understand what's happened . . ."

"Where can we take him, my lord?"

"Let me try . . ." He pressed his hands together at his forehead and then spread them wide, and a portal gaped before us, revealing what appeared to be a plain, tidy bedchamber. Ven'Dar's jaw dropped. "So fast. I've never— Come, let's get him up."

Ven'Dar bearing his shoulders, I his feet, we carried Gerick through the portal and laid him on the narrow bed. Ven'Dar's complexion was flushed, but I didn't think the exertion of the move had caused his heightened color. Gerick was not so very heavy.

The prince gave Gerick a quick examination: head, arms, legs, back, and bleeding shoulder. He threw the wadded bloody shirt on the floor. "Though he's lost blood, the wound doesn't seem all that severe. All other injuries seem older."

Besides the bed and a scuffed wooden chest, the room held only a bare table, two chairs, a well-stocked bookshelf, and a patterned rug of green and yellow. Ven'-Dar's hands quivered as he rummaged in the chest and pulled out a faded blanket of brown and yellow stripes and a clean linen handkerchief.

He tied the handkerchief around Gerick's shoulder. "I'll send someone with food and wine. I doubt I can find a Healer, even if— But I'll send medicine at least. Bandages." His eyes raced over Gerick's huddled form. Reaching down, he yanked a knife from Gerick's boot. He shrugged as he stuffed it into my hand. "Am I right to assume that you're willing to stay here with him?"

I didn't like his air of excitement or the hint of a smile peeking out of his untrimmed beard as he spread the striped blanket over Gerick. Such reactions seemed an unsupportable frivolity in this precarious hour. "As I said before, my lord, if he's a Lord of Zhev'Na, then we're all in a stew. . . ."

". . . and if he is not . . . if the Lady has spoken some truth in her madness . . . then perhaps we find ourselves at a beginning, not an end. I'm beginning to think that's possible. I'm hearing things . . . sensing things . . . more every moment, even with so much uncertainty, such devastation. . . ." He straightened up, shook his head, and blew out a long breath. "But we've some anxious hours ahead, and if we're to protect him, I must get back before someone detects me here. This house is quite secure, this room more so. Keep him here if you can. As soon as I learn anything more, I'll speak with you, if you'll permit. . . ."

"Of course, my lord. I just . . . I can't mind-speak myself."

"I'd say you'd best not assume anything, at this point. Everything's changed." For a moment his face was distracted, as if he heard something else in the room. When he looked up at me again, his eyes had taken on a new

spark, the web of fine lines about them smiling, though
his bruised lips did not. "I feel young, Jen. I feel new."

Prince Ven'Dar stepped through the portal and it
closed behind him.

What did he mean by that? Of course, everything was
changed. I felt tired. I felt confused.

I moved across the room to the window. Proximity to
Gerick seemed to garble my thoughts, and there was
little I could do for him anyway. Hurt's ease, my mother's purification spell, needed three pure elements to create it. I didn't know where I could find anything clean
or pure in this whole blighted universe.

Outside the tall window it was day, though billowing
fog left the sun a gray disk as it hovered over a ghostly
horizon—west, certainly, from the shape of it. Had the
world truly spun a complete revolution since I'd stood
in the colonnade and watched D'Sanya ride out of the
palace? But then who would expect time to make sense?
The Bridge had fallen, and the earth had shaken for so
long my teeth felt loose in my head.

We seemed to be on the third or fourth floor of a
large house. Below the window spread a wide lawn,
hedges, and a long, low building painted white with a
fenced yard behind it—a stable, perhaps. I yanked up
the stiff old sash, stuck my head out, and inhaled . . .
and started coughing. Smoke, not fog.

The city was quiet now, as it had not been those endless hours ago when Ven'Dar had made a portal to take
us from Skygazer's Needle into the palace. By the time
he had found loyal men to reinforce the weaknesses
Gerick had revealed to me, the Zhid had brought up a
ram to smash the palace gates. A few had made it past
the walls and the enchantments and were battling the
defenders. If an entire day had passed, then who had
won the battle for Avonar? The silence and smoke shivered along my back. Perhaps everyone was dead.

Behind me, the bed creaked. I scraped my arm on the
window frame in my hurry to look around.

Eyes still closed, Gerick had rolled to his side, clutching the blanket tight around his neck. His trembling

shook the small bed and the floor. The striped blanket
slipped slowly to the floor, exposing his sodden boots
and breeches.

I felt helpless. What had he done to himself with his
monstrous magics?

*Idiot! This isn't enchantment or madness. He's lost a
vat of blood, has likely not eaten or slept for two days,
and is soaking wet.* Enough to deplete anyone, even if
he'd not just expended magical power unseen in ages of
the world. He was freezing.

I dragged off his boots and leggings and threw the
blanket back over him. As I dug in the chest through
books and bundles and spilled sonquey tiles in search of
blankets and dry clothes, I tried to think what I might
possibly say were he ever to wake up. *Is it part of your
devilish scheme to plant conviction of your innocence in
my head along with your messages, your soul, and whatever else you see fit to put there? What perversion makes
me so sure of you, even after you've broken the world?
I hate this madness you've put in me, when I know I
should put a knife in your heart again, and leave it this
time. Tell me what, in Vasrin's mighty shaping, you've
done to the world. To me.*

The chest yielded only a man's linen—worn, but clean.
No other clothes. No more blankets. I returned to the
bed, and yanked and tugged the bedclothes trapped underneath him until I could flop the thick, slightly damp
quilt and linen sheet over the top of the striped blanket.
After a quick glance at his face to confirm he was yet
insensible, I reached underneath the bedclothes to fum-
ble with the waist buttons on his breeches.

A cold hand clamped around my wrist, twisting just
enough that I was forced to let go of his clothes, kneel
down beside the bed, and look him in the eyes—deep
brown eyes, open pathways to a soul filled with painful
questions.

"F . . . f . . . first things first." His teeth were chattering. "T . . . t . . . tell me what I am, Jen. Please. You
always see the truth."

One might have thought the battle fires had reached

this room and set my skin ablaze. Before answering, I retrieved my hand and sat back on my heels, putting slightly more distance between us so I could breathe. He relinquished my appendage without argument, but not so my eyes.

"I don't know what you are," I said. "The Bridge is no more. The Gate's gone dark. Some kind of barrier—crystal or glass—exists in its place. As to the world . . . the war . . . I don't know that either. Ven'Dar and I are alive, and we're not Zhid. For the moment, he is capable of using power. That's something at least. The prince says that others live. The Lady survived, but seems . . ."

He nodded, his serious expression unchanged. "Truth broke her. I should have let *you* face her long ago."

Unable to comprehend his meaning, I could not remember what I was saying. "I don't know any more to tell you. Someone's bringing food and medicine. We'll look at your shoulder."

"Just cold now." He hunched his quivering shoulders and averted his eyes. "Thank you . . . for believing."

"But I didn't—"

"Felt it the whole time. Remembered what you said; didn't hold back."

So he had used my advice to destroy the Bridge. I wanted to throw something, to explode something. But all I did was yell at him. "How could you do it? I defended you! Yes, I believed in you, but I don't know why, and I still believe in you, but I think I must be mad or corrupt, a traitor to everything and everyone I've ever cared about. Tell me why you did it!"

He swung his legs around to the side of the bed, set his bare feet on the floor, and sat up, chin drooping on his chest as he gathered the bedclothes around him. His eyelids sagged as his violent shaking eased into gentler tremors. For a few moments, I thought he had passed out and might topple onto the floor. I dared not touch him.

After a brief time, he heaved a deep, tremulous sigh. Shrugging off the blankets, he reached for the muddy leggings and boots I had left by the bed.

"I did what I believed necessary," he said, pulling the black hose over his legs with hands that were increasingly steady. "But I don't have time to explain right now. They're going to come for me—the Dar'Nethi, the Preceptors . . . whoever's left. I'll let them do whatever they want with me. I'll help, if they'll allow it . . . if I can. But I must get to the hospice first. My father's dying."

"Are you going to play Lord again? Have you forgotten the firestorm you brought down on Avonar? The Zhid legions that stretch like an ocean all the way to the borders? How do you expect—?"

His glance halted my accusations as decisively as he cinched the buckle on his left boot. His face shone like the horizon just before the sun pushes itself above its boundary. "Just now I ordered the Zhid to stop the attack. No one answered me."

I caught my breath. "Then the avantir is—"

The door slammed inward, bouncing against the wall. Gerick dived into the curtained alcove behind the bed. I had a chair in my hand before the tall man in the black, hooded cloak could drop two bulging leather saddlebags to the floor and stretch his long arms out to either side.

"It's all right. Just me. Everything's all right." He shook off his hood. Paulo.

He caught the chair before it crashed to the floor, and when I flung my arms about his waist and burst out crying like a ridiculous schoolgirl, he wrapped his long arms about me and allowed me to dampen his apparel even more than it was already. "I guess it's been a rough night for everyone."

After a moment I felt the need to regain a bit of self-respect and reassure Paulo that I hadn't suddenly misinterpreted our friendship. Though my arms seemed unwilling to relax their hold, I swallowed sharply and forced my voice even. "Aimee's well?"

"She's off to the palace with Je'Reint and Ven'Dar. You just can't imagine what all she can do." No worries that his attentions had been diverted from brave, insightful Aimee. The new note of assurance in his admiration, an air of privileged knowledge, almost had me smiling.

He waved at the empty bed. "Where's—?"

"Knew you'd get our backs—you and that excessively cheerful lady."

The voice from the alcove spun Paulo out of my grasp and brought a grin to his face. "Knew you'd get into trouble without me. But, demons of the deep, I never thought . . ."

Paulo's smile faded as Gerick kept his distance. Gerick's expression had lost its luster as well. Though his words expressed genuine relief, his body was wary.

Paulo hesitated. "You're all right? You look a right bloody mess. I heard she stabbed you."

"A small thing." Gerick waved at his shoulder halfheartedly. "They've sent you to fetch me, haven't they?"

Paulo breathed deep. "I offered to speak with you. There's a number of folk downstairs waiting. Wicked upset. Needing to understand what's happened and why and what's going to happen next."

"I've got to ride north first, Paulo. My father—"

"You can't go. There's some down below as want to bring this house down on your head no matter who's with you or what questions will never be answered. There's some as would have you trussed up in so much dolemar it would look like plate armor, and locked away in Feur Desolé with your mind like frog spit before you take two breaths more. You set foot in a direction they don't like and they'll do it, no matter what you might do to them in return. Ven'Dar has pledged his word that before the next hour passes you'll answer for what you've done without so much as bending a hair on another man's head."

"Ven'Dar had no right to do that." Gerick turned away from us to face the window. He ran his fingers through his matted hair. "If my father isn't dead already, then he's got only hours left. I've killed him, Paulo, and I've got to tell him why. I've got to tell him what I learned . . . what I felt . . . how I tried to make things right even though I've destroyed everything he fought for. I'll do whatever they want after, but he has to know before he goes."

Paulo walked up behind him. Closer than anyone else in the world would dare go just now. "He knows, my lord . . . my *good* lord. If he felt you inside him—holding on to him, protecting him, giving him strength to survive that upheaval last night—the same way I felt it, the same way Aimee did—"

"Yes! That's exactly what I felt," I blurted out.

Paulo dipped his head toward me as he continued. "—then he understands all he needs to know. He doesn't want you dead, and he'd hate for these good people to bear the burden of killing the one who saved them after all."

Long moments passed. Gerick's shoulders were still.

"It's not fair," he said at last. "My head must already be filled with frog spit. The only morsel of power I managed to scrape together here at the end of everything, and I used it to test the avantir. I could have used it to tell him goodbye."

CHAPTER 39

Paulo had brought wine, water, bread, bandages, towels, a clean white shirt for Gerick, and a clean green tunic for me. I didn't complain that the tunic bagged out of my vest and reached all the way to my knees as if it were an elder brother's. Rather I almost fell into overemotional foolishness again at the thought of washing my face. Perhaps if I could get clean, I could form a clear thought.

When Paulo asked if I could warm the washing water, I clenched my dead fingers as if I could hide their incapacity. I told him my mother had taught me that cold washing was healthier. He very kindly did not refute the lie by mentioning my adamant insistence on hot water for cleansing Gerick's wounds back in the desert.

After we had washed and changed, we sat in the middle of the patterned rug and shared out the provisions. Paulo left the food to Gerick and me, as he had eaten more recently, but he shared the wine and gave us a brief summary of his adventures while we ate.

Evidently Aimee had raised an image of witness so harrowingly clear and indisputable that Je'Reint and his commanders had been jolted into immediate action. Je'Reint's legion had ridden to the succor of Avonar through half a day and most of a night without stopping. From Paulo's account, I estimated that the Dar'Nethi had fallen on the Zhid from the rear only a few hours after Gerick had broached the Gate fire.

"We found more Zhid out there than flies in a dairy herd," Paulo said, "but everyone marveled how so few

Zhid were already inside the walls. Most of the Zhid were still in their camps, waiting for orders to move. Some said a Lord was commanding the Zhid. . . ."

Paulo waited for Gerick to say something. But Gerick was spreading a thick bean paste onto his portion of the chewy bread with Paulo's eating knife. He just shrugged and motioned Paulo to go on, then threw the knife down and ate as if he'd never tasted food before.

The battle had been joined immediately, Paulo said, and continued through the tumultuous night. ". . . then the whole world went dark, a lot like in the Bounded when you stopped the firestorms. But this time I could see maybe three paces from my nose, and nothing else. I was glad I didn't have a light, as I just knew that if I was to shine it past what I could see, nothing would be there. Just nothing. The ground shook so hard, I can't figure how anything in the city is still standing. But when the shaking stopped, and the world came back, the Zhid couldn't fight any more. Some threw down their weapons and flopped down on the ground. Some waved swords around, but as if they'd forgotten what to do with them. Some just took off running. While the Dar'Nethi started taking prisoners and chasing after the runners, Je'Reint and Aimee and me took out straight through the city to the palace. Aimee told us the Bridge was gone, and Je'Reint was afraid everyone was dead in there."

We had scarcely swallowed the last morsels when Paulo stood up and reached for his cloak, well before the critical hour could expire. He offered me his hand, but spoke to Gerick. "The Preceptors want to question you and to take you to the Chamber of the Gate to have you explain what's there. But we have to go downstairs first. People are gathering."

I refused his help. Thoughts of what might come made me instantly regret that I had eaten anything.

Gerick wiped his hands on one of the towels and got to his feet. As Paulo held the door open, Gerick touched my arm gently, staying my steps. He studied my face, starting to speak several times and then stopping himself. His expression had been tight and sober since he had yielded to Paulo. Now his mouth twitched and his eyes kept meeting mine and then glancing away again. The moment seemed very long. "Perhaps it would be best if you—"

"Don't you dare say it!" I wrenched my arm from his grasp. "Don't you dare smile at me as if I were some stupid, naïve country maiden and think you can turn my knees to mush and make me do whatever you like. You're not going to leave me behind when I can give evidence that might help you. Do you think I'm afraid of those people down there?"

"Well, you're certainly no naïve country maiden," he said, "and you're certainly not stupid, so I think you *must* be afraid. I certainly am. I've not a scrap of power, and I don't want to die. There's so much . . . I've just never . . . until recently . . . You're a fine teacher, Jen'-Larie, and I'd not see you brought to account for my deeds."

One person shouldn't feel so many things at once. In the main, I felt as if I were tangled in a briar thicket and would never find my way out. *A fine teacher.* Next he would call me a competent sweeping girl or a healthy child-minder. "Let's just get this over with," I snapped. "We both have people we need to see to. You're not the only one who makes difficult choices."

The expression that took shape amid his weariness and his worries was neither the patronizing smile I feared, nor was it the grin he reserved for Paulo in better times, but rather something different that just touched his dark eyes and the corners of his mouth. I doubted he even knew he'd smiled. The briar thicket tangled me tighter. He bowed quite formally. "Shall we go then?"

His smile vanished as we followed Paulo down the stairs.

To get Gerick to the Chamber of the Gate in one piece was going to take every bit of skill, persuasion, diplomacy, and authority that Ven'Dar possessed. People crammed the lawns and gardens of the Precept House—which I finally recognized as we descended the stairs and crossed the broad foyer. They had spilled out into the street beyond the grounds and were exactly as Paulo had described. Some were grieving. Many were wounded. All were disheveled and dirty and very angry.

Flanked by four people wearing Preceptors' robes over their own untidy garb, and a few other people carrying torches, Ven'Dar stood on the Precept House steps, shouting to be heard over the noise, reiterating arguments he had clearly propounded until he scarcely had a voice left. The Zhid were in complete confusion, as if they had forgotten how to fight or why, he told them. Je'Reint's legion was guarding the walls. No one was being transformed into Zhid. The Lords had not manifested themselves. Though not dead, the Lady D'Sanya was incapable of performing the duties of the Heir . . . however changed those might be now that the Bridge was gone. As always, the Preceptors would determine who would hold D'Arnath's chair. No one knew what had become of the mundane world, but there was no reason to believe it had fared worse than Gondai, which was wounded but not by any means destroyed. Reports were still coming in. The commanders in the east and north reported their own battles won and the Zhid in chaos. Avonar would endure.

Paulo slipped through the door and whispered in Ven'Dar's ear. The prince responded quietly, and Paulo came back inside. "He's got to show you to them," he said to Gerick. "He'll try to protect you, but asks you please not to . . . do . . . anything."

Gerick, sober again, nodded and offered Paulo his hands, wrists together.

Paulo blanched. "No . . . demonfire, no. Of course not. No need for that."

"People, hear me!" cried Ven'Dar. "The world is changed, but we must all search for the truth and light that can be hidden beneath slander, rumor, and shadows. Prince D'Natheil's son, accused of treason, murder, and consorting with our enemies, has submitted himself to the judgment of your Preceptors, claiming that the deeds of this terrible day have saved us from chaos even though the Bridge has fallen. In these past hours, I doubted as you do. I was angry and in despair as you are. But I have seen evidence that his claims are truth."

Paulo stuck his arm in front of me, so I could not follow Gerick through the doors. "Best he do this alone," he said. "He knows we have his back."

I found a window from which I could see Gerick take a position on the broad steps at Ven'Dar's right. His fists were clenched, his body taut. A rabbit's wrong blink would make him run.

As the people realized who he was, sound and sensation struck me like a flaying wind, threatening to strip my bones bare of flesh and my spirit of all harmony. I could hear every word of the crowd as if it had been spoken into my ear and feel every emotion as if each person were a Soul Weaver living in my skin. *The devil! The Destroyer! Why does he live when my son . . . when my father . . . when so many . . . do not? He commanded the Zhid! We all saw him! What's happened? My power . . . My talent . . . Beware the demon Lord . . . The Bridge fallen . . . It's the end of the world . . . Chaos . . .* I was one of them and all of them. Curses, oaths, and questions flew, a fury thundering louder than the Zhid ram and shaking the very stone beneath my feet as if the end had come the second time in one day.

"What's wrong?" Paulo grabbed my arms as I wobbled.

"They're so afraid," I said, willing my knees firm and struggling not to weep. "He mustn't do anything. They're just afraid." Fear made crowds dangerous, of course, so I willed Gerick to keep his temper and stay quiet.

As the storm raged about him, he raised his head, leaving his eyes in some nonthreatening, neutral focus. He clasped his hands loosely in front of him—clearly visible to all. He did not flinch. Did not move again.

Minutes . . . half an hour . . . passed as Dar'Nethi and Dulcé vented the emotions of this terrible day. But I saw no evidence of violence, mundane or enchanted. Of course, if the people believed their power destroyed, then they'd not be able to muster enchantments. Belief was a key to power. Everyone knew that. I looked at my hands that had failed to make a light and tucked that thought away for later exploration.

Eventually Ven'Dar's words of calm, and Gerick's demeanor, quieted the torrent of anger and abuse enough that Ven'Dar could speak again. "The Preceptors and I will summon the finest minds and talents in Gondai to investigate the events of this night," he said. "But I exhort each of you to listen and feel the changes in the universe, for every succeeding moment convinces me that something extraordinary has come to pass—not our doom, but rather our salvation. Dar'Nethi power is not destroyed. Behold . . ."

Ven'Dar raised his right arm and a beam of white light shot out from his fingers, reflecting from broken window glass and shattered lamps, from a toppled bronze warrior maiden, and from hundreds of fearful eyes. The crowd gasped as one when he cupped his hand and the light fell back, flowing into his palm like liquid silver. "Good people, I have not felt such innocence of power . . . such joy and completion . . . since I conjured my first light."

Gerick lifted his head to watch Ven'Dar's magic and his eyes opened wide and his lips parted as if on the verge of speech.

"That's exactly the way I felt when I sang my children to sleep not an hour ago," said a sturdy woman in the front ranks, whose face was streaked with soot and mud.

Ven'Dar motioned her to come up the steps, and had her repeat it where the enchantments of the house could amplify her report for the mass of people. ". . . and that's why I came here," she said. "To see if the tales I heard could possibly be true, for I'd never made such a song as could take their fear away and send them into a dream."

A few others stepped forward and recounted similar experiences, and before very long the mass of bodies had split apart, the fearful citizens gathering around more witnesses and peppering them with questions.

"Share your stories," said Ven'Dar, "and then help each other. Believe. We will come to you when we know more."

As Ven'Dar motioned everyone on the steps back into the Precept House, a tall, graying woman with a sword at her belt stepped forward, her arm about a young man's shoulders. "I'll keep them talking, sir. My son is a Scribe, and he'll take evidence from those who have demonstrated power. I knew Prince D'Natheil, and I know you, Prince Ven'Dar. I trust your word."

"I'm sorry to put you through that," Ven'Dar said to Gerick, as soon as guards were posted and the doors closed and barred behind us.

"Better than I had any right to expect," said Gerick, rubbing his forehead for a moment before folding his arms, allowing his right arm to support his wounded left. "But you were right—" He whipped his head toward me. "No, *you* were right. They were just afraid. I don't claim to have much judgment just now."

Ven'Dar nodded. "Indeed they were. We diffused some of the rumors, at least, to give ourselves time to work."

"And your power," said Gerick. "I didn't think anyone— I don't understand it, but I'm glad."

"Clearly there's much to understand. Come," said Ven'Dar, brisk and serious. "I would like to offer you some rest, but we've some difficult hours ahead of us. Preceptor K'Lan is off working with the wounded; Preceptor J'Dinet is working with the city administrators to provide shelter and food for those who need it. W'Tassa is with the legion in the east. Je'Reint is rounding up Zhid, who seem entirely stripped of their ferocity and purpose—quite differently from five years ago. But these four others and I have decided we must put off other responsibilities. You've left a path of destruction behind you well worthy of a Lord of Zhev'Na, Gerick, and before we can begin to rebuild in earnest, we must understand what you've done and why. And we must know what we face in the future, if it is not you."

Ven'Dar led us down the short wide flight of steps into the council chamber. Two women and two men in dark blue Preceptors' robes had already taken their places behind the long council table that fronted a massive hearth. Only one of them, Mem'Tara the Alchemist, did I recognize. The ancient, plain wooden chair in front of the table—King D'Arnath's own chair, so children were told—sat vacant. Four other chairs had been placed in a semicircle before the table. One was occupied.

Aimee popped to her feet as soon as we entered the chamber, beaming first in Paulo's direction, and then at Gerick and me. "Oh, Jen, and my good lord—Gerick— to find you safe is beyond happiness."

"We're as happy to be in one piece as you are to find us that way," I said, wondering how she had known our identities before we had spoken. We joined her, and she threw her arms around me and kissed me on each cheek, before turning and extending her palms to Gerick. Paulo took a position close to her right shoulder. It would take another earthquake to budge him.

Gerick returned her gesture of greeting. "Mistress."

She bent her head toward him as gracefully as if he had kissed her hand.

Ven'Dar motioned us to take our seats beside Aimee. He himself remained standing. "We need to hear your story from the beginning, Gerick," he said. "Every detail. It's the only way we'll be able to judge you fairly."

Gerick nodded, and as soon as we were settled, he closed his eyes for a moment, as if to compose his thoughts. Then he looked up at the Preceptors. "If I'm to start at the beginning, then we must go very far back indeed. For this cannot be merely a recounting of my own deeds—or crimes, as many of you consider them— but the story of my family. It begins with a king who was a card cheat and a gambler, who loved his family only slightly less than he loved his marvelous kingdom, and it tells of his three children, and his beloved cousin who is my own ancestor, and the three sorcerers who defied his wisdom, to their own ruin and his and very nearly to ours . . ."

He assembled the pieces—D'Arnath and the Bridge, D'Sanya and her tragic coming to power, the horror of her captivity in Zhev'Na, and her father's desperate attempt to salvage his terrible mistake—and laid them in a magical pattern like the tiles and silver bars of a son-quey game. And then he spoke of his own childhood, and his own dreadful coming of age, and the blight of memory he had retained long after his mentors had vanished beyond the Verges. And he spoke frankly and clearly of his guilt and his doubts and what he considered to be his failure in uncovering D'Sanya's madness. ". . . When my father and Prince Ven'Dar asked me to investigate the Lady D'Sanya, the last thing I expected was that I would grow to love her—or rather, the image that I made of her. I feared the seductions of my past, the power I did not fully understand, the memories I had inherited, but the true danger lay in a direction I had no capacity to imagine . . ."

For hours he spoke, softly, telling his tale without averting his eyes. The Preceptors questioned him intensely, often brutally, but never once did this most private of souls bristle or withdraw or attempt to hide his own culpability. ". . . Yes, I knew Dar'Nethi would die in the assault, but I was not strong enough—no one was strong enough—to face D'Sanya alone . . . I had to get to the Bridge and break the link, and I believed the Dar'Nethi would slay me before I could do so . . . and that was before I knew that she was, herself, the link. Yes, I was tempted to take power for myself . . . I chose not. Yes, I fully intended for the Zhid to destroy the Bridge if I failed. If they were capable of doing it at all, then they would, at the same time, destroy their own connection to each other—the avantir. Then perhaps one of you could have picked up the pieces and made the worlds live again . . . I hoped . . ."

As Gerick spoke, scenes flashed through my head in vivid display, people and places and torments excruciatingly real and complete, far beyond his unadorned words. Only when he paused could I shake my head clear of them, feeling foolish at my presumption that I could envision the past through his eyes. Exhaustion had made me silly, for I'd even seen myself—and in a way no mirror could ever show me. Neither foolish, cowardly, nor awkward. Yes, I had a good mind, and I knew how to put two words together to make some sense of matters. But admirable? Insightful? Beautiful? I slumped in my chair and covered my face with my hand, attempting to smother my snickering before someone noticed and read my thoughts. Mind-speaking, limited for so long to only a few of us . . . Ven'Dar hinted that it might be revived in this new world. An uncomfortable consideration when one had thoughts too ludicrous to see daylight.

Aimee's chair was slightly behind my own, so that when I noticed Ven'Dar nodding at her I turned to look. Her hands were raised and held flat in the air a short distance from her temples, a look of exquisite concentration on her face. Aimee the Imager. So, what I had envisioned was her image, drawn from Gerick's words and the knowledge and belief underlying them. . . .

"Mistress Jen!" Ven'Dar. His voice rang sharp and impatient on the ancient stones.

A cold sweat signaled my guilty panic that he had done exactly the thought-reading I feared.

"Would you please give your testimony now?"

"Sorry . . ." *Concentrate, Jen.* As I recounted what I had seen from the moment Gerick had spilled my raspberries in the hospice corridor until I found him slumped beside the crystal wall, a clerk brought us wine. I was pleased because I could focus my eyes on my cup and keep Aimee's images out of my head. Knowing what she was doing made me feel awkward, and I worried that certain muddled thoughts that had no bearing on the case might show up in her work. But no one gaped or snickered, and a sideways glance told me that Gerick was gazing at the floor, expressionless, his mouth buried in one hand.

As most of my tale merely confirmed Gerick's account, the Preceptors had few questions for me. Only a bit about my years in Zhev'Na, and how I could possibly allow someone I feared and loathed to crawl inside my soul.

"By that time I trusted him," I said, impatient with their insistent skepticism. "I can't explain more than that. He didn't trick me, and I'm not entirely an idiot. His testimony is true and complete. You can believe him."

"We thank you for your testimony, Speaker," said Preceptor Mem'Tara, bowing her head quite formally. "The value of your judgment of truth cannot be measured."

"I'm not— I've no such talent. I've no talent at all. I'm a Speaker's *daughter*!" I stammered and fumbled. Were they *trying* to humiliate me? Or had I somehow misled them? To impersonate a Speaker was very serious. In such a matter as this, it would be considered criminal.

But they had already begun questioning Paulo. And soon they turned back to Gerick, probing to understand the results of what he'd done.

"I remember nothing beyond what I've described," he said. "I saw images . . . my family . . . my friends . . . my homelands . . . and I tried to help them endure what was happening, to survive. I knew the Bridge was gone, as I didn't feel the disharmony any longer. I also couldn't feel anything under my feet. And then . . . nothing. I can't tell you more than that. I just don't know."

The proceedings were abruptly adjourned to the Chamber of the Gate. My good intentions of setting my credentials, or lack of them, straight fell by the wayside as we gazed in awe upon the crystal wall, even I who had seen it before. The wall pulsed and gleamed with light, as if it had captured every handlight cast since the world was young.

"I didn't create this," Gerick said, as he walked up and down beside it, the glow illuminating his wonder. "I've never made anything like this . . . so beautiful."

"The Lady says you carried her through it," said Ven'Dar.

"I don't remember that. Is she—?"

"We've taken her away to be cared for. She cannot tell us anything more for the time being."

A scrawny, odd-looking man with thinning hair had been in the chamber when we arrived. Wearing a ragged, dirty robe that had once been yellow, he sat on the floor between two protruding faces of the wall, gazing intently into the smooth surface. It seemed odd that neither Ven'Dar nor the Preceptors acknowledged him. They just carried on with Gerick's interrogation. I wondered if I should mention his presence, in case I was the only one who'd noticed him.

But after a while the man unfolded his long thin legs and popped to his feet. Still facing the wall, he produced the most incongruous of sounds, thoroughly interrupting the dignified Preceptor L'Beres' latest declaration of mystification. A robust, bellowing laughter penetrated my bone and blood. I would have sworn the light of the crystal wall glimmered in rhythm with it.

"By Shaper and Creator," said the ragged man, wiping his eyes with the filthy corner of his robe as everyone fell silent, "do you know what he's done? Have you even looked, my dear and befuddled L'Beres? Come here, young man! Come, come, come." He waved a hand at Gerick, and it felt as if the air itself reached out and drew Gerick from my side to stand beside him.

Though the odd-looking man had yet to even look at any of us, the others seemed to know him. Preceptor L'Beres rolled his eyes. The two I didn't know retreated a few steps, clearly uncomfortable, while Preceptor Mem'Tara, a tall robust woman with an iron-gray braid and a sword at her side, stood her ground, curious and interested. Ven'Dar's solemnity relaxed halfway to a smile.

Gerick looked at the man, curious. My blood rippled with inexplicable hope.

"Touch the wall, Gerick yn Karon," he said. "Go on. It is not painful, especially for one who has known pain in so many forms. At worst its power will repel you as it does the rest of us, but I believe . . . . Well, try it. Show us."

Gerick reached out and pressed his hand to the glassy surface . . . and ripples of brightness shimmered outward. He brushed his fingers across the smooth face.

"There, you see? It knows you in the same way the locks on a man's treasure house know him."

"What does that mean, Garvé?" asked Ven'Dar softly, watching Gerick traverse the convoluted length of the wall, dragging his hand across its edges and faces, causing a cascade of light.

Garvé . . . the Arcanist! Though tempted, I did not step away. Not from someone who laughed as he did.

"First tell me of your talent and power, Ven'Dar . . . L'Beres . . . all of you . . ." The man spun like a dancer, sweeping a pointing finger at all of us. I felt as if a stripe of music had been painted across my breast. He stopped his spin at the exact point at which he'd begun, facing the wall. ". . . and if you've not felt their return, then believe, look inward, and you *will* find them. I am not diminished, but alive as I have not been in my eighty-seven years, my talents become one with my flesh, balanced, stable, more like another sense than a separate skill to be mentored and grown like playing the viol or dancing or climbing sheer cliffs with ropes and hooks."

"I've felt something like," said Ven'Dar, "but I didn't dare hope . . . Is the Bridge not destroyed, then? Or has our understanding been so wrong?"

"D'Arnath's Bridge is gone," said Garvé. "As to what is here, that study may take many hours . . . years, even. For tonight, report to the people the story you've heard in these past hours and what you've seen here—mystery and beauty, the very essence of hope."

He peered over his shoulder. A kind face, smiling, piercing gray eyes that darted from one to the other of the company in the chamber. "But, of course, if you were to forbear a bit longer and service an old man's whims, then perhaps we could learn a bit more. Many talents we have assembled here: Word Winder, Soul Weaver, Alchemist, Speaker"—I would have sworn the man winked at me—"Balancer, Effector, Navigator, and, ah, an Imager. You, Mistress Imager . . . if you would be so kind . . ."

"Sir," said Aimee. He took her hand as she stepped forward, and drew her close.

"So," he said, touching her eyelids with a bony finger. "The unseeing one who perceives so accurately. I've heard reports of your skills. Will you trust me, mistress, and indulge my whims?" He opened his palm, laid her hand on it, and waited.

Aimee dipped her head and used her other hand to fold his fingers around hers.

Garvé then led her around the great chamber, turning her this way and that, retracing steps, until the poor woman could be nothing but confused.

"Take all you know of the Bridge, young woman," said Garvé, when they came to a halt halfway across the room. "Delve deep into your knowledge of all that it has meant for Gondai, and the Breach, and the world beyond, of D'Arnath's great heart as he constructed it, of his Heirs' courage in defending it, of all you know of our people and their will and their bravery throughout this long fight. And I wish for you to build an image of the Bridge—an image we will not see, of course, for the Bridge is an enchantment, thus its essence is not visible. But as your talent allows you to match the image in your mind to the reality it shadows, perhaps you will be able to tell us if the link that binds the universe and maintains its balance yet exists or not."

Aimee held her flattened palms in position, close to but not touching her temples as if shielding her mind from noise and distraction. Paulo stood poised like a cocked catapult, ready to run to her aid if she should falter. All of us had been drawn into Garvé's test; every eye was on Aimee, and when she lowered her hands and lifted her head, we held our breath as if of one mind. Her brow was drawn up in a most puzzled knot.

"Tell us, mistress," said Garvé softly. "Where is it?"

Aimee turned almost a complete circle before she came to a stop, raised one finger, and pointed. "There. The Bridge is there."

Her finger pointed directly at Gerick.

Surely it would take Garvé and Ven'Dar and the Preceptors hours or months or years to understand what Aimee's magic told them. For most of us in the chamber, it was a wonder and a consolation; for one or two, perhaps, it was only a young blind woman's whimsy unworthy of belief. Gerick was not reduced to an enchantment, nor did anyone assert that chaos would descend if he were to die. But certainly in my own mind, the existence of the Bounded gave credence to the concept of a man who embodied the binding of the worlds, a Soul Weaver who had loaned us all his strength and would hold us together until we could do it on our own. Poor mad D'Sanya had understood it first. *He held them. Loved them. Saved them.*

When Gerick, as mystified as any of us, pressed his hand firmly to the surface of the wall and his arm vanished to the elbow, the skeptics were surprised. When he stepped through entirely and then returned a short time later, claiming that he had existed in the mundane world, the skeptics mumbled to themselves. Though none but he could pass the wall or even bear to touch it, he took their hands and escorted them one by one either to the mundane world or to the Bounded and back again. The skeptics were silenced.

After he had brought Preceptor Mem'Tara back, Gerick offered me his hand. "Would you like to see?"

I nodded, speechless since he had first disappeared into the crystal.

The passage through the wall felt like breaking the cool surface of water. He led me through a crystal pathway, glittering with light. We stepped out to stand beside a frozen lake surrounded by snowy peaks. Behind them, the sky was the color of lapis. The air frosted my lungs, but exhilaration and beauty and wonder could have held me there freezing until I was as fixed in place as the mountains themselves.

"This is the place where the Exiles built their stronghold," he said, wrapping his arm around my shoulders to slow my shivering, "and where my father came back—" He released me and stepped back toward the wall, his glow of pleasure vanished. He pressed his fist to his forehead as if a lance had struck him there.

"Are you all right?" I said.

"Gods—" He grabbed my hand and turned back to the cliff where the crystal wall appeared as an exceptionally polished sheet of ice. "It's my father."

"I must go," he said, as soon as we stepped back into the Chamber of the Gate. "I'll come back, if you want, answer more questions and help you understand this, but I need to be at the hospice now. Please, Ven'Dar. My father is dying. Send guards if you wish. Bind me if it suits you. But you've more than enough to think about for a few hours while I'm gone."

Ven'Dar answered first. "Of course, you should be free to go. We've had enough for now."

The Preceptors had not embraced Gerick, but somewhere along the way, they had come to believe in him. Since we had come to the Chamber, they had spoken nothing of punishments or prison, only of study and investigation. The four agreed that Gerick could go, two of them somewhat reluctantly, but they insisted he return to Avonar as soon as possible and work with Garvé and others to determine what this new order might mean. "You have much to answer for," L'Beres pronounced.

Gerick would have agreed to anything to be gone. Even the brief delay as Ven'Dar shut down the portal to the palace and rebuilt one to the hospice had him grinding his teeth. But as he stepped to the threshold, he turned back and extended his hand. "Jen'Larie, would you . . . ?"

"They don't need me here," I said. Even if he had stayed in Avonar, it was time for me to go. I'd been away from my father long enough. I turned to Ven'Dar.

The former prince—whom I suspected would be our prince again—tipped his head toward the portal. "Your service has been incalculable, Jen, both in your testimony and in deep and abiding ways that no story of these days will ever report. Go. Do as you need. And believe."

The night was warm and still as Gerick and I stepped out of the portal at the main house of the hospice, just in front of the porch where D'Sanya had greeted her guests in her filmy white gowns. As we ran up the steps and through the deserted passages, I wondered, unworthily, if Gerick would ever be rid of the image of her. Of course, his thoughts were elsewhere now. The sound of women singing hung on the air as we cut through the unlit library and through the upper courtyard gardens, down the few steps past the fountains and rose arbors, and into the lower gardens. One glance, and I knew he was too late.

The lower garden was a sea of white lights, the small round handlights that Dar'Nethi used in funeral processions. Fifty people or more stood amid the overgrown roses and graceful willows. The men joined the singing with a countermelody. *The Song of the Way,* intertwined melodies of grief and joy, was always sung to celebrate the passing of the Heirs of D'Arnath.

Na'Cyd stood well apart from the crowd, on the steps near the fountain that marked the lower garden. He neither cast a handlight nor did he sing. But he bowed wordlessly to us and led us through the mass of people, parting them briskly with his hand.

Prince D'Natheil lay still on the soft grass, his blue robes gracefully arranged, peace on his handsome features. Lady Seriana sat beside him, holding his hand to her forehead. One might have thought them a Sculptor's creation, set in that garden to remind us of love and mortality.

I hung back as Gerick hurried across the circle of mourners to his parents. As he knelt and laid his forehead on his father's breast, I scanned the faces in the crowd, missing the one I needed most to see. I turned quickly.

"He remains in his apartment," said Na'Cyd, his eyes fixed on the three in the grass.

I sped through the gardens and courtyards, suddenly unable to move fast enough to get there. No lights burned in either garden or residence as I slipped through Papa's door. His breathing, quick and shallow to manage his pain, led me to the open window where he sat in the dark, crooked and bent. The glorious song drifted on the cool air like a promise of spring, though my heart ached with all the griefs of winter. What was happening to me? I said nothing as I knelt in front of him, laid my head in his lap, and let his hand on my ugly hair Speak to me of love.

Gerick

One year from the day my father died, my mother stood before two hundred scholars in the history lecture hall at the University in Valleor wearing the billowing black robe and blue sash of an Honorary Lecturer in Ancient History. With the strong, clear voice of a woman of intellect, education, and experience, and with an intensity that demanded every mind in the room open and every ear hear, she spoke of an extraordinary event in the history of the Four Realms—the day four hundred and seventy years in the past when the King of Leire, one Bosgard by name, had issued a decree that every member of a single race was to be exterminated. They were to be hunted down and burned to death, their lands and fortunes forfeit, their homes laid waste, their names forever obliterated from the councils of the land. Any man or woman who consorted with members of the condemned race or failed to report them was likewise condemned.

By the grace of His Majesty, Evard, the late King of Leire, had this decree been lifted, and at the command of Her Majesty Roxanne, Queen of Leire, had one Karon yn Mandille, a historian, archeologist, and physician of Valleor been required to prepare a history of the decree of extermination, its origins, and its results. On this day, said my mother, she would present the first of twenty-six lectures on the work he had completed before his death.

For two hours, she held the room spellbound in the grip of her story—my father's story—my story—and she had scarcely even begun. When she closed her notes and said, "Until next week," the room erupted into the chaos of excitement and discovery. From every side came questions, demands for more time, more words, more of the truth they had never even suspected.

She remained an island of serenity in the center of the storm, patiently telling them to come back and hear more. They would hear the truth of a universe that was larger than they had ever imagined. They would understand.

Throughout all of this, I sat on the back row of the lecture hall and watched as the circle of admirers and skeptics drifted away, still chattering and murmuring. My mother's eyes roved the empty chairs until they landed on me, not surprised in the least to see me there, though I'd not told her I was coming and had not seen her for almost half a year.

Her smile banished the shadows. "What questions would my students have had if they'd known the King of the Bounded, the most powerful sorcerer in three worlds, was sitting in the hall?"

"A small wonder beside the first woman ever to give a lecture at this University," I said. "Someday we may have a university in the Bounded, and I needed to know if a woman could teach men anything."

She laughed. "This is all your doing, isn't it? How else could Roxanne have known to command the Chancellor to allow it? For me to stand here . . ." She waved toward the vaulted ceiling and the tall windows of colored glass, to the ancient lectern, and to the rows of seats where every scholar of the Four Realms had sat at one time or another. Where my father had once sat.

"I only mentioned it to her. It wasn't my idea." I strolled down the long flight of steps, the stone worn into concavity by the generations of students who had trod them, each step a little too wide to take in one stride, a little too shallow to require two. "But I had to be here. I was asked to give you something when this day came."

Into my mother's hands I placed the long, thin parcel

I'd brought with me, wrapped in green silk and tied with a green velvet ribbon. For one instant her cheeks lost their flush of exhilaration, but as she unwrapped the parcel, her graceful fingers ever so slightly trembling, her soft smile drew the sweet coloring back again. The dewdrops on the soft petals that were just on the verge of opening seemed a reflection of the tears in her eyes.

But her tears did not fall. Rather she inhaled the scent of the flower and glowed with happiness. "He still cheats death," she said after a moment, laying her hand on my cheek. "To see you is to see his best self. He lives."

I had only begun to understand the magic that could create a rose of such glorious perfection and lasting beauty. This one had lived a year already. My father had designed it to bloom fresh and fragrant at my mother's bedside, the first thing she saw in the morning, and the last thing she saw at night, for as long as she drew breath.

"So tell me all your news," said my mother, as she directed me to gather and stack up her papers. She would not relinquish the rose.

"Paulo sends his best. He wanted to be here today in the worst way, but he won't leave Aimee and little Seriana and is terrified to take them traveling as yet."

I put a hand under my mother's elbow as we started up the stair, but she didn't need it. I felt the strength in her steps. "I don't know if I can wait until Seille to see them," she said. "A granddaughter . . . earth and sky . . ."

"You should have seen Paulo's face when Aimee told him she was in that way." I grinned, as always when I remembered that moment. "I don't know whether he was more embarrassed that someone might guess what he and Aimee had been up to since they came back to the Bounded, or more terrified at the prospect of being a father to a human child instead of a foal. He's been working so hard at his schooling for fear of this child being born better read than he, he'll likely be giving lectures here next year."

"And Aimee is happy in the Bounded?"

"She says so. I think she would be happy in a pit if Paulo were there with her. The Singlars adore her, calling her 'the Golden One who Sees All' and she gives them so much—showing them how their ideas could change the world."

We left the lecture hall and crossed the foyer to the heavy outer doors.

"And what of the good king of your land? How does he fare?"

I knew my mother worried excessively, afraid that D'Sanya and the deeds she had forced me to had left scars worse than those the Lords had given me. I had caused my father's death and driven D'Sanya into madness. Avonar would forever bear the scars of my war, and the Dar'Nethi would always fear me. My memories had not vanished and would not. When I worked sorcery, the temptations of power would always require me to choose the light again.

Yet, I had tried to reassure my mother that I had at last begun to understand the Dar'Nethi Way. Pain is life. Scars are life. Guilt and dreadful memory . . . those, too, are part of the pattern we weave as we walk this world. But somehow, when viewed in the vast perspective of a life lived fully, they take on less overpowering significance. Still, she worried, and so on this visit I had brought evidence I thought might alleviate her concerns a little.

I stayed determinedly somber. "Some things have happened. Serious things."

She stopped at the door and looked at me with her stubborn stare that allowed no hiding. All my plans of subterfuge and clever misdirection evaporated, and I started laughing as I shoved open the door and nudged her through it into the autumn afternoon. "He fares exceedingly well, as it happens. On my last visit to Gondai, I devised a way that a few of the most powerful Dar'-Nethi, ones that Prince Ven'Dar chooses, can traverse the wall without my help. Well, a few weeks ago, Je'-Reint came for a short visit to explore the Bounded and to discuss how we should manage it all. And he brought a companion who had stormed the palace, stubbornly demanding to accompany him. His companion, a Speaker of growing influence, drove us to distraction for three lights gathering information and experience for a solid judgment of our land, and then refused to leave the Bounded when Je'Reint returned to Gondai. . . ."

My traveling companion was perched on the top of an ancient brick wall, her knees drawn up, and her eyes closed as the golden sunlight bathed her face. She didn't even move before she started in on us. "And why should I go back when the Bounded is far more interesting, and clearly in need of someone with some proper organizational skills? And certain royal persons seem sadly lacking in the disciplines of mathematics and natural science, not to mention some of the rudimentary applications of true talent."

She blinked her eyes open and smiled at my mother as if I weren't present. "Je'Reint promised to bring Papa on his next visit so that I would be properly chaperoned. Did you hear, my lady, that some mysterious person came to Gondai behind my back and enabled Papa . . . strengthened him . . . so that he was able to endure a healing for his back, and then left again before we could even thank him? That same person has aided every survivor of the hospice in like manner, and even poor J'Savan the Gardener, who now tends a small farm in Lyrrathe Vale. Papa will adore the Bounded. A new life, born of our trials. I can hear him say it even now." She turned her face back to the sun, and though she closed her eyes again, she could no longer hold in her teasing smile.

"Thank you for waiting," I said as I encircled her waist with my hands and lifted her down, kissing the eyes she stubbornly held closed. "Mother, you remember Jen'Larie?"

Seri

I watched them together for an hour, and listened to Jen describe the marvels of Gerick's world and the intelligence, strength, and compassion he brought to his work, as if I had never recognized the gifts of my beautiful son. Gerick said little, as usual, but his eyes never left her and his mouth seemed perpetually on the verge of a smile.

When it came time for them to go, Jen kissed my cheek and whispered, "He sleeps well, my lady, and is at peace. Is he not gloriously dear?"

And then Gerick kissed my other cheek and whispered, "She has brought light to the Bounded, Mother. Is she not a wonder beyond wonders?"

Then Gerick made a small gesture with his hand, and they waved and walked into a burst of light that warmed the day.

They didn't need any answer from me. But I called after them, "Yes!" And as the light of their enchantment faded, I smiled, inhaled the sweet scent of Karon's rose, and strolled down University Hill. Friends were waiting; I had things to do. Life was not done with me yet.

ABOUT THE AUTHOR

Though **Carol Berg** calls Colorado her home, her roots are in Texas, in a family of teachers, musicians, and railroad men. She has a degree in mathematics from Rice University and one in computer science from the University of Colorado, but managed to squeeze in minors in English and art history along the way. She has combined a career as a software engineer with her writing, while also raising three sons. She lives with her husband at the foot of the Colorado mountains.

The truth cannot be silenced.

SONG OF THE BEAST

by Carol Berg

0-451-45923-7

From the acclaimed author of the Rai-Kirah series
comes the epic story of Aidan MacAllister,
a musician beloved by the gods, whose voice and harp
can transform the souls of men.

"CAROL BERG LIGHTS UP THE SKY."
—*MIDWEST BOOK REVIEW*

"A BRILLIANT WRITER."
—*BOOKBROWSER*

R740

Read more in the Rai-Kirah saga from *CAROL BERG*

TRANSFORMATION 45795-1

Enter an exotic world of demons, of a remarkable boy prince, of haunted memories, of the terrors of slavery, and of the triumphs of salvation.

REVELATION 45842-7

Seyonne, the slave-turned-hero from Berg's highly acclaimed *Transformation*, returns to discover the nature of evil—in a "spellbinding" (*Romantic Times*) epic saga.

RESTORATION 45890-7

A sorcerer who fears he will destroy the world. A prince who fears he has destroyed his people. Amid the chaos of a disintegrating empire, two men confront prophecy and destiny in the last battle of the demon war...

"Carol Berg lights up the sky."
—*Midwest Book Review*